WARLORD ARCANIST

FRITH CHRONICLES, BOOK VI OF VII

SHAMI STOVALL

Published by
CS BOOKS, LLC

Warlord Arcanist
Copyright © 2021 Shami Stovall
All rights reserved.
https://sastovallauthor.com/

Cover Design: Darko Paganus

Editor: Amy McNulty, Nia Quinn

IF YOU WANT TO BE NOTIFIED WHEN SHAMI STOVALL'S NEXT BOOK RELEASES, PLEASE VISIT HER WEBSITE OR CONTACT HER DIRECTLY AT s.adelle.s@gmail.com

ISBN: 978-1-7347587-1-9

To John, my soulmate.
To Beka, forever.
To Gail and Big John, my surrogate parents.
To Henry Copeland, for the beautiful leather map and book covers.
To Brian Wiggins, for giving a voice to the characters.
To Mary & Dana, for all the jokes and input.
To my patrons over on Patreon, you're the best.
To my Facebook group, for all the memes.
And finally, to everyone unnamed, thank you for everything.

CONTENTS

THE PUREST MAGIC

Every night since I had bonded with the world serpent, I'd had the same dream.

I swam in the ocean. In the distance, beyond the waves, I could see the gigantic tree where the world serpent had been born. But that wasn't where I was heading. Instead, I swam for a castle poking out of the water—all I could see were the tips of roofs and the heads of fearsome gargoyle statues. However, the closer I got to the castle, the more turbulent the waves became.

Every night, I woke before I reached the structure, my body dabbled with sweat, and my heart racing. I had never seen the castle before, nor did I know why I was swimming there.

And no one was with me. Not Illia, not the world serpent...

Not Luthair.

Tonight, instead of sleeping, I stood on the edge of Gentel's shell, all the way by her head. The cold ocean winds kept me wide awake, despite my exhaustion. I wrapped my coat around my body and buttoned it closed. My thick boots and sailing trousers shielded me from the weather better than my thin tunic and gloves, but it didn't matter. The chill wouldn't force me back to the guild manor house.

Guildmaster Eventide had given me a new room to live in. It wasn't like what I'd had as an apprentice or journeyman arcanist—it was one of the major rooms reserved for master arcanists.

Which was ironic, given the fact that I had just recently bonded with Terrakona, the second world serpent. I might as well have been an apprentice all over again.

But I knew better. I wasn't a normal arcanist anymore. I was a legendary *god-arcanist*, one of twelve individuals bonded to mystical creatures so powerful, they could alter the world. Funny how little that had changed about me.

Gentel, the atlas turtle the whole guild had been built upon, was large enough to host a field of grass, a pond, a giant oak tree, and a three-story building. And when I stared forward and examined the massive size of her head—I could easily fit in her mouth like a cherry could fit in mine—it made me feel small, both metaphorically and literally.

The world was filled with wonders I still knew nothing about, yet *I* was supposed to lead civilization into a new *age of knowledge of magic*.

This was the *turning of an age* that so many scholars had written about.

I stared down at my gloved hand, the moonlight bright enough to highlight the stitching.

"There's no turning back, Volke," I said to myself, my breath a hot mist.

The ocean waters bulged a moment as the world serpent lifted his head beyond the waves. Terrakona's scales were a brilliant jade. Even at night, I could appreciate the depth of the green.

And despite the fact Terrakona was a hatchling world serpent, he was already the size of a full-grown leviathan and a few hundred feet long. When he emerged from the ocean, water splashed onto Gentel. Terrakona didn't attempt to get onto Gentel's shell. Instead, he swam alongside the colossal atlas turtle, matching Gentel's pace with the concertina movement all serpentine creatures were known for.

Terrakona turned his draconic face to stare down at me.

I admired his eyes—the right was scarlet, and the left was sapphire—and his slit pupils expanded and constricted as Terrakona focused on me.

"Warlord," Terrakona telepathically said, his voice so deep, regal, and precise, it was like hearing him speak aloud. **"We have yet to reach our destination. What troubles you? I sense none of our enemies nearby."**

Terrakona didn't have a hood, like vipers. Instead, he had spines made of crystal, clustered like a mane or crest. The crystals themselves were similar to star shards. They glittered with inner power and were a dark black, like the night sky. It was as if he were made of the world—natural gemstones, crystals, and metals, all mixed to form his epic body.

I rubbed the back of my neck. "Nothing is troubling me."

"Why aren't you safe in your den?"

"My... *den*?" I asked. Oh, he meant *bedroom*. I chuckled. "I'm not in my room because I wanted to be alone." I exhaled and stared up into the cloudless night sky. "And I know what you're thinking. Wouldn't I be alone in my room? But you would be surprised by how many people just *barge in* to speak to me."

"Who are these people? Children of Yama? Should they face punishment for their trespasses against you?" Terrakona flashed his massive fangs. They were long and came to a fine point, and some even glistened with venom that leaked from the glands.

I held up both my hands. "Whoa, whoa. I meant my *friends* would barge in. They don't deserve any wrath." I forced a nervous smile. "Trust me."

"Friends?"

"Yeah. Illia—well, she's my sister—sometimes teleports into

my room to speak with me. Usually about Zaxis, or stealing something, or about something she discovered a while ago." I lowered my hands and shrugged. "And occasionally, Fain comes to see me while he's invisible. I mean, I wish he'd let me know." I laughed as I paced the edge of atlas turtle shell. "Half the time, Fain doesn't even say anything. He just stands in the corner of the room like a piece of ghost furniture."

I hesitated a moment as I recalled the many—*numerous*—times people had entered my room without notice or consent.

"Evianna *always* wants to discuss something and just shadow-steps under the door," I said, half-smiling. "Karna disguises herself as my other friends using her doppelgänger magic. Hexa's hydra once broke my door down by slamming its many heads into it." I ran a hand down my face. "And don't even get me started about Adelgis... He hears all of my thoughts, watches most of my dreams, and has seen more of my memories than I can even remember."

I really had zero privacy.

"No one understands the word *boundaries*," I quipped.

Terrakona shook his head, misting the air with salt water. Then his forked tongue darted out for a brief second. Even his tongue appeared highly magical—it was marked with glowing runes, similar to the runestone used to open his lair.

"You have a great responsibility as a god-arcanist," Terrakona said. **"You cannot afford to suffer the company of fools. You should surround yourself with advisors, diplomats, and the most talented of instructors."**

"Master Zelfree has guided me along," I muttered, my chest tight. "Even if he's... rough around the edges. And Guildmaster Eventide has been growing the guild and reaching out to other nations. Everyone knows of the Second Ascension's villainy because of her."

"A tree surrounded by weeds will wither." Terrakona lifted his serpentine head high into the air, his gaze still focused on me. Water dripped from his chin and splashed across the atlas turtle. **"Associate with talent, Young Warlord. You don't have the experience of a long-lived life. Rely on those who can offer you wisdom, not heartache."**

While I wanted to reply to his words, an odd thought struck me.

"Terrakona," I muttered, staring up at him. "Why is it you sound so old, when you've only just been born? I mean, you don't have the experience of a long-lived life, either, yet you have wisdom to offer."

Terrakona growled—a much different sound than his telepathy—and it rumbled through his throat, creating a haunting echo.

"Magic connects all things," he eventually stated. **"From the grass to the blood in your veins to the stars in the night sky. And I have been bathed in the purest of magics since I entered this world. All my knowledge... I have gained by absorbing it."**

I had never been formally educated. My ability to read and write, and my love of history, all came from Gravekeeper William. Those times had been difficult. Every scrap of information, especially from the steps of the Pillar, I had studied hard in order to remember. I couldn't even imagine just *knowing* things.

"If you can just know things, why don't you know what kind of magics I can wield?" I asked.

Terrakona snorted. **"The knowledge I've acquired is not chosen. It comes to me in brief moments of clarity."** The gigantic world serpent flared the scales near his head. **"You have touched the purest magic as well, Warlord. When your knightmare achieved his true form, you should have felt it. Perhaps just for a moment, but it was there."**

When Luthair had achieved true form?

That moment was etched into my memories so thoroughly

that I could relive it whenever I wanted. There had been a fraction of a second in which I had felt limitless possibility—like I had grazed greatness—but then lost it just as quickly.

Terrakona lowered himself into the waves of the ocean, but when I leaned over the edge of the atlas turtle shell, I could still spot the darkened shadow of his massive body. He swam from side to side, staying close enough to the surface to create wakes.

"Wait," I said, holding out my hand. "I think we should practice our magic together. I haven't learned anything yet, and we've been bonded for five whole days."

The guild had been frantically chaotic since we left the lair of the world serpent. My brother—whom I hadn't even known about six days ago—was also bonded to a massive creature of untold magic, and he had no idea what his magics did either. The guild had fought the forces of the Second Ascension, and while the enemy had teleported away, we still had to sail back to civilization. Several of our arcanists were injured, and some infected with the madness-inducing arcane plague. They could be cured, but it took time and tested our sanity.

Everything made it difficult to focus on studying my own magic.

"**You should rest,**" Terrakona said, his telepathy clear, even while he swam under the waves.

"But we'll arrive in Fortuna in roughly a week," I said, half-tempted to leap into the ocean. "I don't have any more time to rest." I *never* had time to rest, it seemed. Our enemies were always scheming and plotting.

And what would Luthair think if he saw me lounging about? I couldn't dishonor his sacrifice by lying in bed when the world needed me.

Terrakona burst out of the water and arced through the air. He crashed back into the water like a dolphin, his serpentine body trailing for a length. His scales glittered under the starlight.

"The magic god-arcanists wield is devastating. Do not take it lightly. Wait until you are fully recovered."

I glanced down at my body. With hasty movements, I patted myself from the shoulders down to my knees. "I'm not injured." I stood straight and motioned to myself. "I'm totally fine. I swear."

"When you lose your eldrin, you carry a wound you cannot see with your eyes. Your soul has been gouged. It will take a little more rest before you are ready, Warlord."

I caught my breath and then ran a hand up my coat. My fingers twisted into the fabric as I remembered the way Luthair had unmerged with me just in time to deal the killing blow to the grim reaper. He had saved me with the ultimate sacrifice. A part of me still couldn't believe it.

We had been through so much together.

I clenched my jaw and tightened my grip on my coat.

The past couldn't be rewritten. Dwelling on sadness wouldn't make anything right. I had to move forward. I had to train myself for the perils to come. I had to...

But the ache in my chest grew worse with each passing moment. I hadn't thought much about Luthair since my time in the world serpent's lair. Whenever I tried to recall his gruff voice, I grew shaky and less confident.

What if I couldn't protect the ones I loved? What if someone else died trying to save me?

But then I remembered the seventeenth step of the Pillar. *Confidence. Without it, we surrender too early.*

I *would* protect those I cared about.

By the abyssal hells, I was a god-arcanist! If anyone could protect the Frith Guild, it was me. I forced a smile and a nod.

"You've got this, Volke," I muttered to myself. "Don't let fear cripple you."

Luthair's final words had been, "*Future greatness awaits you. Don't allow this moment to hold you back.*"

And I didn't intend to.

With a deep breath, I turned on my heel and headed for the guild manor house. The sky had shifted in color with the rising of the sun. Purple night bled into a pink and orange morning. Salt water always smelled different in the morning, and I enjoyed the aroma as I made my way to my room for a long rest.

2

CARRYING THE PAST

Thirty minutes after I had fallen asleep, someone shook me awake.

My eyelids almost refused to open. I forced myself to sit up, even though my body felt like it weighed three times as normal. The heavy curtains were drawn, blocking the morning light. It was odd to be blinded by the darkness. When I had been a knightmare arcanist, my passive magic had allowed me to see through all manner of shadow.

Now I couldn't even see the person standing a foot away.

"Get up," a gruff voice said. "We don't have much time."

"What's going on?" I asked, my heart leaping into my throat. "Is it the Second Ascension? A dread pirate? Are we under attack by plague-ridden creatures?"

A strong hand gripped my shoulder. "Calm down, kid. It's not that kind of emergency."

I'd recognize Master Zelfree's voice anywhere, and it relaxed me to know we weren't under immediate attack. I exhaled and chuckled at the same time, my fatigue returning in full force. Rubbing at my eyes, I shoved my blankets away.

My new bedroom suite was massive. My four-poster bed

filled the upstairs room to the point that barely anything else fit. The bed canopy hung in elegant folds along each post, but I had yet to shut them. I didn't like the idea of having a curtain between me and the rest of the room. What if I needed to spring into action at a moment's notice?

My new wardrobe and dresser were empty. Well, that wasn't entirely true. I had a few trousers, a coat, a couple of belts, and a pair of boots, but otherwise they were empty.

Master Zelfree walked around my bed, his heavy footfalls a clear indicator that he wasn't well rested. When he was awake and lively, I rarely heard him walk around. When he was tired, on the other hand...

He threw open one of the curtains, flooding the room with sunlight. I squinted and held up a hand to shield my eyes. I already missed the darkness.

"We'll arrive at Fortuna soon," Zelfree drawled. He turned around and then leaned against the wall. The dark circles under his eyes had never been so prominent—and that honestly shocked me.

He wore a pair of bangles on his wrist that shimmered in the sunlight. They were his mimic eldrin—Traces—who had shifted her shape to hide herself in plain sight.

"I'm looking forward to Fortuna," I said as I slid my legs off the edge of the mattress. I wore trousers and nothing else, but that was fine. The temperature in the guild manor house was pleasant.

But...

Normal arcanists had their mark on their foreheads. My old knightmare mark was half-faded on my skin in the usual location. However, my god-arcanist mark hadn't replaced my old one. Instead, the mark had appeared on my chest, just over my heart.

I grazed the tips of my fingers over the flesh etching. The twelve-pointed star ran from my collarbone down to the base of my ribs, but the world serpent marking wrapped around my shoulder and torso, with the tail of the beast by the side of my hip. It was a mark that defined my body.

Master Zelfree pinched the bridge of his nose. "I don't think you comprehend the position you're in, Volke."

I glanced over and lifted an eyebrow.

"You haven't even *used* any of your world serpent powers."

I shook my head. "You think I don't know that? I've been trying, but Terrakona says I've been through a lot, and I need to rest first."

Zelfree snapped his fingers, startling me. Then he forced a half-smile. "Listen. When we make it back to land, we're gonna have important people waiting for us. And no one is gonna care what you've been through. I know that sounds callous, but it's true. All they're gonna care about is witnessing your power."

My power?

I glared at the floor, my body tense. This didn't surprise me. I understood. Now that the world was aware of god-creatures, everyone would want to see what I was capable of.

"They're going to be disappointed," I said. "I can't possibly learn all my magic by the time we reach Fortuna."

"You don't have to know all your magic. Just *something*."

"I think everyone will be just as disappointed if I show up with only one trick," I sarcastically muttered. In a mocking tone, I said, *"Hello, I'm the world serpent arcanist, and all I can do is move dirt around into small piles. Don't worry. I'm here to save the world. Leave everything to me."*

Then I gave Zelfree a half-lidded stare.

He pushed away from the wall, his bangles softly clinking together, and he walked over to my side of the bed. Flecks of dust swirled through the morning sunlight, clear evidence this room hadn't been occupied in some time. When Zelfree sat next to me, another cloud of motes rose off the sheets and into the stream of light.

"You don't have to tell them you can't use your other powers," Zelfree said.

"You want me to lie?" I snapped. "That isn't really *my thing*."

"You don't have to lie, kid. You just don't have to tell the complete truth." Zelfree stared at me, his dark eyes focusing on mine. "If we arrive in Fortuna, and you give a good demonstration of at least *one* power, we won't have to say anything else. Everyone will make assumptions—and assumptions will carry you along like a powerful tide, do you understand?"

"Why do we want them to make assumptions?"

Zelfree laughed once, his throat raspy. He coughed and then leaned back. "This might come as a shock to you, but we have enemies. If our enemies realize you can't you use your magic, what do you think is gonna happen?" He tapped the side of his head. "But if they assume you've already mastered aspects of your sorcery... Are you following?"

I nodded along with his words as they sunk in. I had to put on a show so that everyone *thought* I was more of a force to be reckoned with than I was.

"Okay," I murmured. "I'll get up. I'll practice my magic."

Zelfree slapped my back. "Good. Meet me out on the field when you're ready." He stood and left my bedroom without another word.

With what little energy I could muster, I slid off my mattress and dressed. Before I left my room, I glanced at my only personal possessions, which were lying on top of my desk. I had a copper guild pendant. One side was blank, and the other side held the Frith Guild symbol: a sword and shield. Copper symbolized the rank of *journeyman*, but since I was no longer a knightmare arcanist, could I even wear it?

I left the pendant on the desk, uncertain if I should wear it.

My other three items were magical in nature. I took my sword, Retribution, and tied the scabbard to my belt. The black blade had been made from the bone of the legendary and infamous apoch dragon. According to old texts, the apoch dragon was the last god-creature born in a cycle—and the one destined to kill all the others.

It seemed ominous to carry a blade made from his magic-destroying body, but the blade had served me well.

I grabbed my shield, Forfend, and tied it to my left arm. It was an ebony heater shield made from the scale of the previous world serpent and imbued with knightmare magic. Now that I had fixed it, the shield reflected magical attacks. A crafty solution to some problems.

It also seemed ominous to carry around a body part from the first world serpent. The last one had died, despite his powerful abilities and status as *Warlord of Magic*.

The last magical item I had was a cape. But not just any cape.

Luthair's cape.

It hung on the back of the desk chair, the outside pitch black, and the inner lining a picture of the night sky. The stars of the sky still twinkled, betraying the clothing's deep inherent magic. Luthair had said that a knightmare's cape was the most powerful piece of them.

When I ran my hand over the cold fabric, I was reminded of my old knightmare powers.

In theory, I could craft this cape into a magical item—a trinket or an artifact—so long as I had the star shards to do so. But I hadn't yet. I still hadn't learned any of my world serpent magic, and I didn't want anyone else to touch the cape. My father was a talented artificer. He could transform the cape into something amazing, but *I* wanted to be the one to do it.

Luthair deserved the best, and my god-arcanist magic would transform the cape into an epic artifact, I was sure of it.

I left the cape on the back of the chair. I didn't want to ruin it by wearing it while training, and it wouldn't technically do anything magical for me until it was imbued.

After a long exhale, I glanced down at my shirt. Most arcanists kept their marks visible. What should I do with mine? Keep my shirt half-open? Not wear a shirt? Neither seemed appealing.

I kept my shirt completely buttoned to the collar, hiding my mark. Everyone in the Frith Guild knew, anyway. Everyone. The other arcanists, even the apprentices, had helped to excavate the world serpent's lair. Star shards had grown from the massive tree lair, and it had required several hours to find and scavenge them all. Terrakona had helped, and I had been riding on his crystal-mane the entire time.

With all my equipment on my person, I headed down the stairs and out the door to my quarters.

I disliked wandering through the Frith Guild.

That hadn't always been the case, but ever since I had bonded to the world serpent, the others had treated me... differently. Even when I'd had a glowing arcanist mark from my true form knightmare, they hadn't stared as much as they did now. And it wasn't just staring. The other arcanists leapt out of my way if ever our paths crossed. Even master arcanists who were several decades older than me... They all fled the moment I got close.

Were they scared? It bothered me. It reminded me of when I'd had the arcane plague, and people hadn't trusted me.

As I entered the front room of the manor house, Journeyman Reo the Ogata Toad Arcanist almost stumbled into me. He was a few years older than me, but he didn't look like it. Even though he was six feet tall, I had a few inches on him, and while Reo had been training as an ogata toad arcanist for several years, he had never developed any combat skills. I had grown muscular from wielding a sword, and training morning, noon, and night. In all ways, I was more imposing.

Reo straightened his glasses and smoothed his robes. He wore black and dark red, and I suspected he wasn't from the islands. Islanders tended toward trousers and thick coats—my favorite type of clothing—and people from the landlocked cities tended to prefer robes made of finer material.

"P-Pardon me," he mumbled. "I d-didn't mean to d-disturb you."

Reo kept his eyes on his shoes as he shuffled backward.

His ogata toad—a human-adult-sized toad with a bright neon-blue belly and glossy, ebony skin—stood behind Reo on all four feet. Reo half-tripped on his own eldrin in an attempt to distance himself from me.

Ogata toads had lean and muscular bodies, unlike the normal toads at a pond. Reo's eldrin bounded out of the way. "Careful, my arcanist," the toad whispered. Then the toad shifted his golden eyes over to me and stared.

"You don't have to worry about me," I said as I rubbed the back of my neck.

"Uh, w-well, I'm not accustomed to addressing god-arcanists," Reo said, fidgeting with the hem of his sleeves. "Should I c-call you *Your Highness*? Or *Your D-Divinity*? The texts don't discuss th-this level of etiquette."

I shook my head. "Look, I'm just the adopted son of a gravekeeper. I don't need this level of—"

"No, no," Reo interjected. He fixed his glasses, pushing them farther up his nose. "Everyone should've known you were more than just a gravedigger. You w-were the arcanist who joined the guild with a fully grown eldrin."

"That could've happened to anyone," I said with a nervous laugh.

"You w-were also the arcanist who made himself an a-artifact shield, even as an apprentice. Most apprentices don't even c-create trinkets."

"Uh, well, my shield was more of an accident, really. I had to keep the pirates from using the scale..."

"*You* were the one who achieved a true form with his e-eldrin, despite not even being a master arcanist." Reo finally glanced up and met my gaze. "It was o-obvious from the start. Of course you would become one of the g-god-arcanists."

I caught my breath, unsure of what to say. No one had ever listed my achievements like that. Then again, I didn't consider those my finest moments. In my mind, Luthair and I had helped each other achieve everything. It hadn't been *just* me.

"You don't have to treat me differently now," I said. "I'd prefer to just *be normal* for a little while."

"This is your new n-normal," Reo replied.

His words stuck in my mind.

Reo wrung out his hands. "I suppose, as a friend, addressing you in a casual manner w-wouldn't be inappropriate." He narrowed his eyes and frowned. "We *are* friends, aren't we?"

In truth, I barely knew the man, but he had been with the Frith Guild longer than I, and if Guildmaster Eventide trusted him, *I* trusted him.

"Yeah," I said. "We're friends."

"Thank the good winds." Reo chuckled. "Life would be difficult, otherwise, I imagine."

"Uh, right," I muttered as I stepped around them, my hands in my trouser pockets. "Good seeing you, Journeyman Reo."

With sluggish movements, I exited the guild manor house and walked into the ocean breeze. Water stretched out in all directions. Every horizon looked the same. I inhaled and enjoyed the tang of sea salt as I shambled through the garden.

Other arcanists were outside. My sleep-addled mind almost didn't recognize them at first, but I shook away the mental cobwebs.

Hexa and her hydra stood by the Frith Guild's fountain. Her

cinnamon hair, puffy and curly, jostled in the ocean winds. She had most of it tied back, but her locks had a will of their own. Her wild hairdo matched her exuberant expression, and her proudly displayed scars. She embodied the word *untamable*.

Her hydra eldrin, Raisen, had gotten larger again.

He had five heads, and one of them wasn't like the rest. The others were snake-like and covered in prickly scales, but the fifth had massive horns and giant fangs that couldn't be contained by its mouth. When had the last head spawned? All five heads turned their golden eyes to me.

I froze and stared back.

"Hey, Volke," Hexa called out, waving. "You look terrible. Get some more sleep."

She was the only one who hadn't treated me differently since I had bonded to the world serpent. I waved back and forced a smile. Then I continued on my way out of the garden.

The Frith Guild was bursting with new arcanists. Guildmaster Eventide had been busy, and it showed. The entire crew of the *Sun Chaser* had joined our ranks, adding four new arcanists, two of whom were considered master level: Captain Devlin the Roc Arcanist, and my father, Jozé Blackwater the Blue Phoenix Arcanist.

Guildmaster Eventide had also taken the remaining khepera from the city of New Norra. Khepera were the only mystical creatures capable of "curing" the arcane plague, since they had magical abilities that involved rewinding time and soothing souls. As long as the khepera could get to a person who had been infected *recently*, they could remove the effects, making them valuable creatures to the entire world.

Vethica stood on the edge of the field next to the guild manor house, training two individuals who had recently bonded with khepera. Vethica was the most proficient with khepera magic, but she had only been an arcanist for less than half a year. She was an apprentice training other apprentices.

Technically, Master Zelfree was a mimic arcanist. His mimic, Traces, could take the form of the khepera and they could help train the new arcanists, but it seemed he was just too busy.

As I walked out across the back of the massive atlas turtle, far into the emerald field of grass, people from the manor house stared out the windows. I glanced over my shoulder, briefly counting at least twenty faces. I offered them a quick wave, and several people ducked out of sight.

Master Zelfree waited near the opposite end of the field, close to the atlas turtle's head. He wore a shirt with no sleeves, which surprised me. He normally wore multiple layers of black clothing—shirts, coats, heavy trousers, belts, and a scabbard. It was still a black shirt, but it showed more skin than normal. Like Hexa, Zelfree had scars, but unlike Hexa's, his appeared rough and jagged.

His black hair had grown out a bit, but he kept it trimmed and neat, which again, was unusual. Most days, it seemed as though he barely put any effort into his appearance.

When I drew near, the bags under Zelfree's eyes were the only things I could focus on. The dark rings reminded me of a raccoon, or maybe even a trickster coyote. Zelfree ran a hand down his face several times and then yawned.

I also yawned.

It would be a long day.

Zelfree smacked my shoulder. "*Wake up*," he snapped. "We don't have time for this."

"You're one to talk," I quipped.

"I'm personally training your brother, you, *and* Adelgis—and Adelgis's training takes the place of my sleep. Not to mention my new apprentice, Evianna, can't seem to keep out of trouble." He motioned to the field around us. "Arguing about who is more tired is wasting *four* people's time. Just use your magic, and I'll attempt to help you refine it."

I rotated my shoulders. "Are you going to have Traces mimic the world serpent?"

Zelfree shook his head. When he crossed his arms, I took note of his improved muscle tone. He *looked* stronger than I remembered, and I wondered where he found the time for his own personal training. He fidgeted with the bangles on his wrist.

"Traces can't mimic the world serpent," Zelfree muttered. "It's too powerful."

"What if she were true form?"

He gave me a sarcastic glower. "Oh, yeah. I hadn't thought of *that*. I'll fit my own personal training in between everyone else's."

I chuckled once and then shrugged. "The Mother of Shapeshifters is with us now. Maybe she would know how to make your mimic true form."

Zelfree snapped his fingers. "Listen," he said. "Focus on you. C'mon. You've evoked magic before. Let's see it now."

I glanced down at my hands. Then I stepped away from Zelfree and stared out at the watery horizon. After a deep breath, I held up a hand. I attempted to *push* my magic through my body—to have it emanate out of my palm, and into the world—but nothing happened. The straining hurt my chest and arms, but it wasn't a familiar hurt, like using magic with Luthair. This was just... a dull ache.

"I've already tried this," I said, lowering my hand. "Nothing happens."

Zelfree waved a hand around. "Try again."

"I told you—I can't."

"Just humor me, kid. I need to see for myself."

Zelfree stepped closer. With his hair tied back into a short ponytail, it was easy to see the arcanist mark on his forehead: a blank seven-pointed star. Then it changed. An image of a phoenix appeared on his skin, etching itself into his flesh as I stood by and watched.

The bangles on his wrist changed at the same time. At first, they were steel, but then they became red, feathered, and glowing hot. A phoenix formed and spread her wings. With an elegant cry, she flapped her wings and took the sky, littering the field with soot.

Traces. His mimic. I loved the way she shifted her shape. I watched her fly off into the distance. Perhaps she was irritated that Zelfree had forced her to transform. Was her bangle-form comfortable? I didn't know.

Then Zelfree held up a hand. A torrent of white-hot flame exploded from his palm, burning up a small portion of the grass. When he closed his hand, the fire stopped.

"I've seen you evoke your terrors as a knightmare arcanist," he said as he glanced over. "It's the exact same. You can handle this."

I nodded once and held up my hand a second time.

When I had first evoked terrors, I'd had my eyes closed, so I exhaled and did the same. All I needed to do was focus.

Gritting my teeth, I attempted to force my magic through my body and then outward. Again, the strain hurt me. What was this feeling? Why was it happening? I wasn't second bonded to Terrakona. So why the agony? Did it have something to do with my soul being injured because of Luthair's death? That was why Terrakona wanted me to rest.

When I opened my eyes, nothing had happened.

"See?' I asked. "This is what happens every time. Terrakona says I should rest."

Zelfree clicked his tongue in a dismissive, "*Tch.*" With a tense stance, he turned to face me directly. "That's it?" He grabbed my shirt and jerked me forward. "What would you do if the Second Ascension attacked us? What would you do if another god-arcanist came here looking for blood?"

I stared at him, my eyelids heavy, but my heart beating fast. "I'd figure something out," I muttered. "I always do."

"No, you don't," Zelfree said, tightening his grip on my clothing. "Getting infected with the plague to save Evianna wasn't you *thinking of something*."

I curled my hands into fists.

Zelfree scoffed. "And all of us barely making it out of the world serpent's lair wasn't *brilliant strategizing*. You might think well on your feet, but you can't rely on that." He released my shirt and pushed me away. His shove had angry force behind it. "Do you remember when I said *don't practice until you get it right —practice until you can't get it wrong*?"

"Yes," I said as I rubbed at my chest. "I do."

"Then why haven't you listened? Sacrificing yourself—*or quitting*—neither of those are options anymore. The only option is to win. That's what it means to be the world serpent arcanist—to take the title of *Warlord*."

Zelfree's fatigue mixed with his naturally gruff voice, gave him a tone of jaded seriousness. And he spoke with such gravitas that it took me a moment to remember we were still on the back of the atlas turtle and not in the midst of a life-or-death battle.

Was he really speaking to me? Or was he speaking to himself? For a brief moment, I wondered.

"Maybe I should start with something besides evocation," I said. "It's too painful. Maybe I should manipulate something. The last world serpent could change the terrain, right?" I glanced around. "Can I manipulate Gentel's shell?" I half-laughed at my own question. "Does it even count as *terrain*?"

After a long exhale, Zelfree waved away the comment. "Yeah, that's a good idea. We should start somewhere else. I doubt you can manipulate the soil on Gentel, since it's actually part of the atlas turtle, but—"

"*Volke, Master Zelfree,*" a telepathic voice said, echoing in my mind like a shout down a long hallway.

I shook my head. "Adelgis?"

"*Captain Devlin has spotted something off our starboard side,*" Adelgis continued. "*Two airships and a pair of merchant vessels.*"

"Airships?" Zelfree asked, his eyebrows knitted together. "What kind of airships?"

"*The kind flying black flags with roc insignias.*"

I clenched my jaw, my heart hammering hard.

Those were the flags flown by sky pirates.

3

GALLUS THE GRAY

"What flags are the merchant ships flying?" Zelfree asked aloud, despite the fact Adelgis was speaking to us in our minds.

"*The merchant vessels have flags with dragons and roses,*" Adelgis replied matter-of-factly.

"They hail from the Argo Empire," I muttered. "Should we intervene?"

Zelfree crossed his scarred arms. Then he motioned to the guild manor house with a jerk of his head. "Eventide will determine that."

"Those airships will destroy two normal sailing ships with ease," I said.

"The ships could have powerful arcanists of their own aboard."

I turned my attention to the starboard horizon. The ocean waves, as well as the glare of the sun on the water, made it difficult to see anything without a spyglass, but when I squinted, I could make out the faint black dots of ships not far from our location.

What would people say if they knew the world serpent arcanist ran from a couple of sky pirates?

"Adelgis," I said. "What has Guildmaster Eventide said?"

Before he could answer, Gentel turned her massive turtle head in the direction of the ships. The whole guild had altered course, and we were now heading north to fight the pirates.

"Guildmaster Eventide has asked that I telepathically request everyone go to their rooms," Adelgis said. *"Except for the master arcanists."*

I took a deep breath. "What about me?"

"Eventide asked me to request your assistance in this matter."

Request my assistance?

I gave Zelfree a quick glance. He smirked and replied with, "You *are* a trained fighter. Stick close to me and Terrakona, and perhaps you can discover your magic through experience."

He was right. "I'll help," I said.

"I'll let Eventide know your decision."

The reply confused me. Eventide had never done anything like this before. She was the one who gave orders, not gently requested them. Would this continue now that I was the world serpent arcanist? Would she always separate me from the others?

After a moment of staring at the grass, I turned back to Zelfree.

"Eventide won't think less of you if you sit this one out," he said.

"No, you're right. I need to do this." I placed my hand on the hilt of my blade. "Even if I can't use my magic yet, Terrakona is powerful, and I've trained for years with the sword." And as the world serpent arcanist, I didn't have the luxury of sitting it out. Everyone would be watching.

Gentel cut through the ocean waves with the ease of a dragon's claw through flesh.

The only individuals out on the atlas turtle's shell were Captain Devlin, Master Zelfree, Guildmaster Eventide, my father, and Gillie the Grand Apothecary. Their eldrin—except for the guildmaster's—stood out more than the arcanists.

Mesos, the giant golden-feathered roc, was the largest of the bunch. Well, not larger than Gentel, but not even Terrakona was larger than the atlas turtle. As a full-grown roc, Mesos weighed as much as eight horses, and had a wingspan of more than forty feet. Her black talons and beak shone in the sunlight, each sharp enough to rend flesh. Rocs were known as *the dragons of birds*, and I could see why. Mesos could eat a man in a few small bites.

My father's blue phoenix, Tine, on the other hand, was much smaller. She was peacock-shaped and weighed nearly a hundred and fifty pounds. Her sapphire feathers glittered with her movement, and the fire of her body pulsed with inner life.

Gillie's caladrius—another bird creature, amusingly—was named Alana. She was the smallest of the feathered eldrin, but her glistening golden beak made her seem just as mystical as the others. Alana sat on Gillie's shoulder, her feathers whiter than snow.

Zelfree's mimic, Traces, circled around his feet, now in her cat-form. She rubbed her feline body along his calves, purring the entire time. Her tail was long enough that it reached up to his hip. Her gray fur shimmered with each step.

Ocean winds rushed over the shell. Guildmaster Eventide stepped toward the edge of her atlas turtle's shell. She had all the swagger of a swashbuckler. Her knee-high boots, sword, pistol, and tricorn cap almost gave her the appearance of a pirate. Her guild pendant, however, dispelled that misconception.

Her glowing arcanist mark, shimmering white, reminded

me that she had a true form atlas turtle. I had once had such a mark...

Her long coat, stitched together in odd patches and made from various mystical creatures, was unique. I didn't know for sure, but if I had to guess, I would say it was a powerful artifact she kept on her person at all times.

I wasn't sure what it did, though. Given the phoenix feathers, unicorn fur, and griffin teeth, the coat was eclectic. Could multiple mythical creatures be made into a single item?

"We'll be on top of them in a matter of minutes," Eventide said.

Although arcanists lived unnaturally long lives due to their magic, most never seemed to age much. Eventide, however, had gray hair tied back in a tight braid. She appeared much older than I suspected she was, but when she spoke, she had the vigor of someone still in their prime.

"What's the plan?" Captain Devlin asked.

He stroked at his beard—it had once been neatly trimmed into a chinstrap, but it had grown out over the past few weeks, leaving him scruffy. It reminded me of men who had been on a ship a few weeks longer than they had intended.

"The sky pirates are likely roc arcanists," Eventide stated. "We'll be fighting in the sky. Most pirates aren't masters of their magic, so I doubt they'll be using hurricane auras."

Gillie, a shorter woman with a wide smile, tilted her head. "Your atlas turtle magic will shield us, won't it?"

"Yes, but I might not be able to defend the two merchant ships in time."

"Why go after them?" Jozé asked. "You said we had to reach Fortuna as soon as possible. Stopping to fight these dastards is just wasting time."

Guildmaster Eventide shook her head. "It's become clear that several dread pirates have allied themselves with the Autarch, and the Second Ascension. For all we know, these sky pirates are out here spreading the arcane plague on their command." Then she turned on her heel and offered my father a smirk. "And I won't leave a group of innocent people in the hands of pirates. It's not in my nature."

I caught my breath and smiled. I had always admired Eventide's bravery. She was the reason the Frith Guild had become so famous.

With the midmorning sun shining down around us, Eventide waved her arm and motioned to Devlin. "Captain," she said, "you'll head to the airships with your roc. Distract them. Don't get close enough to actually fight."

Captain Devlin—a tall and muscular man—gave our guildmaster a sideways glance. He had once been the captain of his own airship, and I was certain he knew a thing or two about aerial combat. He held himself with a fighter's stance, his feet set apart and his movement fluid. He carried two pistols on his belt.

"I'm not weak," Devlin spat. "I can fight a couple of nobodies."

Eventide lifted an eyebrow. "Don't worry. You'll get your chance. But only *after* the merchant ships are safe."

"Heh. Fine." Devlin crossed his arms and leaned his head back. "I'll play the waiting game."

Eventide glanced over at Gillie. "I need you to help the merchant ships. Heal them and guide them away."

"Of course, Liet," Gillie replied, her voice filled with jovialness. "It would be my honor."

"Jozé, I want you to stay here," Eventide said. "I know your leg causes you problems, and for this fight, mobility will be key. If any of our enemies attack Gentel, or somehow manage to breach my barriers, you'll be our surprise defense."

My father nodded once. "You know me so well." Then he tipped his tricorn cap. "Surprises are my specialty."

The guildmaster turned her attention to me. "Volke, I'm

asking that you and Terrakona help protect the merchant ships. I know your world serpent is powerful, but unless he learns to fly, you'll need to keep your focus on the water."

"I understand," I said.

"And what about me?" Zelfree asked. He pointed to the airships—both of which were much easier to see now that we were closing the distance. "You want me to fight some pirates like we used to?"

Eventide shook her head. "No, Everett. I want you to use your chimera aura."

For the first time in a long time, Zelfree tensed and seemed at a loss for words. His mimic perked up her pointed ears and then arched her back.

"Are you sure about that, guildmaster?" Traces asked. "I, uh, don't have much control when I become a chimera..."

"A mimic arcanist's chimera aura is a powerful tool," Eventide said in a gentle tone. "Our foes are constantly inventing new ways to gain the edge in this battle. We cannot afford to avoid using some of our strongest abilities."

A while back, Adelgis had shown me some of Zelfree's memories. In them, Zelfree had failed to create his aura properly, and Traces had had to be stopped through the use of Calisto's manticore venom, which interfered with magical abilities. We didn't have a manticore with us this time, though. What would happen if Zelfree really lost control?

I glanced over. Zelfree stared at his boots, still tense. Then he rotated his shoulders and replied to the guildmaster with a casual smirk. "I won't disappoint you."

Eventide smiled. "You're one of my most reliable arcanists, Everett. Even when you don't quite follow commands, you always manage to come through."

I could tell Zelfree's smile was only for show. An awkward stillness came over the man, and I wondered if he doubted his own magic.

I also found it ironic that Eventide had called him out for operating by the seat of his pants. Not because that was bad, but because Zelfree had *just* scolded me for the same damn thing. Perhaps I had learned the behavior from him? I shook my head. No. I had always been impulsive. Even Gravekeeper William had said so.

"Any questions?" Eventide asked, her braid fluttering in the powerful wind.

We were close. The two airships tore through the sky, fueled by magic. And just as suspected, the captains of these sky vessels had roc eldrin. The two rocs blazed through the clouds and dove for the merchant ships. One roc smashed into the mizzenmast and ripped it clean off the deck. The other roc slammed into the waves. At first, I thought it had missed, but then I noticed the ten giant tentacles just below the surface.

They belonged to a kraken, a gargantuan mystical creature of the sea.

"Wait a minute," Eventide said as she tilted her cap back. "Is that Gallus?"

"Who?" Devlin snapped.

I stepped forward, my excitement building. "That's Gallus the Gray's eldrin! He's a kraken arcanist and a member of the Frith Guild."

"A kraken arcanist? Out here in the middle of nowhere?" Devlin shielded his eyes from the sun and then snorted. "And why hasn't *he* been sailing with us?"

Eventide lowered her cap. When she spoke, it was with a hint of genuine amusement. "I ordered Gallus and Yesna to answer requests for the Frith Guild while we handled the bigger problems. If Gallus is here, it's likely because he's looking for us."

Yesna? The Ace of Cutlasses?

I had met both Gallus and Yesna before the Sovereign Dragon Tournament, but I still got chills at the thought of fighting alongside them. I had read so many stories about their exploits. They had swashbuckled their way through countless dangers!

"Yesna isn't with them," Zelfree stated. "I don't sense her siren magic."

Eventide pointed to the merchant ships. "Just Gallus, then. He'll need our help." She motioned to Zelfree. "What other mystical creatures do you sense?"

"I can sense roc, wyvern, hippogriff, kraken, and mermaid magics. I can't tell how much of each, though."

"Safe to assume the mermaids and kraken—all creatures unable to fly—are with the merchants." Eventide smiled. "No more wasting time. Let's go."

Mesos threw back her head and screeched. The vicious shriek blasted my ears, and I flinched as she spread her massive wings. Devlin didn't flinch. He smiled and then leapt onto her back, his movement aided by a gust of wind that lifted him high enough to land on top of his eldrin.

"Last one there is lost to the abyssal hells," he said with a chuckle.

Then Mesos flapped her wings and took to the sky. Her wingbeats sent powerful bursts of air across the atlas turtle shell. With amazing agility, she headed straight for the nearest airship. Would Devlin hold off on fighting, like Eventide wanted? Devlin wasn't an arcanist from the guild system—he had run his own mercenary group for some time.

"Let's get closer, Traces," Zelfree said. He ran to the edge of the shell and then jumped off the side.

His eldrin chased after, her fur standing on end. "You know I hate water! Get back here!" Despite her protests, she, too, went off the side of the atlas turtle. Just before she disappeared from my sight, her body bubbled and shifted, her fur shimmering with magic. A couple of squid-like tentacles sprouted from her body, and I knew that Zelfree was mimicking Gallus's powerful kraken.

Not a bad a plan. Krakens were kings of the waves, just short of leviathans.

I ran to the edge of the atlas turtle shell. If we managed to regroup with Gallus, we'd have another master arcanist to help fight against the Second Ascension. And Gallus was known for his cunning battle style, his charismatic charm, and his ability to find hidden treasures lost in shipwrecks. I had read stories about how he had defeated master arcanists in ship combat using his knowledge of the island rocks to his advantage.

Once reunited, we would travel together for a long while, which meant I would have an opportunity to speak to Gallus the Gray about all his many adventures. Was everything they had written about him true? Was his brother, Gali the Red, really as terrible as the stories made him out to be?

But I gritted my teeth and refocused on the immediate. I had to help fight the pirates and protect the merchant ships. After a long exhale, I secured the buckles of the shield on my left forearm and checked to make sure Retribution was in its scabbard.

"Terrakona!" I shouted.

The ocean shuddered as the world serpent swam toward the waves. His jade scales caught the light as he rose to the surface, glittering like lost treasure. The crystals that made up his mane, however, were as black as night and absorbed the rays of light that drew near, creating darker shadows around his head.

"You have called for me, Warlord?" Terrakona telepathically asked.

"We ride for those ships," I said as I leapt from the atlas turtle. "Let's go!"

4

A NEW STYLE OF COMBAT

I hit the water and plunged a good ten feet deep. The fall from the atlas turtle shell had been further than I had expected—perhaps a good twenty feet—and it took a bit of effort for me to curve toward the surface. The ocean had a way of being deceptive. Tides and large waves took swimmers by surprise all the time, but I was an islander with a lifetime's worth of experience. Despite the flow of water, I broke the surface and whipped my head back to keep my messy hair from clinging to my face.

If Luthair had been here, we could've flown to the airships...

I shook the thought from my head before it could take root in my heart and blossom into despair.

Terrakona didn't need any further instruction. He twisted through the water and then lifted underneath me so that I sat on his crystal mane. I held on as tightly as I could. Then Terrakona lunged forward through the water. He raised his head above the waves, taking me with him, and wind whipped through my wet hair as we rushed forward.

The speed...

We were keeping pace with Devlin's roc, racing toward the merchant ships. The waters weren't hindering the world serpent's movement. What would the pirates think of the approaching god-creature? They'd probably assume he was an odd-looking leviathan and nothing more. After all, no one had seen a world serpent in thousands of years. Why would these dastards recognize my eldrin?

We passed Master Zelfree and Kraken-Traces. He gave me a sideways glance from his perch on the tentacle of his eldrin, but I just smirked and waved.

"Terrakona," I said as we closed in on the ships. "We're to protect the merchants from the sky pirates. The men and women aboard are our top priority."

"As you say, Warlord."

My chest twisted into a knot of anxiety. Without magic, how would I fight? I released one hand from Terrakona's mane and placed it on the hilt of Retribution. I'd have to rely on my swordplay. My blade could cut through magic, even barriers and other types of artifact armor. I wasn't useless.

Once we were a hundred feet from the merchant ships, Terrakona veered to the side and stopped his approach. His scales flared as he roared at the vessels. His screech sent a shiver up my spine.

"What's wrong?" I called out.

"Corruption," Terrakona telepathically replied. **"It's all around us. In the water... In the breaths of these villains... It warps magic and drives all insane."**

I leaned forward, almost slipping from Terrakona's mane. My heart hammered against my ribs as I searched for any signs of the arcane plague—it was the ultimate corruption, and I had seen dozens of individuals fall to lunacy while twisted by its influence.

Counting their eldrin, I could tell there were five sky pirate arcanists. They had two rocs, two wyverns, and a hippogriff, each adorned with leather armor and wearing a black bandana. Rocs were considered man-eaters, which meant they were immune to blood diseases, and thus, the plague. But wyverns and hippogriffs weren't man-eaters, which meant they could be twisted by the plague. The wyverns were too far away for me to see any details of their bodies, but the hippogriff flew close enough for me to examine. The pirate's eldrin was just as distorted as I had feared.

Hippogriffs typically had the head, wings, and front legs of an eagle, while having the back end of a horse. The pirate's hippogriff looked as though it were vomiting its own skull—a second eagle-like beak jutted out of the hippogriff's mouth, the new beak jagged and serrated and coated in blood. The hippogriff's milky-white eyes bulged and jiggled, similar to those of a dead fish.

Each time the hippogriff cried out, its voice was laced with psychotic laughter. Its crazed cackling was more disturbing than the whistle of storm winds or the crack of freshly broken bones.

When I'd had Luthair in his true form, I couldn't be twisted by the plague, but...

"Terrakona," I whispered. "Can you be infected with the arcane plague?"

"This weak corruption cannot taint my magic."

Relieved by the information, I unsheathed my sword.

"Then we'll handle the hippogriff," I said. "We can't let anyone else get infected." We had someone who could cure it, but I didn't want to take any chances. What if something happened to Vethica? Better to be cautious.

"That tiny creature is but a distraction," Terrakona stated, anger in his telepathic voice. **"It's the ancient guardian of the depths we should be concerned about."**

The guardian of the depths?

Before I could solve his cryptic statement, a man burst out

of the water—straight up, propelled by the waves themselves. He wore a long cloak that fluttered behind him like a shadow of a dragon, but it was his necklace that drew most of my attention. The silver pendant glinted in the sunlight, the shine contrasting harshly with the black coat.

It was a guild pendant.

The Frith Guild.

"Gallus!" I said with a wave of my hand. "Over here! We've come to help!"

The man turned to me with a quick snap of his head. He fell back into the ocean a moment later, falling faster than the water and mist he had created with his initial jump. Gallus hit the water and plunged deep, disappearing from my sight. When he burst out of the waves a second time, it was in my direction. Kraken arcanists could easily manipulate water, and Gallus used his ability to leap high into the air. Kraken arcanists could also breathe while beneath the surface, and they jetted through the waves without moving any part of their bodies.

Gallus leapt high enough to land atop Terrakona. But the world serpent flared his scales a second time and hissed with the rumble of thunder. A moment before landing, Gallus swiped his hands in front of him and evoked storm winds— gale-force winds, hail, and frigid water, all at once.

I lifted my shield, but not fast enough. I blocked the storm winds from freezing over my face, but the gust of powerful wind knocked me off Terrakona. I tumbled off his crystal mane and fell a good fifteen feet before hitting the water. I lost my breath from the force of the impact. My vision blurred as I sank into the ocean waters, half-paralyzed from the terrible sensation.

Ocean water stung my eyes, but I had long since become accustomed to the bite of salt.

Gallus dove in after me. In half a second, he was on top of me, close enough that I could finally make out more details.

He had a white beard but a thick, black mustache. His bright-blue eyes locked on to mine, his gaze so intense, I could *feel* his hatred. His salt-and-pepper hair fluttered in the water, and bubbles escaped the corners of his mouth, but the ocean didn't seem to bother him in the least. He grabbed the collar of my shirt and twisted his fist, dragging me close.

His arcanist mark was a seven-pointed star with a ten-tentacled squid wrapped around the points—a kraken. But it was different. It glowed, but unlike Guildmaster Eventide's mark, Gallus's shimmered with a crimson hue, sinister in all regards.

The deeper we went, the darker the waters became. Soon, wiggling lines of abstract light and Gallus's mark were the only things I could see. I grabbed Gallus's arm and attempted to swing my sword, but the ocean fought against me. It was *difficult* to get any force behind my swing, but I did it anyway.

Gallus, on the other hand, moved with the grace of a divine fish. He spun away from my attack and then withdrew a blade from a scabbard on his belt. When he slashed, he clipped my stomach, leaving a crimson line across my body.

I had forgotten how much getting hit hurt. With Luthair, I had always had armor...

I coughed and the last of the air rushed out of my lungs. Water slipped in. I hadn't known water could burn so badly until that moment. It seared my throat, my nose, my chest, and my gut. Salt water had a distinct taste, but my tongue didn't work with so much fire in my body.

Gallus swam around and stabbed at me again, this time aiming for my kidney. I spun and slashed with Retribution, and my black blade sliced his sword clean in half. He could probably still use it as a jagged weapon, but instead he released the sword and allowed it to sink to the bottom of the ocean. I thought he would retreat, but I was badly mistaken. Gallus punched me in the center of my chest—an entirely new type of pain.

Despite my agony, I lifted my shield. It pulsed with light amounts of magic. Forfend could reflect attacks, and I had blocked at least *some* of Gallus's initial storm wind attack. With my jaw clenched, I unleashed the stored evocation and blasted Gallus away from me. He swirled through the ocean's tides, obviously caught off guard by my action.

My heart slammed against my ribs so loudly, it reverberated in my ears.

Where was the surface?

Panic clouded my thoughts.

I flailed my arms.

Terrakona!

My eldrin's thoughts lingered at the edge of mine, and I could sense his concern. Although I hadn't been able to sense Luthair's proximity, with Terrakona, it was different. I knew where he was. I knew where he was going.

Getting closer.

And closer.

But I tried to breathe again, and I couldn't. The burning intensified.

My vision darkened.

If I were still a knightmare arcanist, I could slip through shadow, manipulate darkness, evoke terrors—fight in ways I could expect—*but now it was different.* What was I doing?

Something wrapped around my body. An instant later, I was yanked upward. The moment I was pulled from the ocean, I hacked up water and a bit of blood. My sight returned in short waves, slowly becoming clearer as I focused.

Terrakona had dragged me from the depths. Willow trees grew from his body at various locations, each with long limbs and vines. The vegetation moved with a will of its own. The vines pierced the water and grabbed people who had been thrown from the merchant ship, carrying them to safety.

"Terra...kona..." I said through my wheezing. "Thank you..."

"We are the earth and tides, Warlord. A wave does not drown. A rock cannot breathe. Stop fighting against yourself."

Master Zelfree's voice rang in my head. He had given me similar advice for my knightmare magic.

A shadow can't fall.

Was I misunderstanding my magic, just as I had with Luthair?

Gallus shot out of the ocean and flew twenty feet into the sky. When he started to fall, he laughed and evoked his storm winds again.

I raised my shield, but it wasn't needed. Terrakona lifted his tail out of the ocean and blocked the blast.

"We need to stop him," I said through my coughs. "He's infected with the plague!"

And if his arcanist mark was glowing red, it meant he was too far gone to help... The red glow indicated his eldrin had transformed into a *dread form* of itself. A product of the arcane plague. A wild monster with no hope of being saved.

When had Gallus been infected? Had it been after the Sovereign Dragon Tournament? It had to have been. Had he been looking for us since then? Had he been hoping we could help him?

Terrakona tensed to attack, but it was too late. Gallus had been a distraction. Tentacles burst from the water all around us. The gigantic kraken snared Terrakona in his grip.

And the kraken was equally infected...

Its tentacles had boils and blisters everywhere. Pus oozed from the open edges of each boil, and the foul yellow liquid looked—and smelled—like lumpy, curdled milk. As the tentacles tighten, blisters constantly formed, as though the creature was boiling from the inside out. Small eyes bulged from the tentacles as well, staring at us with unblinking intensity. For some reason, each time I caught a glimpse, I could've sworn the look they gave us was one of pure agony.

Terrakona screeched as the disgusting tentacles yanked us deeper into the water. His tree-like appendages lashed out at the kraken, but Terrakona was still a hatchling world serpent. His magic was powerful, but a *dread form* kraken was on par with an adult dragon, perhaps more so, since magical corruption was so devastating. And krakens had the advantage in the water.

Even against a world serpent? I didn't know.

Determined to free my eldrin, I leapt down the back of the serpent and slid along his emerald scales until I reached a tentacle. I swung Retribution and slashed clean through the kraken's limb. Black blood splattered across Terrakona and then ran in rivulets into the ocean. A cloud of bloody darkness spread outward.

The kraken lifted its body high enough out of the water that I spotted his beak-like mouth underneath. Normally, the beak looked similar to a bird's. Twisted with the plague, however, it was a maw straight to the abyssal hells. It opened far wider than it should have—ripping the kraken's skin and creating a smile that bled. The kraken's throat was lined with arms and hands, each grasping forward, as if looking to pull something into the kraken's belly.

I had been too busy staring into the void of the kraken's gullet to notice Gallus bursting out of the water next to me. I turned just in time to defend with my shield as he evoked another blast of stormy winds. I tumbled across Terrakona and then went straight back into the ocean. With my breath held, I sank beneath the waves.

I swung my sword. Gallus had already become predictable.

He showed up a moment before I completed the arc of my attack. My black blade sliced through a part of Gallus's arm, but that didn't seem to faze him. He smiled, his beard and mustache distorted with his freakish grin.

Then he swirled his hand around and manipulated the waters.

With all the force of a riptide, I was yanked deeper into the ocean, my breath already burning.

5

WORLD SERPENT EVOCATION

Gallus rushed down to meet me, never giving me a moment's rest. I didn't have another opportunity to slash him with my blade. He punched me and then darted away, keeping his distance and only attacking when he had an opening.

Terrakona!

I sensed my eldrin above, struggling to deal with the plague-ridden kraken. He was preoccupied. Gallus manipulated the waters again, dragging me deeper into the ocean. Through the murky darkness, I spotted a second kraken above me.

Wait, a *second* kraken? Impossible! How could—

I silenced my internal panic and shook my head. No. Focus. I knew the answer. The second kraken was Traces mimicking Gallus's eldrin, but they were so far above me, I doubted they even knew I was drowning.

Unable to reach anyone, I had to handle the problem in front of me: Gallus himself. I had dealt with plague-ridden arcanists in the past. If I wanted to help Terrakona, or even breathe again, I had to fight my way to the surface.

Just as Zelfree had said... Losing wasn't an option.

With superior movement, Gallus slammed another punch into my side. Sharp pain shot through my chest and throat.

I concentrated and forced the magic through my body. For a brief moment, I had forgotten I was bonded to Terrakona—I held out my free hand as though to evoke knightmare terrors. Instead, my body felt hot. Not from a lack of air...

A wave does not drown. A rock cannot breathe.

On instinct, with Terrakona's voice ringing in my head, I took a deep breath, ready for the sting of salt water. Instead, the cold liquid filled my throat and lungs, but it felt... refreshing. Like taking a drink after a long day in the sun. With my heart pounding, I exhaled and inhaled again, elated.

I could breathe underwater.

It wasn't evocation, but an innate ability—those were typically acquired much later in an arcanist's training, yet here it was. Perhaps the first of many?

My momentary celebration cost me. Gallus shot through the water like a pistol shrimp. He punched my kidney, taking away my new "breath" just as fast as I had acquired it. An innate magical ability wouldn't save me here. I didn't know what I could evoke, but I knew I either had to do it *right now* or I was going to die.

And I refused to die.

So, when I focused on my magic a second time, the ocean suddenly began to boil.

Heat ripped through the water so quickly and so intensely that Gallus's smile twisted into a grimace. The water shifted and bubbled. My hearing underwater was bizarre, but it sounded like the waves were crashing near me at an ever-increasing speed.

What had I invoked?

My palm hurt. I pulled it back and held it close to my chest. A pillar of bubbles—superheated and painful—circled around my fingers. I gasped for air and found the water provided me with the breath I needed. I was one with the water.

Whatever I had conjured with my magic, it was destructive. I gritted my teeth and waited until Gallus shot toward me. With as much energy as I could muster, I reached out and grabbed his arm with my burning hand.

Gallus opened his mouth and screamed, the gurgling loud, even underwater. Then he shot toward the surface. I kept my grip tight on his arm, and for some reason, it was easy to hook my heated fingers into his flesh. Gallus dragged me along with him.

He couldn't breathe. He needed to get to the surface.

Together, we burst out of the water and sailed through the sky. I coughed up water as we dropped toward the waves, but I knew I didn't have time to second-guess myself. I swung with Retribution. It was a terrible swing, barely any power and no aim behind it—but I managed to clip Gallus's neck. My sword sliced through him without any resistance. Blood wept from his injury, and as we fell, he smiled.

I let go of him.

"Your magic belongs to me!" Gallus shouted just before crashing beneath the surface.

I hit the water at an odd angle, my shield arm under my body. It hurt as though I had fallen onto packed dirt, but it wasn't enough to rattle me. I swirled through the water and then angled upward. When I broke the surface, I caught sight of Terrakona fighting with the plague-ridden kraken.

"You'll die here," the kraken said, his voice more a deep rumble than anything else. "*I* will be a god in your stead!"

The kraken slammed Terrakona with four tentacles, and when the world serpent lunged forward to bite, the monster used its other tentacles to shove Terrakona away. To my surprise, venom leaked out of Terrakona's massive fangs. The purplish-black liquid splashed into the ocean and a harsh sizzling rang up around us.

For the second I could focus, I noticed Zelfree had used his kraken powers to scoop up the last of the merchants and sailors stranded out in the water. Captain Devlin distracted the pirates with his roc magic. Chills overcame me—Devlin's hurricane aura was building. The sky darkened with his powerful master magic.

The giant atlas turtle, Gentel, had moved close enough that Eventide was able to evoke barriers over the sailing merchant ships. She protected them from the pirates raining down bullets and cannonballs. The balls of metal slammed onto her shimmering barriers and crashed into the water, never harming a soul.

Gallus leapt from the waves and headed in my direction, sliding across the surface of the water, propelled by his stormy winds. As he evoked a gale-force gust, it added to the building hurricane aura, creating winds so powerful that it felt like my skin might tear. I dropped beneath the surface to avoid the attack, and Gallus plunged in after me.

Without thinking, I used my magic again. Scorching heat erupted from my entire body, causing the water to boil. Gallus flailed and twisted and then retreated. What was I evoking? I swam to the surface. Then I brushed my dark hair out of my eyes and stared at my palm.

Molten rock oozed from the creases of my hand. Black rock —obsidian?—had sprouted from my knuckles and the point of my elbow. It startled me, and I tried to rip the rocks from my body, but I couldn't.

What was going on?

Gallus slammed into my back, and I almost dropped Retribution, but I tightened my grip on my weapon. Then the master arcanist got close. He grabbed my throat and squeezed.

Even though I could now breathe underwater, I was *once again* struggling for air.

I couldn't remember what kraken arcanists could augment with their magic—I could barely keep any attention on my surroundings—but Gallus's sorcery stung as it altered my body. In desperation, I used my evocation again, even though I had no idea what I was doing.

Blazing heat unlike anything I had ever felt before flared all around us. The ocean boiled and steamed, my skin oozed with molten rock, and more obsidian sprouted from my body. I burned Gallus with my sorcery, far worse than I had expected. Not because I had touched him... but because he was touching *me*. My entire body had the temperature of a live volcano, and all of my clothes above the waves burned away, leaving me with one sleeve, half a shirt, and my trousers.

"May the abyssal hells curse you," Gallus said through gritted teeth.

He waved his hand and manipulated the waters to drag his body away from mine. His injured hand was seared to the bone. He couldn't uncurl his charred fingers, and he glared at his useless limb for a long moment. When he smiled at me, ice flooded my veins.

"Such power. *Wasted*." Gallus snorted.

I bobbed with the waves, my body more... *jagged*... than I remembered. "Fight that madness!" I shouted. Ocean water splashed in my mouth, and I spit it out as I said, "We have someone who might be able to heal you."

"I don't need healing," Gallus shouted back. "I'm more powerful now than I've ever been. And once I take *your* power, and Eventide's *pure magic*, I'll be able to survive the trek to the abyssal hells."

What?

The battle with Gregory Ruma spun in my head. Ruma had been twisted by the plague, and unlike mystical creatures, who became monsters after becoming infected, arcanists lost their minds. Ruma had attempted to resurrect his dead wife by feeding the plague to her phoenix eldrin. Now Gallus the Gray wanted to survive a trek to the abyssal hells? He likely had an irrational reason fueling his desire for power.

The clouds darkened and gathered overhead. A chorus of roars echoed throughout the area.

Then I saw it.

A gargantuan creature emerged from the waves. It had three heads—one a turtle, one a roc, and one a bulging ball of flesh that resembled a squid.

It was a chimera. One at least half the size of Gentel, perhaps more. Traces? It had to be. This was the power of a mimic arcanist's *chimera aura*. The mimic and their arcanist would gain the magical abilities of three nearby creatures, all combined into one giant monstrosity.

The chimera had a body made of all three creatures as well. It had a twisted shell, flat and cracked in half to allow for two golden wings to sprout from its back. It also had four tentacles jutting from its underbelly, and a tail that was a mix between a lizard's and an eagle's.

Gallus took note of the chimera as well. He kept his good hand on his neck, stifling the blood spilling out into the ocean, while his charred hand remained closed.

I needed to act.

If I'd had my shadow manipulation, I could've used the darkness to wield my sword and slash at Gallus, even though we were a good twenty feet apart. My new evocation wasn't capable of long-range attacks. It seemed localized to my body, radiating from my pores and creating both obsidian and magma.

It gave me an idea.

"You'll never have my magic, Gallus!" I shouted. "I'm far more powerful than you!"

In the stories, Gallus the Gray never turned down a challenge. And even in his crazed state, Gallus slowly turned his full attention to me. Blood soaked the collar of his shirt, but he didn't appear to be concerned.

"My sword can cut through all magic." I held up Retribution. The blade shone in the building storm. "You felt its sting on your neck. Soon I'll have your head."

Gallus chuckled. "Your heat saved you once before, lad, but it won't do you any good this time." He submerged himself in the brine and disappeared from my sight.

I clenched my jaw as I remained above the waves. His tactics wouldn't take me by surprise. I knew what was coming from the many tales I had read. So, when the tides yanked me down, I didn't fight back. When Gallus positioned himself between me and the surface, I didn't attempt to move. And when he reached for my sword, I didn't bother swinging—I kept it close and then wrapped my arms around Gallus the instant I could.

He was faster underwater, but it wouldn't matter as long as I kept a hold of him. I evoked my molten magma and everything burned. I tightened my grip on Gallus as he fought to escape. Obsidian rocks jutted from every joint on my body, like they were extensions of my bone fighting to escape out of the pores of my skin.

The superheated waters, and my contact with Gallus, cooked him right in front of me.

How hot was my evocation? It stung me slightly, but I was obviously immune to the worst of the effects. Perhaps I was just getting used to the heat.

Gallus thrashed and manipulated water and even evoked his winds, which caused whirlpools to form in the ocean, but nothing separated us. My very touch melted his skin and muscles, and the harder I squeezed, the faster Gallus peeled away.

The waters became murky with scarlet clouds of blood. His "chum" unnerved me, but I refused to let go. I closed my eyes and continued to focus on the magic coursing throughout my body. Gallus didn't stand much of a chance. In a matter of seconds, half his body had been liquefied by my evocation. I released him only once he stopped struggling.

Then I headed to the surface, the heat in my chest subsiding. A blast of stormy winds greeted me once I made it above the waves. Luckily, I managed to concentrate.

But I didn't even have time to celebrate my victory over Gallus the Gray.

Terrakona and Zelfree's chimera had both engaged in combat with the pirate rocs, the hippogriff, and the twisted kraken.

6

A CLASH OF TITANS

Tidal waves dominated our tiny corner of the ocean. Not only did we have a hurricane aura, but the gargantuan creatures battling for survival added to the fury of nature.

Swimming on the surface was nearly impossible. Instead, I dove underwater and swam forward with as much strength as I could, breathing easy the entire way. The obsidian on my knuckles, knees, elbows, fingers, and shoulders made me feel... awkward. In my mind, I was some sort of twisted monster, but when I caught sight of myself, I remembered Luthair.

When we had merged, he had covered me in black, shadowy armor. This obsidian... it was different, but familiar. Was it my protection? Was it an offense? A useless byproduct? I didn't know. I'd have to practice with it more.

The stormy waters made it difficult to see and swim, especially with my sword, but I sensed Terrakona and then headed in his direction. Waters with blood were warmer than the icy ocean currents. I swam through warm patch after warm patch, trying not to think about the gore.

I angled toward the surface, ready to fight whatever I came across. Before I reached my destination, vine-like branches from a willow tree wrapped around me and yanked me out of the depths. Terrakona, without needing instruction, lifted me into his crystal mane, all while lashing at the corrupted kraken with his tail.

I tightened the straps of my shield and corrected my grip on my blade.

Rain beat down on everything—me, the ocean, the ships, the pirates—and nothing I did kept the water out of my eyes. Still, I attempted to shield my gaze.

Zelfree's chimera screeched with its roc and turtle heads. The kraken-portion of its body didn't make a noise, but multiple tentacles rose from the waves.

The dread form kraken whipped the chimera with its puss-covered tentacles. The resulting cracks sounded like thunder in the storm. But the chimera wasn't hurt. The beast had access to *atlas turtle* magic, and a barrier shimmered into existence before anything could touch it.

Terrakona rushed forward through the waves. I almost lost my balance, but I kept hold of the crystal mane. Terrakona struck at the kraken, his fangs flashing in the storm. The pirate rocs—both wearing leather armor on their chests and heads—dove for Terrakona's eyes. Their talons were as large as a man and sharp enough to pierce metal. Terrakona stopped his attack and dodged away, but not fast enough. The attacking rocs still drew blood. Their talons punctured the scales on Terrakona's face and nose.

When the rocs flapped their wings, they took to the hurricane skies in an instant.

The hippogriff swooped in to attack Terrakona where he was injured, but this beast was too slow, and too outclassed. Terrakona opened his maw, struck forward, and crunched the hippogriff between his venomous fangs. The plague-ridden creature was dead in an instant.

Cannonballs flew down from the airships, pelting the waves

like hail. Guildmaster Eventide created more barriers—this time, protecting me and Terrakona from the cannons.

Captain Devlin shot down from the black clouds, riding his roc eldrin. Mesos clashed with a pirate roc, tearing into the enemy with her talons. Devlin manipulated the winds to jostle the airships, and the enemy pirates responded with bullets and wind magic of their own.

What was I going to do?

I had to deal with the kraken. It was the threat that Terrakona and I could handle.

Without Gallus the Gray, the kraken didn't have an arcanist, but that didn't cut off its magic. The kraken would just be enraged—every eldrin that lost its arcanist always went through intense pain. And the monster fought like it had nothing to live for. It lashed out in all directions.

And the water...

I caught my breath once I realized the dread form kraken was creating a whirlpool. The waters swirled and swirled, becoming ever more dangerous with each passing moment. The diameter of the vortex grew larger, threatening to take the merchant ships and even the atlas turtle down to the depths.

Master Zelfree and his chimera entered the colossal whirlpool. He tried to counteract the magic, but Zelfree's mimic couldn't copy true form magic, nor could she copy dread form magic, both of which boosted a mystical creature's capabilities. The monster kraken had more power over the ocean due to the corruption running through its veins.

And while they fought for control of the water, Captain Devlin struggled to keep control of the sky. The sky pirates leapt onto their rocs and teamed up against Mesos. They clashed in the wind-torn skies, their talons deadly. Golden feathers, ripped from the giant rocs, got caught in the storm and flew off into the dark clouds.

Eventide and Gentel swam out of the whirlpool, and they

used their barriers to drag the merchants and their ships with them.

With his chimera aura active, Zelfree would have access to three kinds of magic. Eventide was invulnerable. But Devlin only had Mesos, and he was pitted against two mystical creatures and their arcanists. They came at him with pincer strategies—one on the right, one on the left—attacking relentlessly.

"Terrakona!" I shouted. "Focus your attention on the rocs!"

"**As you say,**" Terrakona telepathically replied.

We couldn't fly, but Terrakona was large enough to reach the enemy if he stretched upward. We couldn't swim straight for them, however. The rocs would fly away if they saw us coming.

"Go beneath the waves," I commanded. "We'll jump up at them from underneath!"

Terrakona dove into the ocean with me on his back, and we glided through the water with ease. When Terrakona turned for the surface, I tensed. We broke into the sky and with one hand, I held on to Terrakona, and with the other, I brandished my blade.

We didn't leap out of the water—Terrakona just stretched his body up high enough—and fast enough—that we took the enemy by surprise. The massive rocs flew higher in the storm-filled skies, just out of reach. If we had gone ten feet farther, Terrakona could've sank his fangs into the bird. The pirate arcanist glared down at us, a sneer on his bearded face. The man pulled out three throwing knives and hurled them down.

Two hit Terrakona, and then clinked harmlessly off his scales. The last was aimed at me, but I lifted my shield and deflected the knife, saving myself from injury.

Then I focused on using my new evocation. Heat erupted from me so fast that the rain around me became an unending steam. As molten rock formed in the creases of my palm, I hurled it up at the nearest roc and its pirate rider. It felt like slinging mud, but the bright flash of blazing lava was a far more impressive projectile.

My molten rock struck the roc on the leg, just above its taloned foot. The massive bird screeched and then nearly fell from the sky in pain. I held my breath as it flew in a half-circle and then dove for me and Terrakona. At ridiculous speeds, the roc and its rider rushed us. The bird didn't aim for Terrakona's head—it aimed for the long, serpentine body that was exposed above the water. With deadly talons, the roc slashed open a portion of Terrakona's body.

I never knew the talons of a roc could be so dangerous...

But the roc hadn't cut deeply enough. The superficial wound barely bled, and the roc had made the terrible mistake of getting close.

The pirate threw three more knives—each carried by his powerful wind evocation—and they shot at us like bullets. All of them bounced off of Terrakona's scales. The knives weren't powerful enough, even when propelled with magic.

Terrakona lunged for the roc before it could fly too high. He clipped the gigantic bird creature with a single fang.

I didn't know how deadly world serpent venom was, but in that instant, I had a better idea. The roc shuddered and thrashed, and then it stopped moving, paralyzed mid-flap. It plummeted from the sky, twisting as it went. Halfway to the ocean, the beast went limp, and the pirate leapt off and landed in the water.

With more courage than I than I expected of a sea thief, he dragged himself out of the waves and managed to get on the back of Terrakona's massive serpent body. I stepped off the crystal mane and slid down the jade scales. The pirate spotted my approach and then threw more daggers, but I blocked them with my shield and then rushed forward the moment I had proper footing.

The sea thief wore leather armor—it pulsed with magic—but I didn't care. I swung upward with Retribution, cutting clean through his whole body. His arm. His chest. His shoulder. One upward strike was all it took. My blade didn't even seem to register the man's bones. It startled me a bit how clean the slash was.

But I quickly shook away the feeling. I had seen Retribution in action before. The bones of the apoch dragon tore through anything magical.

One roc and his arcanist were dead.

When I glanced up into the sky. The storm was fading.

Captain Devlin and Mesos were caught up in an intense battle with another arcanist pirate. Captain Devlin had likely lost his concentration and couldn't maintain his hurricane aura. The clearer the skies became, the easier the airships could maneuver through the sky.

At first, I feared they might attack us, but Eventide was still close enough to defend us with her magical barriers. Then I realized their actual intentions—both airships turned and started their retreat.

"Terrakona," I said from down on his lower back. "The last roc! Focus on that!"

Although the storm had waned, the kraken's whirlpool continued to rage. Zelfree's chimera and the plague-ridden kraken slammed into each other, one evoking barriers and winds, and the other evoking hail and yellowish gases. Plague blood circled in the waters, but Zelfree would be fine so long as he had man-eating roc magic coursing through his veins. The man-eater mystical creatures were immune to blood diseases...

I just hoped Zelfree wouldn't die the old-fashioned way.

Terrakona struck upward, but Devlin and the pirate roc were too high in the sky. The trees and vines growing off Terrakona's back shimmered with powerful magics. Vines shot into the sky, all aiming for the enemy bird. But the enemy roc evoked winds and went even higher up, nearly touching the fading clouds.

"Captain!" I shouted. "Here!" I motioned him to our location.

Normally, I'd be too far away for anyone to see me, but roc arcanists had the innate ability to see at long ranges, much like eagles and hawks. Devlin immediately angled Mesos for us. They dove for Terrakona's location, and the enemy roc flew toward the airships, as I had hoped.

When Devlin drew close, I shouted, "Attack the airships! Get them into range of Terrakona."

For a split second, I feared Devlin wouldn't take my commands—he had fought against Guildmaster Eventide, after all—but to my relief, he replied with a curt nod and whistled for Mesos to attack the airships. They took off as a team with no further questions.

My heart pounded, even as confidence fueled me.

Terrakona lowered his head, and I climbed back up his crystal mane. It was difficult climbing with the obsidian rock jutting from various points on my body, but I managed. Together, we swam through the chaotic waves, heading in the direction of the airships. The pirate roc attempted to attack Devlin, but Mesos flew with precision. She and Devlin shot past the enemy bird and used their powerful gale-force winds to rattle the airships.

The enemy roc swooped back around and used its own wind magic, but by this point it was too late. The airships were forced to descend, and Terrakona was ready. With all the power of a coiled snake, he leapt up from the ocean and crunched a portion of the airship in his massive mouth, the wood splintering and cracking so loud, it hurt my ears.

The second airship attempted to ascend, but Terrakona lashed out before it could escape. Again, Terrakona took a bite out of the flying vessel, shattering the wood and magic that kept it afloat. I held on to my eldrin, smiling to myself once I knew they would never be able to escape.

The pirate roc and his arcanist, likely sensing their defeat, shot into the sky, flying as fast as they could.

But where would they go? Without their airships, they had no place to land. We were in the middle of the ocean, after all. They were flying away from us, but straight to their deaths.

"I'm heading back to the guild house," Devlin shouted as he and Mesos flew by.

It was only then that I saw their injuries. Mesos had been injured by the enemy's many attacks. Blood wept from slashes and bullet wounds. Even Devlin looked as though he had been through a tornado of daggers.

When Terrakona turned around to survey the fight, I was able to witness the last of Zelfree's clashes. His chimera caught the plague-ridden kraken before it could escape. The turtle head and roc head grabbed the squid-like kraken on opposite sides. With brutal strength, the two heads ripped the kraken apart, slowly tearing the monster in half.

Blood gushed from the giant body, pouring into the ocean like a crimson lake had been dumped into the waves.

"Let's go," I said, tapping Terrakona.

The world serpent nodded and headed into the dying whirlpool.

The kraken gurgled a bloody scream and then collapsed into the ocean, sinking below the surface until he was swallowed by the darkness. But I hadn't urged Terrakona close because I was worried about the kraken—Zelfree had admitted concern about his chimera aura, and I knew he hadn't fully mastered it.

The final swirl of the whirlpool left the ocean filled with gore. Terrakona swam through the kraken flesh and blood, unconcerned. When we drew closer to Zelfree's chimera, I tensed.

"Be careful," I said, more to myself than Terrakona.

"Agreed," Terrakona telepathically replied. **"We must be ready for anything if we are to be victorious, and occasionally that will require patience. We must act at the correct moment."**

The massive three-headed creature waded through the calming ocean, its kraken head splashing through the waves with four tentacles. When the turtle and roc heads roared, the hair on my body stood on end. Then the chimera thrashed and shuddered. Its two golden wings stretched wide, but I suspected the beast couldn't fly—it was too awkwardly shaped. The atlas turtle portion was heavy and gigantic.

When the chimera turned its three heads in my direction, I knew we would have to deal with it. Its six eyes were crazed.

"Don't use your venom," I said. "Just subdue it!"

Zelfree's eldrin wasn't evil or malicious, and it hadn't been infected with the plague. It was going crazy because Zelfree had created his mimic aura improperly. The three heads were too much for Traces to handle because of the improper magic, and now she thought *everyone* was an enemy.

A low growl rumbled Terrakona's entire body. **"I will do as you say."**

My world serpent sank into the ocean. I sheathed my sword and held on as tightly as I could. We rose up around Zelfree's chimera, faster than I had been expecting. I figured Terrakona would use his vines to hold down the three-headed beast, but I was mistaken. Terrakona did what any good snake would do: he wrapped his body around the chimera.

The chimera's tentacles lashed around, and the roc head screeched. The more the beast struggled, the more Terrakona wrapped his body around the creature. It had a twisted shell, but Terrakona didn't focus on that. The world serpent circled around the massive neck of the chimera. With three heads, all sprouting from the same location, the beast had a large throat.

I could barely see everything from my perch on Terrakona's head, but I felt the fight between the two grappling creatures. I wanted to help, but I didn't actually want to *kill* Traces. I couldn't use my blade or my new evocation.

"Enough!" Zelfree shouted, though I never saw him.

The chimera's body shimmered and shifted... and then broke apart before my very eyes.

7

HELPFUL ALLIES

Zelfree's chimera disappeared from Terrakona's grip. When the beast vanished, there was nothing to hold on to. Terrakona crashed into the ocean, his serpent eyes wide.

I was about to make a joke about another victory under my belt, but I didn't get the chance. Terrakona straightened himself, and then lifted his head into the air. I patted his crystal mane, proud of his courageous attempts to help in battle. He was still young, after all. This was only his second battle ever.

Without warning, searing pain filled my back and shoulder as a roc talon skewered me from behind. The black talon had punctured straight through my body just at the base of my ribs, on my right side—as the roc shot over Terrakona. The beast took me with it, carrying me by its hook-like talon, like a hawk carrying a fish out of the water.

Shock darkened my vision. Hanging from the roc's talon like a fresh piece of meat hurt more than I could have imagined. I held on to the bird's massive foot to alleviate the strain of my weight tearing my own body.

The pirate arcanist and his roc... I had never expected they would return... They really took me by surprise...

Terrakona roared as the roc took to the sky. His anger resonated in me, and it helped me narrow my focus. I concentrated on my evocation. The heat emanated from my whole body, not just my hands. And just as I had hoped, the talon sticking out of my gut *melted*. The enemy roc gasped and thrashed its head.

"It burns!" the roc screamed.

The creature jerked its leg and I fell off of its liquefying limb. With my breath held, I watched the ocean rush up to greet me at startling speed.

Terrakona had said we were the masters of earth and tide, but it didn't feel like that when I hit the waves shoulder-first…

I had that dream again. The one with a castle in the ocean, and Terrakona's giant tree lair in the background. This time was different, though.

Instead of swimming in a turbulent ocean, I managed to use my evocation to evaporate the waters around me. *All* of the waters. The entire ocean just… slowly disappeared into a great cloud of steam. Once it had vanished, I was left at the base of the castle.

The building reminded me of King Drake Castle, located in the capital of the Argo Empire, Thronehold. There were sovereign dragons and leviathans built into the structure and designed into the fountains and shrubbery. Although the place had been underwater, it looked immaculate and beautiful. It was a dream—what had I been expecting? Realistic water damage?

I walked through the gates and then the sprawling gardens of the courtyard.

Alone.

Shouldn't there have been guards or servants or knights around?

But I saw nothing. Instead of dwelling on it, I continued on, my head hazy. When I reached the castle, I held my breath. There weren't any doors or windows. Just... walls. I placed my hand on the cold stone bricks, confused. How was I supposed to get in? I didn't understand.

And then the skies grew dark with storm clouds, and the chill of the wind left me covered in goosebumps.

What kind of dream was this?

It required most of my strength to open my eyelids. Why were they so heavy? I swear I could've fallen back asleep the moment I closed them again, but I didn't want that. My sore body ached as I rolled to my side and groaned. I couldn't see properly. My blurred vision made everything look like abstract shapes and colors. Light streamed in through a window.

Where was I?

"Oh, Volke, are you actually waking up this time?" a familiar voice asked.

The tone was feminine and filled with concern. It wasn't Illia. Her voice had a harsh edge. And it wasn't the Grand Apothecary—she was cheery and bright, even during the darkest of storms. This was... Princess Evianna. Well, not really a princess anymore, since most of her family had died, but still.

Was Evianna okay? I hoped the pirates hadn't managed to breach the magical barriers. I didn't have the strength to ask, however, even though I tried.

"Don't wake him," another voice said. "Let him keep resting."

That was Illia.

"He's been resting for two days," a third voice chimed in.

"He'll get sores if he lies in the same position for too long. It won't be pretty. Volke is too handsome for that."

Another feminine voice, this one sultrier than the others. Who? It had to be Karna the Doppelgänger Arcanist. She'd always had a way with her words that made everything seem... exciting.

Someone placed a hand on my chest and walked their fingers down toward my stomach.

Another person placed a hand on the opposite side of my chest, and then batted away the first. "Please. This is a place of healing. Show some respect."

A fourth person? This person I had known for a long while.

Atty Trixibelle. A phoenix arcanist from my home isle, and one of the most beautiful women I knew. She was here? Healing me?

My vision clarified in small bursts. Atty sat next to me, her eyes as blue as the sky, her golden hair flowing like waterfalls of amber. When she smiled, I couldn't help but smile back. Her white robes matched the clean décor of the infirmary. Even my sheets were crisp and fresh—the place smelled like recovery.

Where was Evianna? I tried to glance around, but my stiff neck refused to comply. I wanted to speak with her.

I had heard her. Evianna was here. I just couldn't see her at the moment.

Illia walked up to my side, into my field of view, and then she stared down with a smirk. "I thought I'd have to reprise my role as a gravedigger." She poked my shoulder and tilted her head. "I'm surprised you're already awake. You didn't look so good when Guildmaster Eventide pulled you from the ocean."

"Well, you look like a swashbuckler," I murmured, my voice weak, but laced with a chuckle.

Unlike Atty, who wore clothes that enhanced her beauty, Illia always wore her sailing coat, knee-high boots, and a thick belt with several pouches. Illia had wavy brown hair—the kind that looked like the wind had styled it for her—which only added to her adventurer's aura. The eyepatch she wore reminded me of home, however. Gravekeeper William had made it for her. A black patch with the design of a white rizzel stitched into it. The ferret-like creature matched Illia's arcanist mark perfectly.

Although it was a tragedy that Illia had lost an eye to pirates, I couldn't imagine her without an eyepatch. It was *her*.

"I brought you extra blankets," Illia said.

I took a shallow breath and managed to reply, "Thank you."

"I also made sure you got the softer pillows."

"Thank you."

"And I tried to keep the others out, but that's impossible these days." Illia rolled her eye.

Atty maintained her bright smile. "I wasn't about to sit outside. Not when I could help with my magic."

Karna sauntered to the foot of my bed and tapped her elegant fingers on the bedframe.

She had a lean body of smooth muscle, long blonde hair that rivaled the radiance of the sun, skin healthy and tan— and all of it enhanced with her doppelgänger sorcery. Nothing was out of place. No flaw visible. When she moved, she did so with the fluidity of a master dancer. She dressed like one, too. A tight fitted top that showed off her stomach, and loose pants that showed off a good portion of her hips.

Then again, I supposed I didn't really know what she actually looked like. Karna constantly changed her appearance. Her doppelgänger magic made it easy.

"When I worked in Thronehold, and the other girls got *an injury*," Karna said the last word with a playful vagueness, and then continued, "we would brew a special tea. It calms anxiety and helps prevent scarring." She motioned to the nightstand near my bed. "I made you a pot."

I tried to glance over, but my neck wouldn't cooperate. "Thanks," I muttered.

Illia leaned down to straighten my blankets, and as she did so, she whispered, "Karna brewed a new pot every six hours since you've been in the infirmary. Maybe something more than a simple *thanks* is in order."

"Right," I mumbled, though I wasn't sure how to effectively express my gratitude. When I was well, I'd do something for Karna to repay her kindness. "Wait, how long have I been...?"

"Two days."

"Oh."

"Don't worry," Atty interjected. She scooted her chair closer to my shoulder and smoothed the wrinkles of my sheets. "You need positivity to recover properly, so don't focus on the negative."

My injuries...

I swallowed hard and then forced my hand up. I was under blankets, but I managed to run my fingers over my chest and side. The moment I grazed my injury, I flinched. My skin was smooth and hot, and I couldn't believe how large the wound was. Roc talons were massive. I closed my eyes and took a deep breath.

I was lucky to be alive.

But before I could relax, I touched my elbow and my knuckles, searching for obsidian protrusions. I found nothing. The rocks had disappeared from my body. Had they fallen off? I didn't know.

"Are you okay?" Illia asked.

I half-smiled. "Yeah," I said, my voice still rusty. "Of course."

But Illia didn't buy it. She stared at me with her eye searching both of mine, like she was digging through my soul for the true answer. But what was I going to say? *Yeah, sorry I almost died. Don't worry. It won't happen again.*

It would definitely happen again. Those pirates weren't the

worst of our problems. And this time, I'd had the backing of the Frith Guild to help me. What would happen when I didn't have them?

Master Zelfree was right. I had to get stronger.

Breathing water and evoking molten rock wouldn't be enough. I needed more.

The door to the infirmary opened, and I managed to turn my head enough to spot the person entering. The Grand Apothecary, Gillie, bounded into the room with her caladrius eldrin on her shoulder. The parrot-like bird had to tilt her head from side to side just to look at everyone properly.

"Is Volke waking?" Gillie asked. She patted down her bright yellow dress and hurried to my bed. "He needs to sleep longer. I'm sorry, ladies. You'll have to leave for the time being."

Illia nodded and then gently patted my shoulder. "I'll see you once you're up."

"Get well soon," Atty said. When she touched me, her magic flowed from her fingertips into my body. It tingled as it helped to alleviate my pain. I suspected her healing had helped me along, but that my injuries had been too great for her to mend all at once.

Karna smiled and then winked. "You'll be better in no time. You always are."

I half-chuckled—even though it hurt my chest. "Thanks."

Evianna finally stepped into my view, seemingly from the darkness, but she didn't say anything. Where had she been this entire time? Hovering around near the corner of the room? Her white hair, especially in the sunlight, reminded me of island clouds. And her bluish-purple eyes... No one looked like Evianna and her family. They were so unique and distinct that I sometimes wondered where their appearance came from.

Her arcanist mark...

It was a sword and cape wrapped around a seven-pointed

star. She was a knightmare arcanist, so of course she had hidden in the shadows with ease.

But why?

Her lingering stare told me she wanted to speak to me, too.

Gillie motioned Evianna to the door. "You can see him again, I promise."

With a curt nod, Evianna exited the infirmary with Atty, Illia, and Karna. I hated to see them go, especially Evianna. Once the door shut, the Grand Apothecary pulled my blankets up to my chin and felt my forehead with the back of her hand. She used her magic, just like Atty had, and the tingle of healing flooded my entire body. Caladrius were birds of medicine and recovery—no mythical creature healed individuals like they did.

"Everything will be okay," Gillie said, smiling. "Just rest up, ya hear me?" She motioned to Karna's tea. "If you get thirsty, don't hesitate to take a sip. It'll have you feeling energetic in no time."

"Okay," I muttered. "Thank you."

After healing me a second time—sending another wave of refreshing tingles throughout my body—Gillie half-closed the blinds on the window and then shuffled out of the room. The silence of solitude lulled me back to sleep, but it wasn't for long.

A minute later, I awoke to the creak of floorboards.

Evianna lifted out of the shadows. Her knightmare magic made it possible to travel through darkness, after all. She stepped upward and entered my room from a shadow under the door. With quiet movements, she snuck over to my bed. Her clothing—tight fitting leather and a dark cowl—made it easier for her to move without the rustle of fabric to give her away.

I half-turned my head. "Evianna?"

I wanted to thank her for returning, but my throat

tightened the more I dwelled on the words. Affection wasn't my strong suit.

Evianna smiled as she quietly pushed a wooden chair to my side. Then she took a seat. "Don't worry," she whispered. "I'm not going anywhere."

"Don't you need to train?"

Evianna shook her head. "I don't care if the monsters of the abyssal hells were invading—I won't leave your side. What if an assassin came for you?"

"That's unlikely," I said, my voice weak. I inhaled and then exhaled. "Eventide protects the whole guild with her magic."

"But what if you woke up and needed something else besides tea? Like water? Or food? Or you didn't know where you were?" Evianna lifted a part of my blanket up—enough to grab my hand and squeeze it in her tight grip. "I'll be quiet. But I'll also be right here, whenever you need anything."

I wanted to tell her everything would be okay—that she could focus on herself—but her dedication to my wellbeing took me a bit by surprise. I didn't want to dismiss her efforts, not when they were so obviously pure.

"What if *you* get hungry?" I asked.

Evianna pointed to the shadows on the ground. "Layshl has been sneaking me in food. Right, Layshl?"

The darkness flickered with life. Evianna's knightmare replied, "Of course, my arcanist." Her dark and regal voice reminded me of Luthair's.

Layshl could easily sneak around and gather food and water without being noticed.

I rested back on the pillow, stress and tension leaving my injured body. "Okay," I murmured. "Just... make sure you're okay. Deal?"

With a gentle squeeze of my hand, Evianna said, "Deal."

I entered a dreamless sleep.

Where was Adelgis? Didn't he normally provide me with entertainment? It seemed selfish to demand he weave my dreams every night, but I did miss them.

But then reality decided I had slept long enough. A crash in the waking world jerked me my sleep. I slowly opened my eyes. The lit lanterns cast harsh shadows around the infirmary. The moonless night offered no other source of light. Again, it took a moment for my eyes to adjust. All the colors and shapes...

"Careful," someone hissed. The voice was familiar. Gruff. Masculine.

"I am!" a second person—a familiar woman—snapped back. "It's not my fault all the beds are so close."

"It *is* your fault for bringing a hydra! Leave your eldrin outside like everyone else."

"Raisen is well-behaved."

"Raisen is a fat dragon with the brain of an alligator and the temper of an irrational chihuahua."

My vision cleared just in time to see Zaxis grab Hexa by the collar of her coat.

Zaxis wasn't a small man. I swear he got bulkier with muscle each time I saw him, and he effortlessly yanked Hexa closer. His red hair—slicked back with oil—made it seem like he was *trying* to look like a well-mannered gentleman, but his red scale salamander armor, near-permanent glower, and tense gait dispelled all pretenses. Zaxis was a warrior through and through.

"You're just jealous," Hexa said, smirking. She fluffed her curly, cinnamon hair, and despite Zaxis's obvious rage, she chuckled. "My eldrin does whatever he wants because no one is going to tell my *fat dragon* what to do."

As if to emphasize her point, Raisen stepped forward and knocked over two chairs, my nightstand with the tea, and a bed. His five heads thrashed around, knocking over a third chair.

The largest head—the one with horns—stopped moving and then the other four, after realizing the other had gone still, did the same thing.

He had to have been close to four hundred pounds. Perhaps five hundred. He *was* a fat dragon with a crocodile-like body. An adolescent hydra that was almost too big to be traveling.

"No one tells us what to do," Raisen's horned head said. His voice was so much more... mature. And deep. Then he turned to Hexa. She patted his spiky head, and he wagged his tail. "Except for my arcanist, of course." A forked tongue shot out of his serpent mouth and then darted back in.

Evianna jumped into view, seemingly from the darkness itself. "Stop! Volke needs to rest! You all must be quieter!" She picked up the chairs and hastily put them back in place. "Don't you know whom you're dealing with? This is no way to treat a god-arcanist!"

Zaxis scoffed and rolled his eyes. Then he released Hexa with a shove. "Look, *princess*, we don't have time for your antics. Volke the Mighty God-Arcanist doesn't need to be coddled."

"You spilled his tea!"

A puddle of greenish liquid slowly spread out across the infirmary, no doubt creating a slipping hazard. Flecks of leaves and petals twirled across the surface. The scent of cinnamon wafted around the room.

"I think he'll live," Zaxis stated. "It's just *tea*."

Evianna ground her teeth loud enough that I could hear it. "Karna made that specially for him. And it's not like we've been to port to resupply—she's using her own tea leaves and time! And you just threw it all on the floor like a brute!"

"Calm down."

"Not until you apologize," Evianna said, practically shouting.

"*Me?*" Zaxis barked. "I didn't knock it over! *And* I wasn't the person who put it in such a terrible spot. I have nothing to apologize for."

I thought their argument would spiral out of control and form its own storm, but Evianna just clenched her jaw and frowned down at the spilled tea. Then she threw her white hair over her shoulder and stood a little taller.

"If no one is going to fix this mistake, I will," Evianna said. "Layshl—can you get some fresh food? I'll brew some fresh tea." She glared at Zaxis, and then at Raisen. "Everyone keep their stupidity to a minimum while I'm gone. Or at least keep it quiet."

Evianna didn't wait for an answer. She stepped into the shadows and disappeared from view. She could slither through the darkness all the way to the cooks and then return to the infirmary just as quickly as she had left.

I rubbed at my face, dispelling most of my grogginess.

"Oh, he's actually awake," someone else said.

I glanced over and found Adelgis standing near the head of my bed. He offered me a small smile, and I returned the gesture.

Unlike Hexa, Evianna, and Zaxis—who all had the aura of fighters—Adelgis was a man of learning. He stood straight, his posture relaxed, and his long robes free of dirt. His shoulder-length hair, ebony and shiny, glistened with fragrant oil. He kept himself neat and proper, but his face... His pale complexion was more wan than usual.

"Come to make me some dreams?" I asked.

Adelgis shook his head. "I apologize. I've been busy helping Guildmaster Eventide most evenings."

"Is she... having trouble sleeping?"

"No. It's—"

Zaxis snapped his attention over to us. "Wait, Volke's awake and coherent?" He stormed over to me. For a moment, I thought he'd drag me out of bed, but he just loomed overhead.

"What's your problem?"

I ran a shaky hand over my face. "Me?"

"Yes, *you*," Zaxis growled. He threw an arm up into the air in exasperation. "Didn't you hear Evianna? You're a *god-arcanist*. Bonded to the world serpent and everything! How did you almost die at the hands of *pirates*?"

"I—"

"If *I* had been the world serpent arcanist, this wouldn't have happened." He motioned to my bed and then glared. "Well? What do you have to say for yourself?"

Zaxis reached for my blankets, but something stopped him halfway. At first, I thought he was frozen in place, but then he jerked his arm away, like he had pulled his arm out of someone's grip. And he had—a man appeared in the room as his magical invisibility dropped.

He was a renegade pirate.

Fain.

He stood between me and Zaxis, frost on his coat, trousers, and the edge of his boots and belt. Most of Fain wasn't noteworthy, but his fingertips were a different story. Black. All of them. Like they had been frostbitten and never fallen off. Fain's dark hair was shaved on the sides of his head, displaying his frostbitten ears as well.

He looked... half-dead. But he wasn't. His fingers and ears worked just fine.

"Volke is trying to rest," Fain said as he curled his hands into fists. Then he turned to Adelgis and frowned. "Moonbeam, why didn't you stop Zaxis?"

Adelgis half-shrugged. "How would I do that?"

"Can't you control people with their minds or something?" Fain asked, his eyebrows knitted.

"In their dreams, but not the waking world." Adelgis shrugged. "I guess I could've put him to sleep, but that feels a bit extreme as well. Besides, Zaxis's thoughts weren't of harming Volke. He just wanted to emphasize his point."

"Oh." Fain relaxed a bit and then rotated his shoulders. "Still."

I forced myself to sit up, despite the spikes of pain that ripped through my chest and gut. With my jaw clenched, I took several deep breaths. The room remained quiet and still as I did so. It wasn't until I had recovered a bit that Zaxis stepped forward.

"Like Moonbeam said, I wasn't going to hurt him," he said as he shot Fain a glare. Then Zaxis returned his attention to me. "I just wanted to show the new god-arcanist what his injury looked like."

I glanced down. On one side of my chest, I had my arcanist mark. On the other side of my chest, I had a star-shaped injury just below the ribs. It was massive, but it had mostly healed—it was now smooth and shiny, like only fresh skin could be.

"You once told me to be less rash," Zaxis said. "But look at you! Take your own damn advice. We're supposed to be helping each other out, aren't we? That means you can't go dying on me, especially not after becoming one of the god-arcanists."

Zaxis ran a hand through his red hair and huffed.

"You could've been quieter and gentler about it," Fain muttered.

"Yeah, well, people always pay more attention when I yell." Zaxis held up a hand and a flash of fire brightened the room for half a second. "They also pay more attention when I'm throwing flames around."

Four of Raisen's heads hissed. "I agree," the main one said. "People pay *way* more attention when I'm being loud and dangerous."

"It isn't dangerous if you know what you're doing." Zaxis snapped his fingers, and another wisp of fire left his hand.

I took a deep breath and then exhaled. The others waited, like they wanted me to speak. I shook my head, dispelling the last of my grogginess.

"Zaxis," I said.

He widened his stance and crossed his arms over his broad chest. "Yeah?"

"You're right. I really need to be better."

Fain and Adelgis both frowned.

"You did amazingly for a new arcanist," Fain said, his voice naturally quiet. "*No* arcanist could fight pirates a week after bonding."

I half-smiled and offered a light laugh. "Yeah, well, I still need to be better. That's the reality." Then I gave Zaxis my full attention. "Which is why I need your help."

"My help?" Zaxis asked, one eyebrow raised. "*You're* the god-arcanist, not me."

"I have a problem that only you and Atty can help me with." I glanced at the dying embers fluttering around the room. They snuffed themselves out before landing on the wood floor. "You both evoke fire," I muttered, not asking a question, but stating a fact that had given me an idea.

Zaxis frowned. "Everyone knows that. What's your point?"

"I think... I evoke some kind of fire as well. And I'd like you and Atty to help me master that."

8

ALTERNATE EVOCATION

"You evoke fire?" Adelgis asked, both eyebrows shooting to his hairline. "But... the world serpent doesn't breathe flame. He has venom strong enough to pollute water for decades. Wouldn't you evoke that?"

I turned to him, my chest aching with even the slightest of movements. "How do you know about Terrakona's venom?"

Adelgis held his breath. For a moment, he was still and quiet, but I didn't understand why he was hesitating.

Fain stepped close to Adelgis and placed one of his frostbitten hands on Adelgis's shoulder. "Moonbeam has been visiting the dreams of the god-creatures," he said. "He's seen all sorts of useful things. Isn't that right?"

"Given the situation, my information isn't nearly as useful as I thought it would be," Adelgis replied in a quiet tone. "I thought for sure I would discover the powers of the world serpent arcanist, but my conclusions are obviously incorrect."

"Only one conclusion is off. The others might be accurate."

"It's nice of you to think that." Adelgis removed Fain's hand and sighed. "But... I need to rethink my observations." He ambled around to the other side of my bed, his eyes drilling holes into the floor. "My father had the magic of his relickeeper to help him identify the powers of the mystical creatures he studied. I only have my ethereal whelk... I can dive into memories, but that doesn't help me predict future powers. And dreams are unreliable. They're more fiction than reality."

Adelgis's father, Theasin Venrover, was indeed a talented researcher and artificer—someone who crafted trinkets and artifacts. I had read one of his books about mystical creatures and had been impressed by the detail and range of information given for each one.

But Theasin was also a fiend of the highest order. He had helped the Second Ascension rise to power and had even created terrible weapons that destroyed magic. As far as I knew, Theasin had found the bones of the first apoch dragon and used them to help the Second Ascension obtain the weapons they needed to fight a war of nations.

Anytime someone made reference to the man, my blood boiled.

I should've killed Theasin the last time we had met—when we had both been at the excavation site. There was no doubt in my mind that the mistake would cost me.

"I would love to help you with your evocation," Zaxis said, smiling. "As long as you're a well-behaved apprentice, you'll be an expert with fire."

Hexa rolled her eyes. "And here I had been hoping that Moonbeam would be right. *I* wanted to help Volke use venom." She hugged one of Raisen's heads. "I've been practicing with it for a while now. It's a sneaky weapon. Perfect for someone with cunning and guile, like Volke."

"Tsk," Zaxis said with a click of his tongue. "Fire can be used in more situations than just *killing someone*. That's why it's superior."

"Really? Wanna try me? We should go out to the field and spar right now."

Adelgis pointed to the dark window. "It's the middle of the night."

"When has that stopped anyone around here?" Fain quipped.

"It doesn't matter what time of the day it is." Zaxis brushed back his hair with a quick motion of his hand. "I'm always ready for anything."

Hexa half-laughed. "You sound like such a blowhard."

While I didn't mind their bickering, my mind drifted back into a state of grogginess. Their taunting challenges and sarcastic statements became a blur of background noise, like the patter of rain on a window, or the howl of wind on a blustery island morning.

Or more like the screech of dozens of caged-up birds.

Raisen moved closer to my bed—careful this time not to knock anything over—and then lowered one of his heads onto my lap. Was he trying to warm me? Hydras were cold-blooded. It didn't do much.

His main head stared at me with intense gold eyes, the lizard-like slit pupils as thin as hair. "You should get some more rest," he said, his voice low and gruff. Perhaps he had been trying to whisper?

"I will," I muttered. "But—"

"Don't worry," he interjected. "I'll protect you."

Another head lowered onto the bed and "snuggled" close. His necks were so long that his heads moved with the concertina motions of a snake. His scales were curled upward at the ends, however. It made his whole body prickly. How did Hexa pet him without cutting up her palms?

I almost asked about Terrakona, but the moment I thought about my eldrin, I felt he was just outside, next to Gentel. Was he swimming alongside her? Most likely. He had gotten hurt during the fight, but not like me. His injuries had likely healed days ago.

"I think I'll be okay, Raisen," I said as I rested back on my bed. A twinge of agony flared through me, but it quickly disappeared the moment I stopped moving. I had learned my lesson. Stay still until I had healed. "You can focus on protecting Hexa."

Raisen wrapped the other three heads around me in an odd hydra "hug." I tried not to move, but his spiny scales caused me to shudder. Another wave of pain passed through me once Raisen was finished and had removed himself.

"Thank you," I muttered through gritted teeth.

"You'll be better soon," Raisen's main head said, flashing his fangs.

I nodded.

The shadows in the room shifted—just slightly—and Evianna lifted out of the ground, stepping from the darkness with a copper pot of tea held in her hands. She offered everyone else a glare as she strode over to the side of my bed.

"I think you all should go," she said as she set the copper pot down on the opposite wooden nightstand. "Volke is clearly tired."

Zaxis opened his mouth like he was going to start something, but I shot him a glower. He sighed but otherwise remained quiet. I thanked the good stars that Zaxis wasn't in a disagreeable mood.

"Pirates have a couple of remedies for people recovering from injuries," Fain said as he moved toward the infirmary door. "Our ship's medic would recommend clams and oysters."

Zaxis crossed his arms and sneered. "Are you serious? We're not going to use *pirate* techniques to help Volke. That's ridiculous."

Adelgis chimed in. "Shellfish have been proven to help those recovering from severe blood loss."

"Wait, really?"

"Yes. One of Gillie's books mentions it extensively."

Fain smirked. Then he grabbed Adelgis by the upper arm and pulled him close. "See? Moonbeam understands. Plus, what does it matter where the information came from? If it's good, we should use it."

"I'm sure Gillie will handle everything," Evianna said. She placed her hands on her hips and flung her white hair back with a jerk of her head. "Now get out. Volke needs his rest, too."

Zaxis followed Fain and Adelgis to the door. Once the other two had exited into the hall, Zaxis glanced over his shoulder. "Volke, whenever you're ready to train with your evocation, just let me know."

I nodded.

Without another word, Zaxis left. Hexa and her hydra went after, but every step Raisen took was its own tiny earthquake. I felt him leave, long after he had entered the hallway. Once the tremors had stopped, I relaxed a bit, comforted by the soft blankets.

Evianna walked over and sat in the same chair next to my bed that she had before. She smiled as she lifted her legs up and wrapped her arms around her knees. "You don't have to worry. I'll make sure it stays quiet for a while."

"Thank you," I said, though it seemed odd that she just wanted to stare at me, and my face heated. "You can get some rest, too, ya know."

"I know. But once Layshl gets back with food, I'm going to tell her to get some shellfish."

I shrugged. "My magic will heal me. We don't need to worry about it."

A part of me wanted to be strong—never weak, never needing help—but Evianna had already seen me at my worst. Should I be worried anymore?

Evianna rested her chin on one knee, her gaze on my blankets. "When I lived in Thronehold, we had a whole team of arcanists who specialized in all sorts of healing. I know the

Grand Apothecary is talented, but... I wish we were in Thronehold. Once we get back to land, we should travel there."

I seriously doubted Evianna wanted to travel there to meet with healer arcanists. In my heart, I knew she wanted the security of her childhood home—of familiar people and sights—and she wanted to know what was happening to her country now that her brother was dead.

"We'll go there," I said. "I promise."

Evianna perked up, her smile shaky as her eyes grew glassy. "I bet everyone in the Argo Empire wants to know more about the world serpent arcanist."

So do I.

But I didn't say that aloud. I just had to focus on learning the *one trick*, like Master Zelfree had said. And it seemed that trick would be my evocation.

Morning.

The hot rays of the sun warmed my face long before I fully awoke.

With all the energy of a ninety-year-old man, I rolled to my side with a groan. I opened my eyes and found Evianna dead asleep. She had crossed her arms and rested her head on top of them, and while it looked uncomfortable, she also looked exhausted. No matter how slumped her posture was, or how hard the nightstand might have been, she remained asleep.

"Hey, uh, would you mind rolling back over?" a tiny voice said from the fold of my blankets. "It's difficult to breathe in here."

I shivered and threw the blankets off—only to grab them again and yank them over my naked body. In a state of confused panic, I simply said, "Whoever you are, *get out.*"

The blankets rustled as a small creature bounded around

under them. The four feet tickled my injured body until the creature finally ran up to my chest and poked his head out, right near my chin.

It was Nicholin, Illia's rizzel.

Normally, I loved to see Nicholin. His little ferret-like body, white fur, silver stripes, and bright blue eyes were the essence of adorableness. Unfortunately, I wasn't in the mood for his antics. He typically brought with him a bag of mischief—or at least a squabble—and I didn't have the energy.

"Good morning," Nicholin whispered. He rubbed at his nose like only weasels could. Once his whiskers were clean, he poked my chin. "Your injury looks better than before. You're healing up nicely!"

"You've been—"

Nicholin put a paw to my mouth. "Shh." He motioned to the sleeping Evianna. "Quiet! Don't be rude."

I narrowed my eyes as he removed his paw. In a hushed tone, I asked, "You've been here before?"

"Of course! You can't keep rizzels out of anything."

With a *pop* and a flash of glitter, Nicholin disappeared and then reappeared on top of the blankets. His teleportation magic made him a tricky little critter, but thankfully, he tended to use his extraordinary abilities for mundane activities. Or jokes. I could only imagine the havoc he could cause if he were motivated and malicious.

Nicholin stood on his back feet.

He had gotten bigger. When Illia had first bonded with him, I would've said he was eight inches long. Now he appeared to be twelve inches—perhaps thirteen!

He patted his little chin with a paw. "So, when are you getting out of bed? Zaxis is being insufferable again, and I need your help."

"Where's Illia?" I asked, ignoring his shenanigans.

"Oh, she fell overboard in the middle of the night,"

Nicholin said with a shrug. "She and the plague-ridden kraken are sharing a watery grave."

"*What*?"

I shot up into a sitting position, my heart hammering against my ribs. Nicholin tumbled into my lap, his whole body like a rubbery spring.

Curse the abyssal hells!

How quickly could I make it to Guildmaster Eventide? Was there still time to jump into the ocean? How had Terrakona not done anything about this? Illia was an excellent swimmer! How could something like this even happen? What would I tell our father? What if—

Nicholin straightened himself and squeaked. "Hm! Now do you understand how Illia felt?"

I glanced down at him, my head spinning. "What're you... talking about?"

"She didn't fall into the ocean, you corn box!" Nicholin disappeared and then reappeared on my shoulder, glitter and a quiet *pop* the only indications he had teleported.

"She didn't?" I asked, my heart calming.

"Of course not. But now you know how you made *her* feel! You were dragged from the ocean with a chest wound! Illia thought you might die. She didn't sleep. She couldn't eat."

"I... I'm sorry."

"You have to be more careful, Volke! If you had died, I don't know what my arcanist would have done." Nicholin shoved his nose in my ear. I flinched, and he backed off. But then he did it again, like it was a punishment. "Don't scare Illia or else next time, I'll bite you in the sensitive bits!"

I nodded. The slower my heart beat, the more I felt my chest injury. With a sigh, I muttered, "I'll try to be more careful."

"Good," Nicholin said with a squeak. "Because—and don't tell anyone I said this or I'll deny it—but I would be upset if you died, too, okay? Think about the cute little rizzel when you do crazy things next time." He stared up at me with his big, blue eyes.

"All right."

I patted Nicholin's soft head, enjoying his white-and-silver fur. He was as silky as a newborn rabbit. He closed his eyes and bathed in the affection.

Then his ears shot up erect. "Oh! Illia is calling me. I've gotta go. Stay safe!"

Another pop. Another puff of silvery glitter.

And he was gone.

I glanced over at Evianna. She hadn't moved. Her even breathing remained constant, and I suspected we hadn't even penetrated her dreams. It reminded me of my own fatigue.

I rested back on the bed. Just a little longer... and I'd be fine.

At least, I hoped.

9

DESTRUCTIVE EVOCATION

It had taken me a total of four days to recover from the roc's attack.

I was surprised I had even lived—while arcanists could heal injuries, that didn't mean *every* wound was capable of being mended. If an arcanist was decapitated, there was no recovery. They just died. And an injury like mine... Well, I suspected many arcanists, especially weaker ones, wouldn't have survived.

It made sense. The stronger the mystical creature, the stronger the ambient magic in the body of the bonded arcanist. Will-o-wisp arcanists couldn't withstand as much damage as a sovereign dragon arcanist. And I suspected none of them could compare to me.

But it still felt weird thinking of myself as a god-arcanist. I had to remind myself sometimes. I felt like an imposter wearing my skin as a disguise.

Before the dawn of the fifth day, I snuck out of the infirmary and returned to my new room. It was located on the first and second floors of the guild manor house. The bedroom was on the second, and the study was on the first, the two connected by a personal staircase. The whole room was positioned alongside the master arcanist suites, which made me uncomfortable. I wasn't qualified to be here, yet here I was.

I passed Gallus the Gray's room on the way to mine. A couple of journeyman arcanists—people Gallus had trained himself—were cleaning out his quarters. They had frowns deeper than the ocean, and I didn't know what to say to them. *Hey, sorry for killing your master. He was driven insane by magical maladies.*

It didn't feel right.

I entered my room, and then found a shirt, an old pair of trousers, and a belt. We hadn't stopped at a proper port in weeks, so it would be a while until I had anything decent. I'd also have to look into having armor crafted for me...

Something that could withstand my new evocation.

Once dressed, I exited the manor house and went straight for the field. A somber stillness lingered over the atlas turtle. We had successfully dealt with the sky pirates, but in the process, we had lost a master arcanist to the insidious plague. Although the Frith Guild had a cure, we were the only ones. People everywhere were still suffering.

How were we going to solve the problem of the arcane plague? Technically, it was the responsibility of the god-arcanists to find a way.

I shook my head. I had other things to worry about. One problem at a time.

The grass that grew on Gentel's shell was always lush. Even if the blades were trampled on—even if they were burned—they grew back a brighter green than before. I walked across the field, my gaze at my feet, amused by the way the grass sprang to life behind me.

Master Zelfree and my brother, Ryker, were busy training.

The breaking dawn illuminated the area. I held my breath when I caught sight of Ryker's eldrin. He had bonded with *the*

Mother of Shapeshifters, a strange mystical creature who few had ever seen. No other Mother of Shapeshifters existed, which meant Ryker would be the one and only arcanist with his set of abilities.

Well, that wasn't entirely true. I had heard that some of his abilities were similar to mimics and doppelgängers. I suspected it was because the Mother of Shapeshifters had given birth to them.

And her appearance was just as unique as she was.

In her undisguised form, she had a terrifying visage. She was a lump of tangled flesh, massive enough to hide an elephant between the folds of her pinkish skin. A light coating of blood covered her entire body, much like mucus and slime covers the body of a newborn child. When she moved, her body jiggled and writhed—did she even have bones?—and the sight always sent a shiver down my spine.

As I approached, eyeballs appeared across her body, like they had floated up through her blood and risen to the surface of her skin. They blinked as they focused on me, each red iris vibrant and glowing.

"Good morning," I said.

"Salutations, Warlord," the Mother of Shapeshifters replied, her voice ancient, but her tone calm. "I'm pleased to see you're well."

"Uh, thank you." I rubbed at the back of my neck. "I'm glad to see you're... still in one piece."

She giggled, her fleshy body jiggling. Was she happy or angry? I wasn't sure if this was the equivalent of a dog wagging its tail or a snake coiling itself for a strike. When she didn't attack, I assumed it was the former.

Master Zelfree huffed. He slowly crossed his arms, as though even *that* was too much effort. The bags under his eyes were darker than the sky, and I wondered if he had rested since our fight with the pirates.

Probably not.

"Curse the abyssal hells," Zelfree muttered, his breath visible in the morning chill. He leaned his head back and stared into the dark sky.

I shoved my hands in my pockets. "Are you okay? You look terrible."

"I'm fine." He sighed and returned his attention to me. "But the doctor said I should be drinking more rum. Also, I call myself *the doctor* now."

My brother, Ryker, snorted and laughed once. His hair, black and thick, just like mine, had been slicked back with pomade, and didn't move even when he chuckled. It gave him a more gentlemanly appearance. My hair was styled by the wind and as free as the waves. It was long enough that it covered half my ears, and I suspected I'd need to cut it soon, if only to keep it from getting into my eyes.

"Volke," Ryker said. Then he took a deep breath. "Shouldn't you still be recovering?"

I shook my head. "My chest hurts a bit, but not much. I'm sure *the doctor* can prescribe me a sleep-aid ale."

"Do you really think it wise to joke about your health?"

"Better than falling into depression."

"Well, shouldn't you rest more, at least?"

"We only have a couple of days before we reach Fortuna. I shouldn't be wasting what little time I have."

Ryker stared straight at me. We were the same height, which was rare. Few people matched me, and I always took note when they did.

He didn't have my physique, though. Ryker had the muscle structure of a scribe, whereas I had been training with a sword and shield for years, keeping me solid.

Master Zelfree stretched for a moment. After an odd cracking noise from his spine, he relaxed. "Volke, your eldrin said you had discovered your evocation, but he didn't say much else. The serpent seemed confused, to be honest."

"How so?" I asked.

"For a while, I didn't understand what he was saying. Then Zaxis started telling everyone you evoked fire. That true?"

"Well, sort of…"

"The world serpent has been unresponsive to anyone since that," Ryker chimed in. "He said he needed to dwell on your path."

My… path?

I glanced out beyond the atlas turtle shell and focused on the dark waves of the ocean. Where was Terrakona? Most likely beneath the surface. Hopefully he wasn't upset. I had thought he would be proud of me. Didn't he want me to develop my magic?

"Zaxis also said he and Atty would be helping you train," Zelfree said, drawing my attention back to the immediate. "Where are they?"

"I told Zaxis to meet me here in the afternoon." I glanced around. "But I told Evianna to meet me here before that. I wanted to help her with her knightmare magic before I focused on my own evocation."

Evianna and I hadn't trained in a long while, and since she had stayed at my side the entire time I had recovered, I knew she hadn't trained with anyone else, either.

"Your evocation is more important at this point," Zelfree said. He pinched the bridge of his nose. "At least we have something to demonstrate if ever anyone asks, but fire wasn't really the ability I was hoping for…"

"It's more like… molten rock," I said, keeping my voice low. "It reminded me of pyroclastic dragons. The ones who breathed lava, rather than mundane flames."

I didn't need to whisper, but for some reason, I felt odd about my ability. Not only had I conjured the molten rock, but obsidian had jutted out of my body. How was I supposed to explain that? No other arcanists seemed to have a bizarre secondary effect to their magic. What was I even supposed to do with it? Atty and Zaxis weren't going to help with the obsidian, either. It was just… an abnormality I'd have to contemplate a bit further.

Zelfree narrowed his eyes. "So, the molten rock was how you defeated Gallus? Eventide said he had been burned, but she had never elaborated. Likely because she didn't want to upset the others."

"R-Right."

"I suppose no one will argue with the destructive powers of a volcano." Zelfree exhaled, his shoulders slumping. His hands shook a bit, and I wondered if he really did need a drink. "Once Zaxis and Atty get here, I'll mimic their abilities and help you train."

I frowned. "Are you sure?"

He shot me a glare. "I'm your master, aren't I? This is my job."

"No, I meant—shouldn't you be working on your chimera aura?"

Zelfree gritted his teeth. "Listen. I'm going to tell you exactly what I told Eventide after that battle. Auras require a calm mind. I think it'll take me a bit longer before I clear my system of mental distractions, so don't worry about me."

I knew Zelfree had a troubled past, but I didn't know it had disturbed him so much that it prevented him from mastering an element of his magic. Was it because he had lost his previous lover? Or perhaps it was because his best friend was now a pirate? Maybe something else. Zelfree rarely shared his darkest fears.

"Is there anything I can help you with?" I asked.

Zelfree crossed his arms and cursed under his breath. "No. *Mind your own damn business.* I'll handle it."

"O-okay."

"I'll train with Ryker until Atty and Zaxis get here."

I glanced over at Ryker's eldrin. "So, uh, Mother of Shapeshifters... You've never had an arcanist before, right? Ryker isn't second-bonded?"

The giant blob shook, and then her many eyes blinked, though not synchronized. Each one seemed to operate independently from the rest.

"We call her MOS now," Ryker mumbled. He walked over to his eldrin. "And she's never had an arcanist before. Apparently, she's been avoiding most of humanity." He perked up, his eyes wide. "Oh! I've been meaning to tell you something, Volke."

"What is it?"

"MOS was around during the time of the previous god-creatures. Her father, the progenitor behemoth, was the tenth god-creature to be born."

I turned to MOS—what an odd name—and tried to focus on a set of eyes. It was too difficult. There were too many, and occasionally a few glanced off in other directions. Instead, I stared at a single eye, and asked, "Do you remember what kind of magics the god-creatures had? Specifically, do you know what the world serpent could evoke, manipulate, and augment?"

Mastering the basics had to come first. I'd have time to develop my aura and other inherent abilities later.

"That is a difficult question," MOS said. "The god-creatures changed depending on their arcanist. Each creature had magic aimed at either destruction or creation, and once one or the other was mastered, the arcanist lost the opposite completely."

"What do you mean?"

"The progenitor behemoth, when young, evoked both a mist that liquefied flesh, and a mist that fortified plants and animals, causing them to become sturdy, healthy, and grow faster than ever before."

"He could evoke *two* things?" Zelfree snapped.

The many eyes of MOS glanced at Zelfree. "He lost the ability to liquefy his enemies," she said matter-of-factly. "The progenitor behemoth and his god-arcanist—the world knew the arcanist as *the Shepherd*—mastered their creative abilities. After that, their destructive capabilities disappeared."

I stared at the ground.

The ancient texts I had read stated that the god-creatures would lead humanity into a new age. They hadn't said a *golden* age, or even a *good* age. Just *new*. Terrakona had spoken at length about being the judge of humanity. Had he been referring to my magic?

No. Terrakona hadn't known what we would evoke.

But maybe... he knew I would need to decide. Would I be destructive? Or would I create? I hadn't known such a choice would be thrust upon me.

Creation sounded the most productive and helpful. Shouldn't I use my god-arcanist abilities to build?

On the other hand, the god-creatures came into existence because of the arcane plague. Perhaps it would be most beneficial to humanity if I learned how to destroy—that way I could clear away this vile disease once and for all.

"I apologize if the information doesn't suit your needs," MOS said.

I shook my head. "N-No. Your information is valuable. Thank you. I'm just... not sure what I'm going to do with it yet."

"You carry the weight of humanity's future on your shoulders."

What was I supposed to say to that? It didn't feel like a weight or a burden, but whenever people talked to me, or about me, it always felt like they were holding their breath, waiting for me to solve everyone's problems with a flick of my wrist.

"Okay, enough chat," Zelfree snapped. He waved his hand. "Ryker and I have training to do."

My brother nodded and walked over to Zelfree. Since Evianna hadn't arrived yet, I stood off to the side and watched. Zelfree's mimic magic allowed him to copy other people's eldrin, but he didn't—or couldn't—copy MOS. Instead, he pointed to the blank arcanist star on his forehead.

"See, whenever Traces becomes a mystical creature, I can feel the magic change within," he said. His star shifted and the image of a phoenix appeared etched into his skin. "I want you to try. You already learned your evocation, and you already said you can sense the magic of others—I think the next step is for some shapeshifting."

"Uh, well," Ryker mumbled. He glanced over at his gigantic, fleshy eldrin. "MOS only seems to transform into an animal. Well, *multiple* animals. But still. She can't become a mystical creature."

Zelfree sighed. "All right. Let's move on to experiment number two."

A twinge of pity shot through me. Ryker was just like me. He didn't know what kind of magics his eldrin would give him, so he had to grasp at the air until he finally found his abilities. It was always so frustrating, and the moment Ryker frowned, I understood his pain.

"What's experiment number two?" Ryker asked.

"*You'll* transform."

"I told you... It's unnerving to think of my body rearranging."

"And I told you that the abyssal hells will open long before I just let you sit on your ass and do nothing." Zelfree snapped his fingers. "You need to push yourself beyond your limitations."

"But what if I can't change back? What if I mutilate myself and I become a vegetable confined to a cot?"

Ryker feared distorting his body? I hadn't ever considered that. I had seen Karna transform so many times that I didn't have any fears about magical transformations. They seemed perfectly safe, so long as the arcanist practiced, I supposed.

The morning shadows around my feet shifted.

Luthair?

My hope swelled and then burst all within the same second. Of course it wasn't Luthair. It had to be Evianna and her knightmare, Layshl. I turned around just as Evianna stepped out of the darkness and stood in front of me. Like Zelfree, she had dark bags under her eyes. Unlike Zelfree, she smiled when she stared up at me.

"I'm here," Evianna said. "Let's get training."

10

KNIGHTMARE MAGIC

I t had taken me a long while to learn my knightmare magic. Knightmares were so rare, that most people knew little to nothing about them. It had made learning my evocation, manipulation, and augmentation difficult.

"I improved upon my terrors," Evianna said as she held out her hand. "Do you want to see how powerful my evocation has become?"

I glanced back at Ryker, Zelfree, and MOS. They were sufficiently far away to be spared Evianna's untamed terrors. With a sigh, I returned my attention to Evianna. "Show me."

She grinned and then narrowed her eyes. After a second of concentration, magic erupted from her body. It wasn't visible, but it radiated off her much like heat radiating off a fire.

Her magic gripped my chest and slithered down my spine. Although I tried to fight it, her fear-inducing powers clawed at my imagination. Images fluttered across my vision. I staggered backward a few steps and grabbed at my forehead. When I closed my eyes, I thought I'd be able to shield myself from the magic, but I was mistaken. It only made the images clearer.

Years ago, I had experienced knightmare terrors. Back then,

the images had been of my family dying. Illia. Gravekeeper William. I couldn't save them. And it was my fault.

But this time...

I...

My body burned like a pyre, and a field of blood and bones stretched out before me. Although the corpses were mangled and dismembered, my terror-induced hallucination included the knowledge of each individual.

Gregory Ruma's wife. The first person I had killed.

Ryllin. The griffin I'd had to slay.

And also...

Zelfree.

Adelgis. Fain.

Atty. Zaxis. Illia.

Karna. Evianna. My father.

I had killed them all with my magic—it raged out of control, and I hadn't tamed it in time. Their blood stained my clothes, my skin, and my soul. Shaken, I tried to step away, but all I found were more bodies. I half-stumbled on the bones of old acquaintances and friends.

It was me. I was *the judgment* that Terrakona always spoke about. I had destroyed everything because it was all tainted. Everything I had loved.

And then—before the terror-dream released me—I spotted a black dragon rising in the distance. A fearsome beast with scales of bluish-black, leather wings, antler horns, and a tail lined with spines.

The terrifying beast held Luthair in his clawed hand. With a flex of his muscles, he crushed Luthair, cracking his armor and shredding his cape. The broken fragments of the knightmare's body disappeared like shadows exposed to light.

Somehow, I knew this was my fault. The guilt burned hotter with each second. I grabbed my clothing, but everything had become sticky and wet with warm blood.

"Volke?" Evianna said. "*Volke?*"

When I opened my eyes, I was on my back, staring up into the morning sky. No clouds—just the gentle pink of dawn streaking over the blue of day. Sweat dappled every inch of my skin.

"Are you... okay?" Evianna asked. She sat crouching next to me, her eyes wide.

"Yeah. I'm fine."

"I told you I had improved my evocation. Powerful, right?"

"Very."

"Aren't you proud?" She grabbed my shoulder and playfully shook me.

I took a deep breath and then sat up. "Yes," I muttered as I rubbed at my temple, "but you need to learn how to shape your evocation next. Right now, you'll just affect people in the nearby area, but with some practice, you'll be able to target foes and spare your friends, even if they are standing next to each other."

"Did you do that with Luthair?" Evianna asked.

I gritted my teeth, the image of Luthair's shredded cape still fresh in my mind. "Yeah..."

Evianna stood and then smiled. "I'll work on it. But also, look! I improved my manipulation." She waved her hand and moved the shadows all around us. They swirled and danced, and then rose up into a physical tendril that split into three others. The level of control was impressive for how young an arcanist she was. "See?"

I got to my feet and nodded. "It's pretty amazing."

Evianna stood a little proud, and when she met my gaze, her cheeks flared pink. "I practice on my own time, in my bedroom."

"What about your augmentation?"

She frowned and shook her head. "Well, that's the one I'm struggling with. I mean, I understand the basic concepts, but..."

Evianna narrowed her eyes and crossed her arms. "But it's very common for arcanists to struggle with at least *one* of their magical abilities, thank you very much."

"Yeah, I know."

"Oh..." She relaxed her posture and nodded. "Good. I just wanted to make sure you knew I'm average or above average in all categories."

I chuckled. "Don't worry. I never think you're below average."

Evianna perked up and smiled. "Right?" She threw her white hair over her shoulder. "Good. Your opinion means the world to me, Volke."

"Okay, but we should practice everything. I think if you have a better understanding, you'll grasp your sorcery easier."

"Okay."

"Evocation is creating magic and throwing it out into the world. Manipulation is controlling the magic in things and objects in the nearby area. Augmentation is *pushing* your magic into something. Affecting it with your skills." I rotated my head. "Illia's augmentation causes things to teleport, because she's pushing her rizzel magic into it."

"I know that," Evianna said, her tone heated. She huffed and then calmed herself quickly. "I'm not trying to be difficult..."

"It's fine." I motioned her close. Evianna walked to my side, and I grabbed her hand and placed it on my forearm. "It took me a while to figure out what knightmare arcanists augment." With a chuckle, I said, "You can help others see in the darkness. It doesn't sound like much, but it's useful." Then I pointed to her hand on my arm. "You need physical contact, like this. Then you should concentrate on your magic entering my body. Think of it like light streaming through a window."

Evianna pulled her hand off my arm. She fidgeted for a moment, her eyes on the grass. "Well, why don't we start with objects first? What happens when a knightmare augments something inanimate?"

I opened my mouth, but then I closed it again. It took me a long while before I managed to say, "Luthair and I never really tested the limits of our magic. We, uh, were never master arcanists. So... you know."

Evianna stared at me with a frown. I didn't know what else to say to her.

"Are you sure you're okay, Volke?" she whispered. Then Evianna took my hand and held it close. She was cold. I closed my fingers around hers, trying to make sure she was warm enough. "I think you should probably rest some more," she said. "You're wan and sickly looking."

With shallow breaths, I nodded. Perhaps she was right. I decided to return to my room.

I paced my new room, from one side to the other, passing my desk and bed.

Luthair's cape hung off the back of the desk chair. Ever since I had lost him, I had attempted not to dwell on his death.

I stopped pacing when I reached Luthair's cape. After a shaky breath, I placed my hand on the cold silkiness of the magical fabric.

"We had a lot of good adventures together," I said. Nothing replied, of course. The fabric shifted with my touch, but that was it. "I wouldn't be the man I am today if it hadn't been for you, Luthair. I still can't believe we made it through so many close calls."

The memories played in my mind's eye, and I visualized every detail, from the fight with the plague-ridden gargoyle to the haunting halls of the world serpent's lair. But when I opened my eyes, it was just me, in a strange new bedroom, with a piece of Luthair's corpse wrapped in my fingers.

Silence descended into the room from all corners. When I swallowed, it sounded like a gunshot. What was I doing?

"Reality says you're gone," I whispered. "Logic says I'm talking to the air." I pulled the cape from the chair. "But sometimes it feels like you're still with me. Somehow. In my dreams, my thoughts, my magic..."

An odd scratching noise came from the window. I tensed and reached for my blade, half expecting the Second Ascension to leap into my room and attempt to kill me. After a moment, I took a deep breath and walked over. The scratching continued, but at a low and steady rate. My bedroom was on the second story of the manor house—who could possibly be scratching the glass?

I threw back the curtains.

The sight of a brilliant phoenix greeted me. His scarlet feathers glittered as he moved. Fire pulsed from his body, as though he were made from flame, and the feathers sprouted straight from the embers. His long tail feathers, flaring at the ends like a peacock's, rustled in the late morning breeze.

I knew this phoenix. His name was Forsythe, and he had hatched on my home isle. Forsythe's gold eyes stared at me for a moment. Then he tilted his head and tapped on the glass with his ebony beak.

"Is everything okay?" I asked as I opened the windowpane.

Forsythe hopped onto the inner sill, his talons just as black as his beak. When he moved, soot fell onto the floor, and embers fluttered out from between his feathers.

"Good morning, Volke," he said, his voice regal. Forsythe held his head high. "Are you feeling well? Atty, Titania, and Zaxis were helping the Grand Apothecary with your injuries."

"Atty and her phoenix?"

"Of course." Forsythe puffed his feathers out, lighting up my room with an eldritch glow. "I helped, too, of course."

"Thank you."

With a hesitant hand, I patted Forsythe's head. The phoenix leaned into my touch. I enjoyed the warmth—it was the exact opposite of Luthair's cold power, but it reminded me of Terrakona, and the molten rock I could evoke.

"Are you here to get me for training?" I asked.

Forsythe nodded. "Yes. My arcanist wants you to meet him at the edge of the field, opposite your brother and Master Zelfree." The phoenix blinked his golden eyes a few times, and then tilted his head in the other direction. "I can tell him you're not feeling well." He held up a taloned foot. "Or perhaps I can heal you a bit first?"

I nervously chuckled. "I'm fine." I ran a hand down my chest. The only thing that would cure me would be sleep. "I can make it to the field."

Forsythe nodded. Then he fluffed his feathers and swished his tail, dirtying my room with soot. "I'm sorry about Luthair," he muttered.

"Uh..." I shook my head. "Don't worry about it."

"Volke, I just want to let you know that... on the Day of Phoenixes, when I first met you and Zaxis, a part of me knew you would make a wonderful arcanist. I thought you would be the one I would bond with." He tilted his head back the other way. "I was always a little jealous of Luthair, to be honest. He had lost his first arcanist, but you saved him from a life of exile in a mire."

Forsythe's words caught me off guard. I tensed and then turned away, a little shaken by the moment. "Thank you," I said, my voice forced. "But we don't have time to reminisce. Let's go meet Zaxis and Atty for evocation training."

"I'm gonna teach you how to use your fire, so from now on, I expect you to call me *master*," Zaxis said with a smirk.

I coughed and laughed at the same time. Then I held up a hand. "Never."

"I'm gonna train you like no one has trained you before." He grabbed at his bulging bicep. "Do you see this? I'm focused and determined. You *wish* you had a fraction of my dedication."

Forsythe, his phoenix, stood a good ten feet away from us, his scarlet feathers fluttering in the breeze. He chirped for his arcanist, singing like only birds could.

"I'm still not calling you *master*," I said.

Zaxis glowered, his green eyes brilliant in the afternoon sun. "That's just disrespectful, really. But you've always been like that."

"We don't need to argue," Atty said. "Fire is my specialty. If anyone is a *master*, it's me. But I'm not a petty tyrant who requires Volke to bend the knee."

"I'm not a tyrant," Zaxis said with a scoff. Under his breath he added, "Everyone is always so damn dramatic."

Ignoring Zaxis's complaints, Atty took a position at the edge of the field, both her arms out wide. Embers sprouted from the tips of her elegant fingers, and when she spun around, they created a ring of light that swirled around her.

The presentation wasn't particularly relevant to combat, but I did enjoy the showmanship and display of fine control she had over her evocation.

"Feh," Zaxis said with a dramatic shrug of his broad shoulders. "Watch this."

He held up his fists. While I wielded a sword, Zaxis wielded copper knuckles. He gave me a confident smirk—the kind I'd be embarrassed to try—and then his knuckles shimmered and shifted in color. In a matter of seconds, the metal of his weapons superheated. Once they were white-hot, he punched the air. Each strike sizzled.

"See?" Zaxis asked.

Atty held up a hand. A pyre of flame gushed outward, nearly fifteen feet into the air. She held the powerful evocation for a second before allowing her magic to fade. She turned around and gave Zaxis a *beat that* look, one eyebrow raised.

"Who cares?" Zaxis said with a growl. "My way also breaks bones."

"We can't measure anything without a ruler," I quipped. "So, let's stop trying to compete, all right? I need help."

Atty's blue eyes grew wide. "Help? I thought we were just practicing your fire evocation."

Instead of explaining everything, I decided to show them. I held out my hand and focused on my magic like I had before. The heat came so quickly, it startled me. Fire erupted off the sleeve of my button-up shirt and I patted at my clothing to put it out.

A small amount of molten rock oozed from the lines of my palm. It was about to spill from my body, but I caught the heated rock before it dropped onto Gentel's shell. What would happen if her shell was burned? Would she even feel it? I didn't want to find out.

"That isn't *fire*," Zaxis barked. He glared at the glowing molten rock cupped in both my hands. "What's wrong with you? You said *fire* and this is... well, it's not fire."

Atty frowned. "This isn't what I was expecting. I think we'll need Master Zelfree's expertise."

"You want to wait for him?" Zaxis glanced over at my brother and MOS. The giant ball of flesh and eyes transformed into a pile of black-furred rats. The rats tumbled outward, spreading across the shell. Zaxis huffed a laugh. "I think Zelfree will be busy for a bit."

"I, uh, thought you might be able to help me control it," I said, glancing down at my burnt clothing.

Zaxis wore crimson scale armor—a magical trinket—

forged from the hide of a salamander. It was immune to flames and all forms of heat, which meant it wouldn't spontaneously combust whenever he evoked too much of his fire.

When I glanced back at my own singed clothing, I knew I needed something like the armor Zaxis wore. With Luthair, I had always had armor, but now I needed to craft something— or have someone craft it for me.

A piece of black obsidian had sprouted from my knuckle. I stared at it for a long time, uncertain why this had happened.

Zaxis noticed my gaze and followed it to the odd, stone protrusion.

"What is *that*?" he asked. "When did it happen?"

"It's a part of my evocation, apparently," I muttered. "So, maybe if you guys have advice about that, too..."

Zaxis snorted and then grabbed my wrist. With all the gentle finesse of an elephant, he scooped up the molten rock from my hand and then hurled it out into the ocean. I watched it sail through the air, leaving a fine trail of smoke in its wake. When it hit the water, white smoke wafted from the surface and a harsh sizzle rang out over the waves.

My magma hadn't burned Zaxis.

"The first thing you need to learn is respect for your flame," Zaxis said.

I narrowed my eyes.

"It'll consume everything around us, so you have to be mindful of that. Unlike your knightmare terrors—which you could shape—your fire will grow a will of its own. It'll even continue without you, if you light the right things up."

Atty nodded along with his words. "He's right, Volke. Fire is a tool, but it's also a force of destruction. Remember that as you train, you risk great damage to everything around you."

"What do you two suggest?" I asked as I slid my wrist out of Zaxis's grip.

Forsythe hopped forward, dropping soot as he bounded

over the grass. When he drew near, he straightened his long peacock-like neck and stared up at me. "When I was a hatchling, I learned something important," Forsythe said. "*Burning logs dream of the forest.* It means an accident can lead to regrets that can never be cured."

I hadn't thought about the gravity of the situation before, but it weighed heavily on my mind now. Of course I would need to be careful. My magic was far more powerful than anyone else's here. What if I had accidentally burned a deep hole into Gentel's shell? What would I have done then?

A loud yell ripped me from my thoughts. I whirled around on my heel and focused my attention on Ryker and Zelfree.

The black-furred rats were attacking them.

11

ISLANDS IN THE DISTANCE

I dashed across the field, lamenting the fact I could no longer step into the shadows for faster movement. Zaxis, Forsythe, and Atty were right behind me, but I slowed my pace the moment I got a better look at the situation.

The rats had leapt onto Zelfree and Ryker, and although they were biting both of them, the rats weren't drawing blood. Zelfree expertly yanked the rodents off and threw them away, but he stumbled backward and tripped over some of the rats in the process, resulting in a tumble onto the grass.

Ryker didn't fare as well. He panicked, threw himself to the ground, and yelled again as the rats dogpiled on top of him. He flailed his arms and legs, but it was clear he had little to no combat training. He wasn't using his body properly—it was as if every limb operated with its own independent thought.

Zelfree quickly leapt back to his feet—before he could be swarmed—and then dodged out of the way of several other rats. Despite their torrent, they couldn't seem to get him. He was too agile, and a few times, he faked them out by stepping in one direction, and then lunging in the opposite direction. He quickly put distance between himself and the horde.

But still... The rats weren't injuring them.

"What's going on?" Zaxis said, his copper knuckles hot again. His eldrin stood at his feet, his feathers flared.

Atty held up a hand, flame already in her palm. "Should we assist you?"

Zelfree stopped his flight and then growled. "*Enough*, MOS. You made your point." He ran a hand through his sweaty black hair. "It's an effective tactic, but one that will only take the enemy by surprise momentarily."

The rats squeaked and chirped as they bounded off Ryker and rushed together to form a little colony of rodents. They squeezed themselves close, so that they remained a tightly packed group. Although I couldn't count them all—they were all the same shade of dark fur—I suspected there were at least two hundred in total.

"I've survived for centuries by using various tactics to scare off arcanists and random hopefuls seeking to bond," MOS said, her mouthpiece a single rat standing in front of the group. "You underestimate me. Check your pockets, Master Arcanist."

Zelfree reached into his trouser pocket and shuddered. He yanked his hand out and stifled a shout. His fingers and palm were covered in insects—centipedes, worms, and needle-nosed beetles. He shook his hand and they fell to the grass. Each one shimmered and shifted, and then they melted back together to form a single rat. The rat scurried back to the group.

"I use tactics to distract arcanists," MOS said. "I break their concentration with their own fears, I evoke confusion to muddle them further, and once they're fully addled, I kill them from the inside with my creepy crawlers and insects. Most arcanists are long dead before they even know it."

Atty snuffed out her flame, her eyes wide.

"Wow," Zaxis muttered as he dropped his hands. "I like it."

"I can protect Ryker," MOS continued. "All he needs to focus on is learning my magics."

Zelfree stared at the rats, and then at Ryker.

Although he hadn't been seriously injured, it still took Ryker a moment to pick himself up off the ground and brush off the dirt and grass from his clothes. With a sheepish look, he glanced around at everyone and then avoided eye contact.

"I apologize," he said. "I grew up on a small island helping my mother... I, uh, never thought I'd need to fight off pirates and brigands. Those weren't skills that interested me."

"It's fine," Zaxis said with a scoff. Then he shrugged and turned away. "Volke, Master Zelfree, and I have enough fighting power for a small army. You'll be fine."

"I can hold my own, thank you," Atty said, still refined, but with a heated edge to her words.

Zaxis turned to her and glowered. "Aren't you locked up in your room most of the time reading about *true forms*?" He motioned to the field. "Where's Titania, huh? Isn't your eldrin in the library right now studying old magical texts and journals?"

"What does that have to do with anything?"

"You're not focused on combat. You're just focused on yourself."

The retort had more anger behind it than usual—and that was saying something, because Zaxis always had a lot of anger.

I stepped between them, disappointed that arcanists in the Frith Guild would be fighting among each other. "Achieving true form with her phoenix would be a great boon," I said, matching Zaxis's narrowed glare. "Atty could develop powerful magics, and she'd be immune to the arcane plague. The Second Ascension wouldn't stand a chance. Not everything has to be about fighting."

For a brief second, everything remained tense. No one spoke. Master Zelfree took a deep breath, as though formulating something to say, but it was obvious his fatigue interfered.

Finally, Zaxis threw his hand up in the air and turned away. "Listen, when I say *Master Zelfree, Volke, and I are great fighters,* and Atty has to interject and demand a spot on the list, I'm not going to put her there *just because.* She has to earn it. And while a true form phoenix could be a boon, she doesn't have one *yet.* She certainly isn't helping anybody or anyone with the amount of time she dedicates to it."

Forsythe glanced at us, then at his arcanist. He hurried after Zaxis when the rest of us remained still.

I wanted to say something, but I couldn't find the words. No path seemed like "the right one."

Atty didn't say anything. She listened to Zaxis's rant with a straight face, no emotion whatsoever. When Zaxis walked away, she turned her gaze to the grass and remained as silent as before. Did Atty believe him? Was she worried she was wasting her time?

I placed a gentle hand on her shoulder. "Hey," I said. "I understand why you've been doing this. You don't have to feel bad."

"Zaxis isn't entirely wrong," she whispered.

A short while ago, when we had last visited the Isle of Ruma, Atty had introduced me to her mother. I had explored their home and discovered the coffins—dead relatives, kept "fresh" and whole. Apparently, Atty's mother wanted a true form phoenix so that the bodies could be resurrected, and Atty felt responsible for following through with her mother's wishes.

The situation wasn't something I had related to then, but now that I had lost Luthair, a small piece of me wondered if Atty's phoenix would be able to resurrect Luthair once she obtained true form...

But I shook my head, dispelling the thought.

Atty's mother was just using her for a goal. I wouldn't be that kind of person.

"Enough, enough," Master Zelfree said as he stormed over to Atty and me. He pushed us apart. "It's true, we'll be fighting a lot of dastards in the future. All the more reason not to fight among ourselves." He glared at Atty. "If you think Zaxis has a point, you can change directions at any time. As a journeyman arcanist, I said I'd let you decide your path going forward, but I'm going to say this to you *again*—don't get obsessed. Obsession is a poison, do you understand me? Obsession may even cost you your life."

Atty nodded once. "I understand. I still stand by my decision. But Volke is also right. If I can just..." She glanced down at her palm. "Maybe I should be in the library right now."

"Perhaps."

The tension remained thick as Atty mulled it over. After a prolonged moment, she took a deep breath and smiled up at me. "I'm sorry, Volke. I thought I'd finally be able to help you with your evocation, but I haven't done much at all, have I?"

"You can still help," I said.

"If I'm going to focus on achieving a true form with my phoenix, I need to make sure all my efforts go there." She stepped forward and pulled me into a tight embrace. She smelled of lavender. "I know Zaxis and Master Zelfree will do well by you."

"Right," I muttered as I returned her affection.

But a part of me knew she was just saying *goodbye.*

"Thank you," she whispered. "For understanding. I think you're the only one who does."

My brother ended his training in the afternoon. At no point did he transform, even when he attempted to use some of his other abilities.

Afterward, Zaxis, Forsythe, and Master Zelfree—with mimicked phoenix magic—helped me train with my molten rock. I evoked it several times, but I had to make sure none of it spilled onto Gentel. The flames that Zelfree and Zaxis used burned the grass, but Gentel restored that within a matter of moments. My evocation was just too destructive to risk throwing around.

After I had gotten comfortable with creating it, Zaxis and Master Zelfree ran me through combat drills. Tossing it from one hand to the other, moving while holding it, using the molten rock defensively—I'd need practice, but it was good to have the first steps in place.

Right as the sun touched the distant horizon, I held up a hand to stop.

My knuckles, elbows, and knees had obsidian jutting out of the joints. Although they didn't hinder my movement, I shuddered each time I caught sight of them. And to make matters worse, I thought they added to my weight. I felt sluggish the longer our training went on, and it wasn't just from fatigue.

My arms were harder to lift above my head.

Zaxis and Forsythe walked over to me.

"You're ruining your clothes faster than I did when I first trained," Zaxis quipped. He pointed to my ripped trousers and shirt. "And are you creating rocks on purpose? They aren't even that sharp." He grabbed my elbow and ran his fingers over the points of the rock. "They're jagged. Totally useless."

I yanked away from him. "I told you. It just happens."

"And do they fall off? What happens to them?"

"I... well, I think they melt away? Slowly. After I stop using my evocation for a while."

Master Zelfree—his eyes half-lidded, and his movements more sluggish than mine—ambled over. "I've seen a few mystical creatures who have side effects to their magic. The most notable are the manticores and the tundra beasts."

"What happens with them?" I asked.

"Manticore arcanists often hurt themselves when they're first training. Their magic gives them superhuman strength, and in the beginning, it's difficult for most to wield. Their muscles rip because they accidentally overexert themselves."

I rubbed at the back of my neck. "So, I'm doing this wrong?"

"I didn't say that." Zelfree sighed. "Look, I knew a guy who would occasionally rip doors off their hinges or crush bottles in his grip because he wasn't used to his newfound strength."

"I just need to get used to this?" I lifted my arms and examined the many obsidian rocks. "They're heavy."

"Yeah, and tundra beasts half-freeze themselves when evoking their ice. They're immune to the cold, so their bodies don't waste away from the temperature, but that doesn't stop the ice crystals from forming across them. The ice becomes a hindrance. It gets in the way of their movement and stiffens their armor."

I hadn't ever read that. Then again, most of the things I read were adventures and legends. Most stories didn't go over the specifics of training.

"How do tundra beast arcanists overcome that?" I asked.

Zelfree half-laughed. "Well, most don't. The ones who do just control the rate at which they're evoking, or they make sure they have trinkets and artifacts to counteract the formation of the ice on their bodies."

"So, maybe I should have something that prevents the obsidian rocks from forming?"

"Potentially," Zelfree drawled. He stared at my hands. "You're not a pugilist, like Zaxis. The rocks will likely get in the way of your swordplay."

I hadn't thought of that.

Zaxis ran his hands over his fire-proof armor. "Didn't we get a whole slew of star shards from the world serpent's lair?" He glanced up at me and smirked. "And isn't your father a master artificer? Once we get to Fortuna, let's ask him to craft you armor that prevents the obsidian from sprouting."

Crafting magical items was a tricky process. It required a piece of a mystical creature, a number of star shards, and the magic of the person imbuing the item. The star shards were the power and glue of the whole process. Without them, no magical items could be made. And the more star shards, the stronger the trinket. If at least ten shards were used, the item became so powerful that it typically couldn't be broken or dismantled. Those were artifacts.

But *what* the item did was dependent on everything else.

A phoenix feather imbued with caladrius magic could create a powerful healing trinket, but a phoenix feather imbued with will-o-wisp magic could create a destructive flame-shooting trinket. My father had imbued salamander scales with his phoenix magic, which resulted in Zaxis's fire-immune armor.

What combination of parts and magic would it take to prevent the rocks from appearing on my body? The problem almost seemed impossible.

"Don't get that look," Zelfree snapped. "Don't worry about this. Jozé will know what magics we need. The man has a gift for crafting."

I slowly nodded. "All right."

"But I think we should call it for today." Zelfree's shoulders slumped, and it was obvious to anyone with a single functioning eye that he might fall asleep at any moment. "We have one more day until we reach Fortuna. We'll dedicate the whole day to mastering a demonstration. Until then, we should rest."

"I'm still filled with energy," Zaxis said.

"I don't care."

Zaxis frowned but didn't offer anything else. I was glad because I didn't think I could continue on in my current state. I followed Zelfree back to the guild manor house and daydreamed of my soft bed.

<hr>

I wished I could focus more.

It seemed as though I had only had two seconds to sleep. In reality, I had slept eight hours, but the time had disappeared in an instant. One moment I had been crawling onto my mattress, getting ready to pull the covers over my body, and the next thing I knew, Evianna's knightmare was shaking me awake, my face in a puddle of my own drool.

I woke, dressed, and stumbled back outside all while half-awake.

Lost in a haze of blurry thoughts, I helped Evianna with terror evocation, and then attempted to go over her augmentation. I barely remembered a thing. By the time the sun was rising, Zaxis and Zelfree were out on the field waiting for me. Evianna hugged me, and I think I hugged back before dragging myself over to the next grueling event.

Twice I almost dropped my molten rock on Gentel, and once I almost burned my last set of whole trousers. It seemed the more magma I created, the hotter the ambient air became. That was why the water around me had boiled when I had been dueling Gallus the Gray. To keep from hurting those around me, I kept my evocation light.

But even if I spaced out the time between each evocation, the obsidian rocks still sprang from my body. It irritated me how often they appeared, but I doubted I could fix the problem in one day's time.

Once the sun had passed overhead, and I was on my last legs, Zelfree turned his attention to the guild manor house as though someone had called his name. I hadn't heard anything, but I patiently waited while Zelfree stared.

Zaxis, on the other hand, jumped close and threw a punch. On instinct, I leaned away. The extra weight of the obsidian made my movement sluggish. Zaxis managed to clip me on the chin, and I staggered backward. For some reason, the blow didn't hurt like it normally did when Zaxis got in a good strike. It felt... a little softer. Had he been going easy on me? Or had something else happened?

I rubbed at my chin. "Zelfree's busy," I said. "Relax."

Zaxis eyed me for a moment, then he stared at his copper knuckles. He never said anything, but the cogs of his mind continued to spin long after our brief encounter.

"We're almost to Fortuna," Zelfree said as he turned back around. He pointed off the starboard side of Gentel's shell. "Look. You can see some islands."

Filled with giddy energy, I snapped my attention to the far horizon. Sure enough, the dots of islands were clear in the beautiful weather. I wiped the sweat from my brow, pleased to be so close to home.

"How long until we reach Fortuna?" I asked.

Zelfree shook his head. "The guildmaster wants us to arrive before dusk. Gentel will be pickin' up speed."

"So, we have a couple of hours?" Zaxis asked. Then he scoffed. "Volke isn't ready. He's barely combat capable."

"I still have my sword and shield," I said.

"But no armor and barely any magic."

I waved my arm at the ocean. "Have you seen Terrakona? He's huge. Unless we're facing a dragon arcanist, I'm sure we'll be fine."

I hoped.

Zaxis shrugged. "I almost got a good hit across your face, and I'm not even a master arcanist. If you don't focus more, I'm sure that—"

"We won't be getting into any combat for a while," Zelfree interjected. "Both of you get back into the manor house. Once we reach the city, the guildmaster will tell you what to do next, understand?"

"Yes," I said.

Zaxis replied with a curt nod.

"Good," Zelfree said with a huff. As he turned on his heel and headed for the front garden, he muttered, "Let's just hope you both follow instructions this time."

TWO HUNDRED ARCANISTS

I arrived in my room and nearly jumped.

Illia, Nicholin, Karna, and Evianna were all lounging about. The entrance room of my vast quarters had a couch, two chairs, a bookshelf, and a massive desk. The stairs up to the second story led to my bed, and while I wanted to head straight up and sleep, I stopped and gave everyone a puzzled look.

When no one said anything, I asked, "What's wrong?"

"Your health," Illia said.

"Your clothes," Karna said at the same time.

"Society," Nicholin quipped afterward.

Evianna stood up from the couch and walked over to me. With both eyebrows raised, she gave me the once over. "Volke, I'm sorry to say this, but you look like a man who has been lost at sea for thirty days."

At a complete loss for words, I glanced down at myself. Black singe marks, tears in my clothing, and smears of blood covered my entire outfit. Even my boots looked as though they had been chewed by a dog. Had obsidian been protruding from my feet? I wasn't sure. I had been entirely too tired during training.

Some of my obsidian still jutted from my body, but most of it had already dissipated.

"I think you should get some sleep," Illia said as she stood from the chair. "But Evianna did bring up a good point. This will be the first time you introduce yourself as the world serpent arcanist. Perhaps you shouldn't look like a vagabond."

"A vagabond?" I repeated in a whisper.

Karna smiled as she sauntered over. She stood on the opposite side of me, avoiding Evianna as she tugged at a lock of my black hair. "You'll need to get this cut." Then she shifted her critical gaze to my shirt. "And this will have to go. We want something that says *warlord*."

"I think his health is still important," Illia interjected, narrowing her eye. "His clothing isn't."

"Of course his health is important. But nobody in Fortuna will care about that." Karna combed her golden hair with her fingers. "Trust me. People judge you more by your appearance than any other trait. We can hide the bags under his eyes, and Volke can conceal the fatigue in his bones, but people will take note of his clothes no matter what we do."

"We're going to reach Fortuna in just a few hours," Evianna murmured. She stroked her chin as she stared at the dirt on the back of my hand. "Will that even be enough time?"

Karna shook her head. "We'll be cutting it close."

A few *hours*?

I stepped away from them, my face hot. "Whoa, whoa. I agree, I should be presentable, but I should also take a nap."

"You can nap in the bathtub," Karna said. She grabbed my upper arm and pulled me back into position. "And trust me..." She inhaled deeply and then frowned. "You'll need to soak for a long time."

My new bedroom had an attached bathing area. It wasn't objectively large, but since I never really had my own bathing room before, it was subjectively gigantic. The porcelain tub stood in the middle of the room, with a drain underneath. The water—heated by magic imbued into the tub itself—was kept warm. Not too hot, not too steamy. Somehow, despite my exhaustion, I had stripped off my clothes and crawled inside.

The tub was deep. I sat on the bottom and the water came up to my chin. It took some effort to lift myself up to the edge and glance over. I had towels, soap, and scented oils, but I didn't want to bother getting out to get them.

I closed my eyes, and time slipped away. Apparently, Evianna, Illia, and Karna were gathering up suitable clothing for me. Where was this *mythical outfit* coming from? We didn't have a tailor and cloth aboard Gentel...

The quiet of the bathing room made it easy to fall into a deep sleep. And it wasn't like I needed to fear drowning—I could breathe underwater. Maybe I could even sleep underwater? That was a fun thought that floated around my head while I slowly lost consciousness.

"Volke," someone said.

I jerked awake, shaken. I glanced over the edge of the tub, my heart pounding.

Fain.

He stood next to the tub, his blackened fingers gripping the white porcelain—it made for a distinct sight. I glanced up and met his gaze. He, too, seemed tired. I supposed most people were still on edge from the nonstop fighting and constant vigilance. Never any time to relax.

"I've been meaning to speak with you," Fain said, his voice rough.

I sat up in the tub, and modestly tried to cover myself. When I realized that wouldn't work, I gestured to the soap. "Would you mind?"

Fain walked over to the washbasin, grabbed the soap on the table, and then ambled back over to me. The soap smelled of honey, and the moment I had it in hand, I plunged it beneath the warm water and rubbed it between my hands. The bubbles and suds rose to the top of the water, creating an ivory foam.

"What did you want to talk about?" I asked, my eyelids heavy.

Fain knelt next to the tub and leaned his weight on the side. He didn't say anything. I waited, confused. Seconds turned into minutes.

Finally, I said, "Good talk."

"Lately, I've been... lonely," Fain muttered.

I leaned back in the tub, the water lulling me back into a relaxed state. I rubbed the bar of soap over my chest and arms, hoping to the stars in the sky Fain wasn't about to court me. I already had troubles with relationships. I didn't need another.

"What do you mean?" I asked.

"I mean, I'm often by myself."

"Where's Wraith?"

Fain's eldrin, the deadly wendigo, appeared inside the bathing room. He hadn't teleported—he had just been invisible. His wolf-like body, along with the wolf skull Wraith "wore" over his head, gave him a menacing appearance. Normally, wendigo also had deer antlers, but Wraith's had been cut off to make plague-immunity trinkets...

Now he had no antlers.

Wraith's emaciated body also made him appear more like a corpse than a mystical creature. When he wandered over, he looked like a dog with mange.

"I'm right here," Wraith said, his deep voice quiet. "I'm always with my arcanist."

"I meant, why aren't you two keeping each other company?"

"Wraith and I are close," Fain replied. "But that doesn't

mean I don't crave human interaction." He patted Wraith's head, and the wendigo let out a contented sigh.

Then Wraith took a seat next to his arcanist. He wagged his fluffy, gray tail, but otherwise his skull-face was damn near emotionless. After a short while, he cloaked himself back in invisibility. A silent wolf, always nearby, their bond steadfast, though quiet.

I slowly nodded. "Where's Adelgis?"

"Moonbeam is with the guildmaster," Fain said with a long sigh. "He's been with her for a while now."

"Why?"

"He's using his dreamweaving and dreamwalking to sense the other god-creatures, or something." Fain shook his head and glared at the bubbly water. "I'm not sure of the specifics. All I know is that he's constantly busy. He's tryin' to... find his father, and find the fenris wolf, and a dozen other things."

"That does sound important." And my statement was anything but profound, but my sleep-addled mind made it difficult to form meaningful comments.

Fain glanced up. I stared at him for a long time, and he lifted an eyebrow.

"You can blink, ya know. Blinkin' is free."

I rubbed at my eyes. "I haven't been? Sorry." I splashed some of the water across my face. "I'm awake. I swear. What do you want me to do about this?"

Fain sighed again. He touched one of his black fingers to the surface of my water. An icy rime sprouted from his touch and lightly coated a small portion of the water. The moment he removed his finger, the magically warm water melted his evocation.

"I'm not sure," he muttered. "You and Moonbeam are the only ones I ever speak with."

"What about Karna?"

"Well, yeah, I sometimes talk to her, but she's made it clear she wants little to do with me."

"Oh." I splashed more water across my face. "Uh, what about... Zaxis?"

"He's always training."

"Zelfree?"

"I don't care for him. He's the *Faceless*, an infamous renegade pirate. I get nightmares about the guy."

"What about Captain Devlin?"

"He's takin' care of that little girl. Plus, he and Vethica are tryin' to figure out ways to use her magic to help people with the plague as fast as possible."

"Have you ever considered that your standards are too high?" I joked.

Fain glowered. "You're right. I should be content to spend time with the brooms in the broom closet. One of them is missin' half its bristles. I'm sure there's an interesting story there."

"There is. The mop got jealous."

"I'm bein' serious," Fain snapped. Then he quieted himself and glanced away.

"What do you and Adelgis talk about?" I asked. "Just discuss the same kinds of things with other people. I'm sure you'll find someone."

Fain shrugged. He remained tense, his teeth gritted. "Nobody talks like Moonbeam. Yesterday, when he woke, he told me he had a feeling this week would be haunted." Fain turned and met my gaze. "What in the abyssal hells does that even mean? All I could do was laugh. And then he laughed. And *then* we started talking about the different types of breakfast we had during our travels."

"Adelgis is unique, I'll give you that."

"Nobody really appreciates him, ya know." Fain stood up and crossed his arms. His posture remained combative, and he refused to look at me. "That's why he's so obsessed with helping the guildmaster. I know it. He wants to prove himself. Prove he's *useful*." He paced around my tub to the other side. "When I ran with Calisto's pirate crew, men proved themselves by killin' other men, or shootin' well... I don't have anything to offer Moonbeam, so he goes off, chasin' glory."

Fain was talking to himself more than me. I listened, though I wasn't sure what the point was.

After a few moments of mumbling, Fain stopped and frowned. When he glanced over, his eyebrows were knitted. "I'm sorry. You've got a lot of troubles already. This is... petty."

"I don't mind," I said. Then I chuckled. "A sprained ankle isn't as bad as a broken leg, but you still shouldn't walk on either. In all honesty, dealing with someone else's minor troubles is a welcome change."

"You're a good man," Fain said, so earnest I could feel it. "You're the reason I wanted to join the Frith Guild, ya know. I could tell you were different." He pointed to the god-arcanist mark on my chest. "And I guess my gut was right."

I hesitated. It still felt odd to be the focus of such reverence.

"Is there anything I can do for you?" Fain asked.

I shook my head, but before I said *no*, I caught myself. "Wait," I said. "There is something. Can you help me train? I think your ice evocation might help control my obsidian."

"Those rocks that come out of your body?"

I nodded. Then I furrowed my brow. "How did you know about that?"

"I watch you train sometimes."

Ah. Always invisible. I should have just assumed Fain was with me more than my own shadow.

"But... I'll handle my own problem. Somehow." Fain shrouded himself with his invisibility. "Someone is heading this way. Wraith says it's... Illia."

Someone knocked on the door before I could reply. With

hasty movements, I rubbed the soap under the water a second time, covering the surface of my tub water in bubbles and suds. The door opened—even though I hadn't said anything—and Illia and Nicholin walked straight in.

Illia jumped the moment her one-eyed gaze landed on me.

"You're awake," she muttered.

"Y-Yeah." I ducked down until my chin was under the water. "Did you come in here before?"

"Just to put the towels over there." She pointed, but I didn't look.

Despite the awkwardness, she hovered around the door, neither walking in, nor walking out. My whole body reddened, and I silently contemplated ducking beneath the water until she was gone.

"Are you okay?" I asked.

"Yes."

The door to the bathing room slammed against the wall and swung a bit. Illia jumped, and backed away, and Nicholin's white fur stood on end. What had happened? My gut knew. Fain and Wraith had left the room, and one of them had accidentally slammed the door on the way out.

"It's fine," I said with a nervous chuckle. "Just the wind."

There wasn't even a gentle breeze, but Illia didn't question it. She turned back around, one eyebrow lifted.

Nicholin ran along her shoulders, his little ferret body a ball of springs and bounces. "Let's go in! I want to help trim his fur."

Illia shook her head. "Evianna said she would handle that."

"Boo. No fun."

Illia stepped closer to the door, her hand on the handle. Right as she was about to leave, I sat up a bit and said, "Uh, Illia. Wait a moment."

She hesitated, half-outside. "Yeah?"

"Have you seen Fain around?"

"No. Not really."

"Would you, uh, check up on him from time to time? Since Adelgis has been busy, I think he hasn't had many people to interact with."

"Why?" she said, her tone shifting from embarrassed and apologetic to mildly outraged. "You know I can't stand him."

Her hatred of pirates ran so deep, even the mere mention of one seemed to put her on edge. I suspected even parrots might agitate her, though it was irrational. Everyone understood why, but I still wished Illia would move on.

"Fain left that life," I said. "And I know if you're not with Zaxis you're just off by yourself."

Illia swept her wavy brown hair back. She had cut it shorter again. It barely touched her shoulders. "*Why* though?"

"He's feeling alone."

"He pillaged and murdered."

I really didn't know the totality of his crimes, but Fain had run with the Dread Pirate Calisto, so I assumed his sins numbered in the dozens. "He's our ally now," was all I could say.

"So?"

"So, I'm saying you could forgive and help him out."

Illia glared, and Nicholin half-hid behind her shorter hair. I thought I was in for an argument, but she took a deep breath and calmed herself.

"Master Zelfree says I should either confront what haunts me or let it go," she muttered. "He says it's holding me back from mastering my magic. It was why... I had such a difficult time with my manipulation and why I can't create a magical aura." She took another step out of the room.

Both Illia and Zelfree couldn't master their auras because of Calisto? That had to be it. Zelfree blamed himself for the way Calisto had turned out, and Illia hated the man because he had taken her eye.

What could I do about this? I didn't have an easy solution.

"Does that mean you'll spend time with Fain?" I called after her.

"We'll see," Illia said as she shut the door, leaving me alone in the warm water.

I figured that was a tiny victory. A part of me wanted to solve everyone's problems, but the reasonable bit of me knew if I accepted every issue that came my way, I'd be swamped. Still, I liked that I could help Fain. And maybe Illia as well.

I really wished she would get along with Fain. Maybe they just needed to spend time together.

<hr>

I fell asleep again, but I woke up the moment I slid down the side of the tub and water got into my nose. I sat up, my heart pounding. I'd have to leave the bathing room soon. I dreaded the idea of getting out of the comfortable, soapy water.

I glanced around. The quiet of the bathing room didn't sit right with me.

"Fain?" I whispered.

Nothing. It was rare that he wasn't nearby.

"Adelgis?" I asked.

He, too, didn't reply. How strange. He usually had his telepathic abilities homed in on me.

I wasn't dreaming, but part of me wished I was.

After a long exhale, I asked, "Terrakona?"

"Warlord?" my eldrin replied, his telepathy a soothing reassurance.

"Sorry," I said aloud. Then I leaned my weight on the side of the tub. "Help me wake up, would you? We're almost to Fortuna."

"We are docking now. This is a city built by the Children of Balastar. It should prove amusing."

"W-We're already docking?" I leapt from the tub and scrambled to grab a towel. I patted my body as fast as I could, half-focused on the moment and half-focused on everything I still needed to do in order to be presentable.

"You should rest," Terrakona telepathically said.

"I will. Later. Right now, I have to meet the arcanists waiting in Fortuna."

"There are close to two hundred arcanists here. Some have traveled a great distance."

My heart nearly stopped. Halfway through drying myself, I stood straight. A mirror hung near the washbasin, and I walked over to get a better look at myself. The god-arcanist mark on my chest reminded me why so many arcanists had gathered here.

They had come to see me.

"How can you tell?" I whispered.

"The arcanists of your guild have already investigated. The mimic arcanist—and the Mother of Shapeshifters—can sense mystical creatures."

I calmed myself by closing my eyes and tilting my head back.

"Are you anxious, Warlord?"

"Well, I nearly died from fighting a roc pirate," I said with a forced chuckle. "So, yeah. A little nervous."

Terrakona's telepathic tone shifted to one of haunting seriousness. **"Death is breathing down our necks, but I'll keep it from catching you for as long as I can."**

I nodded and smiled to myself. "Thank you."

"It is my duty. We will face oblivion together."

Oblivion?

For some reason, I thought of the dark and sinister dragon I had seen in my terror-filled delusions. Would the apoch dragon be our oblivion, like it had been for the first world serpent arcanist? I hoped not.

"I need to get ready," I said as I wrapped the cloth around my waist and headed for the door. "Terrakona, can you please watch after the guild while I'm in the city? I don't want anything to happen to them."

"I won't be accompanying you?"

"No. You're too big. I don't want to cause a scene."

"As you wish, Warlord. I will defend the guild and atlas turtle until your return."

WHERE THERE IS FEAR, YOU WILL FIND POWER

I wandered into the front room of my quarters, expecting to find Illia or Karna. After a deep breath, I made sure my towel was secured around my waist. I already had an awkward time with women—I still needed to speak with both Atty and Evianna about serious matters—and I didn't want to make anything more complicated than it already was.

"Finally," a gruff voice said.

"Huh?" I asked as I snapped my attention to the corner of the room.

Master Zelfree leaned against the wall by the window, one foot hooked around the other ankle. He rested his weight so heavily on the wall that I was tempted to make a joke about them being a married couple.

"Get dressed," Zelfree said. He motioned to a neatly stacked tower of clothes on the edge of the couch. "If you need help with anything, I'm here."

I half-laughed. "I don't mean to brag, but I've been successfully dressing myself since I was two—that's nearly sixteen years."

Zelfree lifted an eyebrow halfway, like he didn't even have

the energy to return my sarcasm. "This is different," he said. "We're dressing you to impress, not for utility. Tell me, when you were apprenticing to be a gravedigger, did they ever teach you how to fold a handkerchief? Or the proper way to lace your sleeves and boots?"

"Lace my... *sleeves*?" I repeated. "Why would I do that?"

After a deep sigh, Zelfree pushed away from the wall. "Okay, listen up. History lesson. Fortuna is run by a gaggle of *old* arcanists who live in a damn clock tower."

"The Astral Tower," I interjected.

"Huh?"

"The name of the clock tower. It's called *The Astral Tower*."

Zelfree narrowed his eyes, fatigue apparent in every line of his face.

"Sorry," I muttered. "Continue the story."

"The arcanists of Fortuna formed a council after the Argo Empire was removed from power over the northern islands. Since then, those wizened arcanists have done little more than issue new laws and dole out justice from their supreme court. Most of them never leave the city."

"Okay. And?"

"They're relics frozen in time, and that time was a few hundred years ago." Zelfree ran a hand down his face. "Which means their fashion sense is frozen in time as well. Back when *sleeve laces* were proper and collar frills were all the rage. And since we're meeting with them in a few hours, Eventide thought it important you make the best impression possible."

"So, I have to wear antiquated clothing?" I gave the stack of clothing a sideways glance. "Where did this outfit even come from?"

"Trust me. You'd rather not know."

The ominous way he said the statement got me thinking unpleasant thoughts.

"They belong to someone who's dead, don't they?" I stared at Zelfree, never blinking.

Unfortunately, Zelfree maintained his emotionless—and exhausted—demeanor and revealed nothing. He didn't even skip a beat when he replied, "Guessing won't do you any good, kid. I'm not gonna say a damn word." Then he snapped his fingers. "Go on. Trousers first."

I walked over to the clothes and dragged out the trousers. At first, I thought they would be frumpy and baked in dust. I had imagined something pulled from the coffin of a man who had died two hundred years ago.

Instead, the trousers were slick, ivory white, with buttons up the sides. They reminded me of a naval uniform I had once seen Gravekeeper William wearing. I slipped the trousers up under my towel. Then I grabbed the large belt poking out of the clothes pile and secured it in place. The buckle had to be half the size of my fist. The silver on the belt shone with a beautiful luster.

I tossed my towel to the side and then picked up the shirt. The collar resembled a crumpled napkin. The frills weren't a look I appreciated, and I tried to flatten them before tugging it over my head.

The fluff of the collar was so massive that the top touched the bottom of my chin.

"Seriously?" I asked.

Zelfree chortled. "You should've seen some of the high fashions in my time."

I picked up a royal blue doublet. Gold trim lined the collar and pockets, and laces with flakes of actual gold were tied on the sleeves. Unlike a normal sailing coat, this doublet was padded and fitted tight around the waist and chest. While I pulled it on, I asked, "What time period did you grow up in?"

"It was long ago now," Zelfree murmured. His gaze unfocused as he stared at a spot on the floor.

"Are you okay?"

My new doublet fit surprisingly well, and I wondered if someone had tailored it to my size.

Zelfree glanced up. "I'm fine. And what did I say about asking personal questions?"

"Why not? We've known each other a while."

After a short sigh, he said, "I suppose. But still. I'm tired. I fear that whatever I tell you will be too much—or perhaps too depressing. Maybe talk to me once I've had three weeks to sleep."

I chuckled to myself. "Fair enough."

Due to the magic coursing through their bodies, arcanists had extended lives. When I was younger, I thought that meant a couple of years, but after I had seen Gregory Ruma—still in his prime—hundreds of years after his exploits, I had changed my thinking.

Zelfree was a few hundred years old. A lot had happened in his life. One day, I hoped he would tell me everything.

I picked up a pair of thin socks and pulled them over my feet. "It feels like we've known each other longer than three years." Just like it had with Luthair. Curiosity got the better of me. "Who would you say has known you the longest?"

"I..." Zelfree's voice became distant. "Probably Eventide."

"What about—" I stopped myself before I said the name. Instead, I forced a cough and then said, "You don't have any childhood friends?" Last time I had mentioned *Lynus* to Master Zelfree, it had caused an argument.

But Zelfree must've realized who I had been referring to. He turned to me, his body tense, even as he crossed his arms. "Lynus is dead," he stated. "He died when he fully assumed the mantle of the Dread Pirate Calisto."

"I didn't mean—"

"I know." Zelfree grabbed the last of the clothing—a gold

sash belt and a pair of knee-high boots—and threw them at me. "I just don't want to talk about it."

I nodded and continued with my outfit. Part of me wanted to help, but another part of me remembered I couldn't be the one to solve *everyone's* problems.

Then again, I suspected I cared about this issue because of Calisto himself. He really *was* the cause of Zelfree and Illia's distress. Something would have to be done, but Calisto ran with the Second Ascension now. When would we see him next? And would we have to fight through an army of arcanists to get to him?

And could my god-arcanist powers beat him? Illia would likely insist on killing Calisto herself. Last time she had tried, we *all* almost died.

"You're tying the sash all wrong," Zelfree growled.

I jerked my attention up, embarrassed that I had descended so far into my own thoughts. "Sorry," I muttered.

My golden sash was twisted and wrinkled. Zelfree ambled over, untied it, and then fixed it back into place with a quick loop around. When he was done, I admired the way the metallic gold complemented the royal blue of the doublet.

"It does look... fancy," I said, unable to think of a better word.

"The problem is your arcanist mark," Zelfree said, glaring a hole into my shirt. "Most clothes aren't made for someone with a mark on their chest."

I unbuttoned the doublet and shirt underneath. It seemed unprofessional—or perhaps pirate-like—to walk around with everything open, but there wasn't a better solution. If people were going to see my mark, I had to look a little sloppy. That suited me fine. The frills of the collar no longer tickled my chin.

Thank the heavens for tiny favors.

Zelfree adjusted the belt again, this time tucking in parts of the loose shirt around the back so it didn't flutter everywhere, but still remained open in the front.

"Try not to get assassinated from the front," he quipped, tapping me in the middle of the chest.

"Last time the roc came from behind."

Zelfree honestly smiled. "Yeah. That's how it'll be. Always from behind, and right when you least expect it." He sighed. "Now let's deal with your sleeves and get you out there. Everyone is waiting. This is your moment."

I allowed Zelfree to fix the gold laces on my sleeves, my heart beating faster now that the moment was upon me. Fortuna was a large city. So many people would be here. And they had all come to see me.

Once everything was laced and tied, I pulled on my boots and secured them as well. Zelfree walked around me, giving me the once over. When he finally stopped in front of me, he smiled. "You look good."

"Thank you."

"Don't let it go to your head."

"I'll try not to." After taking a few steps to get accustomed to the soft leather of the boots, I turned to Zelfree and asked, "Is there some other reason we need to make such a good impression?"

"You mean, besides the many numerous reasons I've already given you?"

"Yeah." I rubbed at the back of my neck as my anxiety built. "It seems like everyone is concerned about it. And not just for my sake."

"Eventide has her reasons."

Perhaps it had something to do with the runestones we had?

Most people didn't know, but the Frith Guild had five other runestones in our possession. They were the key to opening the lairs of the god-creatures, and the only way someone could prove themselves in the trial of worth. Now that the god-creatures were spawning around the world, there was no doubt in my mind that people would be willing to pay exorbitant amounts of gold to get their hands on one.

But as long as we kept that fact hidden, there shouldn't be any problems.

In theory.

"Who will the Frith Guild give the other runestones to?" I asked.

Zelfree grabbed my upper arm and yanked me toward the door. He had a strong grip, despite his obvious fatigue. "Are you serious? *Focus*. What in the abyssal hells did I just tell you? We need to make a good impression."

"I will."

"Not if you're daydreamin'."

Zelfree took me into the hallway for the master arcanist quarters. To my surprise, Karna and Evianna waited for me, one with a pair of scissors, and the other with a small bowl of water and a towel.

"Last step, then we're heading out," Zelfree stated.

No one had cut my hair properly in a long time.

I hesitantly ran my fingers through the short cut on the sides and eventually grazed the longer locks on the top. My wild black hair had been tamed with a generous amount of pomade, giving it a slicked-back and wet appearance. I hardly recognized myself when I glanced in a mirror.

Somehow, I looked good. Dashing, even.

Like a hero arcanist of legend. Or perhaps an epic swashbuckler.

The faint outline of my old knightmare arcanist mark was still visible on my forehead, however. I traced the thin lines with a shaky hand. I'd have this scar for the rest of my life, and I wouldn't have it any other way.

Before I left Gentel, I made sure I had Retribution and Forfend. With my sword at my hip, and my shield tied to my left forearm, I resembled a heroic knight from the old tales of chivalry.

With my thoughts lost in a haze, I exited the guild manor house to find almost every single apprentice, journeyman, and master arcanist outside and heading toward the dinghies. The smell of salt water and flotsam eased my nerves as I strode toward the small boats.

I didn't get far, though. Guildmaster Eventide had been waiting for me in the courtyard. She stepped close and smiled wide. "Volke. Perfect. We need to talk."

I held up my arms. "I think I'm all dressed."

"Hm. Very handsome." She placed a hand on my shoulder and met my gaze. "Listen, I was hoping you could make a dramatic entrance. Something stylish and noteworthy."

"Really?" I asked. "Why? Shouldn't I just... walk into town? And try not to trip?"

"You're a god-arcanist, which means you're larger than life. Do you remember Gregory Ruma? When he arrived at Fortuna, he always made a splash. Forgive the pun."

I nodded along with her words. I did remember. Ruma had changed the weather and splashed the docks with playful waves. His leviathan had circled through the waters, creating gentle whirlpools. Everything about his arrival had stirred up energy, hype, and anticipation.

Eventide wanted me to do the same thing?

"How?" I asked.

"Sail into the docks while riding Terrakona."

"Just like Ruma rode on the back of his leviathan?" I asked, my heart racing. "Really?"

Eventide nodded.

"Okay," I said as I brushed myself off. I couldn't help but smile. I had always wanted to do something as stunning and as spectacular as Ruma. This was my moment.

"Just remember you represent the Frith Guild," she said as she motioned to the edge of the atlas turtle. "Don't do anything to make the people worry about you." Eventide patted my shoulder and gestured me off.

"I won't." I stepped around her and hurried off. "Terrakona!"

His presence in my mind stirred. Unlike Luthair, who had to be merged with me to speak with me telepathically, I always had a link to Terrakona. Muttering his name was enough to summon his attention, and the waters around the gigantic atlas turtle rumbled with his movement.

I walked toward the edge of the grassy shell. "I need to get to Fortuna. Can you take me, please?"

"A simple task, Warlord," Terrakona telepathically said.

With a crowd of arcanists watching, I leapt from the shell and sailed toward the water. Ever since I had flown with Luthair, heights didn't bother me. A part of me felt as though I'd sprout wings at any second and take to the skies, or that I'd land in the shadows and dive beneath the surface of the darkness.

Instead, Terrakona lifted up to meet me, slow enough that I didn't collide with his head and shatter my legs. I landed on the very top of his skull, above where his scales became his crystal mane, my knees buckling, but I managed to keep my balance.

The Frith Guild arcanists gasped and pointed, their excited murmurs infectious. I laughed the moment Terrakona swam for the Fortuna docks, the ocean winds disturbing my perfectly cut hair. Smiling from ear to ear, I knelt and held on as Terrakona picked up speed. In less than a minute, he arrived close enough to slow and veer toward a pier.

The denizens of Fortuna had gathered on the streets, piers,

and rooftops of Fortuna. Their many bodies blurred together in my vision, like a shimmering school of fish, where it was impossible to pick out a single individual. They wore festive clothing, some with ruffled collars, some with fancy coats.

It really did remind me of the celebration the city had held for Ruma's arrival. I never thought I'd have such a reception. That, too, was infectious. In my mind, I played out my arrival—jumping off the head of the world serpent, declaring the destruction of the Second Ascension—and striding through the cheering crowds with my hands held high.

It'd be a long walk.

Fortuna was a city that was as tall as it was wide. It had been built on a giant hill, with buildings on every step-like terrace to the very top. Farms and smaller homes dotted the base and certain terraces, creating a beautiful mix of industry and rural life.

On the top of the hill, like a crown on the head of a king, was a gargantuan clock tower—*the Astral Tower*. A representation of the night sky had been etched into a steel dais that rotated with the seasons. Bells hung around the outside, some large, some so small I couldn't see them from the docks, but each with enough sound to ring out across all of Fortuna.

It was a legislative building, a home to the ruling arcanists, as well as the city's keeper of time. And, also, my destination.

Terrakona lowered his serpentine head near one of the crowded piers. I thought I'd have to push my way through the citizens, utter dozens of apologies, and slowly make my way down the main street. To my surprise, the people of Fortuna leapt away from me.

Some were so desperate to flee my presence that they threw themselves into the water.

The gasps and silence that followed didn't remind me of Ruma's reception *at all*. Fortuna had cheered for him. He had made it snow with his ability to control weather, delighting the adults and children alike. They had claimed he would solve their problems.

But when the people of Fortuna looked at me...

Their wide eyes and trembling stances were anything but delighted.

Fear?

Panic?

Confusion?

I hadn't... expected any of that. It bothered me. It always bothered me when people were afraid. Guildmaster Eventide had said not to make them worry, yet here I was...

They pointed at Terrakona, and then at the mark on my chest. I was the first god-arcanist in thousands of years, so I understood why they'd be hesitant, but I had thought, because I was a member of the Frith Guild, they'd trust me.

But they didn't. I took a step toward the city, to tell the dockmaster to get dinghies for the people in the ocean, and even more of the crowd hastily backed away. The fishermen, the dockhands—even the city guards—dared not approach.

"Terrakona?" I mumbled under my breath.

"Warlord?"

"Can't you... hear the thoughts of others?"

"Only inside my lair," Terrakona telepathically replied. **"In my lair, I can hear the thoughts and desires of all who enter. Out here, bathed in the glow of the oldest light, I can only hear the voice of my arcanist."**

I walked forward, and the sea of people split all the way to the main road. They knew where I intended to go.

"Why are they afraid?" I muttered under my breath. "I thought... the god-creatures were born to help guide humanity into a new age. I thought...."

"Where there is fear, you will find power." Terrakona slipped down beneath the waves, his emerald scales glittering like gemstones in the afternoon light. "**The power to usher humanity into a new age is unlike what they have seen before, and things that are *new* only amplify the fear.**"

I continued down the pier, and then onto the main thoroughfare of the dock. The planks of wood creaked under my boots—I never knew an entire city could hold its breath. When I glanced at the people in the crowd, they flinched and moved away.

"But why?" I whispered. "I haven't done anything yet. And I'm not here to kill them. I'm here to make things better."

"**I cannot provide the reasoning behind the actions of a few hundred thousand individuals. All I know is that change frightens them. Some people won't move on from *good enough* to *greatness*. Sometimes people won't let go of *bad*, for fear of *something worse*. That is why you must guide them.**"

A shadow washed over me, and I turned my attention to the cloudless sky. Mesos flew overhead, her massive wingspan enough to create a fair amount of shade. She screeched as she headed toward the Astral Tower. Two people were on her back —one had to be Captain Devlin—but who was the other?

A second roc streaked across the sky. For a moment, I thought the pirates had returned, but then I realized it had to be Master Zelfree. His eldrin had mimicked Mesos so they could travel to the clock tower faster.

The citizens of Fortuna watched the two rocs go with *oohs* and *ahhs*.

It was only then that I spotted the myriad of other mystical creatures. Fairies fluttered overhead, as well as a few pixies and grifter crows.

There were two hundred arcanists here, after all. Their presence reminded me of my responsibilities.

After a deep inhale, I headed into town. No one stopped me. No one crossed my path. No one even spoke to me. It might as well have been a funeral—the populace observed with half-bowed heads and silent stares. A few children, unbound by society's pressure, attempted to approach, but their parents yanked them away and fled shortly afterward.

I didn't let it stop me, though. With my head held high, I set my sights on the Astral Tower and didn't glance back.

THE ASTRAL TOWER

A part of me wondered how news of my bonding had traveled so fast.

How did the people of Fortuna already know?

Then again, how *wouldn't* they know? When I had bonded with Terrakona, the entire sky had gone black, probably across the entire world. And after the attack on Thronehold, I was certain everyone knew of the Second Ascension's intentions to get their hands on the god-creatures. News was spreading faster than any fire.

But was the information they circulated accurate? Maybe the people of Fortuna thought of me as a tyrant.

I had imagined walking down the main road of Fortuna all the way to the Astral Tower, but the moment I spotted a narrow alleyway, I ducked into it, despite the gasps and pointing of all those watching me. I ran down the narrow and twisted walkways behind shops and tall buildings, careful to avoid people and even dodging a bucket of dirty water as a woman threw out her old washbasin.

Once certain I had evaded the main crowd, I leaned against a rough stone building and caught my breath.

My flashy new clothing fit in with the festive citizens. I buttoned up my shirt and doublet, hiding my god-arcanist mark, and with a quick yank, I undid my sash belt and tied it around my forehead, creating an impromptu bandana.

With my new "disguise," I wandered onto a different street and continued my trek toward the Astral Tower. As I had suspected, no one recognized me. I hadn't yet become so famous that people would know me by my face, and without an arcanist mark, most would assume I was mortal.

"The world serpent arcanist disappeared," someone told another.

"Like a thief, he ran off into the shadows, he did," a woman added.

I didn't care. Zelfree had said to make a good impression, but I figured disappearing was better than frightening everyone. I wanted our *foes* to fear us, not the people of my island nation. And Eventide didn't want me to cause anyone anxiety.

This was for the best.

With haste in my step, I hurried for the Astral Tower. Fortuna was a large city, and avoiding the main road made the trek longer. I remembered when I had first set foot here and thought this city was too gigantic to be real. Living on an island... my world had been so small. Now my eldrin was larger than the Isle of Ruma.

My pace slowed.

Fortuna buzzed with commotion. The guards were looking for me. People rode horses up and down the main thoroughfares.

"*Volke?*"

The telepathic communication caught me off guard. I almost tripped on the bricks of the road.

"Adelgis?" I said aloud.

"Where have you gone? The people of Fortuna say you disappeared. They claim you have invisibility."

"Oh, no," I muttered. Then I shoved my hands into my doublet pockets. "I just couldn't stand their frightened stares. I'm on my way to the tower."

"I'll let the guildmaster know."

"Thank you."

"And I'll send Fain to follow you."

"Why?" I asked, almost indignant.

"You shouldn't be alone, Volke. Fain can follow you discreetly."

It amused me how Adelgis coordinated things. His telepathy had become so powerful. Just like his dreamwalking and weaving. I dwelled on it as I headed toward the tower. Everyone said Adelgis's magic would be stunted due to the abyssal leech he had carried in his body. Was he achieving this greatness *despite* the leech? It made me wonder how powerful he would've been if he hadn't carried the monstrous creature.

"Where are you?"

"By some sort of bakery," I said, the aroma a pleasant distraction. "Tell him to search for the scent of bread."

"He'll be with you shortly."

I didn't bother to wait. I pressed forward. Of course, the rest of the Frith Guild would be worried. I probably should've waited for them, but the idea of making an impressive entrance had just taken hold of me. It had probably been foolish. I cursed to myself as I went.

The uphill roads made the walk difficult. My legs burned by the time I reached the wrought-iron fence around the building, but it wasn't something I couldn't handle. I had gone through worse. Much worse.

The fence surrounding the Astral Tower stood fifteen feet tall. The main gate was a few feet taller than that, and the metal bars were twisted into designs—owls, stars, and ships. Two guards waited on the outside of the fence, while two stood on the inside, closer to the gate.

One on the outside had a star etched into his flesh on his forehead. An arcanist. And when I got closer, I noticed the mystical creature woven throughout the mark was a troll. The muscular form, and pointed ears made it distinct.

Troll arcanists had increased strength, and I was fairly certain they could see through darkness and were immune to things that paralyzed creatures or turned their flesh to stone. Was this troll arcanist the captain of the guard?

"Hello," I said as I approached the gate.

The main gate was positioned in the shadow of the massive clock tower, and I didn't have to shield my eyes as the troll arcanist straightened his posture and stared down at me. Not too many people could do that. He had at least three inches on me, and his muscles were barely contained by his leather armor. Even his brown hair seemed prone to wild growth—it was thick and flowing and went past his shoulder blades.

I didn't see a troll around, and I suspected the mystical creature was inside. Trolls didn't care much for the daytime. They were nocturnal.

"The Astral Tower isn't open to the public," the troll arcanist said, his voice low and deep enough to intimidate stone.

"I'm not *the public*," I said. "Everyone in the tower is waiting for me."

The troll arcanist chuckled. And then the other guards joined in. One guard even murmured, "Did you hear that? *This guy.*"

Another shook his head. "He's drunk."

"I hope all the eldrin heard that," the troll arcanist said. He glanced up and smiled.

I tilted my head back and stared up at the massive tower. A single roc sat atop the tip of the intricate machine. But it wasn't just Mesos. My eyes widened as I noticed the two dragons perched alongside the giant bird.

Both had dazzling wings, but one had feathers and the other had thin leather.

The feathers... They drew my attention right away.

Only a few dragons had *feathered wings*. And this dragon was unique because it had two heads. It wasn't a hydra—the two heads of this dragon were identical, with bright blue eyes alight with intelligence.

This dragon was white, with hints of blue on its scales.

A twilight dragon.

A juvenile twilight dragon, in the flesh. Probably only *half* the size it would become once it was fully grown, and already it weighed as much as Mesos.

Twilight dragons were bright white during the day and bluish-black at night. A dual creature that changed with the time of day. They were so rare, some books I had read said there were only three left. Was that true? I never thought I'd see a twilight dragon in my entire life.

The other dragon was impressive, sure, but when it sat next to the twilight dragon, it just didn't compare.

The other was a cliffside dragon, the kind with copper scales and green eyes. It was bulky—almost looked fat, but I knew better. Cliffside dragons could hold their whole weight on the side of a mountain for multiple days in a row. They were strong, and their wide mouths could bite through quartz. What looked like fat was just muscles.

And this one was an adult, unlike the juvenile twilight dragon.

Dragons were some of the most powerful mystical creatures. According to Theasin Venrover, they were *tier 4* out of a 5-rank system. But they weren't as powerful as the god-creatures. Still, dragons were impressive, and I couldn't let my guard down, not when I barely had any of my powers. If those dragons swooped down, I was certain they could kill me, or at least get real close.

"Gawking?" the troll arcanist said with a smirk. "What's wrong, doorknob? I thought you said everyone was gathered here for you?"

"I..." I couldn't help but nervously laugh. "I know what this looks like. I can explain."

He offered me a faux bow, one arm held out in sarcastic fashion. "Are you lost, *Your Majesty*? Have you come to introduce yourself to the world serpent arcanist like the other princes, kings, and queens?"

Other princes, kings, and queens?

More nervous laughter escaped me. "Wait, what? Princes, kings, and queens?"

The troll arcanist and other guards chortled louder.

"That's right," the arcanist said as he stood tall. "I, your faithful servant, Gustav Wern the Troll Arcanist, will escort you into the banquet hall, where you can mingle with your peers until the world serpent arcanist arrives."

I stared up at the dragons. Most monarchies were formed around the bonding of certain dragons. Only sovereign dragon arcanists could rule in the Argo Empire—other nations had similar requirements. Dragons had some of the hardest trials of worth, so most people equated that with an individual's ability to govern.

"Are those dragons the eldrin of kings and queens who have come to meet the world serpent arcanist?" I asked. They had to be.

Gustav dramatically lifted both of his bushy eyebrows. "You must be the *Prince Doorknob of the Amnesia Kingdom.* Don't you remember? You said everyone's expecting you."

My mouth went dry. I had known this would happen. Master Zelfree had even said so. I was here to make a good impression. I had thought I'd have more time to practice, however. The ruling arcanists of Fortuna were supposed to be my *practice round*, but instead, multiple kings and queens were already here?

I hadn't seen their knights in town or their boats at port.

I gave the dragons another quick glance. The kings and queens had flown here, just as the master arcanists of the Frith Guild had taken the rocs. It was a faster form of travel, and since most of them would've been given short notice of my arrival, flying was the only way to get here in time.

"Uh, well, I have an amusing confession." I couldn't suppress the awkwardness in my tone.

"Oh? I can't wait to hear this."

The other gate guards exchanged bemused expressions.

I tugged off the golden sash wrapped around my forehead. The guards stopped their chuckling and examined my old knightmare mark. It was faded but still visible.

"You used to be a knightmare arcanist?" Gustav asked. His amusement vanished in an instant. "You must be from the old Steel Thorn Inquisitors Guild."

"Well..." The story was so long, I didn't know where to begin.

Gustav rapped his knuckles on the gate and the two guards inside pulled it open. "Go on in. The others are waiting for you."

"Really?" I asked. I had been prepared to open my doublet and show them my god-arcanist mark. I hadn't expected this.

"The last of the knightmare arcanists already went inside." Gustav gestured with a thumb. "I apologize for my tone earlier. I thought you were a drunkard." His dark brown eyes hardened a bit as he stared at my old mark. He frowned. "It must be difficult, losing your eldrin."

I held my breath, conflicted. I didn't want to explain myself. His pity hurt, and the mere mention of other knightmare arcanists got my hopes up.

"Thank you," I said.

Gustav replied with a genuine bow of his head. "Welcome to the Astral Tower, Inquisitor."

The title got me nervous, like I was lying to the man. But I replied with a curt nod and headed for the main double doors.

The Astral Tower had been constructed with the utmost care. The pathway to the door was made out of bricks with names of all the workers, designers, and arcanists who had helped to build it. The garden and shrubs around the massive building were kept trim and neat. The doors themselves had bronze knockers in the shape of owl heads.

And the sound...

The click and clank of machinery softly trickled out of the tower. How did it work? Was it powered with magic? Was it louder inside? Although I had seen the Astral Tower several times from afar, this was the closest I had ever been.

I yanked open the left door and strode into the building, my throat tight. Several dragon arcanists, the council of Fortuna, and dozens of other arcanists were waiting for me.

Curse the abyssal hells! I hadn't even thought of what I would say.

THE TWILIGHT DRAGON ARCANIST

The inside of the Astral Tower took my breath away.

Exposed gears and cogs covered the ceiling, each turning at a steady pace. The clang of operation echoed in the long hallway before me, and I stood for a long minute admiring the atmosphere. The brass, copper, and steel of the machine all shone with care. Oil from the rotators and twisting mechanisms tarnished the luster around the connecting points, but otherwise, everything appeared as though it were cleaned thoroughly, perhaps daily.

I slowly strode down the entrance hall, my attention on the ceiling and not my feet. I almost tripped on a gray rug, and I stumbled a bit before catching myself.

Unlike the castle in Thronehold, or the libraries I had seen in the city of Ellios, the Astral Tower wasn't elaborately decorated. There were images of owls and feathers etched into the thick glass of the windows, but otherwise, there was a utilitarian presence to the tower. No decorative plants. No vibrant colors. Just wood, stone, and metal gears.

It felt like I had shrunken down and was walking around the inside of a clock.

With unsteady hands, I unbuttoned my shirt and doublet. Then I tied my sash belt back in place.

I almost laughed. Despite everyone's efforts, I had disheveled my hair, smeared pomade on my sash belt, and then tied it sloppily around my waist. I probably looked worse than before.

"I'm the vagabond prince," I muttered to myself.

Clang... Clang... Clang...

The machines above me kept perfect rhythm as I wandered the hall. On the left side of me, windows. On the right side, doors. Where was everyone? I didn't see anyone attending the hall—or even guarding the entrances. Should I poke my head into every room? Would that be considered snooping?

Gustav had mentioned a banquet... A room like that would be larger than the others. That was my destination.

"I think you need to head this way," someone said.

I had a hand on the hilt of my sword before I managed to recognize the voice.

"Fain," I said as I slowly turned around. He remained invisible. "I forgot you were there."

"Most people do."

"That's not what I meant." I glanced around. "Uh, which way do you think it is?"

"This way."

He tugged on the sleeve of my doublet, guiding me to one of the doors. I followed his suggestion, but once I touched the handle, I hesitated.

"Why this door?"

"The symbol above it. That one there. It matches the one on the front door."

I turned my attention to the doorframe. Above the door, fitted into the construction of the building, was a silver cog. At first, I thought it was part of the architecture, but after I examined it, I realized it was decorative. The other doors had symbols above them as well—one with a feather, one with a book, another with a table...

"Keen eyes," I said.

Fain didn't reply.

I took a deep breath and opened the door.

Another hallway.

I exhaled and continued. The door slammed shut behind me, and I turned, thinking I'd see Fain, but of course I didn't. Hoping he was with me, I walked a good fifty feet before arriving at another door with a silver cog. This door was bluish-black—nullstone infused. Nullstone made it impossible to use magic on it. Was this a barrier? Beyond this had to be the banquet hall.

Soft murmurs of voices leaked out from under the door.

If Luthair were here, I could've sent him into the room before me. He could've played scout and reported back.

"What're you waiting for?" Fain whispered.

I shook my head. "Trying to think of my first words." I turned to face thin air, approximately where I had heard Fain. "You wouldn't happen to have heard any motivational speeches before, have you?"

"Oh, yeah. Tons."

"Really?" I smiled. "Which one was the most moving? Or better yet, which one motivated you into action?"

"Probably the speech where Calisto was gutting a man for stealing one of his magical trinkets." Fain's tone slid further into sarcasm with each word. "It really motivated me not to steal from a dread pirate, ya know? Very inspirational."

"That doesn't help me," I said, turning away and gritting my teeth.

"Trust me. If you gutted someone, there would be a lot of motivation to do *something*."

I replied with a sardonic *ha, ha* before grabbing the door handle a second time. The voices filtering out from under the door had stopped. Were they waiting for me inside?

With a forceful push on the door, I entered the banquet hall.

The smell of smoked fish and beef assaulted me in full force. I took a deep breath as the many occupants of the room turned in my direction. More than thirty people sat at a U-shaped table. I recognized a few—Captain Devlin, Master Zelfree, Guildmaster Eventide, the Grand Apothecary—but most of the people here weren't familiar to me.

Eventide stood out in this crowd. In all crowds, really. She was the only one who had a glowing arcanist mark—the only one with a true form eldrin.

Two dozen mystical creatures were in the room, but most were small and half-hidden by the furniture. Six pillars helped support the ceiling—free of cogs and gears—and a couple of creatures ducked behind them before I could identify anything.

Five mongwu owls were perched on the backs of chairs. I could tell they were mongwu owls because of the "horned" feathers that grew on their heads. Their black talons and the red tips of their wings cemented their identities. They were mystical creatures of wisdom and death, and they supposedly had powerful clairvoyance.

Plates filled with delicious food sat on smaller tables near the walls. Scribes in long tunics stood by every table, each with serving utensils in their hands. While the room had been built for grand gatherings, it was obvious from the dust on the windows, the cobwebs in the upper corners, and the odd assortment of chairs around the U-shaped table, that everything had been hastily thrown together.

How much warning had been given to the arcanists of Fortuna? A single day? Perhaps less?

Everyone stood from their chairs, their eyes wide.

Guildmaster Eventide forced a smile. "There he is. Volke Savan the World Serpent Arcanist of the Frith Guild." She waved me over and then gestured to an empty seat by her side. "Come. We've just begun."

The tension in the room was so thick, I could've choked on it. But I couldn't show weakness. With my head held high, I strode forward, pushing down both my anxiety and my hammering heart.

Everyone watched me.

Their eyes followed my every move.

I didn't meet anyone's gaze. I stared straight ahead and held my breath until I reached the seat. It was near the back end of the table and positioned so that Eventide would be on my right, and someone I didn't recognize would be on my left.

Once I sat down, everyone else took their seats again, though it was slow and cautious, as though I might strike out at any second.

"Volke, let me introduce you to the arcanists who care for the City of Fortuna," Eventide said. "This is—"

"Who is that?" someone yelled.

I turned my attention to the door. Fain had appeared just as he had crossed the threshold. The nullstone door wouldn't cause his magic to fail, so long as he wasn't touching it. What had happened?

He stood, confused, his eyes wide and his black-fingered hands trembling.

Before anyone from the Frith Guild could explain, a man at the table stood. His plated armor was layered and flared at the shoulders and hips. He wore chains and flexible gauntlets, all with fragments of bones and teeth forged into the metal. Dragon teeth? They were large, and I suspected his entire suit of armor was highly magical.

A large, two-handed sword was tied to his back.

The man waved his hand. "Subdue him."

A white tiger leapt out from behind a pillar near the far wall. The tip of its tail was see-through, like a ghost, but the closer the tail was to the body, the more solid and opaque it became. Muscles rippled under its majestic and glistening fur.

A star tiger. They weren't found anywhere near here!

The 900-pound creature tensed in preparation for a lunge just as Eventide stood from her chair.

"Stand down," she stated. "He's an apprentice from the Frith Guild."

But the star tiger didn't listen. It lunged for Fain, its white claws outstretched.

Eventide created a shimmering barrier of magic around Fain. The tiger crashed into it as though it were a wall, but the beast wasn't so easily jarred. It hit the floor on all fours, its hackles raised. Then it disappeared in a puff of glitter.

Just like Nicholin.

Star tigers also had the ability to teleport!

I stood, fearful it would get past Eventide's barrier. But it didn't. The tiger reappeared on the opposite side of Fain and then roared in frustration. It couldn't get through the barrier?

"What is the meaning of this?" the star tiger arcanist asked. His voice was smooth but authoritative. Not rushed—but clearly agitated.

"You'll find that true form atlas turtles can repel even the craftiest of magics," Eventide said with a smile, as though we were all having a great time. "No need to worry. I'm certain my apprentice was just acting as an escort for the world serpent arcanist." She faced Fain, her cheerfulness never waning. "You may wait outside, Fain. Thank you for making sure Volke arrived safely."

Fain, who seemed frozen in place, took a long moment before nodding. "Y-Yes, Guildmaster."

He walked backward out of the room, like he couldn't stand the thought of turning his back on the tiger. I didn't blame him. The tiger watched him go, its fangs bared, a guttural growl rumbling from its massive chest. Once outside, Fain cloaked himself in invisibility.

The star tiger arcanist was a man with a wide jaw and a prominent nose. His black hair was tied back—long enough to create a short ponytail, but not long enough to then reach his shoulders. His facial hair was cut short and kept meticulously even.

"We agreed that only master arcanists would attend this gathering," the man stated. "I suspected someone would try to sneak others in, which is why I insisted on the added protection."

"Do you not have accidents in the Kingdom of Javin?" Zelfree quipped.

"You think me a fool? The great Frith Guild would never allow such a mistake to happen. You insult yourself, and my liege, King Odion, with such an explanation."

A man at the table—sitting next to the star tiger arcanist— held up a hand and smiled. "Tarik, we shouldn't begin these talks with animosity and distrust. If the guildmaster says it was an error, then it was an error."

"But, my liege," the man, Tarik, said. He turned and frowned. "Your safety is my top priority."

"I'm not made of porcelain." After a quick laugh, King Odion added, "I think I could've fended off a single wendigo arcanist, if an attack had happened."

King Odion...

I hadn't heard of him, but I knew the Kingdom of Javin had long suffered from one revolt after another. A king and a queen had both been assassinated, resulting in knightmares, and almost any news from the southern region was filled with strife and famine. My information was out of date, however. The Isle of Ruma never had anything up to date. Was King Odion the latest one to take the throne?

He was impressive, though. His armor was similar to Tarik's—plated and layered, resulting in a flare at the shoulders. Odion's was white and sparkled with the scales of the twilight dragon.

And his hair reminded me of Evianna's. It was white, with strands of metallic silver, beautiful in a mythical way. Evianna's hair had a purplish-blue hue, but not King Odion's. He kept it short, and it seemed bristly. It contrasted nicely with his dark tanned skin and matched the icy blue of his eyes.

While he sounded older and confident, he kept his face shaved, giving him a youthful appearance. He appeared to be in his mid-twenties, but I knew arcanists' ages could be difficult to determine. Odion had an easy smile, and when he turned his attention to me, I didn't get a sense of fear.

If the twilight dragon outside was his, that meant he probably wasn't a master arcanist. His eldrin wasn't old enough. They had likely only been bonded a few years. In guild terms, he'd be a journeyman arcanist, but I still couldn't let my guard down.

Twilight dragons were powerful.

"Thank you, Your Majesty," Eventide said. She placed a hand on my shoulder, and both of us sat. "Volke, please, let me introduce you to everyone here."

All I managed was a nod. I still didn't know what to say.

"Pardon me, Guildmaster," King Odion said, lifting a single finger. "While there are several important arcanists among us, none is more important than the world serpent arcanist himself." He turned his intense gaze to me, the light blue of his irises striking. "Please, God-Arcanist Volke Savan, do us all the favor of introducing yourself. What life did you lead that brought you to the world serpent?"

The question stewed in my thoughts, and I found it difficult to remember anything that had brought me here. It wasn't a complex question, and when I glanced over to Master Zelfree and Guildmaster Eventide, they both offered reassuring nods.

"I..." I took another breath and steadied myself. Why was this worse than fighting a plague-ridden arcanist in the middle of the ocean? "I found the world serpent in his lair. It was a giant tree. I had the runestone, and..."

Odion leaned forward, and it was enough that the simple movement stopped my story and got most people's attention. He had a *presence*. It was difficult not to pay attention to him.

"Where were you born?" he asked, no hesitation in his voice.

"Born?" I half-smiled. "The Isle of Ruma."

"How old are you?"

"Seventeen."

That answer caused several arcanists in the room to flinch. One lady even gasped.

I laughed once and then quickly added, "I'll be eighteen soon."

Did they think me too young? There wasn't much I could do about that.

"And your parents encouraged you to become an arcanist?" Odion asked.

"N-No. My parents... They abandoned me."

It sounded harsh when I said it like that, and I almost corrected myself with something kinder, but King Odion seemed ready to move on.

"Who raised you?" he asked. He laced his fingers together and watched my every move as I spoke.

I forced a chuckle. Why did anyone care about this? "I was raised by Gravekeeper William. I was his apprentice. A gravedigger."

The other arcanists in the room—monarchy from distant lands, even the mongwu owl arcanists who ran Fortuna—exchanged looks and words, but nothing I could hear. They all seemed hyper focused on my movements and statements.

King Odion pointed to my forehead. "I see from your old mark that you were once a knightmare arcanist. How did that happen?"

"Luthair came to our island after his first arcanist was murdered." I rubbed my neck, surprised at how much I was sweating. "I bonded with him. Second-bonded."

"How did you complete his trial of worth?"

"Uh, it wasn't an official trial. I was... Er, there was this plague-ridden white hart, and I helped my friend's brother escape. Luthair saw the whole thing. He bonded with me, saving my life, really."

My first meeting with Luthair... It was a memory burned into my thoughts. But would everyone here want to hear that? I wanted to keep my answers short and to the point.

"And then?" Odion asked. "Did you kill your knightmare to bond with the world serpent?"

"Oh, no. Nothing like that. Luthair died protecting me from a grim reaper. After that... Well, I was taking my brother to the world serpent, but he wasn't worthy. I, uh, bonded in his stead."

Well, it hadn't been exactly like that, either, but I didn't like recalling the details of the story. The dark tree, and the horrors within, were a waking nightmare. I thought I had lost so much. It had taken all my strength to make it to the world serpent.

Silence.

I glanced around.

Everyone stared. Waiting. Like they wanted something more from me.

"Why did the world serpent pick *you*?" King Odion asked, this time each word said with suspicion.

"I don't know," I muttered, trying to be honest. "Terrakona

said I have what it takes to pass judgment, but even that... I'm uncertain of what he means."

Terrakona spoke in a bizarre way, and he often referenced things I knew little of. He mentioned the *Children of Balastar* and *Luvi*, and I really didn't know what he was trying to say. It was almost like he was so old, that everything he knew had long since died, and now he was making references that no one could relate to. But he wasn't old. The magic was just talking to him.

"Judgment?" the star tiger arcanist asked. "What does that mean?"

King Odion shook his head. "It's all right, Tarik. Let the man finish."

I sighed. "That's it. I haven't been the world serpent arcanist long, so there isn't much to say." I chuckled, but no one else joined in.

"What he means," Zelfree added, his voice distinct and loud, "is that Volke needs to pass judgment on the Second Ascension."

"Hasn't your entire guild been dealing with them?" Odion asked. His intense gaze shifted to Zelfree for a short moment. "But none of you were chosen by the world serpent."

"I was the only one there," I said. "In the lair."

"The only one?" Odion asked. For the first time during this meeting, his cool composure slipped. He almost sounded angry.

"Well, my brother was there," I said, trying to gather my thoughts in a coherent manner. "And so was Evianna. We were the only ones. It was dark and difficult to reach the serpent."

The knowledge didn't seem to sit well with the other arcanists. I leaned back in my chair, stiffer than I thought I'd be. The other arcanists—even their eldrin—continued to whisper among themselves, each one taking a moment to glance in my direction. What had I said that had upset them so much?

Guildmaster Eventide leaned in close to me. When she smiled, it was reassuring, like she had everything under control. "See those five arcanists sitting in the chairs with the owls?" she whispered. "Those arcanists sit on the Fortuna Council. Once we're done with introductions, they want to discuss your role as protector."

Protector? Me?

I liked that idea. I wished we could've discussed that first. Talking about my history seemed to do more harm than good.

The mongwu owls also turned their giant, golden eyes in my direction. Their heads turned around while their bodies remained motionless. They muttered things—more like whispering hoots—but never said anything to me directly.

When King Odion straightened his posture, everyone silenced their side conversations.

"Volke Savan," he said. His serious tone reminded me of combat.

"Yes?" I asked.

"I think there has been a mistake." He stood from his chair. "I've heard nothing but legendary tales of the Frith Guild, but clearly, there has been a lapse in judgment on their part. Somehow, they allowed a seventeen-year-old boy—a gravedigger from a nowhere island who second-bonded with a pitiful knightmare with no trial of worth—to meet with the world serpent."

Guildmaster Eventide tensed in order to stand, but I had already shot out of my chair. I could handle him speaking poorly of me. Lots of people had. I had grown up an orphan on a small island that hated anyone who handled dead bodies.

But I wouldn't let him speak poorly of Luthair *or* the Frith Guild.

"No matter what you think, the world serpent has chosen," I stated, no warmth in my words.

King Odion smirked and narrowed his eyes. "Mistakes can be corrected, *child*. The last King of Javin learned that lesson the hard way." He pushed his chair to the side, and it crashed to the floor. "You're unworthy to be a god-arcanist. Even if I have to second-bond with the world serpent myself, I'll see this mistake corrected."

UNWORTHY

I held my breath, my hand on the hilt of Retribution.

Guildmaster Eventide stood and then the rest of the room followed suit. Before anyone else could speak, Eventide said, "Come now. Making hasty declarations is the fastest way to make irreparable mistakes. Volke Savan has my full backing. He's proven himself time and time again."

Her words meant the world to me, but I couldn't take my attention away from Odion. His gaze was locked on mine.

"I do nothing in haste," Odion stated. He smiled, a picture of confidence. "Volke has a history."

He waved his hand, and an arcanist stepped out of the shadows in the corner of the room. I recognized the new arcanist—a knightmare arcanist by the name of Lucian Nellit. I had met him in the city of Thronehold. He had been the Grandmaster Inquisitor's apprentice.

Lucian hadn't changed a bit. He was about my age, and he wore a dark, tight-fitting shirt and loose, white pants that flowed outward. He kept his head shaved short, but not bald, and his face was as smooth as polished stone, same as Odion's.

"Lucian fought Volke in the Sovereign Dragon

Tournament," King Odion said. "Volke didn't even reach the end of the competition. From everything I've heard, Volke wasn't focused enough to offer much of a challenge. *This* is our new world serpent arcanist?"

Master Zelfree scoffed. "Don't be a fool. The god-arcanists have more on their plate than combat."

"And if *Volke Savan* had anything impressive to display, perhaps I wouldn't need to step in. But look at him. His clothing is haggard, his hair disheveled. No thought in anything he does." Odion slammed his hand on the table, drawing everyone's attention. "I've heard enough. We came here to make an alliance with the backing of the world serpent arcanist. From what I've seen, this will never work."

"I agree," Tarik said.

Other arcanists in the room nodded, even Lucian, who I had thought would have backed my position since we had both been knightmare arcanists, but I supposed that was foolish. We never had much in common.

And now I knew why Zelfree had been so insistent on making a good impression. The attitude in the room had shifted. At first, they had feared me. Now, they thought me a joke. They wanted to kill me so they could take my power for themselves.

It would be like this forever—until I had made a reputation for myself. And we didn't have much time for that. How I handled this situation would reflect on me forever. I couldn't let Odion paint me as incompetent.

King Odion glowered, his calculating gaze challenging me long before he voiced it in words. "Volke Savan—the fate of the world is on the line. I won't follow a child into battle. I challenge you to a *magi cross*. Refuse, and the Kingdom of Javin leaves, no alliance."

A magi cross? That was a duel between arcanists, but not the normal kind. Usually, an arcanist's duel involved both the arcanist and their eldrin. A *magi cross* was a duel between only the arcanists, no eldrin. Magi crosses took place in Kingdom of Javin, and rarely in other locations.

"If the Kingdom of Javin leaves, then so will Antihelm," a woman stated.

She wore robes that were tightly wrapped around her body and held in place with long sashes on her waist and shoulders. They looked expensive, since they were made of silk and woven in with pearls and gold, but I didn't recognize the style.

Her arcanist mark had the cliffside dragon wrapped around the points of her star.

She had to be a queen—the Queen of Antihelm. A smaller nation to the west of Javin, both of which were so far south, they were beyond the Lightning Straits. They were nations on the ocean, though, and trade took place around the straits.

"We must have unity," one of the mongwu owl arcanists stated. He sounded old, even though he only appeared to be in his late thirties. "Guildmaster Eventide said the Second Ascension has already infiltrated places like the *Argo Empire*. We cannot stand against a nation of that size on our own."

The conversations in the room erupted all at the same time. It was difficult to tell one voice from another, but I didn't care. Odion waited for my reply. Everyone else argued and made statements, but not him. He remained still and focused.

A magi cross was a serious challenge. Arcanists would fight each other with only their magics and the trinkets or artifacts they had created themselves. No eldrin. No outside help. Just the two arcanists.

And they would fight to the death.

Was that what Odion wanted? Of course. He thought he could bond with Terrakona if he killed me first.

But did I have the magic to face a juvenile twilight dragon arcanist? I barely understood the scope of my evocation. There was a good chance Odion could end me, depending on his skill level. He wasn't a master arcanist, that much I knew. His eldrin was too young, and he had likely just taken the throne. Perhaps I did have a chance.

Terrakona.

"**Warlord?**" Terrakona replied, his telepathy a comfort.

I didn't have telepathy to speak back, but he sensed my thoughts, and I wanted to know if he'd bond with someone else if I were killed.

"**Our destinies are intertwined.**"

When I thought about the rules of the magi cross—about how eldrin weren't allowed—there was a *hissing* in my mind. Was Terrakona disgusted?

"**Antiquated practices. Barbaric. Disgraceful.**"

He didn't approve. Would he allow such a duel to take place?

Terrakona didn't reply. He hadn't done that before, and I wondered if it was because he *would* allow it, even if he didn't like the idea. If that were the case, I didn't have much of a choice.

"Your fear is louder than the noise around us," Odion said, his voice low. He shook his head. "Someone like you isn't suited to be a god-arcanist. You should've stayed with your previous pathetic eldrin."

"I accept your challenge," I said through gritted teeth, loud enough to cut through the commotion.

Zelfree snapped his attention to me, his eyes wide.

"Don't throw your life away, Odion," Guildmaster Eventide said. "I've seen Volke's magic. He defeated Gallus the Gray."

Her sheer confidence was amazing. She almost made *me* think I was more powerful than I actually was.

Odion didn't seem to have a wide range of emotions. He kept himself controlled, that much was obvious. So, when he hesitated, I knew Eventide's statement must have unnerved him, especially when the other arcanists in the room all turned their judgmental gazes on him.

"I issued the challenge," Odion finally stated. "I'll stand by it."

A piece of me knew he wasn't entirely confident.

Odion motioned to his scaled armor. "I assume you know the rules of a magi cross, Volke. The Kingdom of Javin penned them, if you didn't know."

That made sense. Javin was militaristic, from what I had read. A bloody history. A nation shaped by wars and infighting. Of course they had made rules for their combat and duels.

"I know the rules," I said. "We can use our own magical items." I placed my hand on my sword and shield.

Odion reached into his armor and removed a necklace with a fragment of a unicorn horn. It was likely a trinket that made him immune to poison and venom. He handed it to Tarik and then held out both his arms.

"Everything else I'm wearing was made by me," he said. "Tarik has my weapon, which I also imbued myself." He slid a hand down his armor. "This was the first magical item I ever crafted, and it's helped me through every war I've ever fought."

He had more trinkets than I did, but both of my items were artifacts—powerful and capable. I'd have to rely on them to win this fight. There was no other way around it.

"When?" Guildmaster Eventide asked. "Tomorrow morning?"

"Now," Tarik said as he stood by his king's side. "We needn't drag this out."

Had they planned on issuing this challenge from the beginning? It seemed like it. Lucian had probably told them about me, and once they had heard about my performance in the Sovereign Dragon Tournament, they had thought I was weak.

They didn't know I had thrown that tournament.

Anger still pulsed through me. I couldn't believe what Odion had said. I wouldn't stand for it. Although I still feared he would win, I had fought far scarier villains and won. And everyone here would apparently abandon Fortuna and my island nation unless I accepted this challenge.

I had to win. And I would.

"Now is fine," I said. "Outside?"

Odion smiled widely, his excitement plain to see. A bloodthirsty king, for a bloodthirsty people.

"We'll fight in the shadow of the Astral Tower," he said. "Before nightfall, one of us will be dead."

* * *

We walked outside, but I wasn't paying attention to my surroundings. I focused on my magic and what I had done to kill Gallus. Could I duplicate that here? We weren't in the water, but perhaps my molten rock would melt him.

Twilight dragons didn't breathe fire, after all. Odion probably wasn't immune to my extreme heat, unlike Zaxis and Atty, with their phoenix eldrins.

Dozens of arcanists had gathered around the outside of the Astral Tower, including arcanists from the Frith Guild. Fain, Adelgis, Zaxis, Illia, Hexa, Karna—even Evianna stood amid the crowd, just beyond the wrought-iron fence. They struggled to get a good view behind the many creatures who had gathered as well. Griffins, unicorns, yetis, and a few pegasi made everything difficult. So many people were here, but the fence kept them at bay.

King Odion waved his hand. "Listen," he commanded. "No one can interfere once a magi cross has begun."

Electric excitement and palpable dread washed over the crowd in equal amounts.

"A magi cross?" someone shouted. "A duel between arcanists?"

Another person asked, "Why challenge the world serpent arcanist? Is King Odion a fool?"

A phoenix flew into the sky and headed for the docks. Was it Forsythe or Titania? Had one of the Frith Guild arcanists sent word back to the manor house?

They were probably warning my father. I didn't see his blue phoenix amid the crowd.

I hoped I'd be able to tell him the whole story myself, once this was all over.

A giant troll—ten feet tall, with a gut that could fit three barrels inside—lumbered around the tower garden. It snarled at the crowds, keeping them from getting too close to the fence. Hair grew out in wild amounts on his back, shoulders, and chest, almost giving him a bear-like coat, but his human-shaped face, giant horse-teeth, and massive hands gave the troll a human-like appearance.

"Stand back," the troll growled. "*Back.*"

"Volke!" someone in the crowd yelled.

I recognized the voice, but I couldn't pinpoint it. The thick crowd made it impossible to spot who had yelled. And then they started chanting my name.

Volke. Volke. Volke.

A small smile crept into the corners of my mouth.

King Odion didn't seem to care. He kept his cool composure —and his excited expression—even as his underling, Tarik, walked over. Tarik unslung the two-handed sword off his back and then handed it to Odion.

The moment Odion had his sword, the crowd stopped their chants. I could feel their collective worry.

I gritted my teeth, about to say something, but Odion shook his head.

"This is my sword, The White Curse," he stated. "I forged it from the corpse of a hex albatross."

He gripped the long handle with both hands and kept the tip of the blade pointed at the ground. Two-handed weapons were devastating. I had seen them in action enough times to know that Odion's strategy would be to end this fight quickly. He didn't have a shield, which meant his fighting style would be aimed more for one-hit strikes and crippling blows.

I didn't have room to make any mistakes.

Tarik leaned in close. Despite the crowd, I could hear the exchange between them. "Are you certain, my liege?"

Smirking, Odion replied, "I defeated the previous king, didn't I?"

After a long moment of silence, Tarik stepped away. While Odion had enough confidence for ten people, Tarik lingered close, his movements stiff. He gave me an odd glance. Was he nervous?

I shook away the thought. I had to focus on the duel.

The troll and the other arcanists from the Astral Tower moved away from us. Master Zelfree tried to get my attention by holding out a hand, and I glanced over. He seemed concerned, but he didn't voice anything. Then he pointed up—a slight gesture, so that no one else saw.

When I followed his point, I spotted the twilight dragon looming overhead. The two-headed beast examined us but didn't get closer. It remained perched on top of the Astral Tower, its white scales gleaming in the light of the setting sun. Then it flashed its two sets of fangs.

"Enough, Hasdrubal," Odion said with a wave of his hand. "I will handle this."

Was Zelfree trying to warn me? I knew about twilight dragons. It would have the powers of light and darkness—and I was *very* familiar with darkness.

Eventide stepped closer but remained at a distance, a good

ten feet away. "I'll give you one final chance, Odion. Surrender now, and we can return to the tower to negotiate an alliance that will benefit everyone."

She spoke in such a convincing tone. For a moment, I thought it would work.

"We'll return to the tower soon enough," Odion eventually replied. "This child has more teeth than talent. It'll be a quick fight."

I pulled out Retribution and belted Forfend to my left arm. The gravity of the situation weighed on me. If I died, Odion would attempt to bond with Terrakona. That was a relief, honestly. At least the Second Ascension wouldn't get their hands on the world serpent.

But I hardened myself. Zelfree had said I no longer had room to make mistakes. I refused to lose.

"A magi cross is about to begin," Tarik yelled out. "King Odion Hayes and God-Arcanist Volke Savan." Tarik patted the head of his giant star tiger.

Our "arena" was a large walkway lined by waist-high bushes, no longer than thirty feet, and only twenty feet wide. Odion stood at the far end, his two-handed blade at least three feet long. The white of the sword reminded me of snow. If it were crafted from the body of a hex albatross, it would probably bring bad luck to those it injured.

It didn't compare to Retribution. My black blade was the exact opposite of his.

"You may begin," Tarik said.

His star tiger roared.

I held my sword tight and focused on my magic.

Odion threw up a hand. "This is over."

He evoked his magic. A flash of light burst in the sky a few feet above Odion's head. It was so bright, it burned my eyes. I turned away, my jaw clenched. Was it just a flash? No. The light never waned. It remained vibrant and powerful and anytime I tried to open my eyes, it hurt all over again.

I'd never be able to see in this condition. It was like... a reverse orb of darkness. Odion was essentially blinding me.

And then I heard him running forward. I couldn't see, but I knew his fighting style. He would swing with a heavy overhand, allowing gravity to help him cleave me in half.

I feigned confusion until he was close and then I lunged for his waist. With molten rock oozing from the palm of my shield hand, I collided with Odion. I had guessed correctly. His arms were above his head, exposing his middle. We both went crashing to the ground, hitting the rock of the stone walkway.

I ran my molten rock across his body. When I touched his armor, it felt as though the scales repelled my heat, but when I managed to graze Odion's neck, he cried out.

Odion hooked a foot underneath me and then kicked outward. He was strong enough to send me off, and I stumbled backward into a standing position. I opened my eyes and instantly regretted it. The dazzling light created by twilight dragon magic wouldn't go away unless I broke Odion's concentration.

I evoked more of my molten rock and the temperature in the nearby area went up. Gasps rang out from the crowd. When I managed to open one of my eyes, I noticed smoke wafting off the closest bushes. The smell of burnt fabric stung my nose. My own clothes were in peril of my magic.

Unable to see, I threw molten rock outward in an arc.

After a scuff of boots on the walkway, Odion shouted. His blinding orb of light flickered and then collapsed. My attack must have interrupted his focus—just as I had hoped.

I opened my eyes in time to see him rushing for me. I couldn't repeat the same evasive maneuver. He would be expecting it now.

Instead, I leapt backward, and it was a good thing I did.

Odion swung in a wide half-circle around him. Had I lunged, my skull would have been in two pieces.

Before I could formulate an attack of my own, Odion threw *another* orb of light into the air. He could repeat this trick forever if I didn't figure out a way to counter it permanently.

I shut my eyes before the pain got to me, but when I rubbed at my face, I felt obsidian stone protruding from my skin. It scratched my face and drew a trickle of blood on my eyebrow.

Damn.

Would the stone get in the way of my combat style? I had to remain focused on Odion. With the light so bright, I doubted Odion could use his darkness-controlling abilities. What other magics would he use, then? I wasn't an expert on everything twilight dragons were capable of.

Odion stepped forward, this time slower, but I could hear his cautious footfalls.

He knew I was listening.

I held my shield up, ready for the next attack. Odion would try to end this soon, and if I wasn't careful, he would succeed.

MAGI CROSS

I evoked more of my molten rock, filling the area with heat so intense that even the giant troll grunted and moved away. A part of me wondered if anyone could see through Odion's light—but even if they could, would they also be capable of resisting my magma enough to stay close?

Odion approached me, sliding his feet across the walkway as he went. Why? To confuse me? He made more noise than just walking, but by making irregular movements, I couldn't picture them in my mind's eye.

Desperate to keep him at bay, I threw more molten rock in half-circles. My clothes caught fire in a few places, and my elbows felt awkward as even more obsidian jutted out of me. The crackle of new flames reached my ears, and I knew my powers were going to burn down this garden in a matter of minutes.

Odion's light ceased.

I opened my eyes, but had to squint again, due to the smoke from my molten rock. Where had Odion gone? He wasn't in front of me, and he wasn't where I had heard him last.

My heart stopped for half a second.

The smoke had created a great deal of shadows.

I leapt to the side so quickly that I almost tripped over my own feet. Stumbling into a burning bush, I dodged just in time to avoid Odion's sword. He had swung from some place behind me.

Shadow-stepping—the ability to move through darkness as though it were a second realm of void-like liquid—was a magical ability I'd had when I had been a knightmare arcanist. Appearing *behind* someone was a winning tactic. Few people could react fast enough to dodge, and those who didn't, usually ended up dead.

Odion had drawn my attention, waited for the smoke to thicken, and then dropped his own light to shadow-step behind me. Clever, especially because shadow-stepping didn't create any noise.

But none of this came as a surprise to me.

"I should've known I couldn't surprise you with this," Odion said, chuckling. "Not a former knightmare arcanist."

I said nothing.

Odion lifted his hand and a bright beam of light shot out of his palm, so fast, I had no hope of dodging. The beam struck my shoulder, searing my clothes and clawing at my skin. It didn't burn me—I was immune to the worst forms of heat— but it did tear my flesh. I realized this was an evocation that was made both light *and* sheer wind force. The burst of air had cut me, not the heat.

I staggered away from Odion, worried he would knock me to the ground with the force of the wind.

Odion leapt forward, closing the distance between us. Then he pointed his palm at me again.

I held up Forfend. The light beam—and blast of air— struck the front of my shield. Power pulsed inside of it. Forfend captured magical abilities and allowed me to unleash them at my leisure. When Odion stepped forward again, I pointed my shield at him and triggered his own beam of magic. A ray of white light shot straight for him.

It did nothing but push him back a few feet. Odion was immune to the harsh effects of his own solar winds. Twilight dragon arcanists wouldn't be harmed by such tactics.

His attack hadn't felt as powerful as I had thought it would be... Was he a younger arcanist? I had my suspicions.

Odion stepped into the darkness, dropping into the shadows and disappearing from sight. Once he vanished, practically melting into the ground, I only had a few seconds to prepare. While he was within the protection of the shadows, I wouldn't be able to strike him. Would Odion come from behind again? Or did he know I'd jump to the side, like I had before?

I didn't move.

Odion rose up from the darkness by my side. He moved as though anticipating my dodge, but my stiff stance threw him off. His two-handed sword required room and time to swing. He had it up and ready, but he had misjudged my positioning, which caused him to hesitate.

I took advantage of his surprise. With a powerful thrust of my sword, I attacked Odion. He barely tried to move—he shifted his weight from one foot to the other, angling his scaled armor in the way of my sword.

But Retribution effortlessly sliced through his armor. I punctured his side, just below the ribs, cutting deep. Blood gushed from the injury when I withdrew my sword.

Another surprise for Odion. His eyes widened—not just from pain, but from disbelief. He had been counting on his armor to protect him. Nothing could have been further from the truth.

To my shock, however, he gritted his teeth and then placed his hand on my chest. A blast of light struck me square in the chest. It knocked me away and I fell onto my back a few feet away, winded. Retribution slid out of my grip and clattered onto the cobblestones.

Few people could fight through the pain of a sword wound, but Odion was clearly experienced with life-and-death combat.

His white scale armor glowed a vibrant bluish-ivory. The glow centralized on the injury to his gut. It rapidly mended itself, but by the time the glowing stopped, the wound hadn't completely healed. Blood ran in small rivulets down Odion's body, and I suspected if the fight ended quickly, he'd be able to get himself healed and never even scar.

Odion rushed forward. I tried to get to my feet, but he was already swinging with his two-handed sword. I lifted my shield arm and blocked with Forfend. Odion struck my shield hard enough that it hurt my arm.

Then he kicked me, the heel of his boot striking my chin.

Gasps from the audience rang in my ears as I fell back to the ground.

"It's over," Odion growled through clenched teeth.

He swung his sword from the other direction—aiming for my neck from my unshielded side. If he decapitated me, I'd die. There would be no healing that.

In the split second I had to act, I lifted my arm. Even if he cut my hand off, it was better than my head. I could, in theory, recover from losing a limb. I'd take the hit, get back to my feet, and once I had Retribution, I could—

Odion's sword slammed into my arm, carving through my skin and muscle, but then it struck my bone hard and stopped. Odion had swung with enough force that my whole arm had collided with the side of my head. Despite that, my bones hadn't been broken by his white sword.

"What the?" Odion asked.

I slid away and jumped to my feet, my head pounding, my arm bleeding. I had been knocked around too much. My vision blurred.

When I glanced at my arm, the dark crimson made me anxious. I would live, and my limb was still intact. But my bones... They weren't obsidian, like the rocks on my knuckles. They were a darker basalt—the sturdy kind of rock left over from ancient volcanoes. Obsidian had a tendency to shatter, after all. If my bones had been obsidian, they wouldn't have stopped Odion's attack.

I had seen tons of basalt on the Isle of Ruma. I recognized it easily. Had *all* my bones hardened into this strange, volcanic rock?

Odion hefted his weapon, his icy eyes locked on my wound. "What are you?" he asked under his breath.

His own gory injury had opened a little from the violent movements he had been making. Blood coated his white scale armor, soaking his pants, protective skirt, and boots. With a shaky hand, he touched his armor.

"This is impossible," he growled, his words laced with rage. "No one has ever damaged my magical items."

While he held on to his wound, I rushed over and picked up Retribution. With my black blade in hand, I turned to face King Odion. I straightened my posture and rotated my sore shoulder.

"With every word and action, you show how little you know," I said.

Odion glowered at me, his blue eyes as cold as death.

"You want to know the truth?" I asked, my volume increasing as I stepped closer to him. "I was willing to die to protect others. *That* was my trial of worth for my knightmare."

I swung wide with Retribution, hoping to clip Odion. He stepped away, narrowly dodging.

"I was infected with the arcane plague while rescuing a princess of the Argo Empire," I practically shouted as I swung again. "*I* was the one who kept half of the runestones from the clutches of the Second Ascension."

Odion gripped his bleeding injury but said nothing.

"You're proud of your armor?" I asked with a dark chuckle. "I crafted my sword from the bones of the previous apoch dragon, stolen from the artificer of our enemies."

The statement elicited a prolonged moment of silence, as though everyone, including the arcanists of Fortuna, held their breath.

I didn't care. Anger fueled my speech—fueled my need to explain everyone's foolishness in underestimating me.

"Where were *you* when we were rushing to find the world serpent's lair before the Autarch and his minions?" I yelled. "Where were you when King Rishan and his grim reaper arcanist came for the world serpent? You didn't pay the ultimate price to keep the god-creature safe. *Luthair did.*"

I evoked more of my molten rock. It oozed from the lines of my palm, but also from the base of the rocks jutting out of my knuckles. The magma dripped from my hand, splashing onto the walkway and melting a furrow into the stone.

Embers fluttered through the air and more smoke wafted up from the shrubbery. The heat and ambient fire were hitting new levels. The rocks jutting from my body were curved and pointed, like claws and spines. The temperature matched my anger, rising and dangerous.

I took a deep breath, and exhaled some of my rage.

"My name is Volke Savan," I said, loud and clear. "I cured myself of the plague by achieving a true form with my knightmare. I fought and hindered the Second Ascension long before the world knew them as a threat. The world serpent didn't bond with me because of a fluke or accident. I'm the next Warlord of Magic."

I lunged forward and slashed with Retribution.

King Odion couldn't move as quickly with his injury. He stumbled to the side, but I still caught him with the tip of my blade. Retribution sliced through anything magical as though it were air. Odion's armor offered no protection. I cut through his defenses and lightly slashed him across the chest. He caught his breath as he stepped away.

Then, with bloody hands, he choked up on the hilt of his two-handed sword and put all of his strength into one quick thrust. I leaned to the side. His white blade sliced me along the ribs, but not deeply. I took that opportunity to stab him in the upper arm on his dominant side.

Odion flinched and half-collapsed.

Then he knelt on one knee, his body trembling. He didn't cry out or whimper. He gritted his teeth as more blood spilled from his new injury. His armor glowed again, but this time not as brightly. His wound half-closed itself, but that wasn't enough. Odion scrunched his eyes closed, his breathing rough.

When Odion tried to stand—and heft his sword—I slashed the back of his hand. He grimaced and dropped his weapon. It slammed to the ground, heavier than I had thought it would be.

The tension and worried murmurs from the crowd drifted to my ears. I had half-forgotten that they were even there, my attention had been so focused on Odion. But now we were at the end of our duel. The rules dictated my only course of action.

I lifted Retribution.

Out of the corner of my eye, I noticed Tarik inching closer. He kept his arms crossed, his hands gripping his arms so tightly, I suspected he was hurting himself.

Odion took a deep breath and kept his eyes shut. Up close, I could admire his twilight dragon arcanist mark. The two-headed dragon was wrapped around the star, but the most interesting details were the cracks. His mark... it was different. Familiar. It was similar to my old knightmare mark.

The temperature got to me. It didn't hurt, but I knew it was influencing my actions. I felt angrier than normal, and I hated that. Did Odion deserve death? He had insulted Luthair and the Frith Guild, but...

"You said you know the rules of the duel," Odion said, his voice low. "Finish this."

He *wanted* me to kill him? "Are you that desperate to get to the abyssal hells?"

"Don't disgrace me, and yourself, by dragging this out."

I almost laughed. "You really don't know me at all."

Odion finally opened his eyes and glanced up at me. He said nothing, but he searched my gaze, as though looking for the answer to an unasked question.

"We shouldn't be fighting among ourselves," I said.

I lowered my sword, the heat around the tower garden waning. The molten rock I had evoked had hardened and cooled, becoming oddly shaped obsidian around the area.

"You're young," I said, half a question.

"Twenty-five," Odion replied.

Older than me, but young in arcanist terms. If he had bonded with a dragon when he had been fifteen, the twilight dragon above us would have been much larger.

"You haven't been bonded with your dragon long," I said, another half-question.

"Only a year."

"You're very capable for how little time you've had. It took me years to overcome the pain of second-bonding."

Odion stared. "You can tell?"

"The mark." I motioned to his forehead. "And the way you fight. I could just tell. You haven't mastered these powers."

He was a new arcanist. He didn't have an overwhelming amount of magic, even though he had bonded with a dragon. The last King of Javin could've been a twilight dragon arcanist, and Odion had taken his eldrin for himself. Most dragons had trials of worth that involved killing, after all.

I sheathed Retribution. That one action garnered more

whispers and gasps from the arcanists and mythical creatures around us. A pair of pegasi whinnied.

The fires and embers around us died. The tower garden was in shambles, but at least the building hadn't been damaged too badly.

"This isn't necessary," I said. "Even Terrakona thought a duel was barbaric. We have real enemies whom we need to focus on, and I would be a fool to kill someone as talented as you."

I held out my hand.

Odion slowly placed his hand on mine. I helped him to his feet, though his injuries made that difficult. He kept one arm tightly across his stomach, his armor glowing occasionally as though trying to fix the last of the wound. He was healing, but it would take several days of recovery, no doubt in my mind.

His silver hair fluttered in the ocean winds. He kept his intense gaze on me, and I forced a smile.

"Why didn't you tell me of all of your great deeds to begin with?" Odion asked.

I laughed once and then shrugged. "I didn't want to put everyone else to shame."

It was an arrogant statement, but I hoped it would convey some levity.

It must have worked, because Odion cracked a smile. "I see. You're a humble knight from a small island. I think I have a better picture of you, Volke Savan."

To my surprise, he grabbed my shoulder and pulled me into a partial embrace, using his free arm to pat my back. I hesitantly returned the gesture, taken aback. More whispers and comments floated around the group of people beyond the fence.

"So, just in case it wasn't clear, I'm calling off the magi cross," I said as I ended our embrace. "We need your help, King Odion. The Kingdom of Javin should join us in an alliance."

Odion nodded once. "I'll do better than join an alliance."

"Better?" I narrowed my eyes. "How so?"

Despite the fact that I had *just* helped him to his feet, Odion knelt once more, grimacing as he leaned his weight onto one knee. He bowed his head.

"I, King Odion Hayes of the Kingdom of Javin," he said, loudly enough for the others to hear, "hereby swear my loyalty to the world serpent arcanist—the Warlord of Magic—Volke Savan."

FEALTY

I didn't know what to say.

No one had ever sworn themselves to me before. In my mind, I had pictured it as more of a ceremony performed in a castle, not an impromptu gesture done in the charred wreckage of a battleground.

My clothes were half-ashes, half-charcoal. My trousers were still on me through the sheer willpower of my belt. I didn't *look* like a god-arcanist who would be accepting sworn oaths of fealty from kings and queens.

But nothing about my journey felt like the stories I had read as a child. Perhaps that was the difference between reality and fables.

"We may be a smaller kingdom of islands, but our warriors, and navy, are not to be trifled with," Odion said, still kneeling. "With my fealty, they will sail to fight your enemies."

The soldiers of Javin were said to go through rigorous training. A single mortal Javin soldier could hold their own against a dozen others, or so the rumors said. And their arcanist warrlors—people said they were an unstoppable force once they committed themselves to an attack. Despite Odion's inexperience, he had fought with impressive magics and tactics, proving the tales of his nation were at least somewhat true. Javin was a land of warriors.

"Well?" Tarik asked, standing close to my side. "Do you accept Odion's fealty?"

I unsheathed Retribution and placed it gently on Odion's shoulder. "I accept."

Pushing through the pain of his injuries, Odion stood. He did so in one fluid motion, impressive and graceful, like he was showing off for the crowd. It wasn't a bad idea. I wish I had thought of it.

"Let's return to the tower," Odion said as he placed a bloody hand on my shoulder. "We have much to discuss." He turned to Tarik. "Gather my weapon and help the city guard clean up. It's the least we can do for the inconvenience."

Tarik didn't complain or grumble. He simply nodded and said, "Yes, my liege."

I turned to head for the tower. Guildmaster Eventide and Master Zelfree immediately approached, both giving me the once over. I wanted to make a quip about how our surroundings had taken more damage than I had, but the slice to my ribs still ached. I thought I would've healed by now, but that wasn't the case. I held the injury closed with my hand, the obsidian rock jabbing me in the process.

The other arcanists—including the five from the Fortuna Council, and the Queen of Antihelm—regarded me with scrutinizing looks. I didn't mind. Now everyone here knew exactly who I was, and how I had gotten here. If they still had a problem with me, it was on them.

<hr>

We returned to the conference room of the Astral Tower. Everyone sat in chairs around the U-shaped table, and

Guildmaster Eventide retook her seat next to me. King Odion sat on my other side, changing the dynamic of the room. One of the Fortuna councilors had to rearrange the chairs to situate himself at the corner of the massive table.

The murmurs and quiet conversations ceased the moment I glanced around the room.

"Volke, these five are the honorable councilors of Fortuna, all mongwu owl arcanists." Eventide gestured to the five sitting in chairs with owls perched on the backrests. All of the arcanists were older in appearance, each with slumped shoulders. Some even had graying hair, which was rare for arcanists. How old were they, exactly? Eventide was the only other person in the room who had signs of advanced aging.

"This is Walter Gonni, Master of Coin," Eventide said, "and this is his sister, Penelope Gonni, the Grand Justice."

The first two councilors of Fortuna acknowledged their introductions with quick tilts of their heads. They didn't meet my gaze. They both glanced away whenever I tried to meet theirs.

Eventide pointed to the next arcanist. "That is Halladay Lanes, the city's mayor." And then she motioned to the last two. "And then we have Marx Ten, the head of law enforcement, and Veena Yaani, the commissioner of public works."

All five of them wore clothing like mine—blue doublets, gold sashes, laces on their sleeves. Well, what mine *used* to look like. I wore burnt cinders while they wore opulent outfits. Some of them had medals pinned to their shoulders, and Penelope Gonni wore a long skirt half-covered in belts. The frills of their collars puffed up so high, I couldn't see their necks.

"Nice to meet you," I said.

"Thank you," Veena quickly replied.

Her owl hooted and then said, "It is our greatest honor to be in the same room as the world serpent arcanist."

Mayor Halladay Lanes cleared his throat. He leaned on the table and forced a smile. "Warlord Savan, the City of Fortuna, as the capital of the Isle Nation Perphestoni, would like to offer you a piece of land to call home."

The last statement seemed like a non sequitur. Why were they talking about land? And a home?

Silence descended over the room.

Every muscle in my body tensed.

They wanted me to answer? But the Isle of Ruma was my home. Or perhaps the Frith Guild, since I had lived there for the last three years. Why would I live in Fortuna?

As if she could read my mind, Guildmaster Eventide elaborated with, "The Isle Nation Perphestoni would appreciate the world serpent arcanist's protection."

Protection? From what? The Second Ascension? My goal was to protect everyone from their vile deeds. Fortuna didn't need to trade me anything for it.

"I'll protect Fortuna," I said.

The energy in the room doubled with each passing second. People glanced between each other, and they murmured under their breath.

The mayor scooted to the edge of his chair. His wan skin, almost translucent, made it easy to see the dark veins on the backs of his hands. "We've learned from old texts that the first world serpent arcanist could change the terrain. That warlord made islands and turned forests into deserts."

I slowly nodded along with his words. The few stories I had heard of the first warlord told of how he had defeated armies by changing the environment. He made rivers and mountains —apparently with ease.

"I, uh..."

Master Zelfree shot me a glower. I had fought in a duel— and won. I had done exactly what Zelfree had wanted. I had displayed power and confidence, even though I barely knew anything about my magics. If I admitted I couldn't alter the terrain now, I'd undo all of that. Everyone would *know* I didn't have mastery over my god-like magic.

Before I had a chance to continue, the mayor leaned further on the table, getting as close to me as possible without getting out of his chair. "Can you reshape the land around Fortuna? Remove the rocks to the south-west? Create a river and a delta that flows inland?"

Guildmaster Eventide held up a hand. "Mayor Lanes, I apologize. I should've been clearer. The Second Ascension is after Volke. We shouldn't announce to the world where he'll be staying in the long term. It'll make it easier for them to plan an attack against us."

"You can't hide his location," Mayor Lanes stated. "His eldrin is too large, and knowledge of his existence is spreading too quickly. Your enemies already know he's here in Fortuna."

"But he isn't going to stay long," Eventide easily replied.

"She's right," I said, jumping on her explanation. "I can't stay and rework the land. Not until the Second Ascension has been dealt with." I hastily added, "I'll protect Fortuna, and all the nations with which we form alliances, but until we've secured the other god-creatures and drawn the worst of the Second Ascension into the open, we shouldn't declare to the world where I'll be for any prolonged period of time."

I tried to sound confident. I tried. I hoped it worked, but it was difficult to read the room. There were so many arcanists, and they refused to look at me long enough for me to read their expressions. Their whispers made me anxious, but I kept myself stiff and still to hide my uncertainty.

It was all about appearances, as Zelfree would say.

I glanced over to him, and he gave me a small nod. Did he approve of my conduct so far? I hoped so. I really wasn't sure what I was doing.

"But once this war is over, you'll use your magic to change the nations who allied with you?"

The question came out of nowhere, and from the oddly dressed Queen of Antihelm. She stood from her chair, her many silk sashes fluttering with her movements. Her brown hair, practically a chocolate waterfall, flowed over her shoulders and down her arms to her elbows.

"I will," I said, hoping I would have the magic to do so after everything was over.

"Antihelm is a nation next to the ocean," she said. "But unlike Fortuna, and the islands of Javin, our connection with the water is treacherous. We don't have beaches. We have cliffs. They make it difficult to build ports and encourage trade." She grabbed one of her sashes and twisted her fingers into the expensive fabric. "If you promise to change Antihelm into a land of beautiful bays and beaches, I'll swear my fealty to you, just as King Odion did."

Another round of tense silence fell over the arcanists.

I turned to Eventide. She regarded me with a serious expression, one that screamed *think about this*. Did I want to promise away my powers to the first group of people who rushed to me? Then again, what downside was there to gaining another dragon arcanist for our side?

Helping Antihelm was a noble cause, after all. I'd probably do it—if I developed the powers in the future—even without the queen's sworn loyalty.

"Very well," I said. "I'll help Antihelm once we've dealt with our enemies, especially the Autarch."

The queen pushed her chair away, and then walked around the outside of the table. She strode into the center of the U-shape, so that everyone could see her, and then she knelt on one knee, just as Odion had.

A few arcanists in the corners fussed, like they were about to protest. They wore the same sash outfits as the queen, just less elaborate and colorful. Were they her guards? Or maybe her advisors? I wasn't certain.

"I, Queen Callandra Gorn of the Nation of Antihelm," she said, her voice regal, "hereby swear my loyalty to the world serpent arcanist—the Warlord of Magic—Volke Savan."

"Thank yo—"

"*In exchange*," Callandra interjected, "Warlord Savan agrees to alter Antihelm for its benefit, regardless of who may be sitting on the throne at the time. Until then, Antihelm's dragons, wyverns, and wyrms will fight all enemies of the world serpent arcanist."

I waited a few seconds, just in case she wanted to add something else. When it was apparent she had nothing more, I withdrew Retribution and then stood. I pointed the tip of the blade in her direction.

"Thank you," I said. "I accept."

Queen Callandra stood. After a dramatic swish of her sashes, she turned on her heel, walked around the table, and retook her seat. The whispers began again, but they quickly ended once I moved my chair. All I wanted to do was sit, but any movement from me got the whole room tense.

I sat back down, and everyone relaxed again.

"The Isle Nation Perphestoni will also swear to the new Warlord of Magic," Mayor Lanes said. "Once we've spoken to the rest of the islands and we're under full agreement, our navy will fight the enemies of the world serpent arcanist."

Although the council of Fortuna didn't get out of their chairs to kneel, I simply nodded and said, "I accept."

I'd had no idea so many nations would want my ability to alter their land. It made sense, now that I thought about it, and now the pressure to develop that ability would be at the forefront of my thoughts.

Odlon cleared his throat, gaining everyone's attention.

"Since it's clear that we don't have all the information," he said, almost sarcastically, but he reined it in. "Why don't you explain everything you know about the Second Ascension? Who are we dealing with? And how long do we have before they become a force we can't deal with?"

"I'm glad you asked," I said. "The Second Ascension has been plotting for a long time. They started the arcane plague specifically to spawn these god-creatures. And, well, I think it's important to know that they have talented arcanists among their ranks."

LOYALTY BEYOND DEATH

I t took several hours to explain everything, and even then, I didn't cover all of the details.

The Second Ascension had learned that the god-creatures spawned when the world was in turmoil. The first time they had appeared, star shards had been raining from the skies, threatening to destroy the lands they crashed upon. The first set of god-creatures had set things right. Star shards still fell from the sky occasionally, but not in devastating amounts. Plus, people could now use the star shards to imbue magic into items or mystical creature parts, creating permanent trinkets or artifacts. That hadn't been possible before.

And it was all thanks to the previous god-arcanists. They had developed a solution.

I wasn't sure about the details, though. I just knew they had done *something* to fix the problem.

The Second Ascension had created this plague to be the new *problem*. The Autarch—a man bonded with the rare gold kirin—wanted to bond with a god creature himself. And not just one... The gold kirin would allow him to bond with multiple creatures, making him the strongest arcanist to ever walk among us.

If he could find them.

The Autarch had wanted to bond with the world serpent, after all, and I had prevented that. If we could just stay one step ahead of him…

I also explained Theasin Venrover's involvement, and how his knowledge of mystical creatures—and his artificer ability to create magical items—had helped the Second Ascension get to where they were today.

Most people seemed intrigued by this information, but no one commented.

As a matter of fact, no one interrupted my story at all. They kept quiet, and they hung on my every word, especially when I described the vile dig site and the corpse of the previous apoch dragon.

But then I came to the moment in the story when Luthair and I had fought the plague-ridden atlas tortoise.

"I was fighting the Second Ascension," I said, my throat tightening with each word. "And Luthair and I were already plague-ridden, so I thought my life was forfeit. I, uh, wanted to destroy their efforts… I wanted to make sure my friends made it to safety. I just kept fighting—I never quit—and that's when it happened. I achieved a true form with my knightmare, and it cleared away the plague. I killed the members of the Second Ascension and then destroyed their equipment."

I really didn't want to talk about that moment with Luthair, so I had spoken in a clinical and heartless manner, but it was better than getting teary-eyed in front of a bunch of powerful and influential arcanists.

Out of the corner of my eye, I spotted Lucian, the knightmare arcanist. He straightened his posture and furrowed his brow. He looked at me—straight at me—and a slight frown pulled at the corner of his lips.

Did he pity me? I glanced away, fearful his expression would cause me to dwell on the memories.

"So, they don't have access to the apoch dragon's bones any longer?" Queen Callandra asked.

I half-shrugged. "They had already taken bones from the site. I suspect they still have some. And since the dragon was massive, I suspect they'll still be able to create weapons and their item-destroying dust. We can't let our guard down."

"Perhaps we should think about writing an informational packet," Mayor Lanes said, stroking his wrinkled chin. "We could distribute it to the guilds. Then everyone would know who our enemies are, and what they're capable of."

"Can we ask the printing presses to create these pamphlets?" Justice Gonni, another council member, asked.

"We can call a state of emergency and requisition it."

"We must do so right away."

Arcanists around the room rushed to make this a reality. A few spoke to each other in hushed tones and then two attendants hurried out the main doors. I watched them zip around with mild amusement. I was glad everyone was taking this seriously.

While they fussed with the details, Lucian stepped into the shadows, shifted across the room, and then rose up from the darkness near my chair. He did everything slowly—I suspected so as not to startle me—and then offered a formal bow.

"Warlord," he said as he stood straight and ran a hand over his shaved-short hair. "I need to discuss something with you."

I nodded. "Okay."

"Ever since the Grandmaster Inquisitor had been killed by Akiva, the Second Ascension's assassin, I've made it my goal to see Akiva brought to justice."

"I understand," I muttered.

The Grandmaster Inquisitor was one of the greatest knightmare arcanists I had ever heard of. Lucian had looked up to him, especially since they had worked together as master and apprentice.

"I've captured a member of the Second Ascension," Lucian stated, straight to the point. "I've attempted to get him to talk, but after hearing your tale, I think it would be better if you interrogated him. My methods aren't working."

Both of my eyebrows shot upward. "You have someone? Where?"

"He's on my ship. My knightmare is watching him as we speak."

The information made me pensive. I wanted to call an end to these talks and head straight to the ship, but I knew I couldn't do that. Everyone here was of high standing. If I told them to go just to satisfy my own curiosity, I'd be insulting them.

Guildmaster Eventide placed a hand on my shoulder. I glanced over and she smiled.

"Take Zelfree when you go," she said under her breath. "He has a way of getting information out of people. Trust me."

I nodded once. "Right. I will. Thank you."

Lucian shifted back into the darkness and exited from the shadows on the other side of the room. He crossed his arms over his muscular chest and just waited, like this was all a show he had seen hundreds of times before.

He wore no armor. Most knightmare arcanists didn't. Their eldrin was their armor.

I touched my bare chest. Armor was something I needed. Every day I went without it was another day I risked injury or death.

"The Autarch," Queen Callandra said as she turned her attention to me. "Can the Frith Guild tell us what they know about him? I want to hear everything, right down to the clothing he prefers to wear."

The others in the room muttered words of agreement.

I decided to tell them everything.

<hr>

It was night by the time I finished.

I didn't know many hard facts about the Autarch—I didn't even know his real name. The title *Autarch* meant a *ruler above all other rulers*. It probably said more about the man than any other fact I had.

Still, that didn't stop the others from asking a million questions. It frustrated me. They wanted to know his age, his occupation before he took the title *Autarch*, and what his ultimate goals were. I had no answers. I knew the Autarch wanted to find god-creatures so that he could bond with them, and I knew some nations had already sworn their loyalty to his cause—so long as he used his god-arcanist magic to advance their goals.

What ultimate goal did the Autarch strive for? I wasn't certain. And how did he plan on dealing with the apoch dragon once it spawned?

According to legend, it would refuse to bond with anyone. The apoch dragon would simply come into existence and then kill all the god-creatures and their arcanists. It was the dragon's divine duty to clear the world—to reset things—in order to allow for humanity to grow once again without the influence of gods.

So, even if the Autarch bonded with multiple god-creatures, he would still ultimately die from the claws and fangs of the apoch dragon.

"A man as calculating as the Autarch will have a plan to deal with the apoch dragon," Queen Callandra stated. She frowned as she added, "He has been planning everything else for decades. His plan accounts for that accursed dragon, I assure you."

"Perhaps," I muttered.

Guildmaster Eventide held up a hand. Then she pointed to the tall windows and the stars dotting the sky. "I hate to point out the obvious, but it's late. Volke has given you all the information he has. Tomorrow we can discuss more of the specifics moving forward. Like how we intend to find members of the Second Ascension, and what information we should be spreading first to the other nations."

The other arcanists nodded and agreed. When I went to stand, Odion did the same.

"My liege," Odion said with a smirk. "Allow me to offer you safety among the soldiers of Javin."

My liege?

"I don't think you need to call me that," I whispered, hoping the others hadn't heard.

Odion lifted an eyebrow. "It's proper etiquette. And I want to remind the others I was the first to swear myself to the world serpent."

"But I'm not aristocracy," I said as we moved away from the table. My fatigue made my movements sluggish. After the magi cross, my exhaustion had caught back up with me. "I don't want people to call me *Your Majesty* or something." I rubbed at the back of my neck.

Odion half-laughed. "You only address kings and queens as *Your Majesty*. You address princes and princesses as *Your Highness*, and lords and ladies as *lords* and *ladies*, obviously."

His lesson caused my face to heat. I was the world serpent arcanist, but I didn't know the first thing about addressing nobility. It felt shameful.

"Then when do you use *my liege*?" I asked. "Why say that to me?"

"Because I swore an oath to you." Odion stared, his icy eyes piercing straight to my thoughts, unnerving me. "That's how you address someone to whom you swear loyalty. And I won't allow my liege to be ignorant on etiquette. I'd hate it if you embarrassed yourself—and subsequently all of Javin—with the improper use of language."

"O-Oh. I see. Well, I suppose I should be grateful." After a prolonged moment of silence, I asked, "I take it you're disappointed I don't already know this?"

Odion chuckled again, this time more genuine. "You asked me if I was young, right?"

I nodded.

"You're younger than me. Of course you don't know everything. And it's foolish to expect that of someone, no matter their age." He placed a hand on my shoulder and then lowered his voice so that only I could hear. "But don't fret. *I* know a great deal of etiquette, and since we're bound by oath, *my* knowledge is *your* knowledge."

"Thank you," I murmured.

Odion clearly took his oath to heart. He had done it in front of so many witnesses, and he already seemed dedicated to helping me navigate this difficult situation.

"Warlord Volke," Mayor Lanes said. "The property we've given you includes a compound. We would be honored if you called it home, even if just for your short stay in Fortuna. I've given all the details to your guildmaster, and I took the liberty of inviting your guild to operate there as your guardians."

Queen Callandra hastily stood from her seat. "The knights of Antihelm will also protect the world serpent arcanist." She gave me a single sharp nod. "You will have nothing to fear, my liege."

I would never get used to being called *my liege.*

"Thank you," I said, though I almost protested all the "protection."

Wasn't I the one who should have been protecting everyone else?

Zelfree shoved his way through the other arcanists and

stood at my side opposite Odion. "Don't fight against it," he said, like he could read my mind. "It's better if you stay in a place separate from the Frith Guild manor house. And we won't stay here long."

"Right. Thank you."

But before I could go to my new compound, Lucian got my attention from across the crowded room. His dark stare was perfect for a knightmare arcanist. He wanted me to visit his captured Second Ascension member.

"Master Zelfree," I said. "Can you come with me? I have a stop to make before I turn in for the night."

***

When we exited the tower, the crowd of arcanists had dispersed. My heart fell. I had hoped to see some of the other arcanists from the Frith Guild so that I could tell them everything that was going on—and the location of my new "home" on the outskirts of the city.

Perhaps they already knew? Adelgis heard the thoughts of *everyone*, after all. I hoped he would meet me at the compound with everyone else.

Soldiers from Javin and Antihelm patrolled around the Astral Tower, likely keeping mortals away from the fence. I said nothing to them, though I did admire their armor. The warriors of Javin wore the same type of plated metal as their king, though theirs was less intricate. It seemed to move better than full-plate armor, and I wondered how much less it weighed.

The knights of Antihelm stood tall and wore chain and studded leather. The metal on their uniforms had been stained and oxidized to appear reddish-brown, matching the color of cliffside dragons. Or perhaps parts of their uniform were made with cliffside dragon scales? That would be interesting.

Zelfree grabbed my shoulder and pulled me toward the main road. His grip was weak, but I allowed him to direct me. "Gawk later," he said. "Time isn't a resource we can waste."

"Right."

Lucian, Zelfree, and I headed for the docks.

I kept my tattered clothes buttoned, hiding the god-arcanist mark on my chest. The frills on my collar felt like a pair of soft hands trying to tickle me to death. I yanked on my clothing the entire trek.

Zelfree dressed as though he were impersonating shadows. His long, black coat was something new—it reached down to his knees. He walked with a casual gait, but I could tell he was just as tired as I was.

Lucian kept his hands in his trouser pockets, his shoulders stiff. He seemed... on edge.

The white of his loose pants was a harsh juxtaposition against the black of his tight-fitting shirt. He was a mix of light and darkness. It reminded me a bit of the twilight dragon.

I glanced over my shoulder and stared up at the Astral Tower. We were close enough that I could still hear the clank of machinery.

The twilight dragon, Hasdrubal, perched on top, was now ebony, his wings as inky as a raven's. They were creatures that changed with the time of day, and this one fascinated me.

But we soon turned down a street, blocking my view. I returned my attention to the path ahead. The people of Fortuna had turned in for the evening, but the occasional city guard, dockhand, and vagabond still dotted the streets.

Streetlamps lit our path, and a small piece of me hated that I needed them.

"So," Zelfree drawled, his gaze shifting to Lucian. "Are you going to swear yourself to the world serpent arcanist as well?"

"What?" Lucian snapped. He shot Zelfree a glare and then shook his head. "No. Never."

"Why not?"

I held up a hand. "It's fine. We don't need to discuss this."

Lucian huffed as we went down a steep road, heading straight for the docks. The cool ocean winds rushed down the cobblestone streets like they had somewhere to be. I figured I would shiver, but a deeper heat in my body kept the chill away.

After a minute of walking in silence, Lucian sighed. "I swore myself to the Grandmaster Inquisitor."

"He's dead," Zelfree stated, his tone callous.

"You think I don't know that?" Lucian sarcastically replied.

"An oath of fealty ends when your liege dies. You owe the dead nothing."

"I don't think you understand knightmare arcanists." Lucian inhaled, and then he exhaled a line of mist. "But, Volke... You know what I mean. You and Luthair... You understand."

At first, I wasn't sure what he was talking about. Knightmares were knights, after all. They swore themselves to their arcanists. If anyone understood *fealty*, it was a knightmare.

But then I realized what Lucian was talking about. He meant that loyalty didn't end with death. Knightmares rose from the corpses of assassinated rulers, born with the desire to seek revenge. And Luthair had sought revenge on the man who had killed his previous arcanist.

It didn't matter that they had died. The desire to set things right was the essence of a knightmare.

"I understand," I said. "And don't worry. The Grandmaster Inquisitor will be avenged."

Lucian regarded me with a small smile. "Oh, I know." He shrugged as he walked, his gaze drifting to the wrought-iron fence along the sidewalk. "We were only in Thronehold together for a short period of time, but I think I got to know you, Volke. We fought each other. We worked together when the Grandmaster Inquisitor summoned you…" His smile widened. "You're the type of man who will make good on his word."

During the conversation, Zelfree said nothing. His gaze wandered and he seemed lost in his own thoughts. His exhaustion became more and more pronounced as the evening wore on. He probably needed a long rest. I decided to ignore him and focus on Lucian.

"What about this man you captured?" I asked. "Where did you find him?"

"He's a pirate," Lucian replied.

"I thought you said he was a member of the Second Ascension?"

"He is. He's an arcanist who serves under the Dread Pirate Calisto."

Zelfree stutter-stepped and almost tripped over an awkwardly shaped stone fitted into the sidewalk. He corrected his posture and wrapped his coat tightly around his body, never saying a word.

Lucian either didn't notice or didn't care. "I caught the man in Port Crown, away from the rest of the crew. That was when I also received word from Fortuna that the world serpent arcanist would be arriving, so I brought the sea thief with me, interrogating him along the way."

"And you haven't gotten anything useful out of him?" I asked.

"No. But I know the man's hiding something." Lucian gave me a sideways glance. "I hope *you* can get information out of him."

I nodded. "Oh, don't worry. We'll figure out everything rather quickly."

THE FAKE GRIFFIN ARCANIST

An icy breeze greeted us as we arrived at the dock gates. The massive wall had slots between the posts, allowing a clear view of the ocean beyond the piers. The cloudless night sky and waxing moon made it easy to see out past the ships.

Gentel stayed far from land. She looked like a small island from this distance, and I still marveled at the size of a true form atlas turtle. Even Terrakona couldn't compare.

"That's the ship there," Lucian said. He pointed down the dock.

Even though my hair had been cut shorter, the wind still toyed with it as we walked. It did the same with Zelfree's hair, but Lucian had the benefit of a nearly shaved head. I supposed he kept his hair that length to avoid it becoming a problem in combat which was a wise decision—but I never seemed to have the time, or forethought, to keep anything trimmed.

I scratched at my chin, irritated by the slight stubble. I'd have to shave again soon.

Lucian led us to one of several *brig* style ships. They had two masts and were considered some of the fastest and most maneuverable warships. They were smaller, obviously, so they didn't have room for many cannons, but they allowed for a decent amount of storage in the hold, which meant they could double as a merchant vessel when not warring.

"This is the *Midnight Thorn*," Lucian said. "It was a vessel used by the Steel Thorn Inquisitors Guild, but…" Although Zelfree and I remained silent, Lucian didn't finish.

Most of the other inquisitors had died in Thronehold during the Second Ascension's attack, which meant the ship was probably Lucian's now. I wasn't sure how the legal title would pass, but I wasn't about to ask, either.

"The *Midnight Thorn* has a nullstone brig," Lucian said as he led us to the gangplank. "It's the perfect vessel to hunt down those Second Ascension scum."

The gangplank shook under our footfalls. Lucian went up, then Zelfree, and I finished our party, but when I got to the top, I felt the plank rumble again. I tensed, ready to unsheathe my sword, but then I took a breath and half-laughed.

"Fain, are you still with us?"

"Of course he is," Zelfree muttered. "He waited outside the tower for you and has been stalking us ever since."

"I'm not *stalking*." Fain's disembodied voice was odd sometimes. His invisibility remained perfect, though. "I'm *protecting* Volke."

"Are you sure you want to follow?" I asked. "We're meeting someone from Calisto's crew."

"I'm fine. I don't have any loyalty to that crew anymore."

Lucian turned on his heel, his muscles tense. "What was that? *He's a pirate*?"

"A renegade pirate," Zelfree stated, his tone both bored and irritated. "He's harmless. Let's just get this over with."

The word *harmless* hung in the air like a snowflake. A part of me knew that Fain wanted a place in the Frith Guild. Somewhere to belong. He had stuck by me when I had been infected with the plague, and he had kept Adelgis company through the worst of his problems. But he wasn't the strongest arcanist—he only had limited training that had started not too long ago. And he hadn't yet been accepted by the others, especially Illia and Zaxis.

"I want Fain to stick close," I said. "Having an invisible ally has its advantages."

"So be it," Zelfree muttered.

Lucian gritted his teeth and glared down the gangplank. "I'll trust him only because I trust Volke. Scum never truly change their ways, though. You should be careful whom you keep close, *Warlord*."

The temperature around the dock rose a few degrees, and I feared I might lose my temper. Instead, I bit my tongue and exhaled. The heat waned.

When I glanced up, I realized Lucian and Zelfree were staring at me with wide eyes. Slight amounts of obsidian rock had sprouted from my knuckles, like twisted claws. I shoved my hands into my trouser pockets.

"Don't get upset on my behalf," Fain said, his voice floating up from nowhere. "I know I'm scum. No need to pretend otherwise."

He stomped up the rest of the gangplank, announcing his presence. I walked up with him onto the ship, dwelling on his words.

The *Midnight Thorn* was a well-kept vessel. Everything had a place, and everything was in its place. The ropes were coiled perfectly, the rigging secured tightly. All the sails were down and folded, and the wood of the railings was scrubbed to a luster.

Lucian took us to the quarterdeck and then down the stairs to the first deck below. The narrow hallway meant we had to walk down one at a time, and Fain kept close to my back, his breath on my shoulder.

"So, how have you been interrogating this man so far?" I asked.

"Torture methods I learned while with the Steel Thorn Inquisitors." Lucian tensed his shoulders and then glanced at me. "But you're familiar with the Second Ascension, correct? You might know what he cares about—and how to intimidate him."

"Uh... Sure." I crossed my arms, my chest tight with uncertainty.

I had never tortured anyone before, and I didn't intend to start tonight. None of the arcanists I revered would resort to tormenting their foes. It just wasn't... noble.

Zelfree half-smiled. "You want me to handle this?" he whispered.

"No. I have an idea. And if that doesn't work, I know how we'll get our info."

When we entered the brig, the slightly suffocating effects of nullstone caused my skin to crawl, more than the rancid smell of moldy fish that hung in the stagnant air. I wondered... Would my god-arcanist powers be suppressed by nullstone? I didn't want to try it here, but I hoped I'd have time to check it out later.

I held back a gag.

The *Midnight Thorn* had several nullstone cages, all large enough to contain three to four adults. The bars were made from bluish-black rock and the wood in each cell was black.

Only one cage was in use. A middle-aged man sat in the back corner, his posture straighter than I had thought possible for a pirate. He wore a torn button-up shirt and shredded long trousers, both stained with his own blood. His brown hair, clumped to one side, half-hid his black eye.

He also appeared wet and slimy, and I wondered if Lucian had been dragging him behind the ship. That was an old tactic used by pirates...

I shook my head. Lucian wouldn't do that.

Right?

The pirate also had a scar on his neck. It was fresh, and a familiar symbol. Three horizontal lines: 三. Every member of Calisto's crew got it branded into their skin. Even Fain had it—something he kept hidden with ascots, bandanas, and high collars.

But this pirate also had black spots on the backs of his hands... I had never seen anything like that. They weren't burn marks, or stabs, or bullet wounds... Was it more torture? Or some sort of sickness?

With the help of the lantern hanging on the bulkhead, I spotted the man's arcanist mark on his forehead.

I caught my breath the moment I recognized the mythical creature.

A griffin.

That was impossible. Griffins only bonded with people who displayed noble bearings and undeniable courage. I had *never* heard of a griffin pirate arcanist. Ever. Hippogriffs, yes. Wyverns, of course. Sirens. Mermaids. And especially rocs... But not griffins.

I walked to the bars of the man's cell, my brow furrowed.

The man turned to face me. He kept his posture as straight as possible as he leaned against the nullstone bars. "Who are you?" he asked, his eyes squinted. "I demand you set me free! You apprehended me in a free port—this kind of abuse isn't allowed!"

His voice was a little higher pitched than I had been expecting, and he spoke more... *properly*... than any pirate I had known in the past.

Zelfree crossed his arms. He stared at the man, his emotionless face betraying nothing.

"Are you a member of the Second Ascension?" I asked.

The pirate gritted his teeth and quieted down. When he didn't respond, I stepped closer to the bars of his cell.

"If you want to go free, you'll answer my questions."

"And if I *don't* answer your questions? What're you going to do? *Kill me*? That's against guild code! You'll all be thrown from your own organization!"

This man seemed to know the law well, which was surprising, but perhaps pirates would know how the laws work, since they went out their way to break them. I forced a smirk and tried to picture Zaxis. How would he react in this situation?

"I'm the world serpent arcanist," I stated, confidence in my voice. "Laws don't apply to someone like me. So, if you want to leave this brig alive, you'll answer my questions."

The man stood and hobbled over to the bars, his left foot injured and barely supporting his weight. Despite that, he moved with brazen, angry energy. He gave me the once over.

"You don't scare me," he growled under his breath.

After a long stare-down, the man turned on his right heel and hobbled back to his spot at the far side of the cell.

I slowly turned around to face Lucian, Zelfree, and Fain. With a weak shrug, I whispered, "Well, that was my trump card. I don't have any other intimidation tactics."

Lucian deeply frowned. "*What*? That's it? You have to be joking."

"Ask the pirate some questions," Zelfree said, gesturing to the man with a tilt of his head. "See what you can get out of him before I ask anything."

With a nod, I turned back around and faced the pirate in the cell.

What was I going to ask him? About Calisto? The Second Ascension? Their plans?

My gaze went to his griffin mark once again. Curiosity got the better of me.

"Where's your eldrin?" I asked.

"I don't know," the man muttered. Then he shot me a glare. "You tell me. The damn knightmare arcanist won't let me see my eldrin."

"I keep his griffin cub in a smaller cage in the captain's quarters," Lucian said. Then he slammed a hand on the bars of the cage. "You won't see your eldrin again until you give us the information you have. What plans do the Second Ascension have? *Where is Calisto heading?*"

"Wait," I said, holding up a hand. "Back up. A griffin cub? You stole a *cub* from its mother? How did you trick it into bonding with you?"

To my surprise, the pirate hesitated. Not out of anger, but fear. He turned his gaze to the floor, staring at the wood that had been stained black with nullstone. His swollen eye seemed glazed over. "I... I didn't steal the cub. Alexi bonded with me after I completed his trial of worth." The man regained his confidence as he growled, "And I completed it on my own, thank you very much."

I shook my head. "That's impossible. Griffin mothers watch over their cubs during their trial of worth."

Why was I arguing with a pirate? Of course he would lie. This line of questioning was pointless.

I stood a bit taller and decided to just cut to the chase. "Listen, if you cooperate and answer our questions, we'll let you leave."

"Never," he said.

"The Second Ascension has nothing for you. They're dastards. Why protect them? They aren't here, fighting to free you."

The pirate ground his teeth loud enough that I could hear. "I don't care about the *Second Ascension*. They can rot in the abyssal hells for all I care."

"So, answer us."

"No."

"Why not?" I demanded, placing a hand on the cell. "You have everything to gain."

A part of me wondered if the man was telling the truth about his griffin. Maybe he *had* been a noble man, but he had been led astray by the Second Ascension. Maybe we could help him, like I had once helped Fain. We didn't need to torture the man any further.

"I won't betray Calisto," the man finally said. "I don't care what you do to me. I'll never talk. *Never*."

He said the words with such certainty. He really didn't sound like a pirate... He even met my gaze with a hardened look of his own, challenging me to question his conviction.

"Are you and Calisto lovers?" Zelfree asked, startling me.

I hadn't thought he would speak. And why did he sound so... jealous?

The pirate turned away, his hand on his blackened eye. "No. Calisto doesn't care about me."

That last statement was unusual. The man didn't have his same conviction. Was he lying? I wished Luthair was still with me. I could've used my magic to sense the betrayal. Was the pirate protecting Calisto? Was he afraid for the other man?

I held my breath.

No. Calisto was a blackheart. Why would anyone care about him? Or was this some sort of sign that Calisto wasn't as twisted as I thought he was?

Zelfree scoffed and then turned away. "This blowhard won't tell you anything. Have Adelgis handle this. Your time is more valuable, Volke."

"Yeah, Adelgis would probably have an easier time," I murmured.

A part of me wanted to have handled this myself, to at least get information on the Second Ascension and *lead* the other arcanists against our enemy. Constantly relying on others, and not even knowing my magic, ate at me. Adelgis could solve this, sure, but perhaps if I had been more intimidating…

"And I've seen enough. I'm leaving." Zelfree headed for the stairs, his long coat billowing out behind him.

I held up a hand to stop him, but I had nothing to say. Was this meeting bothering him? He had run with Calisto in the past, and I knew they had been childhood friends, but what about this upset Zelfree?

"We'll be back," I said as I headed for the stairs myself.

Lucian followed close behind. Once we made it up a couple of steps, and then out the quarterdeck door, he grabbed my shoulder and spun me around.

"What's wrong with you?" Lucian demanded. "I told you that pirate has information. I know it. We can't let him go without questioning him! We'll have to resort to more extreme means."

I removed Lucian's hand. "We won't need to. Once Adelgis gets hold of him, we'll have everything we need. Just let him sit in the cell for now."

"Adelgis?" Lucian ran a thumb over his nose. "Is he some sort of intimidating brute?"

I half-choked, and half-laughed. "Uh, no. Definitely not. But don't worry. His magic will help us uncover everything. I promise."

"I see. Well, then, I'll leave you to it, Warlord."

After giving me a bow, Lucian turned back around and headed down the stairs. I watched him go, my chest tight. A part of me had been hoping to see his knightmare. What was his name again? I had met him in Thronehold.

It was Azir.

I swallowed my desire to ask to see him and instead walked out onto the deck of the ship. No one was here. I suspected the deckhands were below, perhaps sleeping. And Master Zelfree had already left the *Midnight Thorn* so quickly it was as if he had sprinted away the moment he had been out of sight.

A chill breeze rushed over the water, carrying with it the smell of sea salt. It was better than the rotting stench of fish, I supposed.

"Volke," Fain whispered out of nowhere.

I turned in his direction. "Hm?"

"I wanted to ask you something."

"Sure. Go on."

"Will you allow anyone to swear an oath of fealty to you?"

Both my eyebrows shot for my hairline. I had already been tense from my meeting with the pirate, and now I felt strangely awkward.

"Uh, well, I guess," I said with a shrug. "I don't think I can stop anyone at this point. I mean, I could refuse their offer, but I suspect more and more arcanists will attempt to either join me and the Frith Guild, or side with the Second Ascension."

"I don't care about those arcanists."

Fain's invisibility dropped, revealing his sickly self. His wan skin, frostbitten fingers, and blackened ears gave him all the charm of a corpse. He appeared paler than usual.

His wendigo, Wraith, also appeared. The wolf creature with the skull face displayed a surprising amount of emotion when he wagged his tail upon seeing me.

Fain glanced around the empty deck. We were alone.

Then he got to one knee in front of me, and I caught my breath.

"Listen," he said before I could speak. "I've never really been a member of the Frith Guild." He grabbed at his neck and pulled the guild pendant out from under his shirt and ascot. "They gave me this in exchange for my wendigo's horns. I know."

Wraith skulked to the side, his hornless skull weighing on my thoughts.

With a powerful overhand throw, Fain tossed his guild pendant overboard. A soft splash marked the last of it.

"There are few people I trust," Fain murmured, his voice almost too soft to hear. "You and Moonbeam and... Well, that's about it." He bowed his head forward. "I, Fain the Renegade Pirate..." He shook his head and clenched his jaw. "N-No... I mean. I, Thibault Raustin of Whitecrest, hereby swear my loyalty to the world serpent arcanist."

I held my breath. Fain had only ever said his real name once before, when explaining how pirates left their old lives behind when they chose a new identity.

"You don't have to do this," I said, staring down at him. "I know you've got my back. I know you wouldn't betray me." I leaned down and placed a hand on his shoulder. "If this is about what Lucian said, don't worry about it. He's always been like that. He didn't trust *me* at first."

I tried to laugh, but Fain glanced up with an icy glare and I stopped myself.

"It's not about that," he muttered. Then he returned his head to a bowed position. "It's about where my loyalties lie. If I had to choose between being with the Frith Guild or staying by your side, I'd pick you any day. So, that's why. I'd rather swear myself to you than have anyone confused."

I inhaled deeply and then exhaled.

Was this how all my friendships would play out? People declaring their loyalty to me?

For a short second, I was lost in thought, but Fain interrupted my musings when he asked, "Do you accept?"

I pulled Retribution from the sheath and then placed the blade on Fain's shoulder. "I accept." Then I removed my weapon and tucked it back into the scabbard.

Fain stood and half-smiled. "Thank you, Volke. I almost thought you weren't going to accept me because..." He motioned to himself. "I mean, I'd understand."

I placed a hand on his upper arm and pointed him toward the gangplank. "I keep saying you shouldn't talk about yourself like that, but you never listen." As we walked, I tried to keep my tone upbeat. "Look, when we get back to the Frith Guild, we'll speak to Adelgis together, okay? We'll get him to interrogate this pirate through his dreams or... something. However Adelgis does his thing."

"Shouldn't you be going to your new home?" Fain asked, narrowing his eyes. "I thought you had a compound now? With knights and guards?"

"Oh, right." I nervously added a chuckle. "You think the rest of the guild is waiting for me?"

"If I were a gambling man, I'd say a lot more than the guards are waiting for you to arrive."

He was likely right. The others would be there.

"Okay, we'll go there first," I said. "Then we'll get Adelgis."

"Whatever you want, my liege."

Damn. Everyone was going to be calling me that now, weren't they?

21

THE SAVAN COMPOUND

I wasn't familiar with Fortuna. I knew the city, but only by reputation. The smaller streets and narrow alleyways were new to me. I made my way southwest, following the street signs that pointed to residences.

Fain shadowed me, his footfalls a comfort. The night grew colder with each passing moment, and for some reason, I wanted company. He had become invisible again, and so had Wraith. His eldrin was much quieter than him.

"I think it's this way," Fain said, tugging on my sleeve to point me in a new direction.

"Okay."

The midnight winds picked up as we arrived at the edge of the main city roads. The cobblestone streets became hard-packed dirt and wooden fences. The city walls were still off in the distance, and I knew my new piece of land was within them, so I wouldn't get *too* lost, but I desperately wanted to sleep. How much farther was it?

"There," Fain said.

He tugged my shirt, pointing me toward a tall, wrought-iron fence. A small, chest-high brick pillar stood to the side of the main gate. I approached and stared at it. A name had been carved into the side, illuminated by the tall lamp on the street.

All the pillar said was: SAVAN.

"I think we found your estate," Fain quipped.

The gate and fence were nearly fifteen feet tall and topped with spear-like spikes. With my new evocation, I'd be able to break in just fine, but a normal man wouldn't have much luck. I strode to the gate and found two Javin soldiers on the other side, both in the light of a nearby streetlamp. Each held a halberd in one hand and a round shield in the other.

They snapped to attention and then bowed their heads.

"Warlord Savan," one said. "Guildmaster Eventide said you would arrive. The other arcanists of the Frith Guild are already inside."

The other Javin soldier hurried to the gate and unlocked it. They both opened the way for me, haste in their movements.

As I walked by, I noticed something odd about their layered plate armor. They both wore bracelets on their left hands, but they weren't made of metal or precious gemstones. They were bracelets made of colored thread. Under the moonlight, the threads shimmered, telling me they were made of silk.

And the bracelets didn't match. One soldier wore a bracelet of black, red, and blue, and the other soldier had a bracelet of black, silver, and green. Were they a fashion statement in the Kingdom of Javin? It was odd to see them on soldiers. Most nations insisted on strict uniform dress and armor. Decorating the soldiers with jewelry didn't fit with the military-worshipping tales I had heard of Javin.

I said nothing as I passed the soldiers, though. A bed was awaiting me.

Fain and Wraith stuck close enough to sneak in with me. We walked the long, brick pathway to the new Savan Compound. We didn't have streetlamps here.

It was too dark to appreciate the landscaping, but I could

tell from the trees lining the pathway that thought had been put into the design. Each tree was perfectly spaced and the exact same size as the last. They were plum trees, currently in a state of flowering. Fruit trees always smelled sweet to me. It made the walk more than pleasant.

I widened my eyes to search the darkness. In the distance, I saw multiple buildings. How large was this compound? The main house had a fountain and a half-cricle brick road, likely for horses and carriages. It was also two stories tall, with dozens of windows lining the face of the building.

How many rooms were there? Over twenty, which was a ludicrous amount. And if the other buildings on this property were of equal size, I would have way too much space for a single arcanist.

The entire Frith Guild manor house could fit into the main building of my new compound.

The front doors—oversized and crafted from heavy wood and iron—had been designed with an ornate lock and copper knockers. I reached for one of the ring-shaped knockers and then chuckled to myself.

"I'm going to knock to enter my own house?" I muttered under my breath.

With a sigh, I pushed the doors open and stepped inside. The place smelled of dust, but the lit lanterns and glowstones on the walls gave the inside a gentle golden color. I stood in the middle of the foyer and glanced around. The floor was patterned to look like water. Blue, light blue, and white oddly-shaped stones were fitted together in a swirling effect that ended in the middle of the room.

A grand staircase led to the second story, and multiple halls led deeper into the main building. I thought, because the lanterns were lit, that people would be nearby, but I didn't see anyone.

Where were they? The Javin soldier had said the entire

Frith Guild was inside, yet I didn't see a trace of them. How large was this compound?

Fain and Wraith uncloaked themselves from their invisibility and stood with me in the foyer.

"This place is impressive," Fain said, his eyes on the vaulted ceiling.

Wraith lifted his snout and inhaled. "This place hasn't been inhabited for a long while…"

I rubbed my nose, irritated by the dust that lingered in the air. "Yeah," I muttered. "I bet it was empty until just recently."

"All the members of the Frith Guild likely disturbed the dust. After a while, it shouldn't be a problem."

Fain smirked. "And this was just *given* to you?"

I nodded. "Well, yeah. I'm supposed to protect all of Fortuna in exchange."

"You would've done that anyway." Fain crossed his arms. "Those chumps really don't know you at all."

"I suppose."

"Maybe you should ask for something more the next time the head of a nation wants to swear themselves to you. See how much you can get away with."

"Nah. Could you imagine having more than one of these compounds?" I forced a chuckle and headed for the stairs. "I, uh, should probably look for a bedroom and get some rest."

"Hm."

"You both can sleep here as well, if you want." I gestured to the gigantic building. "Uh, my home is your home? I guess you're my knight or something, so it makes sense that you'd stay here."

What *was* I supposed to call people like Fain and Odion—people who had sworn themselves to me?

"Thanks." Fain turned his attention to the halls. "I'll try to find a room suitable for someone like me." He turned and waved his hand at his eldrin. "Come, Wraith. Let's check the compound out."

They headed off down the hall, spring in their steps. I thought he had just been waiting to explore the building. Wraith's tail wagged the entire time.

Fatigue gnawed at me, but I leapt up the stairs two at a time, curious to see the place. When I got to the top, I grabbed the railing and took a deep breath.

"Maybe I really should just get some sleep," I whispered.

I exhaled, and then headed into the upstairs hallway. It was fully furnished with side tables, potted plants, and a long golden rug. This was my place? My steps echoed off the walls. Paintings hung near the windows—paintings of the Astral Tower and of sailing ships. They were pleasant, and nonspecific.

The first room I checked had a bed. A large bed. And a couch. And a... baby bed?

There was a smaller bed on the opposite side of the massive room, with the couch between them, sitting in the middle of the room. It seemed odd, but perhaps this was a room in which to care for small children? One bed for a parent, and one bed for a child?

It was a nursery. The large bed was likely for a wetnurse, someone who would breastfeed the child.

But did that matter? The room was vacant, and it wasn't like I needed to pick somewhere dignified right now. I could find another room later.

I wandered inside, grabbed the white blankets lined with golden thread, and threw them aside so that I could sleep. The second I planted myself on the soft mattress, I lost myself to slumber, despite the fact I still wore my clothes, weapon, and shield.

I dreamt of my home island, the Isle of Ruma. Such wonderful weather and clear skies—the sight made me homesick in an instant. A familiar person joined me on a stroll to my favorite locations.

Adelgis.

His long, black hair fluttered in the afternoon light. We stood on the white sand beach near Gravekeeper William's cottage. My bare feet enjoyed the splash of gentle waves as we strode along the perfect coast. Gulls serenaded our walk.

With each deep breath, my stress melted away.

"Adelgis," I said. "I'm glad you came to see me."

His robes, as white as the sand, shimmered with his movement. "Came to see you? What an odd way of putting it." He chortled as we walked.

This was a pleasant afternoon.

But even in this dreamscape, Adelgis sounded tired. He took short steps, and his energy seemed drained. He clasped his hands behind his back, his attention on the sand at his feet and not our beautiful surroundings.

"I need your help." I turned to him, thankful he had given me a tunic and loose trousers for the dream. The winds and moderate temperature made everything easier.

Without looking up, Adelgis replied, "If this is about the god-creatures, I assure you, I'm trying my hardest to pinpoint their locations."

"No. Not that. I need help with a pirate that's been captured. I'm sure Fain has told you all about it."

Adelgis waved his hand, and the breeze on the island ceased to exist. "No. I haven't seen him. I've been busy."

"Oh." I crossed and then uncrossed my arms as I mulled over his statement. "Well, there's a Second Ascension pirate we need to interrogate. I was hoping you could look into his thoughts."

Adelgis smiled as he finally glanced up. "Consider it done."

"Don't you need to know where he is?"

He tapped the side of his head. "You already told me, Volke. So don't worry about it any longer. I'll unearth your pirate's secrets."

With a nervous chuckle, I turned away. The pristine beaches on the Isle of Ruma were a wonderful backdrop. I admired the island atmosphere as I contemplated the situation. It always felt weird that Adelgis could just *know everything about me* by reading my mind and thoughts.

Then again, at least it was someone like Adelgis. He was a good man, and the more I got to know him, the more I wished he had had an easier life. Adelgis had tried so hard to please the people around him. It almost ate at me when I dwelled on the details. At first, Adelgis had admired his father, who had used him. Then he had tried to serve the rest of his family, who had treated him poorly. And then the Frith Guild... where he had struggled to fit in.

"Please, no more," Adelgis whispered.

I returned my attention to him.

Adelgis stared at me with a blank expression. I couldn't read it. His dark eyes homed in on mine. "What's wrong?" I asked.

He shook his head, his bottom lip trembling. "I apologize. Just... I think it's time for you to wake up."

"But—"

I jerked awake, my breathing ragged, my vision unfocused.

After a long sigh, I pinched the bridge of my nose. I shouldn't have thought all those things in his presence. I had only infected Adelgis with dark thoughts—that wasn't helping anything.

I rolled over and realized the sun was shining, bathing the room in bright, white light. Struggling to motivate myself, I sat up, my back sore. The ruffles from my giant collar tickled my chin, waking me faster than cold water. I scratched at myself and stood.

I was still in the same room with the two beds, but I was now sweatier from a long night's sleep in terrible clothes. I tugged at them—undoing my belt and unbuttoning my shirt.

The room was just... odd. It was long and rectangular, with small toys lined on the shelves. A long table and washbasin were near the window. Perhaps I could clean up?

The door opened. I whirled around and tensed, in a state of undress.

To my surprise, it was King Odion who had opened the door. I locked up, unable to move as my sleep-addled mind wrapped around the situation. I already looked bizarre from yesterday, and now my black hair was squashed to one side, my clothing wrinkled and half on my body, and I likely had an odor he could smell from the door.

And to make matters worse, Odion appeared well-rested and put together. He wore his armor—white scales and plated shoulders—giving him an edged silhouette. The damage done by Retribution had been mended, and he even wore a frilled feather belt, no doubt made from the wings of his eldrin.

He stood with regal bearing.

"H-Hello," I awkwardly said.

Odion smirked. "Good morning, my liege."

It felt sarcastic when he addressed me like that. I wondered if Odion, upon seeing me this morning, regretted his decision to swear an oath to me. I *was* just standing around like a lump, half-awake, half-exhausted. I wanted to be impressive and demonstrate my competence.

Unable to think of a clever follow-up statement, I said, "Uh, welcome to my home?"

For some reason, I motioned to the walls and furnishings, as though showing them off. I hadn't realized until then, but this room didn't have artwork depicting Fortuna or the docks or sailing ships—it had paintings of mothers and children at all stages in life.

One painting was of a nude woman holding a small child in her arms as she fed the babe with her body. The details were unfortunately numerous and realistic, with attention paid to the coloration of their skin and the rosy highlights on their tanned cheeks.

My face grew bright red as heat spread through me. Once I tore my gaze from the painting, I found Odion stifling a chuckle.

More embarrassment washed through me. I covered my tomato face with a hand.

"L-Listen," I stammered out, both frustrated and baffled. "That—*this*—let's just, er, forget we saw this."

I hoped all the way to the abyssal hells this was just an eccentric dream woven by Adelgis.

Please. Let it be a dream.

Odion couldn't contain his mirth. He laughed as he smoothed his silver hair. Then he shook his head, his icy eyes gleaming with amusement. "Don't worry. Your secret is safe with me." He smiled as he held the door open. "I won't tell people about your desires."

"*No,*" I half-yelled. Then I strained myself to control my volume. "This isn't that. I'm not—this isn't—I was just lost." I hurried out of the room, wanting to distance myself from it forever.

Or perhaps burn it down.

It was my home, right? I could do that.

"I really was lost," I said again as I hustled down the hallway. "It's a nursery. I didn't decorate the place."

"It's perfectly natural—"

"Don't." My skin practically burned from all of my blushing. "Just. No more. As a matter of fact, as your liege, I command you to never speak of this again."

Odion full-on laughed. I grew a deeper shade of scarlet, my eyes narrowed.

"It's not that amusing," I said.

"Oh, it is. Trust me." Odion continued to chuckle. Only after he calmed himself did he speak again. "They say you can tell a lot about a leader by the first command they give. I think I learned a little more about you, Volke."

"I suppose." But was it really a good command? Probably not.

I stopped walking, my head spinning. When I turned around, Odion stood right next to me. While he was so close, I noticed a bracelet on his wrist, similar to the ones worn by the soldiers outside. The silk threads were all kinds of colors—black, blue, green, white, and red.

"What is that?" I asked.

"This?" He held up his left hand. "It's a warrior's mark. Beautiful, no?"

"Is it special? I saw some of your soldiers wearing the same thing."

"All warriors from the Kingdom of Javin have one of these." He spun the bracelet around his wrist. "It symbolizes death and serves as a reminder." He tugged on a black thread. "This color here—you add a strand to your mark for every enemy you kill."

I caught my breath, my blood running cold. They... celebrated their kills?

Odion must've sensed my shift in thoughts. He shook his head. "It's a way to honor the enemy. We never forget the people who have died." He tugged at the red threads on his wrist—he had more of those than any other color. "This color is for every brother-in-arms you've seen die. A remembrance."

"Oh. I see."

The colors of his warrior's mark made more sense to me now. I stared at his, looking for the color he had the least number of threads of.

"What's that green one?" I asked.

"You add a green thread for every loved one you've seen die."

I looked away. "I'm sorry for your loss."

Odion half-laughed. "You needn't be. Death comes for us all. In this case, it was peaceful." Then he studied my face. "Tell me, would your warrior's mark have any green threads?"

For a brief moment, I didn't say anything as I considered his question. "Does the death of your eldrin count?" I asked, my voice low.

"Certainly."

"Then, yes. I'd need at least one." But I didn't want to focus on this conversation. Instead, I asked, "Why are you here, Odion? Don't you have other matters to attend to?"

"No one knew where you had gone for the evening," Odion said. "The guildmaster of the Frith Guild wanted to speak to you, so I offered to search."

The guildmaster of the Frith Guild.

His phrasing brought me back to the reality of the situation. It wasn't *your guildmaster was looking for you.* Odion had worded it to make sure it sounded as though I weren't under her command. Eventide was just *a guildmaster of some guild that I happened to know.*

I took a moment to straighten my frumpy coat and trousers. At some point, I had lost my sash. I didn't miss it.

"Why are *you* here?" I asked. "I mean, you could've sent a messenger."

"I'm here to protect you, of course," Odion said, smiling. "Is that wrong?"

I didn't know why, but that statement didn't sit well with me. "I beat you in a duel," I said. "Whatever you can handle—I can handle."

"But perhaps there are enemies that require both our strength. Have you considered that?"

I wanted to protest, but I decided to drop it. The grogginess from my short rest lingered worse than a morning fog.

"Uh, would you mind telling Guildmaster Eventide that I'll meet her in the kitchen?" I asked, combing my sloppy hair with my fingers. "I'll meet you both there once I've cleaned up."

Odion replied with a noble bow of his head. "I'll inform the others. I'll see you in the kitchen, my liege." And then he turned and headed away from me with a confident gait.

I watched him go. Odion never glanced back. He went all the way to the grand staircase and then descended.

Finally alone, I hurried away from the staircase, determined to straighten myself before interacting with anyone else.

22

WE NEED TO TALK

Apparently, my new compound came with servants.

Men and women dressed in plain white tunics and aprons cleaned the rooms and halls as I walked by. A few of them offered me *good mornings* and *good afternoons*, all addressing me as *the honorable world serpent arcanist*.

I avoided them as much as possible as I searched for a bathing room. Once I found one, I locked myself inside and washed off with the cold water stored in buckets near the tub. I probably could've heated it with my molten rock, but unlike with fire, I wouldn't have a way to deal with the byproduct that didn't involve melting the room and building.

I washed myself in record time. Only a few minutes—to avoid anyone else walking in on me—but afterward, I spent an unreasonable amount of time searching for clothing. I threw on my old "fancy" trousers, but after that, I searched the numerous cabinets and closets. How many closets and cabinets did one room need? Four seemed excessive, but this room had six different hideaways.

For some reason, there were already towels, clothes, and

cleaning cloths in all of them, as if someone had stocked the compound, knowing it would be inhabited.

Or perhaps it had once belonged to someone else?

I flinched as the washroom door burst open.

"Volke, where in the abyssal hells are you?" Zaxis yelled, his voice echoing throughout the tiled room.

I poked my head around the closet door. "What're *you* doing here? I'm trying to dress."

Zaxis sauntered into the room, his salamander scale armor clean and sparkling. He held up a stack of folded clothes and placed his other hand on his hip. "Here ya go, *Your Highness*. What else can I get for you this afternoon?" He offered me a sarcastic curtsy.

I stormed over to him and ripped the clothing from his grip. "Don't do that."

"Do what? Show you respect?" He laughed once and then cocked his head to the side. "What's wrong, *Your Grace*? Did your butt-wiping servant miss a spot?"

"*Zaxis.*" I tried to keep the venom from my voice, but I couldn't. "I'm not in the mood."

"Feh." He shrugged and then leaned back against the door. "I just wanna make sure you don't get a swollen head after everything that's happened. Dragon arcanists bowing to you left and right—huge compounds thrown into your lap." He gave me the once over. "Or are you better than all of us now?"

I yanked a new tunic over my head and secured the fine leather belt around my waist with so much anger, I almost burned my clothing with inadvertent evocation.

"You live in a fantasy world, you know that?" I shoved my feet into the silken socks. "Always jumping to conclusions."

"You left last night without telling anyone anything. And then you missed training this morning to sleep in." He motioned to the gigantic bathing room, the many towels, and the large tub. "You're just soaking your godly body in thirty kinds of lavender oil, no doubt. Adelgis contacts me telepathically to say you need your clothes brought to you." He scoffed and threw his hands up in the air.

"See? This is what I'm talking about. None of that happened like you think it did!"

"Oh, yeah?" he snapped.

"I had matters to deal with last night. And yeah, I slept in, sure, but that's because I've been exhausted and this is a strange place, and who was I going to tell to wake me up? I have no clue."

Zaxis narrowed his eyes and listened.

"I slept in a random nursery last night," I continued with a dark laugh. "I've embarrassed myself in front of the King of Javin, I have to interrogate a pirate, fight the Second Ascension, help the Frith Guild locate all the other god-creatures, defeat the Autarch, *and now* I have your whining to contend with." I slammed my feet into the pair of shiny new boots. "Please, for the love of the good stars at night—can you just help me without being an ass? I have no idea what I'm doing!"

I shouted the last part so loudly my words bounced off the walls. I grimaced and stepped away from Zaxis, trying to keep my composure. What was I doing?

Zaxis waited for a moment, probably wondering if I was going to say anything more.

Once I finished dressing, I ran my hands roughly over my body, trying to smooth out the creases of the clothing. I barely saw them—they were better than the old outfit, but still. Who cared what I looked like?

"What're you talking about?" Zaxis asked, his voice quiet.

I glanced up and just stared at him.

"Look around you," he said. "Everything is going well."

I took a deep breath and then held it.

Zaxis stepped close. He grabbed my shoulder, his grip tight. "You managed to get allies against the Second Ascension.

Small allies, sure, but you convinced the rulers of two nations, and the Fortuna Council."

"But... I..."

"You're safe, right?" Zaxis asked. "Another win. The Second Ascension hasn't gotten you yet." His grip tightened. "And you've already learned some of your magic. You haven't mastered it yet, sure, but it's powerful." He forced me to look at him, his green eyes far more serious than normal. "So, what're *you* whining for? Too many servants? So many bedrooms you slept in the wrong one by accident? Get a grip, ya piece of toast."

His last insult made me chuckle for some reason. I rubbed my face and then gave Zaxis a half-embrace with one arm. I broke away shortly afterward, slightly embarrassed I had gotten angry at his antics.

"Sorry," I said.

Zaxis's face flushed. "D-Don't apologize. I just called you a piece of toast. We're even."

"Okay, well, I have to meet the guildmaster in the kitchen." I pointed at the door. "Join me?"

Zaxis scoffed and then smiled. "Of course. Lead the way."

I rubbed the back of my neck. "About that... I have no idea where the kitchen is."

"Eh. It won't matter. Illia will know. Let's go."

Zaxis and I traveled out of the bathing room and down the hall. I was content to walk in silence, but Zaxis smacked my arm.

"I saw your duel, fool," he said. "I know we haven't trained much with your molten rock, but listen up. Odion was blinding you, but you could've blinded him back. Heat near the eyes will dry them up. If you had kept your heat close, he wouldn't have been able to approach."

Memories of Hexa's training filled my mind. She created a poison fog that kept enemies at bay. Could I create a moat of molten rock that would prevent enemies from approaching? Perhaps. And I could blind them with the heat, like Zaxis wanted.

"That's a good idea," I muttered. "Thank you."

Zaxis nodded. "Of course. I'm your master, after all." He buffed his nails against his scale armor. "I've got all the tips and tricks."

"I'm never calling you *master*. Even if you achieve the rank in the guild."

"Tsk. You'll call me master one of these days, I guarantee it."

"Maybe in one of Adelgis's homemade dreams."

We reached the staircase, both of us chuckling.

Illia and Nicholin were there waiting for us. Illia wore no coat, just a loose white shirt, fitted trousers, and boots to her knees. Today she also wore a white eyepatch, which I hadn't seen before. She turned to face me, her wavy hair bouncier than normal.

Nicholin scampered across her shoulders, poked his head through her hair, and stared at me with his little ferret-like eyes.

"Volke," Nicholin said. "There you are! We've been looking for you everywhere. Did you know this compound has *four* buildings? One for the servants, and three for the family. It even has a barn!"

"You've been to them all?" I asked.

Illia grazed her fingers over her eyepatch. "We ported around."

Ported?

"You mean, you teleported?" I asked.

She nodded. "We went to the main rooms of all the buildings. Apparently, this used to be a summer compound for some sort of city councilor, but he hasn't been here for over a decade, so the land was reclaimed and given to you."

"*Ha,*" Zaxis crowed. "You got a hand-me-down compound. Hilarious."

I slowly turned and glowered at him. Didn't we just have a pleasant conversation? How had he already reverted back to his usual self?

"We also ported to some of the master bedrooms, but you weren't there!" Nicholin raised his fur. "You weren't in some girl's bed, were you? Don't lie to us!"

Illia placed a hand over his face. "You don't have to answer that."

"He was in a baby's room or something," Zaxis said with a shrug. "It doesn't matter. Let's get to the kitchen."

Nicholin's ears twitched. "Baby's room? You mean a nursery?"

"Let's go," Illia said, holding out her hands. "Everyone is waiting."

Zaxis and I each grabbed a hand. She concentrated and her magic pulled me at my core. I felt yanked in a direction, and my sight disappeared. After a short, but intense, thrust forward, I stumbled around as my sight returned. We were inside a large kitchen, complete with several stoves, countertops, and stew pots.

So many other people were here, it made the kitchen feel much smaller than it actually was.

Eventide, Devlin, my father, Zelfree, Gillie, Odion, Queen Callandra, Karna, and Vethica...

And not to mention so many of their eldrin. Traces, the mimic. Alana, the caladrius bird. Tine, the blue phoenix. And Akhet, the scarab-like khepera. They were the only ones small enough to fit in the kitchen. Well, technically, Karna's doppelgänger could've fit, but he was never around, for some reason.

"It's been a long time since I've called a gathering of master arcanists," Eventide said with a smile and laugh. "I remember...

when Ruma and I had to call together multiple arcanists to deal with some threats. It was always the start of something epic. And dangerous."

Her gaze became distant, like she wasn't here, but rather, deep in a memory.

Captain Devlin licked his thumb and smoothed it over his chin-strap beard. "You know I'm more of a mercenary, right? I don't usually play the hero."

"Then be prepared for a new chapter of your life," Zelfree said as he sat up on a stone countertop. "Our enemies are already on the move."

Zaxis, Illia, and I approached the group. The others turned to us. Karna immediately smiled, and Zelfree met my gaze for half a second before looking away.

Before anyone said anything else, Eventide turned her vacant gaze in my direction. Then she focused and forced a smile. "Ah, there's our world serpent arcanist." She held out a hand. "We need to talk."

I stopped at the edge of the group and nodded. "Okay. I'm here."

"No," Eventide stated. "Just you and me. Please, join me out in the courtyard."

"You have a courtyard?" Zaxis muttered under his breath.

I held my breath as I nodded a second time. I followed Eventide out of the kitchen, walking past the other arcanists, including King Odion and Queen Callandra. They gave me odd looks, but I didn't know them well enough to interpret them. Instead, I ignored their nonverbal communications and stuck close to the guildmaster.

The kitchen led out to a square courtyard bordered by waist-high brick walls. White flowers, more plum trees, and vibrant green grass filled the area. A couple of gardeners were busy pulling weeds at the far end of the courtyard, nearly two hundred feet away.

Guildmaster Eventide led me away from the building and far from the compound's servants. Once safe in the shadow of an overgrown plum tree, she turned to me. Her glowing arcanist mark, combined with her intelligent eyes, reminded me why there were so many stories about her.

Her eclectic jacket—an artifact, no doubt in my mind—was covered in scales, odd patches of leather from strange mystical creatures, phoenix feathers on the shoulder, and caladrius feathers on the collar. Were they all part of the construction? Or were they souvenirs from past adventures?

Eventide untied her gray hair from its usual braid. Her long hair flowed free and wavy afterward, though it was still trapped under her tricorn hat.

"Volke, we've never really had a very long conversation between us," she said.

I shook my head. "No. But we've spoken earnestly to each other."

"True. But I fear that we're running out of time."

Hot winds rustled the leaves above us, but the plum tree protected us from the breeze.

"What's wrong?" I asked. "Has something dire happened?"

"We have a situation on our hands. Two, really." She combed her hair with her fingers, a slight smile still on her face, despite the gravity of her words. "First, it seems Theasin will be heading to Thronehold in the near future. Adelgis has determined that he, too, is a god-arcanist. He's bonded with the soul forge."

I clenched my jaw, unable to think of anything to say. What *was* a soul forge, anyway? I had no idea what it looked like.

"We've also determined that the sky titan and fenris wolf have both spawned. The Second Ascension has some way of detecting them, and they have the marble runestone, which is used to unlock the sky titan's lair."

"Don't they also have the shale runestone?" I asked. "I

thought King Rishan had it—and that the Second Ascension took it after our fight near the world serpent's lair. Can't they gain access to the fenris wolf lair as well?"

"Rishan *did* have it. But it's ours now. That means we just have to get to the wolf and find someone worthy enough to brave the trial, and I believe it's near Thronehold, where Theasin is heading." Eventide twisted her hair over her shoulder and braided it again without even looking.

The fenris wolf would be in the Argo Empire, and Theasin was heading there. We'd have to face him. No—*I* would have to face him. Another god-creature couldn't fall into their hands. I had to protect it.

"Volke, I have a request."

I straightened my posture. Eventide's tone—serious but casual, somehow calming—told me this was important beyond anything that had come before.

"You should call me Liet," she said.

I awkwardly sputtered out a laugh. "Uh, okay. I'll do that. Liet."

Eventide smiled. "You should also entrust the planning to me. On everything. You need to focus on your magic—and your training."

The first request was more of a joke. This was the real one.

"King Odion and Queen Callandra—and all the other arcanists who will soon arrive to test your mettle—will want the honor of serving as your second-in-command. They'll want to *help* you." She said the word with a bit of sarcasm. "But what they really want is the honor, fame, glory, and prestige. They may not be qualified, and you need to be careful of individuals with large egos. If you deny them, they're far more likely to take it personally."

Her comments reminded me of Terrakona's advice.

"My eldrin said I should surround myself with high quality people," I said, repeating my eldrin's words.

"Terrakona advised me to keep experts around so that they could help."

"Fine advice," Eventide said as she finished her braid. She tied off her hair and threw it over her shoulder. "The route I'm advising is to allow me to operate as the tactician, and the one ultimately in command under you."

"Under me?" I said, almost in disbelief. "You're already in charge. Fully." I rubbed at the back of my neck and found it sweaty. Why was I so nervous around her? "I know everyone keeps implying that I'm not really in the Frith Guild anymore, but I don't think that way."

Eventide softly chuckled. She stepped closer to me and kept her voice low. "Volke. You've outgrown the Frith Guild, as shocking as that might be." She met my gaze, and I was surprised to find I was taller than her. Just slightly. "The Frith Guild is about defending the defenseless and fighting against those who would take the freedom of others. But the world serpent arcanist has a calling far above that."

"I..." My chest twisted in agony. "I know."

"But I'm also painfully aware of your age. You're seventeen. This is overwhelming. You've never done anything even halfway on this scale before, and it shows."

"I know," I stated through gritted teeth.

"You need someone to lean on who has experience. You need someone you can trust completely."

"I know." I hardened my stare. "I trust *you*."

Eventide snorted and held back a dour laugh. "I'm glad. And if we were being realistic, *I* would swear the guild's loyalty to you."

"N-No," I said as I shook my head. "I don't think that's necessary."

"What I'm proposing is this: allow me to handle information, strategy, and planning. You don't know Odion or Callandra. They could be agents for the Second Ascension—as could anyone else who comes seeking your power and magic. Don't trust them completely. Tell them to come to me, and we'll discuss the many details of their alliance. Keeping them at a slight distance will allow you the freedom to do whatever it is you need to do to stop the plague and prevent the Second Ascension from winning."

I breathed a sigh of relief.

Liet Eventide spoke like a person who was confident beyond the normal. The stress of the situation had been quietly eating at me, but having her to lean on was a blessing. I was lucky to have her.

"Thank you," I said. "I'd like that."

"Back in the day, I had Ruma, Yesna, Zelfree, Sevrin, Dravon, and Gallus to help me out of dire situations." Eventide's gaze became unfocused again. She turned her attention to the leaves above us. Her smile... it was sad. When she spoke, I felt the pain. "Over the years, our numbers have dwindled. It's just me, Yesna, and Zelfree now... and I haven't seen Yesna in over a year. As far as I know, she might also be infected with the plague."

I swallowed hard, angry with myself. I hadn't thought about how Gallus's death would affect Eventide. All these arcanists were her friends. Her family. She had sailed with Ruma, Zelfree, and all the others, for decades, perhaps centuries. Longer than I had been alive. And now more than half of them were dead.

"I'm sorry," I said. I wanted to reach out, or pat her arm, or do *something* to show that I understood, but I didn't know what would be appropriate.

Eventide stepped away, closer to the tree, perhaps because she could feel my apprehension. "I appreciate your sympathy, Volke, but you have too many other problems on your plate to think of mine. Focus on your magic. This compound will be a safe place for you. I'll create barriers around the walls and fences. No one will get in or out without my knowledge."

"Really?" I asked.

She nodded.

"How long will we be here?"

"I don't know. The moment Theasin moves for Thronehold, we'll have to meet him. We don't know his plans, but since he's been a major force for the Second Ascension, I'm assuming he'll do something both monumental and terrible."

"What if he is after the fenris wolf? How will we stop him from letting someone bond with it?"

"As long as we have the runestone, we'll be able to control who gets to enter the lair. I'll send Zelfree to find someone to bond with it. If Theasin really is going to Thronehold to find it, we'll have to defeat him there."

I slowly nodded along with her words. "I see."

A quiet moment came between us. Eventide dwelled on her memories while I dwelled on the future. There was no turning back. She was giving me the option to focus on just getting better while she handled the other details.

"Are you sure you're okay with this?" she asked.

"I am." I inhaled and then exhaled. "I really appreciate this. I feel like... you're the only one I could trust to do this."

"Perhaps Terrakona meant you need people like *me* at your side," Eventide said, playful and arrogant. But then she laughed. "Or perhaps your eldrin meant something else entirely."

I didn't really know.

"I'll speak to the others," Eventide said. She motioned to the main compound building. "I'll be here, discussing strategies. Whenever something is decided, I'll inform you. If, for whatever reason, you need something to change, let me know."

"I will. Thank you... Liet." I shifted my weight from one foot to the other. "But... do you mind if I stay in the Frith Guild?"

"Why?"

"Well, I *am* still young, and I've always idolized the arcanists of the Frith Guild. But more importantly—why must I outgrow it? Why can't the Frith Guild grow to meet me?"

Eventide's eyes widened, and for the first time ever, I thought I surprised her. "What do you mean?" she asked.

"You say the guild just defends the defenseless and fights injustices, but why can't it become more? Why can't the Frith Guild become an organization that fights corrupted magic? Or strives to bring balance to a world of chaos?"

"We could," she whispered.

"You said you wanted to expand the guild. What better way than having a god-arcanist member? We can do this together."

Eventide tried to hide her smile, but couldn't. "You've got moxie, Volke. I like it. I'll discuss it with the other members of the guild. In the meantime, I'll also have someone craft a pendant worthy of a god-creature."

CHANGING THE TERRAIN

I sat alone in the corner of the courtyard, staring at my hands.

The obsidian rock protruding from my knuckles still baffled me, but if it hardened my bones as well, perhaps it was a type of protection. It wasn't the only mystery, though. Apparently, I had two kinds of evocation.

"Terrakona," I whispered.

"Warlord?"

His response was quick and fluid, as if he were always attached to me and just waiting to be summoned into my mind. It was a comfort, and an odd feeling. Terrakona was otherworldly and difficult to understand.

"I have two kinds of evocation," I whispered. "I thought about it a lot. Those trees you grow on your body... That's a type of evocation, isn't it?"

"Yes. I evoke the vegetation."

"One type of evocation is destructive, and the other one isn't."

"Correct."

I clenched my hand so tightly, I could feel my pulse

through the fingertips digging into my palms. Was I supposed to develop destructive evocation? Or was I supposed to develop something more wholesome and constructive?

"How do I evoke the plants, like you?"

"When you evoke molten rock, you seek to destroy. If you are to evoke vegetation, you should seek to create."

What did that even mean? I unclenched my hand, willing my magic to flow through me. When I had evoked terrors, my aim had been to cripple my enemy. When I had evoked my molten rock, my aim had been to kill. Now, I focused on my hand and tried to imagine creating something to help me— something to produce.

Small sprouts erupted from the lines of my fingertips. They were tiny at first, like fresh clovers, and then they bloomed upward, transforming into thick vines and fragrant flowers.

At first, I was happy, but the longer I stared at my garden-hand, the more it disturbed me. I shook my arm, dispelling the odd growth. To my confusion, I could *feel* what the plants felt, including when they hit the courtyard pavement.

They had been an extension of me until they broke from my fingers and withered at my feet.

"But be wary, Warlord. Once you master either your molten rock or vegetation, you will lose the other. As a god-arcanist, you must decide on the best course of growth."

I didn't have an answer for that yet. Instead, I took a deep breath. "First, I need to learn how to manipulate the terrain. I've promised the rulers of nations that I would help shape their countries."

"Beware the consequences. Rivers can run through multiple nations."

"What do you mean?" I asked, my brow furrowed. "What does it matter?"

"Perhaps you can alter the terrain, but when you do, you will affect every nation connected. Rivers flow in one

direction. What if you craft a lake, and kill the river? What happens to the nation that loses their water? Will you help them? What if you can't? Even if you create a river, it might be unsustainable. Can you make good on your promise? Can you harm others to make one nation great?"

His words sank deep into my thoughts. "I hadn't considered any of that," I muttered.

"It comes as no surprise. The Children of Balastar are prone to quick decisions."

I rubbed at my chin. "Terrakona, if manipulating the terrain is a constructive use of my magic, what would a destructive manipulation be?"

"I'm uncertain, Warlord."

"Help me figure it out. Please."

"As you wish."

All day, I focused on trying to manipulate the dirt. I sat on the bench in the courtyard, staring at the mud, sand, and rocks under my feet.

Nothing worked.

But I had come across this before, even with Luthair. Every step of mastering my magic had required me to grasp a new concept. What concept was I missing here? Why was this so much more difficult?

"Why are you by yourself?" a feminine voice asked.

Not just any voice.

Illia's.

I glanced up and she stepped around the trunk of a plum tree, her one eye on me. Illia wore casual clothing—a tunic, loose trousers, and sandals. I had never seen her in sandals before. Even when we lived by the beach on the Isle of Ruma. Illia had preferred boots or bare feet.

"I'm trying to focus on my magic," I said with a shrug. "I thought it'd be easier if I could focus."

"Oh." Illia walked over and took a seat on my bench. "I won't stay long, then."

I clasped my hands together and glanced over at her. "Are you okay?" I stared at her for a long moment and realized that Nicholin wasn't with her. Her little rizzel eldrin was *always* with Illia. "Where's Nicholin?"

"He's doing things for me," Illia cryptically replied. "Nothing to worry about. I came here to speak to you about the captured pirate, though. Master Zelfree said he's a member of Calisto's crew."

"That's right."

"Good." When she smiled, it was cold—almost malicious. "Can you ask Adelgis to get information on Calisto for me? I can't seem to find Adelgis, but I know his magic can pierce into that sea thief's mind. Adelgis will know all the man's secrets soon enough."

"Why do you want them?" I asked.

Illia glowered. "You know why. Don't play dumb. It doesn't suit the *world serpent arcanist*."

Her sarcasm ate at me.

There was no point in arguing, though. Illia had a legitimate reason to hate Calisto and want revenge, and no matter how much I pleaded with her to let it go, she just couldn't. Perhaps I could persuade her through other means.

"I'll ask Adelgis to get that information," I said.

Illia lifted the eyebrow over her one eye. "What's the catch?"

"I won't give you the information unless you spend time with Fain."

"*What*?" She glowered at me and then reached up and touched her eyepatch, her fingers unsteady. "That's not funny, Volke."

"You already said you would. Once you do, I'll give you the information."

Illia turned away from me with a sharp movement. "This is cruel."

"So, you were lying to me before?"

She didn't answer, but her unspoken words were loud enough.

"Illia, please," I said. "I know Fain was once a pirate, but he's different now. He swore himself to me, like Odion and Callandra did."

She perked up and slowly relaxed against the bench. "Anyone can swear themselves to you? I thought it was only a custom that rulers of nations did. You're allowing sad sack pirates to serve you directly now?"

"Do we have a deal?" I asked, ignoring her dismissive attitude. "You spend time with Fain, and I'll ask Adelgis to get all the information he can on Calisto." I chuckled. "Especially any of his weaknesses."

Illia half-smiled. "And if you could get his schedule, and a list of his fears, that would be perfect."

We shared a laugh. The fading sun brought the darkness, and although I wasn't a knightmare arcanist anymore, I still enjoyed the comfort of the shadows.

Then Illia sighed. "You're worse than Zaxis sometimes, ya know that? Stubborn. The both of you."

"Sorry."

She shook her head. "I guess I have a type." Then she abruptly stood and brushed herself off. "But fine—I'll spend time with your *pirate knight*. And don't stay out here too long. You need your rest, and it gets cold at night."

"Thank you," I said. "You needn't worry, though."

"You put everyone else's needs before your own. Just... focus on your own wellbeing sometimes, okay?"

I had that same dream again—the one where the ocean had drained, and I stood before a castle with no windows or doors. The brick walls prevented me from entering, and I just stared at the gigantic edifice, confused.

I placed my hand on the side of the fortified structure. My molten rock had evaporated the ocean, but it couldn't harm the castle. Why not? I just didn't understand. Something was inside, and I couldn't reach it, but my dream-logic told me it was important that I try.

On the edge of giving up, I had a realization.

What if I manipulated the stone of the wall? But would I be able to? The castle had been constructed with purpose. Brick by brick. I could only manipulate dirt, right?

I didn't know.

Within the dream, I concentrated on the brick wall, my focus homing in on the tips of my fingers. To my surprise, and joy, my hand sank into the bricks and warped them. Was this the magical technique I had been looking for? Why was it different here? I had tried manipulating the dirt for hours before I had gone to bed.

With a kick of my leg, I awoke.

I sat up, my heart pounding. Where was I? Why was it so dark? I couldn't see...

Panicking was beneath me. I slid off the side of my bed and stood. Where had I gone to bed? In my new compound. In one of the master bedrooms. I had been so focused on my magical training, that I couldn't even recall what the room looked like.

Wait—there was a fireplace on the far wall. I carefully made my way over, feeling the smooth tile floor with my bare feet. When I reached the fireplace, I reached inside and allowed magma to seep from the creases of my palm. It oozed out, lighting up the room, and then dropped on the dry logs, sizzling the bark and bursting into flames.

With the fire lit, I could see.

My opulent room had a bed large enough to fit two horses on top of it. The windows were ten feet tall, and the center of the room had a table, chairs, and couch. This room was practically its own house, and I had stumbled in only a few hours ago to sleep.

I rubbed at my temples. My dream... I had manipulated the stone in my dream.

I knelt and placed my hand on the tiles. I focused and attempted to warp the floor.

But nothing happened.

Why?

I gritted my teeth, trying to control the frustration. What had I done in the dream that I wasn't doing here? I tried to remember.

In my dream, I had realized the wall had been constructed. Piece by piece, the bricks had been laid by human hands. But what about nature? In my mind, it was nothing but chaos. But was it really? No. Beaches didn't appear on mountainsides. Trees didn't grow in salt water. Nature had its own laws and rules and order.

The wind carried the clouds that carried the water. Piece by piece, nature built itself with skill and finesse. Just because it didn't look like a human civilization didn't mean it wasn't orderly.

The tiles in the room were cut marble, but the stone itself had been crafted from thousands of years of the earth refining itself. When I pressed my palm on the tile this time, I understood what I was trying to do—I hadn't considered the tiles to be rocks, I had thought of them as something created by mankind. It wasn't true. The tiles were still made of rock. They were still bits of nature, even if they were in a new shape.

I held my breath as I pressed harder with my palm. My magic tingled, but...

It worked.

I gasped and half-laughed as my hand sank into the marble floor. This was it! My ability to manipulate the terrain!

"Do you see this?" I said as I glanced up.

The flicking fire barely illuminated my empty room.

I was alone. Who was I even talking to?

"You're distressed, Warlord," Terrakona telepathically said, his presence like my clothes—always there, but never consciously on my mind.

I shook my head. "I'm fine." Then I smiled. "And I know you can't see this, but I managed to manipulate marble. So, I'm actually quite happy."

"A fleeting bout of elation isn't happiness."

I sighed. "Thank you for bringing me down a notch. That's what I needed. A hard shot of reality."

"You have my loyalty, power, and wisdom—frivolous celebrations are not my specialty."

Holding back a laugh, I said, "And you're honest. My last eldrin was just like that."

"Your knightmare was an honorable creature."

"You knew him?" I asked, glancing up, staring at nothing.

"No, but I saw his sacrifice in my lair. His thoughts were of your safety first and foremost."

The mere mention of Luthair's sacrifice got to me. I tried to stand, but my hand was embedded in the marble. I half-stood, then lost my footing, and stumbled back to the floor. I yanked my arm, but my hand was stuck. Apparently, I had stopped focusing on my manipulation, trapping my fingers in the stone.

The shadows fluttering at the edges of the light hardened and changed. I watched as they coalesced into a partial suit of armor that resembled leather and scale. The cape of the armor appeared like dragon wings, and I knew this knightmare belonged to Evianna.

Layshl.

A moment after the knightmare stepped out of the shadows, Evianna followed. She wore black clothing—her trousers, shirt, boots, and gloves—and her white hair had been secured back with a dark bandana, cloaking her in makeshift shadows.

"Volke?" she asked. "What're you doing here?"

"I live here now," I quipped.

"I know that! I meant, why are you in this room? I slept here the other night."

"Oh, uh, I didn't know that. I couldn't sleep in the other room because I was, uh, in the wrong place." I yanked my arm again, but my hand was still rooted in the floor. "Why are you just now going to bed?"

Evianna's face reddened. She turned away and shrugged. "I was just training. I lost track of time."

Her knightmare said nothing.

With my free hand, I straightened my hair a bit. Still unruly, but I tried. "Okay, well, do you mind if I have this bedroom tonight? I'm quite attached to it."

I hated myself for that pun.

Evianna stepped closer, fidgeting with her fingers. She glanced around the room, glaring at the corners. "You're alone in here... right?"

"Well, I think so," I said with a shrug. "Fain? You here?"

No reply.

"Yeah, I'm alone."

She narrowed her eyes, her eyebrows knitted. "Volke, why are you kneeling like that? Are you okay?"

With my free hand, I rubbed my face. It felt like I was cursed by the abyssal hells to make a fool of myself. I was the world serpent arcanist, yet here I was. Trapped in the floor. Through my own magic. Should I explain that to Evianna?

"This is your own doing, isn't it?" Evianna asked, sardonic. She stared at my hand and giggled. "You were manipulating the marble before I got here, and I scared you, right? Your concentration broke when I expertly exited the shadows."

With a nervous laugh, I shrugged again. "Your training is really paying off. You were very quiet."

I wasn't lying. Until her knightmare had formed, I hadn't known she was nearby.

Evianna hurried to my side and knelt. She placed her hand on the marble tile near mine. "Let me help you."

The shadows hardened and moved, and with the fine precision of small knives, they chipped at the tile around my hand, slowly carving out gaps big enough for me to wiggle my fingers and free myself. I had feared she would cut me with the darkness, but fortunately, that never happened.

As I pulled my hand out of the floor, I smiled. "I'm impressed, Evianna. Thank you."

She nodded once, and then stood, her posture regal. "It wasn't a problem, Warlord. I'm devoted to helping you win against the Second Ascension."

I got to my feet and frowned. "Please. Don't. Everyone has been doing that lately, and it gets annoying."

"What're you talking about? It's not annoying." She crossed her arms. "It reminds me of home. People addressed me as *Princess Evianna* and *Your Highness* constantly. Here at the Frith Guild, I'm only known as an apprentice." She tilted her head to one side and sighed. "I miss the respect people used to pay me."

"Calling me *warlord* or *world serpent arcanist* doesn't feel like respect," I muttered as I wandered over to the foot of my luxurious bed. I sat on the silk sheets and stared at the fire I had created. "Well, that's not entirely true. When *some* people say it, I can feel they mean it. But with others... It feels like *fear*. Like they're saying it just because they think I want to hear it. They say it to avoid getting on my bad side."

Evianna quickly walked over, her footsteps inaudible. She sat next to me on the foot of the bed, her weight light enough that she barely disturbed the bedding. "You're probably right," she said. "But shouldn't they fear you? I saw your duel with King Odion. You were amazing! You're barely an arcanist—only a few weeks—and already your magic can destroy entire gardens and alter the terrain. You don't think that deserves respect?"

I shrugged. "I guess I just don't want people to think that I'll be upset if they don't. I'm here to help them, not to subjugate them."

Silence.

"Everything okay?" I asked, glancing over.

"You sound like my sister," Evianna murmured. Her posture grew stiff as she glanced at her hands. "Anyone else would be *thrilled* to be called *Your Highness*, but she hated it."

"Lyvia?" I asked.

Evianna slowly nodded, her attention still on her hands. "Yeah. You're so similar. Even while I watched your duel with Odion. It was like... I was about to see someone I care about die all over again." She clenched her hands into fists.

Before I could say anything, Evianna leapt off the bed and stood. Her knightmare shifted through the shadows, ducked into the darkness, and then rose up from her feet. Armor formed over Evianna's body—sleek and inky, coating her in leathery scale armor with a wing-like cape.

The two had merged together as one.

"I should let you get some rest," Evianna and Layshl said, their voices combined. "I've taken too much of your time as it is."

"Did you want this room?" I asked, motioning to it. "I can

find another. Apparently, each building has twenty-eight bedrooms. I can find a spare."

Evianna hesitated for a moment. When she glanced back—Layshl forming a cowl over her head and face—she smirked. "I miss being a princess, and being addressed as *Your Highness*, but it occurs to me that perhaps I should earn that right again." She swished back her cape as she headed for one of the windows.

"You need your rest as well," I called after her. "Just relax tonight, okay? Take care of yourself."

She stutter-stepped near the sill, and then glanced over her shoulder. "Okay. I will. Thank you, Volke."

I didn't know why that affected her so much, but I was glad she had taken my advice seriously. When Evianna stepped into the darkness and disappeared into the void, I took a moment to breathe deeply.

Where was Luthair's cape? Back at the Frith Guild on the atlas turtle.

I'd have to get it and bring it here.

PIRATE DREAMS

I would've given away all of my worldly possessions for a single night of solid sleep.

Unfortunately, it felt as though the abyssal hells had cursed me. Every night, there was something new. Either my dreams were restless, someone woke me too early, or the nightmares drained me of energy for the next day, sapping away my willpower.

And this night was no different.

My dreams melted away and then reformed into something crisper and clearer. I was still dreaming, but I had experienced this hundreds of times before. Adelgis was a master at weaving dreams, and he could allow people to "live" the memories of others. I had seen many of Zelfree's memories through his eyes, all while I had slept.

Why was I here tonight?

Was this because of the captured pirate? Perhaps Adelgis wanted me to know the pirate's secrets. Calisto helped the Second Ascension, after all. If I could glean something valuable from these memories, perhaps it would help me fight our enemies.

The chill winds of night whipped across the deck of a man-o-war ship. The gray wood of the deck and mast betrayed the ship long before I heard anyone speak her name. This was the *Third Abyss*—the Dread Pirate Calisto's flagship. It was made from ghostwood, and the ship created its own bank of fog that protected it from view.

Sure enough, a thick mist swirled around the outside of the ship, creating a veil that prevented me from seeing the ocean or horizon.

The deck was devoid of life except for me.

But when I glanced around, it wasn't because I had willed myself to do so. I watched someone else's movements through their eyes.

The creak of the deck caused me to jump—or caused my body to jump, I should say. I had no control over the movements. I simply observed everything, as a passenger in the head of another.

I turned around and spotted Calisto himself. He strode onto the quarterdeck, his coat collar high, and his breath hot enough that it came out like mist as thick as the fog around us. His copper hair, wet from the evening air, was stuck in clumps around his face and head. He slicked it all back with a stroke of his hand, giving him a more composed look, even if his expression was murderous.

He stared ahead—beyond me—as though glaring at some location on the opposite side of the ship. When he walked, his leather boots slammed on the deck, betraying his anger.

I recognized his boots.

They were the ones I had crafted as a knightmare arcanist...

"Calisto," I said, my voice familiar.

I was right! This *was* the pirate—the one Lucian had captured! Adelgis was trying to tell me something.

Calisto glanced over, his teeth gritted. For a second, he was tense, like he would lash out, but then he seemed to rein himself in. "What is it, Markus?" he asked, his tone terse.

Markus? I supposed I knew the pirate's name now.

"I fed the mythical creatures, like you wanted," I said. Then I pulled my coat tight around my body, blocking out some of the cold, but not all of it. "They're still fine. Still alive."

"Good." Calisto withdrew a copper flask from his inner coat and took a quick swig. When he was done, he twisted the cap back on and tucked it away. "Let me know if they turn back into corpses. I bet that would surprise our new soul forge arcanist."

"They seem healthy and happy," I replied. When I stepped closer to the dread pirate, I shoved my hands into my coat pockets. Apparently, I carried a few cards, a ring, and a small blade. "They don't even remember being corpses. I tried asking the griffin, but he says he can't remember being reborn."

Calisto scoffed and forced a dark laugh. "Yeah, I bet it's a hard memory. It was darker than the abyssal hells in the soul forge's lair."

The conversation intrigued me. Creatures being reborn? Corpses given life again? Mystical creatures with no memory? What kind of bizarre creature was the soul forge that it could do such a thing?

"Is there anything else I can do?" I asked, obviously eager.

Calisto lifted an eyebrow and stared down at me. Apparently, Markus was a few inches shorter than me—about five or six inches, to be precise. It seemed odd, seeing the world from a shorter height.

"What else could you possibly do?" Calisto growled. "You're terrible at swabbin' the deck, useless when it comes to the riggin', a terrible cook, and a piss-poor sailor. This is why I hate noblemen like you. Pampered layabouts. Useless."

I turned my gaze to the deck of the ship, my breathing shallow. "I studied magic," I muttered, anger lacing my words.

"When I joined the Second Ascension, they said they'd make me an arcanist. They said they'd control the world and give everyone who served a mystical creature."

Calisto took another long swig out of his copper flask. Then he coughed once and exhaled, smiling. "Good news. Your father was some sort of hippogriff arcanist, right? Bond to the damn reborn griffin, they're almost the same thing. You seem to have taken a likin' to it anyway."

I glanced up, my chest tight. "Are you sure?" I asked, my tone already back to hopeful.

He shrugged. "What do I care? We're not headin' to a port to sell it, and Theasin—*oh, mighty soul forge arcanist*—says we shouldn't let anyone else examine it, lest they find out that the soul forge gave it new life. Bond with the damn creature, for all I care. Then maybe you might be able to serve without embarrassing yourself."

My breathing grew faster, and excitement coursed through my veins more than blood. "But what about the trial of worth?"

"I don't care. Pass it or don't pass it. We have other corpse creatures if you fail that one."

Calisto shoved past me, hitting his shoulder against my own and almost causing me to fall. I stumbled aside, my footing a bit unsteady, but I was still bristling with elation.

"Thank you," I whispered to Calisto.

He growled something I didn't hear and then glanced over his shoulder. "What did I say about that? Stop thanking me. I already regret your presence here."

"I a-apologize," I muttered. "It's just... I really do appreciate everything you've done for me."

The way I said it—or rather, the way *Markus* said it—sounded more genuine than anything else had before. The words came out thick with emotion.

Calisto continued his trek across the deck, his gait stiff, his breath still hot enough to see. He didn't say anything else.

Then the dream faded.

No. It reformed. The colors swirled and melted and then pieced themselves back together to form a coherent environment. Well, it wasn't entirely coherent.

It was dark. Too dark. I could barely see anything.

But I could feel Markus's body again. I rode with the man in his head as he traversed a long corridor down into the depths of darkness. Something wasn't right. The air was stagnant and smelled of rot. Nothing about the wide corridor was warm or inviting. This was a place of death.

Why was Markus even here?

Deeper and deeper I walked, seemingly down the throat of an enemy. Three other people were with me. Maybe four? No, three. And one large creature walked behind us.

Then someone cleared their throat. They were up ahead—at least thirty feet—but it was too dark to see. "Calisto, have you brought what I requested?"

I recognized the voice hidden in the shadow. Theasin Venrover. He sounded just as icy and callous as ever. He was waiting for Markus?

"I got you some men, yeah," Calisto called out from behind me.

"Bring them inside," Theasin said. "And don't allow them to leave."

"Wait, what?" I asked, a terrible shiver running down my spine.

Something shoved me and the other three people forward.

I fell face-first onto the ground, and it was only then that I realized it was covered in bones and rotting flesh. These were corpses. Some of them popped and exploded, as though sacks of blood had been kept deep in their chests and were waiting to burst.

I was covered in the vile gore of dead mystical creatures.

And then something else happened. My flesh... rotted away?

No. As I writhed, I realized it was being *torn away* from the inside. Something was draining me—devouring my life, one piece at a time. My skin fell off in chunks, the pain so unbearable, my vision went white with agony.

I tried to stand, but I couldn't. The bodies underneath me were *moving*. The zombie-like mystical creatures stretched out bone claws toward my flesh, hungry for whatever life essence I had. When I tried to walk, I tripped, and when the pain intensified, I knew I wouldn't be able to stand.

"Help!" someone called out.

"*What's happening?*" another individual in the room screamed. "*What is this?*"

"It hurts! It hurts so much!"

The haunting shouts disturbed me. I wanted to wake from this memory. I wanted Adelgis to take me out of it. I got it. They suffered. Why did I need to hear it? Couldn't he make this part go faster? Couldn't he mute the screaming? Dull the pain?

I didn't want this. Why wasn't anyone helping Markus and the others? Was Theasin watching them die? Was Calisto?

"Calisto!" I managed to call out. "*Help me!*"

What was Markus thinking? Calisto wasn't going to help him.

"Please!" I shouted, my voice weak, my body weaker.

"Get him," Calisto commanded, his voice sharp. "*Now.*"

Thankfully, something lifted me off the corpses. The pain remained, as did the rot, but the intensity waned the moment I got away from the blood and gore. I took deep and steady breaths until I was lowered to a portion of the floor without monsters crawling over it.

"Thank you," I rasped. "Thank you..."

Somehow, I knew it had been Hellion who had saved me—

Calisto's manticore eldrin. Its scorpion-like tail stroked my back, soothing me for a moment as light shone over the corpses in the other room.

I could barely see. My vision was blurred by pain and injury.

There were hundreds of corpses of young mystical creatures, and three dead men among them. But there were also three newborns, alive and well. A griffin. A unicorn. A caladrius. They weren't zombies or rotting shambles. They were... creatures. Normal mystical creatures. Just young. Confused. Each one calling out.

"Fascinating," Theasin said, his voice so far away, fading in and out. "Just as I expected... The soul forge can... manipulate life itself."

Calisto said something. I couldn't make it out. My hearing and focus blurred with my injuries.

Then something struck me. *This* memory had happened before the memory on the ship. Why had Adelgis shown them to me out of order? The griffin cub that Markus had been caring for... Was *this* the same griffin? This corpse creature?

I tried to stand, but I couldn't. My arms shook.

"Thank you," I wheezed. "Thank you."

Calisto growled something, but my ears were still ringing with pain. All I could tell was that Calisto was leaving. Why?

I held up a weak hand. "Wait... Don't leave me. Please... don't leave me."

Calisto shouted down the corridor. "*Hey.* Come get an injured man!"

I whimpered. "No. No, not them. I want to stay with you..."

Again, my tone—*Markus's* tone—was genuine. And I didn't know why, but Calisto seemed to take it to heart. Instead of giving me to the other men, Hellion picked me up and placed me on his back, right between his leathery wings.

And then the memory faded.

The colors melted away. The shapes drifted apart.

But I could still hear the screams in my mind. They echoed in my thoughts, bouncing around with the phantom pain I had experienced in the corridor.

When the colors coalesced again, I stood in a new memory.

This time wasn't like the others. It was warm and pleasant, and while there was mist, it was a hot steam created by coals and water. I sat in a room made of bright golden wood with tall walls and no windows. A coal pit was in the center, a square stone structure the height of a man's waist. I wore nothing—I just sat on a wooden bench, staring at the embers. Multiple benches were built into all four walls.

A small, narrow door was the only exit.

I rubbed my forehead, and the arcanist mark I felt told me this was a memory that took place after the other two. Markus was a griffin arcanist now.

There were three others in the room with me. I recognized two of them.

Calisto. He sat on the tallest of the benches, in the corner of the room. Sweat dappled his body. He wore a necklace with a shard of a unicorn horn as the pendant—and nothing else. He didn't seem bothered or uncomfortable, and it was easy to see why. The man had strength-enhancing manticore magic, and his muscles were defined enough for a statue.

Calisto's glowing arcanist mark shimmered in the steam of the airtight room. He glared at the coal pit, his breathing steady. Perhaps he didn't care about modesty, because he leaned back against the wall, his legs apart.

I really didn't want to get to know Calisto in this way.

I would need to have a long talk with Adelgis about the proper etiquette of sharing memories with me. No nightmare-inducing trauma. No nudity. The basics.

The other person I recognized was Spider, Calisto's first mate.

She... also wore nothing. But unlike Calisto, who didn't seem to care who looked or didn't, Spider sat in the opposite corner, her arms tightly crossed over her chest, her knees up, and her back planted against the wood wall.

Her black hair, heavy with steam, clung to her body, hiding her shoulders, upper arms, collarbones, and side. Her sharp features were angled and pronounced with each glower she shot toward everyone else in the room.

Her arcanist mark sickened me. It was a fish man with claws and needle-like teeth. A kappa. A man eater mystical creature that feasted on children. From what I had heard, only women who had sacrificed their own babies could bond to a kappa...

The last man I didn't recognize at all. His arcanist mark was faint, but it was a sea serpent wrapped around the seven-pointed star. He was gaunt, his skin riddled in tattoos, most of which seemed unfinished. To my chagrin, he also wore no clothes.

This lanky man smiled, revealing the fact that most of his teeth had deserted him long ago.

"You look nervous, *nob*," he said.

I cracked my knuckles. "I've been inside steam rooms many times, just never here in Port Crown."

"Don't answer to *nob*," Calisto growled, drawing everyone's attention with his anger. "What kind of man are you?"

Spider snickered, her smile oily. "Maybe that should be his pirate name? *Nob* fits him. Short for *noble*."

"Or maybe we should call him *Gas Bag*," the taller pirate said, gesturing to me. "Ya look way older than ya should? Ya do. Weird lookin'."

I ran a hand down my face, unsteady and shaking. "It was... a side effect."

Spider pointed to the tall one. "Or—and hear me out—his name is *Wit*. Maybe Markus should go by the name *Nit*."

A loud *bang* caused me to jump. I snapped my attention to Calisto, who had slammed his fist so hard against the wall, he had cracked the wood panels. "What in the abyssal hells is wrong with you? You want my crew to be laughingstocks, is that it?"

Spider turned away, hiding her face behind a curtain of wet hair. "Tsk. It was just some fun. I wasn't serious."

The tall, tattooed man—Wit, I supposed—shrugged. His short blond hair tangled on one side, making his head look like a trapezoid. "When are we shovin' off? I've got men to meet before we go."

"Tomorrow evening," Calisto said. "And if you're in such a hurry, *get out*. I came here to relax, not deal with your shit."

Wit stood and stormed from the room, the steam swirling around as he passed by. I didn't watch him. I just listened, and once the door slammed shut, I turned my attention to Calisto. To my confusion, I didn't say anything. Markus stared for a long moment, which meant I did as well. When I finally returned my gaze to the floor, I was ready to thank the good stars.

"Why did we take that man on?" Spider asked. She wrapped her arms around her legs, keeping her body curled in a ball. "I swear, each new arcanist we hire is worse than the last."

"I'm gaining a reputation for death," Calisto muttered. He tilted his head back so that he stared at the ceiling, his focus distant. "Ever since we carried that plague-ridden gargoyle, I've had trouble. I can't seem to shake it, and everyone here knows."

"So, you go with whatever sad sack will sign with us?"

"That's right. Sometimes we need fodder. Especially with all the danger flying around now. You never know what kind of crazy magic you'll see next."

Spider cleared her face of her wet hair. "Is that why we're draggin' around dead mystical creatures? Some sort of crazy magic?"

"That's right."

The steam helped my muscles relax, but the conversation got me tenser than ever before. I perked up. "I know where we can get some hippogriff bones. My father cares for a whole flock of them, and there's a tomb for the hippogriffs and their arcanists."

Calisto smirked as he leaned his head to the side. "That right? Well, the hold is almost full, but I suppose a couple more bodies won't hurt."

"You're always so eager to please," Spider taunted, her dark eyes pinning me in place. "Maybe your new name should be *Kiss-Up.*"

Although this wasn't my memory, I couldn't help but feel pent up frustration. I stared at Spider, and she made a kissy face in my direction. Calisto didn't comment or even seem to care. He returned his attention to the ceiling, no doubt trying to relax.

"Better a kiss-up than a waste of a room," I said as I leaned forward, my elbows on my knees. "If you had stayed behind, we could have filled your quarters with even more corpses. That would have been more useful than carrying your worthless hide from one port to the next."

Spider yanked back a good portion of her inky hair, her hand shaky. "*What do you know*? The only reason the crew can see through the fog is because of the trinkets I made!"

"We have plenty," I drawled. "Even some spares. Just another reason to leave you behind."

Although I didn't know Markus that well, from the three memories I had of him, I could tell this conversation was just him posturing. He was *trying* to fit in by taunting this other pirate. He kept glancing in Calisto's direction, like he was checking to make sure he wouldn't upset their captain.

"I've sailed with Calisto for *years*, nob," Spider practically hissed. "I'm not about to be upstaged by some pompous blowhard. Isn't your eldrin one of those corpses? Maybe you should sleep with them, and then we'll use *your* room for extra cargo."

Her voice got louder with each word, like she couldn't contain her irritation.

Calisto ground his teeth as he returned his attention to Spider and me. "I don't want to hear anything else. Either sit down and shut up or I'll be throwing a body on the coals instead of water."

A cold quiet came over the steam room. Spider poured another bucket of water into the grooves of the coal pit, causing a fresh burst of hot mist to waft into the air. It washed over my skin, causing me to sweat, but in a pleasant way. I relaxed back, one arm on the bench, the other in my lap.

Then Spider stood. She kept her arms over her chest as she walked to the narrow door. Thankfully, Markus had some decency, because he didn't stare long. He turned his gaze to the floor until the door slammed shut.

Alone with Calisto.

For some reason, it felt tenser than I had thought it would.

The embers on the coals flickered.

"Are you gathering the creatures for the soul forge arcanist?" I asked.

"What do you think?" Calisto sarcastically replied.

"But we have so many corpses... More than you have members of your crew. What would we do with them all? Or what will the soul forge arcanist do with them all?"

Calisto shrugged. "I don't care. They don't pay me to think about their plans. I just do as they say."

His tone this time was distant. Callous. Uncaring. It was

different from the last time I had seen him—when he had taken me on a ship ride to the dig site. I barely knew the man, but he had hurt both Zelfree and Illia, which was all I needed to maintain my rage. A part of me hoped he was discontent with life. His was a vile existence. He was the Autarch's dog.

"Is there anything I can do for you?" I asked. "Maybe add more water to the coal pit?"

Calisto didn't answer.

"Griffin arcanists can sense the loyalties of individuals. If you want, I can make sure Wit isn't a man who will betray us. I can—"

"He'll betray us if he gets the chance," Calisto interjected with a scoff. "I don't need magic to know that. I've got two workin' eyes."

"Why keep him if—"

"Why do you keep talkin'?" Calisto spoke over me, his jaw clenched. "I said I came here to relax. You're the educated one, remember? You should know the definition."

I bit my tongue and kept to myself for a moment. With each passing second, I fidgeted with my hands, lacing and unlacing my fingers or rubbing at my own knuckles. Why was Markus so nervous? I wish I could've asked, but as a passenger, I just had to wait for the memory.

Then I broke the silence with, "I heard of your fight with Redbeard, and how you defeated him. Impressive. Killing a reaper arcanist is no small feat."

Calisto sighed as he sat forward.

A part of me wondered how Markus had survived this encounter. Was he asking to get killed? Calisto had made it clear he didn't want to speak.

"Word has already gotten around about that, huh?" Calisto asked, a little more jovial than before. "I'm surprised a nobleman like you even heard of it."

"My father keeps close track of dread pirates. I know a considerable amount about them."

Calisto rotated his shoulders, his back popping and cracking, as though he hadn't moved in quite some time. "What's with you? I keep tellin' you to leave. You don't have to be part of my crew. You clearly don't belong here."

I shook my head. "Do I need a reason?"

"Don't play the fool. It makes you look weak."

"I just..." I shook my head a second time, water dripping off my hair. "You're different than I thought you'd be. I want to repay you for all your... All the times you've helped me." I looked back up at him, tense. "My father says civilized men crave hierarchy. They want lords, laws, and leadership. Maybe it's just in my *noble* blood. I'd rather serve you than the Autarch. Or my father. Or my homeland."

Calisto didn't reply. He rubbed at his nose and rested against the wall. "Fine. Do whatever you want. I gave you a chance to leave. Don't come cryin' to me a second time when we're caught in the fires of war, inches from the abyssal hells."

"You don't think the soul forge arcanist will win?" I asked. "Theasin says he has plans with the Autarch. That we'll kill the world serpent arcanist and then finally get all the runestones. You don't believe him?"

"Oh, he'll probably win," Calisto said with a shrug. "No one is as conniving as Theasin. But that doesn't mean *I'll* survive. Those are two different situations, and Theasin is willing to burn anyone to make smoke, if needed."

I exhaled and rubbed my hands together. The heat of the steam helped ease the tension in my chest. "No matter what happens, I'd still rather serve you than anyone else. I don't care if your first mate thinks I'm a kiss-up, or some bumbling noble —I'll do whatever I can to help you."

The statements were filled with confidence and conviction.

I was surprised. Then again, I supposed Calisto *had* saved him and helped him become an arcanist.

"I said you can do whatever you want," Calisto muttered. He sighed and then added, "If you really want to help, get me star shards and other crafting components before we shove off. I wanna craft some things on the trek."

"Can we get what you want in Port Crown?"

"We can get *anything* in Port Crown."

MAGIC AND FAMILY

I jerked awake, my breathing shallow.

The dreams hadn't been too frightening, but they had been vivid enough that I felt as though I had been subjected to trauma. I rubbed at my arms, remembering the terrible sensation of the corpse creature draining my life and rotting my flesh.

Markus's life. Markus's flesh.

In the last memory he had said he looked older because of a side effect. Was it from the soul forge? Had that terrible monster's magic altered Markus for the worse?

Could Theasin do all this with soul forge magic?

I understood now why Adelgis wanted to show me the dreams.

Fear made me tense. I glanced around, my eyes wide. The master bedroom was so... strange. The wide-open space, the ample number of cushions, blankets, seats, and pillows... I had never owned anything so luxurious. I didn't feel like I deserved it. What had I done to earn such a magnificent place?

The fireplace had gone dead in the middle of the night.

I slid off the side of the bed and stood. The cold tiles

bothered my feet. I stretched, my body stiff. For once, someone didn't burst out of the shadows, or unshroud themselves from invisibility. I took the moment to savor the tranquil silence.

But after a few seconds, the quiet became a torture.

My shadows didn't move—empty of life. No one else was in the room—it was just spacious.

"Adelgis," I said. "I know you're there."

"Yes, Volke?" he replied telepathically. "I'm nearby."

His voice comforted me a bit, dispelling the worst of the lonely anxiety. I took a calming breath and then exhaled. "Have you found out everything we need to know about Markus?" I asked. "Is there anything more I should know?"

"Unfortunately, I'm not sure. He seems to know quite a bit. Calisto pulled him from the lair of the soul forge, and I've been sifting through those memories, but it's slow going."

"Why?"

"They're painful, as you experienced."

I nodded along with his telepathic words. The memories had been painful. I could see why Adelgis would take his time learning everything.

"Do you think Markus has a secret that could turn the tide of battle?" I asked the air. My voice echoed in my spacious room. "Knowing what the soul forge is capable of is important." The more I know about the enemy, the better.

I didn't want any surprises.

"I think this pirate has information that will be useful to us, but he wasn't important enough to join the other arcanists in the planning. What little I learn, I will pass to you, but I doubt it'll be significant."

"How long will this take?"

"Just a little longer, I apologize."

"All right," I muttered.

But something didn't sit right. Adelgis's telepathic voice

seemed dour and strained. Was he okay? "Everything all right on your end?" I asked.

But this time, Adelgis didn't reply. His mind had left me. Where had he gone? To give someone else dreams? Or perhaps he was having a physical conversation.

I decided to dress and find the others. Guildmaster Eventide had said she would handle the plans for the future, and that I needed to focus on my magic. Perhaps that would be best. I could find Master Zelfree and Zaxis, train for a few hours, get some food, and then train again until evening. Perhaps—once the sun went down—I could even help Evianna.

With energy in my step, I changed my clothes. It was easy—every closet and dresser had something for me to wear. Had they been stocked with my size? I considered myself tall, but everything fit perfectly. And the fabric wasn't the rough wool I had become used to. It wasn't silk, either. It was something practical *and* breathable.

Silk had a tendency to catch fire—and fast.

My bright white shirt, open in the front, and dark trousers, gave me an *officer's* appearance. The leather belt, woven to look like the world serpent itself, was a stunning touch. I wandered over to the vanity mirror and gave myself the once over.

Not bad.

And it felt great to be myself, rather than a pirate in Calisto's crew.

Satisfied with my appearance, I exited the master bedroom and traversed the hall with my attention on the elaborate architecture, windows, and decorative rugs. Everything felt meticulously placed.

The sound of additional footsteps got me excited. Someone else was here? Thank the good stars! I didn't want to be alone anymore.

I rushed down the hallway and turned the corner, almost

running into my father and brother. Jozé used a cane to get around, helping him stand when his weak leg couldn't hold his weight. If I had bumped into him, he would've surely fallen.

Jozé half-laughed and then smiled. "Oh, there's the man of the hour. My son." He held out a hand. "In case I haven't said it lately, I'm really proud of you."

I hadn't realized until then, but his blue phoenix stood at his feet, her sapphire feathers glittering, even as soot fell from her body and sullied the floor. Tine's peacock-like tail feathers shimmered when she moved.

Then Tine bowed her head and held out her wings. "Good morning, Warlord."

I rubbed at the base of my neck. "Ah, yeah, good morning."

My brother, Ryker, was clothed in a tunic, trousers, and anxiety. He wrung his hands, his breathing quick. I would've said he was the spitting image of me, but not when he stood with a slumped posture. Was it dread that kept him trembling?

"Are you okay?" I asked.

He let out a long exhale. "It's nothing." Then he inhaled and added, "It's my magic. I hate it. I transform, and I don't know what to do."

He reached into his pocket and withdrew a white mouse. Its red eyes stared up at me with glittering intelligence.

I stared at the rodent. "MOS?"

"Hello, Warlord," the mouse said, her voice adorably small.

"I just don't like... the sensation of my bones warping," Ryker muttered, sweat dappling his brow. "That isn't crazy, right?"

I turned to my father. Jozé replied with a small shrug. "I decided to take Ryker on a stroll through the compound to ease his anxiety."

"This place is gigantic," Ryker muttered as he tucked MOS back into his pocket. "I don't know if it's helping."

"Well, there are several washing rooms." I pointed down the

hall. "And if you want a nice bed to nap in, there are five bedrooms down this corridor alone."

"What're you going to do with all this space?" Ryker furrowed his brow as he glanced at the tall windows. "Surely, you can't live here all by yourself after this war is over?"

That thought hadn't occurred to me, but now that Ryker had mentioned it, I knew he was right. Did I need all this space for myself? The massive compound could house four families. What was *I* going to do here? I was lonely after a single morning without human interaction.

It wasn't like I had an extended family I could—

"Wait," I said aloud.

Jozé lifted an eyebrow. "Wait for what?"

"Sorry. I just realized what I can do with the compound." I smiled as I imagined everyone's reaction. "I'll send for Gravekeeper William."

"Who is that?" Ryker asked.

"My—" I gave Jozé an odd glance before continuing, "—adopted father. He raised me on the Isle of Ruma, along with my adopted sister, Illia."

"Ah. I see." Ryker stopped his nervous fidgeting as he withdrew into his thoughts. For a long moment, he said nothing. Then he faced me, frowning. "What about... our mother?"

Jozé snapped his attention to Ryker, his dark eyes narrowed. He kept his expression neutral, but I could tell by the way he gripped the head of his cane that he feared seeing my mother. But did that mean I shouldn't invite her?

"Is our mother okay?" I asked.

I hadn't seen her since I was young. Very young. I couldn't even remember her face. A bit of shame crept into my thoughts when I realized I hadn't asked much about my mother since discovering Ryker was my brother. I should've asked him this sooner—was our mother okay? Was she safe? Did she have food and shelter?

Why hadn't I done so sooner?

"We lived a modest life," Ryker replied. "Nothing fancy. She was... branded as a thief. It made things difficult, but a local silversmith helped us make ends meet."

I gritted my teeth as I nodded along with his words. "Right. Well, I'll invite her, too, then. And the silversmith, if he wants to live in a city like Fortuna."

"Really?" Ryker asked, his voice barely a whisper.

Again, I nodded. Then I motioned to our surroundings. "Look at this place. She can have her own building, and Gravekeeper William can have another." Another thought struck me. I half-smiled as I said, "Maybe there are more orphans on the Isle of Ruma... I'll invite them here, too. I'm sure William wouldn't mind watching over them, like he did with me and Illia."

Jozé stood a little straighter. "Listen, I know we don't talk much about our pasts, and perhaps that's for the best, but... When I first heard there would be god-arcanists in the world, I dreaded it."

His phoenix glanced up at him. Ryker and I remained quiet.

"In my opinion, power makes people crazy," Jozé continued. He closed his eyes for a moment, recalling something. "I've never trusted bureaucracy and legislation. They feel like tools to oppress, rather than to keep order." When he opened his eyes again, he smiled. "But you make me proud, Volke. Maybe you don't care, but I figured I needed to say it."

His words meant a lot, and they fluttered in my chest, giving me a light and peaceful feeling. I gripped my open shirt, unsure of what to say in response. Ryker also smiled—perhaps for me?—and I wondered if this kind of over-the-top praise of his older brother made him feel shunned or jealous.

"Thank you," was all I managed to mutter.

Jozé patted my shoulder, as if he didn't know what to say, either.

His eldrin, Tine, lifted her heron-like head. "Warlord, let me take the message. I can tell the councilors of Fortuna that you wish to send for people on the islands. They can provide boats to retrieve your adopted father, and your mother."

"I would greatly appreciate that," I said.

"Anything for you, Warlord."

Tine spread her blue wings. My father, with the aid of his cane, made his way to the nearest window. It took him a solid shove and grunt to get the glass open. He pushed the window open wide, allowing his phoenix to take to the sky. Her inner body—deeper than her feathers—was a ball of white flame, pulsing with her life. She soared to the clouds, her bright blue body almost blending in with the azure of the sky.

The thought of Gravekeeper William and a group of orphans living in my compound brought a renewed sense of vigor. What if, once the Second Ascension was defeated, I started a school for orphans? What if I could help children who had a hard life, like myself?

But a sharp spike of pain shot through my chest.

The apoch dragon—the last god-creature to be born— would kill me. I'd never get to see a compound full of orphans getting a second chance at life.

I shook away the agony and focused on the present. If I left this compound to William, he would know what to do with it. He was a wise man, generous with his resources and time. If anyone could make the world a better place with just a couple of buildings, it would be him.

Everything would be okay.

I offered Jozé and Ryker a quick bow of my head. "Listen, as much as I'd love to continue catching up, I need to train with my magic." I gave my brother a hard stare. "I know being an arcanist is new for you, but relax and give it time. You should take smaller steps."

"But the war with the Second Ascension…"

"That's my responsibility, remember? Just improve at your own pace."

I would protect my brother like I would protect everyone else. I'd carry their burdens. Ryker wasn't a fighter, and while his eldrin was powerful, without proper training, he wouldn't be a suitable arcanist to help me take on the Second Ascension.

"Father," I said as I walked by. "Once my belongings are brought in from the Frith Guild, I was wondering if you would help me craft something?" I stopped and regarded him. Although he was weak, he stood tall to meet my gaze. I continued, "Perhaps you could gather some star shards for me? We'll need them for the item."

"Of course," Jozé said.

"Thank you."

For some reason, thinking of Gravekeeper William living at my compound made my training easier.

It was as if the knowledge that everything would be okay once I was gone brought with it an inner peace that I hadn't known I had been missing. Everyone would be cared for—I just had to make sure the Second Ascension didn't ruin that.

Zelfree and Zaxis had been sparring with me, improving my combat. With my sword, I cut through all magic. With my shield, I deflected their attacks. When I used my molten rock, I did so in strategic ways.

Today was the time to practice something new.

Zaxis snapped his fingers, signaling the start of our match. I evoked molten rock and threw it in front of me, creating a circular "moat" of heat and fire. The magma stayed in place, burning the ground, and causing smoke to fill the courtyard.

With expert athleticism, Zaxis leapt over my lava defenses and then threw a punch for my jaw. I leaned to the side, dodging his attack. We had gone through this maneuver a hundred times—it was ingrained in my muscles. Now I had to improve upon it. I planned to knock Zaxis back, tripping him into my molten rock.

Since Zaxis was immune to fire, he wouldn't be harmed through this training, but most of my enemies wouldn't be as lucky. In theory, I would knock an enemy arcanist into my deadly moat, burning their feet and hobbling them.

I evoked more molten rock, hoping to throw it, but then vine-like plants sprouted from my hands. I lashed out, almost unintentionally, using the vines like a whip. I hooked Zaxis, and the sheer surprise of my new attack caused him to lose his footing. He fell into the fiery puddles around our sparring circle, just as I had wanted. The heat burned my plants, but not Zaxis or his armor. It was nothing but a mild inconvenience for him—his phoenix magic kept him protected.

Zaxis yanked his arm out of the molten rock moat, sending embers into the sky. Then he stood and brushed off the last of my vines, mumbling a curse under his breath.

The plants I had evoked...

I felt them burning.

It didn't hurt, I just sensed every leaf and twig as they became cinders and ash.

Once Zaxis had scraped the embers and heated rocks from his body, he exhaled, his breath laced with smoke. He ran both his hands through his red hair. "You make plants now?"

"Yeah," I said, forcing a nervous chuckle. "Sometimes, at least."

I had evoked the plants along with the magma—not completely intentionally.

Our impromptu sparring ring had been made in the center of my compound. All three buildings had a view of the courtyard, and from the windows, other members of the Frith Guild watched with rapt attention. Especially Hexa. She and Vethica sat in a ground-floor room, both leaning on the windowsill and admiring the action.

Hexa's puffy cinnamon hair complemented Vethica's auburn, as though both their hair colors had been stolen from a dusty sunset.

"Surprising your enemy is a good thing," Hexa called out, smirking. "And trust me, you'll surprise 'em."

Vethica always had a harsh expression. Today was no different. She regarded me with a frown. "Don't bother using plants on our enemies. They don't deserve it."

I didn't want commentary. I almost wished I had gone somewhere private to train.

Master Zelfree stood outside the circle, his feet set apart. He watched with a critical eye, and although he wasn't getting much sleep, he seemed alert and prepared. With slow and careful steps, he wandered around the courtyard, examining my molten rock before it dissipated.

The mark on his forehead was a star and a phoenix—he had mimicked Zaxis's powers, which meant he was now immune to heat and fire as well. Zelfree didn't need to be careful around my powers, but I suspected he didn't want his clothes to catch fire.

"Listen, Volke, I don't think you should change course," Zelfree finally said. "It's great you can summon plants, or whatever it is you do, but that can come later. Just focus on the molten rocks. You see some of these clumps you evoked? They're a different shape and temperature. You should strive to be more consistent, or at least, to have control over them."

"But if I focus too much on the molten rock, I'll might lose the ability to create the plants altogether," I said.

Zaxis brushed himself off. "Who cares? Those aren't as useful as the magma. Trust me. Fire is always a win. You don't need plants."

While I wanted to argue—just because arguing with Zaxis was sometimes amusing—I didn't disagree. The molten rock *was* more useful. Why would I ever try to master the vegetation? That alone wouldn't defeat the Autarch.

I exhaled. "Maybe we can try manipulating the terrain now? I need to master that as well."

"You said you had a breakthrough," Zelfree stated. He returned to his original spot and resumed his observation. "Show us."

With a smile, I knelt and placed my hand in the center of the sparring ring. My magma slowly cooled around us, sending more embers into the air. Zaxis waved his hands around, snuffing out any tiny fires that arose.

I pressed my palm on the dirt and closed my eyes. With as much focus and concentration as I could muster, I willed my magic into the ground. This time, it wasn't difficult. I could "see" the formation of the dirt and the hardened rock just underneath.

My hand sank into the ground all the way to my wrist.

When I opened my eyes, I smiled wide. "Do you see this?" I exclaimed.

Both Zaxis and Zelfree walked over to me, their arms crossed, and their eyes narrowed. They waited, silent. I said nothing—I just stared up at them.

Weren't they impressed?

"And?" Zaxis finally asked. "Your hand is in the ground." He scoffed. "Give me enough time, and I can do the same damn thing with punching."

"This took a lot of hard work," I said.

"Look, you might have an adoring crowd when you walk around outside, but I don't clap for you just because you got out of bed in the morning. You have to do something impressive first."

Zelfree shot Zaxis a cold glower. "What did I say about becoming a master arcanist? You're never going to get any apprentices if you can't even utter even *one* encouraging word."

"Pfft. People will want to be my apprentice no matter what." Zaxis flexed his muscular arms and smiled. "Have you seen me? I'm amazing."

"And so humble," I quipped.

Before I could pull my hand from the ground, Hexa banged on the windowsill. "Hey," she called out, her boisterous voice easy to hear, even half a mile away. "Stop bickerin'! Guildmaster Eventide has returned, and she has the Ace of Cutlasses with her."

THE ACE OF CUTLASSES

Yesna, the Ace of Cutlasses, was legendary.

She dual-wielded cutlasses—curved blades, sharpened on one side, and fitted with wide guards on the hilt. They were often used on boats, especially by pirates, because they were robust enough to cut through rope, canvas, and wood, while being short enough to use in the narrow corridors found belowdecks.

It was often said that learning to wield a cutlass was easier than learning to wield a short sword or a rapier, so people often associated cutlasses with amateurs or thieves. Yesna was different, though. She had developed her own fighting style that involved quick, dance-like movements.

Her siren eldrin helped her as well. Its enchanting song befuddled her enemies.

A powerful combination.

I yanked on my hand in the ground and half-laughed when I realized I had once again gotten myself stuck. Determined to free myself, I manipulated the ground and somehow turned the hard dirt and rock into a fine sand.

It startled me—had I changed the structure of the land? I

turned to show Zaxis and Zelfree, but they had already gone. With a deflated sigh, I stood and headed out of the courtyard, catching up to the others.

A part of me was glad that Yesna wasn't plague-ridden, like Gallus the Gray. Another part of me hated that we didn't have Gallus to count among our forces.

I shook away the terrible thoughts.

We had Yesna now. Our numbers were greater. That was what we needed. An army to fight against the Second Ascension. And since Yesna was a master arcanist, this was a major boon. At least we had *one other* arcanist who hadn't died somewhere or gotten themselves infected with the arcane plague.

"I haven't met Yesna yet," Zaxis said, practically hopping along. "I heard she has two blades, one made of surgestone and the other made of froststone."

"That's right," I said, excited. "She uses them to cripple her opponent's movement." I couldn't help but move my hands around as I spoke, imagining the epic battles Yesna would find herself in. "The surgestone crackles with lightning, harming muscles. And froststone coats the body in rime, weighing down an individual and hindering their joints."

Zelfree laced his fingers together and placed his hands on top of his head. "She calls her blades *Tempest* and *Glacier*, and I've always given her a hard time for that."

"Why?" I asked. "Those are amazing names."

He shrugged. "When we were younger, she would get agitated." Zelfree chuckled. "You wouldn't believe how many duels we had. All for jest, of course. Nothing like your combat with Odion."

"Duels?" Zaxis asked, an eyebrow raised.

"Those were the days." Zelfree smiled, obviously lost in some beautiful memories.

I didn't quite understand it myself. My magi cross with

Odion had been intense and stressful. Who would want to do that for fun?

We exited the courtyard and found ourselves at the front of the estate. While most of the Frith Guild was staying here—the arcanists, anyway—it still felt devoid of life. Guildmaster Eventide, the Ace of Cutlasses, and two Javin soldiers stood by the main gate, but there was no one else. Even the street beyond the fence was empty. I figured people would be gathered there constantly, hoping to catch a glimpse of what was happening, but I saw nothing.

Perhaps the soldiers of Javin and Antihelm had shooed them away?

Before I could approach, Zelfree grabbed me by the upper arm and spun me around. He withdrew a handkerchief from his pocket and wiped the sweat from my brow and face. Then he smoothed my shirt, slicked back my black hair, and brushed off my shoulders.

"Make a good impression," he muttered under his breath. "You need to take your appearance into consideration at all times, understand?"

I nodded along with his words. "Sorry. I'll try to remember."

Zaxis patted away the last of the dirt on my side. Then he gave me a thumbs up.

"Good," Zelfree stated. "Now let's go."

He turned me back around and we headed over.

While Eventide had an older appearance, marked with graying hair, Yesna appeared to be in her prime. She didn't wear islander armor—or the typical armor worn in the Argo Empire. She wore something unique. She had armor over her chest, upper legs, and shins, and nowhere else. Her stomach was bare, as were her arms and feet. The grooves of her muscles, especially her abs, were hard to ignore. She almost matched Zaxis, though her arms and legs seemed leaner rather than bulging with untamed strength.

And she wore gold that accented her island-tanned skin. I doubted her armor was actually made of gold—that metal was soft, and not suitable for war—but it could be gilded or stained to look gaudy.

Her long, black hair had been tied in a messy bun atop her head. The strands of loose hair had more energy than a pack of children. And when Yesna smiled, it seemed like she had two too many canines—sharp fangs, like mini-swords.

Her arcanist mark was a seven-pointed star with a half-human, half-bird woven throughout it. A siren—a mystical creature of the seas that was said to lure men to their deaths. They were strange beasts that specialized in singing. I had only ever seen one in my life... and it had been plague-ridden.

I shook my head, dispelling the thought.

Yesna's two cutlasses, both in ornate scabbards, hung at her sides.

"There he is," Eventide said, motioning me over. "The world serpent arcanist."

Yesna glanced over, her skilled eyes running up and down my body. "Oh," she murmured. "You must've been training." Then she turned her attention to Master Zelfree. "With you? The boy must be clever. Or filled with patience."

"Something like that," Zelfree stated.

Yesna snorted and crossed her arms. "I see you haven't kicked your habit of training redheads."

Zaxis's face brightened to match his hair.

"*It's not like that,*" Zelfree growled, and then he dismissively waved his hand. "I wasn't even technically supposed to be his master. Ruma was. I just took over when there weren't enough masters at the guild." He gestured to her. "*I* wasn't off gallivanting across the world, unlike some people."

"The Frith Guild had important work for me."

"Well, now that you're back from your vacation, maybe you can start pulling your weight."

Yesna tapped the hilts of her cutlasses. "Have you kept up on your sword work, you old buccaneer? Perhaps we should cross blades, for old time's sake."

"Trust me, I haven't rusted." Zelfree offer her half a smile. "Perhaps I'll give you another haircut."

"You wouldn't."

For a second, I thought they'd actually start fighting. Zelfree walked over to her, and Yesna stepped forward, her stance stiff. But the moment they drew near, Zelfree held out his arms and Yesna did the same. They embraced, patting each other on the back.

"You look better," Yesna said as she broke their hug and stared at him. "Not healthy. Just better. Did you finally get over your old pirate friend?"

He frowned deeply. "We don't need to talk about it."

"Ah, the usual response! Maybe you're not as better as I thought you were." Yesna tilted her head and offered me a smile. "Well, I'm here to help the Frith Guild expand. Liet told me you suggested we broaden our horizons and become *keepers of magic and freedom*. It has a nice ring."

"It does," I said, already in love with it. "I'm excited for our future."

Eventide threw back her gray braid. "So am I. We have one more master arcanist in our ranks."

Yesna patted Eventide's shoulder. "I can see us becoming a guild that protects the greater fate of magic. Starting with the Second Ascension, obviously."

"With the world serpent arcanist, I'm sure we'll be attracting the most powerful of arcanists," Zelfree added. "At some point, we might have too many people to keep track of on a personal level."

Everyone mulled it over, and the prospect truly excited me.

Even Zaxis, who was normally prone to making everything about himself, seemed taken by the idea. He fiddled with his guild pendant, turning it over in his fingers.

Yesna fluffed her messy locks. Then she stared at me. "So, everyone keeps calling you the *world serpent arcanist* or *warlord*. What should I call you? *Sweaty-Open-Shirt-Man*?"

"My friends just call me *Sweaty*," I quipped.

"Ha! I'm gonna like you."

"My name is Volke Savan," I said, bowing my head.

Yesna straightened herself. "Oh, well, don't bow to me. You *are* still the world serpent arcanist." She bowed her head deeper than I had. "I'm your humble servant."

I gritted my teeth, disliking the way she spoke to me. She and Zelfree were so casual—picking on each other, being friendly without trying—but when she lifted her head and met my gaze, I could tell she wasn't about to start anything with me.

"If you need a real master of the blade to help you train, remember that my door is always open," Yesna said.

"Perhaps," I said.

Zaxis grabbed my shoulder and yanked me back a step. "What he meant was *yes, definitely, once I understand more of my magic.*"

I thanked the lucky stars that Eventide was handling outside matters.

For the next few weeks—fifteen days—I trained. I could evoke vegetation and molten rock, and I started manipulating the ground not with my hands, but with my feet. It had been Zelfree's suggestion, and it was so brilliant and obvious, I didn't understand why I hadn't thought of it earlier.

I knew why. When I had manipulated the shadows with Luthair, I had moved them with flicks of my hand and wrist, and I had imagined the darkness as limbs detached from my body.

But I couldn't do that with the ground. The soil, rocks, and plants weren't my limbs. They were too massive and all-consuming. If they were part of me, they were the *majority* of me. My body was the tiny extension, and that made everything I had tried before seem foolish.

On a bright afternoon, I stood in the middle of the courtyard, my feet bare. I stared at the ground, watching it shimmer and warp. I could break down stone into sand or harden dirt into pebbles. I couldn't believe the amount of power I had. It baffled me.

"Everything okay?" someone asked, their voice half a purr.

I turned around and found Karna sitting on a bench in the courtyard. She leaned back, her legs crossed, her silk dancer's dress semi-transparent. With a gentle flick of her wrist, she threw back her blonde hair, catching the light with the distant strands.

"You look lost," Karna said. "You were staring for a few minutes without doing anything."

"I was just... thinking about my powers," I said, turning my attention back to the ground. "When I was with Luthair, I understood my magical abilities. I controlled *the darkness*. I was an arcanist who could detect lies and right injustices. But now..."

"But now you use fire, create plants, and shuffle the dirt around?" Karna finished. She stood from the bench, sultrier than necessary, her hips swaying. "Are you saying you don't know why they're connected?"

"Well, they're all related to the world," I said with a sigh. "And I get it. He's a world serpent. Ha, ha. But what am I supposed to do with these? How am I supposed to extrapolate the next step of my magic? Like creating an aura, or..."

Karna held a hand over her mouth as she giggled. "Give me

a moment," she said as she walked back toward one of the compound buildings.

Everything she did was heightened. Her movements were fluid, her skin beautiful in the afternoon light. I knew she agonized over her real appearance, but I still didn't know why she kept up her charade with me. At a few points, she had made it clear she wanted to be with me—and maybe I could return her affections—but I kept getting the feeling she was hiding something from me.

It wasn't about her appearance. I wouldn't care what she really looked like. It was something else she kept hidden from me. Something I couldn't describe.

When Karna returned, she held a cup of tea with both hands. She walked over, presented it to me like I was a king, and then gave me a curtsy once I took it.

"For you, Warlord," Karna whispered.

"Uh, thanks," I said, staring at the soft steam rising from the liquid. "But what does this have to do with my magic?"

"Tea perfectly represents your new magics," she said. Then she placed a finger on the rim of the cup and swirled it around the edge. "You see, tea is grown in soil. Water allows you to extract the essence. Heat removes the bitterness and keeps the flavor."

I laughed once as I examined the liquid in the cup. "Since when did you become a master tea brewer?"

"I've made tea for myself for years," Karna said. She stopped toying with my cup. "But only for me. I don't usually give anyone my special brews." She leaned in closer. "You're the exception, of course."

"How do you think this tea analogy will help me?"

"Tea is only made whole when all the elements come together. It seemed like you were trying to master everything separately and confusing yourself because you didn't understand how they connected."

Her simple statements drilled into me. I *had* been thinking of them as separate things, but for good reason. Terrakona had said I could only go down one path: destruction or creation. If I needed *all* the elements to be whole, how was I supposed to do that? If I mastered the molten rock, I'd lose the vegetation.

"How long have you been watching me?" I asked.

Karna snickered. "When am I *not* watching you?"

"Hey, uh, I know this is going to be a bit selfish, but—"

"I love selfish requests." Karna placed one of her hands on my chest. "Ask away."

"Can you help my brother?" I finished. Then I removed her hand. "He's having a hard time with transforming. Apparently, he dislikes the way it changes his bones."

Karna lifted an eyebrow. "He's the one who looks just like you, right? Tall? Dark hair?" She placed a finger on her red lips. "Although he's always trembling when I see him. A nervous little thing."

"Yeah, him. His name is Ryker."

"He *is* handsome," Karna said. "But what do I get out of helping him train?"

"Eternal satisfaction?" I said with a shrug.

"Boring."

"Okay. What do you want?" I held up a hand. "Nothing to do with me or my time. I have too much to do. Legitimately."

"Do you have time for a celebration?" Karna asked. She combed her blonde hair with her fingers. "What I miss most about Thronehold is the constant parties and soirées. Besides, isn't it your birthday soon?"

I opened my mouth and then closed it. When was my birthday?

"Why?" I asked. "Why ask for that?"

Karna widened her eyes and pouted. "Volkie, I like you. I remember dates that are important to you, and I want to celebrate them."

"Uh... thank you."

"Plus, your dear sister has been planning something, but I think it's far too modest." Karna rolled her eyes. "And that princess wants to do something as well. So, this will make everyone happy, ya see."

I stared at the cup of tea. Karna had been useful, and I knew she could help my brother as well. Perhaps it was my destiny to help certain people find each other. Wasn't that the essence of being a leader? Knowing who was suited to the task and then having them complete that task?

"All right," I muttered. "You can make plans. Just... tell Eventide about them, all right?"

"Really?" Karna's voice went up in high-pitched surprise. "You'll let me?"

"As long as you train with my brother."

"Oh, of course. Don't worry about that. It'll be done." She threw her arms around me and offered a quick hug. "You won't be disappointed."

A MASTER OF TERRAIN AND NIGHTMARES

"It's getting late," Zaxis said. He wiped his forehead with the back of his arm and turned his gaze to the starry night above.

Master Zelfree stood at the edge of the mangled courtyard. He surveyed the destruction with narrowed eyes, an almost bored expression on his face. Rocks jutted from the ground at odd angles, sand pits littered the walkways, and one bench was upside down and half-burned.

Then he stared at the many pools of molten rock. Steam wafted off the crusted black surfaces of my evocation. The byproduct of my magic wouldn't last forever. Without star shards, evoked magic eventually faded, which would result in scorch marks on the ground and nothing more.

My manipulation was a different story, however. Manipulation was just magic altering something that existed, which meant the land would retain the shape I had left it in.

A red phoenix flew down from the roof of the nearest building, its body a lantern light in the night sky. With a few flaps of its elegant wings, it landed next to Zelfree. A moment later, its body shifted and shimmered until its wings became legs and its peacock tail became thin and feline.

I recognized the gray fur long before it finished morphing. It was Traces, Zelfree's eldrin. Once back in her cat form, she leapt up to her arcanist's shoulders and purred.

Zelfree's arcanist mark went from containing a phoenix to having nothing but a star. Empty. It would change the moment his mimic transformed once again.

"You've really gotten the hang of this," Zelfree said as he petted Traces. "You're a natural with your manipulation."

"You think so?" I asked.

"Let's see." He snapped his fingers and pointed at an area of grass next to a small blueberry bush. "Why don't you alter the terrain around the bush without disturbing it? And this time, try to make something pleasing."

I spread my stance and exhaled. With the shift of my foot, I focused on the ground around the blueberry bush. My magic gripped the dirt and I shuddered with anticipation. Unlike with my previous shadow manipulation, I had to think more about what I'd do with the terrain once it was under my control. The possibilities seemed endless.

Should I create mud? Or sand? Or harden it to rock? Shift it around? Drop it down, creating a pit? No. I needed to make something *pleasing*. Maybe a small moat? I couldn't create water, but I could create a furrow.

With a clenched jaw, I gripped at the ground.

The dirt twisted and swirled, like a whirlpool on land. It shifted around the bush, and then hardened into diamond-like stone. It crushed the roots of the bush and then yanked it halfway underground, smashing the leaves and squirting blueberry juice across a small portion of the courtyard.

"Beautiful," Zaxis quipped.

I sighed. It had taken me forever to master detailed manipulation with shadows as well. "Maybe I should just focus on what I can do," I muttered. "I can make changes to the ground. That's great, right?"

Zelfree scratched at the stubble on his chin. Then he mulled over the situation and smiled. "Or... hear me out. You're often motivated by people and situations, not simply mastery for mastery's sake."

I nodded along with his words, agreeing with him. My entire life, I had wanted to become an arcanist—not because I had wanted to master magic, but because I had wanted to be a heroic legend. I admired swashbucklers, and those who gave their lives to defend people who didn't have the power to defend themselves.

Magic was a tool to help others, not the goal.

"Let's try this again," Zelfree said, smirking. "This time, alter the ground around Zaxis."

"*What*?" Zaxis snapped. He wildly motioned to the crushed blueberry bush. "Did you see what happened the last time?"

"I did."

"And you're okay with *Zaxis juices* being squirted all over the courtyard?"

Zelfree groaned as he pinched the bridge of his nose. "Curse the abyssal hells, boy—never utter the phrase *Zaxis juices* ever again. That's an order."

"Does it matter how I describe it?" Zaxis walked over to the decimated bush and kicked the crushed branches. The plant fell to the side, pathetic and dead. "I. Don't. Want. To. Die."

"You're not going to die," I said. "Now who's the one being dramatic? Calm down."

Zaxis left the bush alone and stormed over to me. "Are you serious? You're a *god-arcanist*. In just a few weeks, you've gone from having no manipulation abilities to rearranging the whole damn courtyard. Of course you could accidentally kill me! Or at the very least, maim me."

With a casual shrug, Zelfree said, "Don't worry. If a life is on the line, Volke won't fail you."

There was a long pause, and my throat tightened. I didn't think I would kill Zaxis, but I could easily crush his leg. I doubted he would forgive me if he couldn't walk.

Then again, he was a phoenix arcanist who specialized in healing. He would be fine.

Right?

"You have a lot of faith in my abilities," I said, chuckling and rubbing my neck.

"I have a lot of faith in *you*," Zelfree stated.

His confident tone shook me.

After another tense moment, Zaxis straightened himself. He sighed as he said, "I have faith in you, too. Just... get this over with and don't crush any part of my body. If you do, Illia will be angry."

"I'll try," I said.

"Don't *try*, you lunatic! Just do it right the first time."

Zaxis walked to the center of the courtyard and stood in the middle of a sandy patch. He crossed his arms and closed his eyes, like he didn't want to see what was coming. I didn't blame him. After that blueberry bush incident, I was nervous myself.

I inhaled and then slowly exhaled. Again, I widened my stance. With all my focus, I pushed my magic through the ground, clawing my way to Zaxis's feet. To my surprise, I could sense Zaxis's body, not just the rocks, dirt, and sand. His... feet. And his pulse through his boots.

The sensation rocked me. I lost my focus.

"Are you okay?" Zelfree asked. Traces tilted her head and grimaced in a feline frown.

Zelfree somehow always knew when I was disturbed. Was I so easy to read?

I shook my head. "I'm fine. I just need to concentrate."

Again, I shifted my stance and prepared myself. With my

magic, I sensed the ground—the minerals, as well as Zaxis's presence. When he shifted his weight from one foot to the other, I felt that too. It was bizarre, but I didn't let it affect me. I imagined my moat, like I had with the blueberry bush.

The dirt swirled around him and then lowered into a shallow furrow. I gritted my teeth as I hardened the ground into solid rock, creating the decorative moat I had wanted to in the first place.

I gulped down air and relaxed. "I did it!"

Zaxis opened one eye and then the other. He stared down at my tiny creation and then breathed a sigh of relief. "Thank the good ships at sea."

"Don't worry," a feminine voice called out. "I was watching."

Illia stepped out from behind a lopsided tree. She rubbed at her eyepatch as she walked over to Zaxis. When she reached his side, she took his hand and caressed his knuckles with her thumb.

"If Volke had messed up, I was going to port you to safety," Illia said.

Zaxis wrapped his arms around my sister, smiling. "Thank you, my starfish."

Illia's face reddened faster than I had ever seen it before. She jabbed Zaxis in the side, right in the liver. "*What did I say about calling me that in public*?" Illia hissed under her breath.

With a grimace, Zaxis nervously chuckled. "Ah, it's no big deal. No one here cares."

"Maybe next time I *won't* save you from one of Volke's training accidents."

Illia teleported out of Zaxis's grip, disappearing in a puff of silvery glitter, followed by a soft *pop*. Zaxis almost fell forward. He stumbled and then corrected his stance.

With a sigh, he turned to face me. "This is your fault. Somehow."

"What?" I asked. "Why me?"

"The only time we fight is when we're talking about *you*." Zaxis dismissively waved his hand. "Never mind. It's late." He stormed off toward the main building, muttering under his breath. He never glanced back.

Zelfree walked to my side and placed a hand on my shoulder.

I turned to face him, and he half-smiled.

"I knew you could do it," Zelfree said. "You just need the right motivation."

"Thank you." Then I narrowed my eyes. "But if you knew I could do it, why didn't you volunteer yourself? Why have Zaxis stand still while I used my manipulation?"

Traces flicked her tail around and chuckled. "It's much funnier to get Zaxis riled up."

"True," Zelfree said. "Besides, he needs to learn to calm himself from time to time. This helps him build trust in you."

"I hadn't thought of it like that," I muttered. "I have a lot to learn."

Zelfree patted my upper arm. "For a kid with the weight of the world on his shoulders, you're doing fine."

"I have a long way to go..."

"Zaxis is right." Zelfree glanced around the ruined courtyard, his eyes lingering on the crushed bush and upturned bench. "After just a few weeks, you're capable of all this. Gargoyle arcanists usually take a year or two to master manipulating stone... Which means your potential—your capacity to manipulate and alter the terrain—will be far greater than I was expecting. This is just the beginning."

"Y-Yeah..."

He turned back to me, and his gaze hardened. "You may have a long way to go, but you're talented. Bright. Resourceful."

"It's a lot easier when I'm not second-bonded," I said with a laugh.

"Whatever the reason. I'm impressed. Let's keep this up." He glanced toward the sky. "But not tonight. Get some rest."

In my room, I trained with Evianna.

Moonlight streamed through the windows, illuminating the wide-open area in the center of the bedroom. Evianna held a short sword and practiced her steps as she manipulated the shadows. She lunged forward, stabbing straight, and then used the darkness to lash out at her imaginary opponent.

"You need to think of the shadows as an extension of yourself at all times," I said.

She nodded once and performed the maneuver again. Thrust. Stab. Darkness.

Her stance was solid and her grip tight. Her knightmare, Layshl, stood like a suit of armor in the corner of the room, watching without a face or eyes. Her empty cowl and armor-like body hung midair as though draped over an invisible soldier.

"Do I have to practice these simple steps?" Evianna asked. "I think I have them mastered."

"The goal is to do them without thinking." I walked over and pointed to her feet. "Once you don't have to correct yourself on your footing, you'll be ready."

Evianna sheathed her sword and then pulled back her white hair. With quick movements, she braided her long locks and tied the end with a black ribbon. Once finished, she threw the braid over her shoulder and placed one hand on her hip.

"I can practice this on my own time." She tilted her head. "Why don't you tell me more about knightmare magic? How do I create an eclipse aura?"

I rubbed at the back of my neck. "That's a more advanced

technique, really. Even I shouldn't have tried it as early as I did. Auras are difficult to create."

"Why?"

"You need to focus. Quiet your mind. Concentrate on all your magic at once." I walked around the room, trying to remember the first time I had created an aura. It had strained my body. "A lot of arcanists still can't do it properly," I muttered, recalling the many times I had seen them fail. "Master Zelfree still can't do it."

Evianna shrugged. "Yeah, but apparently, his lover died not too long ago."

I stutter-stepped to a stop. "How do you know about that?"

"Everyone in the guild knows. I just spoke with a few of the cooks one day and they told me all about it." She narrowed her eyes. "Apparently, he and his old apprentice were together, and that displeased some people."

I waved away the comments. "I know all about it." With an exhale, I returned to my pacing. The moonlight comforted me, but the fatigue wouldn't leave. Every step hurt, but I knew if I sat down, I'd instantly fall asleep. "Let's not focus on Zelfree. Why don't we talk about Captain Devlin? He always creates a hurricane aura without fail."

Evianna crossed her arms and smiled. "I already spoke with him. *He* said I need to have a clear mind."

"Oh. Well, yeah. That sounds about right." I stopped and turned to her. "Zelfree has a lot of guilt. I think, when he's alone—even if just alone in his mind—he tends to dwell on his past mistakes, which interferes with his focus and magic."

"I thought you said we weren't going to talk about him."

I ran a hand down my face. "You're right. Sorry."

Silence fell between us. I didn't know what else to talk about. Why couldn't she just run through her drills? That required little thought from my exhausted mind.

Evianna relaxed and shifted her gaze to the floor. With a

slight frown, she whispered, "When I'm by myself, I'm more focused than ever. But... when I'm with the others, I feel out of place." She glanced up and met my gaze. Her bluish-purple eyes searched mine. "Do you ever get that feeling?"

"I had it all the time on the Isle of Ruma," I said with a forced laugh. Then my legs stiffened, and I retreated to the foot of my bed. With little grace, I plopped down on the mattress, yearning for sleep. "When I was alone, or with Illia and William, I was just a normal kid. When I was with anyone else, I was *the gravedigger*. Something disgusting. They all hated me, and I couldn't ever shake the feeling. I never felt right."

Evianna listened as she walked over and took a seat by my side. She barely disturbed the bed. She just sat and then scooted closer to me.

"When I'm with you, I think of my sister," she said, her voice low and distant. "Lyvia was so important to me. I wish I could've been stronger. For her." Then Evianna turned to me. "And for you, too."

"Me?" I asked. Then I chuckled. "I'm plenty strong."

She jerked her gaze away, unable to meet my eyes. "Maybe... if I had been stronger in the world serpent's lair... you wouldn't have lost Luthair."

Her statement stung. I waited for anything else, but she offered nothing. Once I took a breath, I exhaled, allowing my sadness to go with my breath.

I placed a gentle hand on her shoulder. "Step thirty-five of the Pillar taught me something valuable. *Forgiveness. Without it, we allow hate and sorrow to consume us.*"

Hesitantly, Evianna returned her gaze to meet mine. "Are you saying you forgive me? Or that I should forgive myself?"

"Both."

After a short moment of staring, Evianna threw her arms around me. She pulled me close and squeezed me tightly, her finger twisting into the fabric of my button-up shirt, her face pressed against my chest.

"Whoa," I muttered as I patted her back. "It's okay."

She shook her head and refused to let go of me. With slow and soothing motions, I ran my fingers along her spine. Evianna remained silent. No sobbing. No words. She just held on. I closed my eyes, and I swear I slipped in and out of sleep.

Finally, she said, "I'm focused and peaceful with you." Evianna released me, but she didn't move away. Instead, she stared up at me. "I'm sorry I take up so much of your time. You... You're so selfless and helpful. Someone needs to look out for *you*."

"I don't mind helping you train."

Evianna jumped up and motioned to my bed. "Lie down. You're so tired, you can barely keep your eyes open."

I lifted my eyebrows, but eventually scooted down the mattress and rested back on the pillows. Evianna waved her hands and the shadows rose up to pull the curtains down over the windows. The beautiful moonlight disappeared, obstructed by the thick fabric.

Evianna walked around to the side of my bed. She tugged the blankets and threw them over my body. The warmth made everything seem tranquil. I snuggled into my cozy bed, and even though I was fully dressed, I didn't care.

"I'm going to try my hardest to help you, too," Evianna whispered.

I couldn't see her through the darkness, and the statement sounded a bit ominous, but I didn't mind. I knew Evianna meant it.

Minutes passed in silence. Evianna could slip in and out of the shadows. She didn't need to open the door to leave my room. Had she gone already? I couldn't tell. Anxiety kept me awake longer than I wanted to be, but eventually, sleep clawed at the edge of my thoughts, slowly dragging me away from the waking world.

Half-asleep, I heard Evianna say, "My thoughts are free to go anywhere, but they always return to you, Volke."

Was I dreaming? Or was she actually speaking?

"I'll never be able to do as much for you as you've done for me... But I'm going to try."

I wanted to reply, but I slipped into unconsciousness.

That dream again.

I was in an ocean, but then my molten rock evaporated everything, revealing the castle. There were no doors or windows, but it didn't matter. I used my manipulation to create a hole in the brick wall—turning a portion of it into loose sand. Confident in my abilities, I stepped inside. A vacant castle greeted me.

Why? I thought the inside would be more profound. Instead, I wandered through an empty foyer, and then into a hallway devoid of furnishings. No windows meant no light, and the deeper I went, the more confused I became. I couldn't see. When I found a set of stairs, I almost fell down them.

Was I supposed to continue downward? The chill of the darkness reminded me of...

In the next instant, I awoke in a pool of my own sweat. I gasped and sucked down air, my hands shaking. When I sat up, it felt as though I were drained of all energy. The blankets of my ginormous bed were twisted around my legs, and I struggled to free myself.

Frustrated, and in a mild state of panic, I heated my bedroom, evoking molten rock from my very being.

The bed caught fire.

The dressers went up in flames.

The fireplace burst into momentary glory before raging out of control.

The curtains withered away, the rugs became ash, and my bedframe charred all before I could contain myself. The shock of setting everything on fire only added to the panic, making it more difficult than before to cease the destruction.

I leapt from my bed and shook out my hands, ending my magic. The molten rock in the room ceased its increasing heat, and the room crackled with lingering flames.

What was wrong with me?

I rubbed my face, still soaked in anxiety. What had been in the depths of the castle? Why did I feel this way? Obviously, the more I learned my magic, the deeper I progressed. Would I see the last rooms of the vacant fortress once I had everything together?

The last of the fire died, leaving my room a blackened husk.

At least everything didn't burn down. It was mine, anyway. I didn't have to answer to anyone for the damage I had done.

"Terrakona," I said, uncertainty in my tone.

"Warlord—you find yourself distressed yet again."

His telepathic voice comforted me a bit. I took in a breath and then coughed. The smoke in the room clung to my dry throat and clouded my lungs.

"Terrakona," I repeated with a hoarse breath. "There's this castle and... It's, well, I don't know. It's haunting. I dream of it... Not every night, but frequently."

"Dreams are a realm of their own. The Children of Balastar were never adept at understanding them."

I shook my head as I staggered to the door of my room. Coughing and wheezing, I slammed out into the hallway. It was still night. Where was I going? I didn't understand Terrakona's cryptic statement. Children of Balastar? Realm of their own?

In a haze of my own thoughts, I pushed forward. The clean air in the hallway helped, and as I traveled through my own compound, I felt a bit better. Where was everyone? I needed to find someone. I wanted to talk to *someone* about my dreams and how to handle them.

I searched the rooms, opening one door after another, trying to find anyone. Fortunately, one door several halls away had light shining from underneath. It gave me some relief—at least someone was awake.

Without knocking, I opened the door.

Glowstone lanterns kept the room illuminated. I froze in the doorway, however, when I realized three individuals were in the room. Adelgis was under the covers, sitting with his back against the headboard, Fain sat at the foot of the bed, and Illia tucked in a shadow corner—sat on a chair.

My eyes grew wide, my eyebrows heading toward my hairline.

"Volke?" Illia asked, her one eye as wide as mine. "What're you doing here?"

Nicholin sat on her shoulder, his little ferret-like arms crossed over his furry white chest. "It's rude to barge into a room, mister."

"What... is going on?" was all I could choke out.

It seemed odd for them to all be together, and in the middle of the night. No one had told me about this. Was something happening? Had I interrupted?

Illia glanced at me, and then Fain, and then Adelgis, and then back to me. "I'm spending time with Fain," she said, like I should've known right away.

She hadn't. I knew in my gut. She had come here to see Adelgis, and Fain *happened* to be here as well. But I didn't want to call her on it. I didn't feel like arguing.

With his frostbitten hand, Fain grabbed a pillow on the bed and used it to rest back on. "I guess we were all drawn here tonight. Adelgis summoned me because his dreams have troubled him. Illia… she just arrived." He shot her a pointed look.

Illia touched her eyepatch, but otherwise didn't respond.

"Volke, what happened to you?" Nicholin asked. He waved his little paws in my direction. "Are you smoking? Do you set yourself on fire to sleep?"

I glanced down and almost laughed. I hadn't thought about my own attire. My trousers and button-up shirt were singed, and one leg was slightly smoking. With a few quick smacks, I patted it out.

"I had a nightmare," I said.

"We all know you were bonded to a knightmare," Illia said. "That doesn't explain your clothing."

I laughed once. "Er, no. I meant, I woke from a nightmare, and then I burned my room down." When no one said anything, I sauntered over to the side of the bed and took a seat. "You know. A typical night for the world serpent arcanist."

The tastefully decorated room was done in blues and whites. Even blue lilies were positioned by the open window, sitting between ivory curtains. It was a fifth the size of my master bedroom, but it reminded me of the small guild rooms. I missed them.

"Did you come seeking my advice?" Adelgis asked. He pushed back his long, inky hair. "About your nightmare?"

Now, in the company of others, the dread of my dream seemed insignificant. Why had I been so terrified and destructive? Perhaps all I had wanted was company. When I was a knightmare arcanist, Luthair was always by my side…

"Didn't Fain just say *you* had a nightmare, Adelgis?" I asked, wishing to change the subject. I leaned back on the bed. "Are you okay?"

Adelgis frowned. After a long exhale, he said, "I was trying to find my father—to see if he had headed for Thronehold yet.

I thought he would've been there by now... All this waiting is driving me insane."

I knew exactly how he felt.

"But dreams of my sister called me," Adelgis said, his voice strained. "I hadn't been able to see hers before. And now that I can, I see they're filled with pain and suffering."

"Wait, the sister I met in Ellios?"

Adelgis nodded. "Cinna has always been sickly, and my mother would complain about the tedium of caring for her. I fear... Cinna might die."

BIRTHDAY BALL

"Die of what?" I asked.

Adelgis said nothing. Neither did anyone else. I bit my tongue, waiting for some sort of explanation, but not even Illia would look at me directly.

Cinna...

I had seen her briefly before the start of the Sovereign Dragon Tournament. Apparently, Adelgis had six siblings, but Cinna was the only one who had been home with their mother in Ellios. Niro, Adelgis's brother, had fought in the tournament and stayed with his father in Thronehold.

Niro had been helping his father with his heinous research.

But then a terrible thought struck me.

"Is Cinna dying because of something that Theasin did?" I asked. "Would her own father hurt her?"

Fain shot me a glare. "He put an abyssal leech in one of his sons. What do you *think* Theasin is capable of?"

"I have no proof," Adelgis interjected, his tone detached and defeated. "Cinna's nightmare was of death, nothing more. It startled and worried me. Her sickness could very well be just a mundane problem."

"Didn't you say even the most talented of healers couldn't help her?" Fain said. "If caladrius arcanists and their legendary healing do nothing for her, obviously, it's not an illness of the body."

The glowstone lanterns didn't flicker—their glow was constant, but not bright enough to illuminate the corners of the bedroom. The dark spots around us seemed sinister when we were discussing grave matters of life and death, like the light was just barely keeping dark thoughts at bay.

Adelgis stared at his lap, unseeing. "If I had to guess, I would say my father had a hand in Cinna's weakness." He dragged a hand over his side, his fingers running along the grooves of his ribs. "I doubt she has anything like a leech, but my father was often obsessed with how mystical creatures grew."

"What do you mean?" I asked.

"Mystical creatures grow older and stronger when bonded to an arcanist. They feed on the arcanist's soul—the inner essence of a person. This *soul* is much like our blood." Adelgis placed a hand over his wrist. "We can bleed and then recover from it. But if we bleed too much, we die."

Illia leaned back in her creaky chair. "That's why we can't bond with multiple mystical creatures, right? Because then our soul would bleed too much, and we'd die?"

Adelgis nodded once. "But my father is never satisfied until he can break the laws of nature and bend everything to his will."

"Yeah. We've seen."

"Well, I think he might've tried something with Cinna when she was younger. Perhaps bleeding her soul to feed mystical creatures who weren't bonded to her, in an attempt to make them grow without an arcanist. I just... I remember him talking about that possibility."

"Did you ever see him experimenting on her?" I asked, my brow furrowed.

Adelgis shook his head. "Never. Which is why I can't say it's his fault... but I have a hunch. And I'm afraid. I have been for years. Cinna is a gentle soul. Even though she's been sick her entire life... She's never grown bitter, despite having every right to hate the world for cursing her with a weak body. I don't want her to die."

"Maybe you should write her a letter," Nicholin said, swishing his tail. "There are couriers in Fortuna. I know because I challenged one to a race and beat his pixie butt all the way across town." He stood tall on Illia's shoulder, his nose in the air.

"*That's* where you were all day?" Illia placed a hand on Nicholin's face. "You've lost your *city watching* privileges."

"Aww!"

"Writing her a letter is a fine idea," Adelgis said with a forced smile. "I'm sorry I worried you with my fears. I know you're dealing with a lot."

"It's okay," I said. "You're my friend. I want to help."

"Cinna's dream is just that. A dream. If caladrius arcanists can't heal her, there's nothing I can do that will help her recover." Adelgis gripped the blankets, his fingers twisting into the fabric, his eyes icy and emotionless. "I couldn't even help myself when the abyssal leech was consuming my soul."

"It wasn't your fault," I'am said in a quiet voice.

"Even so, it doesn't dispel this feeling of being completely and utterly useless."

I wanted to reassure Adelgis that everything would be okay, but even as a powerful god-arcanist, I didn't have the ability to mend people's souls. Could it even be done? Technically, I had healed Adelgis's soul by feeding him the sand of a dead khepera—those scarab creatures had bodies made of powerful inner healing.

"Maybe Vethica can do something to help," I said. "Once she's mastered more of her khepera magic, she might be able to mend someone's soul."

Adelgis weakly nodded. "Perhaps."

He didn't seem convinced. After all, what if Cinna died before then? If her dreams were filled with death, it was probably weighing heavily on Adelgis.

The shadows in the corners of the room seemed darker than before.

"I apologize for my bleak musings," Adelgis said as he lifted his gaze to mine. He had a look of exhaustion, with dark rings under his eyes. "These are just unsettling thoughts brought on by other people's dreams."

I shook my head. "Again, I'm your friend. I don't mind listening to you voice your concerns."

"You're much too kind, Volke." Adelgis tried his best to put hopeful emotion into his voice, but he wasn't fooling me. "You should rest. I can tell you're still tired."

"I burned my room down, remember?"

"But you're not thinking about your nightmare anymore. And there's another bedroom down the hall. Four doors down, past the personal library. It has a window to the courtyard."

It almost felt like Adelgis wanted me to leave. My body was heavy with fatigue, though. Especially my eyelids. I yawned as I stood and stretched. Perhaps I could help Adelgis further once I was more awake.

"Are you sure?" I asked. "I can stay and talk, if you'd like."

"Actually, I'd rather get some sleep myself." Adelgis tossed his inky hair over his bare shoulder and half-shrugged. "As a dreamweaver, I should be capable of altering my dreams for the better. I'm just overreacting. Cinna will be fine."

"I'll stay close," Fain stated.

Illia stood and then cradled Nicholin in her arms like a spoiled cat. "I should've left a while ago, honestly. It's late, and I want to get some good sleep in before we leave Fortuna."

"Good night," I said.

Fain and Adelgis both nodded.

With another puff of silver glitter, followed by a *pop*, Illia vanished from the bedroom. I wondered where she was sleeping. It couldn't be far—her teleportation didn't span long miles, just short distances. If I had to guess, she was likely on a floor below, but I didn't know.

"She's down the hall as well," Adelgis said, answering my internal thoughts. "She and Zaxis share a room."

I held my breath for a long while. "I didn't know they were that close," I finally said.

Fain slid off the side of the mattress. "Does them sharing a room bother you?"

"Hm? Oh. No. It's fine."

"I could make sure it doesn't happen."

I narrowed my eyes into a skeptical squint. "How?"

"Trust me. If I wanted, they'd never have another peaceful night of sleep." Fain became invisible, perhaps to demonstrate his ability to sneak in and out of most areas with ease.

What would he do in their room? My childish thoughts envisioned him "haunting" Zaxis and Illia. Pushing books off bookshelves. Scratching the glass window with his fingernails. Making eerie noises. But the more realistic part of me knew that Fain had once been a pirate who had ran with Calisto. He had the capacity to thoroughly mess with their comfort and security.

"Like I said—it's fine." I held up a hand. "Good night, you two. I'll see you both tomorrow." I turned for the door and shuffled out, my legs like lead.

Their muttered *good nights* followed me into the hall, and I shut the door behind me with a soft click. Then I turned and headed four doors down, determined to find yet another room to call my own. As I wrapped my fingers around the handle, Adelgis's door opened a second time.

Fain stepped out into the hall. He shut the door and headed in my direction, his dark gaze on the rugs. When he reached my side, he glanced up, his eyebrows knitted.

"What's wrong?" I asked. "You want to sleep in my bed now?"

I was being sarcastic, but Fain didn't even crack a smile or laugh. He sighed.

"Is it acceptable for a knight to ask something of his liege?"

I tensed and felt more awake than I had a couple of minutes ago. "What do you need, Fain?"

"It's Moonbeam. He's really worried about his sister."

"I know," I whispered. "He was the same way when we visited his home last time. He went straight to see her before doing anything else."

Fain slicked back his hair, his black fingers shaky. "Would you... send for her, too?"

"What do you mean?"

"I know you sent letters to bring your adopted father, and your mother, to this compound. Could you—as the world serpent arcanist—have Cinna brought here? For Moonbeam. If she were here... if he could just see her for a little while... I think he would be happier."

Fain thought I could make people travel to Fortuna just because I was the world serpent arcanist? I didn't have that kind of authority. I couldn't force Cinna anywhere and given how contentious her mother had been last time, I doubted she'd take kindly to a demand.

What if I just invited them to live here? Again, I doubted Cinna's mother would approve of that. Adelgis's family estate was luxurious—more so than my compound—and it already had everything that Cinna needed for her treatments. What benefit or advantage would they gain by coming here? They would never do it willingly.

"Listen," I muttered, hating myself for rejecting Fain's request. "Adelgis's mother probably won't go for it."

But before I voiced the last of my statement, I thought the situation over one more time.

I didn't need to force Cinna here.

"Wait," I said, pulling Fain a bit closer. "I know how to get them here."

Fain stared. "Commanding them?"

"No. I'll invite them to a party."

"Huh?" He snorted. "Where did that come from? Who cares about a party?"

"No. Listen. Cinna won't come, even if I send a request for her. Adelgis's mother hates the Frith Guild, hates Master Zelfree, and is obviously in love with that maniac, Theasin. I can't force her to come here—Adelgis would never appreciate that anyway."

Fain clenched his jaw and balled his hands into fists. "How does having a party solve this?"

"Adelgis's mother is a socialite of the highest order. She loves wealth and prestige and looking important."

"But if *you* invite her to a party, we'll run into the same problems," Fain snapped. "Remember? You just said she hates the Frith Guild. Even if she would normally attend opulent balls, she won't if your name is attached to the invitation. Right?"

I smiled and then shrugged. "Fain—*I'm* not going to invite her. King Odion is."

Fain took a long moment to mull over my statement. But then he relaxed and returned my smile with a smirk of his own. "Oh. I see. Trick her into coming here." But his amusement faded. "What if she doesn't bring Cinna?"

"If Odion says he wants to meet her family—the Venrover

house is famous, after all—it might work. I'll ask him to do it for me. As his liege, I'm sure it won't be a problem. Even if they don't show, I'm willing to take the chance just so Adelgis can see his sister."

The City of Ellios, Adelgis's hometown, was on the road to Thronehold. In theory, we would pass through on our way to confront Theasin. But we wouldn't have time to visit or socialize—Guildmaster Eventide had made it clear that we would need to confront Theasin as soon as possible.

This was probably the only way we could get time for Adelgis to spend with his sister.

"Thank you," Fain said, bowing his head slightly. "I'm sure Moonbeam will be happy that you even tried."

"No problem."

If my new room had lanterns or lights, I didn't bother looking. I groped around the darkness until I found my bed and then— still wearing my burnt clothing—collapsed on top of it. Everything was so soft.

When I dreamt, I knew Adelgis had a hand in it.

Everything was beautiful and perfect. I sailed on a ship of my own, the wind in my sails, the sky dotted with dragons, drakes, and colossal white clouds. The smell of salt water and adventure was enough to bring a smile to my face.

When I awoke to the sun shining in through the courtyard window, a part of me knew I had slept better than I had in months. Something about the relaxing nature of a dream with no purpose reinvigorated me.

I threw myself out of my bed, dressed for training, and then headed out into the destroyed courtyard. The quiet halls of my compound also helped me relax. By the time I made it outside, I felt better than ever.

To my surprise, Zaxis, Zelfree, and Fain were waiting for me. Each of them stood around the toppled tree, Zaxis leaning on the trunk, his laughter loud enough to wake people. They chatted among themselves—didn't Fain hate Zelfree?—and they only stopped once I approached.

When I reached the tree, they smiled.

Zaxis patted my shoulder. "Good. You're awake. Now let's get sparring."

I turned to Fain. "Are you here to watch?"

"You said you wanted me to evoke ice, remember?" Fain asked. "You thought it would help with your obsidian."

"O-Oh. Right. Thank you for remembering."

I took my position at the opposite end of the courtyard and then assumed a combat stance. After rotating my head and arms, I motioned for Fain to attack me. "Just use your frost and cover everything. I think the chill might prevent my obsidian."

Fain nodded once. Then he lifted his hand, his blackened fingers outstretched, and evoked a wave of ice. It covered everything in a harsh blast, coating the ground, benches, and trees in a light layer of frost. When he waved his hand again, another layer formed over that one, creating a thick rime. The chill covered me as well, hindering my movements.

After a deep exhale, I evoked my magma. The heat and ice didn't care for each other. Steam and smoke went everywhere, and when I threw the molten rock onto the ground, a foul fog sprang to life, humid and smelling of burnt grass.

Unfortunately, the cold didn't stop the obsidian from jutting out of my skin at my knuckles and elbows.

"Wait," Zaxis said, stepping forward. He slipped around on the ice and almost fell, but he caught himself just in time. "Hear me out. Didn't you say your *bones* became basalt? That weird, hard volcanic rock?"

"Yeah," I muttered, staring at the pillar of steam. "So?"

"Why would you want that to stop? It's a form of defense."

"It slows me down."

"You can train to mitigate that," Zelfree interjected. "If you run, move, and exercise with the obsidian in your body, you'll become used to it. Then it won't feel like extra weight."

"Do you think that's wise?" I asked. "What if these protrusions get in the way of something? They already make sword fighting harder."

Zaxis, Zelfree, and Fain all mulled over my statements. It seemed like, no matter what I did, there was always some sort of drawback. I stared at my hands again, at the black rocks. As I stared, I had a chilling thought.

They reminded me of Luthair.

I closed my hand into a tight fist.

The obsidian didn't seem like such a nuisance after that.

"Wait," I said aloud. "Zaxis is right. These basalt rocks... They're an inner armor. They protected me from Odion's blade. He couldn't cut through my arm. Well, he probably could, but it would take more effort than cutting through bone."

Zelfree scratched at his stubble. "Then I highly recommend you take my suggestion and train with the rock all the time. If you get used to the weight, you'll never notice it when you're fighting."

"But the obsidian goes away once I've stopped my evocation for a short period."

"You can wear weighted clothing, to simulate the effect."

That was a clever idea.

"Okay," I said. "But how?"

Master Zelfree glanced around the compound and then held up a hand. His arcanist mark went from blank to having a rizzel laced around the points of the star. With a soft *pop* and puff of glitter, he disappeared from the courtyard, leaving me, Zaxis, and Fain alone with the rubble and busted trees.

Zaxis took a seat and Fain cloaked himself in invisibility. The morning sun sparkled down on us, saying *good morning* with a gentle increase in temperature. I waited with bated breath, wondering when Zelfree would return. I wanted to get stronger, I really did, and this plan seemed crucial to that goal.

I rubbed at the obsidian on my hand, thinking of Luthair.

Could I somehow use his cape to create an artifact that enhanced the rock? Become some sort of armor? The thoughts filled my mind with creative musings. I got lost in them and jumped when Zelfree finally reappeared with another pop of glitter.

He tossed me a coat. I grabbed it and stumbled forward, caught off guard by the weight.

"What is this?" I asked as I lifted the piece of clothing. Metal clinking rattled around in the sleeves.

"It's heavy, right?" Zelfree said. "Put it on."

I did as he had instructed. Once I got it on, I realized that small metal rings had been sewn into the sleeves and hem of the coat. It had to weigh nearly fifty pounds, but it didn't strain my shoulders like a backpack full of rocks would have.

The sunlight didn't feel so gentle anymore.

"I might get too hot," I said. "Which is ironic, given that I create magma."

"I can keep you cool," Fain said from nowhere. "Don't worry about that."

I smiled and nodded. "That's true..."

With this, I felt like training would be more productive, but I knew it'd drain the last of my energy. Before I could resume my harsh schedule, one of my compound servants rushed into the courtyard. At first, I thought we were under attack, and my veins filled with an icy rage, but the moment the servant girl smiled, I knew I had overreacted.

"Pardon the intrusion, Warlord," the servant said with a deep bow of her head. "But King Odion and Guildmaster Eventide told me to inform you of the good news."

"What good news?" I asked.

"Your birthday ball will be held here at the compound in fourteen days."

"His *what*?" Zaxis snapped.

The servant offered a nervous smile as she said, "The warlord's birthday ball." She bowed again. "All the invitations have been sent. Several guildmasters, kings, and queens, have already sent back confirmation of their attendance."

29

MARKUS THE PIRATE

"Who approved this?" I asked.

"Guildmaster Eventide of the Frith Guild," the servant girl said, her voice becoming less certain with each word. "Is this news upsetting? I thought it would be well-received..."

"It's good news," I said.

Sort of.

"King Odion wanted me to reassure you that he invited your special guest of honor." The girl bowed her head a second time and then inched toward the edge of the courtyard, away from me. "The compound will be prepped and ready for your celebration. You needn't worry about a thing."

I nodded. "Thank you."

Then she hurried off, her brow furrowed. I suspected she thought I'd be elated to hear about the party, but it really didn't sit well.

"I thought I was supposed to be hidden?" I asked as I turned to Master Zelfree. "Having a huge party is the exact opposite of that. We could just have a small one."

Zelfree sighed as he ran a hand through his dark hair. "Yeah. It seems reckless. Unlike Eventide."

"Right?"

"Or perhaps she wants more allies, and fast. We'll be heading to Thronehold soon. Perhaps she wants arcanists here and ready to march with us."

That was a logical excuse, but it still seemed reckless. I wasn't that afraid for myself, but I was worried about the runestones in our possession, as well as the weaker members of the Frith Guild. What if our enemies captured them or took them as bait? My father could barely walk and wasn't a combatant. What if he was targeted in an attempt to get to me?

I stepped close to Zelfree and then lowered my voice. "We should call this off."

"Oh?" Zelfree cocked a brow. "According to Karna, you asked for a birthday celebration. Eventide might've even gotten the idea from her."

"Er, well, I didn't *ask* for a birthday celebration. Karna just wanted to do it."

A cool wind from the nearby ocean rushed into the courtyard. I enjoyed it—my new coat was hot, even when I wasn't moving—and I waited while Zaxis, Fain, and Zelfree mulled over the information.

"I'll go speak to Eventide," Zelfree said, stepping around me. "Just train while I handle this."

I watched him go, worried that Eventide had put us all in jeopardy. What if the Second Ascension came here? I had invited Gravekeeper William and my mother to move here—they would be easy targets for my enemy. What was I going to do about this?

Eventide had atlas turtle barrier magic, but that wouldn't be enough, not when our enemy had bones from the apoch dragon.

"Everything will be fine," Zaxis said, as if he could read my mind. "Trust me. When you train your muscles, you won't even think about your problems. It works for me every time." He grabbed his upper arm as he flexed.

Was he trying to cheer me up? It worked a bit, but only because Zelfree had said he would handle the problem. Zelfree managed to do most things he said he would, even if it took a terrible toll on him.

"Okay," I said as I lifted my arms to practice my evocation, obsidian protrusions, and basalt hardening. "Let's train."

Without needing to be instructed, Fain evoked ice over the courtyard, keeping us cool while we worked.

Zelfree didn't return.

The sun left us, and by then, my whole body ached. Zaxis healed me throughout the training, easing the tear of my muscles, but it never lasted. After half an hour of moving in that weighted coat, I couldn't stand and needed another round of healing.

Weariness got to me. When I finally made it to my bedroom —the one I hadn't burned down in a fit of panic—I threw off my clothes and collapsed asleep.

My last thoughts were of my birthday.

Why have a massive celebration? Why invite other guildmasters, kings, and queens?

Before I could concoct some theories, I drifted to sleep.

My dreams were vivid, and I was once again someone else.

I watched from behind their eyes as they patrolled the deck of the *Third Abyss*. The fog from the ghostwood kept the horizon a mystery, but the moment I put a pair of magical glasses over my eyes, I could see through the mist without problem.

I took the glasses on and off as I stared into the distance.

There was an island I could only spot with the glasses on. The lantern hanging from the main mast messed with my ability to spot details, but I could still clearly see the island.

"I didn't know there was an isle so close to Port Crown," I said, my voice strange to my ears.

Markus. This dream was one of his memories.

Calisto stepped close. I didn't flinch, so I suspected Markus wasn't surprised, but *I* was. Calisto wore a new coat—something with shiny copper buttons and bright threading. His knightmare boots and unicorn necklace, as well as a few new bracelets on his arms, all caught my attention. Had he been collecting even more trinkets and artifacts? It seemed so. How many did one person need?

His glowing arcanist mark—a star with a manticore woven throughout—always confused and impressed me. How had Calisto gotten a true form eldrin? I wished I knew.

"That island is uninhabited," Calisto stated.

"Are there mystical creatures there?" I asked, embracing the glasses and wearing them fully.

"There used to be."

"Oh?" I turned to Calisto, smirking. "More corpses?"

Calisto's copper hair shone in the lantern light, almost as much as his white canines when he flashed a cruel smile. "That's right. But these ones are special."

"How so?"

"They're extinct."

The information intrigued me. Although this was a memory, I tried to ask follow-up questions, but I was only an observer. If Markus didn't ask questions, I couldn't do so in his place. Frustrated, I just waited as I stroked my chin, my gaze on the far island.

"They aren't king basilisks, are they?" I asked.

Calisto chortled. "Heh. Those aren't extinct *yet*." He pointed to the beaches of the far isle. "I'm talkin' about the charybdis.

They're freakish worms that create whirlpools in their mouths to sink ships."

"I-I've heard about them. They could melt metal and wood with their saliva."

"And their scales repelled heat and ice." Calisto smiled. "They were dangerous. Powerful."

I shivered and then glanced down. To my surprise, a griffin cub sat between my feet. It glanced up at me with a lion's face. A boy, then. Female griffins had the heads of eagles. His golden fur and feathers rustled in the midnight winds.

I leaned down and stroked the neck of the little griffin. "And all the charybdis are dead? Did someone go out of their way to kill them?"

Calisto shrugged and then replied with a click of his tongue, "Tsk. I thought you were educated? Isn't that what you told me? Daddy paid for your book-learnin'?"

"We didn't learn about mass killings," I said as I stood straight.

The griffin between my legs pawed at my trousers, trying to get my attention. He meowed softly and then stretched out his needle-like claws, hooking onto the fabric of my clothes. I ignored the creature and kept my focus on Calisto.

"The island used to belong to strange people," Calisto said. "The original island-dwellers. Somehow, they had been living there for hundreds of years. They were backward."

"What happened to them?" I asked.

"Killed." Calisto huffed. "Privateers thought they might have valuables hidden on the island, so they fought with the island arcanists. Apparently, those islanders worshipped the charybdis, so to break their fighting spirit, the privateers poisoned the waters near their nesting grounds and killed the lot of them."

I gritted my teeth and took a deep breath. "The charybdis are susceptible by poison?"

"It's damn near their only weakness. Or so they say."

"Was this the only place the charybdis lived?"

"That's right." Calisto hardened his gaze. "The only island."

"And no one came to collect their bodies to make into trinkets?"

"They couldn't find them." With a casual shrug, Calisto laughed. "But don't worry. Hellion will find our gravesite. That's what he's good at. Well, that and killin' people."

The ship creaked and I turned my attention to the massive manticore that came walking from the mizzenmast. It was Hellion. I would recognize his white fur and black leather wings anywhere. His scorpion tail, curled upward, glistened in the lantern light, but it wasn't the most intimidating factor about the beast.

It was the face mask.

The manticore wore a mask that gave him a human face. The eyes and mouth, curved to look like a smiling face, didn't move as he spoke. "We're getting close," Hellion said, his voice low and dark. "Blood lingers on the air here."

The griffin cub scurried away from my legs and ran to the manticore. Hellion was nearly the size of an elephant, and the cub was the size of a small dog. The griffin spread his tiny wings and flapped around the monster's massive claws. I thought Hellion would try to devour the cub, but no such thing happened.

Instead, Hellion fell to his side, like a dog wanting scratches, and playfully batted the griffin into his grip. With gentle movements, the manticore toyed with the griffin, even messing up its golden fur.

"I'll get you!" the little griffin shouted, his childish voice adorable.

The happy face on Hellion's mask grew wider and more "joyful."

But to me, Hellion's expression bordered on the insane.

How could anyone stand such a monster? The griffin snorted and played as though the manticore were its fun, albeit disgusting, uncle.

"You'll never be a mighty warrior if you can't escape me, Alexi," Hellion said, his voice still gruff and dark, but somehow lighthearted. It was a strange juxtaposition. "Fly. Use your teeth."

The griffin, Alexi, giggled and struggled harder, never managing to free himself from Hellion's grasp.

I pulled my gaze from the two mystical creatures playfighting and returned it to Calisto. He stared off into the distance, and I just stared at him. After a prolonged moment, I cleared my throat and Calisto gave me a sideways glance.

"Why are you up, anyway?" he asked.

"I was trying to think of other locations where we could find mystical creature corpses." I straightened my posture and forced a smile. "You were excited by the hippogriffs we got, weren't you?"

"Don't get too excited," Calisto growled. "After we gather up the charybdis, we won't be packing any more bodies onto the ship."

"Why not? We still have some room."

"Because. Theasin says he has enough. Once we deliver them to Thronehold, the Autarch wants me to help with the sky titan. Apparently, the little girl destined to bond with it needs her nappy changed."

I knitted my eyebrows. "What do you mean?"

Calisto wheeled on me, his body tense. "*I mean I've been summoned to watch over her, like a dog.*"

He dismissively waved his hand, and it was close enough to my face that I flinched away.

"I'm not gonna strike you, *fool*," Calisto said through gritted teeth as he crossed his arms and turned away. "Unless you get on my bad side. Then I'm not responsible for what happens to you."

The cold mist lingered between us. Instead of backing away —or running from this madman—I stepped closer, limiting the distance between us.

"If it upsets you to serve the Autarch, why bother?" I asked.

"He provides me with trinkets and artifacts."

"You have plenty. Why not go?"

Calisto growled something I didn't hear, his gaze locked on the distance. Then he said, "It's all just a game of power. If I serve the Autarch, and he wins, I'll live a life of luxury. If I leave, and he wins, I'll be hunted down for my betrayal. And if I leave, and he loses, then I'm just a pirate, same as I've always been."

"But as a pirate, you're free," I said. "The trinkets aren't worth fighting all the Autarch's enemies. He's just using you as a shield. He doesn't care about your life."

Calisto honestly laughed. With a crooked smile, he glanced over. "*I* don't care about my life, so who cares if the Autarch does? At least now, things won't get dull."

While I hated the man, it felt... sad, somehow, that he didn't value his own existence. Like the trinkets and artifacts were worth more to him than living. With an attitude like that, no wonder he could harm so many people and not feel a thing.

I shivered and rubbed my arms. "Captain, why don't we turn in for the night? We'll need our rest if we're going to dig up charybdis bodies tomorrow morning."

"You needn't worry about me."

"Someone has to," I said, defiant.

Calisto relaxed a bit. "Why are you always like this? There's nothin' between us."

"It didn't seem that way last night. Or the night before. Or the night before that."

"I just needed somethin' physical," Calisto said with a dark smirk. "Don't go readin' into it."

Hellion and the griffin cub stopped their play tussle. They both stood and headed for the quarterdeck, their movements sluggish and tired. Were they turning in for the night? Or were they avoiding the conversation? I didn't know.

"Let me stay with you again tonight," I said.

"I'm not in the mood," Calisto snapped.

"Just to sleep. Please."

He glanced over and glowered.

I didn't flinch.

Calisto eventually turned away, his expression softer. "Do whatever you want," he muttered. "I won't stop you."

So, Markus *had* been lying about his relationship with Calisto. Had Zelfree known? Was that why he had gotten upset when we had spoken to Markus in the brig?

The dream ended abruptly.

Someone shook me.

With heavy eyelids, I opened my eyes. Morning sunlight illuminated my room, creating a warm and beautiful hue of gold that lingered over everything. I stared at the ceiling, admiring the rays of sunshine that streaked over my bed.

"What the?" I murmured.

"Wake up, Warlord," someone purred.

I slowly rolled to my side and then nearly jumped out of bed. Karna was lying next to me, her golden hair spilling over the pillows and sheets like a gorgeous pool of liquid wheat. She stared at me with blue eyes and a glorious smile.

"Sleep well?" she asked as she pulled the blankets up to her shoulders.

Thankfully, I could see she wore clothing.

I wasn't as decent.

I grabbed the sheets and blankets and tucked them around myself, my body red and my heart rate heightened. "What're you doing?" I asked. I didn't bother getting out of bed. I figured that was what Karna wanted.

"I came here to talk to you about your birthday, obviously," Karna said, rolling her eyes. "No need to get excited. I assure you, this will be brief, but you're going to want to hear it."

After a long inhale, I relaxed. "Okay. What is it?"

"Everything is all set for your birthday." Karna's smile never waned. "Food, guests, presents—you can't even imagine the guest list. I'm stunned, really. It'll be bigger than the gala in Thronehold."

I stared, blinking only a few times. "Why?" was all I managed to choke out. "Why would we hold a huge event? I thought I was—"

"Supposed to keep a low profile?" Karna said, finishing my sentence. She reached out and poked my nose with a single finger. "Oh, how cute you are when you're confused. I could stay here forever."

I narrowed my eyes into a glare. "No games."

"Fine." Karna grabbed a pillow and held it tight. "I went to Guildmaster Eventide and told her about my plans for your birthday. It was originally going to be a modest affair, I promise, but Eventide insisted that she be allowed to help in the planning."

"Okay. And?"

"And then apparently you told Odion to invite people here for a party. Eventide mixed these two events together—on purpose, mind you—and sent out invitations to half the known world. The council of Fortuna has also pitched in. They're the ones providing the food and entertainment."

I sat up, suddenly filled with restless energy.

"But why?" I demanded. "It doesn't make sense."

Karna gave me a *calm down, I'm getting to that part* kind of glance. I bit my tongue, but I couldn't stop my mind from running through a million explanations, none of which were good.

"I wanted to know why as well," she said. "But Eventide refused to tell me. So... I used my doppelgänger magic and disguised myself as Master Yesna. Apparently, Eventide trusts the Ace of Cutlasses enough to discuss plans and tactics for capturing the assassin with her."

"*What*?" I asked.

"That's right. The assassin already knows you're here, and he's been sneaking around, apparently. No one can catch him —not even Eventide. Thankfully, the barriers she's created keep the assassin from getting into the compound."

I nodded along with the story, too tense and confused to add any words.

Karna twisted some of her golden hair onto a single finger. "Eventide is throwing this ball in an attempt to catch the assassin. And you're the bait."

30

SOCIAL ACUMEN

"You're sure of this?" I asked.

Karna nodded. "I found out about the assassin last night." She stretched and forced a yawn and then tucked her hand behind her head. "I wanted to know if Eventide had told you yet. Apparently not."

I turned away, my thoughts bogged down with doubt. On the one hand, why would Eventide keep this from me? Was it to shield me from fear and stress? On the other hand, I trusted Eventide. If she thought keeping this from me was important, perhaps it was. Perhaps there was some detail I was missing.

Karna rolled onto her side and faced me with a smile. "And look." She lifted the blankets, revealing her dancing outfit and lace-up sandals. "I'm here fully dressed. See? I listen when you say some things are important to you."

"Thank you for keeping your clothes on," I sarcastically said.

Why was that a need I had to voice with some people? Sometimes I forgot how strange my life was.

"What're you going to do about the knowledge of this assassin?" Karna asked.

I shook my head. "I need to think about it. Depending on who it is, I might need to handle this before my birthday. Maybe I can sneak past Eventide's barriers. Somehow."

"Eventide seems convinced she's going to capture this man when he comes for you during the party." Karna tapped her red lips with a single finger. "For the record, I'm not a fan of that plan."

After a long sigh, I fell back on the bed, my gaze up at the ceiling. I still couldn't figure out why anyone would keep this from me. Did they mistrust me? Or maybe they didn't want me to reveal to the assassin I knew of his presence, for fear he would run off?

Karna stared at me for a long while, and when I said nothing, she puffed her breath, moving some of her blonde hair out of her face, and then smiled again. "Anything you want for your birthday?" She ran a hand over her side. "I'm willing to entertain all sorts of requests."

I slowly turned to face her. "You know I don't like it when you get so aggressively suggestive."

With a huff, Karna rolled her eyes. "You're still courting someone else, I presume? Is it Atty? Or has Evianna made more of a move on you yet?"

My face reddened and my stomach twisted. "It's complicated."

"Most people don't have as much trouble as you do, Volkie."

I ran a hand down my face, remembering what Evianna had said to me the other night. "I know. But... I'm not sure what I'm doing wrong. No matter what I do, my love life has always felt off. Like wearing a shirt with the buttons misaligned. Or wearing a boot without a sock."

"What an interesting way to describe that," Karna said as she fluffed her pillow. Then she gave me a sweet grin. "I think if you spent one night with a high-quality *companion*, all your problems would be solved."

"Companion?"

"A whore," Karna stated. She waved her hand around like she was holding a wine glass. "That's what all the noblemen in the Argo Empire would say. *I need a companion for the evening.* No one wanted to admit they were with a harlot, after all."

I ran a hand down my face. "I don't need a harlot."

"Once you get this out of your system, you'll understand." Karna sighed, as though my naivete was too much to deal with. "You should be with *someone*. Stop denying yourself this. I don't know why you do it, but it's clearly a mental obstacle you need to face."

A mental obstacle? That was how she saw my love life?

"You want me to get past this obstacle so that I'll be with you, right?" I drawled. "What a beautiful romance."

Karna clicked her tongue in disapproval and then glared at me. "Youth is wasted on the ignorant. All I'm saying is that you won't know a good relationship until you've had at least *one* yourself. Then you'll realize what you're missing—what *I* bring to the table."

"Hm."

I ignored Karna's suggestions and instead tried to focus my thoughts. What would I do about this assassin? Go out and get him? And now a part of me also thought of Atty and Evianna. But what was there to think about? Atty had made it clear she was more concerned about obtaining a true form phoenix than anything else.

In no uncertain terms, Atty had always rebuffed my advances.

"You're thinking of a girl, aren't you?" Karna whispered. "I know that look."

"I probably should be thinking of an assassin," I said with a dark chuckle. I got out of bed—holding one of the blankets around my waist—and headed for the dresser. As I searched for clothing, I glanced over my shoulder and asked, "Karna, let's say you're right. I need a relationship. Can I ask you a hypothetical question?"

"Of course," she purred.

"If, uh, I were to declare my... uh... *affection* for someone, what would you suggest I say? In theory, of course."

Karna's eyes went wide with excitement. She leapt out of bed and hurried to my side. "Oh, I have a million suggestions. Where do I even begin?" She grabbed a shirt out of the dresser —a white one with black stitching—and handed it to me. "Come now. Put this on."

Keeping the blanket around my waist, I pulled on the shirt. Karna handed me a pair of black trousers, and I yanked those on under the sheet. Once clothed, albeit poorly, I released the bedding and brushed myself off.

"All right," I said. "So, what do you think I should say? Should it be sweet? Or caring? How romantic is *too* romantic? Should I just declare my love?"

Karna placed the back of her hand on her forehead. "Oh, Volkie. You're too much." She yanked my hand and dragged me back over to the bed. We stopped before hitting the mattress, and she stared up at me with a calm smile. "Listen to me. Women want someone strong. A tough man who will be callous to everyone else, but not to his lady."

"O-Okay," I said as I rubbed the back of my neck. "Should I just tell someone that? *I'll be tough on everyone but you.*"

Karna's amused demeanor shifted to slight annoyance. "No. Just relax and do exactly what I show you."

I loosened my shoulders and tried to keep my stance casual. "Okay. I'm ready."

"I need to tell you something," Karna whispered. She maintained eye contact and kept her expression neutral. "As the Warlord of Magic, I have a responsibility to the world. But..."

With a gentle touch, Karna placed her delicate hand on my

shoulder and guided me backward. When the back of my legs hit the mattress, I sat down.

"But I also have a responsibility to my heart," Karna said as she leaned down, our faces close, her breath on my chin. She ran her hand over my shoulder and up my neck until she cupped my cheek with her palm. "Swear yourself to me. All of yourself. Your mind, your soul—" Karna brought her lips to my ear, "—your body."

I held my breath, my chest and throat tight.

"In return," Karna whispered in a husky tone, "I'll swear myself to you, and only you. The Warlord of Magic will be your knight for the rest of your days."

I wanted to say something, but my face was too hot, and I feared making a fool of myself.

Karna didn't say anything more. She released the side of my face and stood straight.

"*That's* what I should say?" I asked, my eyebrows at my hairline. "Really?"

With a wink, Karna replied, "Oh, trust me. Any woman would swoon if you managed to pull that off without breaking character."

The way she said that last statement broke me out of her seductive trance. I didn't want to have a *character* or a *persona* when interacting with someone I cared for. No matter how convincing the lines or how smoothly I conducted myself, it wouldn't be *me* if I were simply acting.

Perhaps asking Karna for advice had been a bad idea from the start.

My skin was still flushed from her demonstration, though. It had been fairly convincing.

I stood from the bed, startling Karna. "I have to go," I stated. "Thank you, though. For the advice."

"That's it?" Karna asked, placing one hand on her hip. "You

don't want any more advice? I can get you some valuable information if you tell me who you're aiming for."

"N-No. That won't be necessary." I made my way to the bedroom door, my thoughts shifting back to my *birthday assassin*. Why did I even bother thinking about my personal life? I really did fumble every step of that.

"I'm going to keep planning things for your big day," Karna called out as I opened the door. "You'll love it, I promise."

"Thank you," I said as I exited the room and entered the long hallway. Then I stopped and glanced over my shoulder. Karna wasn't leaving. Did she intend to stay there?

I shook my head, dispelling the thought. No point in telling Karna to give me personal space. She had never taken my demands seriously in the past, and I doubted she would start now. Better to save my breath and energy for training my magic.

The long hall wasn't nearly long enough. By the time I reached the end, I still hadn't finished thinking through my problem. I turned around, took a deep breath, and walked it again, all the way to the other end. But still—I felt conflicted on the best course of action.

What was I going to do about the assassin? Pretend I had never heard anything? I had to deal with him. I had to.

Echoes from down an attached hallway drew my attention. They sounded like feminine voices, and I recognized one of them, though just barely.

Yesna. The Ace of Cutlasses.

A strange thought occurred to me, and I headed in her direction. I turned down one hall, and saw her at the other end, speaking to one of the Javin soldiers. Yesna pointed to another long hall. "I think more patrols need to take this path," she said.

"I will relay this at once to King Odion, Master Yesna," the soldier replied before bowing and then walking off down the hallway.

With my head held high, I made my way over. It also occurred to me that my god-arcanist mark wasn't visible, so I unbuttoned my shirt a bit before nearing Yesna. I wished I had more suitable armor—perhaps something with my mark on it. My father would know how to craft such a thing, and as soon as I had time to craft it with him, I would.

Yesna's gold armor still amused me. It revealed a good portion of her skin, but I understood why. Some fighting styles required more mobility—especially movement-intensive styles, like those of the whirl blade users of the Amber Dunes, or the cliff knights of Regal Heights. Wearing heavy armor while moving around the battlefield would sap an arcanist of their strength too fast to be practical, and most metal armor wasn't flexible enough to keep up with the flowing stances of those styles.

Yesna turned on her heel and smiled at me. "Oh, Warlord. Nice to see you again." Then she offered me a deep bow, though it didn't feel like a gesture of respect, but rather more of obligation. "How fortunate we met. I have something to discuss with you."

I forced a smile. "Good morning, Master Yesna. What is it?"

"Eventide and King Odion have decided to host your birthday celebration on these grounds." Yesna stood straight and then motioned to the empty halls around us. "We'll be gaining as many allies as we can before heading out to confront Theasin in Thronehold. In the meantime, I've been tasked with improving security. If you have any ideas to improve our defenses, please let me know."

"With Eventide's barriers, shouldn't we be safe?"

"Zelfree and Eventide insisted on it," Yesna said matter-of-factly.

"And about this celebration," I said as I crossed my arms. "Apparently, dozens of people will be in attendance. Don't you think that's a security risk? We probably shouldn't invite anyone into the compound."

Yesna shrugged. "Oh, I'm not in charge of planning. I'm just here to tell you the details."

"What details?"

"It'll take place fourteen days from now, and Liet thinks it'll be the perfect opportunity to solidify alliances and perhaps gain new arcanists for the Frith Guild." Yesna patted the hilt of her left cutlass. "She said no magi crosses, though. So, if you get the urge to have a duel, just spar with me instead. I'll show you how a master wields a blade."

"Why isn't Eventide telling me this herself?"

Yesna frowned. "She's off doing other business. Talkin' to people. Making connections. You know her. She's never *not* busy."

"What if someone from the Second Ascension sneaks in during this party?" I asked, a little frustrated that Eventide wouldn't bother to tell me any of this herself.

But Yesna was right. Eventide was always busy, no matter the time of day or the calm of the waters. I admired that about her.

"I seriously doubt anyone will sneak in," Yesna replied. She took a few steps away from me, inching toward the next hall over, like she wanted to exit the conversation now that we were discussing potential threats. "The Javin arcanists have ways to dispel invisibility and illusions. Plus, we have Eventide's barriers, even if they'll be open for a short period to allow guests in. Worryin' is for the birds. Don't bother."

Worrying was for the birds? I had never heard that expression before.

"There aren't any known threats I should be worried about?" I asked. "Like someone in town who might want to do me harm?"

"Nope. You're fine. Just focus on your training."

I held my breath, disturbed that Master Yesna would lie to me so brazenly. Then again, she had said everything so smoothly that it hadn't sounded like a lie to my ears. But I knew otherwise. Yesna was aware of the assassin, yet she avoided telling me.

"I need to go," Yesna said with a half-shrug. "Duty and all that. I'm sure we'll speak again, Warlord. And again, if you think of any areas in which we can improve your protection, let me know."

I nodded to her as she went. Once Yesna disappeared down the next hall over, I decided to find Master Zelfree. Wouldn't he be waiting for me in the courtyard? I rushed my way there— through the hall, down the stairs, and out the door.

Sure enough, Zelfree stood in the morning shade of a busted tree. He had a book in one hand, his eyes narrowed as he read. Once he spotted me, he put the book down on the broken bench.

I walked over to him, trying to control my gait so that I didn't betray my motives.

"Zelfree," I said once I drew near. "Did you manage to speak to Eventide about the celebration?"

The man gave me the once over. "Why aren't you wearing any boots?"

"To get in touch with the dirt or something," I said. "But that's not as important as this celebration. Apparently, the Frith Guild and I will be making alliances."

Zelfree nodded once. "That's right."

"And remember how you said you thought it was a security risk? I'm perfectly content *not* having a celebration. We can make alliances the old-fashioned way."

"Marrying into their families?"

"N-No," I stammered. My love life was already a wreck. "I meant by letter and messenger. I'm worried our enemies will infiltrate the celebration and hurt someone."

For a split second, I thought Zelfree would say the exact same things as Yesna. *It's fine. Don't worry. Eventide will handle this.*

But Zelfree's eyes hardened. He grabbed my shoulder and pulled me close. Before he said anything, he glanced around, as though to make sure no one would hear.

"Listen," he whispered. "Eventide wants to have a large celebration not only to ally ourselves with several guilds and arcanists, but also to sniff out an assassin."

I tried to act surprised by lifting an eyebrow, but I didn't know what to say without giving myself away. I remained silent.

"Don't tell anyone I told you," Zelfree said, his tone beyond serious. "Eventide doesn't want you to worry about the issue, and she's afraid the Second Ascension might have an ethereal whelk arcanist on their side as well. If an enemy reads your thoughts, we might have a lot more problems on our hands."

With my breath held, I nodded once.

Thank all the good stars at night that Zelfree had told me. A part of me had feared I might not be able to fully trust anyone anymore, but obviously, I was wrong. Some people would be with me no matter what happened, and Zelfree was one of them.

"Thank you for telling me," I said.

Zelfree glared. "What did I just say? Don't acknowledge that. Ever. Eventide debated for a long time whether or not to tell you, and ultimately decided against it. However..." Zelfree pinched the bridge of his nose. "I know you better than she does. I remember when you *ran off* to save Illia from Calisto. If you think you can handle it on your own, sometimes you just do, so I have to curb that instinct right now."

"What do you mean?"

"I mean, if you somehow found out about the assassin beforehand, you probably would've gone after him yourself."

I nervously chuckled and waved away the comment with

both hands. "What? Me? No. That was a reaction a younger me would've had."

Zelfree narrowed his eyes into a sarcastic glower. "Uh-huh."

"I won't go after the assassin," I said. "You have my word. Plus, I need to do a lot more training. I don't have time to worry about this other stuff."

The morning was still young. If I trained until nightfall, I'd probably have a good eleven or twelve hours to practice. I was ready for it, too. I wanted to improve my magic. I had to keep going and pushing as hard as I could.

"Okay," Zelfree said as he patted my upper arm. "Let's get some practice in."

FOREVER LOYAL

Training blurred together.

For ten days straight, I woke up, wrecked the courtyard a bit more, met Evianna at dusk, helped her with some of her knightmare magic, and then took an hour-long bath. The soldiers of Javin and Antihelm stayed close, but I never saw King Odion and Queen Callandra. I assumed that had something to do with Guildmaster Eventide. She had probably involved them in her scheme to catch this assassin.

It was hard to concentrate when I knew someone was out to get me, but I pushed it aside to focus on my magic.

My magma was interesting. The obsidian and basalt were still heavy, but Zaxis's help with training made the ache of my new weighted clothing easier. And the plants I could evoke had fascinating properties. I could *feel* them, as though they were part of me. Even once the leaves were ripped off the vines, I could still feel them, too.

How could I use this to my advantage?

Manipulating the ground had become easier. I couldn't do much with it, but changing the properties of the dirt and stone around me meant I could control the battlefield. Fighting on sand was much harder than on flat stone. When I fought with Zelfree, I changed the ground under his feet to disorient him. Unfortunately, Zelfree was resourceful. I only caught him with my tricks half the time—Zelfree often steadied his stance in a matter of moments.

I wanted to be a better warrior, like him. I tried watching his footwork, and something interesting happened. Just as I could feel things through the plants I evoked, I realized I could feel people on the ground I had my magic hooked to. And it wasn't just them, it was the tremors they created—the vibrations of their every movement.

It made it easy to predict what they would do.

If someone shifted their weight to their left foot, it meant they were going to step with their right. If they shifted their stance to rely on the front of their foot, they weren't going to lunge. If they rested on their heel, they would pivot.

But learning so much in such a short time left me physically and mentally fatigued. When I helped Evianna at night, I was barely there. I hardly remembered what I had taught her. All I knew was that I had to tell her of all my experiences with Luthair.

From what I could recall, Evianna was learning quickly. I was surprised, not because she wasn't capable, but because I didn't know what fueled her drive. When her brother had still been alive, Evianna had sworn revenge, but now he was dead, so what pushed her forward at such break-neck speeds?

Was it me? I wasn't certain. She seemed extremely determined, though.

On the tenth day, while training with Zaxis and manipulating the ground, I remembered part of my fight with Gallus the Gray. He had used his water manipulation to drag me into the depths.

What if...

Zaxis ran at me from the other side of the courtyard. I had

seen him do this before. He'd jump up when he got close, to keep his feet off the ground, and then he'd slam at me. Instead, I held out my hand and imagined the dirt as water.

The earth twisted and pulsed. Before Zaxis could jump, he lost his footing. A whirlpool of sand and rock sank downward in the middle of the courtyard, trapping Zaxis's feet up to the ankle and dragging him with it.

"What in the abyssal hells?" he shouted.

With blazing-hot knuckles, he punched at the ground, but the sand and rock swirled around him, sinking more of his body into the earth. I kept my manipulation going, thinking he wouldn't go far, but to my shock, Zaxis plunged beneath the dirt like a drunken sailor dipping below the waves.

"What's going on?" Master Zelfree yelled from the edge of the courtyard. "Volke, is that *you*?"

Most of the courtyard had distorted into a sandy crater of rocks. The slope was steep, and Zelfree didn't dare jump in to save Zaxis.

Where was Illia *now*? Teleporting Zaxis to safety would've been preferred!

Forsythe screeched and took to the sky, but even he didn't dare touch the ground. He circled like a panicking vulture, his soot wafting through the air.

I halted all my magic use, but that only seemed to make things worse. The sand hardened into stone, becoming smooth and bowl-like. I stared at my own creation, my heart slamming against my ribs. What if I had killed him?

"I... I didn't know this would happen," I said, my voice shaky.

He was just gone. No sign of Zaxis anywhere.

Buried alive.

Zelfree exhaled and calmed his voice. "Concentrate," he commanded. "Don't panic. Just reverse what you did. Zaxis is a strong phoenix arcanist, with above-average healing—

especially for himself. If you can get him out of the ground, I'm sure he'll be fine. Don't think about the alternative."

I nodded along with his words, my blood running cold with guilt. Zelfree was trying to remain composed so that it would be easier for me. And it worked. His confidence and logic spread like fire, melting the icy feeling of dread.

With my feet steadied, I used my manipulation on the ground and altered the terrain. Instead of imagining Gallus pulling me into the ocean, I remembered how Gallus had used his water manipulation to jump straight out of the waves and high into the sky.

I waved my hand, and the ground cracked open. The crater split in half, and air trapped under the dirt burst upward. Then the ground followed, jutting into the sky like a tiny volcano, with Zaxis at the top, his whole body covered in mud, dirt, and scrapes.

He coughed up a mouthful of sand and then continued to wheeze for a full minute afterward. His phoenix flew to the top of the mound I had created—nearly ten feet in the air—and landed next to Zaxis.

"Are you okay?" Forsythe asked. "Can you breathe, my arcanist?"

Zaxis hacked up another round of sand before replying, "I'm... fine..." He patted his own chest and then choked out, "I had that under control. In just a few... minutes... I would've freed myself."

Zelfree laughed once as he climbed the side of the rocky hill. "You nearly gave me a waking nightmare. What's wrong with you?"

"*Me?*" Zaxis spat. "*I* knew something like this would happen! I tried to warn you. Volke is a god-arcanist now. You think this will be the last time this happens? He learned his evocation and killed a man. Now he's learning his—" Zaxis coughed and wheezed another round of dirt from his lungs, interrupting him mid-tirade.

I took a single step backward and surveyed the courtyard with a more critical gaze.

Everything was destroyed. The dirt, the benches, the walkways, the trees... They had all been twisted together in the whirlpool of earth I had created.

And this was barely my fourth week of training. It had taken me *years* to master powers this destructive as a knightmare arcanist.

"I think we should take a break," I said.

Master Zelfree helped Zaxis to his feet and assisted him as they walked down the hill. Forsythe flew around them, his golden eyes locked on to his arcanist.

"I think it's time for a break, too," Zaxis muttered. He rotated his shoulders and then his neck. "I'll heal up, and the next time we spar, I'll be ready for that little move."

"You'll keep sparring with me?" I asked, shocked. "Even after that?"

Zaxis replied with a single nod. "Someone has to do it. And let's face it—I'm your perfect training partner. Well, and Zelfree. No one else has the spine and healing magic to handle you."

<hr>

I sat in my bathtub, staring at the ceiling and dwelling on the terror that Evianna's knightmare magic had created for me. The one where I had killed everyone I knew...

The silence of the bathing room didn't help my mood. After a powerful exhale, I focused my thoughts on how I had manipulated the ground to be like water. It had been so devastating.

"Terrakona," I whispered.

"Yes, Warlord?"

"Do you think manipulating water would be a destructive force or a constructive one?"

"Water is a force that changes everything it touches. Rivers cut through mountains. Lakes flood into valleys. A simple glass of water can dissolve salt and sugar. The Children of Balastar often underestimate the power of erosion and dissolution."

I had never thought of water like that, but Terrakona was right. Water could erode rock. Hail could cut through trees.

"But water also brings life," I said.

"And fire provides warmth," Terrakona replied. **"Water and fire are more similar than some would admit."**

I dwelled on his words for a long time. With a flick of my wrist, I splashed the water in my tub, wondering if I could use my magic to control anything in it. Much like how I concentrated with the rocks out in the courtyard, I focused on the ripples of my bathwater.

Could I actually fight like Gallus the Gray? He had been a monster in the water.

I waved my hand, hoping to move a tiny bit of the water in my tub. Unfortunately, I wasn't prepared for how powerful I had become. With a mere flick of my wrist, the entire tub's worth of water splashed out onto the tile floor of the bathing room. The splash and echo almost made me laugh.

"Not what I was expecting," I muttered to myself. "But at least I was right... I can manipulate the earth and water."

"Impressive," a voice rang out through the washing room.

I turned around, my hands on the side of the tub, ready to jump up if this were the assassin. Instead, it was Adelgis. He stood by the door, calm and collected, his long hair as straight as a ruler. While he normally wore fine robes, tonight he had a tunic and trousers and nothing else. Had he just woken up? It was late—nearly midnight.

"What're you doing here?" I asked.

Adelgis stepped into the bathing room, his footfalls splashing in the water on the floor. He made his way to my porcelain tub without slipping. Then he stood by the side and laced his fingers together.

"Hello," I awkwardly said as I stood and reached for a towel on a nearby stand. With a hasty movement, I wrapped it around my waist and just stood there. "A fine evening we're having, right?"

"Indeed."

I halfheartedly chuckled. "What're you doing here, Adelgis?"

"I came here to thank you for inviting my mother and sister to your celebration. A messenger confirmed their attendance."

I stepped out of the tub. Adelgis didn't move, even as I grabbed a second towel to dry myself. "No need to thank me. Fain requested it. You should thank him."

"I did."

With a smile, I added, "I'm glad they accepted. Hopefully, you'll be able to speak to Cinna again." I meant it, even if I did find Adelgis a bit unsettling at times.

Adelgis stared at the water on the floor for a moment before turning his attention to me. "Fain also told me about swearing himself to you."

"Yeah, well, it's getting weird," I said with a sigh. "I didn't think so many people would do that." I laughed once. "I didn't think anyone would do it *at all*."

"People swear themselves to causes, nations, and royalty all the time. Why would it come as such a shock to you?"

"I don't know." I rubbed down my hair, then my chest, and stopped when I realized I still had a faint scar from the roc talon that had pierced my body. I should've died from that attack, but here I was. "Maybe it's because, not too long ago, I was *no one*. A simple gravedigger on a small island. It feels strange to have people bow and say *my liege* all the time."

"You should think of it as a tool," Adelgis said. "That's what Eventide said to me. If you have the right people on your side, then fighting the Second Ascension won't be so difficult. There are plenty of nations with powerful arcanists. When King Odion swore himself to you, he also swore his armies—and the arcanist knights who swore themselves to him."

I nodded as he spoke. He was right, of course. If the right people swore to me, we'd have the resources and strength to scour the world.

"Volke, I really appreciate that you invited my sister," Adelgis said. "And I was hoping to ask a favor of you."

"What favor?"

"We'll meet my siblings on this journey, there is no doubt in my mind. My brother, Niro, is one of my father's soldiers, and I'm afraid my other siblings are in the same category." Adelgis turned his gaze to the floor. "Volke, would you spare my brothers and sisters? My father pressured them into this, I know it. Just like he used me to nurse his abyssal leech. I... I want to save them from my father's abuse."

"Of course, Adelgis. I'll do whatever I can to help you."

Adelgis glanced over, his eyebrows knitted. "You don't want to think that over for a moment longer?"

I shook my head. "No. I mean, I don't like Niro, but I'll still help you."

There was a long moment of silence between us. Adelgis glanced away, a slight smile on his face. "You really are different, Volke. I understand why the world serpent thought you would make a good judge."

"Why do you say that?"

"Even though we just talked about how you could have arcanists swear themselves to you, that thought never crossed your mind when I asked for your assistance." Adelgis laced his fingers and used them as a rest for his chin. "You just agreed to help. No hesitation. Even though... I didn't tell you about Eventide's ploy to catch the assassin."

I tensed, holding back my anger. Of course Adelgis knew about the assassin. He could hear everyone's thoughts, including Eventide's. And he *hadn't* come to tell me. But after a moment of thought, my rage died.

"I know what it's like to have a lot of pressures," I said, meeting Adelgis's gaze. "I know you struggle with your magic a lot, too. Hearing everyone's thoughts all the time—with no way to stop it—must grate on your nerves and sanity. And Eventide is your guildmaster. It's only natural to do as she asks."

Adelgis stared, unblinking, as I gave my reasoning.

"Plus, I know you've been searching through far-off dreams to gain information about our enemies," I continued. "We only know about your father because of your ceaseless efforts. I'm sure you have your reasons for not telling me things. That's fine. I trust you. And if you need help, I don't need you to do anything for me in return—we're friends."

To my surprise, and shock, Adelgis searched my gaze, his eyes glazing over with tears.

"What's wrong?" I asked, tossing my second towel to the side. "Are you okay?"

"Of course," Adelgis said, faux confidence in his tone. He rubbed at his face with the back of his arm. "I just... I need to thank you. Again. I feel like... you and Fain are the only ones who ever see me. All of me. Even the parts I try to hide from others, like my struggles."

With a nervous chuckle, I shrugged. "Don't worry about it. We've been through a lot, right?"

"You saved my life," Adelgis whispered. He leaned on the side of the tub, his gaze distant, even though he stared straight at his hands. "You let me confront my father, even though..."

The light from the lanterns shimmered and shone bright.

Pieces of it—like rays of sunlight—broke away from the lanterns and then coalesced in midair, a few feet from Adelgis. They formed into a spiral shell the size of a human head, with long tentacles that hung from the shell's opening.

It was an ethereal whelk—Adelgis's eldrin, Felicity.

Her iridescent body glittered in any amount of light. She was a strange creature that floated through the air, spinning and twirling, untethered by gravity. Ethereal whelks had the power over light and dreams, and I could see why. Even their movements seemed dream-like.

"Don't cry, my arcanist," Felicity said, her voice tranquil and happy. "You said you needed your strength to search farther tonight, remember? You mustn't get upset."

Again, Adelgis rubbed at his face. "I'm fine, Felicity. Thank you."

"Fain and Volke might know you well, but I'm with you always," Felicity said. Her tentacles reached out and played with Adelgis's silky black hair. "Whatever hardships you face, I'll be by your side."

Her statements reminded me of Luthair. He had said something similar, and a piece of me felt guilt for being here without him. I knew that was crazy. Luthair had died protecting me. He didn't want me to join him. But still—Master Zelfree was right. I had to be better. If I had been better in the world serpent's lair, I would've been able to save Luthair...

Adelgis took a deep breath and then turned his attention square on me. "Volke, please. No more dark thoughts. I have something else I wish to say."

"Okay," I said. "What is it?"

After another breath, Adelgis stood and then knelt in front of me, the water soaking into his trousers. "I, Adelgis Venrover of Ellios, hereby swear my loyalty to the world serpent arcanist—the Warlord of Magic—Volke Savan."

"You couldn't have waited until after I was done bathing?" I sarcastically asked, motioning to the tub, the towels, and my complete lack of a sword.

Adelgis lifted his head and smiled. "I apologize. I don't need any formalities. All I need to know is whether or not you accept."

"I accept. Of course. All of this wasn't even needed."

Adelgis stood and brushed off the knee he had been kneeling on. Felicity floated around, orbiting his head a few feet in the air.

"Technically, these oaths of loyalty aren't binding unless there are witnesses," Adelgis said matter-of-factly. "Mystical creatures aren't considered suitable for the purposes of being witnesses, so Felicity doesn't count."

I lifted an eyebrow. "Do you want me to go get someone for this bathing room ceremony?"

"No. I was just letting you know for the future. If you have any other arcanists swear to you, make sure they do so in front of others."

"I'll keep that in mind."

Adelgis grabbed my clothes next to the washbasin and handed them to me. "Thank you, Volke. I'm sorry my father has caused the world such hardship, but I swear I'll do everything in my power to make it right."

"Thank you," I said as I took my new outfit. I slipped the tunic over my head and then put the trousers on under the towel.

"Eventide asked me to keep the assassin a secret because she's worried about your ability to concentrate," Adelgis said. He held his hands behind his back and frowned. "I agreed to keep it secret because of two things I learned while observing the soul forge's dreams."

"The other god-creature?" I asked.

Adelgis nodded once. "Firstly, my father has been bonded to his god-creature longer than you have, and he's a natural for developing his abilities. If you're too unfocused or concerned about trivial matters, you might fall significantly behind."

"R-Right."

"And secondly, I know the identity of the assassin outside of your compound. Their magic is preventing my ability to hear their thoughts, but the assassin and mystical creature have slipped up twice, and that's when I learned about them. I haven't told anyone, for fear of what might happen."

"Who is it?" I asked, already fearing the answer.

"My older sister, Venae Venrover."

EIGHTEENTH CELEBRATION

Now I understood why Adelgis had asked me to help him protect his siblings—and why he had hesitated to tell me any of this. He didn't want to kill his sister, the assassin skulking around the compound.

"Is she an arcanist?" I asked.

Adelgis nodded. "She's bonded to a white hart."

Curse the abyssal hells...

I had disliked white harts ever since I had faced a plague-ridden one in the Endless Mire. Normally, they were legendary creatures of stealth and avoidance. White harts were some of the most difficult creatures to locate, and their breeding grounds had been a mystery for hundreds of years. With their invisibility and lack of footprints, most occult hunters couldn't find them.

No wonder Eventide was having problems locating Venae.

I paced the room, my bare feet splashing in the water, my thoughts on distant things. How could I subdue a white hart arcanist? Perhaps if I just killed her eldrin—taking away her magic—I'd be able to bring her in without taking her life.

With a quick swipe of my hand, I brushed back my hair.

Part of me wanted to laugh. Fighting a single white hart arcanist wouldn't be difficult. Another part of me knew I shouldn't jump to conclusions.

"Can you tell me anything about your sister?" I asked.

Adelgis rubbed at his arm. "I don't know much about her, and even when I search her dreams, they're fleeting. Her magic obfuscates her presence, so I've only been able to hear her thoughts for brief periods of time."

I turned to face him, my eyebrows knitted. "You don't know your own sister?" I couldn't imagine not knowing a thing about Illia.

"Venae is much older than I am. She and my brother, Yevin, are twins, and they were very close, almost inseparable. I think my father was more hands-on with their education and childhood than he was with me or Cinna. The two of them have always been distant, and of the pair, Venae rarely spoke. Yevin and I occasionally exchanged words, but those were only at family celebrations or at the start of the new year."

"What kind of arcanist is Yevin?"

The darkness beyond the windows told me it was late, but I didn't feel the least bit tired. A part of me felt powerful—especially after I had almost killed Zaxis—and I wanted to end this problem once and for all.

Adelgis walked to my side. "Yevin was once a sibyl arcanist, but his eldrin tragically died." He shook his head. "My father was upset... He said he would help Yevin become an arcanist again, but I never heard anything further. Yevin is too old to participate in a normal trial of worth. That was many years ago, though... He could've found something to bond with. I just wouldn't know."

"Okay, so Yevin probably isn't helping Venae?" I scratched at the stubble on my chin. "Do you think any of your other siblings would be nearby? Like Niro?"

"I doubt it. I think I would've seen their dreams if they were nearby. Or perhaps heard their names in the fleeting glimpses I get of Venae's thoughts, but I've seen nothing."

"She's all alone?" I asked, skeptical.

Adelgis nodded once. "I believe so."

"A single white hart arcanist thinks she can kill a god-arcanist?" I almost laughed. "Do we really need to be worried? I'm being serious."

White harts weren't known for their fighting or destructive powers. They didn't have poison or fire, and while they had golden antlers, their arcanists didn't have any notable combative abilities. They were creatures capable of great secrets, not strength.

"She'll likely have weapons made of the apoch dragon," Adelgis whispered.

I held my breath. The apoch dragon *could* kill a god-arcanist, that was certain. Retribution cut through *anything*. What if she had a similar weapon? I had been so confident about beating her two seconds ago, and now I felt as though my arrogance could've cost me my life.

I couldn't underestimate the Second Ascension.

No matter who they sent after me—a will-o-wisp arcanist to a pyroclastic dragon arcanist—I had to take it seriously. I had to assume they had some way to end my life, even if it seemed ludicrous.

"If you find out anything from her thoughts, please tell me," I said.

Adelgis slowly nodded, but he frowned at the same time. "I've been trying, but I've also been attempting to follow my father's movements as well as sift through that pirate's memories."

"Markus?" I asked.

"Yes. There isn't much information, but he clearly knows my father needs the corpses of mystical creatures."

"He's going to give them a new life or something," I

muttered, recalling the strange dreams where the griffin had spawned. "I'm not sure how he does it—or how many he can do it to—but according to Markus's memories, your father wants hundreds of corpses."

"Every moment I try to focus on my sister is a moment I'm not concentrating on those other tasks."

I hated that our enemy seemed to have the upper hand. They were so many steps ahead of us, likely because they had had decades to plan their schemes. As the world serpent arcanist, wasn't I supposed to handle this? Yet I still didn't have a full grasp on my powers.

I stared at my hand as I clenched it into a fist.

"Don't worry about keeping an eye on your sister," I said, glaring. "I'll handle her—even if she comes wearing a whole suit of armor made of the apoch dragon. You need to focus on watching Theasin."

"You'd rather me focus on my father than the pirate?"

"Markus has served his purpose. I understand more about our enemy now. We need to focus on moving forward, and Theasin is our biggest threat currently."

Adelgis shook his head. "That pirate said that Calisto is going to deliver corpses to Thronehold and then travel to the sky titan arcanist. We'll probably end up seeing Calisto when we confront Theasin. The pirate could potentially have other information for us."

"One major world-ending problem at time," I said with a half-smile. "Maybe he knows something about the sky titan's location, but let's just survive my birthday—words I never thought I'd have to utter—and then we'll move on to the next problem on the list."

"As you wish," Adelgis said with a slight bow of his head. "But please don't focus on my sister. Eventide is right—if you can't concentrate on your training, you won't develop your magic properly."

The last ten days had been rough. I had felt apathetic and lethargic. If I wanted to advance faster, and properly, I had to push all of these negative thoughts from my head. Just like Zelfree and Illia—who were caught up on past grudges with Calisto—if I allowed myself to dwell on outside factors, I'd only hinder myself.

"Thank you, Adelgis," I said. "I'll try to keep everything you've said in mind."

He replied with a tired smile. "Thank *you*, Volke. I appreciate you being willing to forgive my sister, even if she's come to take your life."

"Don't mention it."

The next four days were better.

My magic wasn't unusual to me anymore, but I was afraid of using it too much while sparring. Zaxis continued training with me, like he had said he would, and now he seemed more prepared than ever. He started jumping more—leaping off the broken trees and benches, and relying less on solid footing to fight. He used *gravity* to help with his overhead swings. Metal knuckles to the face hurt a lot more when they came from above.

My basalt bones didn't seem to break under the force of his blows, though.

And when I punched him back, the obsidian on my knuckles shattered and remained in his skin, like tiny flakes of knives. My rocks grew back, but his injuries lingered.

The information was beyond useful.

The night before my birthday, there was no training. The compound servants said they needed to beautify the place, so the courtyard was off-limits. It didn't matter, anyway. Apparently, I needed to beautify myself as well.

I was starting to hate these rituals. Well, except the bathing part. I didn't mind sitting in the warm water after a long day of sparring matches and magic use. The heat eased the ache in my sore muscles, and it reminded me of Karna's analogy of my magic.

When I slept this time, it was gloriously peaceful. No dreams. No interruptions. I woke when I naturally would have and stretched across my bed, happier than I had been in a long time.

I sat up, surprised by how much light streamed in through my window. It was nearly noon. I calmed myself with the fact that the celebration wasn't supposed to begin for several more hours. It was an evening party, after all.

Determined to dress myself without anyone's assistance, I grabbed my *birthday clothes* and hastily pulled them on.

I didn't know who had designed them or picked them out, but my outfit was sleek and black. Stars had been stitched onto the edges of the sleeves, and the phases of the moon had been etched into the silver buttons of the shirt. I kept it slightly open to reveal my god-arcanist mark, but I took a long while admiring the odd details.

Since there was an assassin after me, I secured my sword to my waist with my belt and sheath. The brown leather clashed with the rest of my outfit, but I didn't care.

Someone entered my room—not through the door, but through magic. I felt them long before they made their presence known, and I remained tense, wondering what they would try. They walked up behind me, silent and slow.

Was it Venae?

"Do you like the outfit?"

I smiled to myself as I turned around to face Evianna. A part of me *wished* it had been Venae, though. If I dealt with her first, I wouldn't have to stay vigilant at the celebration.

"I do like it," I said as I showed off the sleeves. "I'm not really into clothing, but this reminds me of Luthair." I glanced over at his cape hanging on a hook by the door. My father had brought it over from the atlas turtle, and just having it close was a comfort.

Evianna wore a similar outfit—sleek, black cloth with some stars stitched onto the hem of her tunic. She also had a cowl and scale-like gloves, both a darker shade of darkness than the rest of her outfit. It contrasted nicely with her white hair, which had been styled in curls.

"I asked the tailors to add those details," Evianna said as she walked to my side. She placed her hands on the long sleeves and smoothed them out. "It's your first birthday present."

"First?" I asked.

Evianna clapped her hands together once. "That's right. I mean, I'm sure *tons* of people will have gifts for you, but I'm trying to make mine useful."

"You think people will have tons of gifts?" I walked over to the bed and grabbed my fancy boots—the ones I had never worn before. "I don't think anyone knows me well enough to get me a gift."

Evianna rolled her eyes and laughed. "Oh, it's adorable how much you don't know about being royalty. First off, *everyone* will get you a gift, and they're all going to try to outdo each other."

I glanced up, my eyes narrowed. "This happened to you?"

"Of course. Every birthday we'd had diplomats and nobles from all over come to King Drake Castle. They wanted my *favor* —" Evianna said the last word with a long sigh, "—or my mother's favor, or they just wanted to look *impressive* in front of all the other nobles, like gift-giving was a contest and only the biggest gift won."

Evianna paced around the room, her attention on the far wall.

"Well, there are worse things in life than tons of gifts, right?" I asked with a shrug.

"They didn't care about me," Evianna said as she came to an abrupt halt. Then she turned on her heel and faced me. Her expression softened as she continued, "They had no idea what I liked or disliked. They got me gilded dolls and ivory bedframes." When she sighed again, it was melancholy. Then she shook the gloom away and faced me with a smile. "But I wanted my gifts to you to be different. Something meaningful."

I glanced at the sleeves again as I stood. "You did an amazing job. I love this. Thank you, Evianna."

Her face grew pink as she smiled widely. "Of course, Volke."

When I strode over to her and held out my elbow, her ears grew a darker shade of red. My cheeks burned slightly, but I felt ten times lighter the moment she wrapped her hand around my arm.

"Let's go to this birthday celebration, shall we?" I asked.

The Savan Compound had transformed overnight.

The old sailing paintings had been replaced with tapestries of the world serpent. The dusty windows and furniture had been cleaned and polished. Fresh flowers of every color sat in vases in every corner of every room, providing the rich scent of the countryside.

The best part of the decorations were the glowstones, though. They had been placed throughout the compound, and several hung in nets, creating makeshift chandeliers. The glittering lights also reminded me of the stars, even in the afternoon.

And the courtyard—I didn't know how many people they had brought in to fix it, but it had to have been a couple dozen. There were new trees, stone benches, a tiny waterway down the center, and topiary bushes cut in the shape of the world serpent. Unless someone had magic that grew entire landscapes in the blink of an eye, all this had to have been brought in from the outside.

The worst decoration, by far, was the clusters of soldiers. Javin knights and Antihelm spearmen stood in groups of three in every room and hallway. They regarded me with bows and muttered greetings, but they never moved out of their designated positions.

It seemed like an extreme amount of effort for a single night of celebration.

"There's the birthday boy," Zaxis shouted as I entered the courtyard.

He and Illia strode together along the newly created granite walkway. To my surprise, Zaxis had ditched his salamander scale armor and donned red robes with phoenix feathers sewn onto the collar. They reminded me of the clothing people sometimes wore on the Isle of Ruma, but he had gotten so big and burly, his outfit didn't quite fit. Still, the plumage of the phoenix feathers drew the eye away from that.

There was also a tuft of white fur on the edge of his robe's right sleeve. Was it rizzel fur?

Illia wore a white dress that pooled around her feet, like a liquid puddle of snowy sand. Silver lines were stitched on the sides, giving her a rizzel-like appearance. It fit her well, though she moved as though the gown were limiting her movement in an irritating way.

Illia's dress had a single phoenix feather stitched onto one of the straps, the only spot of color on the pure white outfit.

Nicholin sat on her shoulder like always, but this time he had a tiny red vest on. When he caught me staring, he lifted his head high.

"Nicholin said he needed some *panache*," Illia muttered, rolling her eye. "So we had the tailor make him a little outfit."

"I'm beautiful, I know," Nicholin said, buffing his paw on his chest. "Everyone can admire, but no one can touch."

Without any prompting, Zaxis's phoenix came hopping down the path, his wings wide. He, too, had a little outfit—a tiny top hat and little bracelets on his long, heron-like legs. A line of soot followed him as he wandered to his arcanist's legs.

"Do I look okay, my arcanist?" Forsythe asked. "Appropriate for this festive occasion?"

Zaxis leaned over, adjusted the top hat to fit a tad better, and then stood straight. "There. No one is more dapper than my phoenix."

Nicholin instantly deflated, his body practically liquid as he jellified on Illia's shoulder. "I'm dapper, too," he whispered, his voice nearly a warble.

"You definitely are," I said.

Nicholin perked up and wagged his tail. "Go on. How dapper? The *most* dapper?"

"Uh, sure. In my opinion, the most dapper."

Nicholin stood straight again. "Perfect. The world serpent's judgment trumps a phoenix arcanist's! I'm the best now!"

The phoenix and rizzel gave each other odd looks, their feathers and fur raised. I'd had no idea it was such a competition.

I turned my attention back to Zaxis and Illia. "I'm surprised you're both dressed up so nicely."

They shot me glowers.

Then Zaxis huffed and lifted a hand into the air. "Have you forgotten who you're talking to? I'm Zaxis *Ren*, from the *Ren* family on the Isle of Ruma. I have a reputation to maintain." He glanced between me and Evianna. "You guys decided you want to match as well, huh? It's not as clever as Illia's and mine, but I guess it's fine."

Illia jabbed him in the ribs. Then she turned to me and said, "Gravekeeper William will be here tonight." She straightened her rizzel eyepatch. "I wanted him to see us looking our best."

I slicked back my black hair and nodded. "Oh, good."

Hopefully, he wouldn't see me get assassinated.

Evianna tightened her grip on my arm. "Your adopted father, right? I want to meet him. A proper meeting."

"All right. I'm sure that can happen."

A trumpet sounded near the gate of the compound.

Illia fluffed her wavy, brown hair, like a delicate lady preparing for an elegant soirée. "Your guests are arriving, Warlord. We should go greet them."

33

GIFTS

Z axis, Illia, Evianna, Nicholin, Forsythe, and I made our way to the foyer of the main building, guided by the many tapestries of the world serpent. When we arrived, Guildmaster Eventide, Master Yesna, Captain Devlin, and Master Zelfree were waiting, like silent castle guards. The front doors were held open by Javin soldiers, and a line of people waited outside, ready to enter.

"I think Zaxis and I should mingle with the guests as they enter the courtyard," Illia whispered. She patted my arm and motioned me forward. "We'll see you later."

I nodded, and the two of them left the foyer the same way they had come in. A part of me wanted to go with them.

"Do you want me to leave as well?" Evianna asked, her voice distant.

I took her arm and held tightly. "No. You were with me in the depths of the world serpent's lair. Why shouldn't you be with me here?"

Evianna's face reddened once again. She said nothing—she just tightened her grip on me. The shadows around her feet shifted, and I knew her knightmare was happy as well, showing it in her own shadowy way.

Before we could say anything else, Guildmaster Eventide motioned me over. The moment I got to her side, she grabbed my shoulders and positioned me in the middle of the room, with Master Yesna and Captain Devlin on one side, and herself and Zelfree on the other. Evianna stayed close, and no one protested her presence.

I didn't even really get to look at Eventide's or the others' outfits—other than they were all clothed in black, similar to my own attire.

"Your guests will be arriving shortly," Eventide said under her breath. "Accept their gifts, but don't speak with them. You can socialize afterward."

I didn't get a chance to reply. Eventide faced the front doors, and then the soldiers allowed the guests inside.

They came in a line. Each one bowing and then having their servants or porters place a gift on the floor of the foyer. Evianna had been right about one thing: There were a lot of gifts, and they were huge.

"I'm Lady Hawke, the ruler of Whitecrest," the first woman inside said. She bowed deeply, her fur-lined clothing giant and impressive. Her porters carried in a large blanket, obviously magical with its glittering chill. A trinket? It probably wasn't an artifact. It was made from the fur of yetis. "This blanket will remain a cool temperature, no matter the heat around it," she said.

The "blanket" could accommodate ten people, and the porters had to roll it into a giant swirl in order to fit it all inside.

The second attendee also wore furs and leather. "Ah, Warlord, it's a pleasure to meet you. I'm Lord Feron, the ruler of North Peak. I've brought you a statue for your eighteenth birthday." Servants carried in a statue of the world serpent so large, it almost didn't fit through the front doors. "It's made from the bones of whales and covered in scales of jade and ruby."

Feron bowed so deeply, I thought he might kneel and place his head on the ground. I wasn't sure how to respond, other than with a curt nod of my head.

I knew North Peak was a region rich in ores, gemstones, and deadly rocks. Whales traveled to their shores to die, or so I had read. According to old poems, it was an honor to keep the remains of a whale nearby.

I stared at the gaudy statue that twinkled under the glowstone light.

Lucky me.

The parade of guests was a bit overwhelming. The next few were introduced so quickly, I barely remembered them. Even their gifts all seemed to blur together as the pile grew larger and more extravagant.

Guildmaster Renshaw of the Trapper Guild came bearing bags of star shards. When the porters presented them, I had to stop myself from gasping. The guild handed over nearly forty shards—an outrageous amount—before the guildmaster headed into the courtyard for the festivities.

I couldn't wait to use those to create more trinkets and artifacts, but I knew I couldn't break away from the party to go do that—even if I fantasized about doing so.

Guildmaster Tillis of the Shikara Guild had men bring in three full sets of armor, each one more magical than the last. They had been made from the scales of tempest dragons, one copper and steel, one made of bone, and the last one had an aquamarine coloration. Images of the world serpent were painted on the half-plate scales, creating intricate designs.

King Hessan brought five curved magical swords.

Empress Cao presented me with three hundred gold coins.

Guildmaster Jonah of the Southern Flier Guild presented an entire glass cage of star moths.

That gift caught my eye for some time. It had been years since I had last seen a star moth. They were so beautiful, and they could warn when corrupted magic was nearby.

I tried to acknowledge everyone who presented themselves and their gifts, but I stuck to Eventide's directions, and I spoke to no one. The guildmasters and world leaders seemed a bit disappointed, but everyone headed inside, toward the courtyard, probably hoping to speak with me later.

I wouldn't let Eventide down. Although I had never studied diplomacy, I would make sure I did whatever it took to gain allies against the Second Ascension.

Just when I was preparing myself to head into the party, King Odion stepped through the front doors.

He wore a cape made of white and black feathers, no doubt made from the wings of his twilight dragon, Hasdrubal. It flowed behind him, creating a long train that swished across the ground. Underneath he wore the same armor he had worn during the magi cross, and I wondered if he knew of the assassin.

Odion ran a steady hand through his white and metallic-silver hair. "I come with well wishes for your birthday, my liege." He stepped closer to me than the rest had, and when he was within a few feet, Eventide sidestepped in the way, blocking Odion from getting to me.

"I mean no disrespect," Odion said. "I merely wish to give the Warlord of Magic his gift."

"The gift table is there," Eventide said, motioning to the pile so thick that the table couldn't be seen.

"It's something more personal than that."

Odion held up a hand. In his palm was a delicate bracelet made from silk thread. It was the same type of bracelet worn by all the Javin soldiers.

"It's okay, Guildmaster Eventide," I said. "Odion swore

himself to me, remember? I think it's okay if he gives me a gift personally."

She nodded once and then stepped aside.

King Odion drew closer and held out his hand. The bracelet didn't have many colors—just two. One thread of green, and one thread of black. What had Odion said? The black was for kills, and the green symbolized the death of a loved one.

Luthair.

"This is worn by all Javin warriors," Odion said as he undid the clasp and carefully placed it around my left wrist. "It is to honor everyone who came before us. To remember our victories and our losses. A *warrior's mark* for all to see."

Then he bowed to me, fluttering his feathery cape out behind him as he did so.

"I have one final birthday gift," he said as he remained in the bowing position. "Potential colors for a warrior's mark are rarely added to our official list, but I think we've reached a new age of magic that requires an additional thread. Gold will be added—a warrior will add a gold strand to their warrior's mark for every god-arcanist or god-creature they kill."

I held my breath, and the others in the room tensed.

Although I knew I'd have to fight Theasin, and likely kill him, I hadn't been thinking about it. And I certainly hadn't been thinking about how I would immortalize the event.

Odion stood straight and smiled, seemingly undisturbed by his own proclamation. His icy eyes were vibrant and focused— they always drew my attention. "I hope you have a wonderful evening, my liege." He shot Evianna a sideways glance, but it was fleeting. He never acknowledged her beyond that.

Then Odion headed off into the courtyard, confident in all regards. His many attendants— as well as his star tiger arcanist —followed behind, protecting him like a swarm of bees guarded their nest.

I exhaled and hoped this would soon be over. Maybe I could enjoy the festivities and relax, if only for one evening.

"Wait," I said, turning to Eventide. "I thought Adelgis's mother and sister would be arriving?"

The guildmaster nodded once. "They confirmed their attendance, but Zelfree says they haven't yet arrived. Perhaps later tonight, I can introduce you."

With a sigh, I turned my attention to the front doors. Nothing. The last of the guests had filtered in, including the many assistants and servants. Hundreds of people were here, but not Cinna.

But before I exited the foyer, one last guest hurried through the door, almost late. How had I almost forgotten? Gravekeeper William had been my father, and one of my greatest supporters, throughout my entire life. Unlike these royals and guildmasters—who hadn't known I existed, or even cared if I lived or died until I had become the world serpent arcanist— William had been there for me.

He walked into the foyer, not surrounded by attendants, servants, or porters, but still, he had a presence. I was over six feet tall, but William was a good six inches taller than I was. I had lean muscle and a confident stance, but William had tree-trunk legs, arms crafted from years of hard labor, and the commanding aura of a naval officer.

I walked forward, breaking free of Eventide's formation and even Evianna's grasp. William rushed to meet me, and we embraced in the middle of the foyer, his mountain of a body reminding me of days spent on Ruma as a child.

"Come 'ere," William said as he tightened his grip around me. "I can't believe what you've been up to, Volke. No one on the Isle of Ruma can believe it, either. The second I got your letter, the whole city was abuzz."

I released him but kept him at arm's length. "I would've loved to see that."

"Ha!" William shouted, his voice rumbling up from his gut. "The looks on their faces. My boy, the gravedigger—the world serpent arcanist."

"I know. I can barely believe it myself."

He yanked me in for one last embrace and then quickly released me. With an exhale and a wide smile on his clean-shaven face, he relaxed. "I wasn't sure what to get ya for this fine celebration... Everything I thought of seemed too small, ya know? I'd hate to be the rube who brought something embarrassin'."

"Don't worry about it," I said. Then I pointed to the pile of gifts. "I have more than I know what to do with. Trust me. Your presence here is gift enough."

When I turned around, Evianna was right behind me. I stopped myself from running into her, but then I wrapped an arm around her waist and pulled her closer. Her eyes went wide as I held her close. "William, I have someone you should meet. This is Princess Evianna Velleta, of the Argo Empire. And she's a knightmare arcanist."

His eyebrows slowly traveled upward, straight for his hairline. "I see. Ya really have come a long way in the world, lad. A *princess* by your side?"

Evianna broke free of my hold to stand straight and proper. "It's a pleasure to meet you, kind sir. Volke holds you in high regard, which means I do as well."

While I had never dreamt of introducing Gravekeeper William to a princess of another nation, this moment felt right. I savored the interaction and feeling, wishing it could last longer. I knew the rest of the night wouldn't be quite as pleasant.

Guildmaster Eventide reminded me of her presence by clearing her throat. She motioned to the long hallway that led straight to the courtyard.

"Warlord, it's rude to keep your guests waiting. I suggest

you mingle with the others, at least for a short while, to let them know how much you appreciate their presence and gifts."

I nodded once, my peaceful moment already over. "Of course," I said as I headed in that direction.

But when I went to pass her, she stopped me with a raised finger. "As a guildmaster myself, I feel it's only appropriate I give you a gift as well."

"I think I already have enough."

"This is different." Eventide held out her hand, her fingers curled around a small object.

I took the item, and the moment it touched my palm, I knew it was deeply magical. Something pulsed within it, like a faint heartbeat. I stared for a moment, wondering what tiny object could have such power.

It was a guild pendant. But unlike the others, which were copper, bronze, and silver—this pendant was made of tannish bone. On one side it read: Volke Savan the World Serpent God-Arcanist. On the other side was the Frith Guild symbol, an ornate sword and shield design, but it was different. A star of magic was carved between the two symbols.

"What's this?" I asked.

"The Frith Guild has evolved," Eventide stated. "And now our symbol will reflect that. We're knights who stand against corruption, both mundane and magical."

I secured the guild pendant around my neck, proud to display to the world that I still belonged. The pendant hung to my collarbone, just above my god-arcanist mark. When I grazed my fingers across it, I felt a subtle shift of magic.

"I crafted this myself," Eventide said. "It's made from the shell bone of Gentel and imbued with my true form magic. When you hold it, and concentrate your magic, you can summon forth a barrier that will surround you. Very few things can penetrate atlas turtle shields, but remember that you won't be able pass through it, either."

"Thank you." I held the pendant tightly in my grip. "It's a fantastic gift. I'll treasure it forever."

"Now it's time for you to enjoy the party," Eventide said, motioning me on.

With William and Evianna on either side of me, I headed toward the courtyard, my mind almost distracted enough to forget about Adelgis's sister who had come to kill me.

I had forgotten most people's names, which was unfortunate.

The individuals I personally admired were adventurers. Most rulers and guildmasters weren't on my list, for a variety of reasons. Not all guilds fought pirates and saved people. The Shikara Guild was filled with architect arcanists—which was a mouthful. They designed boats of all types and imbued magical items and artifacts to help with travel.

What was the guildmaster's name again? Despite the fact she was standing right in front of me, I couldn't recall. I had only gotten a few feet into the courtyard when she ambushed me. The entire time, she spoke about boats and houses, and the rivers of the Argo Empire.

William and Evianna had left to obtain their food, but they hadn't returned.

My stomach grumbled.

"We have several plans drawn," the guildmaster of the Shikara Guild said. She held a small glass of wine close as she stared up at me—she had to be five feet tall. "If the rivers running into the Argo Empire were wider, we could sell our designs to the many noblemen there. That's where you come in. Helping to improve the river system."

"That sounds fascinating," I said. "But I'm sorry, I'll have to look at the plans a little more closely before I decide anything.

Rivers run through multiple nations, after all. Consideration has to be taken."

"By all means, please think over my plans." The guildmaster smiled wide. Her arcanist mark was a seven-pointed star with a mermaid woven between the points. "We could make an alliance and improve the world at the same time. I'll leave my proposal with the guildmaster of the Frith Guild."

"Thank you. If your plan is as ingenious as you say, I'm sure an alliance would be advantageous."

I moved around her and headed into the courtyard. The mystical creatures were a little more exciting to me than the people. Dragons weren't in attendance—they were too large—and neither were any creatures confined to the waters, like the mermaid. But there were others, including a golden sphinx!

With enthusiasm in my step, I attempted to cross the beautifully lit courtyard, but I only made it ten steps in before I was stopped. A tall man with an imp arcanist mark on his forehead, and his blond hair slicked back, smiled down at me. He was as tall as Gravekeeper William, but he was a twig in comparison.

His imp sat on the man's bony shoulder. It was an emaciated creature with black skin, bright red eyes, and a smile that literally stretched from one ear to the other. According to legend, imps were creatures of laughter and mischief, but also strategy and scheming. The greatest imps had served legendary tacticians.

"I see you're interested in my eldrin," the man said, his gaze wandering my body, starting at my feet and ending at my head.

I lifted an eyebrow. "I've never seen an imp in person. Does he have a name?"

"Never mind that." The man—maybe he was a ruler of some sort?—stroked his chin. "You're a handsome man. Sturdy. You will suffice." He dismissively waved his hand. "I accepted the invitation because I heard the world serpent arcanist was unwed."

I nodded but stopped halfway. "What?"

"My daughter is a talented singer, painter, scholar, and athlete of extraordinary beauty. She deserves only the best. I've denied every other man who has come to court her, but I think you might do." He motioned with a quick twist of his wrist. "Fraya, my sunflower, let me introduce you to *the* god-arcanist of Fortuna."

The woman he wanted stood in a group of people across the courtyard. The man pointed, but his daughter never saw, apparently.

The imp's smile dominated its whole face. "We can seal our alliance with family. Good deal, ain't it? Wait till you see her."

"I'm flattered," I drawled. "But I have somewhere important to be. Maybe we can talk later."

With fast footwork, I shifted around the man. Was the imp arcanist a king of some sort? No. He didn't have a dragon. He was likely a duke or marquess or some other high nobleman. I wasn't interested in marrying his daughter, even if she was talented and beautiful. I knew plenty of extraordinary women —most of whom I considered gorgeous—and none of them were faking their interest in me now that I was a world serpent arcanist.

I managed to get fifteen feet away from the imp arcanist when *another* man practically rushed me. He was stockier than most—heavy around the belly, though he wore tailored robes that fit him well. Even the necklace he wore around his neck had been linked together to fit just right and not look tight.

"Excuse m-me," the man said, bowing his head several times, "I need to speak with you."

With a deep breath, I tried to remain regal and confident. I could feel everyone's collective gazes following my every movement.

"One moment," I said as I tried to step around him and head for the food. Maybe if I had something to nibble on, I would have the energy to persuade these people into helping us. I didn't want to appear tired in front of anyone.

"Wait," the man said as I tried to dodge him.

He held up his hands. I stopped dead in my tracks, shocked by his appearance.

His hands were scarred—from the tips of his fingers down to his wrists. They were fading white scars, like hundreds of tiny knives had cut into him all at once.

With a frown, the man said, "Please, listen. For just a moment!" He motioned to his forehead, and I examined his arcanist mark. A dragon was laced around the star points, but it wasn't a dragon of flesh and scales. It was a dragon made of patchwork pieces.

"You're a relickeeper arcanist," I said, lifting an eyebrow.

He nodded. "My name is Santonio Gerrero." He stepped closer—limiting our distance to a few inches—and then lowered his voice. "Please, Warlord. I need to discuss something important with you. I'm in charge of archaeology for the Finders Guild."

"I don't remember meeting your guildmaster," I muttered, thinking back.

"That's because he wasn't invited." Santonio grabbed my shoulder and held tight. "I came as a guest to another guildmaster." He held up his scarred hand again, and I realized he couldn't use his fingers properly. The scarring had damaged his muscles and tendons. "I've been trying to uncover a building for a long time. It's submerged underwater. But it's important. I need your help, and *only* your help."

"There he is!" someone from across the courtyard shouted. "We told you to wait inside!"

I spotted four Javin knights pushing their way toward me and Santonio. They glowered underneath their plated helmets, and all of them had pistols and swords hanging from their belts. One was a salamander arcanist, and a small flame sprouted in the palm of his hand as he approached.

Santonio pulled me closer. "It's a f-fortress," he said, so fast, he tripped over his words. "Or maybe a castle! It's an old structure from a time long gone. It has no windows or doors. I need help getting inside. It's protected with powerful magic. If I can just get inside—*all my focus and research*—I know it has something to do with—"

The Javin knights took hold of Santonio. One grabbed his left arm, another grabbed his right, and the third stood behind him. The salamander arcanist shoved Santonio away from me.

Santonio's words buzzed through my thoughts. A castle with no windows or doors? Like in my dreams? Was he talking about the same thing? Or was I grasping and imagining because of my fatigue?

Or perhaps he was trying to trick me.

"I apologize, Warlord," the Javin arcanist said with a deep bow. "This man is part of Guildmaster Tillis's group. We told all the attendants to wait inside for the performance part of the evening, but some have refused to listen."

There was a *performance scheduled* for the evening? A part of me was impressed this entire celebration could be thrown together in a few weeks. Another part of me wished I had practiced my etiquette with King Odion. I needed to seem more... regal. Somehow.

"Thank you," I said to the knights, trying hard to sound confident and decisive. "I appreciate your vigilance."

The soldiers shoved Santonio away.

"Please come see me," Santonio said, desperation in his tone. "Only you can help me! It'll be a great discovery from an age long thought lost!"

"Should we throw him out of the party?" the Javin arcanist asked.

I shook my head. "No. Just return him to the guild he came with."

I didn't know what Santonio was talking about, but I did know that relickeepers were creatures drawn to magical items, places, and materials. Perhaps Santonio *had* found something interesting. What did he want me to do? Travel with him to that fortress and alter the terrain so he could get inside? Perhaps after this was over, or I had better control of my powers. Then I could go to all kinds of archaeological dig sites and maybe solve a couple of mysteries.

Determined to escape the arcanists slowly closing in on me like sharks on chum, I hurried to one of the many tables serving the guests. Platters of crab, fish, and shrimp were served on thin sticks. Hundreds of glasses and several jugs of wine were out and ready for new owners.

An attendant manning the food spotted me examining the plates. He straightened himself, reached for a bowl on a side table, and then handed it to me over the piles of the other food.

"This is for you, Warlord," he said, bowing his head.

I took the bowl, confused. They had made me my own special dish? What was it?

To my surprise, the bowl was filled with fish stew, along with a single metal spoon

My favorite.

"Your sister instructed the kitchen to prepare your favorite meal," the man said. "I hope the cooks captured the flavors of your home isle."

Illia...

I stared at the ceramic bowl for a prolonged moment. An ironic chuckle escaped me. Out of all the gifts I had gotten today, the stew had touched me the most.

Then again, what if the assassin knew I would come here and had this set aside in order to poison me? Was I being too paranoid? No. It was unlucky. The assassin wasn't going to strike when there were so many arcanists around who could potentially save my life. In the crowd I could see a caladrius arcanist—renowned healers—and two phoenix arcanists. Poison wasn't the way to kill me.

I held the bowl close and tried to walk away from the table, but the moment I turned around, there were already several arcanists waiting for me, hovering around with eager expressions. Even if the bowl was poisoned, my rumbling stomach yearned for the nostalgia of my youth.

"Warlord," one woman said. "If you have time, I brought maps with me. We should discuss beneficial weather patterns."

A man sidestepped in front of her, his tricorn cap adorned with a black feather. "Warlord, I think I have more important things to talk about than *the weather*. And I have more arcanists under my command than this woman."

"*How dare you*," she growled.

I held up a hand. "Please, calm down. No need to get upset. We have all night."

The celebration was scheduled to last until dawn, or so I had heard.

"Before I commit to anything, I want my demands met," the woman bellowed. "I demand to be heard."

I gritted my teeth.

Damn. It was probably my own fault. I had set a precedent by offering the Fortuna Council protection and then giving the Antihelm queen my word that I'd alter her land. Now everyone expected something from me.

I wished they would just wait until I had the privacy and space to hear them all out. Before I could voice my concerns— mainly about hashing out matters of diplomacy around a buffet table—I was stopped by Evianna. She rose from the darkness, stepping out of the shadows like only a knightmare arcanist could.

A few nearby individuals pointed and gasped.

I didn't blame them. It was an impressive sight.

Evianna threw back her white hair, ignoring the people at the celebration. She held out her hand and motioned me close with a tilt of her head.

I grabbed her open palm and then she yanked me forward. We both fell, but instead of hitting the dirt of the courtyard, we plummeted into the darkness. Evianna's knightmare magic enveloped me, allowing us to travel through the shadows at rapid speeds. When I had been with Luthair, I could mildly sense where we were traveling, but when traveling with Evianna, she was in control of our destination.

My fish stew... would it be okay?

Within a matter of seconds, I stumbled forward, my footing unbalanced. Harsh ocean winds whipped around me as I staggered out of the darkness. It took me a short moment to realize I was now on the roof of the main compound building.

I sucked in air and waved my arms to steady myself. To my relief, most of the stew was still in the bowl. It had shadow-stepped with us as easily as my clothes.

The slant of the tile roof made it difficult to get comfortable. I leaned forward and then admired the clear sky above. Stars twinkled throughout the dusky evening.

The bustle of my celebration echoed in the courtyard below, but up here, it was calm. Serene.

Evianna stood next to me, smirking. "Gift number two. Saving you from the crowds."

"As much as I enjoy spending time with you, I probably shouldn't abandon my own celebration," I said.

"I told you. I've had to deal with stuffy celebrations my whole life." Evianna ran up the roof to the very top, right where the two sides of the roof connected. She gracefully balanced on the rounded portion of the roof. "This is the plan—you stay up here for an hour, and then you return to the celebration. But don't walk among the guests. Summon them a few at a time to a private room."

I opened my mouth to question her, but I stopped before I formed any words. Having private meetings would likely make things easier.

"It'll make your guests feel special." Evianna tapped the side of her head. "Tell them you wanted a chance to talk to them in private, because they're *so* important." She chortled as she continued, "Trust me. Everyone here thinks they're the most distinguished guest. If they think you're treating them extra special, they'll be more inclined to help you. Trust me."

"That just might work," I muttered.

Evianna nodded. "Plus, most of your guests will tucker themselves out searching for you in the meantime. It's *much* easier to handle everyone once they've had their drinks and food and their feet hurt."

I laughed at the thought of the guests tiring themselves out while searching for me. Perhaps it was a clever idea to wait. At least then I could gather my thoughts and enjoy my food.

"Thank you," I said as I scooped some of the stew. It smelled and tasted like scarlet snapper, a wonderful and flavorful fish. "So good."

Evianna's hair fluttered in the ocean winds. She motioned me over, and I climbed the roof to get to her side. She pointed to the far end of the building, on the opposite side of the roof. She had set up a blanket with a couple of wine glasses, held on the roof with shadowy tendrils, no doubt her magic at work.

"We can relax there," Evianna said.

We walked along the top of the roof, three stories up from the festivities below. The chill of the wind cut through my clothing. It didn't matter. My enthusiasm shielded me from any negative thoughts.

I ate more stew, actually enjoying myself for once today.

Evianna stayed close to my side, and as we walked, I could

hear the conversations of those below me. With confident steps, I slid closer to the edge so that I could glance down. I couldn't make out the chatter of those in the courtyard, but to my curiosity, groups of people stood around on the second and third story balconies. Their conversations were easier to hear, and as I made my way to the blanket on the roof, I slowed my pace. I recognized individuals from the Frith Guild.

Karna and my brother, Ryker, milled about a balcony covered in flowers. Although it was difficult to see them fully when I was standing so high above, it wasn't hard to make out Karna's sparkling dress. It drew all attention to her—and it was cut to reveal more skin than most would consider tasteful.

Ryker wore a fine vest of some sort. I only knew because he tugged on it constantly while he spoke.

"Your shapeshifting skills are impressive," he said, his voice faint, but distinct.

Karna slowly combed her golden hair with her fingers. "You like that? I can show you so much more, you know."

Ryker's nervous laugh drifted up on the evening winds. More tugging on his vest. "I'm surprised someone like *you* would want to spend time training *me*. Any bachelor would consider himself lucky to have your attention."

With a single laugh, Karna fluffed her hair. "Have you actually met Volke? I feel like you don't know him well."

"We've only just discovered we're siblings. I... don't know him much at all. He's extraordinary, though."

Karna let out a wistful sigh. "I suppose I would agree."

My face heated. Should I be listening to this?

Ryker held the balcony railing. "Thank you for agreeing to see me in private. I'd rather we were alone."

"Oh?" Karna turned to him, her movements quick and sharp—she was annoyed, I could tell. "What does that mean? Let me guess. You have a special request for my shapeshifting. You think I'll perform for you on command, is that it?"

"Oh, n-no," Ryker hastily said. "I apologize, I meant nothing like that. I'm just glad I know a master doppelgänger arcanist, because I'd like to ask you to train me... I just didn't want to do it in front of everyone else." He exhaled. "My struggles with magic are embarrassing. Especially when I have a god-arcanist brother."

Karna relaxed and leaned on the balcony railing. "Oh. In that case, I'm the one who should be apologizing. I'm not a master arcanist. I can augment myself and change shapes, and I can manipulate people, but I can't evoke anything. Perhaps we both struggle with our magic."

Ryker perked up and stepped closer to her. "Manipulate *people*?"

"Oh, yes. It's an amusing ability. I should show you some time."

"Of course," he said, probably not even fully thinking that through. "And I can show you my evocation. I seem to cause confusion in the minds of those around me. Maybe... maybe we can help each other."

"Interesting." Karna placed her hands on Ryker's. "I'd like that."

"G-Great. Excellent." His nervous chuckling almost interfered with his words. He slowly pulled his hand away from hers and then rubbed at his knuckles. "I, uh, don't want to give anyone the wrong impression. I'm sure your husband wouldn't want us alone for so long."

Karna genuinely laughed, her head tilted back. It took her a moment to calm down, but once she did, she turned to Ryker. With a smile in her voice, she said, "You remind me a lot of Volke."

"Thank you."

"And don't worry." She placed her hand on his again. "I'm not married."

Evianna grabbed my arm and tugged me toward the

blanket. I shook my head and moved away from the edge of the roof.

"What were you doing?" she asked, one eyebrow raised.

I half-shrugged. "Uh, well..."

"Eavesdropping?"

"Yes," I stated. Then I rubbed at the back of my neck. "Sorry."

Evianna narrowed her eyes and smirked. Then she gently tugged me in a new direction. We walked across the slanted roof, and while we traveled, I finished my fish stew. Delicious.

We reached another edge on the opposite side of the building. This balcony didn't overlook the courtyard—it faced out into the garden. It was quieter here, and Evianna stepped lightly as we moved to the edge. She placed a finger over her lips.

I glanced down but immediately regretted it. Hexa and someone else were sitting on a balcony bench, their hands exploring each other's bodies. Hexa's fluffy mane-like hair was a dead giveaway, but the red hair of her companion was more of a mystery to me. It wasn't Zaxis, but others in the guild had similar fiery hair.

Even from twelve feet above them, I could hear their gentle moans as they kissed like only lovers could.

A glittering scarab—a khepera—fluttered around the balcony, as if keeping watch. In the garden below, Raisen's five heads remained vigilant.

Without making a noise, I quickly moved away from the edge and shook my head.

"I don't want to see this," I whispered to Evianna.

She frowned and tugged me toward another portion of the roof. "Sorry, that wasn't what I meant to show you," she said under her breath. "Here."

We crossed over the roof again and returned to the balconies overlooking the courtyard. When we reached the edge, I hesitantly glanced over, already regretting my decision to spy on others.

"Tell me about yourself," someone demanded.

Illia.

I knew her voice with utter confidence.

"Yeah, tell us about yourself," Nicholin said, his tone stern.

My sister stood on the balcony below me. Her white dress with a single phoenix feather was an odd look for her, but I knew her stiff stance. She always stood like that when she was annoyed or irritated.

To my surprise—and delight—Fain stood with her. His blackened ears were easy to notice, even from above.

"I already told you everything," Fain muttered. He stayed away from the balcony's railing and instead leaned against the wall of the building, his arms tightly crossed. "From my childhood, to Calisto's ship, to right now."

"That was just a history," Illia said. She stood on the far opposite side of the balcony, as far away as she could be without being in a separate room. "I meant... tell me about your likes and dislikes." She struggled for a moment, as though debating what to say. "What's your... favorite color?"

"Why do you care?"

"I don't," Illia snapped. Then she gritted her teeth and turned away from him. "But maybe we can get to know each other better if you just answer my questions."

Nicholin's white fur glittered in the star light. "Yeah. What my arcanist said. Just cooperate and maybe you won't be so insufferable."

Fain scoffed. With a dramatic shrug, he said, "Why don't you just ask me what you really want to know?"

"What do you mean?" Illia asked, her voice low and threatening.

"You wanna know more about Calisto, right? You wanna kill him for taking your eye?"

"And my parents," she snapped. "He took them from me as well."

"Whatever. You want revenge." Fain growled something inaudible and then continued, "This isn't about *me*. You wouldn't care if I were swallowed by the abyssal hells—I can tell by the way you glare every time I enter the room."

Illia said nothing. She kept her back to him, her gaze on the active courtyard below.

"Just don't pretend you're my friend," Fain stated. "Ask me what you want. I'm not gonna lie."

"What did you see in the man?" Illia gripped the balcony railing. Nicholin, wrapped around her neck like a scarf, snuggled close, as if hugging her with his whole body. "Why call Calisto *your captain*?"

"You wouldn't understand."

Illia forced a dark laugh. "I thought you said you'd answer my questions?"

"Fine," Fain said, his voice growing louder with his anger. "You wanna know? I'll tell you. You're not the only one who lost their parents, but *unlike you*, I didn't get a loving adoptive family to take me in. I had my brother, and my brother had Calisto."

Fain took a moment to calm himself and control his volume. Still, Illia didn't move.

"And ya know what?" Fain continued, shrugging. "Calisto wasn't taken in by a loving family either. He... understood sometimes. When we sat around and drank, and talked about our past, and about the future... He knew. Calisto knew that life was unforgiving and relentless, and sometimes it felt like he was the only one who would do whatever it took to make sure *our* lives weren't terrible. He fought for *us*. His crew. His ship. *We* mattered. Nothing else did."

I held my breath, my chest tight.

"Calisto didn't care what we had done in our past," Fain

said, his voice getting softer. He turned away from Illia. "We were a new family. It was a terrible family—but a family nonetheless. And that's why I called him captain."

Illia didn't respond. Neither did Nicholin. Silence took root between them, and never let up. I waited for a minute with Evianna by my side, but the two of them just sat there on the balcony, never bothering to follow up with any statements.

I moved away from the edge, and then almost slipped on a tile. Evianna waved her hand and caught me with physical shadows.

"Thank you," I whispered.

Evianna smiled in response.

Once I got my footing back, we headed to the blanket and wine glasses she had prepared on the roof. It overlooked the massive gardens, but it was too dark for me to appreciate them. Glowstone lanterns kept the garden paths lit, but those were for someone strolling the stone walkways.

Evianna had gathered the blanket from a random bedroom —the blue hue and embroidery told me it was expensive. It had probably been awkward stealing it from a random bed.

I took a seat on the blanket—I leaned to one side, to compensate for the slanted roof—and then placed my empty bowl on the nearby gutter. "Thank you for this."

Evianna sat next to me. "I have one more gift for you, by the way." She threw back her hair and sighed, her formal outfit glittering in the starlight. With a frown, she said, "It's nothing fancy."

I waved away the comment. "That's fine. I didn't do nearly as much for you on your birthday."

"You kissed me."

The statement gave me pause. That was true—we had kissed. It hadn't felt awkward or forced, or like I had a boot on without a sock. Maybe Hexa had the right idea. Maybe I should be in the throes of passion and love, enjoying my youth, like Karna had said.

But did I have that luxury? I was a god-arcanist. When would I get a chance for that?

Maybe I should just enjoy every quiet moment I had.

I leaned over the blanket, closer to Evianna. She stared at me, her breath held, her body tense. What was I supposed to say? Karna's suggestion danced in my head. Seductively ask Evianna to swear herself to me?

I had as much seduction as a squishy tomato.

The truth then...

"Evianna," I whispered. We were so close that talking at a normal volume seemed too loud. But what else was I going to say? It ate at me. I turned away, my jaw clenched.

Evianna touched my upper arm and I glanced back. She leaned in closer, her face close to mine. "Volke."

I waited, unmoving.

"You're important to me," she said, her voice strained, her face pink. But she never looked away. "I know this might sound pathetic, or maybe you'll think me childish, but... I can't be happy if you're not happy."

I stared for a long moment, unsure of how to respond.

"You could be with anyone!" Evianna said with a frustrated sigh. She ran both her hands through her shimmering white hair. "You're the *Warlord of Magic*. Everyone wants to be with you. And I'm just..." She sighed. "I don't even have my home anymore."

"Why're you bringing this up?" I asked, my words slow. "Obviously, I'm here with you now. Not someone else."

"Because... I wanted to tell you something." Evianna dropped her hands and took a deep breath. "Even if you don't pick me because you want someone more... beautiful and prestigious... I'll be okay as long as you pick *happiness*. Does... does that make any sense?"

"Yeah," I whispered.

Evianna fidgeted with her dress for a short while. "Good. And just to be clear—I'll be fine with whatever outcome you decide. No matter what." She forced half a smile. "You're a good man, Volke. You deserve someone who will make you happy."

Evianna's words struck me as genuine, and the sincerity melted away my frustration and exhaustion. Perhaps a dozen people called me friend, and several were my family, but I hadn't yet experienced someone who I would call my *partner*.

I brought my hand up to Evianna's neck and caressed her cheek. She felt warm to my touch. If we were being honest, I knew what I had to say now.

"Whenever there's a crowd, I look for you in it," I said. "When you're in danger, I think of nothing else until you're safe. Lately, you've been there for me. I want to be there for you, too. I'm done being indecisive. I won't know what makes me happy unless I make a decision and—"

Evianna leaned in and pressed her lips to mine, cutting me off. I held my breath, caught off-guard. After a short moment, any sort of tension between us drifted away on the wind. I closed my eyes and gently pulled her closer. She smelled of lilac perfume and tasted of beef skewers. She must have eaten before taking me from the celebration.

Most thoughts left me. All I focused on was Evianna's presence.

She wrapped her arms around my neck, her kiss becoming gentle as she slowly separated from me. Then Evianna pushed her hands on my chest, guiding me down until I was lying on my back, staring up at the sky. She leaned half of herself onto me, the weight of her body a mild excitement.

I hated that we were on a roof. The slant made it difficult not to tumble off into the garden. When Evianna rested most of her weight on me, I had to brace myself on the roof tiles to prevent us both from slipping.

Evianna kissed me a second time, and the difficulties of our positioning seemed insignificant. Roof? What roof?

I ran my hand along her back, trying to be as gentlemanly with my thoughts and gestures as I could.

Lying under the stars, wrapped in bliss...

I enjoyed the beating of Evianna's heart. It quickened whenever I brought my hand up to stroke her silky hair. We stayed in each other's arms for so long, I couldn't imagine *not* hearing her heartbeat.

With a slight laugh, Evianna stopped our kissing and braced her hands on either side of my head. Her white hair fell around us, creating a curtain that blocked out the world. All I could see was her smile.

"You make me happy," I whispered, running my knuckles along her cheek.

Evianna's eyes went glassy. A tear fell from her face and landed on mine.

I furrowed my brow, unsure of what to do. "What's wrong? Why're you crying?"

She rubbed at her face, clearing away the tears. "I'm just..." Evianna hardened her expression, caging her other emotions with playful anger. She laid down on my chest and curled herself on top of me. "Don't ask ridiculous questions."

I wrapped my arms around her, holding her close. "Do you want to go inside?" I rubbed at her arms, feeling the chill on her skin.

"We can't stay here forever?"

"It'd be a little awkward, but maybe if we found a sustainable food source..." I chuckled at my own terrible joke.

Evianna poked my ribs and I flinched. "Let's... stay here for a while longer. I want to remember this moment forever." She held on to my shirt and closed her eyes. "Please?"

I smiled at her words and used my embrace to shield her from the cold. "I'd like that."

The time we spent on the roof came easy.

Ten minutes.

Thirty minutes.

An hour.

I knew the party continued without me, but it was worth it. Evianna's presence wasn't difficult. It didn't feel off. I just enjoyed it, and I suddenly understood why Zaxis and Illia found time to just be alone together.

"I'm not going to play nice with anyone who tries to take you from me," Evianna stated matter-of-factly.

"That's... aggressive," I muttered, half-chuckling.

"You're too nice. One of us needs to be aggressive." She nuzzled my chest.

"I've killed a lot of people," I said, quiet and distant. "I'd say that's at least somewhat aggressive."

Evianna sat up, a slight frown on her face. She stared down at me, like she wanted to say something. Then her eyes widened. "Oh! Wait right here. I'll be back." Evianna stood, the shadows flickering around as though restless. "I have one more gift, remember?"

"I'd rather you just stay," I said, motioning to the blanket on the tiles.

"No, no. I have to get it! You'll love the gift. I promise."

Before I could respond, Evianna slipped into the shadows and used the darkness to travel across the roof. Alone, I exhaled and stared up at the moon. With nothing else to do, I took deep breathes, trying to bleed some of my excitement and anxiety.

Maybe I really did have a mental block. It felt so freeing to just be with someone. To enjoy the moment. To feel affection in physical form.

A creak of roof tiles caught my attention.

"Back already?" I asked. "That was fast. Not that I'm complaining."

Searing pain shot through my neck as someone ran a blade across my windpipe, just under the chin.

At first it burned—the fire of knife injuries was familiar—but then it spread faster than fire, up through my jaw, and down to my shoulders. I tried to stand but couldn't. Instead, I rolled to the side and half-slipped down the roof. With a shaky hand, I held the injury on my neck, trying to stifle the blood flow.

Curse the abyssal hells!

Unable to breathe, I frantically glanced around.

No one.

Just me and my own blood, soaking into my shirt.

But I wasn't fooled. This was the work of Adelgis's sister. She had finally come to kill me.

34

VENAE VENROVER

I got to my feet, barely balancing on the roof.

Heat enveloped the area, but I clenched my jaw and held back my magic. If I set the whole building on fire, I'd cause a panic. There were so many arcanists here—master arcanists—that Venae would surely be killed in the ensuing battle.

I had promised Adelgis I would save his siblings. I couldn't allow her to die.

Although I was at a disadvantage because of my injury, *I* had to handle this alone. Instead of heading into the party with Guildmaster Eventide and Master Zelfree, I steeled myself to the reality that I couldn't rely on them.

Blood soaked into my formal shirt. With my free hand, I pulled out Retribution, the black blade shining in the moonlight. I typically fought with a shield, and keeping one hand pressed hard on my neck injury would hinder me, but I couldn't change that.

Someone swiped at me. I felt the wind of the attack, and the sharp point of a dagger near my shoulder, but I managed to step away. I concentrated, hoping to feel her movements like I could with Zaxis.

But nothing.

I felt no steps or shifts of weight.

Why? Did her white hart magic prevent me from feeling her footsteps? Perhaps that was how they avoided trackers. They didn't touch the ground. Perhaps white harts had an ability to walk without touching anything—a light-footed ability to avoid leaving tracks. Perhaps it was similar to a knightmare's shadow-step.

But how had she gotten into my compound without getting caught? King Odion and his knights had a way of dispelling invisibility—they had used it on Fain. Yet Venae had managed to infiltrate the celebration?

It didn't matter. I'd deal with that later.

Before Venae could attack again, I sheathed Retribution and leapt off the side of the roof. I landed on an unoccupied third-story balcony, rolling to my feet. Then I grabbed the railing and leapt again, this time onto the second-story balcony.

I reached for the railing again. Venae slashed at my arm. My sleeve ripped open and so did the skin. My invisible assailant had cut me from my wrist to my elbow, but not deep enough to incapacitate me. The injury burned like the one on my neck, the agony seeping into my hand and shoulder.

Poison?

When I grabbed the railing and tried to leap over, my elbow buckled. I hit the wrought-iron and tumbled down into the garden, slamming into the cobblestone ribs-first. I grunted and scrambled to my feet, still unable to breathe. The slash on my neck went deep.

I feared my vision would blur, or my lungs would hurt, but those side effects never happened.

A rock didn't need to breathe.

Or perhaps I just didn't need air as much and as often as I used to. Not only that, but the injury on my neck was quickly healing, my skin stitching itself together at a furious rate, as though magic itself didn't want me to die.

"Warlord?" Terrakona asked, his telepathy harsh in my mind.

I couldn't speak, but I shook my head, trying to impart my confidence. I had this handled.

"Your thoughts are tinted with desperation and panic. I'll come to your aid."

That was the last thing I wanted. Terrakona was gigantic. If he smashed his way through Fortuna, he would cause the biggest commotion the town had ever seen. Venae was just a white hart arcanist. I could handle this.

"I can travel across land as easily as I travel across the seas. Nothing will stop me from reaching your side if you're in danger, Warlord."

Still determined to keep my fight secret, I shook my head.

With shaky legs, I backed away into the garden, away from the people in the party. My blood spotted the walkway, dripping from the hem of my clothing. I felt lightheaded, but I had an idea.

Venae pursued me. I couldn't sense her steps, but twice she swiped with a sharp dagger. She caught my shirt, slicing off a moon-etched button and then again on my trousers, cutting a hole near the knee. She wasn't aiming for a killing blow—not after the attack to my neck—now she was just trying to bleed me out or riddle me with so much poison that I couldn't function.

As soon as we were away from the main compound building, and away from any other people, I stopped. My knees shook, but I steeled myself and waved my hand. Plants in the area grew—from my palm, from the ground, even off the rocks. Ferns. Vines. Shrubs. With another motion of my hand, leaves shook off all the nearby vegetation, even the trees of the garden. They danced on the evening winds, flooding the area with a hail of greenery so thick, it could've been fog.

Leaves wouldn't hurt anyone, but that wasn't why I had created them. I couldn't sense Venae's footsteps, but when the leaves made contact with her invisible body, I felt her location. She stood in the garden, just a few feet from me, and so did her massive eldrin. The white hart pranced alongside her, its body as large as a moose and its antlers twice the size of any deer's.

Venae must not have known how my powers worked. She didn't even move, she just shielded her face from the leaves.

Then I imagined the ground dragging her under, like a whirlpool of dirt. But just like as it had been with Zaxis, I didn't seem to have much control on the force used. The ground fell away, creating a crater. Venae slid into it. Her eldrin tumbled into it as well.

Then *I* fell into it.

The stone shifted to sand. Venae sank into my trap, but her agile white hart leapt from the pit before it could be trapped. I dug my hand into the ground and hardened everything before I could be buried.

Venae gasped and struggled. Her concentration broke, and her invisibility faded. She was half-buried in the ground, her waist and legs now held in place by solid stone. She clawed at the slanted dirt all around her, trying to pull herself free, but unable to get anywhere.

Like Adelgis, Venae had black hair. Unlike Adelgis, she kept it short and pulled back in a tight ponytail that resembled the fluff of a wolf's tail. Her dark eyes made her pale skin seem even paler, like she was a member of the undead. Her thin fingers, sunken cheeks, and narrow jaw gave her the visage of a skeleton.

She resembled her father, Theasin.

I tried to call out her name, but my chest seized with pain. I coughed and blood splattered across my trousers and boots. The pain from Venae's stabs burned hotter than before.

"My arcanist," the white hart said, masculine in voice. "Get up."

The legendary beast dropped his invisibility. His pure white coat and golden antlers reminded me of my time in the Endless Mire. This would be the second time a white hart had almost killed me.

With golden hooves, he leapt into the crater and lowered his head to nuzzle Venae. She grabbed the white hart's antlers and the beast attempted to pull her free. When that didn't work, her eldrin turned his attention to me.

His golden eyes reminded me of a phoenix's, and they shimmered with a metallic sheen. He lowered his head, angling his twelve antler points in my direction. The sharp tips were unlike anything a deer was capable of. They were deadly.

Unable to speak, I pulled out Retribution just in time to slash at the white hart as it charged. My blade effortlessly sliced off one antler at the base, but that didn't stop the other antler from piercing my thigh.

If I could've yelled, I would have. The white hart lifted me a few feet from the ground and shook. I hit the dirt and slid down the crater's side, tumbling closer to Venae, my blood smearing across the twisted rocks and sand I had created.

If I had just wanted to kill them, I could've done so by now. I could've buried Venae and her eldrin alive, or I could've melted them like I had melted Gallus. But I couldn't.

And now my thoughts blurred. I got to my feet and then fell to one knee. Whatever poison Venae had used, it had taken a toll on my strength.

"Arthur, kill him while he's weak," Venae said. "Quickly!"

She used her dagger—a thin stiletto, a type of weapon used

for deep stabs and quick strikes—in an attempt to dig her way out of the ground. The stiletto was too narrow to dig with, but Venae stabbed at the stone as hard as she could, chipping the granite.

Arthur, her white hart, shook his head. He was lopsided without the other antler, and when he turned his golden eyes toward me, he snorted and stomped his cloven hooves. Then he leapt into the air. Literally. He stood on the air, a few inches from the ground, like he was hovering. That was how he had avoided my tremor sense.

Then the white hart shrouded himself in invisibility.

The leaves I had created were long gone. When the beast lunged, I had no way of detecting it. Panic took over.

I had promised Adelgis I'd save his siblings—not their eldrin.

Unstable heat washed throughout the area as I evoked my magma. It oozed from my palms and injuries, burning most of my clothes. The obsidian jutted from my knuckles just as the white hart stabbed at me again. His golden antler pierced into my side. And then Arthur began to melt.

The white hart screamed. I reached out and grabbed him. Although the beast was stronger, the moment I placed my hand on the hart's shoulder, its leg crumpled and half-liquefied into pink and red foam.

Everything smelled like cooked venison.

"*No!*" Venae shrieked. She lifted her hand, holding the stiletto to throw it. Without my shield, how was I supposed to defend myself?

With expert skill, Venae flung the dagger at my chest. In that split second, I grabbed my guild pendant. The magic within pulsed and a shimmering shield burst around me, a complete bubble. The stiletto smashed against the barrier and fell to the ground, harmless. The white hart, injured from my sword and magma, attempted to flee, but he couldn't jump from the crater. And with his injuries, he couldn't seem to concentrate enough to activate his magic.

"Arthur!" Venae shouted. She used her hands, gripping at the stone, her fingernails bleeding from the strain. "*Get away from him!*"

My atlas turtle barrier faded.

I still couldn't speak.

The white hart stumbled back to his arcanist, whining and burned across half his body. The once white fur no longer shimmered, and the remaining gold antler was slashed, melted, and covered in crimson.

"You must... flee," the white hart said, his voice strained.

Venae wrapped her arms around his neck. "I'm so sorry. Please don't die. I wasn't told he could do this. I didn't know."

With the last of his strength, Arthur slammed his antler into the rock around his arcanist. A crack opened up, and Venae managed to yank herself free from the stone. Her hands shook as she hugged her eldrin, but the white hart could no longer stand. He collapsed into the crater, his blood running into the cracks and the holes in the stone.

"Arthur, get up!" Venae shouted as she shook the corpse of her eldrin. "Get up!"

Without warning, blinding light flooded the area. I had to look away, and I shielded my face with my injured arm. Was this King Odion? The magic reminded me of his twilight dragon. When the blinding light faded, I opened my eyes and found Master Zelfree standing at the edge of the crater.

He waved his hands and shadow tendrils lashed out from the darkness all around us. They attacked the unmoving white hart, as well as Venae, whipping with such force as to slash through her thin armor and cut through skin. She hit the dirt, obviously taken by surprise.

Without magic, she wouldn't stand a chance against Zelfree.

And without the ability to speak, I couldn't call him off.

A dozen more tendrils emerged from the darkness as Zelfree manipulated the shadows to his will. He waved his hand, but I concentrated on my magic and altered the garden landscape around us. In an instant, jagged rocks jutted up around Venae, stopping the shadows from striking her. Then the crater reversed—it lifted skyward, becoming a small hill filled with rough pebbles and lopsided boulders.

The rumble of my magic shook the whole estate, and even smashed part of the garden, as dirt, rock, and cobblestone mashed together.

Venae, at the top of the hill, glanced at the rocks that had saved her, and then to me, her fright and confusion mixing in equal parts.

Her white hart tumbled off the hill and hit the ruined garden, unmoving.

As Master Zelfree ran around the side—just as confused as Venae—Adelgis's sister took off into the decimated portion of the garden, physically hiding herself behind world serpent-shaped shrubs as she fled. I didn't have the strength to chase her, and to my relief, Zelfree decided to help me, rather than pursue her.

My injuries... I still couldn't breathe, and now my chest flared with pain. Too long. I hadn't taken a breath for far too long.

Zelfree ran to my side and helped me stand. He offered a shoulder, and I took it without question. His arcanist mark carried the two-headed symbol of the twilight dragon. He had mimicked King Odion's powers.

"You're okay," Zelfree said. "Calm down."

I didn't know how. The panic set into my thoughts. More magma oozed from my body, to the point where Zelfree had to hold me awkwardly. Embers lit up the air around us, like sinister fireflies. It was just like my nightmare. I had woken up and burned my whole room down. Now I felt like I'd do it again.

Rumbling started again. It shook everything. The trees. The garden. The buildings.

Was *I* doing this? It only added to my uncertainty. Could my magic rage out of control? What if I couldn't contain it? What if I burned all of Fortuna to the ground?

Zelfree manipulated the shadows, attempting to stifle the smoke and fire. The flames of my molten rock singed some of his clothing, but he didn't flee. "You have to get this under control," he commanded, no fear or hesitation in his tone. "*Discipline. Without it, we are not masters of our own destiny.*"

The third step of the Pillar?

Just hearing the words helped me focus. I relaxed, and my evocation settled. But then I didn't have the strength to stand. I had lost too much blood, and the quaking made it difficult to keep my balance.

Zelfree tightened his grip on me. He kept me on my feet, despite the shaking.

"It's okay," he said. "I've got you."

I held on to his long coat. But the rumbling didn't cease.

It wasn't me. It was Terrakona.

Then the rumbling stopped.

I glanced up, sensing his presence. There he was! At the edge of the Savan Compound, his massive serpentine body large enough to block out a portion of the moonlight, shrouding the garden in thick darkness. His crystal mane glittered with starlight, and his emerald scales appeared black at night.

Terrakona turned his gaze down, his slit-pupil eyes narrowing into thin lines until he spotted me. Then they widened, and his hot breath washed over the garden. I stared up at him, unable to speak, but I wanted to convey my gratitude.

His concern for my wellbeing flooded my thoughts.

"**Warlord**," he telepathically said. "**I promised I would fight death itself for you.**" He lowered his head, his tongue darting out. It was large enough to knock me over, but it didn't. He snaked it around me, tickling my skin, and then pulled it back. "**You frightened me.**"

I wanted to tell him I was sorry for worrying him. Terrakona must've known. He poked his giant nose against me, nudging me a few inches.

He seemed much younger when he was scared, like the hatchling world serpent he actually was. It was cute.

Zelfree held up a hand. "Everything will be fine, world serpent. I have him."

Terrakona didn't speak to Zelfree. He simply lifted his head and observed from above us, his eyes never leaving me.

"*Volke?*" Adelgis spoke to me telepathically. "*Thank the good stars you're all right.*"

I couldn't respond.

"*I apologize. I didn't realize Venae was so close until after her invisibility dropped. I contacted Master Zelfree and told him to investigate. I should've expressed more urgency, but I didn't want to cause a panic. Unfortunately, your eldrin has done that now.*"

Sure enough, arcanists from the celebration had rushed to the garden. My head spun. I couldn't count them all.

Master Zelfree, oblivious to the silent conversation in my head, half-carried me toward the main building. "Gillie is close. She'll help with your injuries. Just hang on."

"Twice you've survived mortal injuries," Gillie said with a slight frown. "Your self-healing is amazing. And it seems it's impossible for you to asphyxiate. Or rather, you can go extended periods of time without breathing."

I sat on a lounge chair in the middle of the personal study room on the second floor. Lanterns kept the room bright, which I was thankful for. The celebration continued in the courtyard and garden. Apparently, Guildmaster Eventide had told everyone that I had summoned Terrakona here as a gift for my guests.

It wasn't difficult to see Terrakona from the study window. He waited on the wall bordering my compound, his body half in the garden and half on the outside of my estate.

To my surprise, he hadn't created a gigantic furrow through town. There was no damage at all, actually. No trees upturned. No hills destroyed. How had something as massive as Terrakona traveled here without destroying everything in his path? I would have to ask him.

Gillie touched my throat.

"Thank you," I said, my voice rusty. But her fingers pressed on my skin, and a stabbing pain shot through me. "It still hurts, though."

"That's why you shouldn't thank me yet," Gillie muttered. "That assassin's blade was coated in something."

"Poison?"

"No. I can cure poison." Gillie's celebration gown—once a vibrant yellow and blue—was now stained with my blood. She didn't care. She stayed close, healing me with her powerful caladrius magic. Her eldrin sat on her shoulder, a little white parrot with a golden beak.

"What is it?" I asked. "If it's not poison…"

Gillie clasped her hands together. "Volke, you were the one who told us about the Second Ascension's use of apoch dragon bones. The substance in your system… It reminds me of that. It seems specifically immune to magical effects."

I grabbed at my neck, my hand shaky. Whatever Venac had used to hurt me, I felt it scratching at the inside of my veins.

Had she used something Theasin had created? He had concocted so many insidious things already…

"It might leave your body naturally," Gillie said. "I'm not sure. My best advice would be to wait and see. If it starts to hurt, you should come see me."

The door to the study forcefully flew open and slammed into the wall. Zelfree and Odion stepped into the study, their glowers locked on each other.

"I told you there was no reason for you to be here," Zelfree said, curt.

Odion clicked his tongue in dismissal. "Tsk. I swore to protect him. I don't care what the guildmaster of the Frith Guild says—his world serpent came here because of an attacker."

"No one ever said that."

"I'm no fool, *renegade*. I know all about how your guildmaster keeps secrets. She may be legendary, but that doesn't give her the right to hide my liege behind a curtain of subterfuge."

Odion's white and metallic silver hair shone in the lantern light, reminding me of Evianna. Where was she? I hadn't seen her since the fight.

The moment Zelfree and Odion turned to me, all thoughts of Evianna temporarily vanished. Odion's icy eyes examined the blood on my clothing—and on Gillie's. Whatever Eventide had said, he knew it was a lie for sure now.

He crossed the study, his gait controlled and smooth. When he reached my side, he stared down at my person. Gillie smiled, but Odion didn't return the gesture.

"Excuse me," Gillie said. "I'm the one in charge here."

"Gillian Dravon," King Odion said as he bowed slightly. "The Grand Apothecary of Fortuna. Such a pleasure." Then he stood straight. "I'll only be a moment. I think it's best that my knights and I know what happened so that we can prevent it from happening a second time. Especially since the assassin wasn't captured."

"*Enough*," Zelfree barked, closing the door. "You needn't concern yourself with that. I'll handle it."

"My captain of the guard can help you," Odion stated. "Tarik has teleportation abilities, and he's an excellent tracker."

"Wasn't Tarik the one who set up the defensive perimeter? Eventide was counting on your ability to negate illusions and invisibility. *What happened*? This attack is practically your fault."

When some people got angry, they were a fire. Heat. Destruction. Yelling. But Odion wasn't one of those people. When he got angry, he was ice. No reaction. No movement. His breath even became cold, and I felt the tension in the room thicken as everything froze in an icy rage.

"We almost lost our god-arcanist," Odion said, his words slow and precise. "And Eventide decided to cover it up. And you dare to accuse *me* of not being trustworthy?"

Zelfree leaned against the door, his arms crossed, his clothing still singed from the fight out in the garden. When he smirked, I knew this wouldn't end well. "I noticed you didn't bother to even explain your mistake." Without missing a beat, he continued, "And I know how *you* keep secrets. Why don't you tell Volke all about how you took the throne? Then we'll see who's trustworthy."

Before this conversation could go any further, Gillie stepped between them, her hands up. Her caladrius had her white wings spread, helping her arcanist break up the tension.

"Please," Gillie said. "I don't care about who is keeping what secrets. All I care about is Volke's health and safety. This discussion won't help him recover."

King Odion took a deep breath and then turned to face me. With a deep bow, he said, "I apologize, my liege." He stood straight. "But now that I know you were attacked, I would suggest you check your belongings."

"My... what?" I asked. "Why?"

"Any magical artifacts you have should be checked. I'm sure this assailant likely rummaged through your possessions."

I stood from the lounge chair, my heart racing. None of my possessions really mattered to me—except for Luthair's cape. Everything else could be replaced or duplicated, if I wanted. Not Luthair. What if Venae had taken it?

"But she came here to kill me," I said, trying to talk some sense into myself. "Not to steal from me."

"Don't be absurd," Odion said. "Any trinkets or artifacts made with world serpent magic will be prized above all. It's only logical that an assassin would look through your things. Your sword, if nothing else, is a wonder."

My sword?

I glanced down to my half-burned belt. Retribution had been made from the bones of the apoch dragon. It cut through any magical object or being.

"My sword isn't imbued with world serpent magic," I said as I placed my hand on the hilt. "I made it while I was a knightmare arcanist."

One of Odion's eyebrows lifted. He regarded my blade with a long stare, and I wondered why.

But I couldn't get the newfound fear out of my head. What if Venae had been greedy? What if she had rummaged through my things? Luthair's cape was here, after all. I had it brought over, to keep it close.

Zelfree relaxed and gave me the once-over. "Volke? What's wrong?"

"I should check my room," I said. "There is something there..."

I wanted to rush out of the study, but Gillie stepped in my path and placed a gentle hand on my shoulder. She squeezed and then smiled as she always did. "You need to take it easy. You're no longer in danger of dying, but whatever the assassin used on her blade is still in your veins. If you feel weak or you start to hurt, you come straight back to me, understand?"

I nodded once.

"Good."

Then Gillie released me.

I headed out of the study and turned down the long hall. Zelfree and Odion shadowed my steps, following me at a good distance in utter silence. Unfortunately, I didn't know where I was going. I turned down another hall, and the echoes of my celebration floated up the nearby stairs.

"Where's my room?" I asked. "My third room. I, uh, destroyed the other two."

Zelfree pointed. "This way."

We turned as a group and continued through my expansive compound. The farther we got from the central area, the less I heard the guests discussing the situation. A part of me was glad Eventide had hidden the truth. Another part of me hated it— everyone would expect me back soon, and my head still hurt. I couldn't explain myself. I just had to hide it.

"Why are you accompanying us?" Zelfree asked.

"To protect the world serpent arcanist," Odion replied.

I tensed, remembering what they had discussed. "Odion, why don't you tell me how you took the throne?"

That got them quiet.

But it didn't last long. Before we reached my room, Odion huffed. "I killed the previous king."

"In a magi cross?" I asked.

"No. I wasn't an arcanist."

"You beat the previous king without magic?" A *dragon* arcanist? I had known Odion was talented, but that seemed extreme.

"The previous king had only been bonded for a few

months," Odion casually said. "He hadn't yet developed many of his magics."

I slowed my walking. "You assassinated him?"

The shadows in the hallway flickered and fluttered, like bats in the darkness. Odion ground his teeth loud enough that I could hear. "I didn't *assassinate* him. If I'm going to take a man's life, I want him to know. I want him to fight back. I want the world to see *I* beat him—that I'm stronger and more capable."

His passionate conviction didn't surprise me. Odion had tried to kill me the first time we had met, after all. This level of fixation on power seemed commonplace among dragon arcanists.

"So, you beat an arcanist even though you weren't one?" I asked for clarification.

Odion replied with a single nod.

"And then you bonded with Hasdrubal, the late king's twilight dragon," Zelfree stated. "I heard it was quite the spectacle to see it all in person."

I hadn't thought about it much, but that tiny bit of information revealed more than I thought Odion wanted me to know. The previous King of Javin had likely been young. Most bonding ceremonies took place when an individual was fifteen. Odion was clearly older, but he hadn't been bonded long, which meant he had likely killed a fifteen- or sixteen-year-old in order to take the throne and the man's dragon.

Without prompting, Odion added, "Javin has been ruled by only one of three families for centuries—the Hayes, the Setett, and the Jorn. I killed a member of the Jorn family, but his father had killed my grandfather, and my grandfather had killed a woman of the Setett family in order to claim rulership. Almost every king or queen of Javin has been second bonded to their twilight dragon. It's damn near a tradition."

"Really?" I asked. Second-bonding had hurt. Luthair and I

had taken longer to master our magics because of it. "It seems a waste." So much death.

Odion darkly chuckled. "Twilight dragons have two heads. Some Javin citizens think it's symbolic. The creature needs two arcanists to fully realize its strength."

I rubbed at the back of my neck. "I don't think that's true."

"It's just the murmurings of mortal citizens who don't understand the complexities of blood dynasty and thrones. Give it no further thought. It's all rumor."

"Why don't you tell him about Tarik?" Zelfree asked.

Odion narrowed his icy eyes. "In exchange for the backing of the knights, I made Tarik the Knight Captain."

"By ending the last captain." Zelfree scoffed. "And throwing his body into the gates of the abyssal hells."

"More *tradition*, I assure you. Besides, Javin was close to becoming a puppet for the Second Ascension, and I couldn't have that. I prevented the one other twilight dragon arcanist from taking the throne. Whatever I did to achieve that... I think it's all worth the price."

I really didn't know much about King Odion. The Kingdom of Javin sounded more and more like a nightmare wasteland built upon murder. I had known it was bloody from seaside stories told by sailors who had stopped at the Isle of Ruma, but hearing it straight from the king...

And Odion didn't seem remorseful at all. That chilled me more than anything.

I grabbed at my wrist. Somehow, the gift he had given me, the warrior's mark bracelet, was still intact. It hadn't burned like most of my shirt. Lucky?

Terrakona had said to surround myself with talented individuals. Odion certainly seemed talented, but could I trust him? He had sworn himself to me, but the citizens of a kingdom were technically sworn to their lords or ladies.

We reached my room in silence, and I preferred that. Once

inside, I went straight to the opposite wall. The chair near my bed had Luthair's cape draped over the back. I breathed a sigh of relief as I walked over and touched the cold fabric. He was still here.

Odion glanced around. "Is that it? Your only prized possession?"

"Yeah," I muttered. "It's a piece of my previous eldrin."

"Something sentimental? That's it?"

I held the cape close. Perhaps it was. "It could be powerful," I said. Once I learned to imbue my world serpent magic. Luthair was... a true form knightmare, after all."

King Odion examined the cape from afar. He stared, and leaned in closer, but he never touched it. "I could help you create something with it. A piece of a knightmare mixed with the magic of a twilight dragon could produce something powerful—an artifact with control of the shadows."

I held Luthair's cape close. "No." I hadn't meant to sound so harsh. I exhaled and started again. "It has to be my magic. Luthair deserves that much."

Master Zelfree walked over and gently touched the edge of the cape. "They say a knightmare's cape is pivotal to its magic —it's their very heart, after all. Whatever you make from this, I'm sure it'll be powerful."

"You should have more protection," Odion stated. He glanced around the room, glaring at the windows and doors. "This place is just a room with no fortifications. Tomorrow we should get to imbuing you some defenses. And perhaps we should make you armor."

"I'm not sure if I'm ready for that yet," I muttered.

My shield, Forfend, had been created in haste. I remembered having a half-broken shield until I had managed to correct it. Theasin and others had told me it was because of my inexperience with creating items.

Artificers were the masters of item creation, and I only knew one person with that title.

My father, Jozé.

"After the celebration, I'll speak with an artificer." I placed the cape back on the chair, content that it hadn't been stolen. "Perhaps it is time I got some better protection."

35

WORLD SERPENT IMBUING

Odion left my bedroom, but before Master Zelfree and I could follow, Zelfree grabbed my upper arm and held me back. His grip was tighter than necessary.

"Why did you protect her?" he whispered, his tone gruff.

Oh. He meant Venae. I had protected her from Zelfree's killing blow.

Without removing his hand, I said, "I promised Adelgis I would help his siblings. I told him I wouldn't kill Venae."

Zelfree said nothing. I hated his haunting, troubled gaze. When I couldn't tolerate it anymore, I finally yanked away and turned my attention to the floor.

"I know what you're thinking," I said, clenching my hands into fists. "She's the enemy. Adelgis is being foolish. His siblings are all grown adults who are making their own decisions. I shouldn't protect them because of familial ties. I can't afford to make mistakes."

I had thought of all this, but I still couldn't bring myself to deny Adelgis. He was also right about their father's influence. Venae had probably been ordered here at some level. What could she do against her god-arcanist father? Perhaps if I could offer her another way, she could finally be free.

Zelfree fidgeted with the edge of his coat, his intense gaze drilling a hole through the floor. The only other time I had seen Zelfree so conflicted was when we had been facing Calisto.

As if he could hear my thoughts, Zelfree exhaled and said, "I know everyone has been asking you for favors."

I caught my breath and waited. Zelfree wanted something from me?

"If I asked you to spare someone for me, would you?" Zelfree asked with such seriousness, I didn't know how to reply.

"I will," I finally said. "I owe you so much, and I trust your judgment. If you think someone deserves a second chance, I'll try my damnedest to make that happen."

His pause after my statement unnerved me.

"Who is it?" I asked, my voice low.

Zelfree scratched at the stubble on his chin, never looking at me. "Lynus."

My gut twisted and my shoulders tensed. "Why?" I forced myself to ask. "Just a few weeks ago, you told me Lynus was dead—that he died when he fully took up the mantle as the Dread Pirate Calisto."

"You wouldn't understand."

"Didn't he torture you?" I motioned to Zelfree's coat collar, where I could still see some scars poking up beyond the edge of his clothing. "You had so many injuries... You almost died."

"*I don't want to talk about it,*" he growled.

"You *never* want to talk about it, even though you're clearly still struggling!" I hadn't meant to raise my voice, but my anger couldn't agree with my patience. "How long are you going to let this fester, huh? Another decade? If you ignore it long enough, it'll go away?"

Zelfree was like this with other problems. His lover had been killed, but instead of facing it, he had wasted away, drunk and miserable, for several years. Why couldn't he see his own destructive tendencies?

"I want to help you," I said, calmer than before. "Why won't you just let me?"

Still and strained, Zelfree was silent. His gaze remained distant, as though he had walked hundreds of miles away from me in his own thoughts.

I waited, hoping he would choose to allow me in.

Finally, Zelfree took a deep breath. "Lynus thinks I betrayed him." Then he exhaled, strained and darkly smiling. "And maybe he's not wrong." The last of his words had an icy edge to them.

"What happened?" I quietly asked.

"I left him. I should've helped him like he had helped me. I should've gotten him into the Frith Guild instead of using him like a tool. If I had been there, he wouldn't be in this situation." Zelfree's breathing returned to a shallow harshness. "I'm to blame for what he is."

"He's a grown man," I stated. "You can't take responsibility for his actions because you feel bad about his circumstances."

Zelfree didn't reply.

"It's not your fault."

He wheeled on me, rage in his motions, though he kept his expression controlled. "If I don't try to make this right, I won't be able to live with myself, do you understand? Maybe I'm just tired of losing literally everyone who has ever been important in my life." He threw an arm up, as though beseeching the stars. "I know fate and chance are cruel, but *every single person* I've felt close to has vanished. I have Liet left. *That's it.* Lynus... I wanted to write him off, but maybe that was just me being a coward."

When Zelfree exhaled, his shoulders slumped.

"Illia wants Calisto dead," I intoned. "And I don't think I can convince her otherwise."

With a weighted and resigned expression, Zelfree met my gaze. "If it's in your power, let me take Calisto's punishment in his stead."

I couldn't believe what I had just heard. I didn't even know how to respond to that. With nervous movements, I glanced around, waiting for someone to jump out from the darkness and declare this all a joke.

"Calisto isn't worth it," I said, on the verge of anger.

Zelfree half-laughed, half-scoffed. "Listen, kid. This isn't all about Calisto. It's about making up for mistakes. For... not being there when I should've." He motioned to himself. "For abandoning someone who needed my help. Especially since... Well, it doesn't matter anymore."

"Why bring this up now? You've never asked for this before."

He motioned to our surroundings in a dramatic fashion and then the window, like I hadn't seen the world serpent outside. "You're a god-arcanist, and apparently, you're doling out pardons. I wasn't going to ask my knightmare arcanist apprentice to spare a dread pirate on my behalf." He tapped the side of his head. "*Think*, Volke. You're the one calling the shots now. I answer to you as much as I answer to Liet."

"I hadn't thought of it that way," I whispered.

"I know. You need to change that."

"S-Sorry."

Zelfree pinched the bridge of his nose. "Don't apologize. Just understand you have the power to change things. *Everything*." He turned away and headed for the door but stopped before he reached for the handle. "I know you don't understand, but..."

"I understand," I muttered. "I understand that you and Calisto

—Lynus, whatever—have a long history. But after everything that's happened, I didn't know you still wanted to help him. I didn't see *all* your memories, so I'm missing part of the picture."

Zelfree silently waited. He kept his back to me, and I wondered what would be best in this situation. Could I really spare someone like Calisto? He was a dread pirate. He didn't deserve mercy.

Then again, some of Adelgis's siblings were no doubt wrapped up in Theasin's plotting. They had helped a madman kill and destroy, yet I hadn't hesitated to spare them.

Calisto was different. He had hurt Illia.

"I don't know if I can," I finally said. "I won't... deny Illia her revenge, even if I wish it wouldn't consume her."

"Then I'll speak to her," Zelfree replied.

"O-Okay. If you can convince her... I'll try my best to grant your request." I held up a hand before he could reply. "But unlike Venae, I'm not going to let Calisto get away. Whatever happens—whenever we face him—that'll be the end of the line. He either dies or repents, and one of those is *way* more likely than the other. You know that, right?"

Zelfree slowly nodded along with my last statement. With movements devoid of energy, he placed his hand on the door and then glanced over his shoulder at me. "Thank you, Warlord."

After changing into less-than-impressive clothes—trousers, an open shirt, and a coat—I went back to seeing guests.

My birthday couldn't end soon enough.

I hurt from the bits of the apoch dragon swimming in my veins. I hadn't seen Evianna since our time on the roof, and I feared she was upset with me. To top it off, every arcanist who had come to see me demanded my full attention while they laid out elaborate schemes and alliances.

The only people who really grabbed my attention and held it were the guildmasters.

All guilds were overseen by the Grandmaster Guild Hall. Each guild was registered at the main fortress, and the arcanists at the Grandmaster Guild Hall were the ones who made negotiations with nations to ensure that the guilds could operate across borders. That was why the Frith Guild could sail the seas of the Argo Empire and also my island nation without answering to either navy. They had the authority to fight pirates and help cities and towns.

Apparently, several guildmasters wanted me to change the status quo. According to Guildmaster Tillis and Guildmaster Jonah, the negotiations with nations were being undone by the Second Ascension. Our enemies had poisoned things with their unrest. Guilds weren't allowed across some borders. Naval ships had been detaining arcanists, and according to the horror stories, some guilds had been intentionally infected with the arcane plague as punishment.

They wanted me to solve this.

It made sense. This was why I was here. To deal with the plague and the Second Ascension.

I agreed, and both guilds swore their efforts to our cause.

The other guests wanted *things* in exchange for fighting the good fight. I agreed to most—altering land and imbuing magical trinkets and artifacts with world serpent magic once I had the strength—but I denied all marriage proposals and agreements to eliminate other nations.

That was surprisingly common. Apparently, several smaller islands wanted to be bigger than their neighbors—and then they wanted their neighbors to be absorbed into their control.

I denied those requests every time.

After all negotiations were made, five smaller territories, all run by dukes and marquises, also swore themselves to the cause. Their soldiers would add their ranks to our own.

By the end of the night, my throat burned, and my head throbbed. I sat in a lounge, waiting for the next guest to be ushered in. With a sigh, I silently thanked Evianna. It was an ingenious idea to have the guests brought to me one at a time. At least I had time between each visit to recuperate a bit.

We were stronger than before. More arcanists. More soldiers.

Would it be enough? I hadn't thought diplomacy would be a skill I would need.

The door to the lounge opened and closed before I sat up to get a good look. To my surprise, Guildmaster Eventide had come to see me. She gave me an easy smile as she crossed the room and took a seat on a giant chair across from me. Her guild pendant shone in the lanternlight, silver and elegant.

"Volke, you seem well," she said.

I glanced down. Everything felt sore. "I'm glad I can fool someone."

"Do you need anything to eat?"

"No." I shrugged. "I'm full... of exhaustion."

Eventide cracked a smile. "I'm glad to see the assassin didn't kill your sense of humor." Then she leaned forward and braced her elbows on her knees. "I apologize for not warning you sooner. There were reasons for my actions, though."

"You wanted to catch her," I said.

Eventide held up a finger. "I wanted to see if our defenses were as good as promised." She lowered her hand. "Our enemy is cleverer than we thought, and because we allowed this one assassin to get through, I now know what to look for in the future."

"You mean, you allowed the assassin to roam around unchecked because you wanted to test our defenses?" I asked. Adelgis hadn't told me that.

"Something like that," Eventide said, one eyebrow lifted. "It didn't go as I wanted it to. Fortunately, you were able to handle the situation. The assassin's eldrin was found dead."

I nodded once. "Have you... found her?"

"Not yet. But we will. Yesna and Captain Devlin are out right now."

"We shouldn't kill her," I said. I didn't know if Adelgis had informed Eventide of his desires, so I knew I had to make sure his sister would be safe. "Please. Just capture her."

"So Adelgis can hear her thoughts and inspect her memories through her dreams?"

"Er, yes. Exactly."

Eventide leaned back in her seat, silent for a short while, mulling over my statement. Then she said, "It's handled. Adelgis has relayed the command."

"Thank you."

With a gentle smile, Eventide added, "I apologize. Your injuries are my fault. I should've been more attentive after the assassin broke past our line. If I had been there, we could have—"

"Don't worry about it." I waved away her apology. "I understand that sometimes guile requires covert actions."

Guildmaster Eventide laced her fingers together and then rested her chin on top. "I'm fortunate to have someone so understanding. Let me tell you about the many times people didn't take kindly to my plans."

"I like to think of myself as reasonable," I said, softly chuckling.

"Perfect, because I need to speak to you about your guests."

That sounded ominous. "What about them?"

Eventide narrowed her eyes. "Volke, there are ten other god-creatures who will need people with whom to bond. Another reason I wanted this celebration to happen, was because I was hoping we might find someone we could trust."

I tensed, my mind abuzz with thoughts.

Of course! Why hadn't I thought about this? Why hadn't Adelgis mentioned this? I should've been paying attention! Who were the individuals we could trust? Who could bond with the fenris wolf, the sky titan, and all the rest? I wouldn't be the only god-arcanist fighting the Second Ascension.

"I hadn't thought about people who could bond with the god-creatures," I said, my guilt thick in my words. "I'll try to remember that in the future."

Eventide tapped her guild pendant. "I know it's difficult to keep so many problems at the front of your thoughts, but this one is important. It could make or break our fight against the Autarch."

She wasn't outright scolding me, but I could read between the lines. Eventide was disappointed. I hadn't used this opportunity properly. I should've been using my position as the world serpent arcanist to feel out other arcanists and individuals from all kinds of nations.

"Why don't we have other members of the Frith Guild bond with the god-creatures?" I asked.

"We could," Eventide said, her words slow. "But bonding with a god-creature would require losing your eldrin." She gave me a slight frown. "I'm sorry about Luthair, but he died protecting you. If we asked someone in the Frith Guild to bond with a god-creature, they'd have to kill their eldrin."

"There's... no other way to unbond?" I asked, my chest tight.

"There are stories, but nothing reliable. Nothing I could replicate. The only surefire way would be death, and I can't ask that of anyone."

Damn. She was right. Who would I ask? Illia would never kill Nicholin. Zaxis would never murder Forsythe. Hexa loved Raisen. Atty wanted her phoenix to grow into her true form no matter what. Zelfree had been with Traces for centuries. Adelgis...

He wouldn't. That wasn't Adelgis.

Gillie had already lost an eldrin. She wouldn't want to do that again.

Who else?

Fain? Never. My father? He had killed a man to save Tine. He wouldn't abandon his phoenix, not after that.

Karna? No.

Vethica had just bonded to a new eldrin. Same as Ryker.

Captain Devlin loved Mesos.

Yesna? Like Zelfree, she had been bonded for centuries.

Evianna's knightmare had come from her own blood relative.

No one would. Absolutely not. I knew in my gut.

"We need to find people," Eventide said. "That's the conclusion I've drawn. I thought we could ask the sybil arcanists again—the ones who had predicted you or your brother would become the world serpent arcanist—but we've had trouble contacting them."

She sighed, and for the first time in a long while, I could hear the strain of the situation on her breath. Eventide did a lot. She never quit.

"I'll try to find people," I said. "I'll make it a priority."

There was nothing else I could promise but that. Starting now, I'd have to evaluate people in terms of bonding to one of the most powerful creatures the world had ever seen.

"Well, I'll let you get back to seeing your guests." Eventide stood. She had a confident presence and demeanor, even after her tired exhale. It eased me to know she would be handling some of the other tasks for me, like capturing Venae.

"Thank you," I muttered, preparing myself to meet with the next few arcanists.

Well beyond the midnight hour, the celebration finally came to an end.

None of the other guests I saw were individuals I considered trustworthy or dedicated to our cause. They were here for themselves. It was a little disheartening.

I didn't meet with everyone, however. Some stayed to watch Terrakona or watch the entertainment.

Apparently, Odion and Karna had prepared several performances for my birthday celebration. Musicians from across Fortuna had come to play their drums and horns. A theater troupe that traveled from isle to isle on their ship known as *The Merry Band* performed a skit that depicted my bonding. And Karna sang and danced.

I didn't get to see any of it. I stayed in my lounge, safe and comfortable in my chair, unwilling to risk the crowds to see the entertainment that had been set up in my honor. I heard about it all from Adelgis and Terrakona, both of whom had telepathic links to me and wanted to describe every detail.

"Warlord, the Children of Balastar are just as impulsive and rowdy as ever. They revel in drink and laugh at the cheapest of tricks."

"It's called having a good time," I said, leaning back in my cushioned seat. "You should try it."

"We do not have sufficient amounts of alcohol to unravel my standards."

I laughed out loud. "I need to tell that to somebody," I said, rubbing at my eyes. "Maybe we should take you to a winery. We can throw a few barrels into your mouth."

Terrakona telepathically sent me a grumpy sound of displeasure. It made me laugh a second time. But once I had finished, I realized I didn't have much strength to carry on. I stood, stretched, and decided to head to my room.

Perhaps I would find Evianna on the way there? She still hadn't come to see me.

Or maybe she would be waiting for me there. Evianna had slipped into my room more times than I could count.

I wanted to see her again.

With heavy limbs, I shuffled out of the lounge and into the hall. Javin knights waited outside, one on either side of the door. A giant star tiger, a good 700 pounds of muscle, also stood waiting. Its white fur and silver stripes made me think of Nicholin. I stared for a long time, admiring how the beast practically glittered in the light of the glowstone lamps.

The tiger examined me with sapphire-blue eyes.

I offered a tiny bow of my head. "Good evening."

"Warlord," the star tiger said, his voice a rumble.

I walked by the knights and the tiger and then went straight for my room. I knew its location only because I had marked the way. All the vases in halls leading to my room were turned so that their decorative markings were facing the direction I needed. I knew I was in the right hall because I had torn a single leaf on each plant in the vases. Not the most clever way to find my way around, but at least no one knew I had marked the hallway.

Following my own bizarre path, I found my room and entered it with hopeful energy.

Inside, I found my father, Jozé, and his blue phoenix, Tine. Jozé stood with a cane supporting half his weight, his attention fixed on something out the window. When I shut the door, he flinched and glanced over.

"Ah, Volke," he said with a chuckle. "There you are."

His phoenix tilted her heron-like head. "You look tired."

I walked over, sluggish in all regards. "What're you two doing here?" I tried not to sound disappointed, but the way Jozé frowned told me I hadn't been successful.

"Well, I know your old man hasn't been in your life, but I

was trying to sneak in some father-son time before the day was up." He motioned to the window and pointed out to the crowds of individuals funneling out the gate. "I know you're popular, but perhaps you wouldn't mind hearing me out?"

"Of course not," I said, trying to be more enthusiastic.

"Good. Because I brought you something." He reached into his coat pocket and withdrew a leather pouch. Then he opened it up and revealed a small pile of star shards. They twinkled with an inner light.

Magic.

Raw, beautiful magic.

I stepped closer and gave them a long look. Each was no bigger than my thumb. Small items, but they contained a wonderful essence. I picked one out of the pouch and examined it more closely, admiring the swirl of stars within.

"I'm not the best father," Jozé muttered. He frowned as he placed the pouch of star shards on the nearby dresser. "But I'm a damn good artificer. Let me help you make a trinket or two. Adelgis should be joining us shortly."

"I'll help if I can," Tine said, flapping her wings and spreading soot around my room.

"Why Adelgis?" I understood why my father and Tine would help, but Adelgis had never been talented at creating magical items.

I had never seen him make *any* magical items, now that I thought about it.

Before my father could answer my question, the door to my room opened and shut. Adelgis slipped in, his long hair loose and straight, hanging down beyond his shoulders. He smiled as he strode over.

"*Thank you, Volke,*" he spoke telepathically.

"I wish you a happy birthday," he said aloud.

I wanted to say *you're welcome* and *thank you*, but in my sleepy state, I mashed them together and said, "You're you."

My father cocked an eyebrow and frowned.

Adelgis genuinely chuckled. "I am me, thank you." Then he waved his hand. "But we have other things to discuss. Felicity? Can you show yourself, please?"

The light from the glowstone lanterns flickered with life. Then a spiral shell formed in the air from the glitter and rays. Felicity's snail-like body took shape, her tentacles hanging from the underside of her iridescent shell.

I liked the way she floated in the air, with no earthly attachment.

Tine stared at the whelk like a bird watching a worm.

"Volke, I spoke with your father about the possibility of creating trinkets," Adelgis said. Like my father, he reached into his trouser pocket and withdrew a small linen pouch. He opened it to reveal shimmering shell pieces, obviously broken off Felicity.

I turned and examined her closely, looking for cracks or damaged pieces of her otherworldly shell. I found nothing. Every inch of her was pristine and glittering.

"How did you get those?" I asked.

"Ethereal whelks don't discover new shells when they grow larger," Adelgis said matter-of-factly. "They make new ones from a special type of light. Recently, Felicity broke her old shell to create a new one, so I gathered up the fragments to make trinkets."

He handed over the pouch. I took it and stared at the shell pieces.

"They're beautiful," I said.

Jozé tapped at the side of his head. "I thought the same damn thing. Actually, I thought, *these are fit for a king.*" He plucked a single fragment and held it closer to the glowstones. The shell piece sparkled even brighter. "Every order of knight, every guild, and every ship crew has a way of marking their own."

I slowly nodded along with his words.

Knightly orders had banners, nation symbols, flags, and distinct armor.

Every guild had a crest, and every arcanist wore theirs on their guild pendant.

And most ship crews had a symbol and name on the ship that they wore with the pendant. Pirates often marked themselves, typically with brands or tattoos.

Jozé placed the shell piece back in the pouch. "Volke, I thought I could craft you something with these fragments. Maybe make you pendants for your knights, or another kind of item they could carry with them in order to mark their allegiance to you."

"It's customary," Adelgis said with an approving tone. "And you have no way, currently, to distinguish those who have sworn themselves to you yet. I know you only have four knights, but still. It's better you make a symbol for yourself now, rather than wait."

"What do you think my symbol should be?" I asked, trying to imagine all the crests and banners I had ever seen.

"Not a serpent," Jozé stated. "Think of something that better suits you as a person. To let people know *you're* the warlord, not Terrakona."

"Okay." I crossed my arms and stared at my boots. A part of me already knew the answer. Why wait to announce it? "I want it to be a cape and shield, around a twelve-point star."

Adelgis half-smiled. "So... A knightmare symbol over the god-arcanist mark? An interesting choice."

"Well, I was a knightmare arcanist first, and if it weren't for Luthair, I never would've reached Terrakona. If there's anything that represents *me*, it's this."

Jozé clapped his hands together once in actual excitement. "That's my boy. Stayin' true to yourself. I like it. I really do."

"Since these are ethereal whelk bits, it will contain magics relating to light, dreams, and thoughts," Adelgis said, excitement in his tone. "If your father imbues blue phoenix magic into it, we'll likely create a magical item that uses light or fire to damage things. Or perhaps a resistance to such damage. No more sunburns." Adelgis waited a moment and then chuckled. "That last part was a joke."

"We don't want that," Jozé said.

"I agree. It wouldn't be the most impressive." Adelgis's eyes went wide. "However, if we imbue ethereal whelk magic into ethereal whelk bits, we could improve the item. Perhaps it could be an item that links the wearers telepathically to one another."

Jozé rubbed at his stubble. "Very useful. I could use my blacksmithing to shake these little bits into Volke's crest, and then you could imbue them."

"What if *I* imbued them with world serpent magic?" I asked.

The two of them exchanged odd glances. Even their eldrin looked perplexed, and that was impressive for a sea snail and phoenix.

"I don't know," Adelgis said. "I've never seen someone imbue world serpent magic into an item. And it's not like the previous Warlord of Magic ever did that. He existed in a time period before star shards could be used to imbue items."

I hadn't thought of that. It made my mind race with ideas.

I had used a piece of the previous world serpent to create Forfend, but that wasn't the same. World serpent magic seemed to be about earthly connection and concentration. And maybe a bit about never dying, I wasn't sure.

But if I wanted these items to be symbols of my knights, it made sense for me to make them.

"Who all has sworn to you?" Jozé asked, his brow furrowed.

"King Odion, Queen Callandra, Fain, and Adelgis," I said. "Technically five, if you count the City of Fortuna. Guildmaster

Eventide has also agreed to serve as my second-in-command, basically, but she didn't swear fealty, like the others."

"So, we need four, but probably a dozen more. There were so many guests here tonight..."

I shook my head. "We'll see. Eventide is right. I should be a little more discerning about who I allow close to me. All these people just want to use my magic and power for their own gain. Most of them aren't even concerned about the Second Ascension, and I can't allow them to influence my decisions. The Autarch must be stopped—that's my top priority."

Jozé grabbed one of the shell fragments and handed it to me. Then he grabbed a star shard and placed it on top of the fragment, both in my palm. "Here. Imbue this. Let's see what it makes. If the trinket is useful, that's what we'll do with all of them."

"Do you think... I'll be able to do it?"

My father nodded once. He wrapped my fingers around the two objects. "The key is concentration and imagination. Visualize what you want in your mind's eye. You have to see your magic melting into the object, and you have to see the star shard as a sort of glue. Also, it'll help to think of an aspect of your magic. Something you want in the trinket."

Then he removed his hand from mine.

I had done this before with Luthair. I could do it now.

After a deep breath, I closed my eyes and tried to do exactly as instructed. Concentrate. Visualize. Focus on the magic.

But what aspect of my magic? The destructive or the creative? That was a difficult choice. Perhaps I wanted my knights to have a part of my magic to use defensively, or perhaps I wanted my knights to have ways to help others.

Mostly, I wanted them to be safe. What could I give that would protect *them* from harm?

The basalt bones? The ability to breathe underwater? Tremor sense?

My magic oozed from my being and dove straight into the ethereal whelk shell fragment. They combined, much like flour and water, slowly at first, and then smoothly afterward. I scrunched my nose as I felt the star shard liquefy and merge with the shell.

A glue.

Somehow, the first world serpent arcanist had altered these star shards to be useful.

Could I do that with the arcane plague?

I gasped and lost focus. When I opened my eyes, sweat dappled my skin. I stared at the shell fragment in my hand, my fingers shaky.

What had I created?

A KNIGHT'S CREST

I handed the item over to my father.

Tine flapped her wings around his legs, stretching her neck up in an attempt to see what was happening. Felicity swirled around us, a slight giggle passing telepathically to me as she moved.

Jozé flipped the object around on his palm. Then he clutched the shell piece firmly in his grip. A subtle light shone through his fingers. He took a deep breath and then opened his hand to reveal the shimmering shell fragment. It lit up the room like a firework caught mid-burst and frozen in time.

"This is invigoratin'," he said with a smile. The light emitting from the fragment slowly waned. "For a split second, it was like... I had grazed something with limitless potential. Something pure."

I took the fragment from him and stared at it, my eyes squinting. "What does it do?"

"It's just a trinket, so not much, but once I felt the light, my leg didn't hurt as much. Also, and I know this is crazy, but it seemed like I didn't need to take a breath."

The magic was defensive! The trinket would allow people

access to my unbelievable self-healing and perhaps even let them survive without breathing for longer periods of time. Was it super useful? Probably not. Only one star shard had been used to make it, after all. The more shards I used, the more of my magic could be permanently bonded to the shell fragment.

"This is what I wanted," I said, holding the fragment close. "I wanted something that would benefit my knights."

Adelgis crossed his arms. "I think you accomplished that. Perhaps we should use one more star shard per trinket, however. To make sure it's potent enough to help an arcanist recover from a dire situation."

I turned to my father. He was the expert.

Jozé nodded. "I think that's for the best as well." He held up the pouch of fragments and shook them around. The jingling inside sounded like broken glass. "What should I make? Bracelets?"

"Why not pendants?" I asked, touching my new pendant from Eventide.

"Eh." Jozé waved away the comment. "I've never been a fan of the guild ways."

"A ring, then." I stared at my hand, my thumb grazing the underside of my pointer finger. "That way, it'll be close, making skin contact for easier activation, and it'll be displayed for all to see."

Jozé tossed the pouch and then caught it. "Perfect. I can make that."

Plus, rings could easily be worn as pendants, if someone didn't fancy wearing something on their hand. But I didn't voice that explanation.

Jozé patted my shoulder. Then he hobbled toward the door, his steps surprisingly filled with energy. His blue phoenix hopped after him, her inner fire flaring with life whenever she moved. She kept her silvery eyes on her arcanist, and I wondered if she worried about my father's injured leg.

Blue phoenixes couldn't heal, after all. Their flames burned brighter and hotter than any other, but if my father had an accident, she wouldn't be able to mend him.

Adelgis waited. Once the door had shut, and we were alone, he turned to face me. "Thank you," he said. "My mother and sister arrived safely not too long ago."

"Cinna is here?" Although I didn't know her well, it made me happier to hear that Adelgis had been reunited with her. "I hope she's feeling well."

"Would you like to meet her?"

"Yeah, of course."

Adelgis straightened himself and then hurried to the door. He opened it and then glanced over his shoulder. "Are you coming?"

"Wait, right now? It's well into the night." I stared at the darkness beyond the window. "Dawn will arrive soon."

"No need to worry. Cinna is awake, and she'd love to meet you."

Although I wanted to sleep, I didn't want to deny Adelgis's request. He cared about his siblings. The least I could do was meet her and make sure she was safe in my compound.

I followed Adelgis out of my room and into the hall. Most of the lanterns had been snuffed, resulting in thick shadows and dark corners. Nothing about the gloom bothered me. The opposite, in fact. Luthair would've loved the small amount of light.

"Is Evianna still awake?" I quietly asked Adelgis.

He probably knew all about our time on the roof. Why hide it?

Adelgis nodded once. "She is. While searching for you, she ran into King Odion, and the two of them are near your world serpent in the gardens. They're having a pleasant conversation, though it's lacking in anything substantial. Evianna is convinced she'll see you sooner if she waits near Terrakona."

"Is my eldrin okay?"

"The lingering crowds from your birthday celebration clap for his every movement. He's amused." Adelgis slowed his walk as we rounded a corner. Then he glanced over. "He's telepathic. You could reach out at any time."

"I was actually wondering if you could hear his thoughts," I said with a shrug. "He seems... resistant to magics."

"He's also just a hatchling. As he grows older with you, he'll become stronger. Right now, his thoughts are a swirl. It's mostly emotions, much like a child."

"He's hardly a child. Terrakona knows a great deal of things."

Adelgis sighed. "Knowing things isn't the same as maturity or experience."

Before I could rebut the statement, Adelgis stopped and pointed to a door.

It opened and a young woman stepped out, her footing shaky. Her long, inky-black hair hung to her waist. It reminded me of Adelgis's. Her dress—a simple white-and-pink garment that went to her knees—couldn't hide her weak arms and legs. She struggled to stand properly and even leaned on the wall once she was fully out of her room.

"Cinna," Adelgis said as he approached, his arms wide. "I'm here."

Cinna's face lit up. She embraced Adelgis the moment he was close. "I'm so happy to be here, brother. Fortuna is just as wonderful as all the books said. It even smells of fish and salt water. I couldn't believe it."

I almost laughed. Why was that so special? Most cities by the water smelled heavily of marine life.

Adelgis took a long moment before releasing his sister from the hug.

Her round face and button nose gave her a cute and soft expression. Her dress didn't have many frills or decorations, but it was well cared for and hung light around her thin body. Although I didn't know what illness Cinna suffered from, her sunken eyes and trembling hands told me a long tale of hardship.

"Let me introduce you to Volke Savan, the Warlord of Magic and Second World Serpent Arcanist." He gestured to me, as if I were an impressive painting. "He's an invaluable friend, and now my liege. I've sworn fealty to him."

Cinna's already wan complexion faded into a deep white. She stared with wide brown eyes, first at me and then at her brother. "Mother isn't going to like this."

"It wasn't her decision," Adelgis stated, no hesitation or regret in his words.

After a moment of contemplation, Cinna smoothed her dress. Then her cheeks flushed a deep pink. "Oh! I'm sorry." She half-smiled. "It's a pleasure to meet you, Volke Savan. I'm Cinna Venrover. I hope... you and my brother are safe on your travels."

She bowed, her black hair beautiful as it fluttered over her shoulder. When she straightened herself, she reached out for Adelgis, who helped to balance her. Every part of her seemed more delicate than an eggshell.

"The pleasure is mine," I said, smiling. "Adelgis has told me all about you."

Again, she blushed. This time, she couldn't seem to meet my gaze. She mumbled something I couldn't hear and then her shoulders bunched around her neck.

"Are you okay?" I asked as I stepped closer.

"Oh, yes," Cinna said, grabbing Adelgis's arm. "Thank you for taking the time to visit someone like me. It's an honor." She tugged at the short sleeves of her dress. "This wasn't the outfit Mother wanted me to wear... I have nicer things. I wasn't prepared." She playfully tapped her brother on the shoulder, her hand balled into a fist in a pretend punch.

"Forgetful brothers." Cinna ended her statement with a nervous laugh.

I had never had any brothers until I had met Ryker, but my thoughts went immediately to Zaxis. He would surely be a forgetful brother. And so irritating at times. I sighed the moment I realized he *might* end up being my brother.

"Cinna!"

The shout came from inside Cinna's room. We all turned to the door, and I wondered who could be there. I didn't have to wait long to figure it out. The door swung open and a tall woman with harsh features stepped out into the hall. Her sharp chin and pointed eyebrows were familiar. It was Ketsa Venrover, Theasin's wife. I had met her before the Sovereign Dragon Tournament, though only briefly.

Her curly, black hair, just as inky as Adelgis's and Cinna's, was pulled back in a tight ponytail. It showcased her minerva owl arcanist mark. They were mystical creatures of study and knowledge, often found near cities with books.

With an elegant gait, Ketsa walked around and placed a hand on her daughter's shoulder. Cinna shuddered.

"What's going on here?" Ketsa asked. She stepped between Cinna and Adelgis, breaking their hold. "Adelgis, what have I told you? Cinna needs rest. You shouldn't have visited her at such a late hour."

Adelgis said nothing, his expression so neutral and still it might as well have been an oil painting.

Ketsa wore a sapphire dress embellished with actual gemstones around the collar. It was tight around her curves, showing off her natural beauty in a way that drew attention to it. Even a blind man would be drawn in by the flair of her outfit.

She turned to me, and her pale blue eyes held no recognition. Ketsa didn't remember me.

For a split second, she sneered, and I thought she would

dismiss me as a servant, but her gaze dropped to my chest—to my open shirt and god-arcanist mark—and she froze.

"Oh," she whispered as she brought a hand up to her collarbone. "Oh, my. You must be the world serpent arcanist."

I forced myself to smile. "That's right. Welcome, Ketsa Venrover. Thank you for accepting my invitation."

Ketsa's entire demeanor shifted in an instant. She beamed at me, smiling wide and fluffing her curly hair. "Where are my manners? Forgive me. The travel was long, and my daughter is ill." Ketsa pulled Cinna close, holding her like a precious object. "We tried to arrive days earlier, but I didn't risk it because of the rains."

"Don't worry about it," I stated.

She bowed her head. "Such an honor. Thank you. Odion's invitation to join in your festivities will be a prized family possession for years to come. I'm humbled, and so is my daughter. Aren't you, Cinna?" She straightened and then motioned Cinna to bow to me in the same fashion.

"We must be on our way," Adelgis said, stepping close to me. His movements and words were so curt, it was almost startling. "Cinna needs her rest, right, Mother?" He shot her a pointed glare. Then he placed a hand on my shoulder. "The Warlord has important matters to attend to."

"Of course. I understand fully. I have matters of my own."

Ketsa bowed a second time as Adelgis and I turned down the hall in the opposite direction. I glanced over my shoulder, getting one more look at the sickly Cinna. She watched me go with wide eyes but glanced away the moment she caught me staring.

I hoped she would be okay with her controlling mother.

Adelgis pulled me into a room, and I didn't protest. Once he shut the door, he leaned his back against it and sighed.

"Why wouldn't your mother be happy to hear you've sworn

yourself to me?" I asked. "She seemed elated that she was invited to the party."

"She wants me to help my father," Adelgis stated. Before I could ask questions, he quickly added, "My mother doesn't know about my father's involvement with the Second Ascension. All she knows is that my father is being paid a handsome sum for magical research, and that most of my siblings already fall under his employ. She never wanted me to join the Frith Guild. She just wanted me to do whatever my father wanted."

Adelgis grabbed at his ribs, his brow furrowed.

"Are they planning to stay here?" I asked.

He nodded once. "Arrangements have been made. Guildmaster Eventide told my mother that you're looking for powerful political connections, which was why she was invited, thus stroking my mother's ego." Adelgis clenched his jaw. "My mother also thought that you were in the arena for a wife, and because my father is *so talented*, she figured you wanted a connection with the Venrover family."

Eh. Nothing could be further from the truth.

Adelgis glanced up with a slight frown.

I kept forgetting he could read my thoughts.

"I don't want a connection with your family," I said, rubbing at the back of my neck. "But you're a good friend. You know that."

"I understand." He shook his head. "And I apologize. Apparently, my mother filled Cinna's head with thoughts of becoming your *lisque*."

A lisque?

That was an old-world term for the mortal spouse of an arcanist. It was mostly used in a derogatory way. An arcanist married a mortal for the specific reason that the mortal would die long before the arcanist would. Mortal lives weren't extended by magic, after all.

From the tales I had read, the arcanists had never been kind to their lisques. It had been a power dynamic—arcanists had kept lisques to use as they had seen fit. The mortal would die, and the arcanist would find a new one to wed, and then repeat the whole process over again.

"Your mother was okay with Cinna doing that?" I asked, more shocked than anything else.

Adelgis took a moment to control his breathing. When he was calm, he said, "My mother also helped convince me it was a good idea to raise an abyssal leech. She's not the best source of wisdom, I would say."

It still hurt to hear that she wanted her daughter to become a lisque.

"She wants the prestige," Adelgis said, obviously answering my thoughts. "My mother has always been shrewd in that regard." He pushed away from the door and shrugged. "I know you would never hurt Cinna. And I suspect this will never be an issue, but just so you're—"

Adelgis cut himself off.

I waited for a long moment, wondering if he would pick up the conversation. Adelgis just stood still, his eyes searching but obviously distant, like he was seeing something I couldn't.

"Volke," he finally whispered. "The Knights Draconic are here to see you."

I sighed and threw a hand up in the air. "*What?* How many more people will come to see me?" I motioned to the window. "It's dawn!" Sure enough, the sun crested the ocean, lighting up Fortuna in a heavenly pink glow. "Contrary to popular belief, I have to sleep at some point."

"You don't understand. These visitors are different."

"How so?" I snapped. "Let me guess. They want me to marry the prince this time, instead of the princess." I ran a hand down my face. "Just tell everyone they only get my time and rewards based on the amount of effort they put toward defeating the Second Ascension. That's my new policy."

Adelgis shook his head. "You don't understand. The Knight Captain of Thronehold is here to see you because there are two sovereign dragon arcanists fighting over the capital. Both have legitimate claims to the throne—to rule over the Argo Empire —but only one can win."

My irritation disappeared as the impact of the statement sank into my thoughts.

"The knights are coming to see you," Adelgis continued, "because they want your support. Apparently, the other sovereign dragon is being aided by the Second Ascension."

POWER STRUGGLE IN THE ARGO EMPIRE

D amn.

Theasin was on his way to Thronehold. So was Calisto.

It all made sense. They weren't just going because the fenris wolf was in the area, they were going to help the new sovereign dragon arcanist take the throne. *Then* they would search for the wolf with the aid of the Argo Empire army.

And we still hadn't found someone to bond with the wolf.

"Can you tell Eventide about this?" I asked Adelgis.

He replied with a curt nod. "I will."

"And tell the Knight Captain that I'll help. I don't want the Second Ascension to get their claws on Thronehold again. That already happened with King Rishan, and he was a madman."

"I understand," Adelgis said. "I'll relay the message."

I clenched my hands together and cracked my knuckles. Every fiber of my being wanted to rush to Thronehold, but I knew I'd collapse ten feet outside the Fortuna gates. I hadn't slept in so long, and the after effects of the fight with Venae still wore on me. The bits of the apoch dragon swirled in my blood like crumbs of food in a glass of water.

"You should just get some rest," Adelgis said as he placed a hand on my shoulder. "When you wake, I'm sure your father will have your rings, Eventide will have assembled the guild, and everyone will be ready to depart for the capital of the Argo Empire."

"Are you sure?" I asked.

"Well, we're all mostly experienced arcanists. I daresay we're competent enough to handle packing for a long trek without your help."

I chuckled and then sighed. "Thank you, Adelgis. I really appreciate this." I returned the gesture and patted him on his shoulder as well. "Wake me if anything dire happens."

I slept, but I didn't have that strange dream.

It was a little disappointing. I wanted to see what was inside the castle. Perhaps I wouldn't until I mastered more of my magic? I seemed to get deeper and deeper the more I had control of my powers. Or perhaps it was something else?

Hadn't someone at my celebration mentioned it? What was his name?

I tossed and turned in my bed, my mind restless. Despite my fatigue, my body didn't want to cooperate. My legs twitched, my thoughts raced, and my stomach twisted around itself. How could I sleep when the Second Ascension was in the Argo Empire already? We had to get on our way.

The moment the sun from the window bathed me in warmth, I threw off the blankets and leapt to my feet. A few hours had been enough. We had to be on our way.

"Terrakona," I said, my voice rusty.

"**Warlord?**" he telepathically replied.

"You said you can travel over land, right?"

"**With ease.**"

"Then we need to head to Thronehold. Are you ready?" I stumbled around my room, grabbing clothing and yanking it on one piece at a time. I had kept my new guild pendant around my neck, just in case something happened in the middle of the night.

"If you want us in Thronehold, then no force will stop me from taking us there."

I loved his confidence. I wished I had more of it.

With Retribution and Forfend on my person, I hesitated. Luthair's cape remained on the back of the desk chair. What would I do with it? Leave it here? Take it with me?

No part of me wanted to leave Luthair behind. I had to take his cape. Besides, I had star shards, I had my father with me—as soon as I thought of the artifact I would make, I would need the cape close.

I gently folded the cold garment and placed it within a carrying pouch. Nothing too large—just enough to carry objects such as the cape and the eventual rings my father would craft. I would need these on my journey.

Then I attached the pouch to my belt. It bulged a bit, but I didn't care.

Groggy and only half-aware, I turned and slammed into a nightstand, bruising my knee, and then limped to the door. At least no one had seen me do that. *Volke, the Warlord of Magic, hobbled by his own furniture. The world was doomed.*

I chuckled at my own internal joke as I opened the door. With haste in my steps, I traveled down the hall and made my way to the front foyer of the main building. The decorations from the celebration remained on the walls. Pictures of the world serpent helped my mood. I wouldn't lose to the Second Ascension. I couldn't.

When I exited the hall, I stopped. To my surprise, a dozen knights stood near the front door. Their silver full-plate and half-plate armor bore the mark of the Argo Empire: a dragon and a rose. They were all unicorn arcanists, which meant these were all members of the Knights Draconic, a noble order of soldiers who answered only to the sovereign dragon arcanist.

Two ivory unicorns even stood inside, their twisted horns nearly a foot and a half in length. They also wore silver armor, stamped with the nation's symbol. Their tails and manes had been cut short and trimmed neatly.

Guildmaster Eventide and Master Zelfree waited for me as well, each dressed in their usual swashbuckling flair. Zelfree's long coat and hat gave him a sailor's look. Eventide's eccentric coat, dotted with feathers, fur, and odd bits of mystical creatures, clashed quirkily with the uniform styling of the knights.

A single knight stepped forward. He wore a red cape with his armor, unlike the rest, his unicorn mark prominent on his large forehead.

"I am Knight Captain Alrick," he said as he placed three fingers over his heart—his thumb, pointer, and middle. "It is a pleasure to be in the presence of the world serpent arcanist."

It was an odd gesture for a greeting, but one I recognized. The people from the Amber Dunes used that to show respect. And Alrick looked the part. His darker-tanned skin, sandy brown hair, and amber eyes all reminded me of my time in New Norra.

"You're from the Argo Empire?" I asked, an eyebrow raised.

It was probably rude for me to blurt something like that out, and I instantly regretted it. I should've just accepted his greeting and moved on.

"I originally hail from the Amber Dunes," the knight captain said. Then he lowered his hand and offered me a bow from the waist, common to the Argo Empire. "Forgive me. I sometimes mix up etiquette." Then he straightened himself, his hard gaze locked on mine. "But there's no time for that. The guildmaster of the Frith Guild says you've been informed of the situation, is that true?"

I nodded once.

"Then my queen awaits," Knight Captain Alrick said. He gestured to the front door. "My knights and I will escort you straight to her encampment outside of Thronehold."

"Er, wait. A queen? And an encampment?"

"Yes. Thronehold has been attacked. The castle hadn't yet been fully repaired from the last attack, so Queen Ladislava set up fortifications on the lands surrounding the wall. She's been fighting her cousin and the Second Ascension, for over a month now."

"Her cousin?" I asked, dread clawing at my thoughts. "He's a sovereign dragon arcanist?"

"He is," Knight Captain Alrick replied matter-of-factly.

"And he's trying to claim the throne?"

"Correct. He calls himself *King Cardozo*, though he's never been coronated. It's a disgrace and an insult." The knight captain scoffed and brushed his hand to the side. "He drew support from a small fraction of Queen Ladislava's court, and that was how they helped him infiltrate the city."

Curse the abyssal hells.

I really had no idea what was happening in Thronehold. Sure, it was a power struggle, but I had never met anyone involved in these fights. Even the knight captain, Alrick, was a replacement for Knight Captain Rendell, a man I had seen die in the last attack on Thronehold.

I knew no one there. All I knew was that I couldn't let the Second Ascension get the Argo Empire. Whoever Queen Ladislava was, I had to protect her and her claim to the throne.

Damn. I wished I had more time. I wished my magic were better. I wished I'd had more rest.

But I couldn't have those things. Destiny was testing my

mettle, and if I didn't rise to the challenge, everything would be lost.

"Let's go," I said, pointing to the door. "Any enemy of the Second Ascension is a friend of mine."

"Thank you, Warlord. The Argo Empire owes you a great debt."

Knight Captain Alrick snapped his fingers once and the Knights Draconic fell into lined formation. They hurried from my compound in an organized fashion, marching with precision until they were outside. Then they mounted their individual unicorns and galloped toward the front gate without hesitation.

Their platoon of knights was a sight to see. Their silver armor shone in the morning light, and Alrick's scarlet cape fluttered behind him as he rode, leading the way.

Guildmaster Eventide and Master Zelfree walked up to either side of me.

"Are you rested?" Zelfree asked, his eyes narrowed in suspicion. "We told the unicorn arcanists we weren't going to leave until you were ready."

"I'm fine," I stated. "We should head out now."

It would take us ten days to reach Thronehold from Fortuna, and that was *if* we followed the roads and didn't have trouble with rain. From the sound of things, Queen Ladislava had already been fighting for some time. How much longer could she hold out?

"Theasin is heading to Thronehold," Eventide intoned, breaking me from my thoughts. "We need to be prepared for his arrival."

"And under no circumstance can the queen's dragon be killed," Zelfree added.

I glanced at him. "Why not?"

"Only sovereign dragon arcanists can rule within the Argo Empire. If her dragon dies, so does her claim to the throne. It's the same for the pretender king. If we kill his dragon, this fight is over. That should be our number-one priority."

Sovereign dragons weren't the most combat-capable creatures, but they were still *dragons*. Killing one—especially if it was an adult—would be difficult. Would one fall to my magma? Probably not. Most dragons were immune to heat and fire.

And what about Theasin and Calisto?

A thought struck me.

"Zelfree, can you bring the assassin's eldrin with us? The body of the white hart, I mean."

He gave me a sideways glance. "Yeah."

"And can you bring Markus? The pirate that's being held in the ship, the *Midnight Thorn*. We should take him with us as well."

Theasin wanted corpses, didn't he? Now we had one of our own—the white hart. Maybe, if we were lucky, we would see this *zombification* process that Markus was so scared of.

Plus, having Markus nearby might give us an advantage against Calisto.

"I'll get them both," Zelfree stated.

I half-expected him to follow it with *my liege*, but it never came. Of course—Zelfree had never sworn to me—but now things felt off when people didn't say it after a direct command.

What was wrong with me?

While the rest of the Frith Guild prepared to travel by carriage and cart, I went straight to Terrakona. He hadn't left the garden of my compound. Thankfully, I found Gravekeeper William standing by a topiary of a world serpent. He examined the shrub with scrutinizing eyes, his large body almost as big as the plant.

"William," I said as I hurried over.

He wore casual clothing—a simple tunic and trousers, both dark in color—but when he turned, he did so with military precision. William relaxed upon seeing me, and then offered a wide smile.

"Come 'ere," he said, motioning me close. When I did, he patted my shoulder. "Happy birthday. I know you had other guests to see, but I missed ya. Hopefully you got everythin' you wanted."

"Almost," I said, my face growing hot as I thought about the gift Evianna had never brought me.

"I heard you were leavin'."

I nodded once. "That's right. I'm sorry I couldn't stay longer." I stepped back and hardened myself to yet another farewell. "Can you please look after the compound while I'm away? Adelgis's mother and sister will be staying as well... And so will my mother, whenever she gets here."

I wanted to speak with her, but I supposed fate just didn't have that in the schedule.

William crossed his massive arms over his barrel chest. "I don't know if we have room for so many people here."

With a chuckle, I said, "Good one."

Everyone practically had their own massive building to live in.

He gave me the once over and then shrugged. "You're tense, boy. I wanted to loosen you up before you left, but obviously, it ain't workin'. I'm not sure what troubles you have to face, but I'm sure they're numerous."

"They are," I said, trying to keep the strain from my voice. William didn't deserve to worry. "I'll handle them, though. I'll be back before you know it."

"I'll be here, holdin' down the fort."

Once again, he patted my shoulder, this time in a gentle manner.

Although I wanted to do a million more things while in Fortuna—spend time with William, relax and enjoy life, properly mourn Luthair, or even meet a number of other people—I had to go. I returned the pat and ran over to Terrakona, his massive serpentine body half-resting in the garden, and half on the other side of the compound wall.

His crystal mane, tinted black, reminded me of Luthair's shadows. The interior of the crystals fluttered with shadows, even in the daylight.

Terrakona lowered his head. His forked tongue snaked out to greet me, like a puppy wagging its tail in excitement. His tongue had runes etched into it. An interesting sight, but I shook away the thought as I ran up to his snake-like snout.

"C'mon," I said as I hopped up onto his nose. "We need to hurry."

"As you say, Warlord."

He lifted his head, taking me with him. The rush of wind and the force of gravity almost knocked me off my feet. My neck and arm burned for a moment, reminding me of Venae's attack.

We still hadn't found her.

A part of me knew that would come back to haunt me.

Another thing I had to push aside.

I pointed southwest, toward the mountains in the far distance. "You need to cross over those to get into the Argo Empire. Then it's just a few short days to Thronehold."

"Foolish," Terrakona telepathically said. He snorted as he added, **"We are masters here. The travel will be swift and easy."**

Before I could protest, he slithered forward, his gigantic body rumbling the ground around us. I held my breath, fearful he would inadvertently destroy everything in the nearby vicinity. To my amazement, when Terrakona moved across the garden, the dirt shuddered, and the trees twisted.

The very earth moved around him—splitting apart to allow him through and then stitching itself back together after he left.

I could hardly believe it. With careful movements, I crawled into Terrakona's crystal mane and wedged my boots between the larger rocks, giving me some steadfast footing. I held on, watching the ground beneath us shift with the world serpent's motions. When I glanced back, I noticed the garden was in one piece, though slightly different than before. The trees and walkway had stitched back together in zigzag patterns, creating the same landscape, just jagged.

Terrakona slid across the hills surrounding Fortuna, moving with fluid speed, never slowing or altering his path for clusters of trees or rocks. They moved around him—he truly was the master of the terrain. I thought nothing would stop us, but Terrakona snaked around a large boulder jutting out of the ground.

I glanced over my shoulder as we passed it. The boulder protruded thirty feet into the air, like a reverse-carrot.

"Why didn't you move that?" I asked, the wind whipping through my trimmed hair.

"My power is not yet potent enough. Perhaps with age—with your help—I can alter such terrain. But not yet."

So some objects were outside of Terakona's capabilities? Interesting. I'd have to keep it in mind.

With lightning speed, we dashed across the outskirts of Fortuna. Farmlands stretched before us, and I tightened my grip on Terrakona's crystal mane as he headed straight for them. I held my breath as he slithered through terraces of rice paddies.

Just as in the garden, the ground split apart, allowing Terrakona to pass without crushing the vegetation. Unlike the garden, the water in the field sloshed around, making more of a mess than I would've hoped. Thankfully, when the earth knitted itself back together, the terraces were in one piece, if a bit uneven. The rice would survive.

It took us little time to reach the wall of Fortuna.

Half a dozen carriages awaited us, along with several carts. Arcanists from my celebration all lingered nearby, and everyone gasped and pointed as Terrakona and I rumbled toward them. The moment we arrived, several individuals fell to one knee, acknowledging my presence with murmured praise and awe, their heads bowed.

I tamed my windswept hair with a hand and then waved to the people far below me. Terrakona slowed and circled around the carriages, as if protecting them, but the horses didn't see it that way. They reared up and neighed, their eyes wide. The drivers had to rush to calm them.

The distance Terrakona had traveled—from my compound to the edge of the city—wasn't considerable, but he had been ten times faster than any cart or carriage. I suspected we could reach Thronehold several days ahead of schedule as long as we traveled alone.

But was that wise? Guildmaster Eventide and the others would be needed to help me fight the Second Ascension. I could take a few people on Terrakona's back, but not an entire army.

Terrakona lowered his massive head. People leapt out of the way, both mortals and arcanists alike. They left me plenty of room to dismount, and I slid off Terrakona's emerald scales and landed on the brick road just outside of Fortuna's walls.

People still seemed afraid...

Where was Evianna? I still hadn't found her. Surely, she was nearby.

"There you are, Volke!" Hexa hustled over, her curly hair bouncing with each step.

The other arcanists—either strangers who didn't know me or the Knights Draconic—held hands to their open mouths as

Hexa went straight to my side. She playfully punched my shoulder and motioned to a carriage at the front. "I'm supposed to help you find your seat." She leaned in close and half-opened her coat. At least a dozen knives hung in small holsters. "I'm here to poison any fool who opens your carriage door without knocking first."

I eyed her weapons. Throwing daggers, four inches in length. "Are you sure that's wise?"

"Hydra venom is potent and fast acting." Hexa leaned away and closed her coat. "Besides, I've been training, and my magic is better than ever. You'll see."

My brother also wandered over. He wore a black vest and a white shirt, but his baggy pants didn't seem to match the rest of him. Ryker's black hair—just as unruly as mine—was held down with liberal amounts of pomade.

"Volke," he said as he approached. Then he cleared his throat. "Uh, I'll also be with you during the trek, along with Karna. We have a plan—she and I will shapeshift to look like you. That way, in case there's an attack, the blackheart will be confused."

"Wait, you can shapeshift?" I asked. "I thought you were having trouble with that."

Ryker tugged at the collar of his crisp shirt. "Yeah, well... Karna said I should start with people who were similar to me in appearance and build. I've, uh, shapeshifted to look like you a few times now. It works." He forced an awkward smile. "I hope you don't find that disturbing."

I slowly shook my head. "I guess not?"

"Oh, good." He exhaled and genuinely smiled. "I thought you might become angry."

Something about how he had said that... It made me wonder what he had done while wearing my face. I didn't question him, though. It had likely been harmless.

To my amusement, *I* walked over to me from the front

carriage. Second-Me had a similar coat, a black shirt—open in the front to display my god-arcanist mark—and thick trousers sailors wore on long treks. Second-Me also had a nice pair of boots, but he was missing my sword and shield. Instead, he carried an ornate flintlock pistol.

Visible confusion spread through the crowd like a wind. Some pointed, some muttered. Second-Me was so convincing, some individuals thought *I* was the imposter.

Second-Me sauntered over and smirked. "Oh, someone is looking good this morning." He pointed two fingers at me and then slid to my side. In one smooth motion, he wrapped an arm around my back and pulled me close. "Men like us should stick together."

He had my voice.

It was... off-putting.

"Uh, Karna?" I asked.

Second-Me just shrugged. "I bet you wish you had the comfort of knowing." He patted my cheek. "I could be anyone."

"I can tell," Ryker stated. "That's Karna's doppelgänger, Karr."

"You can *tell*?" Karr-Volke asked, an eyebrow raised.

It was bizarre looking at myself. Like staring at an unruly mirror.

Ryker replied with a nervous chuckle. "Uh, yeah. MOS said that I'd be able to see through all mimicked and shape-changed individuals. It's an innate power."

Karr-Volke rolled his eyes as he slid away from me. "You're taking all the fun out of this. Why haven't you molded yourself yet? We're scheduled to leave as soon as the guildmaster arrives."

I glanced around, surprised I had beaten Eventide and Zelfree here. Terrakona really was fast traveling over land.

"Warlord! Over here!"

A man struggled against a group of Javin knights. His round

silhouette and perfectly tailored clothing looked familiar. I stepped forward and squinted. The scars on his hands... Was that the relickeeper arcanist who frantically tried to tell me about a building underwater?

"Santonio?" I asked.

The soldiers glanced over their shoulders. "Do you know this man, Warlord?" one called out.

I nodded. "Uh, yeah. You can let him go."

With a rough shove, the soldiers released Santonio from their hold. The man stumbled for a bit before regaining his footing. Then he brushed the dirt from his clothes and hurried over. His face was rather friendly now that we were out in the daylight, and I could get a better look at him. He had laugh lines around his eyes.

Santonio glanced between me and Karr-Volke. I pointed to myself, to let him know I was the real one.

"Warlord," Santonio said with a hasty bow. "Please, I need to speak with you! It's about the castle. Do you remember? From the celebration? I told you about it?"

He spoke so fast, it was difficult to get a word in.

"I remember," I managed to say, though Santonio kept talking regardless.

"That castle is thousands of years old! And it's resistant to all forms of magic I've used to get in. Gargoyle arcanists couldn't mold the stone. Iron golems couldn't warp the metal. I know it's from the time of the first god-arcanists, and I've spent years trying to unravel the mysteries from the outside, but if *you* come with me, I'm sure we'll be able to discover everything together!"

His excitement couldn't be contained. Santonio's volume increased with each word, to the point I figured all of Fortuna had heard his speech.

"Where is this castle?" I asked.

"In a lake," Santonio stated. "Crystal Lake. To the west of here. Nestled in a valley. Not too far!"

In my dreams, the castle had always been in the ocean. Was this the same place? I was starting to have my doubts.

Karr-Volke nudged me with his elbow. "This man is *desperate*. What's the price for your time again? It's not cheap."

"I can pay you," Santonio said before I could respond. "Whatever amount of coin you want! This discovery is more important than wealth."

Hadn't this man seen the pile of gifts? I didn't need his money, and he couldn't give me anything I truly needed. But his offer to solve this mystery did intrigue me.

I held up a hand. "Stay close. I need to speak to the others."

Santonio opened his mouth as though he would speak again, but when I stepped around him—and the others followed—he swallowed his words and remained silent.

HEADING TO CRYSTAL LAKE

I waited by Terrakona, keeping my attention on the road, hoping to meet up with the others.

Still no sign of Evianna. The others said she had been up and awake with them. Where was she?

Jozé arrived before Eventide and Zelfree. He hobbled to the carriages, a tricorn hat on his head pulled down to block most of his face. Once he caught sight of me, he straightened his walk and carried himself with a stiff gait. His blue phoenix stood between us, as if blocking the sight of his leg.

I had seen it a million times before. Why hide it?

As I walked to him, I noticed the stares of the many idle arcanists. They stood in groups on the side of the wide cobblestone road, their eldrin gathered near the trees beyond the fences. Guildmasters, rulers, and several attending arcanists watched as I strode by.

The adolescent twilight dragon turned both his heads in my direction, his scales white to reflect the day. He spread his feather wings, casting a dark shadow on the road. Hasdrubal's eyes never left me.

Was my father worried about their judgmental gazes?

"Oh, Warlord," Jozé said as I approached. "I'm glad you're here." He untied two pouches from his belt and handed them to me. Then Jozé backed away, moving closer to the cobblestones. "That's everything you'll need to make your knights' trinkets." He gave me a bow and then turned to leave.

"Wait," I said, holding up a hand.

Tine leapt in the way, blue embers wafting from her feathers. "Please, Warlord. It's our pleasure to serve you." She bowed until her beak touched the road.

"Why're you doing this?" I asked under my breath, my tone harsh.

Jozé shot me a glower. "You don't want to be seen with the likes of me." He grabbed his coat, his hand balling into a fist as he clutched his clothing. "C'mon, kid. Think. I'm actually a scoundrel, and if anyone recognizes me, it'll be rough for you." He forced himself to walk straight until he reached a carriage door, then he leaned on the vehicle, his hand shaking. "It's better if we don't associate. I'm not an impressive companion."

I didn't know what to say about that.

It was true, my father had been convicted of murder on the Isle of Ruma, but from every account, it had been self-defense. He had been protecting Tine from men who had wanted to steal her away from the island. But that didn't matter—the official record had his name black marked.

Jozé was a talented artificer, though.

When I opened the pouch of rings, I took a moment to admire his work. The rings were various sizes, but all wide enough to fit the emblem I wanted. A twelve-pointed star, a cape, and a sword. They were small, but the rings shimmered with an iridescent color, like oil on the surface of water. They were beautiful.

He had likely used his phoenix fire to warp the shell fragments, and then with skillful hands, had carved the emblems.

How long had it taken him? All night?

Jozé entered the back carriage—away from me.

"You okay, Volke?"

I jumped and wheeled on my heel. Fain allowed his invisibility to drop, appearing next to me. He had an ascot tied tightly around his neck, hiding his pirate tattoo. He also kept the collar of his coat up and walked closer with his hands in his trouser pockets.

"I'm fine," I answered. "But I'm glad you're here. I have something for you."

He patiently waited as I searched through the iridescent rings. I plucked one out at a time until we found one that fit Fain. Once we had it, I withdrew two star shards from the other pouch. I had twenty inside—eighteen now—and I placed two shards in the same palm as the ring.

I closed my eyes and imagined the defensive capabilities of my powers. I wanted to protect my knights. If they were going to fight for me, I wanted a part of my magic to be with them in their most dire moments.

The star shards flared to life, glowing brightly as they acted like an adhesive. My magic was imbued into the ring, garnering more gasps from the surrounding crowds. Even the twilight dragon kept his attention on the item creation, as though he were jealous.

With a powerful exhale, I opened my hand and smiled.

Creating that *one* trinket had taken a lot out of me. Imbuing items was difficult, and although I wasn't doing too much, I was still a brand new god-arcanist. This level of creation was damn near painful.

"A gift," I said, loud enough for the others to hear. "To one of my knights. A man who has sworn loyalty to me." I handed over the sparkling ring.

Fain's eyebrows shot to his hairline, his mouth slightly open. For a prolonged moment, he didn't move. He just stared.

I had to narrow my eyes at him before Fain realized he should have been acting.

"O-Oh," Fain stammered. "Thank you, my liege." He bowed and then did it a second time before finally taking the ring from my palm. "I'm greatly honored."

That last part felt forced, like he had had to fill the silence with some sort of speech.

"Don't worry about it," I said. "Now the world will know you're with the world serpent arcanist."

The murmurs spread away from us like ripples. Everyone would be talking about this for days, there was no doubt in my mind.

"What does it do?" Fain whispered as he slipped it onto his finger. "Is this... from Moonbeam's eldrin?"

I nodded once.

"Tsk." Fain gritted his teeth. "That damn idiot is too selfless." He closed his hand and admired the emblem on the outside of the ring. "A knightmare's mark..."

"It'll protect you," I said. "Add healing, light, power... It's, uh, meant to be defensive."

"Thank you, Volke."

Wraith appeared from nowhere, also dropping his invisibility. His tail wagged as Fain showed off his new trinket. The ring sparkled in the sunlight, catching everyone's attention. I suspected people would wonder why I had knighted a wendigo arcanist, but I didn't have to answer to them. Fain was loyal through and through.

Someone emerged from the crowds, and the rumble of whispers caught my attention.

King Odion.

He walked across the cobblestone road with utter confidence. When he approached, he smiled and gave me a deep bow. His white-and-silver hair sparkled almost as much as the ring.

"My liege," he said as he stood straight. "Hasdrubal has informed me that you're giving your *knights* gifts."

Jealous?

I didn't say it, but it struck me as amusing. Odion had been the first to swear his fealty. I supposed I should've given him a ring first. I hadn't thought of it, though.

I searched for a ring, removed two more star shards, and did the imbuing ritual all over again. This time was more painful, though. Draining my magic into the item was difficult, and by the time I finished, it felt like I was a spring without any water. I gulped down air and wiped sweat from my brow. I hadn't been running, but it must have looked like I had just sprinted across Fortuna.

"Odion," I said between deep breaths. "This is a gift. For my knights. Please wear it with pride." I handed him the ring, and Odion carefully held it between two fingers as he held it up to the light.

Hasdrubal stepped closer, his body larger than one of the carriages. The nearby arcanists moved to allow the dragon access to the road. Both his heads leaned over and stared at the new ring. His two dragon heads seemed to move in sync, unlike Hexa's hydra. They weren't two personalities, but the same cooperative being.

"Beautiful," Hasdrubal said from one head, his voice young, like a teenager.

Odion nodded. "It's an elegant gift. Perfect for royalty." He slipped it onto his right hand and showed it off to the arcanists gathered around. "Thank you, Warlord. Your magic is a priceless gift. I'm glad you're pleased with my loyalty."

The way the crowd reacted made me think I'd have a lot more people swearing to me in the future.

"You want to visit Crystal Lake?" Guildmaster Eventide asked.

The cramped carriage wasn't the most comfortable of location to discuss our future plans, but there were few other options. I sat on one side while Eventide, Zelfree, and Karr-Volke sat on the other. I disliked the doppelgänger plan, mostly because I didn't want anyone else getting harmed in my stead, but also because I hated staring at myself. It wasn't like I was hideous—although I was a bad judge of my own appearance—it was just awkward glancing over to see myself.

"A relickeeper arcanist by the name of Santonio thinks it has some sort of special significance to the god-arcanists." I sighed and leaned back on the cushioned seat. "I have dreams of it. And Crystal Lake is on the way to Thronehold. With Terrakona's speed, I could explore it without wasting much time."

Zelfree rubbed at his chin. Traces purred and walked along his shoulders, her tail wrapping around his neck like a scarf. "How fast is Terrakona?"

"He can get me to Thronehold in a few days," I said. "Well... Probably. No longer than three."

Eventide turned to Zelfree. The two shared a knowing moment. When she turned back to me, it was with a deep frown. "You should take a small group of arcanists and head to Crystal Lake. Then you should go straight to Thronehold afterward. Everyone else will meet up with you as quickly as possible."

"I'm not sure how many people Terrakona can take." I glanced out the window of the carriage, trying to estimate his carrying capability. He could easily take me and a couple of others. Maybe a total of seven? Eight if we pushed it. And that was only if their eldrins were smaller.

"Zelfree should be one of them," Eventide said, placing a hand on his shoulder. "His eldrin is compact and he's a valuable asset."

Traces turned around, showing her feline backside to Eventide. "Hm! I'm more than compact. I'm adorable."

"I'll take Adelgis," I said. "His telepathy and dreamwalking could help us keep in touch."

Eventide held up a finger. "Take someone else capable in combat."

"Evianna," I quickly stated. I followed it up with, "She's my apprentice, after all. I need to help her with the rest of her knightmare training."

"I was going to say Yesna."

Ah. That would make sense. Yesna was a master arcanist renowned for her combat abilities.

But she didn't trust me. We barely knew each other, so that was no surprise, but it made me wonder if I was making a mistake. Perhaps I should protest and ask for someone else?

No one would compare, though. Yesna was a master siren arcanist.

"I'll take Yesna," I said. "But what about you? Your barriers could keep us safe."

"My magic will get weaker the farther we travel from Gentel." Eventide grazed her fingers over her glowing arcanist mark. "Even with my heightened true form abilities, Thronehold is too far away. I won't be able to help if the fighting gets intense."

Curse the abyssal hells. That had been a problem the last time we had visited Thronehold.

After a short sigh, I said, "I'll also take Zaxis and Illia. They're capable, even if they're not master arcanists. Illia's teleportation can help us escape if something dire happens. Zaxis's healing can save someone from death."

Eventide mulled over my explanation and eventually nodded. "All right." She threw back her gray braid and sighed. "I can ask Captain Devlin to take me and a few others to

Thronehold, just as quickly—perhaps faster—than Terrakona."

Devlin's roc could fly at amazing speeds. That meant we'd still be leaving several people behind.

"I need to give Queen Callandra a ring, and then I'll head out," I said.

Zelfree snorted. "She left this morning. Apparently, she's returning soon with more of her army."

"Hm." I rubbed at my neck. "I see. Well, then I'll travel to Crystal Lake with Terrakona, and meet everyone on the outskirts of Thronehold in three or four days."

Before I headed off to meet with my group, I noticed a cart carrying a nullstone cage. It was at the back of our long caravan, closest to the tall walls of Fortuna. Inside the cage was a griffin cub—one with a lion's head. Male, then.

I walked over, my heart rate high. Everyone moved aside once they noticed my mark, even the city guards who normally patrolled the roads. The smell of spices and horse manure reminded me there were merchants looking to trade their goods in the city, but most of them hadn't yet gone in—they were all too busy admiring Terrakona.

Ignoring everything else, I reached the cage. I knew who was inside.

Alexi. The pirate's griffin. The one he had claimed had been the result of bizarre soul-forge magic.

To my added surprise, I found Atty standing on the other side of the cage. She had one hand on the nullstone bars, her eyes following the little griffin as it paced the inside. Her golden hair fluttered in the gentle breeze.

"Atty?" I asked as I approached the opposite side. I stared through the bars and met her gaze as she glanced up.

"Volke? What're you doing here?" She frowned and fiddled with her hands. "I thought you were supposed to head to Thronehold immediately?"

"I'll be leaving soon."

The griffin arched his back, his hackles raised. Even his eagle feathers flared. "Get back," he said in a voice too cute to be threatening. "I'll cut you with my claws!" He extended his little claws and growled, but even that almost made me smile.

"Hello, Alexi," I said as I reached a finger through the bars.

The griffin swiped at me, cutting a small line of blood on my pointer finger. I jerked away, disappointed he hadn't calmed down. I had been hoping—since he was a griffin, who were typically reasonable—that he wouldn't lash out randomly.

Atty walked around the nullstone cage and stood by my side. She tamed her hair with a simple ribbon, tying everything into a loose ponytail. "I've heard a strange rumor," she said as she finished working the ribbon into a bow, "that this griffin was once dead."

"I'm not dead," the cub said, flashing his adorable fangs.

"Yeah," I muttered, my thoughts already dark. "But you heard how it happened, right? Something in the soul forge's lair killed some members of the Second Ascension, and that's what gave the creatures life."

Atty's eyes went wide. "What? I hadn't heard that."

"Well, I'm not entirely sure." I had only heard and seen it through the eyes of Markus. It was all so vague, but I was fairly confident that the deaths of others had fueled the rebirth of the griffin. "From what I know... It's horrific. And a piece of me wonders if it'll even last..."

Normally, magics didn't last without the help of star shards. The imbuing process bound the magic to the object or person permanently. Without star shards, the magic would eventually fade. At least, that was what I had been taught. Would life leave this little griffin?

"I hadn't heard any of that." She closed her eyes and rubbed at her temple.

"Are you okay?"

"I just... I thought maybe there was another way." She pushed away from the cage and hurried toward our caravan, never even glancing back at me. "I'm sorry, Volke. I have more studying to do. I can't speak with you right now."

She could never speak to me.

I watched her go until she disappeared into one of the rear carriages. After a long sigh, I turned to face the aggressive griffin. He glared at me with amber eyes. Alexi didn't yet have a mane, so he appeared more like a large cat, his wheat-colored fur gorgeous.

"Alexi, do you remember where you come from?" I asked.

The griffin's growl trailed off into confusion. His fur relaxed and he stared at me with round eyes. "Come from?" He tilted his head.

"The dark cave?" I had seen it in Markus's memories. "Where you met Markus."

"My arcanist?" Alexi's nose twitched. "I do remember the darkness..."

"You don't remember anything before that? Having a mother or a father? Having siblings?"

Alexi remained quiet, his gaze becoming unfocused. Could he really not remember anything before the cave?

"Most griffins have families," I muttered. "They live in aeries. That's what they call large nests up on tall places, like cliffs and towers. Do you remember anything like that?"

"I..." Alexi replied with a feline frown. "*Most griffins*? I've never seen another griffin." He glanced at his paws. "I'm not just a different type of manticore?"

The question disturbed me.

Alexi really didn't remember anything from before. What a terrible fate. He had been raised on a pirate ship with Calisto and his crew. He knew nothing else besides the darkness of the twisted soul forge cave.

"Don't worry," I said, leaning onto the bars. "Once this is all over, we'll set you free."

My statement didn't sit well with Alexi. He arched his back a second time and flashed his fangs. "You better not hurt my arcanist! I'll never forgive you!"

I didn't know what we would do with Markus, but I knew I had to keep him close if we were going to deal with Calisto. Unwilling to tell the griffin that, I tapped on the bars as I pushed away. Hopefully, he would be okay in the cage until we could figure out what was going on.

Zaxis, Illia, Yesna, Zelfree, and Adelgis all gathered around Terrakona's serpent body. Their eldrin were all portable. Nicholin stayed on Illia's shoulders, his weasel-sized body easily mistaken for a scarf. Forsythe would fly alongside us. Traces, no larger than a sailing ship tabby, stayed close to Zelfree's feet no matter where he walked. And Felicity was a creature who could hide in light itself. Like Luthair, she was always nearby, even if I couldn't see her.

Yesna's siren could also fly, though she was much larger than Forsythe.

Sirens were cruel mystical creatures that rarely sought to bond. They were aggressive carnivores who delighted in watching foolish people perish. From what I had read, they loved to decorate with bones, and their nests were made from the carcasses of the people who had attempted to bond with them and failed.

I knew sirens well, only because several famous dread pirates and swashbucklers had been bonded with them. Sirens had the ability to lure people, after all. Pirates would use that to attract merchant ships, and some hero swashbucklers would use the siren to lure pirates from their hideaways.

"This is my eldrin," Yesna said to our small group. She motioned to the siren. "Her name is Pellah. Don't worry—she won't bite."

Pellah stood a good five feet tall and reminded me of a satyr. Her lower half was the bird—an albatross, specifically—with giant, white wings on her back. Her chest, arms, and human head were equally as beautiful. Pellah's grayish hair matched the charcoal color found on the tips of her tailfeathers. She wore leather armor studded with bone fragments over her torso and shoulders, giving her a warrior's appearance.

I had seen a plague-ridden siren once, several years ago. The crazed beast had almost killed me. It had been an owl siren, and its screechy voice occasionally haunted my nightmares.

Pellah, surprisingly, offered me a bow. "Warlord," she said in a singsong voice. "It's a pleasure to meet you."

"Good to meet you as well," I said.

Yesna patted her siren on the shoulder. "Don't worry. I won't have her do anything to you."

"I'd like to see her try," Zaxis said under his breath.

Whenever my world serpent moved, the ground trembled a bit. Terrakona shifted as he turned his head and stared down at us. His eyes—one scarlet, one sapphire—examined Pellah. The siren shuddered and leaned away, like a bird being sized up by a snake.

Yesna leapt between them, even though she was so much smaller than Terrakona. "Hey, now! Throw your anchor down and let's stay calm."

The crystals of Terrakona's mane, while normally black in coloration, resembling shadows made physical, seemed to glitter slightly when he snaked his tongue out. Then he moved away, returning his attention to the distant hills.

But where was Evianna?

As if summoned by my thoughts, the nearby shadows shifted and fluttered. Evianna and her knightmare, Layshl, rose from the darkness in one smooth and elegant motion. Layshl's wing-like cape twisted in the wind. She walked without a body, her pieces held in place as though strapped to an invisible person.

Evianna wore leather armor dyed black. Everything fit snugly, no doubt to minimize noise and the chance her clothing could get caught on anything. She was... much more alluring than I had thought.

Was it the daylight? Or had I just missed her?

Evianna headed straight for me. I walked over to greet her and threw my arms around her the moment I could. With loving aggression, Evianna ran her hand into my hair and pulled me into a deep kiss.

Everyone just... watched.

My face reddened, but I wasn't about to stop, either. I just held Evianna until she wanted to stop her affections.

"Ugh," Zaxis said, rolling his eyes. "Kids these days. Does *time and place* mean nothing?"

Illia and Nicholin snickered.

"Ah, to be young again," Yesna said, turning to face Zelfree. "Do you remember the good ol' days? When you were like that at every port?" She tapped the hilt of her two cutlasses. "I had a good time getting you out of some prickly situations. Right, Everett?"

Zelfree ran a hand down his face. "Please. Don't ever repeat those stories."

Evianna finally broke our kiss. She smiled up at me, a cunning edge to her expression.

"Didn't you say you had another gift for me?" I asked.

"Maybe." She held a finger up to her lips. "But now isn't the time. Maybe when we're alone again."

My curiosity was at an all-time high.

Terrakona shifted his body, rumbling the ground again. I stumbled but kept my footing. Was he anxious to get going? Probably—I felt the same way.

Before we could leave, I glanced over to the road. Santonio and his relickeeper hustled toward us. Relickeepers were interesting. They looked like piles of trash—broken glass, twisted metal, shattered vases—but they were arranged to appear like a dragon. Magical threads held everything together, keeping it all in place as the creatures moved.

Theasin's relickeeper had been gigantic. Santonio's relickeeper was the size of an adult horse. It moved with surprising speed, clinking and clanking with every step, like a sack filled with metal bars.

Santonio clearly didn't go outdoors often, his pale skin and heavy breathing betraying that fact. His clothes were wonderfully tailored, though. And the red, gold, and sea-green coloration suited him well.

"I'm here," he said between panting breaths. "Let us away!"

I whistled, and Terrakona lowered his head. Then I held out my hand, and Evianna took it long enough for the two of us to climb up to the crystal mane.

"No fair," Nicholin cried. "I wanted to go up there."

Zaxis scoffed. "You can teleport, ya wagon wheel. Get up there whenever you want!"

"It's not the same."

As Terrakona lifted us up, I patted his head and pointed him toward Crystal Lake. "C'mon, Terrakona. Let's get this done."

CASTLE UNDER THE WATER

We traveled across land so quickly, I couldn't stop smiling. Watching the ground split and reconnect behind us never got old. Evianna laughed as we snaked through a forest. The trees moved, disturbing the wildlife. Hundreds of birds took to the sky, flowing up around us. They didn't bother Terrakona, but Forsythe and Pellah flew the skies beside us, and they had to dodge the flocking birds.

"Watch it!" Zaxis shouted from Terrakona's back.

I glanced back, curious as to how the others were handling things. Terrakona's head didn't move around much, but his body moved back and forth in concertina motions. Zaxis, Illia, Zelfree, Yesna, and Santonio held on to the world serpent like their lives depended on it.

"Are you all okay back there?" I asked, practically yelling.

"I vomited on your eldrin," Nicholin shouted back. "Sorry! It's actually *your* fault, but since I'm so awesome, I'll clean it up!"

Laughter escaped me. I couldn't help it. Terrakona growled underneath me, the thunder of his displeasure adding to my mirth. He never slowed, though. His power and speed weren't hindered by the valleys, woods, or hills. We easily sailed over the green waves of grass, passing farmhouses, caves, and watchtowers. From atop Terrakona's head, I could see a fair distance, and I understood how that could be an advantage in a war.

From up here, I could command an army.

"*Volke*," Adelgis telepathically said. "*Santonio would like you to know that Crystal Lake is beyond the western ridge. One day at these speeds, and we should arrive.*"

"Thank you," I said aloud, knowing he would hear.

This probably would've been just as fast with an airship, but since we had a knack for destroying those, Terrakona was our best bet. Random bandits and brigands wouldn't dare attack a world serpent, even if they just thought it was a land-bound leviathan.

I pointed in the direction we should head. "That way, Terrakona." The ridge was made of gray and black stone, but nothing too high or insurmountable.

Evianna held on to my other arm. She wore her knightmare, which resulted in a shadow cowl over her head, hiding her white hair. I didn't mind. Her knightmare was a calming presence, and I was glad we still had one to rely on.

Terrakona slithered up a hill and then down the other side. I laughed as we went, enjoying the ride. The others shouted—though Yesna laughed hard enough to drown out their terror.

***

We rested at night.

Zaxis and Forsythe built a campfire. Illia and Nicholin teleported wood to our campsite. Yesna pulled out her froststone sword—bluish-black and stunning—and then sliced the logs into pieces. Zelfree poured everyone a drink, which he had brought along for some reason.

Santonio's relickeeper was the real champion, though. Its trash body opened up to reveal an iron chest. Inside, Santonio had provisions. Dried meats, cooking oil, and all sorts of seasonings. The relickeeper removed the food and passed it out with hands made of shattered glass. I had to carefully take the jerky from its hand, lest I cut myself.

We sat around the campfire, on logs that had been arranged for seating. Zelfree passed me a small glass, no larger than my thumb. The whiskey inside was potent enough to burn my nose hairs.

"I save it for special nights," Zelfree said as he sat on the dirt and used the log as a back rest. "And this is one of them." He poured another glass and then handed it to Illia. "Cheers."

She took it without hesitation. To my surprise, she threw back the glass, drinking the contents in a split second. Her face twisted afterward, but she managed to swallow.

Illia coughed and patted her chest. "That's rough. I thought it would be smoother."

"I didn't say it was expensive," Zelfree said, half-smiling. "Just that I was saving it."

He poured another one and handed it to Zaxis. Unlike Illia, he stared at the drink and sighed. As Zelfree poured another, Zaxis took a seat on a log and then motioned for his phoenix. Forsythe hopped over, his feathers puffed in curiosity. Zaxis held the glass while Forsythe dipped his tongue into the drink.

Forsythe hiccupped and spewed fire into the air, brightening the area.

The others laughed, but Zaxis reached out for Forsythe. "Are you okay?"

His phoenix eldrin nodded. "Of course. It wasn't that good, though." He shook, spilling soot everywhere.

Yesna slashed another log and threw it closer to the campfire. Her siren lingered on the outskirts of our gathering.

From what I could remember, sirens weren't social creatures. They liked solitude and often didn't get along with people.

When Yesna was done cutting, she sauntered over to the campfire, her muscled body and gleaming armor impressive, even in our humble setting. "You said this was a special night?" Yesna asked, eyeing Zelfree. "Why's that? Seems like an ordinary night, if you ask me."

Santonio lifted a hand. "We're about to unearth an amazing secret. It's a special night."

Without answering, Zelfree poured himself another helping of whiskey. "Forget I said anything." He threw it back just as fast as Illia, but unlike her, he never flinched. The man's liver practically had its own alcohol-absorbing magic.

But why was he drinking so much? I knew he still occasionally had a drink, but he hadn't indulged in heavy drinks in a long while.

Adelgis, sitting on the other side of the fire, contacted me with his telepathy. "*He's worried about seeing Calisto. He and Illia have been thinking about it for a while—ever since Markus was taken from the* Midnight Thorn. *He sarcastically means it's a special night because he doesn't have to deal with the problem yet.*"

I stared through the flames, trying to act natural while Santonio cooked up some food and Evianna took a seat next to me. The orange and yellow flames warmed the area, but they didn't chase away the dread.

Calisto would be in Thronehold. So would Theasin, the other god-arcanist. So would the fenris wolf, another god-creature. So would the Second Ascension. Sure, Illia and Zelfree would need to deal with the dread pirate, but I had to deal with the rest.

I stared down at the drink.

Although I didn't particularly like alcohol, I threw back the drink, allowing the whiskey to burn my mouth and throat as it clawed its way down into my body. It felt like swallowing my molten rock. It took all of my willpower not to spit it out over the fire.

"You okay?" Evianna asked, her eyes narrowed.

I placed my glass in the dirt near my feet. After the burning stopped, I exhaled. "Yeah. Fine. Everything is fine."

When I turned my attention to Illia, I realized she wasn't herself, either. She toyed with the empty glass in her hand, her one eye staring a hole through it. I knew her well, and she always got this way when she was tense and agitated. This was her behavior right before she did something reckless.

Zaxis scooted down the log and then threw his arm around her. He pulled her close. "What's that look for? We're in the middle of a specialized mission—helping the world serpent arcanist save the world."

"We're investigating ruins," Santonio said from the other side of the fire.

"*Was I talking to you*?" Zaxis barked. "I'm trying to cheer up my girl."

"That's right," Forsythe said, spreading his wings.

"M-My apologizes, phoenix arcanist." Santonio bowed a bit, but when some embers jumped to his fancy clothing, he leapt away. His relickeeper patted the singe marks with a flat iron piece on its tail.

Now that we had a moment, I untied the pouches with the rings and star shards. Adelgis needed his emblem. I withdrew a ring and then two star shards. While I had looked for sizes before, I didn't have the mental energy to remember this time. I had started the imbuing process without even considering the ring.

Magic filled my being, and I closed my eyes. I imagined it rushing into the ring and then being held there with the power of the star shards. They absorbed my essence and latched it permanently to the ring size.

Gasping for air, I stopped the process and glanced down at my palm. The iridescent ring was complete.

When I looked up, everyone had their eyes on me. I held my breath, wondering if I had done something wrong. No one moved. Even Yesna, who seemed prone to high-energy antics, didn't budge.

"Adelgis," I said, trying to break the silence. "I made you this emblem. It's so everyone knows you've sworn yourself to me."

Adelgis stood from his log and walked over. "Thank you, Warlord. Did you ever find out what it did?"

"I mean, vaguely," I said, chuckling.

Santonio leapt to his feet, rather quickly for a man his size. "O great world serpent arcanist. If you can't identify your item, please allow me."

I stared at him for a short second. Then I remembered—relickeepers could touch magical objects and immediately know their purpose and function. Relickeepers were obsessed with permanent magical phenomena. Their arcanists made excellent artificers, since they could always intuit everything they created.

"Okay," I said, handing Santonio the ring.

With shaky hands, the man closed his eyes. He closed his grip around the item, holding it like a precious piece of glass that might break if he squeezed too hard.

Then Santonio opened his eyes. "Oh! What amazing properties. It momentarily links the wearer to the lifeforce of the world serpent himself."

"Wait, what?" I asked. I hadn't thought any item could do that. "How?"

Adelgis caught his breath. He held up a hand. "It must be the ethereal whelk element to the ring." For the first time in a long time, he smiled and ran a hand through his long, black hair. "Ethereal whelks are born from dead children!"

Everyone waited for further explanation.

None came.

Nicholin coughed.

"Adelgis," I said. "What does that matter?"

"They're linked to life and death." Adelgis paced a few times near the fire. "You see, dreams are said to be the landscape closest to a person's death. When you're asleep, you're barely alive. Half-breathing. Your heart slows. The magic of an ethereal whelk mixed with the world serpent creates something powerful. A link. The serpent prevents you from dying."

"For a short time," Santonio added, one finger up. "It lasts for only a few seconds, but during that time, a person could draw from the powers of the world serpent. It's truly amazing. I've never seen anything like it. The power—it's raw. If you used more star shards, this could be extraordinary."

Santonio handed the emblem ring to Adelgis, his scarred hand trembling, as though he didn't want to let it go.

"God-arcanist magic draws out the most powerful elements of the items they imbue," Santonio whispered in awe.

"Thank you, Santonio," Adelgis said.

"Thank *you*, ethereal whelk arcanist."

Zaxis leaned back on his campfire log. With a smirk, he asked, "You don't know any of our names, do you?"

The man fumbled with his ornate clothing, nervously chuckling. "There are so many of you. How could I be expected to remember *all* of your names? I can only grasp a few." Santonio pointed to Zelfree. "That's Charlie." Then he pointed to Yesna. "And that's, uh, *Yanni*."

Zelfree lifted another glass. "Cheers to Charlie," he sarcastically said before downing the whiskey.

"The Frith Guild is *massive*," Santonio said with a frown. "And it's not like I'm just remembering one name. Everyone has their own eldrin. You want me to remember both names? Of twenty people? That's asking a lot for a man who just wants to study ancient and powerful magic."

Nicholin rubbed his little chin with a paw. "That's fair. Carry on, random relickeeper arcanist."

While the others laughed and joked about potential new names, I let my mind wander. I stopped hearing their conversation and just stared at the embers of our quaint fire.

The reality of my inevitable situation wouldn't leave me. In moments like this, when I doubted, Luthair had always comforted me with his advice. Master Zelfree had done the same occasionally, but as he threw back a fourth drink, I knew I couldn't turn to him.

Illia...

She had been there for me, too. But this wasn't her moment. She was preparing herself for a showdown with an arcanist who was more powerful than she was. Calisto's true form manticore could easily rip her and Nicholin apart. He almost had, back when we had been on his ship.

"Warlord—stop drowning in a mire of hypotheticals. The Children of Balastar have occasionally defeated themselves in the battlefield of the mind, long before the actual war."

I ran a hand down my face, unable to shake the doubt. "I'm sorry, Terrakona."

Evianna placed her hand on my shoulder. I jumped and turned to face her.

"I'm here for you," she said, quiet but determined. "Whatever problems you face, we'll face them together. I've been practicing all my magic for this very moment. So I can protect you—so that you can rely on me—when the time comes."

"For me?" I asked. "But... you should do this for yourself."

"Maybe I always wanted us to do this together." Evianna tightened her grip on my shoulder. "Don't worry. We can do it. No one stands a chance."

I half-smiled and nodded. Without saying another word, Evianna leaned her head on me. The crackle of the campfire seemed distant then.

I wanted to revisit that strange dream with the castle, but instead, I went back into a memory.

Markus's memory.

Rain battered me from above. The sound of shovels slamming into dirt assaulted my ears. I stood in a hole, at least ten feet into the ground.

With bloody hands, I picked up bodies from the mud. Mystical creatures. Wyrms of some sort. They had been buried in stone boxes, but the tops were shattered, and I had to shove the stone away to reach their lifeless corpses.

A fat wyrm—no legs, twelve feet in length, its scales decayed—ripped in half as I struggled to free it from its coffin. The insides had become a jelly, but without air, they hadn't yet rotted to the bone. The mucus of its cadaver splattered across the rocks.

The laughter of pirates rang out round me.

I shielded my eyes as I glanced up, preventing the rain from blinding me. Calisto stood at the edge of the hole, staring down. He motioned to his manticore, and the beast growled down at me, his face mask contorted into a frowny face.

"We need to hurry," Calisto yelled, mirth in his voice. "Theasin sent word that we don't need as much. Thronehold will have the rest. Get out of there."

"Can't we take this anyway?" I called back up, Markus's voice weaker than my own. "If not for the Autarch, for ourselves."

Calisto crossed his arms. "You mean so we can sell them?"

"Or make them into our own trinkets."

After a moment of contemplation, Calisto laughed. He tapped the side of his head, his wet, copper hair sticking to his skull. "Good plan. Take it. When we stop in Port Crown, grab some shards. We'll make these into trinkets that'll make us immune to hypnotic calls. That way, Theasin won't be pulling us along, either."

I nodded along with his words. "Or you can let me use my griffin magic. Griffins are immune to mind-controlling magics. Their fealty can't be broken." Hasty to add another part, I said, "If I'm close to you, I can use my augmentation to break you of any hypnotic calls."

Calisto shrugged. "I prefer the trinkets."

"But the decay dust..."

"Tsk." Calisto growled something to himself. Then he stared down at me. "As soon as I find a way to deal with that, I'll be unstoppable."

I nodded with his words. "Of course, Captain."

I jerked awake, my chest tight.

The campfire was out, and I swallowed hard, trying to control my own evocation before I set the whole area on fire by accident. Calisto would definitely be in Thronehold, and he would have everything he needed to help the Second Ascension take the city. If we were going to have any hope of protecting the city, I would have to secure one of those trinkets for myself.

Charybdis were similar to sirens. They called people to them, and while they were entranced, the charybdis would kill them.

Evianna slept on my shoulder, unaware of my panic. Zaxis, Illia, Nicholin, and Forsythe had created a little cuddle-family, all four of them wrapped around each other. None of them were bothered by my deep breathing and slight movement.

Santonio, Yesna, and Zelfree were all awake, along with their eldrin, the relickeeper, Traces, and Pellah the siren. They stood away from the camp, giving everyone else privacy while they talked.

"You're up, Warlord?" Santonio asked, keeping his tone quiet. He hustled closer, smiling wide. "Oh, by the mercy of the abyssal hells, this will be amazing! Please, let's pack our things and head out as soon as possible."

I glanced up at the sky and found hues of pink and blue. Dawn. This fool wanted us to head out right away. But I couldn't complain. The Argo Empire was relying on me.

Everyone was.

And Zelfree was right. I couldn't lose.

With determination as my sole fuel, I got to my feet and prepared for another day of travel.

We reached Crystal Lake much faster than I had expected.

And when Terrakona arrived at the top of the ridge, and we could stare down at our destination, I knew how the lake had gotten its name.

Crystal Lake twinkled in the sunlight, a glorious glittering testament to nature. The edges and banks of the lake weren't sand or rocks—they were crystalline boulders, transparent and reflective. The light bouncing off their surfaces was almost like staring at the sun itself. Rainbows sprouted in all directions, filling the area with a riot of color.

The nearby landscape...

It was like the lake hated everything around it. Scorch marks covered all the surrounding mountains. Maybe there had been forests here, once upon a time, but the light refracting through the crystals had caused wildfires. Now there was no grass, no shrubs, no trees, and no life. Everything was black and burned, with no hope of ever returning.

Crystal Lake was a beautiful graveyard.

It made sense why no one lived here, and why no one would've thoroughly investigated the underwater structure until now.

"There it is," Santonio shouted from Terrakona's back. "See that point in the center of the lake? That's the structure!"

Terrakona didn't need instructions. He slid down the mountainside, straight for the body of water. I shielded my eyes as we drew closer. Even the surface of the water—undisturbed by fish or birds—created a mirror-like surface that reflected the sun. We reached the crystal-covered bank within a matter of minutes. The devastated countryside offered no resistance to our travels.

Forsythe and the siren flew in after us. They landed on nearby glassy rocks, though they had to perch in the shadows of other boulders.

With no people or structures to worry about harming, Terrakona quickly curled up around the largest of the crystalline rocks. His emerald scales shone across the surface of the boulder. Terrakona's mane resembled our surroundings—crystals, like giant star shards, glittering with extraordinary wonder.

What was this place?

Santonio rolled off Terrakona's back, as did his relickeeper. The trash dragon slammed against the crystals, the clink and clank of its body echoing off the crystalline structures, and then across the mountains that surrounded us on all sides.

Despite looking like glass, the rocks were rather solid.

"This place is otherworldly," Illia said as she used a hand to cast shade over her one eye.

Zaxis leapt off Terrakona and landed on his feet. "Let's get this over with." He rotated his shoulders and stared at his own reflection on a nearby crystal. "I don't like this. We could easily be ambushed. There are plenty of places to hide in all the cracks and rocks and *rainbows*." He waved his hand through the air, like he could fan the rainbows away with enough force.

While I wanted to get off Terrakona and look around, I waited. Master Zelfree hadn't moved since we had gotten here. He kept his eyes shielded from the glare, but his attention was on the far edge of the lake, beyond our destination.

"There are grifter crows nearby," Zelfree said.

We were lucky to have someone like Master Zelfree with us. His mimic magic allowed him to sense nearby creatures, and if we needed it, Zelfree could always mimic their powers for our benefit.

Grifter crows were weaker mystical creatures with minor illusion capabilities, though. Their arcanists usually became the ringleaders in circus troupes, or thespians in theater houses. I was a god-arcanist. We had nothing to worry about from *grifter crows*.

Yesna must have thought the same thing because she laughed loud enough to create her own echo. "Who cares, Everett? If they flock over here, we'll handle them." She leapt from Terrakona and landed next to Zaxis. I swear they were cut from the same cloth.

Standing next to each other, it was like they had practiced the same training regime. Both muscular, both smiling, both overconfident.

Yesna threw back her long, black hair and tapped her cutlass. "Time to get us some answers."

Zaxis punched one of his fists into the palm of his other hand. "That's what I'm talkin' about."

"C'mon, Everett!" Yesna motioned for Zelfree to join her on the ground. "It'll be just like old times."

Although Zelfree hadn't slept much last night—and had stayed up drinking—he seemed more alert than ever. When he slid off Terrakona, he did so with careful movements. He landed on the ground and then knelt to examine the structure of the crystals, and the slight amount of dirt found between them.

This place was an unknown. Gathering information was a sound decision.

Terrakona lowered his massive head so that I was closest to the water. I stepped off and stood atop one of the crystal boulders. Evianna did the same, landing next to me and smiling. The glass-like boulders were slick, and I suspected if I touched the pointed edges, I would cut myself.

Santonio dragged himself over a small pile of cracked glass-like stones, slicing his clothes as he went, proving my suspicion. He almost tumbled as he neared the water. His relickeeper grabbed him and steadied his footing.

"There!" Santonio pointed to the tip of a tower jutting out of the lake. It was at least two hundred feet away, and the glare of the sun made it difficult to focus on. "It's a fortress-castle under the water. There are no doors or windows... I had a gargoyle arcanist attempt to mold the stone, but that never, ever worked."

"How did you ever find this place?" Zaxis spat. "It's in the middle of nowhere!"

"Mystic seekers found the location while searching for rare mystical creatures." Santonio held up his scarred hands. "But it was my magic that identified the structure as magical. And since relickeepers can determine what kind of magic is imbued into something... *I* determined this whole castle was imbued with world serpent magic. A discovery for the ages!"

THE FIRST WORLD SERPENT
ARCANIST

"I believe *you* can open it, Warlord!" Santonio shouted from the crystal nearest me, his excitement apparent in his volume. "Once inside, we'll discover all the secrets! I'll record them and spread them throughout the land!" He turned to me, smiling wide enough to show off all his teeth at once. "We'll have to swim. Are you up to the challenge?"

"I can breathe underwater," I said, turning my attention to the smooth finish of the water.

Zaxis scoffed. "Seriously?" Then he threw his hands up into the air. "What *can't* you do?"

Ignoring Zaxis's complaints, I headed for the lake. There wasn't an easy incline that led into the water. I reached the end of my crystal boulder and stood a good ten feet above the lake. A rainbow shone between me and my destination.

Terrakona stuck his tongue out. **"This place is comforting. You have nothing to fear here. Someone awaits you inside."**

"Someone?" I asked aloud.

"Yes. Their thoughts... I can almost hear them. This lake feels like my lair. A structure I created."

"Everyone," I said, turning back to the group.

They had assembled on the crystals, each one attempting to get in the shade as much as possible. Even Nicholin had leapt off Illia's shoulders and scurried along the boulders, sniffing at the edges of the water.

I held up a hand. "Wait here."

Santonio scoffed and held a hand to his collarbone. "*Excuse me*? This is the greatest discovery of our time! *I* brought you here!"

"I'm sorry. I think... I need to go inside alone."

My dreams of this place hadn't been filled with danger, but they had been personal. If Terrakona sensed someone inside, I suspected they wanted to speak with me and not the rest of the group. And if I was wrong, I could always exit and gather everyone inside.

It was better for me to err on the side of caution. Why would I dream of this place if it wasn't important?

Evianna clenched her hands into fists. "You want *me* to stay here?"

"Please," I said. "I swear I won't be long, but I want to do this by myself."

Although I feared she would argue with me, Evianna just nodded once.

"Don't be a hero," Zaxis shouted. "Just let us help you and—"

Evianna wheeled on her heel. "*Hey*! Volke said he needs to do this alone. Are *you* a god-arcanist?"

The tension between them only lasted a second. Zaxis exhaled and then smirked. "If I were, I would've defeated the Second Ascension by now." He slicked back his red hair, the sparkling light of the lake playing across his salamander scale armor, practically making him glow.

The groans from the others made me chuckle.

"We're going to wait here," Evianna stated. Then she shot

Santonio a glare. "Your relickeeper is nothing compared to my knightmare. You'll wait here as well."

Santonio—obviously not a man of battle—grimaced. Then he glanced between me and Evianna at least three times. I felt for him, but I couldn't wait any longer. I took a deep breath, and then I leapt into the water.

With a splash, I broke the surface and plunged deep. It was hotter than I had thought it would be, but the farther down I went, the colder it became. A part of me wanted to laugh at myself. Why had I held my breath? I inhaled and enjoyed the sweet freshness of the lake. It filled my lungs and concentrated my focus.

And not only could I breathe underwater, I could also see…

The murky depths weren't a problem. The light that shone too bright above the surface couldn't penetrate low enough to reach me.

This place…

It reminded me of the many times I had visited it in my dreams. This wasn't the ocean, but the sight was the same. But the solution in my dreams had been to evaporate the water. Could I do that here? No. I manipulated the water to drag me down—all the way to the bottom.

When my feet touched the sandy depths of Crystal Lake, I took another deep breath of water and continued forward. The castle was here, just as I remembered it. I swam forward, trying to imitate Gallus the Gray. When he had manipulated the water during our fight, his kraken magic had sent him darting through the depths.

I tried that and smiled to myself as I zipped closer to my destination.

The castle.

With no doors or windows, it was impossible to see inside, but I didn't care. I swam to the base and placed my hand on the stone bricks. Just like in my dream, my magic seeped into the wall, and the castle opened.

Unlike in my dream, I was dragged inward as the lake rushed to fill the empty structure. A deluge of water exploded into the empty hallway. I slammed into the castle and tumbled through the torrent. With my teeth gritted, I waved my hand and willed the wall to shut.

My manipulation worked. The wall slammed shut, keeping the water out.

I spun for a bit as the water carried me a few more feet. Then it petered out and I came to a halt at the end of the hall, soaking wet and probably looking ridiculous.

Thankfully, it was just me and the smell of salt water.

I stood, and my eyes immediately went to the pale, green lights near the ceiling. Spook lights? They were mystical creatures that inhabited abandoned buildings. Unlike some mystical creatures—who were born from a mother and a father —spook lights were born through circumstance. These "fable" births meant that they could spawn into existence at any time, so long as the requirements were met.

Knightmares spawned when the sole ruler of a nation was assassinated.

And spook lights spawned in abandoned buildings that had once been of extreme importance.

There were dozens of spook lights here. They didn't move to greet me, though. They clung to the ceiling, like semi-corporeal jellyfish, each one a pale green and giggling.

They were smaller than my fist.

Had Terrakona sensed these things? I doubted it. The spook lights didn't react to my presence, so I ignored them and picked myself up off the floor. After wringing out my clothing, I continued deeper into the castle. But just like in my dreams, there was nothing here. Even the spook lights had vanished.

Empty.

Barren.

Cold.

It was a maze of halls and deserted rooms. Where was I? Searching the castle hadn't been this difficult in my dream. Without the glow of the spook lights, I had to grope around, slowing my pace even further.

No. I shook my head. The solution in my dreams had been my magic. Instead of panicking, I evoked molten rock in one hand and leaves in the other. The magma gave me light, dispelling the eerie darkness. The leaves gave me clarity. I threw them into the hall and willed them to search out the building.

The leaves traveled through the windless corridors on the strength of my magic. When they hit the walls, I felt it. When they collided with the floor, I sensed that, too. In a matter of moments, I mapped out the whole building, sensing everything at once, as though seeing it from a bird's eye view.

Now I knew where the stairs were.

With my heart pounding wildly in my chest, I hurried forward. I wanted to see this mystery solved. What was here?

I ran faster than before and smiled when I reached the stairway down. Taking the steps three at a time, I hustled to the bottom.

Terrakona was right. It felt familiar. Cold. Protective. Almost like... Luthair.

I shook the painful thought from my head. Now wasn't the time. Obviously, it wouldn't be him.

When I reached the bottom, I held up my handful of molten rock, allowing the light to shine across the walls. I caught my breath. Blood stained the stone walls, and bones littered the floor. White dust, tattered clothing, and clumps of undefined gray matter covered everything. The stagnant air was difficult to breathe. I coughed and wheezed and then held my breath as I pressed forward.

The corridor of abandoned, nameless bodies haunted my thoughts. What had happened here? I saw no weapons, yet the bones were scattered, and the dark crimson stains on the wall looked like they had been splattered there.

My boots crunched some of the brittle bones.

"Warlord?"

"It's okay," I said aloud with a cough.

"If you need, I will destroy that building—and this lake."

I tried to project reassurances. Santonio would be devastated if the castle were destroyed, and I wasn't in any danger yet. The bones were just disturbing. They had put me on edge.

The long hall ended in a single wrought-iron door. The black metal had been forged with a twisting surface. It gave the door a unique, wavy appearance, like the surface of water. I placed my hand on the cold door, and with a grunt, pushed it open.

Light poured out from the inside. Again, I had to shield my eyes, but after a moment, I realized it wasn't as bright as the outside. This circular room was just lined with glowstones, illuminating the room with a steady light.

A man stood in the middle of the strange room.

I stepped inside, and the wrought-iron door slammed behind me, sending a shudder throughout the castle.

This man was unlike anyone I had seen before. He was tall and muscular, but his armor was strange and awe-inspiring. He wore the large bones of a dragon, all of which had been cracked and forged into pieces of armor. His pauldron—armor over a single shoulder—had been crafted with the fragments of unicorn horns and wendigo antlers. His legs were covered in the heavy fur of yetis. And on his back, he carried a two-handed battle axe, the kind seen in the far north.

The axe seemed far heavier than normal. It had a thick, metal haft, etched with serpents. The head of the blade wasn't anything I recognized—it was a reddish metal with a black hue when the light hit it just right.

The rest of the man's body was exposed. Blood paint had been used to mark him—swirls and handprints were on his bare shoulder.

His blond hair, long enough to reach his shoulder blades, was pulled back in a wolf's tail. His beard, just as blond as his hair, had been tied in front. His eyes—they stared at the door as though he had known I would be coming.

I had no idea who this was. None of the arcanists I had read about matched his appearance. He seemed barbaric, and from a time long forgotten.

"Hello?" I asked, confident in my tone.

As if jolted to life, the man shivered and then rubbed at his bearded jaw. "Ah. There ya are. Finally." He lifted both hands, his arms twitching with bulging muscles. "Long have I waited." The gruff timbre of his voice matched his rugged appearance.

Once he lowered his arms, I stepped forward, ready for anything, even a fight. "I'm Volke Savan, the Second World Serpent Arcanist and a member of the Frith Guild. Who are you, and why are you at the bottom of an empty castle?"

"Empty?" the man said, lifting a blond eyebrow. "We have a way of fixin' that." He waved his hand and the circular room—once barren of furnishings—populated with pillows, blankets, curtains for the walls, and paintings of the world serpent. The color scheme reminded me of Terrakona. Green. Black. Red. Then soft music played from the ceiling, as though a band were on the floor right above us.

The hazy smoke of incense wafted through the air, twisting around me and filling my nose with the scent of spice, ginger, and resin.

"What is this?" I asked, glancing around.

"Illusions, Volke Savan." The man placed both his hands on his chest. "The same as I. An illusion."

"Really?" I asked, my eyes wide. "You're an illusion?"

"Aye."

"But who are you?"

The man smirked, his wolf-like teeth giving him a feral look. "You may call me Luvi, the *First* World Serpent Arcanist and King of the Spire Isles."

I... I didn't know what to say. At first, I thought it might be a jest, but Luvi pulled off his shoulder armor and wiped away the blood paint, revealing the twelve-pointed star on his chest. A world serpent wrapped around the points, and his ribs, almost matching my own god-arcanist mark.

Then Luvi pulled the armor back on and secured it in place.

"You made an illusion of yourself to stay here?" I asked, motioning to the windowless room we found ourselves in. "Why? For what purpose?"

I had so many questions! A part of me wanted to word-vomit them all at once, but I knew I had to take a breath and slow down. One question at a time.

"Simple," Luvi said. "I built this fortress so that the next world serpent arcanist wouldn't struggle like I did." He tapped his chest with a fist. "Though we likely share no blood, yar my brother now. We look after each other. Ya must hear my warning."

"I... I don't know what to say." I rubbed at my neck. "Thank you. What's your warning?"

Luvi clapped his hands together once, sending a thunderous boom up to the tall ceiling. The illusions shifted and shimmered until they became a map below our feet. I stood over a battlefield like a giant. Men and horses and mystical creatures were only a few inches high, all to scale as they dashed between trees and charged across fields. Their shouts, war cries, and drums were loud—I could practically feel the reverberations through my body.

Luvi stepped across the battlefield, his feet passing harmlessly through the little illusions of soldiers. "In my time, disaster struck."

Illusions dotted the ceiling. Hundreds of stars fell from the sky and crashed into the battlefield. No, not stars. *Star shards.* The glittering crystals rained down with tremendous force. They blasted the fields, trees, and men, ripping the land—and flesh—apart with ease.

The war cries became screams, and then it all eventually became silence.

Luvi motioned to the room. "The sky turned against us, Volke Savan. And then the ground did as well."

The star shards continued to fall. They hit the mountains and then another valley. The illusion of the map panned away, showing more areas. The star shards fell on them, too, kicking up dirt into the air, and blotting out the sky with clouds of dust and debris.

Luvi slammed his foot down. "That's when fate brought me to Jörmungandr, the first world serpent. We set about fixin' the mistake of the heavens." He turned his attention to the cloudy ceiling. The illusions swirled into a storm of black chaos. "But everythin' we did was never enough." He pointed as even *more* star shards crashed to the ground.

I couldn't believe it. I knew star shards fell from the sky, but they had never been this numerous or deadly. They were destroying everything. Nothing would be left.

"There were others," Luvi muttered, his gruff voice dark and serious. "Other god-arcanists, like me. Astros went into the abyssal hells to bond with their abyssal kraken. Uther tamed the fearsome garuda bird. The shards of the heavens didn't harm our creatures."

The illusions in the room shifted. A hundred more shards shot toward the ground, glitter streaming behind them as they went. They passed through a mini illusion of a world serpent wrapped around the peak of a mountain. No harm.

"We searched for an answer," Luvi said with another stomp of his foot. When he turned toward me, it was with a deep glare. "But the years dragged on, and the sky never grew healthy. The sun couldn't pierce the clouds. The rivers filled with dirt and ash. So many women, babes, and men died from the *blight of the sky.*"

Again, I'd had no idea it had been so terrible. No wonder the old scholars had called this time period a *turning of the age.* The devastation and calamity were beyond anything anyone had ever seen before.

"I have the answer now," Luvi said, a chuckle in his voice. "But it was long and difficult, and every mistake took lives. Then the infighting began. The other god-arcanists and I warred against each other."

I slowly nodded, uncertain of what to say.

"We eventually cured the sky—and the world—but Jörmungandr said we wouldn't be the last of the world serpent arcanists. He warned, he did, that somethin' like this might happen again, and that I wouldn't be there to help stop it."

"That's why you built this place?" I glanced around again, impressed with the ingenuity. "You built it after you stopped the blight of the sky?"

Luvi smirked. "I won't be defeated. Not by men, not by arcanists, not by time. And just like Jörmungandr said, there *is* another world serpent arcanist." Luvi pointed at me, almost accusingly. "Ya've come to take my place."

I nodded, my mouth dry. I swallowed and took a deep breath. "That's right. We don't have a blight of the sky, but my home is being ravaged by the arcane plague. It drives arcanists mad and twists mythical creatures into monsters." I shook my head. "We won't die from polluted skies and rivers. We'll die because everyone will kill each other."

"The source of this plague is magic, no?"

"Yes," I said. "It's magical. Er, *corrupted* magic. It's not natural. It's something heinous."

"The blight of the sky was corrupted magic, too."

I hadn't known that. No one had ever said that star shards used to be corrupted magic. I couldn't help myself—I paced around the illusionary room, staring at the terrain on the floor. The tiny illusions of decimated villages and ruined castles sent a shiver down my spine. This would be *my* future if I didn't learn Luvi's answer to the solution.

The plague would drive the world to lunacy, but that wasn't even the worst of our current problems.

"I want to fight this corruption, but there are other problems as well," I said, struggling to find the words to explain. "Other god-arcanists are out to rule the world and bring about destruction of their own kind."

"We god-arcanists fought, too. That's why the blight of the sky carried on for a decade, killin' and destroyin' everythin'." Luvi stroked his blond beard. "The longer you take to make peace, the longer the world will suffer."

"Really?" I shook my head, hating this line of conclusions. "Why?"

"The answer is the auras of the god-creatures," Luvi stated. "But like yar other magics, there'll be a choice. Ya must pick between yar *armageddon aura* and yar *salvation aura*. In my time, the armageddon aura shattered the shards and prevented them from ever falling again. The salvation aura changed them into powerful sources of energy for the arcanists to use to make permanent magical items."

Two auras? One destructive and one creative? Just like my evocation and manipulation. I had two of each.

"In my time, we couldn't agree," Luvi said, his voice loud in anger. He stomped his foot again, sending a ripple through the illusions. "Astros and I wanted to end this misery—destroy the blight once and for all—but Balastar refused. Headstrong and touched in the head, he was. Balastar insisted we change the world. He convinced us. But not everyone."

"What happened?" I asked.

"Balastar and his *fenris wolf* created a powerful salvation aura. But it couldn't work. Not when others had created armageddon auras. The magics clashed and made the blight of the sky worse than ever before."

"So all the god-creatures can create the same two types of auras?" I asked.

Luvi grunted. "Aye."

"And if even one god-arcanist picks differently than the rest, it'll intensify the corrupted magic? It'll make things worse?"

"That was our problem." Luvi shook his head. "We made things worse. Our indecision and infightin' brought about more graves. That's why I had to warn ya—why I made this monument to the past. Why I tried to reach you in your dreams."

This was... terrible news.

Maybe if I had been the first god-arcanist, and the Second Ascension hadn't given Theasin the soul forge, I could've warned everyone of the consequences. But what if we couldn't agree? What if we needed *all* god-arcanists to solve the arcane plague? What if—by killing Theasin—I would doom the world?

"What happened?" I asked, shaking away the mire of doubt. "You said Balastar created a salvation aura, but others didn't. What happened then? Did they change their auras?"

Luvi laughed once. When he smiled again, it exposed his fang-like teeth. "Whenever anyone chose to create an armageddon aura, Balastar ended them. Their battles tore the ground apart. Everyone called him *the Hunter*. He tracked the other god-arcanists down until only those with salvation auras remained. But that took years. The world suffered until then—until we could come together to end the blight of the sky."

"And that worked?" I asked, hoping beyond reason that I could still solve the problem of the plague without needing to rely on the members of the Second Ascension.

"Four god-arcanists died to Balastar," Luvi said. "And when the fifth one—*the Monster*—tried to kill those with salvation auras, Jörmungandr and I handled it. My tactics and strategy are unmatched. The Monster fought with legions of soldiers, thousands more than I had. But I still won. That's why Jörmungandr and I are *Warlords*."

"Five god-arcanists died, and you were still able to solve the blight of the sky?"

"Aye. Our magic was strong enough. We prevailed." Luvi pointed to me. "This is yar legacy. Be wary, though. If too many of the god-creatures are slain, the auras won't be able to cover the world. That was another thing Balastar feared. We'd have killed too much."

The gravity of the situation weighed heavily on me. This was my legacy. I had bonded with the second world serpent, and now it fell to me to make sure the world didn't collapse into ruin. The illusions across the floor intrigued me. This could easily be the Isle of Ruma, or the Argo Empire.

"I haven't been a world serpent arcanist long." I ran a hand through my hair. "I barely have a grasp on my powers. How long did it take you to master everything?"

"Years," Luvi replied, no jest in his voice. "The more I developed my magic, the more powerful it became. I thought there was no end to what I could do."

"Do I choose between destruction or creation for each part of my magic? Evocation, manipulation, augmentation, and my aura?"

Luvi nodded once. "Aye. Once ya master one, the other

leaves ya. Too powerful for a single man to have both. They were devastatin'."

All of his statements gave me pause. I felt like time was an enemy.

"Can you tell me anything about the apoch dragon?" I asked. "I need to know more about it. I thought it had killed *all* of the god-arcanists. I'm surprised that five had died before he was born."

The illusions in the room didn't change. They remained locked on the apocalyptic past that Luvi and the first world serpent had had to face.

"I know not of an apoch dragon," Luvi said.

I wanted to hold up a hand and claim he was a liar, but I stopped myself short. If Luvi had made this place, then he had still been alive while he had done so. Maybe he didn't know about the apoch dragon—so his illusion wouldn't know about it, either.

"Okay, wait a minute," I said, staring at my feet. "*Balastar*?" That was the name Terrakona kept throwing around. *I* was a Child of Balastar. "Did he have a large family?"

"Balastar ruled his clan on the mainland," Luvi replied. "His blood ran from coast to coast. His consorts were many and fertile. He protected them from the blight of the sky. When others perished, his blood did not. Only those with the protection of a god-creature lived to tell the tale after—Astros, Yama, the others... We tried to protect our blood as much as possible."

Did that mean I was somehow descended from the first fenris wolf arcanist? Were the people of my time somehow all descended from the many god-arcanists who had come before?

I turned my attention to the devastation shown through the illusions. Perhaps so many people had died during this calamity that only those who had served or followed or were descended from the god-arcanists had been left alive at the end.

"Ya must tell the others," Luvi said, his tone serious. "Yar aura will get rid of the corruption or change it into somethin' else. Yar kind—those who bond to god-creatures—must decide together."

"But not all of them," I muttered. "You said that you and Balastar killed five god-arcanists who didn't agree."

Luvi replied with another curt nod.

Which meant I could still kill Theasin and his soul forge, and I wouldn't harm our chances of ridding the world of the arcane plague. I knew now what I had to do, but there was still one question that remained.

"Why would anyone pick the armageddon aura?" I asked. "It seems needlessly wasteful. You said yourself that the star shards could either be destroyed or turned into an energy source for making items. What's the downside to that?"

Luvi grunted a laugh, then he crossed his massive arms. "Ya sound just like Balastar. Never thinkin' it through."

He waved his hand and the illusions in the room changed one more time. The terrain changed to forests and fields. Luvi and I towered over the tiny illusions. Little men ran between the trees, chasing what looked to be a white hart, but it wasn't normal. Instead of having golden antlers and white fur, it was silver. Entirely silver. Even its hooves and eyes. The beast glittered whenever it ran into the sunlight cutting through the leafy canopies.

"After we changed the star shards, men began huntin' the mystical creatures." Luvi sighed, his dark blue eyes locked on the silver hart. "They needed the pieces to make items. That hadn't been the case before. Now everyone wanted those bits. Some creatures had been hunted to oblivion."

I caught my breath, my thoughts buzzing.

Several mystical creatures had been hunted to extinction

because people had wanted their corpses for magical items. The all-seeing sphinx used to be common in the Amber Dunes, but now it was no more. Their third eye had been a prized component for items.

"The silver harts didn't last long," Luvi said as the illusionary people stabbed the beast to death. "And I can't help but think, that was *us*. The god-arcanists. The blood is on our hands." Luvi turned to me, just as serious as ever, perhaps more so. "Every choice ya make will change the world, Volke Savan. That's what it means to be a god-arcanist."

That was what it meant to usher in a new world. To see the turning of an age.

If Luvi and the others had just destroyed the star shards, then people wouldn't have hunted all those creatures. Then again, we wouldn't have magical items, either.

"Thank you, Luvi," I said with a bow of my head. "If you hadn't created this place, I think it would've taken me a long time to figure all of this out." I stood straight and met his harsh gaze. "I don't have a master to help guide me through this process. You're the first person—er, *illusion*—to help me get a grasp on this."

He smiled and patted his chest. "We're brothers bound by magic. Jörmungandr would have felt the same." Luvi held up a fist. "I planned our second victory thousands of years in advance when I made this castle. To ensure the new world serpent arcanist knew everything he would need to know to prevent disaster in his time. I never lose."

I smiled, knowing what he meant. Nothing would defeat him, not even death. He would protect this world from corrupted magic, even from beyond the grave. What an inspiration. Luvi and the others—even my long-lost progenitor, Balastar—had done this world a great service.

Now it was my turn.

SIREN SONG

I left Luvi's illusion room and walked back through the hall of bones and dust. With my thoughts on the future, I climbed the stairs and made my way into the corridor of spook lights. They giggled slightly when I passed, but none came to speak with me. If they wanted to inhabit this sacred place, I didn't mind.

When I reached the outer wall, I braced myself for the water and placed my palm on the bricks. With my manipulation, I opened a hole. The lake rushed in, and then I used my water manipulation to yank me—and the water— outside of the structure.

I swam up to the surface, my mind still fluttering with thoughts and ideas. Deciding between destruction and creation was more important than ever. I would need to convince the others.

Not Theasin. He would never side with me. Nor would the Autarch. I had to convince every other god-arcanist.

The surface glittered above me. Harsh oranges and reds told me that dusk had arrived. Soon it would be night and then we'd have to rest. Afterward, we could head to Thronehold and finally confront the soul forge arcanist.

I broke the surface of the lake and threw my head back to clear my hair from my face. I spit out a line of water and squinted to block the sparkles of the crystalline boulders. Everyone waited by the charred shores, but they weren't staring in my direction. I followed their gazes to the opposite side of Crystal Lake.

Hundreds of birds were circling in the sky, their black wings forming an ominous cloud of feathers. They cawed and screeched and giggled and laughed.

I tensed, knowing that sound.

They had been driven insane by the arcane plague.

"Terrakona!" I shouted.

My massive world serpent turned his head. He snorted steam and then lunged into the lake, creating a wave of water that splashed against the crystal shores. With lightning speed, he zipped to a position underneath me. Only then did he lift his head out of the water, catching me with his crystal mane. I patted him as he turned his head to face the flock.

Grifter crows. All of them.

Tiny illusions of fireworks and colored paper swirled around in their flock. Their magic was technically enhanced by the arcane plague, and the longer they stayed together, the larger and more confusing the bits of illusions became.

"*Volke,*" Adelgis telepathically said. "*Master Zelfree says the crystals around this lake amplify illusion powers. He believes the plague-ridden crows are here because of the ambient magic.*"

I patted my world serpent again. "Terrakona, let's destroy them."

"By your command, Warlord."

Terrakona swam across the lake. The wind whipped through my hair, and I pulled Retribution of its sheath. When we drew near, I noticed that the twisted birds didn't fly quite right. Some had three wings, others had bulbous heads, and a few had melded together into a single creature, their four legs sticking out at odd angles and their two heads laughing the entire time, as though becoming an abomination was worth a chuckle.

Terrakona opened his mouth wide. Smoke and steam billowed out, rising into the rainbow-filled sky. Then he vomited molten rock. Most of it splashed into the water, creating hard rock and waves of white clouds, but some of it splattered across the plague-ridden crows. They laughed as they burned and melted.

And then hundreds of them darted for me. I held up my sword and slashed as they drew near, but there were too many. An individual grifter crow wasn't harmful, but dozens of them swarmed my face and attempted to peck out my eyes. Some of their beaks were razor-sharp and coated in hot blood. Some of them had their intestines hanging from their open stomachs, dangling like ropes on the side of a ship.

I slashed and cut three in half. Four more took their places, their claws angling for my hands.

Illusions popped in and out of existence. First there was a second me. Then there were seagulls. Then flashes of stars and light. The crows were out of control, and the more they created their illusions, the more the crystals of the lake twinkled with inner power.

I grabbed Forfend and held it up, trying to shield my face, but I was too late. A crow swooped in and slashed me across the left eye. A burning sensation filled me, starting with my throat. It was the "poison" that Venae had infected me with. It inhibited my healing—made it painful.

With my teeth gritted, I held a hand over my eye, hating how the blood wept down my cheek.

Terrakona batted at the flock with his tail, but there were too many. He swatted dozens, and they died instantly—

splattered into tiny bird chunks—but even *more* crows flew up from around the crystals, swarming us with an ever-growing intensity.

"We need… *your magic*," one cackled.

Another laughed. "I *will* become *perfect!*"

The odd cadence of their speech was common among the plague-ridden. They were all insane.

I would have to burn them.

But before I could evoke a wave of magma, an odd sound rang out over the lake. It was a song. A blissful, peaceful song. I held my breath, the pain of my damaged eye no longer a concern. I lowered my hand, and my shield. With shaky breaths, I turned to face the other shore. Yesna stood atop the highest boulder, her siren by her side.

Pellah the siren sang louder.

"*Come, little crows, the time's come today! Here in the light, we frolic and play!*"

Her voice was haunting and slow. The lyrics weren't even about me—I wasn't a crow at all—but the longer the music went on, the more I saw myself as a bird. My mind got lost in the playful nature of the enticing melody. I wanted to frolic and play with the illusions the crows had to offer.

The hundreds of birds, wrapped up in the same desire, flew across the lake as fast as they could. The siren continued her song, her albatross wings spread wide, and her half-human body holding her hands up like a passionate songstress.

"*Follow, sweet crows, I'll show you the way! Here in my arms, you can't get away!*"

The grifter crows laughed and giggled as they fell into line. One by one, dozen by dozen, they swooped down and circled the siren. She sang with such vigor that I couldn't look away. Why wasn't I joining the line?

"*Volke!*"

Adelgis's telepathic voice shook me.

While her siren sang, Yesna pulled out her two cutlasses. One crackled with lightning and the other shone with glittery frost. She leapt up to the crystal boulder and sliced through the crows, decapitating them and striking them with thunder from her blade. They died—they were too small and weak to live through a single strike—but none of them ever stopped circling the siren.

The magic of Yesna's siren was too powerful. The crows were hypnotized. They continued to obey the siren without a second thought, laughing and attempting to sing along, even though they were terrible.

"Come, little crows," one screeched. "The time's... come... *today!*"

Zaxis shook out of the same trance and then fired a shot at the flock. Illia also broke free, and I suspected Adelgis had to break people out one by one. Once Illia had her mind back, she held up a hand and evoked white fire. It broke apart any crow it touched, ripping them to shreds by teleporting tiny bits of them away at a time.

Evianna was freed and managed to manipulate the shadows into physical whips. With precise strikes, she slashed a dozen crows into chunks of flesh.

Yesna and the rest of our small troop made short work of the flock. The grifter crows never stood a chance against her siren. When the last bird fell, their blood coated the entire rock, but Yesna and her eldrin hadn't been injured. The siren smirked down at us, and Yesna leapt back to the charred ground, the same smirk clear on her face.

At least they hadn't gotten infected.

"You saw that, didn't you?" Yesna asked.

I thought she had been talking to me, but she just elbowed Zelfree. He chuckled, but then moved away from her.

"You've still got it," he replied, almost sarcastically.

Zaxis jumped to her side, his breathing filled with excited

huffs. "How did you do that? What was the siren doing, exactly?"

"She evokes mind-controlling songs." Yesna tapped the side of her head. "The lyrics dictate the targets, and those drawn in follow a siren's orders, even if it results in their own deaths. Pretty amusin' if you ask me."

"There's no way around it?"

"The more targets, the weaker the song. The more determined the individual, the less the song works." Yesna shrugged. "Most people are caught off guard. Never see it comin'. If they have high willpower, they usually break free quick, though."

Terrakona snorted. "**Tricks of the mind are lethal. Be cautious, Warlord.**"

I nodded. "I'll try." Then I pointed him to the shore. The sun hadn't yet set. "Let's go. Maybe we can make it a good way to Thronehold before the sun fully sets."

"**Certainly.**"

***

We left Santonio at the lake. He didn't want to leave—he said he had a place to stay nearby—and he politely asked me to return once the fighting in Thronehold was over. I agreed and told the whole group about my adventure. Santonio wrote everything down, and I suspected he would kiss the paperwork throughout the night, he was that excited.

In the morning, after we had rested, we headed for Thronehold. As we traveled across land, Evianna returned to my side. I held her close as we sat on Terrakona's crystal mane. Her knightmare used her magic to help keep us positioned between the points. The shadows were used as pillows— something I had never seen a knightmare do.

"So," I said to Evianna, pulling her closer. "Do you... know anything about these two sovereign dragon arcanists? The ones fighting over Thronehold?"

I couldn't even remember their names. I knew Eventide had told me, but I had just met so many guildmasters and rulers that each name bled into the other, all becoming one. A part of me figured I needed to improve my memory. If I could memorize all one hundred and twelve steps of the Pillar, I could remember names.

Step twelve. *Knowledge. Without it, we fear our surroundings without hope to understand.*

"Ladislava?" Evianna asked. "She used to come to our castle from time to time." She rested her head on my shoulder. "She wouldn't speak to me, though. She said I was too much of a child."

"To your face?" I asked.

Evianna chuckled. "No. I would listen to her conversations with Queen Velleta."

"Your great-great-great-great grandmother?"

"You missed a great. Or two." Evianna shrugged. "It's not important."

"So you don't know anything about her? Well, if not her, what about the other sovereign dragon arcanist? Cardozo, I think his name was?"

Evianna shook her head. "I know nothing about the man. Maybe he'd be a good ruler, but that's not my decision anymore."

Her voice had become distant and icy. This wasn't a conversation she wanted to have. I didn't know what to do about that, though. I needed to know more before we threw ourselves into the fray.

"How many sovereign dragon arcanists are there?" I asked.

"About twelve," she replied, nuzzling against me. "At least, twelve is the number I remember counting last time I was in

Thronehold. I've been away for a while, though, so I don't know anymore. Maybe some of them have died."

"Are you worried about returning home?"

She didn't answer.

Which was answer enough for me.

"You could head to the City of Ellios," I said, pointing to the east. "It's not far from here. There's a great university and library. Once everything is finished, I could come to get you with Terrakona."

Evianna wrapped her arms around one of mine and held me close. "No. I'm here to help you. Thronehold *was* my home, but not anymore." She scrunched her eyes shut. "The moment I bonded with Layshl, I knew I wasn't going to follow in my sister's footsteps. I was never going to rule the Argo Empire."

"Do you have to rule it to call it home?" I whispered.

She dug her fingernails into my arm. "Thronehold is nothing more than a grave for my family. Everyone I cared for died there. Why would I call it home? Just because I stayed there when I was younger?"

The shadows around us flickered and danced. Evianna's knightmare rose from the darkness, her cape fluttering as Terrakona continued forward. Layshl's cowl—empty—stared down at Evianna. "My arcanist," she said, her voice cold but comforting. "*I* met you in Thronehold. I consider it a place of destiny."

Evianna chuckled, though there was no mirth in it. "Thank you, Layshl. I guess... I met you *and* Volke in Thronehold. You two changed my life, but you're the only positive things to come from all those terrible memories."

"Celebrate the little moments. Every happiness is worth cherishing."

With half a smile, Evianna rubbed at her face.

I didn't know what to say. I still considered the Isle of Ruma my home, despite the fact I hadn't lived there in years. Our circumstances were different, though. I had enjoyed most of my days on the white sand beaches.

"If seeing Thronehold bothers you, just let me know, okay?" I glanced down at Evianna, hoping I could be a comfort to her somehow. "And if you remember anything else about Ladislava or Cardozo, please let me know. We'll be there soon."

Evianna exhaled and loosened her grip on me. "Thank you, Volke. I'll try to remember something if I can."

QUEEN LADISLAVA

Another night, another campfire.

My eye healed slowly. I hated feeling it through my eyelid and realizing the eyeball had a furrow through it. My sight returned after a long night's rest. I think it bothered Illia. She had had her eye cut out by Calisto before she became an arcanist. Magic didn't heal scars, just active injuries. By the time Illia had bonded, it had been too late. She would never have her full sight again.

But I didn't discuss it with her. I tried to maintain a leader-like presence throughout the trek. This was a good time to practice.

Two days ago, we had crossed over the Clawdam Mountains, the northern edge of the Argo Empire. Soon we would be back on the main road to Thronehold. At least, that was what Evianna had said. I had only ever been to the Argo Empire once before, and I didn't recognize the territory.

Illia and Nicholin found useful plants in the surrounding countryside with Evianna's help. Apparently, gulletberries were difficult to find, since the fruit was hidden inside a sac-like pouch that grew on the bushes. Gulletberry leaves, dark and thick, made even locating the sacs an arduous endeavor. Evianna knew how to locate them, however. She said she had often snuck out of the castle to gather some before large parties.

"I used them to scare the guests I didn't like," Evianna said, her face reddish-pink as she recounted the story. "The little sacs look wet and throat-like, so I would stick them in bowls with other fruits and just wait for one of the haughty ladies to find them nestled between the grapes."

Sure enough, the gulletberries were the stuff of nightmares. Holding the sacs meant there was a high likelihood the berries inside would get crushed, resulting in their red juice oozing out the sac, sticky and sweet. And it didn't help that the sac was a dark purple, like a liver or spleen.

They made each meal delicious, though. Yesna used her frostblade to chop them up, resulting in chilled berries for the group.

Despite the fact that we had to sleep on the dirt—and not one of the seventy-two beds in my new compound—I was excited to retire for the evening. Not because I wanted the rest, but because I enjoyed my time with Evianna. We didn't really have *privacy*, but we did lie down on the opposite side of the logs, away from everyone else. We weren't close to the fire, but we were close to each other, and that provided enough heat.

Evianna kept her arms wrapped around me, our mouths never more than a few inches apart at any given moment.

When anyone walked by, we leapt apart, feigning interest in the surrounding trees. I felt juvenile for wanting to spend every moment of free time with Evianna, but on the other hand, being in her embrace felt right.

Why couldn't we get longer than an hour or two to be together? Why did everyone insist on seeing me? Or patrolling the campsite? We didn't need constant vigilance. Terrakona was nearby.

I knew that was foolish, but still.

The moonlight wove through Evianna's hair, giving it a pleasant glow. Her purplish-blue eyes put most gemstones to shame. I couldn't bring myself to say any of it, but I felt it each time we gazed at each other, unspeaking.

Once the campfire had died down and most of the others were asleep, Evianna stroked the side of my face with her hand. I enjoyed the soft graze of her fingers.

"Evianna," I whispered. "Being with you… it isn't like wearing a boot without a sock. If that makes sense."

It probably didn't. I regretted the words as soon as I had spoken them, but it was too late to take them back.

She stifled a giggle. "I agree. We go together like a boot and a sock."

Her analogy made me smile. At least she wasn't disappointed by my lack of seduction and experience. If anything, the *newness* of the relationship made everything feel significant and monumental. Even things like falling asleep in each other's arms—which most couples enjoyed on a nightly basis—felt special and wonderful.

"I need to get a drink," Evianna said with a sigh. She stood and dusted off her trousers with her hands.

"Can't Layshl get you a drink?"

Her cheeks reddened and she turned quickly on her heel. "I have to do something else, thank you very much. I'll be back in a moment." When she walked away, the shadows fluttered around her feet, shifting as though alive.

I rested my head against the unforgiving log. The bark poked at my scalp. It wasn't comfortable, but it was better than the ground. Then a thought struck me. I placed my palm on the dirt and closed my eyes. With as much imagination as I could muster, I pictured soft, white sand, the kind found on the Isle of Ruma.

The cold dirt became chill sand underneath me. I relaxed into it, thankful for my new powers.

Without warning, Zaxis sat down on the log, right near my head. I flinched away, startled by his close presence so late at night. His red hair seemed brown in the moonlight. His green eyes, however, were alight with vibrant color.

I sat up. "What're you doing here?" I kept my voice low, trying not to wake the others.

Zaxis lifted a leg up and rested an arm on his knee. "I think it's time we had a talk. Man to man."

I waited, completely baffled by his statement.

"You see, when a man loves a woman very much…"

I held up a hand, somehow angry, embarrassed, and disgusted in a matter of seconds. Only Zaxis had that effect on me.

"*Zaxis*," I growled. "Get out of here!"

He leaned in closer and lowered his voice. "I'm being serious, Volke. Everyone has seen you giving Evi those longing eyes." Zaxis motioned to the sandy dirt patch far from the campsite. "Even a blind man could see what's going on over here."

My face grew hot and red. I wanted to tell him to jump into the abyssal hells, but he was right. Everyone could see what was going on between us.

"Wait," I said. "Did you just call her Evi?"

"Yeah."

How did *Zaxis* already have a nickname for her when I *didn't*? And why was I so jealous? I ran a hand down my face, trying to remain calm. This wasn't worth arguing about. Everything was fine.

"Am I being too crude?" I whispered, fearing his answer. "Should I be more discreet with my affections?"

"Hey, I don't mind." He patted my unruly hair and smirked. "I kinda like watching."

"Did you seriously just come over here to mock me?"

Zaxis rolled his eyes. "You're missing the point. I'm just trying to look out for you. Everyone's watching your every move, right? Just... don't only have eyes for Evi. You might miss something important."

Even though I loathed to admit it, Zaxis was probably right. "How do you do it?"

"Do what?"

"Stay so dispassionate about your relationship with Illia?"

He scoffed and huffed and turned away. "Illia and I are *very* passionate, I'll have you know." Then he scoffed a second time. "So passionate, it would rock you to your core. *Worlds* more passionate than anyone we know, as a matter of fact. We're all over each other when we're alone."

"You do remember that you're talking about my *sister*, right?" I quipped, anger in my words.

"We're just not overly affectionate in public," Zaxis finished. He smoothed back his hair with a quick motion of his hand. "It's classier that way."

A tiny giggle caught our attention. Zaxis and I glanced over. Nicholin stood a few feet away, half-hidden by a small shrub. His eyes reflected the light like mirrors, giving him a haunted expression, one twisted with his mischievous ferret-grin. His silver stripes sparkled as he bounded over to us and leapt onto the log.

"How long have you been watching us?" Zaxis asked.

"Long enough to hear about all that *passion*." Nicholin held his little paws to his mouth. "I can't wait to tell Illia all about that one."

"You better not, you little gutter weasel." Zaxis stood, his body tense and embers wafting from his knuckles.

"Hm. Maybe if you apologize really nicely to me for eating the last biscuit after I clearly said it was mine—then I'll keep it a secret." Nicholin snickered. "But you have to kneel first. Yes.

Kneeling while you apologize." He rubbed his front paws together. "Pretend I am a god-creature."

Zaxis grabbed Nicholin and yanked him up. "I'll pretend you squeak if squeezed hard enough."

Before things could turn ugly, Nicholin huffed—and then disappeared in a burst of silvery glitter. A soft *pop* followed his disappearance, and Zaxis gritted his teeth in frustration.

"When I get my hands on that rat," he muttered as he stormed off, completely forgetting about our earlier conversation.

Once Zaxis was gone, I rested back in my sandy spot and placed my head on the log. Evianna stepped out of the shadows next to me, rising out of the darkness with confidence and purpose. I smiled and motioned to our new surroundings. Without another word, she leapt back to my side and wrapped her arms around me. She was cold, and I pulled her close, offering my body heat for her comfort.

I fell asleep without trouble. We only had a day's travel left before we reached the walls of Thronehold, and I wanted to get a good night's rest before I dealt with even more problems.

But my sleep was restless.

I didn't have dreams, my mind just wouldn't cooperate. I kept thinking about Luvi, the blight of the sky, and how not even the previous god-arcanists could cooperate. Seven of them had lived, only to be cut down by the apoch dragon. At least they had dealt with the corruption raining from the sky.

I silently cursed to myself when I realized I hadn't asked Luvi about his experiences with world serpent magic. I had been too excited to report my findings to the others—and rush to Thronehold—to even think about asking.

It didn't matter. I would return there soon enough, and then I could ask.

With my back on the ground and my gaze on the sky, I tried to imagine Santonio as the fenris wolf arcanist. I laughed to myself. Santonio wasn't a brave man, but at least he was persistent. That wasn't enough, though.

So who would bond with the fenris wolf?

The sounds of footsteps caught my attention. I lifted myself onto my elbows and glanced around. Our campfire had become dull embers. Illia slept on Zaxis's chest, and Nicholin slept on top of the both of them, like a little tower. At some point, Forsythe had wandered over to me. He slept only a few feet away, his head curled around most of his body, his scarlet feathers vibrant, even at night. When he exhaled, a soft birdsong whistled from his beak.

With careful movements, I unhooked Evianna's arms from my body. Her knightmare didn't need to sleep, but she also didn't need to leave shadows. I suspected Layshl was in the surrounding darkness, ready to be summoned at a moment's notice.

To my amusement, Terrakona had curled himself around most of the campsite. He had left an opening so that people could leave if they wanted, but otherwise we had three scaled "walls" all around us. When Terrakona snored, it sent slight rumbles through the ground.

Yesna and Zelfree were also asleep.

Odd. They had said they would take turns watching the camp. Had they forgotten? Or had they gotten drunk?

I pushed off the ground and stood. Where was Adelgis? I glanced around, noticing both the siren and mimic were asleep as well.

Although I hadn't seen any danger, a strange dread welled inside of me. I grabbed Retribution and pulled the black blade out of its sheath. No one moved. They remained sleeping, as though under a trance.

I walked around Terrakona's massive body, my hand on his scales as I went. The surrounding woods welcomed me with a chill breeze. Despite that, I walked out into the trees, my sword in hand. I searched as well as I could, but without the aid of dark sight, the gloom made everything difficult.

The farther I strayed from the campsite, the more worried I became about Adelgis. Where was he?

As if answering my question, I heard his voice further in the woods. I hurried in his direction, hoping everything was okay. Then a second voice floated through the trees. I stopped in my tracks and waited. A woman? Adelgis was speaking with a woman.

I crept forward, careful not to disturb the twigs and leaves.

"Please, Venae," Adelgis said, his tone quiet. "Listen to me."

"*You know nothing*," she growled.

"You must trust me. I can hear thoughts. Even yours."

"Not when I had my white hart, you couldn't! He protected me from such things!"

Her voice grew louder, but we were far enough away from the camp that I doubted she would wake the others. Determined to see what was happening, I continued forward, one slow step at a time. Once I found them, I stayed behind a large tree trunk, unwilling to sheath my sword.

Adelgis and his sister, Venae, stood in the middle of a small clearing. Moonlight streamed down around them, illuminating their tiny portion of the woods. The two siblings were eerily similar. Long black hair, thin frames, and narrow faces. Venae wore a cloak and trousers, and Adelgis wore long robes of black, but otherwise, they were strikingly close in appearance.

"You don't have to report anything to Father," Adelgis said.

Venae stepped back, glaring. "*Stop reading my thoughts.*"

"You don't know what you're doing. Father doesn't care about that. He only cares about his experimentation and magic."

"He's a god-arcanist, Adelgis. What's wrong with you? He's already won!"

"Cinna had horrible stories to tell me." Adelgis's tone

shifted from serious to calming. He stepped closer to Venae. "Please let me help you."

Venae hugged herself for a moment, her hot breath forming a cloud of mist whenever she exhaled. Her shoulders were bunched at the base of her neck, and she shivered when another gust of wind whipped past.

"Father will forgive us if we return with something he wants," Venae said, her rage waning. "Help me capture the mimic. I know you're traveling with it." She glared as she hugged herself tighter.

"We'll never be able to stroll into camp and walk out with the mimic," Adelgis said.

"Can't you put them all to sleep? If you really want to help me, you'll do this!"

Had Adelgis put everyone to sleep in order to speak to his sister in private? He could hear thoughts, after all. Perhaps we had stumbled upon Venae on our way to Thronehold. And ethereal whelk arcanists could touch people and augment their wakefulness, sending anyone into a deep sleep.

Or perhaps the only people he'd had to manipulate into sleep had been Yesna and Zelfree, since they had been on guard duty.

"One mimic won't do," Adelgis muttered.

A mimic? My mind wandered for a moment. When I had been Theasin's prisoner, he had kept MOS in his little experiment room. He had been intent on doing something with her, and he had always had a fascination with mimics in general.

But why? I knew the motive was sinister, but I couldn't deduce the reason.

There was a long moment of silence. Venae relaxed a bit, her eyebrows knitted.

"You're not going to help me, are you?" she asked.

Adelgis frowned. "This isn't the type of help you need. Our

father will never be satisfied, no matter how many tasks you complete for him."

Venae shook her head, her long hair fluttering about. Twigs and leaves poked out of her locks, and I suspected she hadn't bathed in quite some time. Had she been on the run since being chased away from my party? Her ratty cloak and dirt-stained trousers told a bleak story of rugged camping.

"No one is going to stop Father!" Venae shouted as she threw her arms to the side. "He has the backing of the Autarch! He has the bones of the apoch dragon!" She stepped backward, trembling. "If we anger him now, when he catches us, it'll be a lot worse." She shook her head. "We should make sure we're in his good graces."

"Venae..."

"Stop!" Venae grabbed her head with her hands. "Stop fighting against it! I don't want to have to kill you."

"What have I told you? I can hear your thoughts." Adelgis stepped close, his hands shaky. "You're afraid. Not for me, but for yourself and Yevin."

"That's not true." She shook her head again as she repeated, "That's not *true*."

Adelgis managed to reach his sister and place both hands on her shoulders. "I'm not going to betray the Warlord of Magic. You can't take me back to our father. Stay with us instead. Let me protect you. I promise our father won't hurt you ever again."

Venae stared into his eyes. Adelgis didn't move. They remained an arm's length apart, quiet and pensive.

I held my breath, hoping their conflict could resolve on a happier note. Adelgis had had so much trouble with his family. Couldn't this one time turn out differently for him? I wished on all the good stars it would be the case.

Then Venae clenched her jaw, and her mouth curled in a sneer. "*Protect me*? You're weak, Adelgis. Worthless. You always have been!" With surprising speed and skill, Venae pulled out a dagger and stabbed Adelgis in the stomach.

Her four-inch blade sank into his soft flesh, all the way to the handle. Blood blossomed from the injury, soaking into his dark robes, changing them to a darker black that matched the gloom all around us.

The sight sent ice through my veins.

I leapt out of my hiding place long before I thought about my actions. Heat engulfed the area, catching the nearby leaves on fire and charring the loose bits of detritus on the ground. Obsidian sprouted from my knuckles as I thrust with Retribution, hoping to end this fight in one devastating surprise blow.

"No, don't!" Adelgis shouted.

He shoved his sister out of the way, and my blade slashed him deep in his side.

Venae tripped backward and hit the ground, her eyes wide. Adelgis stood between her and me, now bleeding from two injuries. His sister's dagger remained in his gut. Adelgis couldn't stand straight. He was slightly hunched over, clutching his stomach, his breathing raspy and wet.

"You promised you'd let her live," Adelgis said as he held up a hand, his palm covered in crimson.

I stepped back, my sword in my hand, my conviction shaky. I had almost killed him. He had *leapt* in front of my weapon, hoping to protect his murderous sister. Venae had tried to murder him, right here in this forest clearing.

"She's confused," Adelgis whispered, answering my thoughts. He furrowed his brow. "Please. Don't hurt her."

I still couldn't believe it. Venae didn't deserve mercy at this point. She had made her choices. Theasin was her master, not logic or reason.

But I wouldn't kill her. Not if Adelgis didn't want that.

"Are you okay?" I asked him, my attention drawn to the

injury on his side. Despite the fact I had held back, I had still cut a deep gouge from his flesh.

Adelgis held my emblem ring close. Light shone from the trinket, illuminating the clearing and the woods around us. Venae wildly glanced around, her panic obvious.

As the ring grew brighter and warmer, Adelgis's injuries mended themselves. He tugged the dagger from his flesh, and his guts sewed themselves in place. The gouge across his ribs threaded together with powerful magics, helping him recover at three times the rate he otherwise would have.

Then the light died, and the emblem ring returned to its dull state. Despite the fact it had given Adelgis intense self-healing capabilities, he still hadn't fully recovered. His stomach and side were sore enough that he couldn't stand.

He wouldn't die, though. And that was all I cared about. My emblem ring had fulfilled its purpose.

"She isn't worth it," I said aloud, only for Venae's sake. "Adelgis, your siblings aren't children. You shouldn't feel obligated to protect them."

Adelgis shook his head, his shoulders trembling. "Please, Volke. You're upsetting her." He looked up at me, a slight smile on his face. "*I* used to think my father was an amazing man worth imitating. I even let him put the abyssal leech inside of me, all because I thought doing what he wanted would earn his respect and attention. I thought... he would treat me kinder afterward." He took a sharp breath. "I want... to help the rest of them. I want to undo my father's terrible influence on this world. Before it's too late."

What a messed-up situation. I was surprised Adelgis felt so strongly about it. Then again, he *had* been very excited about his father several years back. Perhaps only he could know the awful truth behind his siblings' suffering. If he wasn't going to help them, who was?

Venae didn't try to stand. Perhaps she knew she couldn't

run away, not when I could manipulate the ground around us. She just glowered at me, her brow furrowed in anger.

"You killed my eldrin," Venae finally said, her words laced with venom.

"You slashed my throat and tried to assassinate me," I stated. "I think we're even."

With an unsteady hand, Venae touched the faded arcanist mark on her forehead. The white hart was still visible between the points of the seven-pointed star.

I felt sorry for her. I knew what it was like to lose an eldrin. But it had ultimately been her choice. She didn't have to fight me out in the gardens. She didn't have to follow her father's orders. My pity died completely when I thought about the fact that she had almost killed Adelgis.

With my jaw clenched, I held out my hand. "You're our prisoner now. Get up. We're going back."

Venae leaned away. "*Never.*"

"She thinks you're going to kill her," Adelgis whispered, still hunched.

I glanced down at her, irritation replacing my hate. "You have my word that I won't kill you."

She laughed once. "You think I'll believe that? You're the world serpent arcanist—you're above all the laws and rulers and nations. You could kill whomever you wanted and get away with it. Why would I ever believe your word?"

"If Adelgis doesn't want you dead, I'm not going to kill you," I said matter of factly. "You can either believe me and take my hand, or you can disbelieve me, and I'll drag you back to camp. Either way, you're coming with us."

"My father is going to wreck your little snake and your life," Venae stated, cold and malicious.

"Pleasant," I quipped.

Then I held out my hand again, ready to end this evening.

She waited for a short moment, but she eventually pushed

herself to her feet and stood. Then Venae knocked away my hand and returned to hugging herself. "I want the dignity of walking myself."

Did Venae deserve dignity after her murder attempt? I could use the plants to create vines and tie her down, but Adelgis gave me a pleading look. I sighed and let the thoughts pass unacted upon.

Together, we ambled back to the campsite. Whenever Adelgis needed help, I offered it to him. He smiled, but it was pained and short. A part of me wished the world serpent had active healing powers, like the caladrius or phoenix.

"Where is Yevin?" Adelgis asked.

"My brother isn't here." Venae offered nothing else.

He frowned as we passed a grouping of trees. With his hand on each trunk, Adelgis slowly made his way over the roots. The red maple trees were known for having roots close to the surface, which made travel difficult. Thankfully, we had Terrakona.

"Yevin is trying to develop a poison for the god-creatures?" Adelgis asked out of nowhere.

Venae said nothing.

I lifted an unamused eyebrow. Would I have to worry about another assassin? Was Yevin, her twin, coming for me?

Adelgis shook his head. "No. My brother is a researcher, much like our father. Apparently, he's trying to improve upon the arcane plague."

I smiled to myself. "Perfect, because I already have a solution for that."

Venae, finally interested in the conversation, shook her head. "You're a fool if you think you can beat Yevin. He's just as clever as our father." The way she spoke about Theasin reminded me of Adelgis when we first met.

Venae dismissively waved her hand. "There's no stopping

my father's plans. He has everything figured out. You. The soul forge. The Autarch. Even the apoch dragon."

I wanted to end her—to be rid of this. But I controlled my breathing and tried to focus on pleasant thoughts. As soon as Theasin was dealt with, this would all be over.

To my shock, Venae pulled out another dagger. In a split second, she went to throw it. Not at Adelgis. At me. But she wasn't fast enough. I willed the ground around her feet to take her down. The roots and dirt underfoot twisted, throwing off her aim, and then the trees yanked her into the earth all the way to her knees, trapping her there.

Venae gritted her teeth and stifled a shout. Then she clawed at the ground, trying to pull herself free. I kept my manipulation on the ground, using the roots as a framework, preventing her escape.

I walked over, knelt, and jerked the dagger out of her grasp. If this were a warzone, I would've stabbed her with it. But Adelgis wanted mercy.

I tried to exhale my anger. It wasn't working like I had hoped.

"I know it frustrates you, but could we please take her to Thronehold with us?" Adelgis asked, ignoring his sister's struggle. "She can be a prisoner like the pirate, Markus."

After a moment of quiet contemplation, I sighed. "Fine."

Adelgis smiled, much to my confusion.

His murderous sister meant that much to him? Maybe Adelgis's home life was worse than I had thought.

"What's on her blades?" I asked, rubbing at my throat. "Whatever she used last time is still lingering in me."

"It's some of the apoch dragon," Adelgis said, confirming everything we had suspected. "Apparently, she was sent to weaken us, just in case we were heading to Thronehold. My father doesn't want you involved, and he suspects you'll avoid a confrontation with him if you're weak from my sister's attack."

Damn.

Why was Theasin always three steps ahead? He didn't even have Adelgis's ability to read minds, yet he had guessed with expert precision what everyone would do.

"Thank you, Adelgis," I said, knowing he must have read his sister's thoughts.

"No, thank you, my liege," Adelgis said. "I'll always owe you a great debt."

Without her eldrin, Venae wasn't much of a threat. I stripped her of her weapons and had Yesna watch over her during our last day of travel. Venae didn't put up a fight. She rested back on Terrakona and never spoke a word. Her distant gaze and lethargic attitude worried me. What if she was pretending? But I didn't give it much thought. Being devoid of magic had left her at a great disadvantage.

That didn't stop Nicholin from trying to cheer her up, however. A few times during the trek, I could hear his noble—but squeaky—voice drifting up my way.

"Don't worry, you can build yourself a bright new future," Nicholin said. "Crack jokes, not skulls—that's my motto."

"Haven't you killed people with your disintegration breath?" Zaxis asked.

"You can't prove anything."

Venae never responded to everyone's bizarre encouragements.

We reached Thronehold by the end of the day.

The main road was packed with thousands of merchants, traders, and diplomats on their way into the capital, but the gates to the massive city were shut, preventing anyone from getting in. Dust from the travelers wafted on the air, creating a thin haze that lingered no matter which way the wind blew.

Once Terrakona snaked his way over the last of the hills, I got a better look at the glorious city of Thronehold. Even Evianna was excited to see the massive city stretched out before us. She stood on Terrakona's mane, holding my shoulder for balance, her attention on the far castle. Her white hair flowed behind her like a river of milk. Beautiful.

King Drake Castle jutted into the sky, four times as tall as the next tallest building in the city. The flat roof and giant balcony at the highest point of the castle made for a perfect dragon landing, but there weren't any dragons on top. A wall circled the base of the castle with enough fortifications to stop a dozen platoons.

The thousands of buildings that made up Thronehold's city proper had little rhyme or reason. Each district had been built into the city as soon as it had been ready, with no grand architect to plan the roads. The twisting streets created a mild maze throughout Thronehold.

Towers dotted the cityscape, some made of stone, others of black wood. Nullstone towers? Thronehold was famous for its nullstone quarries. Dragons weren't affected by the anti-magic powers, so sovereign dragon arcanists always had free rein in the city.

A river cut Thronehold down the middle. What was its name? I couldn't remember. Bridges crossed the river every half mile or so, and small docks lined the banks. Mystical creatures swam in the waters, including beasts large enough that their giant silhouettes shimmered beneath the surface. Hatchling leviathans? Tempest dragons? I couldn't get a clear look.

Most wore armor, though. I suspected they were soldiers, but for who?

Smoke rose into the air at a steady rate…

Pillars of black and gray rose from the depths of the city, no doubt from the smiths, mines, and mills. Industry had a price, and Thronehold had embraced progress like a lover.

No. Wait. Some of the smoke wasn't from smiths or mills. It was from fire. Several houses were burnt or burning. Were they caught up in the fighting? Or had it just been an accident? I couldn't tell.

When I had first laid eyes on Thronehold, I had been taken aback by its sheer size and power. I had been both fearful and excited, as though I could never search the city thoroughly enough, or that it could never be defeated, not with walls that high.

But now I felt differently. The fires—the swarms of displaced people—and even the empty dragon throne made the city seem fragile. I was here not to gawk in awe, but to protect a place I had once thought didn't need anyone's aid.

"Search for the encampment," I said to Terrakona. "We need to find Queen Ladislava."

"By your command, Warlord."

Terrakona turned and headed toward the city. It didn't take us long to find what we were looking for. Queen Ladislava's sovereign dragon was massive—almost the size of Queen Velleta's dragon, Vercingetorix. It had to have been an adult, which meant Queen Ladislava had likely been bonded a long time and was thus a master arcanist.

Sovereign dragons had black scales on top and red-scaled underbellies. Her dragon rested on the countryside, curled up and asleep. The darkness of his body allowed him to blend in with the dusk, despite his size, which was why I hadn't seen him when we had first discovered the city.

Terrakona slithered in his direction. When he neared the main road, panicked merchants whipped their horses and oxen into motion. Shouts rang up around us. Everyone cleared a path as fast as they could, most pointing and muttering. I waved to the people as we passed, hoping I was making a good impression, like Zelfree had advised.

When we crossed the road, Terrakona's magic split it apart

and then mended it together again once he had gone. The road wasn't harmed by his gigantic size, and that baffled the merchants even more. They rushed to the middle of the road, examining the strange phenomenon.

As the sun set over the mountains, rays of orange and purple streaked overhead.

And so did a two-headed dragon. Its feathered wings and shifting scales—fading from white into a bluish-black—gave away its identity. It was King Odion and his juvenile twilight dragon, Hasdrubal.

"Let me off here," I said, patting Terrakona's head. "Please?"

He offered a rumbling growl and lowered his head. Evianna and I slid off his mane and landed on our feet. The moment I was closer to the ground, though, I had to cover my nose. A mixture of manure, rotting fish, and fragrant onions permeated the area. When I was high on Terrakona's head, the crisp mountain air had protected me from the scents, but no longer.

A few of the merchants shouted and pointed.

"My produce is wasting away!" one man bellowed.

Another added, "We need to get into the city!"

Evianna grabbed my shirt sleeve and pointed. "Volke, I think they're speaking to you."

"Me?" I balked. "Impossible. I just got here."

I glanced around, trying to find the merchants who had shouted. Evianna had been right. They stared right at me, some even motioning to the tall walls around Thronehold. The crowds gathered on the road nearest me, so thick, I couldn't count them.

"Do they know who I am?" I asked.

Evianna frowned. "I don't know. I think because your eldrin is so massive, they believe you're a master arcanist of some sort. Maybe they think Terrakona is a leviathan?"

Or word had traveled from Fortuna. When I had lived on the Isle of Ruma, news had spread fast. If the schoolmaster knew something, he'd share it with the fishermen when he was out collecting his produce for the day. The fishermen would tell the navy ships when they passed at sea. The soldiers would gossip at the ports they frequented. The girls in the taverns and pubs would repeat everything they heard, just to earn a few more leafs from the people from out of town.

In a single day, dozens of islands could know one secret.

Which meant these people probably knew of me. They wanted the world serpent arcanist to fix this situation.

And now agents of the Second Ascension would know we were here. Whatever war was going to happen, it would happen soon, as soon as everyone knew Terrakona had arrived.

I smoothed my clothing. Nothing would make me presentable in time, but I didn't care. Queen Ladislava was in trouble, and if she wanted a pompous blowhard, she was going to have to look elsewhere. I was here to fight Cardozo and end this feud once and for all.

Unicorn arcanists and their steeds rode toward us, their thunderous hooves announcing their presence wherever they went. The crowds were between us and the knights, and it took them a while to push their way through the disgruntled merchants and travelers. Knight Captain Alrick finally made it through and rode his pure white unicorn all the way to my side. When they drew near, the unicorn slowed to a trot and circled around me once.

"Greetings, Warlord," the knight captain said.

"You made it here already?" I asked, glancing around. "Has the entire Frith Guild arrived?" I had thought we would beat them to Thronehold, but perhaps their travels had been quick and easy.

Knight Captain Alrick offered me a reserved smile. His silver armor radiated authority and the merchants on the road had stopped bothering me ever since the captain had arrived.

"A few arcanists of the Frith Guild arrived via roc," Alrick said. "But the majority of your members—including a woman with a giant hydra—had to take the caravans." He motioned to the congested road. "And it's been slow-going. The gates are only open for a few hours every day."

"Why?" Evianna demanded. "That's not how the city guard works!"

Alrick ran his hand along his unicorn's short mane. "Fighting has broken out in the city. We're short on men, and even shorter on patience. The merchants have been smuggling in weapons or messages from the distant districts."

Things sounded rough.

Knight Captain Alrick pulled on the reins of his unicorn. "Follow me, Warlord. I will take you to see Queen Ladislava right away."

I glanced down at my attire. Evidence of our impromptu camping trip covered me from head to toe. Was this how I was supposed to present myself? No. I needed to be better than this. With few options, I opened the large pouch on my belt and withdrew Luthair's cape. The cold, silky darkness flowed through my fingertips as I secured it over my shoulders. The cape fit me perfectly, falling all the way to my ankles. Tiny stars still twinkled on the inner lining.

Evianna's eyes went wide, but she said nothing.

Even the knight captain seemed amazed.

It was a good choice. The cape hid my travel clothing and was an impressive statement, even if I hadn't made it into an artifact yet.

Knight Captain Alrick's unicorn eldrin trotted away from the road and toward the large encampment. I followed, and so did Evianna. The others—Zelfree, Adelgis, Zaxis, Illia, Yesna, and our captive, Venae—didn't chase after me. They slid off Terrakona and searched the area, likely looking for members of the Frith Guild.

The dragon sleeping among the trees didn't move as Alrick

led us down a path near the dragon's clawed feet. The massive beast was still smaller than Terrakona, but I feared the dragon's potent magic. Sovereign dragons were immune to fire and heat, and I suspected my molten rock would have no effect against him.

But I wasn't fighting this one. I would be fighting Cardozo's dragon.

Alrick glanced over his shoulder as we walked by dozens of military tents. "We have a thousand men here. All trained, but no combat experience. Cardozo leads a force of five hundred, but they're mostly sailors. All experienced, but in the wrong type of combat."

I acknowledged him with a curt nod.

"Queen Ladislava wants to move carefully. We haven't engaged in combat for a few days."

"We don't have time," I said. "I think we should move quickly. Another god-arcanist is on his way here. Plus, if we kill Cardozo's dragon, the fighting is over. The smart move is to end this quickly."

For a long moment, Alrick said nothing. When he finally spoke, it was quieter than before. "If you can convince the queen, I'll follow."

His hesitance worried me.

Cannons and cannonballs were gathered near the edges of the encampment. Queen Ladislava had three hundred cannons, and I suspected they could blow a hole through Thronehold's walls if desired. But if Ladislava and Cardozo were fighting for control of the city, they likely didn't want to wreck the infrastructure in the process. It wouldn't make them popular rulers in the long run.

Soldiers throughout the encampment kept themselves busy cleaning armor, mending weapons, or passing out rations. The scent of gunpowder and fresh stew mixed in equal parts in the breeze. Every soldier we passed offered bows—or three-finger salutes, their hands on their chests—as their knight captain trotted by.

Most just eyed me nervously, none willing to meet my gaze.

The largest tent in the encampment was the size of a house. It stood taller than the rest, almost two stories. Two soldiers were posted outside, both with their hands behind their backs. The linen walls of the tent—a dull tan in color—had been pinned and tied down so that they remained taut.

The crest of the Argo Empire, a dragon and a rose, had been stitched into every wall, from the bottom to the top. Queen Ladislava was making a statement. *She* was the proper ruler of Thronehold. Traditional. Reliable.

Alrick dismounted his unicorn.

"Watch the perimeter," he said.

His eldrin nodded. "Yes, my arcanist." Then the unicorn galloped off beyond the tents, heading for the outskirts of the encampment.

The Knights Draconic, always unicorn arcanists, served the ruler of Thronehold. Having the knight captain on her side was also sending a message. She was legitimate. But I didn't see any of the Sky Legionnaires—pegasus arcanists also bound to the throne. Could they be with Cardozo? Fighting flying soldiers would become a problem.

The two guards outside of the war tent stepped forward to open the flap for Alrick. They held it open for both me and Evianna, and I thanked them with a quick bow of my head. The men didn't acknowledge me. They remained as still as empty suits of armor, as though moving would be interpreted as an insult to my honor.

"Alrick, leave us," a woman said from the other side of the tent. "I must speak with the world serpent arcanist in private."

DIPLOMACY

Once Alrick left, it was just Evianna, the woman, and me inside the massive war tent.

The woman stood at the opposite end of a battle table. A map sat on top of it, but the lines of the chart shimmered and shifted. The ink moved, traveling across the giant piece of parchment and forming new symbols and words, even though no one was interacting with it.

Despite that, I kept my attention on Queen Ladislava.

She had the presence of a dozen kings, and her hard gaze pierced right through me. She wore half-plate armor with studded leather between the steel plates. Black dragon scales were woven into her defenses, though only a few. The scales were as large as a person's head. I suspected they had come from Ladislava's sovereign dragon.

And just like her tent, her armor had been etched with the Argo Empire's symbol. Dragons and roses—smaller and intricately designed—covered every bit of metal on her armor. Someone had taken weeks to make it look as spectacular as it did.

Her hair—it was just like Evianna's. White. Beautiful. Silky and otherworldly. Her eyes were the same shade of blue and purple. Ladislava and Evianna were certainly cousins, and I wondered if all of Evianna's family shared those characteristics.

Ladislava's skin was a sun-kissed tan, though. Evianna had spent months in the darkness, training her knightmare magic. It showed through her paleness.

"You may leave," Ladislava said, motioning to Evianna and then to the tent flaps.

Evianna took a deep breath and held her head high.

Before she could unleash a tirade, I stepped in front of her. "Evianna is my intended." That wasn't entirely true. *Intended* meant we were scheduled to marry, but it was the first thing that came to mind and now that I had said it, I didn't want to take it back.

Evianna placed a hand on my back, as if reassuring me that everything would be okay.

"I was unaware you were betrothed to my cousin," Queen Ladislava said. She placed her hands on the war table and leaned forward. "Then, for the sake of family, I implore you to help us oust the traitor, Cardozo."

She had the essence of authority as she stared down the long table, her eyes intensely focused on me. Her attention briefly went to my cape, and I suspected it had done as I desired and impressed her. But now I had to take control of the situation. I walked to the table and stood my ground, prepared to be the leader everyone needed.

"Is it true?" I asked. "Is Cardozo being helped by the Second Ascension?"

Queen Ladislava narrowed her eyes. Without moving from her spot at the table, she replied, "Yes. I have proof in the form of intercepted letters. Not only that, but several scoundrels in his employ are known Second Ascension members. We haven't seen any of the major players, however."

Determined to get the whole story, I figured I should start

with the basics. "How are rulership disputes normally handled here? Why haven't you and Cardozo solved this through Argo Empire means?"

"King Rishan disturbed the order of inheritance when he took the throne nearly a year ago." Ladislava spoke with a matter-of-fact authority. "Typically, the oldest sovereign dragon arcanist who has been serving as a province ruler would return to Thronehold and be given the crown. However, since the crown was lost during Queen Velleta's assassination, Rishan was able to pull out some archaic laws and claim *he* should sit as ruler in Thronehold."

"And that worked?"

"Obviously," Ladislava drawled. "Since Rishan has been slain, *I* claimed the throne under the same ancient laws. I have already been accepted, and a ceremony in the castle was held. That was when I chose my new knight captain."

Which explained why she already had the title of *Queen*.

Ladislava continued with a sardonic smile. "But Cardozo appeared with the ancient crown in hand and claimed *he* should be the next ruler of the Argo Empire. No one knew how he got it, but I suspect those Second Ascension *dastards* were the ones who handed it to him."

I held my breath and remained quiet. The crown's disappearance wasn't due to the Second Ascension. Karna had stolen it during the attack on Thronehold, and then later sold it in New Norra. I had no idea the crown was that important for the rite of succession. Karna's actions... Had she been instrumental in all this chaos?

I wouldn't mention anything, but the knowledge weighed heavy on my thoughts.

"I'm older than Cardozo," Ladislava continued, "but he's ruled over his province longer. Now he and his Second Ascension allies are walled up in the city, and since the *official* way to handle disputes has been called into question, it seems our destiny is to handle this like dragon arcanists. One of us will die, and the other will take the throne."

The bloody rite of dragons seemed ingrained in every dragon arcanist I personally knew. Even Odion had thought a fight to the death had been acceptable to claim my eldrin. It had probably stemmed from the fact that all dragon arcanists had to go through a trial of worth that involved death, but I wasn't certain.

I supposed fighting was the only course of action at this point.

"Why haven't you gone into the city?" I asked.

The map on the table shifted again, and Queen Ladislava glanced down. With a wave of her hand, she indicated that I should examine the map as well.

"This is a *Tactician's Charm*," she said. "The ink is made with sibyl blood, and it's imbued into the parchment with sovereign dragon magic." She pointed to a dark line near the edge.

It took me a moment of concentration, but I finally realized that the map detailed the terrain of the surrounding valley. Thronehold, the Clawdam Mountains, and even the city of Ellios were listed within range. The mountains and buildings didn't move, but the clouds did. Weather was displayed across the entire territory, including smoke from the fires in the city. There weren't any troops or people listed, but the map seemed capable of predicting the weather far in advance.

When Queen Ladislava touched the top of the map, the ink shimmered, and a date at the top changed. The clouds rolled over Thronehold and burst into waterfalls of rain.

Sibyls were creatures with minor abilities to predict the future, and sovereign dragons were creatures focused on bringing prosperity to the lands they ruled over. This trinket was the perfect combination of their powers.

"I've been waiting for the perfect opportunity," Queen Ladislava said. "Soon, I'll have my moment."

"Has Cardozo taken control of the castle?"

Queen Ladislava glanced up from the Tactician's Charm, one eyebrow raised. "He raided the city while I was away. The Sky Legionnaires follow his command. They blanketed several districts with decay dust—an insidious smoke that destroys all trinkets it comes into contact with."

"I'm familiar with decay dust," I muttered.

"It hobbled many of my arcanists. Without their trinkets, they were weaker than the enemy soldiers."

"Decay dust is a devastating weapon. One of the Second Ascension's favorites."

She clicked her tongue in disgust. "Cardozo threatened to use the dust on the merchant and magic districts. The weakened knights, no longer with their standard magical gear, forfeited the castle." Ladislava slammed her fist on the table, shaking the Tactician's Charm and rumbling the whole tent. I'd had no idea she had such power—when she lifted her hand, the wood underneath was cracked. "Cardozo hasn't officially occupied it, yet. Many of the city's arcanists won't allow an official shift of power without the proper ceremonies and procedures."

"Why isn't Cardozo's dragon in the city?"

"He's keeping her away from the fighting." Ladislava stood straight. The lanterns around the tent cast warm rays of light that glittered across her etched armor.

"But Cardozo is in the city? You're certain?"

"That's right." Then she walked around the long table, her steps followed by the soft *clink* of her armor.

I didn't say anything, but it was because of King Odion. I remembered how he had handled our first meeting. Odion had asked question after question, seemingly harmless, all with the intent of gathering information that he could later use against me. Now I knew more about Queen Ladislava's situation, but how could I turn it to my advantage in a negotiation? I would remain quiet and listen, then we could discuss alliances.

"Help me defeat Cardozo," she said, pointing to the walls of Thronehold on the map. "We're soon to be family, after all. It benefits all of us if you lead the charge into the city. Cardozo won't stand a chance."

I stood straight, and our heights matched. Her confidence was a lot like Odion's. I could feel it just as well I could feel her breath.

Her arcanist mark was etched deeply into her skin. It didn't glow, but the dragon wrapped around the star was still a sight to behold.

"If I help you, I'd like your help in return," I said. "The Frith Guild needs more master arcanists, and I need more nations to join my alliance. Can you provide me either of those?"

Queen Ladislava half-scoffed and half-laughed. "You want the Argo Empire to join an alliance? With *whom*?"

"Currently, the Kingdom of Javin, Antihelm, the Shikara Guild, the Southern Flier Guild, and five territories have all agreed to fight under my banner."

"Pathetic," Ladislava said with a dismissive wave of her hand. "The Argo Empire is ten times the size of your entire force put together. I won't allow my citizens to become the working dogs of your cause. You should be bending over backward to *me*. I'll help you defeat the Second Ascension *here* —we'll weaken their forces for when your minor nations finally muster enough soldiers to fight them outright."

Her disdainful attitude grated at my patience. I didn't need her to worship me like the rest, but I wouldn't tolerate her insulting me or the brave people who fought by my side.

"I understand that you think the conflict with the Second Ascension doesn't really involve the Argo Empire," I said, trying to remain calm and diplomatic. "But it does. Even if we oust them from Thronehold, they'll return, probably with deadlier and more sinister weapons much worse than the decay dust. I want us to form an alliance for your benefit as much as mine."

"Once Cardozo is finished, and I have the full backing of the Argo Empire, I won't need your help," Queen Ladislava stated. She narrowed her eyes, sizing me up a second time, her gaze lingering on the stars of my cape. "You may be impressive, but my armies, knights, and legionnaires are far more talented and powerful than you can imagine. So, I ask you again: will you lead the charge against Cardozo? You can garner yourself a bit more fame by fighting for *my* cause."

I mulled over her statement, almost amused by her verbal aggression. She wanted to strong-arm me into compliance. I wouldn't let her.

"People spoke my name in reverence *decades* before anyone knew of you," Ladislava added, her tone snide. "I think you should consider your course of action carefully. We're equals in these negotiations."

I half-smiled. Now was my moment. Odion's tactic of gathering information first had paid off for me. Queen Ladislava had given away too many details.

"I don't think we're equals in this matter," I said, curt. "It seems to me that you're losing. You lost your city, and you don't seem to have a plan to take it back." I motioned to the Tactician's Charm. "This is just a map. The power of Cardozo's functioning eyeballs will tell him that dark clouds mean rain is on the way. Knowing a few days in advance is hardly an advantage."

Queen Ladislava smirked. "Heavy rains hinder the pegasi of the Sky Legionnaires. If we strike while they're grounded, we'll strip them of an advantage."

I hadn't thought of that, but I could already feel her going on the defensive, like she wanted to lash out at me for even daring to speak back. Ladislava had expected me to roll over, probably because of my age. It didn't matter.

"I think you sent your knights to get me so that you could have a scapegoat in case something went wrong," I said. "You already fell victim to Cardozo's ploys, and now you're afraid to see what else he has at his disposal." I shrugged. "If *I* lead the attack on Thronehold, whatever happens will be on *my* head."

"How dare you," Ladislava growled. "I would never."

"You did it just now," I said with a sardonic laugh. "You said *the knights* forfeited the castle, but I doubt they did so without your order. It was *you* who forfeited the castle, but you can't admit that, can you? It's easier to blame the knights, and I'm certain they're loyal enough to take the fall for you."

Queen Ladislava held her breath and didn't respond. She waited, unmoving, and with poise enough to absorb my words.

I knew I was right.

"If you have me to blame—if you let me lead the charge, like you suggested—then you can sit back and allow me to take the worst of the casualties." I pointed to the tent flap. "Why aren't you out there right now, rallying the troops or speaking to your citizens? It's because you don't have an answer and you already look foolish. You want me to fix this, but you also don't want to look any worse in the process."

"What are you implying?" she asked, her voice controlled.

"If you give me territory or you swear fealty, people might perceive it as a weakness. They might think, *Queen Ladislava had to pay the world serpent arcanist to help her because she couldn't do it herself.*" I let the words sink in for a moment. "I'm right, aren't I? You don't want to look weak. You want us to be on equal footing when it comes to the victory and the negotiations, but you want *me* to suffer the ill consequences of failure and hardship."

I motioned to the empty tent.

"Isn't that why you sent your knight captain away?" I asked.

"To make sure you could negotiate with me in private? To make your pitch first and then describe how everything went to your soldiers afterward? Paint them a picture about how you dominated me into compliance, or perhaps paint yourself as the philosopher queen who convinced me to risk the world serpent for the betterment of the Argo Empire?"

I was stretching with the last bit, but I knew I couldn't be too far off. Who had a war tent with no advisors in it? Obviously, Queen Ladislava was worried about appearances. She didn't want to look like she couldn't handle the situation. That wasn't a bad tactic—confidence was better than panic— but it wasn't going to help her in these negotiations.

"You would let the Argo Empire fall to the Second Ascension?" she asked, slow and cold with her words.

"It's a matter of priorities," I said with a half-shrug. "The arcane plague is threatening the whole world. The Second Ascension is just threatening this city. I could deal with the plague first and then return to take back the Argo Empire." I stepped back and motioned to our surroundings. "But by then, this tent won't even be here anymore, will it? You'll have been defeated, and I'll be negotiating with someone else."

Evianna gripped my cape, but I couldn't turn back to face her. Ladislava and I were in a duel of wills. She wanted to threaten me—she wanted other options. If she had just agreed to help, this wouldn't have become such a battle, but here we were.

"I'm not asking for much," I said. "Be reasonable."

"Hm." Ladislava walked around the war table again, her harsh gaze on the Tactician's Charm. Then she stopped at her original position—all the way on the other side of the tent— her gait stiff and movements restrained. "You crossed *my* borders, walked into *my* army, and then had the audacity to address me without first paying respects? You never offered an introduction or bowed before the Queen of the Argo Empire—

yet you lie and say we're equals? Equals show each other deference. Am *I* asking for too much?"

She was shifting the subject of our argument to make me look bad.

Although, she did have a point. I hadn't introduced myself or offered a bow. Then again, neither had she.

Was *that* what would ultimately prevent us from making an alliance? Was Queen Ladislava so offended that peace couldn't be our goal? Would she insist on revenge for the slight against her?

Although I didn't want to give in to any of her demands, I didn't want to be rude, either. I offered Queen Ladislava a full bow at the waist. "My apologies. I am Volke Savan, the Second World Serpent Arcanist and the Warlord of Magic. It's a pleasure to meet you, Queen Ladislava Velleta."

Then I stood, but it hadn't changed Ladislava's demeanor. She remained tense and silent.

"Volke," Evianna whispered, her voice almost inaudible. "Tell her it was the Second Ascension who helped Rishan take the throne after the last queen died. She might not know."

"I had hoped to return the Argo Empire to its rightful ruler, since the last had been a puppet controlled by the Autarch," I said loudly, still facing Ladislava. "But I can't ignore my greater duties. If you can't help us—for whatever reasons you have, all valid, no doubt—I'll have to be on my way."

It was a bluff. I couldn't leave, not when I knew Theasin was on his way. But did she know that? I doubted it.

"What do you want?" Ladislava asked. "*Specifically.*"

"Help us fight against the Second Ascension beyond the borders of the Argo Empire," I quickly stated. "Protect the smaller nations to your west. Aid those who swear themselves to me. Allow us to travel through your land without delay or hindrance."

Everything else, we could handle, but as long as the Argo

Empire wasn't a wall that divided the mainland, we would be okay.

I feared that Ladislava might ask me to change the terrain of the Argo Empire after the war was over. The empire was so huge, that altering it would likely take forever and harm all surrounding territories. Besides, several rivers and lakes were located here, and the Clawdam Mountains provided protection from northern attacks. What more could I improve? I had nothing to offer her in that regard.

"You can tell your men that you're swearing an oath of vengeance against the Second Ascension," I said. "Because of how they harmed your family. It would make it seem as though you were *equally* allying yourself with me, rather than just giving in because you had already lost to Cardozo."

This was her out. At least now, she could save face.

I prayed to the good stars in the sky that she would agree.

The seconds passed in slow silence. I hated every moment. Queen Ladislava just stared at me, her shoulders rigid.

Finally, she said, "Well, Warlord, I can see why so many were excited to meet you." Then she motioned to Evianna. "And I can see why my cousin would be quick to marry you."

My face flushed a slight shade of pink. It probably didn't help me look confident.

"I will ally myself with your cause," Queen Ladislava stated, her posture relaxing a bit. "Now can we plan our attack against Cardozo? I want this chapter of my life done with."

INTO THRONEHOLD

I refused to make any plans without the others involved. I wasn't a strategic genius, and I wanted the opinions of people who were better versed in war. Unfortunately, Queen Ladislava demanded an equal number of her people involved. I brought Guildmaster Eventide and Master Zelfree. She invited Knight Captain Alrick and a man by the name of Val Velleta.

I thought Val would be a relative of Ladislava—since they shared the same last name—but when he entered the tent, I took note of his black hair and green eyes. He was much thinner than most people in Thronehold and wore the long robes of people from the northwest, beyond the ice barriers. They had a love for the moon, since their skies were clear most of the year, and his clothing reflected that. He wore crescent earrings and a star-shaped ring.

But he had no arcanist mark.

Val sat as the table and placed books out in front of him. He seemed ready for anything and wrote notes whenever anyone spoke. It seemed rude to ask why he would be included, so I never did.

We planned to attack Thronehold two days from now,

when a monsoon of rain would pour over the city. The grounded pegasi of the Sky Legionnaires wouldn't be able to blanket the city with decay dust, and we'd have a slight advantage since we knew the difficulties of the weather ahead of time.

The soldiers wouldn't know, however. We couldn't risk telling them to prepare for heavy rain, only for one of them to let the plan slip to the enemy. We would just have to prepare as much as possible without their involvement.

Terrakona would attack from the walls of the city—to avoid massive destruction to the infrastructure—and I would be inside, helping at the street level.

At least the three days would give me time to recover a bit from Venae's attack. I didn't know how long it would take for the essence of the apoch dragon to leave my body, but I hoped it would be enough time.

"We should gather information from the inside city," Eventide suggested. "A few of us can enter and make observations."

"They're preventing arcanists from entering," Knight Captain Alrick stated. "We won't be allowed inside."

"Then we'll sneak in."

"We should be beyond careful. If anyone is captured, there's no telling what might happen. We don't know the arcanists they have beyond the pegasi and the sovereign dragon."

I agreed with that point, but it wasn't a fear I thought should stop us.

"We attack with the rains, then," Ladislava said. "You have that all written down, Val?"

He nodded once. "I do. I'll disseminate the information immediately." He stood from his chair, offered everyone around the table a quick bow, and then left the tent without another word. He was so... quiet. And reserved.

Master Zelfree leaned back in his chair and crossed his

arms. Traces leapt from the ground to his shoulder, her gray fur sleek and shiny in the lantern light.

"Is Val your husband?" Zelfree asked, lifting an eyebrow.

He was less concerned about manners, apparently.

Queen Ladislava stood and rolled up the Tactician's Charm. "He's a lisque, nothing more." She said it with such finality that it seemed darkly harsh. Val was just her mortal husband until he died? That was all she thought of him?

No one around the table said anything.

Without prompting—or perhaps because she could sense the tension—Queen Ladislava lifted the Tactician's Charm into her arm and said, "I assure you it's quite common among the sovereign dragon arcanists of the Argo Empire."

That made sense. Out of all the dragons, sovereign dragons were the most power-hungry and autocratic. They didn't share well, and they didn't bond with people who shared well, either. That was why they preferred duels to the death as part of their trials of worth.

If Queen Ladislava didn't have an arcanist partner, she wouldn't have to "share" authority of the territories she ran. The Argo Empire didn't recognize non-arcanist rulers—the nation didn't even recognize *other* arcanists, unless they were bonded to a sovereign dragon.

And now that I thought about it, I remembered that the old Queen Velleta didn't seem to have had a partner. She had ruled with only her dragon. Had she had multiple lisques in her life? Mortals whom she had used for a while and then allowed to die so she could get another?

"I'll speak to the rest of my guild as soon as they arrive," Eventide said, ignoring the previous topic of conversation. "We'll be prepared for the attack."

Ladislava nodded once. "As will I."

Markus the pirate was brought in the next day. His carriage was a magical prison made of nullstone and nullstone-soaked wood. It prevented him from activating his magical powers, though he didn't seem to be struggling. Not even his griffin, who had been placed in a small nullstone cage, seemed interested in escape.

Venae, on the other hand, couldn't stop fighting against us in bizarre ways. She attempted to escape, somehow fashioning herself a knife out of dull silverware. Twice she tricked the guards into thinking she had been under the control of magic, and that was why she had been doing all those awful things.

Eventually, Adelgis used his augmentation to put her to sleep. We couldn't keep her like that for more than a few days, but at least we wouldn't have to worry about her.

With everyone coming in on the main road, and the merchants clogging up the majority of it, there wasn't much for me to do but wait. Zaxis and Zelfree were here—we could continue my training—but I wanted to rest. Evianna was with me, of course, but again, it wasn't like we could get much privacy. Every moment with her, someone was watching.

The clouds gathering overhead reflected my mood.

Soon there would be a battle. The cracks of lightning through the clouds tasted like conflict.

I walked through the crowds of merchants, travelers, and tradesmen, and regretted every moment of it. The people were pleasant—they greeted me with bows and pleasantries—but the overwhelming smell of rotted meat just wouldn't leave.

With my shirt up over my nose, I wandered by a few carts, looking for the worst of it. Perhaps I could burn it to the ground... and rid the world of this stench.

I found a cart with a dirty tarp thrown over the contents. When I walked over, the merchants gave me sideways glances, and the moment I reached for the tarp, a man leapt between me and the wares.

"Don't touch that!" he shouted. "It's ours!"

"It reeks," I said through my shirt. "I could smell it from half a mile away."

"I don't care! I still sell it to farms and cooks. I can still get money for it!"

His frantic attitude was confusing. The man practically trembled as he spoke. Was he afraid? Of me? Or was he afraid I'd steal his cart of decaying meat? He fussed with the high collar of his coat, the kind that went to his chin. Where did this merchant even hail from?

I turned away with a sigh. "I'm sorry to have bothered you. Good day."

The merchants watched me leave, each one of them with furrowed brows. It was odd, but I wasn't about to argue. They could do whatever they wanted with their products.

I spotted Vethica and her khepera at the edge of Ladislava's encampment. Her scarab-like eldrin had an iridescent shimmer that was hard to miss. Its exoskeleton looked like oil on the surface of water, dozens of colors mixing into one.

"If you think you're infected with the arcane plague, come see me," she shouted.

Her khepera buzzed around the tents. "By orders of the queen, you must be cured!"

It pleased me to know that the Second Ascension wouldn't be able to spread their terrible plague throughout the camp. Vethica's magic could reverse the ill effects, so long as she treated the creatures and arcanists in time.

But I didn't have the energy to help her at the moment.

When I wanted to be alone, I headed for Terrakona. He waited on the side of the road, his massive size and imposing presence enough to keep people at a distance. No one got close. Some of them even muttered false rumors about Terrakona rolling over and squishing a child.

I crossed over the main road into Thronehold and headed

straight for his side, hoping to calm my anxious mind. When I arrived, it was to a curious sight. Terrakona had his snake-like snout close to the ground. He sniffed at the tall grass, his serpent eyes wide, and his slit irises huge. He looked more like a cat than a snake.

"Is everything okay?" I asked as I hurried over to his nose.

Terrakona lifted his head a few feet from the ground. **"Warlord, come see."**

I slowed my pace as I neared the grass. The green blades danced in the early winds of a storm. In the grass, I spotted a green tree snake. I held my breath as I leaned over to get a better look. The little animal was in the middle of shedding its skin. The white crest of its former body peeled off slowly.

Terrakona watched with rapt attention, his tongue flicking out occasionally—and close to the snake. Once the little tree serpent had completely shed its skin, it slithered away into the grass, leaving a shell of itself behind.

"Was that fun for you?" I asked.

Terrakona leaned in closer to the dead skin. He was so huge —and the skin so small—that it could have easily fit into one of Terrakona's nostrils.

"She gave it to me," Terrakona telepathically said.

"Her... skin?" I asked, a little confused. "I'm pretty sure snakes shed all the time. Or at least once a year." I wasn't an expert on snakes.

"There may be many like it, but *this* one is mine." Terrakona gently poked the skin with his snout. **"It is a gift I will cherish."**

I rubbed at the back of my neck, slightly confused. Most mystical creatures didn't identify with normal animals, even if they were similarly shaped. Unicorns didn't live with wild horses, and a caladrius didn't dwell among parrots. So why was Terrakona so fascinated by the snake? Had they spoken to one another... somehow?

Terrakona lifted his massive head and then turned it to face me. His forked tongue jutted out for second, evaluating me before returning to Terrakona's maw. **"You have been preoccupied, Warlord. New love is to be celebrated, I feel. But that did not stop me from thinking about my existence."**

"What do you mean?"

"There is only one world serpent." Terrakona tilted his head to the side. **"I will never know another. So, while I can feel your bliss when you are with Evianna Velleta, I am aware that I will never know a similar experience. I should be content to have it vicariously through you."**

The statement left me speechless. I waited, trying to mull it over, but there wasn't much to say. Terrakona was right. He was unique. He would die, and perhaps thousands of years later, another world serpent would be born. He would never be there to greet it.

But it did surprise me to hear he experienced my emotions. He seemed to always know what I was feeling and reached out telepathically when I was hurting.

"The snake provided a momentary distraction," Terrakona said as he lifted his head again, nearly twenty feet in the air. **"But it's late, and the storm approaches. You should rest. The Children of Balastar are known for catching colds in the rain."**

A part of me wanted to know if Terrakona even knew what he was talking about when he had made that statement, but I decided against it. Rest sounded good. I wanted nothing more than to sleep away some of my burdens.

My dreams were confusing and a mix of colors. At first, I thought it was Adelgis, but nothing was clear or coherent. I floated on my back in the coloration, like it was a part of the ocean. The sky was just as bad—a swirl of reds and blues and grays.

"Adelgis?" I whispered as I stared up at the sky.

"*I apologize, Volke,*" he telepathically replied. "*I wanted to show you more images, but it's... difficult...*"

"What's wrong?"

"*There are so many people here. It's hard to focus. I'm losing my concentration, and the voices are invading my own thoughts.*" His telepathy agitated my mind, like a voice reverberating so hard it caused a vibration.

"Can't you get away?" I asked. "Why not leave? Everyone will understand."

Adelgis didn't answer for a moment. I enjoyed the stillness of the colorful water as I watched golden clouds shoot across the sky.

"*There are enemies nearby,*" Adelgis said, rather ominously. "*They're close, but I can't focus on them. All I hear are snippets of thoughts. They're here to kill you. To kill Ladislava. To kill us all.*"

"Right now?"

"*No. But soon.*"

Then we would have to be ready. "What about the fenris wolf? Do you know where it is?"

"*Close. In the mountains. In a... cave... But I won't be able to find it until the voices stop. There are so many... It's getting difficult to even speak with you.*"

"Don't worry. Thank you, Adelgis. I think you should get away from the city. But before you go, tell the others about the enemies."

"*Are you sure?*"

"I'm your liege, right?" I chuckled to myself. "It's an order. Get away from the people until you can focus again. Help from afar."

Adelgis's telepathic voice sent over a laugh. "*Thank you, my liege. I'll do just that.*"

I slept in one of the Frith Guild carriages, thankful a few more of our allies were here outside of Thronehold. Evianna stayed with me—she slept on the opposite bench. They were cushioned, which made for easy sleeping, but it was difficult knowing she was only a few feet away.

Knights of Javin, as well as Fain and Wraith, protected the vehicle at all times. Whenever someone approached, the knights would direct them away, and Fain would stalk them closely, always invisible. When Fain slept, Wraith took up his post. I was never without their protection—an admirable trait for a knight.

A part of me feared I would damage Luthair's cape if I carried it through the fighting, so I left it inside the trunk of the carriage. Then I locked it shut and kept the key. As soon as I had a better handle on my magic—and I knew what I wanted to do with the cape—I would create an artifact that would stay on my person forever.

Luthair...

It had been in Thronehold that he had said he would stay with me no matter what. Even when I had been infected with the arcane plague, Luthair had stayed with me. I had never wanted him to leave.

As I exited the carriage to prepare for the day, I almost ran into Master Zelfree. His mimic sat on top of the carriage, staring down at us with her bi-colored eyes.

"You're awake," Zelfree said as he leaned against the side of the vehicle. The glass on the door—wavy due to decorative design—creaked from the weight. The carriage wasn't in the best condition.

"Are you okay?" I asked, glancing around.

He pointed down the road. I spotted Karna and my brother standing close to the giant walls. The gates were open, and people were being ushered inside. It was still slow-going, but the excitement spread throughout the merchants. Even the ones with rotten goods got inside, and I was happy for me—but happier for my nose.

"Ladislava is sending in some of her soldiers to investigate, but I think we can get some additional information." Zelfree motioned to himself, then Karna and Ryker, and then to me. "It won't be long. We'll get in and out before sunset."

I understood why Zelfree, Karna, and Ryker would make a good team. Zelfree could pretend to be any arcanist, and Karna could be any person. Supposedly, Ryker had the potential for both, but currently, he at least had some shapeshifting, so this would be a good place to practice.

But the guards weren't allowing arcanists inside. How would we make it past them with Zelfree? Karna and Ryker could hide their marks with their shapeshifting, but not Zelfree. Then again, I knew he'd have a solution.

"Are you sure I should go?" I asked.

"Your mark is also easy to hide," Zelfree said, gesturing to my buttoned-down shirt.

"Perhaps I should stay behind... It seems like a needless risk."

"We just gallivanted off to a magical lake so you could speak to a hallucination of the past world serpent arcanist. You had no fear then—why are you hesitant now?"

A part of me didn't want to ruin relations with Queen Ladislava by disrupting her plans. Then again, information was important. I didn't like being in the dark.

"As long as we don't upset Ladislava." I laughed darkly. "I get the feeling she would do something unreasonable if we failed in our actions."

Zelfree smirked. "I've been meaning to tell you—I'm impressed. You handled the situation with her well.

Convincing individuals to act against their nature is a rare trait."

"I'm trying to learn." I had only just begun to be the leader everyone expected.

"You remind me a lot of Gregory Ruma," Zelfree said, his tone softer. He even laughed to himself as he continued, "I don't know how he did it, but he always managed to come out on top, no matter the task given to him."

"That's... what you think of me?"

"You have a rare kind of tenacity that I appreciate. That's all I'm saying." He stopped smiling and stared at me with a stony expression. "Remember that we need an epic leader, not just a guy who can get things done. Don't lose sight of your goal."

He was always so good at giving me perspective. I knew I needed more practice in this diplomatic arena and having outside confirmation at least assured me I could assess myself. That hadn't been the case years ago.

"Having the Argo Empire on our side is a massive boon," Zelfree said. He turned his attention to the carriage. "And since you're with someone related to the new royalty, I suppose that'll help as well."

"I'm not with her because of that," I said as I stepped around him and headed for the wall. "C'mon. We should head in. Thronehold is a gigantic city."

THE JUSTICE DISTRICT

I probably should've told Evianna where I was going before I left. I hoped she wouldn't be too upset by my disappearance. We'd be back by nightfall, though. That wasn't long.

Terrakona remained in the same location, a short distance from the main road, his serpentine body tightly coiled. He was asleep—I hadn't seen that often—and I wondered if he would be safe. I shook the thought away. There were few beasts that could mortally wound Terrakona, and I was certain I would see them coming long before he was assaulted.

Traces leapt from the carriage and landed on her arcanist's shoulder, her balance unparalleled. She purred as she wrapped her long tail around his neck, and we headed off.

As Zelfree and I walked alongside the road, I turned to him and frowned. "What does the soul forge look like?" I hadn't thought of it until just then. "Whenever I picture Theasin attacking, I imagined a bigger version of his relickeeper." A dragon made from broken and discarded pieces.

Zelfree glanced over. "Illia acquired a book a while back

that briefly described the soul forge as a *primordial abomination*." He laughed once. "It fits Theasin."

"Is it gigantic? Like Terrakona?" I had assumed so.

"Probably," Zelfree replied as he scratched the stubble on his chin. "Any and all materials I've seen on the god-creatures indicate they were forces of nature, could be seen from afar, and were feared by all."

"Do you think Theasin will ride it here? Or will he teleport into Thronehold, like the assassin did a few years ago?"

"If I had to guess, I would say Theasin will appear suddenly and without warning." Zelfree sighed. "Which is why we have to stay on our toes." He patted me on the shoulder. "If it makes you feel any better, the soul forge isn't known for being a beast of combat. I think you'll have the advantage in a fight."

The news helped my mood a tiny bit, but it wasn't enough to dispel the anxiety. If I *didn't* defeat Theasin, he would continue to develop disgusting tactics and weapons for the Second Ascension. And what if he developed an aura before I did? There were too many disastrous outcomes to let him roam free.

I glanced at the tall walls that surrounded Thronehold. "Why aren't we teleporting inside?" I whispered. "Illia could get us in without a problem."

"Illia is helping the guildmaster. She'll be in the city, and with my magics, I can mimic Nicholin if we need to. However, teleporting around could accidentally get us caught. I don't want to risk that when we can do it the good ol' fashioned way."

When Zelfree and I approached Karna and my brother, they moved away from the side of the road and led us to a small cluster of trees. Once out of sight, Karna held out a dark brown cloak. The bottom hem was frayed, and it smelled slightly of booze. Zelfree took it and frowned. Then he handed it to me. I threw the cloak around my shoulders and tried to ignore the musk wafting off the wool.

To my surprise, Karna wasn't dressed in her normal dancing attire—a small top made of silk, and a bottom portion crafted from cotton satin. Instead, she wore chainmail with a tunic overtop. A dragon, a rose, and a sword were stitched on the fabric, indicating it was a tunic worn by Thronehold's city guard.

"How do I look?" she asked.

Her soft and curved body practically drowned in the large clothing. Had she stolen them from a man twice her height?

I shrugged. "I'm sure you'll grow into it."

Karna frowned at my joke. Then she tossed back her wheat-gold hair. "Here's the plan," she said, smiling. "My doppelgänger will stay here and pretend to be Volke. I'll look like a city guard and usher the three of you inside. Ryker will be a merchant, and you two will be his guards."

"Why is your doppelgänger staying behind?" I asked.

"So that no one goes asking questions about your location." She winked.

"It would be easier if I mimicked one of the will-o-wisps inside the city," Zelfree stated. "I can be a member of the Lamplighters Guild and stroll in without trouble."

Ryker, perpetually nervous, shook his head. "They have special lamps they wear on their belts. We can't replicate that. We'll get caught for sure."

The Lamplighters Guild was a small organization inside Thronehold. Their members—all will-o-wisp arcanists—maintained the streetlamps throughout the city. They deterred crime, helped with minor disputes, and generally kept the peace. Zaxis's brother had joined them years back, and I remembered appreciating his efforts.

They weren't a guild I wanted to recruit for our cause.

though. Their arcanists, and goals, weren't suited for a war against bloodthirsty blackhearts.

"What do you want me to do, then?" Zelfree asked. He touched the arcanist star on his forehead. It was blank—his mimic had yet to transform—but it was still clearly visible. "If I wear a hat or a scarf, they'll remove it."

"I'll handle this," Ryker said. "I, uh, discovered what I could manipulate thanks to Karna's efforts."

With an unsteady hand, Ryker reached out and touched Zelfree. At first, nothing happened, and I waited, expecting something dramatic to occur at any point. Ryker's eyebrows knitted in severe concentration. After a solid minute of staring straight at Zelfree, a shimmer of magic caught my attention.

The arcanist's mark on Zelfree's forehead faded. The skin stretched, rippled, and froze into place, altering Zelfree's appearance.

"*You* did that?" I asked as I stepped closer to Zelfree. His mark was gone. No trace of it was left.

Ryker exhaled and smiled. "Yes. I can manipulate people's appearances. It's, uh, not permanent. Their natural look will return after a short period of time, but it'll maintain throughout the day."

That was new. Doppelgänger arcanists manipulated people —controlled their actions as though they were puppets on strings—but the Mother of Shapeshifters didn't seem to have that ability. What an interesting development.

Ryker turned to me and placed a hand on my shoulder. Would he hide my god-arcanist mark? A slight sting on my forehead told me he was hiding my old knightmare mark, which wasn't a bad idea. Then pain gripped my chest as my god-arcanist mark faded from my skin.

"I can't do much more," Ryker said as he released another long exhale. He removed his hand. "Hopefully, in the future, I'll be able to disguise anyone or anything. A useful trait, no?"

I nodded as I rubbed my smooth forehead. "A very useful ability."

Traces stopped her purring and leapt down to Zelfree's arm. Within an instant, she transformed into a pair of bangles and wrapped herself around Zelfree's wrist. Her object-form made him seem more like a pirate than before—sea thieves would often wear jewelry from the ships they had plundered, after all.

"Let's go," Zelfree stated.

Karna closed her eyes and forced her body to transform. Her athletic dancer's body became that of a thick, barrel-chested man. She grew into her oversized chainmail and tunic, hair sprouting from all visible patches of skin. Her long blonde hair shrank—practically sucked back into her body, growing in reverse—and only stopped once it was shorter than a fingernail and as black as death.

Then *Guard-Karna* opened his eyes and sighed. "How do I look now?" he asked, his voice ten times gruffer than before.

Ryker softly clapped his hands a few times. To my surprise, a white mouse poked her head out of his trouser pocket and also clapped. The glowing, red eyes of the mouse made the celebration seem sinister somehow. Of course, the mouse was MOS, but she had still surprised me.

Where were the other hundreds of mice? Probably nearby...

Without prompting, Ryker took a deep breath and closed his eyes. His hands shook as his magic rearranged his body. At first, his face only changed faintly, then his black hair lightened and grayed at the temples, aging him forty years in the blink of an eye. A beard sprouted from his chin, wild and unruly, much like a scraggly weed.

His arcanist mark faded as well.

Then Ryker coughed and staggered back a foot, hitting one of the nearby maple trees. After a calming breath, he glanced up and half-smiled. "Do I look okay?" Unlike with Karna, his voice hadn't changed. While Ryker looked different—a new person, for sure—anyone who knew *him* would figure out his disguise in an instant.

He had a long way to go before he was a master of his shapeshifting.

Guard-Karna sauntered over to him. With a smirk, he patted his upper arm. "You're doing well, my apprentice."

Zelfree gave him a sideways glance. "Watch it."

"What? I'm training him in the most important aspect of his magic." Guard-Karna thumped his massive, hairy chest. "He can learn all about your little *copycat* magic when he's done studying at the foot of a disguise artist."

The resulting silence didn't sit well with me. I motioned to the main road around the cluster of trees. The others nodded and headed out of the woods and into civilization. We stepped onto the brick-lined road and walked through the hundreds of bodies crammed together, all funneling to the same location.

I kept the smelly cloak tight around my body, hiding my sword and shield from view. Without a mark on my forehead, most people didn't bother giving me a second glance. I didn't blame them. I had just woken up—my hair flattened on one side—and the smell of a brewery followed me like a stray dog. Who would think *I* was the world serpent arcanist?

Guard-Karna and Ryker led the way. We reached the gates and stood in line for a few minutes before we were allowed to move forward. Guard-Karna handled the talking. He whispered a few things to the men at the gates. It took another couple of minutes, but finally the four of us were admitted.

The smell of the trolley cars brought back memories.

The main street was large enough for a dozen mustangs, but nothing impressed me like the *horseless trolleys*. They reminded me of gazebos—no walls, but pillars and a roof. They were attached to tracks and moved thanks to magic-created steam. The nearby trolleys hissed and headed deeper into the city, but Guard-Karna didn't rush after them. Instead, he waved us to the side and then entered a back alley as soon as he possibly could.

My brother gawked at the machinery, his eyes wide and his mouth hanging open. He looked like such an island bumpkin that I couldn't help but smile to myself. I tugged at his elbow and jerked my head to the side. "C'mon, Ryker. This way."

"B-But did you see those vehicles? They can carry so many people!"

I nodded once. "Yeah. They're great. Stay focused."

He didn't protest, but his eyes never left the trolleys. I had to direct him to the alley Guard-Karna had disappeared into. Zelfree stuck close to me, his skilled gaze examining each and every person who got too close to us.

The buildings had been constructed so close together that sunlight never touched this portion of the city anymore. The chill and stagnant puddles gave the alleyway a new feel all its own. The main road of Thronehold was paved with smooth cobblestone, but this narrow path had nothing but mud, steppingstones, and dirt.

Every building stood at least two stories high, with stone near the base, and wood for the second level. The windows and tiled roofs were the product of expert craftsmen—and although the streets had no order, everything else did. Neat doors. Square windowpanes. Perfectly layered roofs.

"We'll get to the main districts faster this way," Guard-Karna said.

"Taking us to your Moonlight District?" Zelfree asked with a smirk.

"You wish."

"*Ha.* I don't need harlots. Men never say no to me—they say *please.*"

Guard-Karna let out a laugh that echoed down the

alleyway, brightening our gloomy corner of Thronehold. "Such confidence." He glanced over his shoulder. "You should wear it more often."

Master Zelfree snorted.

As we hurried around a pile of trash, I turned to him and frowned. "I asked you for relationship advice dozens of times and you refused to help. If you're so suave, why didn't you give me some pointers?"

"There's a big difference between *manipulative seduction* and *trusting love*." Zelfree shot me a glare. "I'm fantastic at one, and you're fantastic at the other. You never want advice from me, kid."

"Are you all seeing this architecture?" Ryker asked, his eyes more on the second story than the road in front of him. He half-tripped a dozen times.

Again, Guard-Karna laughed. "Oh, Ryker. You're such a sweetheart." His gruff voice made the statement sound amusing.

The smoke bothered my nostrils. We were close to the fires, and the farther we hurried down the alley, the hazier the air became. Guard-Karna led us out onto another street and then into a second alleyway, this one darker than the last.

Men and women went about their lives, despite the chaos all around them. Laundry hung on strings, bathwater was thrown from windows—it sloshed down gutters and spilled into our alley on more than one occasion.

The people of Thronehold were resilient. The people of Ruma lost themselves in a tizzy when I had improperly joined the phoenix's trial of worth. Perhaps the Argo Empire was just used to disasters at this point. Two years ago, their queen had been assassinated, and then a few months ago, their new king. I was certain both events had caused untold turmoil for the citizens. A few fires probably didn't compare.

We exited the second alley onto another street. A metal

sign, nearly ten feet tall, caught my attention. It read, JUSTICE DISTRICT, with a picture of a man in a cage next to the lettering.

Guard-Karna turned and headed in that direction.

"How large is this place?" Ryker asked, spinning for a moment as he hurried after Karna.

I didn't answer him. Three members of the Lamplighters Guild rushed by us, each carrying a decorative lantern made of thin wrought iron and polished glass. Their will-o-wisps dwelled inside those lanterns, and the flames of their eldrins danced as the men ran by. They wore pendants around their necks: two copper and one bronze.

"Another fire!" one shouted, pointing to the smoke in the sky. "Hurry, Bee-Bee!"

He opened his lantern and the will-o-wisp dashed out of it and headed straight for the emergency. Will-o-wisps weren't powerful mystical creatures, but they could snuff out flames, if they were close enough. The greenish-red wisp floated into the sky, moving like a feather caught in an updraft.

"Volke?"

I glanced over my shoulder and spotted Ryker down the street. Guard-Karna and Zelfree were already out of the sight. I had been too enthralled by the will-o-wisp arcanists to even pay attention to the others.

After shaking away the thoughts, I ran after my brother and straight into the Justice District. Unlike in the residential streets, the buildings here were mostly made of gray-striped marble and stone. The windows were protected with bars, and nullstone had been used in the construction of the doors, chimneys, and steps.

"Where are we going?" I asked as I rejoined the others.

"Getting information from your underworld friends?" Zelfree asked.

Guard-Karna chuckled. "No. We'll get more information if

we speak to the judges. They always know what's going on. They speak to the soldiers, the guards, the knights, the lamplighters, *and* the criminals. If there are Second Ascension members here, the judges will know where to look for them."

I nodded along with his words, hoping this endeavor would pay off.

The terrible stench from the main road soared into my nose. I cringed when I noticed the tarp-covered cart being drawn down the road by a single horse. A merchant hovered close to the disgusting "merchandise." How could he stand to be so close? And who in the Justice District wanted any of that foul-smelling meat?

I didn't have time to investigate, however. I continued with the others, shaking away all my tangential thoughts.

Zelfree, Ryker, and I waited outside the Hall of Justice while Guard-Karna went inside. From our position on the nullstone steps, it was possible to see several streets down in three directions. Cardozo's soldiers patrolled the district, each group carrying a flag with a dragon and a rose. Just like Queen Ladislava, Cardozo was likely trying to claim legitimate authority by waving the empire's emblem around as though it were his own.

These men seemed intent on keeping the peace. They didn't bother anyone unnecessarily, and when they passed the Hall of Justice, they barely gave us a second glance. In fact, the soldiers passed out blankets, rice, and flour to groups of downtrodden denizens who were gathered in the Justice District as some sort of protest. Perhaps the soldiers had joined Cardozo and the Second Ascension simply to remain in the city and help the citizens.

"What a fascinating city," Ryker said, watching the soldiers march by. "So many people. How do the rulers keep track of them all?"

"They don't." Zelfree yawned and then stretched. "They have other people to do that. Instead, they focus on the larger concerns of the nation, like food, the might of their military, and the maintenance of their prosperity aura."

A sovereign dragon's aura could make everything in the nearby area more productive, and even increase the happiness and attention of the citizens—only by a slight amount, but that was all it took to make a nation prosperous.

I wanted to go inside the Hall of Justice and see what Guard-Karna had gotten himself into, but my thoughts came to a halt the moment I spotted a disturbing sight.

Calisto.

In the Justice District.

I almost couldn't believe it, but I would know him anywhere. He stood tall, and even though dark clouds gathered overhead, his vibrant copper hair stood out, even among crowds. He wore a bandana over his glowing arcanist mark, hiding his status, but he did nothing else to cover his identity. He wore a long coat, boots of knightmare magic, and thick trousers—a sailor's outfit.

Spider, his first mate, hovered close to him. Her button-up shirt was half-undone, exposing more of her cleavage than was proper, but not so much as to be indecent. Her tricorn cap was pulled down enough to also cover her forehead, and I thanked the good stars that her kappa and Calisto's manticore weren't around.

She fluffed her curly black hair and eyed the streets as she and Calisto walked in our direction.

I grabbed Zelfree's arm, panic fueling my actions. He glanced over just in time. While I was still thinking about the situation, he pulled me up the bluish-black nullstone steps of the Hall of Justice and shoved me behind a group of

Thronehold citizens. They were waiting to get inside, and the ten of them made for great cover.

Ryker never saw us leave. He was too busy admiring the city—his eyes on the far-off towers.

I mingled at the edge of the group of people. They eyed me, but no one said anything. Most kept small piece of parchment close to their chests. Mumbles between them were rare. To my horror, Calisto and his first mate headed up the steps, straight for the doors of the Hall of Justice.

They walked right by Ryker, no care whatsoever. Ryker did look *different*, and his arcanist mark was hidden…

The nullstone likely prevented an arcanist from activating powers. Would it stop mine? Now was a good time to check. I clenched my fist and evoked some of my molten stone. Although the nullstone tried to stifle my abilities, it couldn't chain down world serpent magic. A slight amount of magma oozed in my palm, creating a tiny thread of smoke.

"He's not here," Spider said with a sneer. "Why're we continuing to search?"

Calisto kept his hands deep in his coat pockets. "They might be keepin' him in those nullstone holding cells they have around the courts."

"And we're gonna break him out?"

"Maybe."

Spider dramatically rolled her eyes. "What's wrong with you? We're supposed to be headin' to the sky titan. We've already stayed here too long. We're gonna get caught up in Theasin's surprise."

"I don't *care*," Calisto growled. "I'll do what I please. The sky titan child can wait."

The people milling around the front of the hall didn't give Calisto or Spider much attention. Their downtrodden expressions and ringed eyes told me they weren't in the mood for other complications in their lives.

"Why would he even come here?" Spider asked, bordering on sarcastic.

"He was a nobleman. His hippogriff arcanist father is somewhere here." Calisto clicked his tongue in disapproval. "*Tsk*. Besides, he knew *we* would be here. He likely came here looking to regroup before the *main event*."

"That's in a few hours. We don't have time."

"He's here. Somewhere. I don't want him caught up in everything."

"I'm telling you—he ran off. *The pirate life* was too much for him. Good riddance, I say."

Calisto wheeled on her, tense and intensely quiet. Spider flinched away, her hands up.

"Sorry," she whispered. "If you wanna find him that bad, I'm here for ya, cap'n.'"

Calisto relaxed a bit. He headed for the front door of the Hall of Justice, but he hesitated as he reached for the handle. He inhaled deeply and turned his attention to the crowd of people. I glanced away, trying not to make eye contact.

He was at least twenty feet away.

"We should go," Zelfree muttered.

I nodded and the two of us headed down the steps, away from Calisto and Spider. We made it down the fifteen nullstone steps and then motioned for Ryker to follow, but by then, it was too late. Calisto turned around to face us, his expression a mix of recognition and dark amusement.

Spider's eyebrows shot to her hairline. Then she gritted her teeth and grabbed Calisto's coat.

"They're inside the city," she hissed. "I told you someone would recognize us!"

Ice filled me as I turned to face Calisto. He smiled and headed toward us, his gait casual, and his speed slow. Ryker and Zelfree stood next to me, but it was obvious they didn't want to act.

If we got into a fight now, Cardozo's soldiers would no doubt get involved. And although the sky was cloudy, it was not yet raining, which meant the Sky Legionnaires would be summoned to deal with us.

I could fight them. I could fight them *all*, but I'd probably lose Zelfree and Ryker in the process if I weren't careful.

Calisto was a powerful arcanist.

"I can't believe you're here," Calisto said as he took the steps one at a time. With narrowed eyes, he continued, "Everett, you disappoint me. We were ten feet apart and you *didn't* take your chance to kill me? You've grown soft."

Zelfree smoothed back his hair, both straightening his appearance and calming his nerves. When he smiled, it was with the practiced confidence of a conman. "Well, well, well. If it isn't the Autarch's chump. I guess it means he's close by, doesn't it?"

Once Calisto stepped off the nullstone steps, I reached for my sword under my cloak, but I didn't yet pull it out. This was going to turn into a fight no matter what. I felt that in my gut.

Calisto was a tall and muscular man—everything about him screamed *imposing*. Even as he advanced on us, it was like he was a hungry shark, and we were the small children swimming in the ocean without supervision.

When he turned to face me, his expression shifted, but just for a moment. "You..." He waited as he mulled over my appearance. "You're the knightmare arcanist."

He didn't know I was bonded with Terrakona.

"That's me," I said with a single laugh.

Calisto gave Ryker the once over. When he had nothing to say, he returned his attention to Zelfree. "I hadn't been planning on seeing you today, but I guess I'm just lucky." He threw off his coat, revealing a flintlock pistol and a couple of daggers. He wore a unicorn horn on a necklace, and his gold earrings glittered with inner magic. He loved his trinkets and artifacts. He would have a dozen tricks up his sleeves, maybe more.

Which ones were the trinkets he had crafted to avoid the manipulation of the charybdis? I would have to steal myself one, if needed.

Soldiers and the nearby citizens pointed and whispered.

"I'm sorry I can't stay to play." Zelfree shrugged. "You know how it is."

"It's funny you think I'll let you escape."

"I don't think you have much of a choice in the matter."

Zelfree's forehead shifted and shimmered. His mark had been invisible, but now his skin had a new mark—a star with a rizzel twisted between the points. The bangles on his wrist transformed as well. They had been metal, but then they sprouted white and silver fur, and Traces became an adorable ferret-like rizzel.

With combat reflexes, Zelfree grabbed Ryker, and then me.

But Calisto was faster. His manticore magic gave him superhuman abilities—and his boots allowed him to step into the darkness like any knightmare arcanist. Calisto dropped into the shadows and reappeared *in front* of me.

I thought he would've gone for Zelfree, but clearly, I had been mistaken.

As the rizzel magic grabbed hold of my body and started to teleport me, Calisto reached into my cloak. He didn't punch me, or stab me, or even shoot me.

He pulled Retribution from its sheath just as I vanished, unable to stop him.

46

THE SOUL FORGE APPEARS

I stumbled forward, somewhere else in the city, silver glitter swirling around me.

Calisto had stolen my sword! Why? I shook my head, already knowing the answer. I had ridden on Calisto's ship, *The Third Abyss*, and he had seen what kind of destruction it could do. Calisto was obsessed with magical items, both trinkets and artifacts.

I just couldn't believe it.

With my anger growing, I turned to Zelfree. "Take me back! He stole my sword."

Zelfree gritted his teeth. "Didn't you hear them? The Second Ascension's attack is meant to happen in a few hours! We need to inform the others."

"I can defeat him," I said, throwing my arm out. "Port me back to Calisto!"

We stood in the middle of a road lined by artisans and small schools. Was this the Education District? Lines of children marched by, each led by an adult with robes that bore the symbol of the Argo Empire. The dark clouds rumbled with thunder, frightening the children. They hurried away, which suited me just fine.

"You'll endanger everyone there." Zelfree stepped close and lowered his voice. "Calisto isn't a man who will spare the innocent because you two are fighting."

"We're going to fight him shortly anyway," I said.

Ryker interjected himself between us. "Karna was in the Hall of Justice, remember? We can't just leave her."

"This is Karna's stomping ground," Zelfree said, grabbing Ryker by the sleeve of his shirt. "And she's a doppelgänger arcanist. She's not in danger. The rest of our guild members are!"

Ryker didn't have anything else to say. He opened his mouth to protest, but his courage never formed the words. I agreed with Zelfree—Karna would be fine. But that didn't quell my rage.

"Take me back," I stated. "*That's an order.*"

The last of the children rushed into their tiny schools, leaving us alone on the streets. Ryker and Zelfree said nothing, their tension growing colder between us.

I almost took back my order, but Zelfree's expression returned to a calm neutral as he said, "As you wish, Warlord."

He grabbed my shoulder and his mimicked rizzel magic teleported us away from the Educational District. The magic tugged at my insides and made me queasy, but not for long. I stumbled when we arrived and then turned my attention to our surroundings. I wanted to face Calisto and get Retribution back —I'd be the one to kill him, if I had to, but I knew both Illia and Zelfree didn't want that outcome.

But Calisto wasn't here.

I walked a few feet forward. Then I walked onto the nullstone steps of the Hall of Justice. I found nothing. Even the denizens who had been waiting to enter the hall were nowhere to be found.

"Curse the abyssal hells," I muttered, my body shaking with rage.

Zelfree stood on the street and waited for me, never saying a word. When I returned to his side, I also opted to remain silent. He touched my shoulder again, and we teleported.

We arrived at the edge of our encampment after several teleportations. It was obvious that Nicholin wasn't yet strong enough to port more than five hundred feet, but unlike Illia, who still struggled to teleport multiple people, Zelfree was a master. It didn't require much effort for him to teleport Ryker and me all the way out of the city.

The moment we arrived, Traces reverted back to her cat form. Then she licked Zelfree's cheek, purred a bit, and jumped down to his wrist. She transformed into a pair of bangles, like a safeguard for his hand.

The main road was a few feet away. Fortunately, the stench had disappeared.

Master Zelfree faced Ryker. "Tell Guildmaster Eventide what we heard. And tell Queen Ladislava."

Ryker—still in his old-man disguise—frowned. "*Me?*"

"You have a working mouth, don't you?" Zelfree snapped. He shook his head, and before anyone could respond, he continued with, "I just... have somewhere else to go. Please, do this. I would appreciate it."

He said every word with forced tension, but it was obvious he hadn't meant to lash out at my brother.

Ryker slowly nodded. "Of course. I shouldn't have questioned it. We're in danger." He hurried toward the war tent. "I'll make sure everyone is aware of the attack!"

It wasn't quiet when Ryker left us. Soldiers continued their work, banging on metal plate armor, more merchants drove their carts to the gates, yelling about the crowds, and mystical creatures made unique noises that mixed into the cacophony. Still, the silence between Zelfree and me blocked out all other noises.

"I'm going to speak to Markus," Zelfree stated. "I want to hear what that pirate has to say when I tell him Calisto is in the city." Then he bowed his head and stepped around me.

"Wait," I said.

Zelfree stopped in his tracks, his back to me.

"I value your input on everything." I exhaled. "I was just frustrated. I made that sword with Luthair, and... I didn't want to lose it."

"You're the world serpent arcanist," he said, never facing me. "You're the one making the calls. Don't feel ashamed about picking something someone disagrees with. They don't have to live with the choices. You do."

"I know." Before he went, I held my head a little higher. "In the future, just know that I don't want your obedience, I want your wisdom. You've always been my mentor, and I need that now more than ever. Especially if I'm the one who will pay the price for the decisions."

Zelfree chuckled to himself and then glanced over his shoulder. "Then my advice is that you prepare for battle. Cardozo—and probably Theasin and the soul forge—are probably on their way."

I nodded once. "Thank you, Master Zelfree."

He waved away the thanks. "Just call me Everett."

Guildmaster Eventide had ordered members of the Frith Guild to pack the several suits of armor I had been gifted for my birthday. I had three to choose from, but I ultimately went with a suit of armor made from steel and copper. Magic had been imbued into the metal, making it lighter and easier to wear without sacrificing any of its protectiveness.

The symbol of the Shikara Guild—a hawk over a three-masted sailing ship—was etched into one shoulder, while the world serpent was etched on the other. It was a sign that the Shikara Guild had come to my birthday celebration in the hopes of allying with me.

The half-plate wouldn't get in the way of my fighting style, and the metal wouldn't burn away when I evoked my magma. Not only that, but the copper would become superheated without much effort—a trick I had learned from Zaxis.

Anyone fighting me would quickly lose the ability to touch me directly.

With Forfend on my arm, I had to use another sword in Retribution's stead. I picked a one-handed short sword with the same lightweight properties. Perhaps I could find Calisto in the turmoil and retrieve my weapon...

Quiet.

I listened for a prolonged moment, trying to hear the merchants or the encampment of soldiers. Where had the bustle disappeared to? I leapt out of the carriage and glanced around. People stared up at the sky, their expressions twisted in confusion and worry. When I turned my attention upward, I saw nothing.

"Volke!"

Zaxis hurried over, Forsythe gliding alongside him. His salamander-scale armor was dull in the light sprinkling of rain. His wet hair clung to his head, but he didn't seem to care. He slicked it back with a quick push of his hand, his expression stern.

"There were flashes of light in the sky," he said. "Something's happening."

"He's here."

I grimaced and then turned all the way around, fearing I

would see Theasin or the Autarch. Where were they? "Terrakona? Who is here?"

"The soul forge."

Zaxis grabbed my upper arm, his strength apparent as he yanked me close. "Forsythe said he saw a creature."

His phoenix swooped around and then landed on the ground. Steam wafted off his feathers. The rain evaporated the instant the droplets touched his body.

"It was massive," Forsythe said. He spread his crimson wings halfway out. "As tall as the walls. Perhaps taller."

A gigantic creature? It had to be the soul forge.

"Where is it?" I asked.

"At the southern wall. Outside the city. I could see it from the sky."

Theasin and his soul forge were on the opposite side of the city? My heart beat hard enough that it echoed in my ears and drowned out extraneous thoughts. No one else could fight Theasin. Terrakona and I would have to travel around Thronehold and meet Theasin on the battlefield.

"What was the soul forge doing?" I asked.

Because of the *forge* in the title of the beast, I had always imagined a giant stove or anvil, but I knew that wasn't the case. It was a mystical creature. I just didn't know what kind of shape it would take.

Forsythe snorted, smoke rushing from the small nostrils on his beak. "I don't know. He *appeared* and then just sat there. I'm not sure what it can do... But it wasn't moving."

When I turned my attention to our surroundings, I frowned. No one had attacked us yet. What was Theasin doing?

Queen Ladislava's soldiers gathered at the edge of the encampment, each readying themselves for war. They tied their swords and pistols to their belts, readied their horses, and hurried to get into formation. No one acted yet—no commander had given the signal—but the crackle of combat surged through the crowds.

Even the merchants urged their oxen and mustangs away from the city, fleeing the conflict.

Arcanists from the Frith Guild gathered around the soldiers, including Hexa, her hydra, Atty, and Yesna. They were dressed for combat, in light armor and chainmail, each one wearing their guild pendant proudly.

I wanted to know what Theasin was doing. I couldn't wait here for him to act. What if he assaulted the southern wall?

I turned on my heel, intent on hurrying to Terrakona, but I stopped before I took a step. Wind kicked up around me. I shielded my eyes as King Odion descended from the sky and landed his twilight dragon at my side. He smiled from atop his eldrin, his brilliant armor impressive, even in the rain.

His sword, White Curse, hung in a large sheath on the side of the dragon saddle. It made me envious, but soon I'd be reunited with Retribution.

"My liege," he said, slightly bowing of his head.

"Odion..."

"Shouldn't you be atop your world serpent?" Odion motioned to his twilight dragon. "The soldiers, and your own arcanists, will expect you to fight alongside your god-creature."

The feathered wings of his dragon caught my attention. "The fighting hasn't started yet. Do you think you could take me into the sky? I need to see the soul forge. I need to know the layout of our battleground." We had a map of the city, but if Cardozo had altered the roads, blocked off pathways, or set fire to strategic locations, I wouldn't know that unless I saw the city with my own eyes.

"It would be an honor," Odion said.

I wanted to jump onto the back of his dragon, but Evianna stepped out from around our personal carriage. The shadow at her feet flickered and fluttered at the edges, but her knightmare never appeared. "Volke, if you're going to go into the city, let me help you."

I wiped some of the rain from my face. "I'll be right back."

"No, I mean, let me use my augmentation. I've been practicing."

"You can allow people to see in the dark?"

Evianna nodded as she stepped forward. The rain was kinder to her. Her white hair clung to her skull, but it only highlighted her beautiful heart-shaped face. I tried not to redden in the face, but I couldn't help it.

When she got close, she went to her tiptoes and gently kissed me. She could've used her magic by just touching my hand, but this way worked as well. The sensation of her knightmare magic caused me to shiver.

And then the storm didn't seem so gloomy. I could see in the dark—to great lengths—as though the sun had shone through the dark clouds overhead.

"Thank you," I whispered.

Evianna stepped away and nodded once. "Impressed, right?"

I chuckled and then nodded. "Very."

Odion leaned down from his dragon saddle and offered his gauntleted hand.

I took it and climbed atop his twilight dragon, Hasdrubal. The two heads of the beast regarded me with excited expressions. Their fang-smiles could intimidate the dead. The massive leather saddle wasn't built for two, but it was large enough for me to get comfortable. Odion tossed me a belt, and I strapped it over my legs, keeping myself stable on the dragon's back.

"We fly," one of Hasdrubal's heads said.

The twilight dragon shot into the air with a single powerful flap of its feathered wings. We went straight for the wall and flew over it.

"I need to find Theasin," I said to Odion, touching his back. Our seats were a good foot apart. "Or if you see Calisto… Either one."

Hasdrubal flew higher, his wings beating at a fearsome rate. I gripped the saddle, my breaths shallow. I had flown before—Luthair and I had been able to fly—but riding on a creature was a different story. If we fell, it would be thousands of feet to the ground below.

King Odion patted the white scales of his twilight dragon and pointed to a group of soldiers gathered in the Dragon District, the area right before King Drake Castle. I shielded my eyes from the cold rain and stared. The soldiers were gathering for a fight, and even though I was hundreds of feet above, I could see the mystical creatures around them—pegasi, griffins, wyverns, and a few sirens, all creatures who could fly.

The pegasi were all mystical creatures in the Sky Legionnaires. They were a variety of colors, due to the bird-type for each. Crow pegasi were black in coat and wing. Dove pegasi were white, much like the unicorns. Hawk pegasi had a mix of brown and red feathers, their wings tipped in black.

All of them wore uniform armor with the emblem of the Argo Empire on the chest, as did the griffins and drakes. None of these arcanists were mercenaries or Second Ascension members. At least, I didn't think so.

Where were they?

We flew over four more districts, and just as I had suspected, barricades had been set up across the wider streets. The enemies feared we would invade the city, and they wanted to control the flow of battle. If they bottle-necked us into a narrow street, our superior numbers wouldn't matter. A few of their soldiers could hold off our whole army.

We didn't have many arcanists in our ranks who could fly and destroy the barricades. We would have to be strategic about this

But then all battle prep left my mind.

I saw it. Just beyond the southern wall.

It was a nightmare made flesh.

The soul forge.

It was a creature that stood at least twenty-five feet tall—large enough to look over the walls of Thronehold. And it was a slug in shape. A shell-less gastropod mollusk. Something you would see in the garden. Something eaten by toads. It had no legs, it was just a semi-translucent monster with a gelatinous body. Hundreds of human arms—*hundreds*—flailed about across its back. It reminded me of hair caught in the wind.

With my dark sight, I absorbed every detail. Dark shadows dwelled within the slug-shaped soul forge. There were people, animals, and mystical creatures trapped inside, like flies caught in melting wax. They were frozen in place, unable to escape.

"What is that?" Odion shouted.

His dragon groaned.

"It's the soul forge," I called out. "Don't get too close. I'm not sure what it's capable of!"

The many arms of the soul forge thrashed about, bending at the elbows and wrists at odd angles. Why did it have so many sticking out of its back? What was it doing?

I tried to search for Theasin, but even with the ability to see through the darkness, I didn't have the sight of an eagle. We were too far away for me to make out the identity of a single person on the ground, and Theasin definitely wasn't standing atop his slug eldrin.

Hasdrubal flew us closer, his feather wings fluttering in the powerful storm winds. A few of his feathers were torn off and fluttered behind us. Not only that, but his white coloration slowly drained away. Hasdrubal became purple, then black, shifting with the time of day. It was now evening, and the twilight dragon would have stronger control over darkness.

"Steady," Odion said, patting his eldrin. "Get as close as you can, but if the storm gets too rough, turn back."

We descended, closer to the soul forge, its tannish slug body rippling with slight movement. Its hundreds of arms then went straight. The arms stretched upward, and the fingers trembled as they strained.

Glowing strands of thread lifted off the soul forge's many hands. The threads were attached to its fingers, but they lifted into the storm sky like spider silk. They waved in the wind and then darted out over the city, creating a web of glittering, raw magic.

Hasdrubal had to fly higher to avoid getting caught.

The webs spread outward, rushing into Thronehold at faster and faster speeds. The threads broke away, fluttered down every alleyway, and touched every window. The buildings didn't stand in their way. The threads pierced the walls without damaging anything—they were incorporeal, like ghosts, shifting through bricks and touching whatever they wanted.

What was going on?

"What's happening?" Odion asked, parroting my thoughts.

"I don't know."

He pulled White Curse from the sheath on the side of Hasdrubal's saddle.

"This is evil," he muttered.

It was difficult to see what the threads were doing. *Were they evil?*

"Look there," Hasdrubal said with both heads, his voice practically a growl.

The threads were clinging to people. They flailed about and tried to remove the magic, but nothing worked. Then they crumpled to the street, thrashing about, knocking other people over, screaming so loudly *I* could hear them through the rain.

I knew that tortured screech. I had heard it before...

In Markus's dream. On the day they had found Alexi, his odd griffin. His memories had been filled with pain and anguish, and the screams of his friends had been similar to those in Thronehold.

And it wasn't just *one* person. It was hundreds. Maybe thousands. Their symphony of pain rose up from the streets, filling the sky with wails. Even the thunder didn't compare. They were suffering.

They were dying.

"We have to stop it," Odion stated.

He urged Hasdrubal forward, but I grabbed his shoulder and shook my head. "No! If you touch any of that, you'll start to die as well!"

"We can't do *nothing*," Odion yelled.

"Take me back to Terrakona! We'll handle the soul forge! You tell Queen Ladislava that she needs to stay clear of this danger or else her soldiers will waste away!"

With a curt nod, Odion patted his twilight dragon.

We turned through the stormy sky, battered by rain. I kept my attention on the streets below—on the endless shrieking and calls for help. Hasdrubal flew over two districts, and everything was the same.

Once I tore my eyes from the suffering people, I noticed something else.

Carts and carriages, all with tarps. There wasn't just *one*, there were at least a dozen. Each was lumpy and filled with the same foul-smelling cargo. The strings of magic gripped the carts as well, but instead of killing everything inside, the tarps shook with life.

I inhaled and held my breath, my chest twisting as realization struck me.

The carts weren't filled with rotting fish or manure or expired meat.

They were filled with mystical creature bodies. They were

Calisto's cargo. Dead creatures he and Markus had collected to bring to Thronehold. Calisto had snuck them inside the city by claiming they were the property of merchants.

The "merchants" were probably just his crew.

The tarps flew off with the wind, revealing the mutilated bodies of hippogriffs. They had the bodies of horses and the heads and wings of eagles. Their coats were always speckled, like young deer and certain breeds of horses, but their hooves came in silver or gold, depending.

The corpse-hippogriffs thrashed in their carts, their bodies slowly forming as the life was sucked from the people of the city.

Odion took shallow breaths, and his dragon roared at the horror below.

The entire city was wasting away in the few minutes it was taking us to fly back. But as we soared over the Dragon District, I realized that Cardozo's soldiers weren't affected by the threads. Theasin was helping the insurgent king, but was he *really* helping? Cardozo would rule over a city of corpses by the end of this.

When we neared the northern wall, I kept my composure, determined to lead an assault against the soul forge itself. But then I noticed Queen Ladislava's sovereign dragon near the gates, along with her thousand soldiers and Knights Draconic. The unicorns arcanists were in the front, the vanguard force.

Rain sprinkled across the city and surrounding landscape. Terrakona, alert and awaiting my return, sat by the wall of the city, his eyes wide and on me. The merchants flocked away from the gates and warning bells rang out over Thronehold. In theory, King Drake Castle could activate an anti-magic effect that protected it from outside invaders, but the nullstone didn't affect dragons or their arcanists.

And it wouldn't affect me—which meant it probably wouldn't save people from the soul forge's life-stealing ability.

Cardozo's archers stood on the northern wall. After a shout, they let loose hundreds of arrows. Normally, they wouldn't be shot in the rain, but one of them was a sea serpent arcanist who willed the water in the sky to avoid their shots.

Arrows rained down over Queen Ladislava's soldiers, more than I could ever hope to count. The arrows slammed into trees, the road, and the grass, but Eventide held up both hands and created a shimmering barrier of translucent magic that stretched over the majority of the encampment. The barrier—a magical shield—prevented the arrows from striking Ladislava's men.

But Eventide struggled to maintain her protection. Her arms shook, and she fell to one knee from the strain of her magic. Her eldrin was so far away... It had to be difficult for her.

"Charge!" Queen Ladislava yelled.

Before King Odion and I could reach her, the queen's sovereign dragon—black, red, and mighty—leapt from the road and rumbled the ground as it rushed toward the wall. Queen Ladislava rode on his neck, a long spear in one hand.

With a roar, the dragon spread its wings. In a single bound, it crashed into the top of the gate, crushing a dozen archers, and then leapt into the city. Another rumble and crash shook the earth, the trees, and the buildings.

The portion of the wall Queen Ladislava had "climbed" was now crumbling and cracked halfway down. Her cannon gunners fired on the wall. Dust and debris exploded outward as cannonballs smashed into the stone bricks. A wave of gray particles washed over soldiers.

They had toppled the gate. The archers didn't stand a chance.

"We reclaim Thronehold!" Queen Ladislava said, rushing toward the magical threads.

47

THE ENEMY SIREN SONG

"Warlord, what are your orders?"

This was it. The moment Zelfree and Eventide had warned me about. All decisions here would change the course of history. I could order Terrakona to fight alongside the queen—and hope she and her dragon could live long enough to kill Cardozo himself. I could order Terrakona away from here, on the off chance that the soul forge could suck our lives and kill us both.

But whatever I decided, I couldn't hesitate. I would forever carry the consequences, either fame or ridicule, though I couldn't consider that now. A great leader—a swashbuckler, a master arcanist, a *legend*—didn't weigh how they would be remembered. They just did what they knew was right, regardless of how they would fare through the endeavor.

"Stop Queen Ladislava's soldiers from entering the city!" I shouted.

Without hesitation, Terrakona rushed to fulfill my command. He smashed through another portion of the wall, avoiding Ladislava's soldiers, and filling the roads with more dust and debris. He curved his serpentine body around several buildings until he snaked his way in front of Ladislava and her sovereign dragon.

"What is the meaning of this?" she shouted as Odion and I flew closer.

"Turn back!" I yelled.

"How dare you! Cardozo has attacked! The walls have been breached! Now is the time for attack!"

"It's a trap! The soul forge will destroy your entire army!"

"These are *my* soldiers! I won't let you undermine my authority!" Ladislava waved her hand out in front of her. "*You* move your eldrin or else I will consider our arrangement broken!"

Her dragon roared in protest. Obviously, they didn't believe me, and the mere act of "ordering" her to do anything had caused a rift.

But I didn't care.

"Terrakona, don't let the soul forge's magic touch them!" I yelled.

When Terrakona roared back in acknowledgement, it eclipsed the sovereign dragon's voice and started the ground quaking. The threads of the soul forge's magic crept through the city, slinking toward Ladislava's army. Terrakona pushed Ladislava back, and then swiped his tail at the roof of a building. Rubble tumbled onto the street, causing the queen's men to back away further.

When the sovereign dragon fought against Terrakona, the two devolved into a grappling match. Their giant size—at least two-stories of muscles and scales—caused the street to crack under their combined weight. When the sovereign dragon refused to move, Terrakona bashed his skull against the head of the dragon, knocking the beast onto its hind legs. Terrakona's crystal mane gave him extra protection against bashing. The dragon had horns, but they were small, and it would take a great deal of force to pierce Terrakona's scales.

The soldiers retreated from the city to stay clear of the titans fighting each other.

Odion urged his twilight dragon to the encampment. I clung to the saddle until we neared the ground, but the moment we were ten feet above the road, I unbelted myself and leapt. With a roll, I got to my feet and ran forward, my lightweight armor barely a hindrance.

Evianna. Where was she?

As though answering my unspoken question, the shadows around my feet shifted and swirled. Evianna stepped up from the darkness with her knightmare already merged to her body as a suit of armor. Her wing-like cape fluttered in the wind.

"Volke," she said with her double-voice. "What's happening?"

"The soul forge..." I gritted my teeth, frustrated. It would take too long to explain everything a hundred times over! "Adelgis!" I yelled aloud. "If you're still close, I need you!"

"*I can hear you, my liege.*"

"Can you use your telepathy and inform everyone of the soul forge's capabilities?"

"*It's difficult... to hear so many thoughts...*"

"Please, Adelgis," I said, facing the stormy sky, like he was above me, but in reality, I had no idea where Adelgis had hidden himself. I motioned to the road and then to the merchants who were still nearby. "They all have to escape."

"*I'll try.*"

I reached for my belt and withdrew five emblem rings. Then I grabbed five star shards and held them all in my hand. Normally, I would give these to people who had sworn themselves to me—and use two shards per—but right now, I wanted as many people as possible protected by my magic. I had to make these quick and easy.

I used my imbuing to soak the rings with my world serpent magic. The drain ate at me, but I pushed through the fatigue and closed my eyes as the last of the rings were transformed into trinkets. Once they were done, I gasped and swallowed air at a fearsome rate. Obviously, I needed more practice, but at least I had made five of these.

"Evianna," I said, my voice ragged. "Take this."

She took the iridescent ring and slipped it onto a finger. When it didn't fit, because it was too big, she slipped it onto her thumb.

"It'll help you if you get into trouble," I said. "Healing, light —keep it close." Then I wiped water from my face, the rain relentless.

Rumbling drew my attention. The road shook. Carriages creaked. The horses and oxen couldn't keep calm, and some carriages were toppled and smashed in the ensuing chaos. Terrakona forced Ladislava and her dragon out of the city, snapping at her eldrin and grabbing the dragon with his tail— shoving them the entire way until the dragon was outside the walls.

Little by little, the merchants gathered their belongings. I hoped it had been the doing of Adelgis—if the merchants knew the dire consequences of staying, I was certain they wouldn't want to be here.

Master Zelfree and Illia pushed their way through the crowds and headed straight for me. Zaxis ran out ahead of Ladislava's army—he had been rubbing shoulders with the Knights Draconic—and he also headed for my position. Had Adelgis summoned the three of them? Likely.

The three of them hurried to my side, and before I said a word, I handed them each one of the rings. They didn't ask questions. They each fitted the rings on the finger that matched well enough.

"Volke!" Odion pointed to the shattered wall.

To my horror, threads of magic slipped over the bricks and slinked toward the road. They were thin and numerous, spreading out again like a web, lurching toward life. They were here for the soldiers and the merchants, and I couldn't delay any longer.

"I have to face the soul forge." I glanced around, hoping I could give at least one other person my emblem ring, but there was no one else. "Protect everyone while I'm away."

Zelfree held out a hand. "I'm here to help."

Nicholin poked his head out of Illia's hair. "That's why we searched for you, Volke! We're going to help *you* no matter what."

"C'mon!" Zaxis said, grabbing my elbow and pointing at the wall. "I've been looking for you all day. My brother lives in this city! We have to save it before I never see him again."

Had all three of them—four, if I counted Evianna awaiting my return—searched me out, not because Adelgis had asked them to, but because they had wanted to assist me? For some reason, it choked me up for a moment, knowing they would be there for me...

The threads washed over the carriages on the road, and I knew I had no more time.

"Zelfree, Evianna, and Illia, you're with me," I said, gesturing to Terrakona. "Zaxis, ride with Odion."

Odion smiled wide, and Zaxis gave him a sideways glance. "This is life and death."

"A man only has two genuine smiles," Odion said as he headed for his twilight dragon. "One right before battle, and one while in the arms of his lover."

Zaxis clicked his tongue in dismissal as he climbed into the saddle of the twilight dragon.

"Follow me and Terrakona," I said to Odion.

He shot me the same smile. "Let's earn us some colors for our marks."

Having Guildmaster Eventide, Master Yesna, Atty, Devlin, or Hexa would've been a boon, but I couldn't spot them in the chaotic crowds. Forsythe likely wasn't with us because of the rain. Phoenixes didn't do so well in the water, and if Zaxis was smart, he had probably told his eldrin to wait behind.

Where was Fain? The disorder and frantic panic made organizing an attack difficult. At least they hadn't caught us completely by surprise, but this wasn't much better.

But I couldn't fix that now. We didn't have time to search out more allies—only time for action.

Illia must have thought the same thing, because she grabbed Zelfree, Evianna, and me and then used her rizzel magic to teleport us. The sensation of being ripped through space left me confused afterward, and I stumbled onto Terrakona's crystal mane and almost slipped off. Thankfully, I grabbed one of the crystals and then slid my boots between two others, giving me a solid hold.

The threads had taken the lives of a few merchants and soldiers, but thanks to Terrakona's efforts, they hadn't been trapped inside the city, fighting to flee. As Terrakona turned to head into the city, I noticed Guildmaster Eventide step in front of the merchants and create another one of her translucent barriers. It was costing her—it must've drained her of her reserves and energy—but her magic prevented the threads from getting any closer.

She couldn't maintain that long, though.

In between the crowds, I saw puffs of glitter. The star tiger was teleporting people to safety as fast as he could. The beast couldn't take many with him—the trips were numerous—and I assumed the tiger would also succumb to fatigue before long.

Using magic was much like using a muscle, after all. A person could only run for a short amount of time before their legs gave out. It was the same with magic.

"Retreat," I yelled at Ladislava and her dragon. "But don't go beyond the hills! Once I defeat the soul forge, and the threads are gone, you must attack!"

I didn't know if she had heard me, or if she even would follow my orders, but I hoped she would listen to reason. With a pat on his head, I directed Terrakona into the city. I feared for Illia and Zelfree—what if the soul forge targeted them?—but if I managed to deal with the threat fast enough, it wouldn't become an issue.

"Get to Theasin," I commanded.

Terrakona roared again, the rumble of his voice enough to fill my veins with raw excitement. Zelfree and Illia held on to his mane as best they could, but it was obvious they didn't have the experience. Both clung to the world serpent as we snaked through the city. Evianna, on the other hand, grabbed my arm and stayed close to my side, her knightmare-armor a comforting sight.

Terrakona—still a hatchling—was small enough to fit down the main streets without busting through the buildings. He was too big for the narrow alleyways, however, and he had to keep his head high to keep us from the threads that haunted the roads like malicious ghosts. Just as I suspected, the threads didn't affect Terrakona. God-arcanist magic didn't seem capable of targeting the god-creatures.

Trolley cars had been abandoned on the tracks. Terrakona crushed a few as he hurried to the southern wall. Dead bodies, all aged and rotted, spilled out onto the street. The life-steal threads aged and rotted the people they touched, feeding the resulting "stew" to the corpses of the mystical creatures.

"Terrakona, down this way," I said, pointing to a road near the Dragon District.

"By your command, Warlord."

He smashed through one of the enemy barricades, shattering stone bricks and sandbags as he continued through Thronehold. With the barricade gone, Ladislava's soldiers would have an easier time retaking King Drake Castle, but

Terrakona wrecked some of the buildings on either side, toppling walls and destroying entire chimneys.

Before we could get far, pegasi rose from the streets and rooftops. Two pegasi flew for Odion and me. The sprinkling of rain slowed them a bit, but not enough. The torrent of rain that Ladislava had banked on wouldn't begin for another day.

Both enemy Sky Legionnaires were crow pegasi, and their ebony appearance allowed them to blend in with the stormy sky. Their arcanists wielded lances, and when the legionnaires threw them, they manipulated the winds to carry them farther than any one person could throw.

A lance flew straight for Hasdrubal, but one of his heads struck out like a snake and bit the lance midair, crushing it between his fangs.

"*Kill them,*" Odion shouted.

Hasdrubal's second head opened his mouth. A straight beam of light *shot* from his gullet, too fast to dodge—and almost too fast to see. It was like a bullet made of the sun's radiance. The light beam struck one of the crow pegasi and seared its wing. The creature whinnied and then spun as it hurtled toward the streets.

When the other pegasus and its arcanist flew close to Terrakona, I gritted my teeth and evoked my magma. I had to be careful—Evianna, Illia, and Zelfree weren't immune to my heat—so I made a small amount in my palm and threw it at the wings of the beast as it soared by.

I hit the pegasus in the upper shoulder. The molten rock burned *through* its armor and cooked the flesh within moments. The pegasus screamed and the arcanist rider tried to calm it. My magma burned through the latches of the armor and the straps of the saddle. The arcanist fell from its eldrin, and the pegasus soon followed, crippled by agony.

"Even a small portion of your magic is deadly," Odion said

with an excited laugh, his voice half-lost in the storm. "*Come. We head for the heart of it!*"

"That's what I'm talking about!" Zaxis shouted, laughing as they flew over the city.

"Pegasi have swarmed near the wall."

I glanced over my shoulder. Thanks to Evianna's ability to augment others with dark-sight, I caught sight of the Sky Legionnaires circling the northern wall. I suspected they would attack Ladislava, goading her into attacking a second time. Or perhaps they would pick at the army and allow the threads to wash over everything.

To my surprise, Captain Devlin and his roc, Mesos, flew up into the stormy sky. With gale-force winds, they blew back the pegasi and protected Ladislava's army. He was only one man, though. He wouldn't be able to keep them all away for long.

But still... He was taking a great risk for us.

"We continue to Theasin," I said.

I couldn't turn back to help them. I had a mission.

Halfway through the massive capital, music reached my ears, even through the storm. It was familiar—eerie and haunting. Nothing like Karna's music, or even the kind heard at ceremonies.

"*Come now, sweet creatures! You've just been reborn. No memories, no past, no lives you should mourn!*"

A siren song.

I held my breath, straining to hear the exact lyrics, but Zelfree grabbed my half-plate armor and jerked me enough to get my attention. "There!" He pointed to a distant tower on the edge of King Drake Castle. Three sirens, all wearing the armor of the Argo Empire, continued their singing. Mystical creatures—especially the hippogriffs—flew in their direction, enthralled by the song.

What was going on?

Were the sirens attracting all the newly "born" mystical

creatures so they could deliver them to the Second Ascension? Was that Cardozo's agreement? He would allow people to die for the Second Ascension's plans so long as he got the throne of the Argo Empire?

Thronehold had been a beacon of civilization, but as I watched the conflict develop, it crumbled to ruin, one wall, one soldier, and one building at a time.

Terrakona raced down the road, knocking over another trolley car and breaking one of the district signs as he rushed for the southern wall. A newly born charybdis slinked out of an alleyway in front of us. Terrakona stopped and stared down at the beast a fourth his size.

The charybdis were wyrms—dragon-like creatures with no legs, arms, or wings. Their circle-mouths reminded me of lampreys, and their three rows of sharp teeth were enough to terrify sharks. Even in the rain, their beady eyes glinted like black pearls.

The beast writhed and slinked forward, unaccustomed to movement on land. "Where am I? What is this place?" The magical threads of the soul forge didn't have any effect on the creature now that it was reborn.

Terrakona's scales flared—the creature was large enough to block our path, but he could easily knock it aside.

"Why am I here?" the charybdis cried, its black pearl eyes glistening with tears, its scale-like skin wet with rain.

Then the siren song reached my ears, the same lyrics as before.

"Come now, sweet creatures! You've just been reborn. No memories, no past, no lives you should mourn!"

The charybdis's gaze went vacant, and it turned its wyrm body toward the music, no more shouting or questions. It moved with a hypnotic rhythm, sliding back and forth, heading for another alleyway.

Zelfree stood and grabbed my armor once again. "Volke!

Don't let it get away! That's a charybdis. They're deadly—they should be extinct. We can't let the enemy have it!"

But...

These creatures were all over the city. We would have to stop everything to find and kill them. Not only that, but I didn't *want* to end their lives. It wasn't their fault any of this was happening. They were innocent—their memories gone, their purpose in life lost—and now they were being hypnotized by siren songs to head into the enemy's arms.

Then again, Zelfree was right. There were hundreds of mystical creatures here. Was I just going to allow the Second Ascension to potentially capture them all? Even if the creatures didn't bond with their members, they could be killed all over again, and then their carcasses could be used for trinket and artifact creation. Either way, they were a valuable resource, and I was just allowing the enemy to take them.

Which course of action was the best?

I didn't know—but I knew which one was right.

"We aren't going to kill them," I said as I patted Terrakona. "Keep going!"

"Those are creatures who cause shipwrecks." Zelfree motioned to the charybdis again. "And don't you remember how Yesna's eldrin worked? Once enthralled, the creature won't even fight back! Killing the charybdis now will be effortless."

"The faster we rid the world of Theasin, the faster we can head back to free those mystical creatures." I pointed forward. "We aren't killing them."

Evianna squeezed my arm and nodded once in affirmation.

After a moment to mull over my statement, Zelfree finally nodded. "All right. You're the one calling the shots, kid."

Illia and Nicholin both turned toward me from the other side of Terrakona's crystal mane. Illia offered a small smile, and Nicholin puffed his chest.

"You made the right choice," he said.

My eldrin continued through the city, avoiding the buildings as best he could as he rushed for our destination. I held on tightly, my heart beating faster and faster as the wall grew closer. The icy rain only added to my adrenaline. I reached for my sword and hated that I drew some low-level trinket from its sheath. The lightweight blade wasn't poorly made, it just wasn't *mine*.

The soul forge awaited us on the other side of the wall, its slug-body visible as we neared the southern wall. The many arms on its back waved back and forth, the threads still attached to the fingers and palms. It was like... the god-creature was weaving a tapestry of life and death.

Terrakona didn't slow down as he approached the wall. Instead, he used his magic to manipulate the stone bricks. They split apart, creating a perfect opening for him to escape through—like a double door opening wide to allow us out.

The southern field outside the city was nothing more than mud and thin grass. The dark clouds swirled overhead, and the lightning crackled between them, briefly illuminating the southern road out of the city.

King Odion flew down on his black twilight dragon and landed near the wall. I thought I had brought an impressive force with me, but I had been mistaken.

It wasn't just Theasin and his soul forge waiting for us.

48

A CLASH OF GODS AND MEN

Six arcanists and their eldrin stood in the muddy field.

Terrakona came to a stop a good thirty feet from them, and his scales remained flared. I stood atop his mane, staring down at the horde of villains.

Of all the individuals in front of me, Theasin was the worst of all. He stood next to his disgusting slug eldrin, his long, black hair slicked back with rain water. He wore robes that clung to his wet body—the left sleeve was longer than the other one, and devoid of an arm. When had he lost that? And why?

Then again, I glanced at the many arms on the soul forge and knew where Theasin's missing arm had gone...

I just didn't understand for what purpose.

Theasin's old arcanist mark—the one on his forehead, the one that told the world he had once been bonded with a relickeeper—had faded, but not disappeared. Now he kept the front of his robes partially open to reveal his chest. The god-arcanist mark started just under his right collarbone and resembled a twelve-pointed star with the soul forge interlaced throughout it. The many arms of the creature were apparent, even on Theasin's mark.

Theasin said nothing as I appraised their group. He waited with a slight smile, as though in control of the entire situation.

A jittery man hovered close to Theasin.

Rhys.

He was thin and sickly, and the rain didn't help his appearance. It gave him the look of a vagabond—scraggly hair, muddied robes, and hands that couldn't remain still. He was a rizzel arcanist, or at least, I suspected he was since he could teleport.

It had been Rhys who had teleported the Second Ascension into Thronehold during the assassination of Queen Velleta. Rhys was an instrumental member of the Second Ascension, and one of the right-hand men of the Autarch.

Then there was Calisto, his first mate, Spider, and the other random arcanist he had hired for his crew. What was his name? *Wit*. Wit stood taller than everyone else around, his sea serpent mark, and eldrin, small and underdeveloped. Wit was likely a new arcanist, and his sea serpent was just an adolescent. The beast was barely ten feet in length.

Spider and her kappa eldrin—a short fish man only four feet tall—waited near Calisto. The rain made Spider look like a woman who had drowned and been brought back to life a few hours later. Her kappa, however, smiled a wide needle-tooth grin, his fish scales slimy and vibrant green in the wet weather.

With Retribution in hand, Calisto stood the closest to us. I had seen Calisto in the rain before, and I swear the weather matched the man's soul. He stared at us with a slightly amused intensity, like this might have been one of the most interesting moments of his entire life. His tricorn cap couldn't hide his glowing manticore arcanist mark—the only true form arcanist on the battlefield since I had lost Luthair, and because Eventide remained with Ladislava's soldiers.

Calisto's true form manticore, Hellion, waited next to the soul forge, his black scorpion tail and leathery bat wings a harsh juxtaposition to the white fur of his lion body. The mask over Hellion's face was twisted in a demented happy expression, complete with a large smile and half-circle eyes.

The last arcanist I didn't recognize, but upon seeing his eldrin, I already knew quite a bit about the man.

He was bonded to a twilight dragon. No. That wasn't right. It was a dread form twilight dragon—a twisted monster of its former self, barely clinging to sanity and reason.

The twilight dragon arcanist, unknown to me, wore half-plate armor made of ebony sovereign dragon scales. The mark on his forehead burned a fiery red, visible in the darkest of nights. He had a warrior's mark on his wrist, small silken strands woven together. I was too far away to see the colors, but I knew this fiend hailed from the Kingdom of Javin.

A part of me wondered... Would this twilight dragon arcanist be made King of Javin if Odion died here today? I was willing to bet money that was the Second Ascension's plan.

But who would follow anyone bonded to such an abomination?

The enemy twilight dragon might as well have been undead. One of its two heads was a spine and skull, with blood that wept from the eye sockets. The other head glared at us with eyes that glowed as red and bright as the dread form arcanist mark.

It was night, so the twilight dragon was black, but the scales had fallen off in places, revealing the beast's insides. The ribs of its chest stuck *out* of its body, similar to spines. The once-lustrous feathers were now sickly and covered in pox and blood.

What a terrible night not to have my sword, and to have apoch dragon dust swirling in my veins. In that moment, I felt cursed—this fight would surely kill some of us.

No.

I refused. *They* would run from Thronehold this time. Not me.

Terrakona lowered his head, and I slid off his crystal mane and landed with a soft squish in the mud. The battering of the rain didn't dull the heat in my veins. Zelfree, Illia, Evianna, Zaxis, and Odion dismounted and stood in the mud as well.

I clenched my hands into fists and strode toward the Second Ascension, ready to earn my title as Warlord of Magic.

The soul forge and world serpent towered over the field, their massive bodies in a league all their own. Rain washed off them in rivers, and everyone here knew they stood among gods.

When I came within fifteen feet, Calisto hefted Retribution, no doubt a warning.

"*Theasin,*" I called out.

Although he only had one arm, he still regarded me with a look that screamed *what is a malformed cretin like you doing in my presence?* He gave me the once over and sneered.

With a quick motion of his hand, he slicked back his wet hair. "I thought you would've been here sooner. I overestimated you."

He stood in the center of their group, his "knights" in a circle around him. A hill of bodies sat near Thronehold's wall, and I wondered if those had been men and women of Thronehold who had attempted to stop Theasin. I hoped they would rest in peace.

"This ends right now." I took a deep breath, calming my rage, but the heat in the area was already ticking upward, despite the chill of the storm. "I'm giving you one chance to surrender. The Second Ascension won't win this war."

The collective laughter that followed disturbed me. Every single person chuckled and shook their head, as though in on a terrible secret I had no part of. Calisto ran a hand down his wet face, half-hiding his smirk.

Theasin turned to face me fully, a genuine smile on his narrow face. "You lost before you picked this fight, boy." He waved his one arm toward his gargantuan slug. "Who would challenge me on my terms? Only a fool who thinks they're in the right. I'm a god here, not you."

I held my position, not swayed by his boasts.

But before I could say anything, Theasin continued with, "Our plans have been around longer than you've been alive. The god-creatures, our rise to power—*our new army*." He laughed and motioned to the city. The songs of the sirens wafted over the wall. "They're gathering now, as we speak. Hundreds of mystical creatures, most of which are fully grown, ready to bond with new arcanists. Soon, the Second Ascension will make good on all of its promises. Those loyal to us will bond with creatures, and we'll grow stronger in the blink of an eye. No army will stand against our might."

"You're stealing life from the citizens of Thronehold," I said. "How many died to make these creatures?"

Theasin's eyebrows scrunched in confusion, as if he couldn't believe I had even asked such a question. "Can't you see what I'm doing? Or are you *blind* like so many others?" Theasin frowned. "Those sad sacks stumbling through the streets of Thronehold were doing nothing with their so-called *gift of life*. Mystical creatures add magic to the world, boy. People who bond with them gain powers. A mortal human brings nothing to the world but *filth*. I'm doing the world a favour by repurposing the denizens of Thronehold. I'm recycling their souls and using them to fuel my new creations."

There was no remorse in his words. No care for the people he had killed. Theasin only cared about his creations—about his magical experiments—just like Adelgis had said.

"I'll give *you* one chance to surrender," Theasin said matter-of-factly. "Surrender your mimic arcanist and the Mother of Shapeshifters, and kneel before the Autarch—your true king—and we'll spare your life."

"Your sins are closing in all around you, Theasin." My words were laced with the anger I could no longer chain. "I've come to collect retribution on behalf of those who can't."

Theasin scoffed. "Your vision is narrow, child. The other nations will bend the knee to our newly acquired might. And those that don't will be overrun with the arcane plague and driven to insanity. We've won—you're just a corpse who doesn't know it yet."

That was it.

I tried.

With a wave of my hand, I altered the terrain with my powerful manipulation. I gave myself solid footing, transforming the mud into stone. I swirled the ground under the feet of our enemies, trapping them all in place. Their feet sank into the earth up to their ankles, which prevented them from moving. Then I lunged forward, not for Theasin, but Rhys.

In one brutal swing, I slashed my lightweight sword at the jittery man. The fool wore no armor, and the blade cut into the base of his neck, down into his chest. Unfortunately, my sword wasn't as capable as Retribution. If I had been wielding my own blade, Rhys would've been dead. Instead, Rhys's bones caused my weapon to get stuck in his flesh. Blood gushed from the wound, some squirting up past the blade.

Rhys grunted, and with a puff of silver glitter, disappeared from the battlefield with a *pop*. Although I had wanted Rhys dead, this was still acceptable. Now Theasin had nowhere to run.

"Kill them all!" Theasin commanded, glancing upward at his soul forge.

I glanced over my shoulder. "Terrakona!"

"They will answer for their crimes."

Terrakona lunged for the soul forge. The massive slug created another wave of soul-stealing threads, but most broke apart the moment Terrakona sank his fangs into the forge's semi-translucent body.

To my horror, the slug's body gave way, and Terrakona "fell" inside, being pulled into the jelly of the body. The soul forge's many arms grabbed at Terrakona's scales and crystal mane, trying to rip pieces away. The hands of the forge seemed to have a corrosive effect. They melted bits of Terrakona, removing tiny portions of his body, like a child scooping sand off a beach.

But I didn't have the luxury of watching the fight between my world serpent and the soul forge.

Calisto used his knightmare boots to step into the shadows, instantly freeing himself from the ground. He shifted through the darkness and emerged right next to me. I lifted Forfend to block a strike, but Calisto was tricky. He didn't swing. Calisto stabbed forward, my own sword cutting through my armor and then my abdomen—no resistance whatsoever. The black blade effortlessly cut through me.

"Nice weapon," Calisto said with a dark chuckle.

Then he cut out sideways, splattering my blood across the rain-drenched field. I stumbled backward, the white-hot agony enough to momentarily steal my vision.

"*No!*"

Calisto and I both turned at the sound of the scream.

Illia teleported to my side. In an instant, she grabbed me and teleported away, the silver glitter and popping noise heralding the start of the conflict. We reappeared next to Odion and his twilight dragon, but the enemies had freed themselves from the ground and were heading toward us.

To give us time, Odion held up a hand and evoked a gigantic orb of darkness. A perfect sphere of inky shadows enveloped the entire battlefield, making everything so dark that no one could see.

Except those with dark-sight.

Evianna rushed between everyone, touching them only long enough to use her augmentation and give them the ability to see in the dark. Some of the enemy wouldn't have that ability —but four of them could likely see regardless. The twilight dragon arcanist would be able to see through all shadows. Calisto wore a kappa trinket that allowed him to see through gloom, darkness, and fog. Spider was a kappa arcanist, so she could see no matter how dark the conditions. And I suspected Wit had the same kappa trinket.

But Theasin and his soul forge had no such luck.

And Rhys had already fled.

Our enemies slowed their rush toward us regardless, likely from hesitation that something more was coming. Odion and Hasdrubal rushed into the orb of darkness and clashed with the dread form twilight dragon and his arcanist. I knew they wouldn't win, though. When a creature became dread form, it gained substantial power. Odion and his dragon would be at a severe disadvantage.

At first, the injury in my gut had hurt, but now I was too icy with rage to feel anything other than my own hate. When I tried to move, however, agony flared from the injury as my skin ripped from the strain, my gut hot with fresh blood that rushed out, coating my armor and my trousers. My god-arcanist healing still wasn't back to what it had been...

Without needing a command, Zaxis grabbed my upper arm. His powerful healing—something he had mastered even more than his fire—sent shivers through my body and caused the flesh of my gut to stitch itself back together. The sensation of having my body work to keep itself whole was one that sent a chilling shudder down my spine.

"Don't die on us," Zaxis said.

I nodded. Then I pointed to Odion. The dread form twilight dragon was already trying to tear off the man's head. "Help Odion," I commanded.

"Consider it done." Zaxis rushed out, heedless of his safety, his knuckles already white-hot. When he punched the enemy twilight dragon arcanist, the man was genuinely shocked and knocked back a few feet, his skin burned so badly some slid off his chin.

Then I turned around and admired the sphere of darkness that encased us. Luthair would've loved it. Illia, Nicholin, and Master Zelfree—able to see through the shadows—went for Calisto and his manticore.

Zelfree's bangles jumped off his wrist and transformed into a second manticore, this one different from Calisto's. Since Zelfree couldn't mimic true forms, his manticore was the standard variation. A golden coat, bat wings, and a scorpion tail. The face wasn't covered in a mask, either—Traces had the head of a lion.

But Zelfree now had the strength and speed of a manticore arcanist. He charged forward with impressive celerity.

"*Calisto is mine*," Illia shouted as she unleashed a torrent of white disintegration flame.

But again, I couldn't sit and watch their fight. Both Spider and Wit attacked me and Evianna, one from either side, as did the kappa and juvenile sea serpent.

They couldn't surprise me. I sensed their footsteps long before they got close—every movement vibrated through the ground, every jerked decision, every tiny slip in the mud. Even without my dark-sight, I could keep track of everyone on the battlefield.

I manipulated the ground, but Spider was prepared for my attack. Leaping toward me, she evoked acid from her palm. She struck the chest piece of my armor, eroding it away in a matter of moments.

Wit and his serpent were caught in the ground as it sank around their bodies. I also managed to catch the kappa, but the little fish man puked up acid on the rocks, destroying my stone trap and freeing himself.

Evianna manipulated the darkness and snared the kappa in a *second* trap, lashing it down with tendrils made of shadows. The little fish man writhed and screeched, trying to puke up more acid, but never getting the right angle.

I didn't want to use my molten rock right away, considering what it did to the environment around me, but I didn't have much of a choice. Spider and Wit were keeping me from attacking Theasin. I had no time to waste on them and their weaker eldrin.

I evoked magma from my palms. The rain in the area evaporated as the temperatures soared. I threw large amounts on the ground, creating deadly obstacles. When the kappa was about to free himself from Evianna's shadow tendrils, I manipulated the ground again, trapping his arms and legs. Then I hurled another glob of molten rock. It struck the vile creature on the shoulder, his flesh melting under the blazing heat.

Spider ran to her eldrin.

Then I turned my attention to Wit.

Obsidian spikes sprouted across my body as I threw more molten rock. Wit manipulated the rainwater. He willed the water to strike at me in small, dart-like attacks, but they were never a threat. Each turned to steam long before striking my body.

When I used my terrain manipulation, I probably went too far. The ground sank low into a crater, taking Wit and his serpent with it. At the bottom, the dirt and mud shifted to sand, and the two of them slid into the ground until I solidified the rock around their bodies, burying them completely in the ever-hardening earth.

Evianna attacked Spider with a short sword. Spider lashed back with a cutlass, the clash of their blades ringing throughout the field.

While they were occupied, I rushed for Theasin. I refused to let him get away.

Perhaps Terrakona felt the same way because his duel with the soul forge grew increasingly intense. The ground quaked with each bash and movement. Terrakona was half-absorbed into the slug—his body slowly decaying inside the soul forge—but when he evoked magma from his mouth, it poured across the forge, melting a house-sized hole into the beast.

Rock burst out of the ground, preventing the slug from escaping, and altering the southern field forever.

The roaring and colossal strikes echoed along with the thunder, filling all of the Argo Empire with the pandemonium of our battle.

With rage fueling my actions, I ran straight for the one-armed dastard and swung wide with my sword. Theasin held up his hand and crystal jutted from the ground, evoked into existence by his magic. The crystals he had created weren't magical like star shards, but they did remind me of Crystal Lake...

The glass-like crystals burst from the ground, and a couple of the sharper ones cut my legs. I tried to leap away, but the injuries were enough that I stumbled to the side. Theasin and I were only a few feet apart. I manipulated the ground, hoping to shatter the crystalline rocks, but I couldn't manage to change them. I moved the ground—and the crystals stayed attached—but I couldn't alter anything Theasin had created.

And he kept evoking them. He stood on his own crystals as they formed in nearly every shape and size, and in all directions. The more he created, the less ground I could manipulate.

But that didn't matter.

Theasin wasn't a warrior. He practiced grandiose speeches, not swordplay. So, when he evoked a second round of crystals, I already knew what to look for. *Never become predictable*—a lesson I had learned after many fights—and Theasin was the definition of predictable.

I stepped around them and swung with my sword, slashing down on his one arm.

Theasin gritted his teeth and backed away, blood running with the rain through his slashed robe sleeve.

"Was it really worth it?" I asked, hefting my blade.

Theasin's eyes were unfocused—he couldn't see through the darkness. He had likely evoked the crystals because he had heard me coming. Knowing he was blind would make this easier.

"You should join us," Theasin said. "Together with the Autarch, we would be unstoppable."

"Never." I slowly advanced, my sword at the ready. "I'll never join men like you."

"Your self-righteous declarations are detestable. Stop living in a childish fantasy." Theasin shook his head. "*We're trying to change the world for the better!*" His shouts echoed with the thunder. "With us, *everyone* will become an arcanist. We will watch over a nation that will thrive more than any others before us."

"How many graves do we have to walk over to get to your nation?" I almost couldn't ask the question without devolving into pure rage. "Not *everyone* will become an arcanist. Only those you deem worthy." I glanced at the bodies scattered around Thronehold's walls. "You'll kill everyone else."

"The worthless will be culled so that the rest can survive. It's a calculated tactic to ensure our best future. You're letting your naivete and emotions get in the way of greatness."

I shook away his words. "You have nowhere to run." I stepped closer. "And all of this is just your attempt to stall."

Perhaps sensing his approaching demise, Theasin reached into his robes and threw out a small pouch. A cloud of dust sprang to life, defying the rain and spreading across the battlefield. I covered my nose and mouth and cursed to myself.

Decay dust.

The moment it touched my sword, the blade rusted and broke apart into fine grains of sand. My shield, however, was an artifact, and the dust washed harmlessly over it. To my surprise, the dust didn't destroy my guild pendant, either. Eventide's birthday gift to me—the bone from her atlas turtle—was unaffected by the blackish dust that swept over the field.

Calisto wasn't as lucky, however. Several pieces of his gear, including a few of his earrings, were caught by the terrible decay. They broke apart into sand.

"*Dammit, Theasin,*" he roared. "What did I tell you?"

I hadn't been able to keep track of everyone fighting. I could sense their movement, and I knew none of my companions had been killed, but that was all. When I stopped to glance around—to survey the battle—I took in the details.

Odion and Zaxis used light and fire to bash away the dread form twilight dragon. The skeletal head bit Zaxis on the arm, no doubt infecting him with the arcane plague, but it didn't faze Zaxis. He healed and continued his barrage of punches, even shattering bone when he landed a solid blow on the monster's skull.

Hasdrubal fought both the nightmarish dragon and the arcanist—one head for each—and Odion used White Curse to slash open the enemy arcanist's chest.

Evianna fought both Spider and the kappa, her combat prowess on par with the pirate, if not better. In the darkness, Evianna had all the advantages. She manipulated the shadows and created solid whips, tendrils, and even spikes to shred Spider—practically killing her with a thousand small cuts.

Illia and Zelfree, however...

They had clearly been losing.

Hellion and Calisto had enough combat experience for an entire battalion of men, and before the decay dust, Calisto had had the trinkets to outfit said battalion. But now he was weaker.

Nicholin teleported above Calisto and breathed white flames. Calisto leapt into the air—his strength enhanced by his manticore magic—and slashed Nicholin almost in half with Retribution. The little ferret tumbled through the air and hit the mud.

Illia teleported a dagger and struck Calisto in the back.

Zelfree lunged and also stabbed Calisto with a knife, clipping him in the shoulder. When Calisto slashed with Retribution, Zelfree managed to dodge, but just barely.

And it was obvious that Zelfree hadn't dodged a couple of prior attacks. Several injuries wept blood, including a gouge that ran from his collarbone to his navel.

Illia's right knee had been slashed so badly that she struggled to stand. Despite that, she teleported around Calisto, attacking with her white disintegration flame at every possible angle.

Hellion's face mask split open, and I had to look away. Anyone who gazed upon a manticore's true face would be paralyzed, and I couldn't afford that. Not now.

"Are you ready to die?" Hellion asked with a laugh.

Calisto chuckled alongside his eldrin. "You've made a terrible mistake, Everett."

"It's not *him* you should be concerned about," Illia said, throwing a dagger. It teleported at the last moment, bypassing Calisto's attempt to block it with Retribution. The dagger slammed into his leg, hobbling him. "I said I would return to get my revenge, *and here I am!*"

Hellion laughed. "It'll be amusing to carve those words straight into your flesh once you've lost this battle."

With a deep breath, I blocked out the other fights and

refocused on my target. Theasin backed away, his attention more on his soul forge than on me. The clash happening behind us was still shaking the field and the walls of Thronehold.

Terrakona's molten rock tore through the body of the soul forge, while the slug's many hands scooped at Terrakona's flesh, creating bloody divots throughout his serpentine body.

I didn't have a sword, and I couldn't manipulate the crystals at Theasin's feet. So instead, I ran forward and punched the man with my obsidian knuckles. I struck him across the face, hard enough that my obsidian shattered and stuck in his cheek and facial bones. He staggered backward and hit the ground, completely disorientated.

Then I evoked my magma. Theasin held up his one arm, and to my shock, evoked the life-stealing threads.

He had two evocations, just like I did. One that created crystals, and one that created magic to steal someone's life force.

When Theasin's thread touched my side, I gritted my teeth and groaned in pain. It felt like a leech—or a wasp—had attached itself to my organs. The intense and pointed pain shot through my system, almost blinding me with agony. Parts of me were jerked out through the thread, draining me at a frightening rate. My skin paled, and my injuries burned hotter than ever before.

I collapsed to one knee, my breathing painful.

Theasin stood. His life-stealing thread was connected to my side, and also to his one hand, like a pipe sucking away my energy and giving it to him. Theasin stepped close to me, and I tried to stand, but the burning sensation of the thread prevented me from moving.

With a weak kick, Theasin knocked me over. I curled up, my gut unstitching itself and bleeding once again. Cold mud soaked into my ruined armor and clothing.

Why couldn't I move?

The magic of the soul forge... it ate at my insides.

"You're pathetic," Theasin said as he touched the obsidian fragments poking out of his face. He looked like he had fallen from twenty feet into a quarry. One of his eyes had swollen shut. "You're nothing without your sword. And now you'll witness the many talents of my soul forge. Your snake is a mere beast—useless in the grand scheme of things."

No matter how hard I tried, I couldn't uncurl myself and stand. The sinister thread continued to claw at my soul, stealing my life.

Theasin wiped blood from his broken nose. "I'll use your magic to make something wonderous—perhaps breathe life into an extinct breed of dragon. And then the Autarch will bond with your world serpent. We'll destroy everything you've built so far. Not that you've done much, but I'll still delight in toppling it."

The longer the thread ate at my soul, the louder my heart beat became. It almost drowned out Theasin's voice, each beat louder and slower than the last.

"From what I can tell, the previous world serpent arcanist only rose to prominence because he was a master tactician and strategist." Theasin huffed as he cleaned his shattered face of obsidian fragments. "Obviously, the world serpent's abilities are useless. Even in a fight, the soul forge is superior." He offered me a cruel smile. "You're hardly a master strategist. And soon you'll be nothing but a corpse. Farewell, Warlord of Magic."

Zelfree said losing wasn't an option. He was right.

I gritted my teeth, closed my eyes, and focused on the plants in the field. I couldn't manipulate the crystals or rocks, but that didn't matter. Vegetation—vines, roots, and leaves—sprang up around us. Theasin stepped back, startled.

But it was too late. I used the plants to grab him and knock him down onto his own crystals. The moment his head struck the crystalline rocks, Theasin lost his concentration, and his deadly life-stealing thread faded.

I didn't have much time.

Despite my injuries, I jumped to my feet, evoked my magma, and hurled the molten rock. I struck Theasin across the legs. He screamed, and even though he tried to evoke more threads, he couldn't. Without his focus, he'd be unable to rely on his magical abilities.

Although I could now breathe, and the thread was no longer burning my insides, my body was still wrecked. Everything ached. I could barely stand.

Still, I advanced on Theasin. More molten rock spilled from the lines in my palms, the heat rising, and obsidian sprouted from my knuckles, replacing what I had lost.

"Wait," Theasin said, his one hand shaky. "I'm the only arcanist who can bring mystical creatures back into the world! The khepera, the king basilisks, the abyssal leeches, the silver harts, the all-seeing sphinxes—the soul forge can bring them all back!"

I almost laughed. "I can't believe you have the audacity to include the khepera in that list when you were the one who went out of your way to kill them." I held up a glowing hand of magma, knowing that Theasin would say anything to save himself. The darkness practically danced with anticipation as I closed the distance between us. "But you don't care whom you've killed, do you? You don't care about the mystical creatures, about the nations of the world—or even about your own children, most of whom you personally abused."

Theasin said nothing. His dark eyes stared into mine, despite the rain and the trickle of blood running from his hairline. He fussed with the burning injuries on his legs, obviously trying to regain his concentration long enough to evoke his magic.

Adelgis had never asked me to spare his father. And why would he? Theasin had helped the Second Ascension at every opportunity. He had located the apoch dragon and turned its bones into weapons. He had helped with the assassination of Queen Velleta. He had tortured his children to further his magical research. He had attempted to destroy the Frith Guild.

And yet all of it was justified in Theasin's mind—as if his end goals were far greater than any cost. *His* wants were more important than everyone else's.

Theasin didn't deserve another chance.

Rhys teleported onto the battlefield, still bleeding from my earlier attack, determination shining in his narrow eyes. He had come to rescue Theasin, I was sure of it.

On instinct, I lunged for Theasin and grabbed him. The magma on my hands burned through his shoulders and neck, searing through the god-arcanist mark on his chest. He tried to struggle, but all he could do was yell—until I burned most of his throat, rendering him mute. When he died, I finally exhaled, knowing that I had prevented Rhys from teleporting him to safety.

Unfortunately, it wasn't Theasin who Rhys had come for.

The jittery rain-soaked man touched the dying soul forge. A great deal of glitter lit up the field, and a moment later, the gargantuan soul forge vanished with a loud *pop*. Rhys disappeared as well, his laughter haunting the storm until it eventually died.

Terrakona roared into the night, his frustration swallowed by the storm clouds overhead. His body reminded me of corn that had been nibbled on. Holes covered his entire body, and copious amounts of blood spilled onto the mud. He collapsed a moment later, his breathing deep, his serpentine body shaking.

"*They left me?*" Calisto yelled.

Then, to my surprise, he laughed.

"Of course, they did." Calisto slashed at Illia, but he missed her as she teleported away. "Everyone always leaves..."

The life-sapping thread from Theasin's attack had left me shaky. I wanted to help with the fighting, but I needed rest. My energy had been drained, and even the thought of walking was too much.

"Come at me, *fool*," Zaxis shouted between heavy panting. He threw another punch at the enemy twilight dragon. "I'm not done!"

All I could do was watch as the war raged around me.

49

REVENGE

The dread form twilight dragon puked blood from its non-skeletal head. Zaxis, Hasdrubal, and Odion were covered, the monster's blood mixing with their own.

If they hadn't been infected with the arcane plague before, they were now.

To my surprise, a ray of light shot through the storm. Forsythe swooped down and angled himself at the dread form twilight dragon. Before the beast could react, Forsythe burst fire from his body in all directions, washing the monster dragon in flame.

The dragon vomited more blood on Forsythe, but the phoenix burned brighter and hotter, melting the creature's glowing red eyes.

While the twilight dragon was momentarily blinded, Odion leapt close and upward with his two-handed blade. In one fell swoop, he punctured the beast's skull, killing it instantly.

The skeletal head of the twilight dragon had already been shattered by Zaxis's fists. The twilight dragon collapsed onto the field, rendering its arcanist incapable of using his magic.

That was when Zaxis struck. He unleashed a torrent of flame that evaporated more water and left the insane dragon arcanist a charred corpse.

Hasdrubal roared a triumphant victory, but the bite wounds and charred injuries told me he was in pain. Both his heads took in deep breaths, and his feathered wings dropped. His sluggish movements mirrored my own. He was drained.

Forsythe and Zaxis celebrated together, both covered in the enemy's blood.

Still in the midst of her own battle, Evianna evoked terrors, rendering the kappa and Spider momentarily stunned. Then Evianna attacked with her sword, striking the kappa and almost decapitating the short fish man. Spider broke free of her terror-fueled daydreams and flung herself in front of her eldrin.

"No, don't!" Spider shouted. "I surrender! Leave my eldrin!"

The desperation and panic in her voice rocked me. I wasn't even part of the fight, but I could *feel* her concern for the creature. Evianna must have felt it as well because she hesitated. Then she lowered her weapon and nodded.

"You'll be taken to the Frith Guild," Evianna said in her knightmare double-voice.

Spider replied with a curt, "*Fine.*" She wrapped her arms protectively over her slimy kappa. The beast wrapped its short arms around her and then flashed its needle-sharp teeth at Evianna.

But while the others had finished their duels with the members of the Second Ascension, Calisto and Hellion continued to fight. With Retribution in hand, Calisto cut Manticore-Traces—removing one of her leathery bat wings— and then slashed her a second time, removing her tail.

She screamed and cried and then reverted back into her cat form.

But...

Even in her natural cat-like state, her long tail was severed.

She hit the mud and trembled.

Zelfree threw a knife at Calisto's face, causing the dread pirate to back away and to dodge. That was when Zelfree ran to his eldrin's side, his eyebrows knitted, his hands unsteady.

Illia—alone—stood against Calisto and Hellion. She teleported away from them, and both gave chase, but much faster than a normal individual. They were superhuman fast—and terrifyingly strong—and every time they slashed or swiped with claws, I cringed.

Illia...

Again and again, she just barely escaped, but Illia hadn't made any moves to attack. At this rate, she would just get unlucky and then Retribution would cut her in half. Could I live with myself if my own sword was responsible for killing my sister?

Zaxis ran over to me and placed a hand on my shoulder. "Get up!" His healing filled my being, but no matter how long he held me, it wasn't repairing what Theasin had stolen. My soul felt weak.

"Help the others," I commanded.

After a huff, he ran to Nicholin, placed a shaky hand on the little white ferret, and healed the terrible slash down his body. Nicholin's ears perked up, and with weak movements, he licked Zaxis's hand.

Determined to heal everyone on the battlefield, Zaxis hurried to Zelfree. He healed both him and his eldrin—but Traces's tail didn't repair. When the healing was over, Traces had a nub left, her long tail on the ground, twisted in on itself.

Despite almost losing, I took stock of our situation again.

Thanks to Evianna's knightmare augmentation, giving everyone dark-sight...

And Odion's control of the darkness...

And Zaxis's healing...

And Illia's teleporting...

And Zelfree's ability to mimic the enemies' magic...

If I hadn't had them, I doubted I would've overcome one of the god-creatures. Now, the threads of the soul forge were no longer over Thronehold. Queen Ladislava should be attacking Cardozo, and our sole focus would be on Calisto and his true form manticore.

Unfortunately, I had gotten my hopes up too far.

Hellion turned back around, and everyone who had been paying attention to the fight was suddenly frozen in paralysis—even me. Hellion's true face was a human's—an older man with a short beard and wrinkle lines by his eyes. One look, and I couldn't move my body.

Neither could Evianna, Odion, or Zaxis, each of whom had been looking in the wrong direction when Hellion had turned around. From past experience, I'd be trapped like this for a few minutes, at least.

If Hellion had caught us all, this whole fight would have been over.

Zelfree hadn't looked, though. His mimic transformed herself a second time—she became a knightmare, just like Layshl. Her shadow armor body was hollow on the inside, like all knightmares. She melted into the darkness and then rose up around Zelfree. With masterful control of the shadows, Zelfree created himself a sword and then stepped into the inky void. When he rose up again, it wasn't next to Calisto—it was behind Hellion.

Calisto and Illia were caught in a loop of attacking and teleporting, neither catching the other—but as an observer, I could see Illia separating Calisto from his eldrin. She led Calisto farther and farther away, keeping his attention on her, and not on Zelfree's fight.

At one point, Calisto clipped Illia with Retribution. The black blade went right through her elbow, almost removing the lower half of her arm. Fortunately, she had my emblem ring. It glowed and shimmered, and briefly gave her the healing necessary to repair herself from the injury. Illia continued to flee, obviously shaken by the near-crippling attack.

That was when Zelfree attacked Hellion. He slashed at the beast's face—but since Zelfree wasn't looking, the sword went straight into Hellion's lion neck.

The manticore shrieked and lashed out with his scorpion tail.

Zelfree manipulated the darkness to protect himself. Shadow tendrils rose up and blocked the attack. The scorpion stinger slid across the hardened shadows and slammed into the ground. Hellion jerked his tail up and struck again, but this time he missed outright, smashing his stinger into the ground a second time. Then Zelfree stabbed again, severing more of Hellion's neck. Hellion's white mane and fur were covered in crimson, his human face contorted in pain. Blood spilled across the mud, making everything sticky as the rain continued to drench us all.

When Hellion tried to roar, all that came out was a sickening grunt that sounded wet. He vomited blood and then backed away, practically whimpering.

Zelfree stepped into the darkness, shifted through the shadows, and then stepped out underneath Hellion. He stabbed upward, disemboweling the large beast. Zelfree disappeared back into the shadows and appeared next to Hellion, drenched in the beast's vital fluid.

Hellion's intestines spilled out onto the field. Hellion—still enraged—swiped with his claw and caught Zelfree. He gouged out a large chunk of Zelfree's chest and slammed the man into the dirt.

But that was the last of Hellion's strength. He collapsed backward, vomiting blood, still trying to call out.

"Hellion?" Calisto whipped around, his voice strained.

Using his extraordinary speed, he abandoned his chase of Illia and went straight to his eldrin's side. By the time he reached Hellion, however, he stumbled out of his run. The mark on his forehead stopped glowing.

Calisto fell to his knees next to Hellion's massive body. He dropped Retribution in the mud, completely disregarding the weapon, and then placed both his hands on the body of his eldrin.

"Hellion..." Calisto muttered, his voice so distant, I almost couldn't hear it.

The manticore didn't move.

My paralysis left me, but the fatigue still lingered. I couldn't use any of my magic. I couldn't even sense vibrations in the ground.

Illia took several deep breaths and then walked across the field. Nicholin teleported to her shoulder, his bright blue eyes locked on Calisto. Together, they strode over and scooped up Retribution.

Although Illia hadn't trained in sword fighting, it didn't really matter. Retribution would cut through almost anything as though it wasn't there.

Only magical things, though. Against mortal men, Retribution was just a sword, but sharp enough that it would still slash through most flesh without much effort.

Calisto gently stroked Hellion's bloody mane, seemingly oblivious to Illia and Nicholin standing right next to him. He stared at his dead eldrin, taking in the sight without any visible reaction on his face.

I knew the pain of losing a true form eldrin... But I kept the memories at bay, never focusing on them. Not now. Not when we had pressing matters to attend to.

Zelfree and Traces stood in the rain, unmoving. They remained merged—Traces as the suit of knightmare shadow armor—but otherwise, they just watched.

Although Illia had my sword, she also just... stood there. Waiting. Almost like she was expecting Calisto to attack her so she could finish the fight.

Finally, Calisto stopped petting Hellion. Covered in his eldrin's blood, he exhaled, his shoulders slumped and his breathing ragged.

When nothing happened and no one moved, Calisto glanced over his shoulder at Illia. "*Well?*" he barked.

Illia flinched. She tightened her grip on Retribution, but still, Calisto didn't move.

Then Calisto gritted his teeth. "Listen, lass. Life is just a parade of pain and suffering. I'd rather not have a prolonged finale." He leaned his head to the side, as if to give Illia an easy spot to bury the sword in his neck.

Nothing.

Illia held the sword close, but she never uttered a word.

Neither did Zelfree or Traces. Nor did Zaxis and Odion, who waited a fair distance away. Only the rain had the courage to make any noise.

Without moving from his position, Calisto sighed. "You want my eye?" he asked in a cruel, icy tone. "Cut it out of my skull already. *It's yours.*"

I really didn't understand what Illia was waiting for.

But before she could decide one way or the other, a crack from a firearm echoed into the storm. A bullet slammed into Illia from behind, and she stumbled forward, blood weeping from a hole just above her belt. The blood was dark—she had been struck in some sort of organ—and she shook as she tried to get her footing.

"Illia!" Zaxis shouted.

A lone shooter stood at the edge of the field closest to

Thronehold. He was next to a hippogriff—one of the newly born creatures.

It was Markus. He held a flintlock pistol out in front of him, a rain guard over the powder and muzzle. With deep breaths, he reached for a muzzleloader, preparing to fire a second time.

"Calisto, I'm here!" Markus shouted. "Run!"

Illia regained her focus and teleported.

Calisto managed to stand and turned around, his eyes wide as we all watched Illia reappear next to Markus. She probably didn't know how dangerous Retribution was, because with one slash, she cut Markus clean in half before anyone could do a thing about it. She sliced him through the chest—from the top of one shoulder to the opposite side down to his waist.

That was it. One clean blow.

Illia had seen me use the weapon before, but I suspected she had thought I had just been strong and skilled—not that the weapon would end anything magical.

She leapt away from the vivisected corpse, her hands shaky, but she never lost her grip on her weapon.

The hippogriff who had brought Markus to the battlefield moved away, his eagle wings spread, his hackles raised. When nothing happened to him, he flew off toward the city, confusion written on his eagle face. Markus had probably escaped his cage carriage during the fighting and then used his griffin magic to break the hypnotic trance on the newly born hippogriff. Had Markus asked the hippogriff to fly him here? He had known Calisto was nearby...

Which meant Markus had rushed across the city to help him.

Illia must have put together everything as well. She stared at the body of the pirate, her one eye never blinking or drifting away.

The sound of the battering rain was all we had for our victory celebration.

Calisto finally collapsed to his knees, his vacant gaze unfocused and downcast. I had never before seen someone embody despair. His icy demeanor and bravado were gone—all that was left were the emotions of a corpse.

RULER OF THE ARGO EMPIRE

"Terrakona," I whispered.

Although my eldrin rested in the mud, his eyes opened, and his slit pupils narrowed into a tight line. "**Warlord?**" With a visible struggle, Terrakona lifted his head and turned to face me. His tongue jutted from his mouth, tasting the air around me, as if determining my health.

"We need to return to the guild. It isn't safe here."

Rhys could return with Second Ascension arcanists at any moment. It wasn't likely, since they knew I was still alive, and on the battlefield, but I didn't want to take a chance.

"**By your command.**"

Terrakona forced himself up. Then he moved toward me and lowered his head. His crystal mane made for an easy ladder when I wasn't injured, but in my current state, it was difficult to pull myself onto him.

Odlon hurried over and helped me, however. He carried more injuries than armor, and I knew the plague coursed through his system.

"We need to get you back to the guild as soon as possible," I said.

He nodded once, smiling wide. "It was a pleasure to fight by your side."

I wished I had been better—more capable—so that I could've handled the whole battle myself. But then again, I appreciated his help. Without everyone here, I couldn't have done what I had. Theasin was dead, though I didn't know the fate of his soul forge. Had Terrakona's venom been enough to kill it? Or would the slug recover and choose a new arcanist?

I didn't know.

The rain slowed a bit, returning to a trickle.

Once atop Terrakona, I glanced over at Calisto. I didn't want to intervene, so I just waited.

Zaxis ran to Illia and healed her bullet injury, and he was careful not to touch her with any plague blood. I was surprised by Zaxis's tenacity and stamina. All this healing had surely taken a toll on him, but he pushed forward regardless. He had fought the enemy and kept our team alive, despite the odds.

Then Zaxis took Retribution from Illia. They spoke to each other, their voices too low and far away for me to hear. Once finished, Zaxis hustled to Terrakona. He handed me my blade without a word. I took Retribution and sheathed it.

With heavy steps, Illia strode over to Calisto. They didn't speak. Ilia simply placed her hand on his shoulder and the two of them disappeared from the battlefield in a puff of glitter and a distant *pop*.

Zelfree, Zaxis, Forsythe, and Odion gathered by Hasdrubal, preparing to take flight.

"You can't ride with us," Odion said to Zelfree. "We're infected. We can't risk infecting you, too."

Zelfree backed away, holding his mimic close. "I'll travel through the city, then."

Infected...

They would all need to see Vethica as soon as possible. Her khepera magic could heal them, so long as they did so within a few days. After that, their eldrin would become monsters, unable to revert back.

Evianna shifted through the darkness and appeared on the back of Terrakona. Together with Lashyl, she made her way to my side. Then we headed for the city, Terrakona's movements slower than I had ever seen him.

Queen Ladislava had invaded Thronehold once the soul forge's magic had been stopped, but as Terrakona moved through the city, I realized the fighting hadn't ended. Cardozo's soldiers clashed with the Knights Draconic, filling the night with the clanging of metal on metal.

Captain Devlin and his roc soared through the sky, manipulating the weather, and altering the clouds. Clear skies shone over the majority of the Dragon District, all the way around King Drake Castle. Pegasi flew through the sky, but to my surprise, they weren't attacking Ladislava's men. They were circling around a siren atop one of the castle's towers. The siren sang a haunting song, and the pegasi stayed close, flying in perfect circles around the tower.

"Come now, my beauties! Sweet horses of flight. Show yourself to me, make yourself a sight!"

The pegasi displayed their wings as wide as possible, gliding on the calm winds created by Devlin. They were the Sky Legionnaires—all of them transfixed by the song and unable to fight.

Enemy arrows flew toward the siren, trying to disrupt the song, but they never hit. A shimmering barrier prevented the archers from striking the siren, and once Terrakona got a little closer, I realized it was because Eventide stood on the tower with Yesna and her siren.

I almost laughed. The barrier prevented the enemy from

halting the song, and the song kept the enemy fliers from raining death down on Ladislava's army. It was an interesting combination, but I couldn't help but wonder where the enemy sirens had gone.

They were nowhere on the battlefield. Their songs had ended, and I no longer spotted the reanimated mystical creatures. All I saw were the carts that had carried their dead bodies into the city.

Where had they gone?

"**What shall we do?**" Terrakona telepathically asked. "**The smell of smoke and blood fills the streets with the essence of battle.**"

"We'll help them," I whispered.

Evianna tightened her grip on my arm. "You're in no condition to keep fighting."

"I can't leave." What would it say about the *Warlord of Magic* if I left in the middle of the fight? I had to stay. No matter what. "Let's go, Terrakona."

With a weaker roar, Terrakona declared his intent. Then he rushed forward to enter the conflict.

There were two fights—one in the streets, and one in the courtyard of the castle. The streets were filled with soldiers and arcanists using the city as their cover as they fought one another. The courtyard was a battle between Ladislava, her dragon, and a handful of soldiers against Cardozo, his elite guard, and a dozen hippogriff arcanists.

Streetlamps, and the illumination provided by the moon, were enough to keep the battle alive in the middle of the night. A few soldiers carried torches, but none of them threw anything into the buildings or needlessly caused a fire. They were all soldiers of Thronehold, after all. No one wanted the city permanently harmed if they could help it.

"Help the soldiers," I called out.

Ladislava would take it as an insult if I helped her in this moment. She wanted her own glory, and she could have it.

"As you command."

Terrakona didn't enter the battle directly. He lashed his tail at one of the three-story buildings and sent debris tumbling onto the enemy soldiers. Unfortunately, it drew the enemy's ire. Archers and gunmen turned their sights on Terrakona's massive body. It wasn't difficult to hit him, but his scales deflected most projectiles. The divots in his body, however...

Every bullet, arrow, and cannonball that struck him in an injury was enough for him to grimace. I felt it every time Terrakona shivered in agony.

He couldn't evoke magma, or else he could harm Ladislava's soldiers. Instead, I manipulated the road, lifting up chunks of ground to block off streets or protect Ladislava's soldiers. To my surprise, waves of flames washed over the enemy archers taking aim at Terrakona.

Atty and her phoenix, Titania, targeted the enemies launching attacks at Terrakona, her fire powers intense and pointed. Her fire practically burned blue as she held her hand out and washed everything in a torrent of flame.

On the streets, Raisen the five-headed hydra devastated mortal soldiers. When they approached, they couldn't predict the heads of the beast. They tried to defend, but it was no use, and the moment the hydra bit them, they were done for. Raisen plowed through the enemy, helping Ladislava's soldiers rush in and occupy more of the city.

Hexa evoked poison clouds and used her magic to clear out alleyways or prevent the enemy from sneaking up around them. Her strategic use of her magic would no doubt make Zelfree proud, but I didn't see him. Odion and his twilight dragon had yet to enter the city...

The Knights Draconic leapt over some of my obstacles and went full force into the enemy. The fluid and graceful movements of their unicorns allowed the knights to weave through the enemies like thread through cloth. The unicorns stabbed enemies with their horns while their arcanists attacked with lances and swords.

With Terrakona's help, it wasn't long before the main road was ours.

Some of the enemies even surrendered upon seeing Terrakona. They threw down their weapons and bowed, some shouting for mercy, others declaring their loyalty to the world serpent.

I could barely hear them.

It felt as if I were growing weaker the longer we went on. I didn't know what Theasin had done, but I couldn't seem to recover.

Evianna must've noticed, because she offered her shoulder, and helped me cling to Terrakona's crystal mane.

"You'll collapse at this rate," she whispered.

"I have to continue," I said.

"Even if it costs you your life?"

I shook my head. "The situation's not that drastic. I'll be fine."

The tips of my fingers had lost all feeling, but I refused to voice my concerns until after the fight for Thronehold had concluded.

"Head toward the castle," I commanded.

Terrakona rushed away from the main street and crashed through the gates around the castle. He still bled from his injuries, but unlike me, Terrakona was slowly healing from his injuries. As we surveyed the battle, I realized ice and rime covered most of the walkways. Fain had used his evocation to stop our enemies from approaching the queen. If a soldier got by, Fain attacked from invisibility and manipulated their flesh so that it fell off in chunks.

Wraith struck at soldiers as well, creating a death trap.

I tried to manipulate the ground, but I couldn't. Instead, I allowed Terrakona to do the heavy lifting. He smashed the enemy soldiers and gave Ladislava the luxury of only focusing on the enemy in front of her—Cardozo.

And while I had never seen the man before today, I knew him because of the black crown he wore atop his head. The man was otherwise clad in dragon scale armor that covered most of his body in full-plate defenses.

Without his sovereign dragon, Cardozo was at a disadvantage. Ladislava and her dragon rushed forward and attacked him at the same time. Cardozo was immune to their flame—all sovereign dragon arcanists were—but he wasn't immune to claws and swords.

Then something unexpected and terrifying happened.

The moon disappeared.

The sky went black. The streetlamps dulled. The fires vanished. Everything was blackness—all light gone from the region in a single instant.

A bright glow of light shone on the far northern horizon, like a pyre was set halfway around the world, so massive we could see it from Thronehold. It reminded me of when I had bonded to Terrakona...

Another god-arcanist.

I knew it in my soul.

It wasn't the fenris wolf. The wolf was here, in the Argo Empire. Whatever god-creature that was, it was located hundreds of miles from our location, far beyond the horizon, likely in the ocean.

Then the darkness faded. The moon returned, the streetlamps flared to life, and the fires resumed their destruction. The glow in the distance faded, leaving most soldiers confused.

But not Ladislava. She had taken Cardozo in the darkness, carving through his armor and stabbing him deep in his side.

With Cardozo momentarily stunned with confusion and pain, Ladislava's dragon went in for the kill. With one devastating bite, the dragon decapitated Cardozo, his fangs severing the man's neck with little difficulty.

Which meant Ladislava was now the uncontested ruler of the Argo Empire.

And then my vision narrowed and blurred.

A MISSING FRIEND

Half conscious, I allowed Evianna to keep me tethered to Terrakona. Her shadow tendrils held me in place as the last of the fight died throughout the city. The morning sun brought with it a renewed sense of triumph, and celebration rang throughout the streets.

Devlin and Mesos kept the clouds away from Thronehold, despite the fact the storm raged all around the city. A pillar of sunlight shone on the city like the world itself wanted to celebrate Ladislava's official coronation.

Although the soldiers and the citizens wanted me to participate in the celebrations, I knew I couldn't. It would harm my image if everyone saw me as a half-alive corpse that could barely walk. Instead, I waved to the people as Terrakona moved through the main road. I managed to maintain my consciousness long enough to reach the shattered northern wall, the entire time waving to the people.

When I arrived, Guildmaster Eventide, Yesna, and Devlin flew over to greet me. I slid off Terrakona and tried my best to nod along with their praises and answer their questions. I told them of Theasin, and where to find his body. I tried to tell them of Calisto, but I still didn't know the dread pirate's ultimate fate.

Once I finished my explanations, the tension among us waned. "You're a damn hero," Yesna said, punching me in the shoulder. "The entire city is going to celebrate for a week for what you've done."

Devlin snorted. "What's left of 'em. After we mourn the dead."

"After that, then—once the queen gets her crown, and she declares for the Frith Guild."

Guildmaster Eventide slowly nodded along with the statements. Dark rings lined her eyes, and I knew that being so far from her eldrin was taking its toll. She pushed back her gray hair and sighed. "Volke, thank you. Fighting with the soul forge couldn't have been easy. You've done the entire city a great service. Everyone who's still alive owes their life to you."

My heart swelled with the words. Although we hadn't saved the entire city, I was glad we could save most of it. That was what I had always wanted, even as a child on a small island—I wanted the power to help those who couldn't defend themselves.

"You don't look so hot," Devlin said, giving me the once over.

I half-shrugged, not sure how to answer.

Eventide placed a gentle hand on my shoulder. "Wait for us in the war tent. I'll make sure Gillie treats you right away."

"I think I need Vethica," I said, my breath ragged. "Her khepera magic can heal... injuries related to a person's soul."

We would also need her to heal both Zaxis and Odion, since they had been infected during the fight with Theasin.

Eventide replied with a curt nod. "It'll be done. Just focus on resting for now." She turned to Evianna. "Can we count on you?"

"No one will disturb Volke," Evianna replied, holding my arm with a protective possessiveness.

I sat in the war tent, my thoughts drifting. The patter of rain beat across the canvas roof, creating a pleasant melody of nature.

Hours went by. Early morning became late morning, and then afternoon. The celebrations continued throughout the city, and I wondered if Queen Ladislava would pardon the Sky Legionnaires or if she would have them exiled or executed for treason.

And my thoughts also went to the new god-arcanist. Who was it? Was it the sky titan? The questions were killing me.

Thankfully, some of my strength returned. The empty war tent wasn't the most comfortable, but I managed to rest my arms and head on the giant table and get some sleep. Evianna never left my side. She felt my forehead from time to time and brought me water. Her knightmare unmerged from her and shifted around the room, constantly checking the tarp walls and stakes that held everything down.

When I felt refreshed enough, I stood and stretched. As long as Queen Ladislava upheld her end of the bargain, the Argo Empire would side with us. And with Theasin dead, who would the Autarch turn to now?

We would chase down the Second Ascension and put an end to their villainy. Confidence welled in me, and my hopes soared higher than the clouds outside. If I maintained my powers and prowess, I would stop them—I could feel it.

"Volke?" Evianna walked toward me from the other side of the war tent. "Is everything okay?"

"Yeah." I took her hand and kissed her knuckles. "I'm feeling a lot better."

She blushed and fidgeted with the ends of her white locks. "Should we see what the others are doing? I haven't seen them in a long while."

With a quick nod, we headed out of the tent. The rain had waned, and I wondered if Devlin's interference had stalled the monsoon that Ladislava had so desperately wanted.

The main road into the city was a carriage graveyard. Broken vehicles were abandoned as far as the eye could see. Bodies were left on the side of the road, most rotted and old, a sign that the soul forge had stolen their life. A few Thronehold soldiers were out cleaning up the mess, but there were less than a dozen.

Terrakona waited around the outside of the tent, his injuries mostly healed. He stared down at me as I walked onto the large road.

I wanted to head into the city and find the rest of the Frith Guild, but the sound of a shaking carriage caught my attention.

Then a familiar feeling crossed my thoughts.

Adelgis.

"*Volke.*"

His telepathy was a comfort.

"Where are you?" I asked aloud.

Evianna turned to me, her eyebrows raised. "I'm right here."

"N-No, I meant Adelgis. He's around here. He contacted me with telepathy."

She crossed her arms. "Oh, I see."

"*Volke, I couldn't follow your thoughts when you were on the other side of the city. I would've kept you apprised of the battle, but I'm just not that strong yet.*"

"It's okay," I said, hesitant with my words. Did he know about his father?

"*I know of my father's fate. Zaxis saw the event.*"

"I'm, uh, sorry about what happened."

"You needn't apologize. I know what you truly feel—and I think the same. My father needed to be stopped... But I know his research will continue to aid the Second Ascension. His hand in this war will continue to help from beyond the grave."

Which was unfortunate, but there was little I could do about that.

I stood on the main road to the Thronehold, my attention on the shaking carriage. It was the only one moving, and it had been part of the Frith Guild's caravan. I walked over, and hesitantly reached for the door.

"I have things to report to you, Volke."

"What is it?" I whispered as I tugged on the handle of the carriage door. Locked.

"It's important you hear this."

"I'm listening," I muttered as I examined the lock.

Evianna stood close to me, her brow furrowed. "Wasn't this the carriage where we kept the assassin's white hart in?"

"Firstly, Queen Ladislava has claimed that any god-creatures born in the Argo Empire belong to her—and that she has a right to determine who will bond with them."

I knew there would be a catch. I wasn't sure what to do about it, though. This was a situation where I wanted Eventide's input before I decided what I should do. The god-creatures couldn't fall into the hands of dastards. Theasin had been bonded to the soul forge for a few months and he had devastated Thronehold with his magic.

I shuddered when I imagined what could've happened if he had been bonded with the creature for a few years.

"Secondly, the fenris wolf is awake and eagerly awaiting someone to venture into his lair."

"Fantastic."

"Thirdly, the garuda bird and abyssal kraken have awoken, and the Second Ascension has their runestones."

I almost responded with a second *fantastic,* but my thoughts returned to the carriage. I evoked my magma and placed my palm on the handle. It only took a few seconds for the metal to melt, and the wood of the carriage to catch fire. I patted out the flames as the lock shifted and twisted.

"*Lastly,*" Adelgis continued, his telepathic voice laced with sadness, "*the enemy sirens led the reanimated mystical creatures to a central location within the city. They were teleported from Thronehold, and then I lost track of them. I apologize, Volke. I should've tried harder. This is my fault. I heard the sirens thinking they would present the creatures to the Autarch.*"

Why was he apologizing so much? The enemy would have fully grown creatures, which was unfortunate, but I wasn't sure how we were supposed to have stopped them.

I opened the door to the carriage and a white hart stumbled out of the vehicle. It walked on three wobbly legs. Its last leg didn't look fully formed—it was still an injury that my magma had caused. But the rest of its injuries—even the antlers I had cut off—had healed and were as good as new.

"Where am I?" the white hart asked. His golden horns glistened in the rain. "Why was I trapped?"

His utter confusion reminded me of the other creatures we had seen in the city.

I held my hand up, trying to calm the giant deer. "Whoa, whoa. It's okay. I freed you."

The white hart stomped his hooves for a moment, testing the ground. Then he snorted and shook his head. "I am... My name is *Arthur.*" Then his ears twitched. "Why can't I remember anything else?"

Evianna and I exchanged odd glances. I turned back to the white hart and patted his side. "I don't know, but we'll help you figure it out."

The white hart stomped his hooves a second time, still agitated and restless, but a little calmer. Arthur glanced around the road with his golden eyes, taking stock of the situation.

"My trial of worth…" Arthur snorted. "I feel as though… It's been completed. But where is my arcanist? I can't find them."

"Your trial of worth is completed?" I asked, one eyebrow raised.

The beast nodded. "Where is my arcanist?"

"I, uh, don't know. I'll try to find her."

"I want to meet her."

That was bizarre. All mystical creatures had a trial of worth, but if the white hart thought it was complete, I wondered if he would bond with anyone. Was that how the Autarch planned on *passing out* mystical creatures? Was he banking on the creatures just bonding with anyone, since their trial of worth had actually been completed by someone else?

What an insidious plan—it had Theasin's handiwork all over it.

I caught my breath, my thoughts drifting to my own carriage.

I turned my attention to it on the side of the road. With quick steps, I made my way over, my heart overworking itself with each step until all I could hear was the sound of it slamming against my ribs.

"*I apologize, Volke,*" Adelgis telepathically said again. "*Truly.*"

Evianna chased after me, jogging to keep pace. "What's wrong?"

I reached my carriage and went straight for the trunk. I had kept Luthair's cape there for safe keeping. With shaky hands, I melted away the lock and threw open the container.

To my horror, it was empty.

I couldn't breathe for a short moment, my thoughts falling into place.

Knightmares could move through the darkness. They effortlessly slide under doors or through the cracks of windows. A shut chest wouldn't have prevented a knightmare from escaping, unlike with the white hart in the carriage.

The threads…

They had come this way…

And the cape was the main part of the knightmare—that was what I had been told.

No. It couldn't have happened.

"*I didn't think of it until later,*" Adelgis continued. "*Until it was too late.*"

"Volke?" Evianna asked, placing a hand on my shoulder.

Luthair…

The cape *was* his corpse. That was all that had been left when he died. Had he been given false life from the soul forge? Had the Second Ascension taken him?

Was Luthair with the Autarch now?

I wanted to stop everything and collect my thoughts, but apparently hardship loved company. Captain Devlin and his roc swooped down from the sky and landed on the road. Each wing beat from Mesos kicked up wind and puddles of water. I held up an arm, shielding my eyes, but my heart refused to calm itself.

"There ya are," Devlin shouted as he hopped down from his roc, his breathing heavy. He stormed over to me, sweat soaking his shirt and hair. He wiped away some of it as he neared me, his brow furrowed. "We have a problem."

"What's wrong?" I asked, my voice shaky. "Is it the fenris wolf?"

"No—it's Vethica."

Devlin grabbed my upper arm and then turned toward his roc. He yanked me toward Mesos, his strength noticeable, but I jerked out of his grip and stood my ground. He whirled on his heel and glared at me.

"We don't have *time*," Devlin growled. "We need you *now*."

Luthair needed me.

The fenris wolf needed an arcanist.

"What is it?" I demanded. "Let me prioritize some things."

"It's Vethica," Devlin shouted as he threw one arm into the air. "She's *gone*, boy. During the chaos—during the fighting—she up and vanished, do you understand? The enemies no doubt targeted her. She can heal the plague, and we made that known."

Evianna froze in place, and so did I.

Without Vethica, we couldn't cure Zaxis, Forsythe, Odion or Hasdrubal of the arcane plague.

That... That changed all my priorities.

THANK YOU SO MUCH FOR
READING!

Please consider leaving a review—any and all feedback is
much appreciated!

Will Volke and the Frith Guild face off against the Autarch?

To find out more about Shami Stovall and the Frith Chronicles, take a look at her website: https://sastovallauthor.com/newsletter/

To help Shami Stovall (and see advanced chapters ahead of time) take a look at her Patreon: https://www.patreon.com/shamistovall

ABOUT THE AUTHOR

Shami Stovall is a multi-award-winning author of fantasy and science fiction, with several best-selling novels under her belt. Before that, she taught history and criminal law at the college level, and loved every second. When she's not reading fascinating articles and books about ancient China or the Byzantine Empire, Stovall can be found playing way too many video games, especially RPGs and tactics simulators.

If you want to contact her, you can do so at the following locations:

Website: https://sastovallauthor.com

Twitter: @GameOverStation

Facebook: www.facebook.com/ SAStovall

Email: s.adelle.s@gmail.com